GEORGE R. R. MARTIN

A GAME OF THRONES

THE GRAPHIC NOVEL

VOLUME 2

ADAPTED BY DANIEL ABRAHAM

ART BY TOMMY PATTERSON

COLORS BY IVAN NUNES

LETTERING BY MARSHALL DILLON

ORIGINAL SERIES COVER ART BY
MIKE S. MILLER AND MICHAEL KOMARCK

HARPER
Voyager

Paintings on pages vi and 182 by Michael Komarck.
Paintings on pages 2, 32, 62, 92, 122, and 152 by Mike S. Miller.

Published in Great Britain by Harper Voyager, an imprint of HarperCollins Publishers 2013

All characters featured in this book, and the distinctive names and likenesses thereof, and all related indicia are trademarks of George R.R. Martin.

ISBN 978-0-00-749304-3

Printed in China.

www.harpervoyagerbooks.co.uk

9 8 7 6 5 4 3 2

Graphic novel interior design by Foltz Design.

DYNAMITE®

Visit us online at www.DYNAMITE.com
Follow us on Twitter @dynamitecomics
Like us on Facebook /Dynamitecomics
Watch us on YouTube /Dynamitecomics
On Tumblr dynamitecomics.tumblr.com

Nick Barrucci, CEO / Publisher
Juan Collado, President / COO
Joe Rybandt, Senior Editor
Josh Johnson, Art Director
Rich Young, Director Business Development
Jason Ullmeyer, Senior Graphic Designer
Keith Davidsen, Marketing Manager
Josh Green, Traffic Coordinator
Chris Caniano, Production Assistant

A GAME OF THRONES

THE GRAPHIC NOVEL

VOLUME 2

CONTENTS

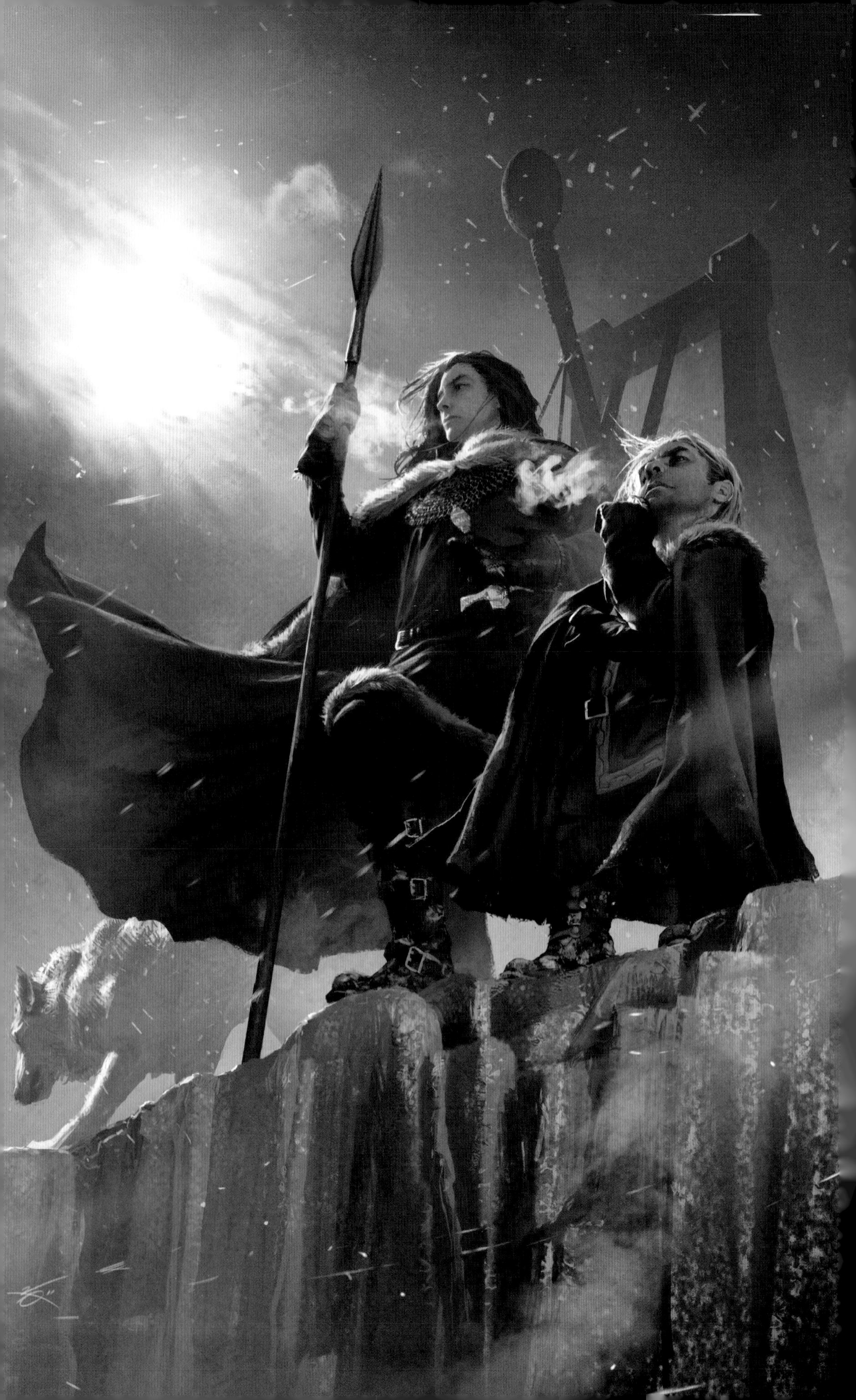

A GAME OF THRONES

THRONES

THE GRAPHIC NOVEL

VOLUME 2

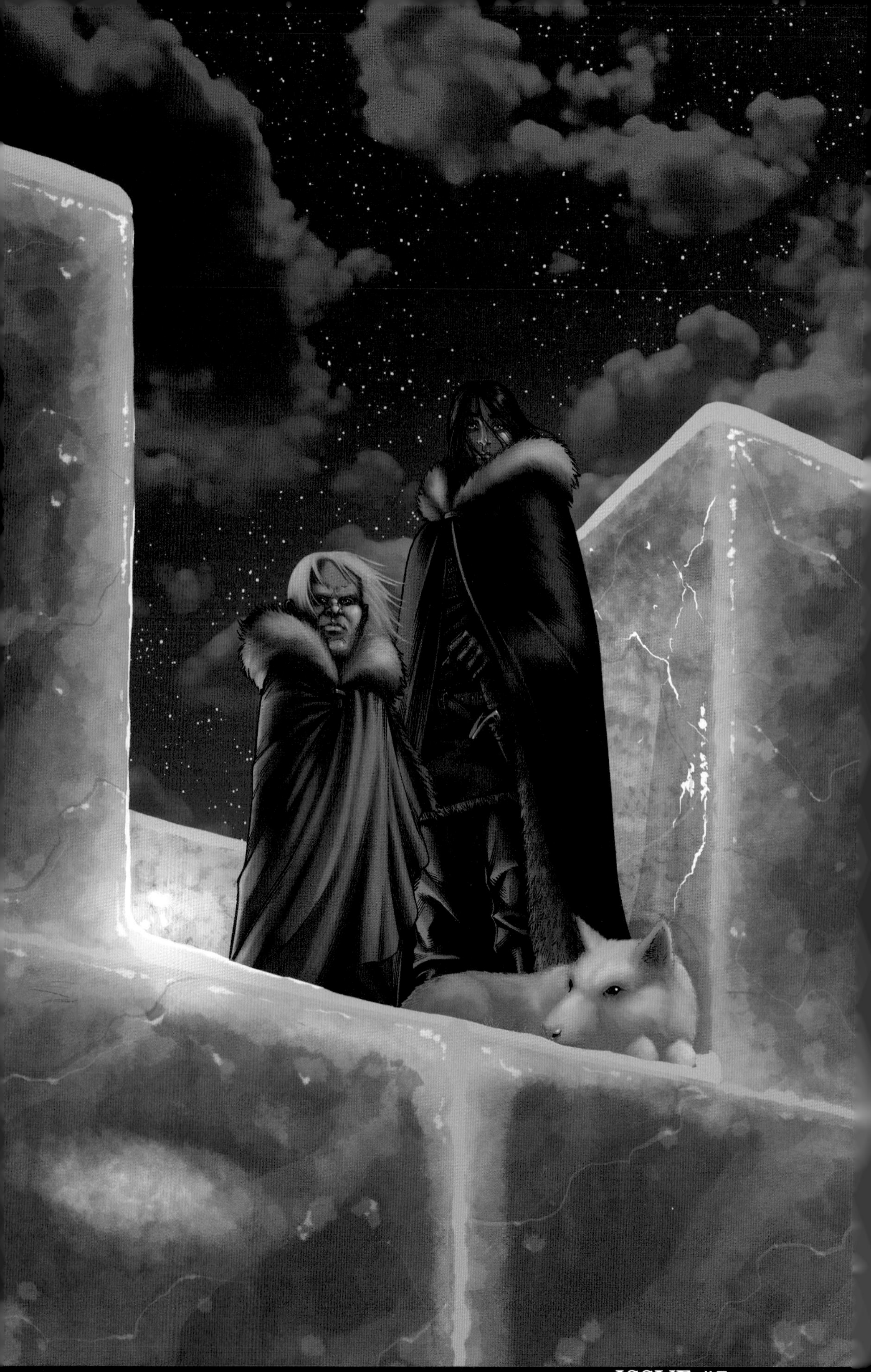

ISSUE #7

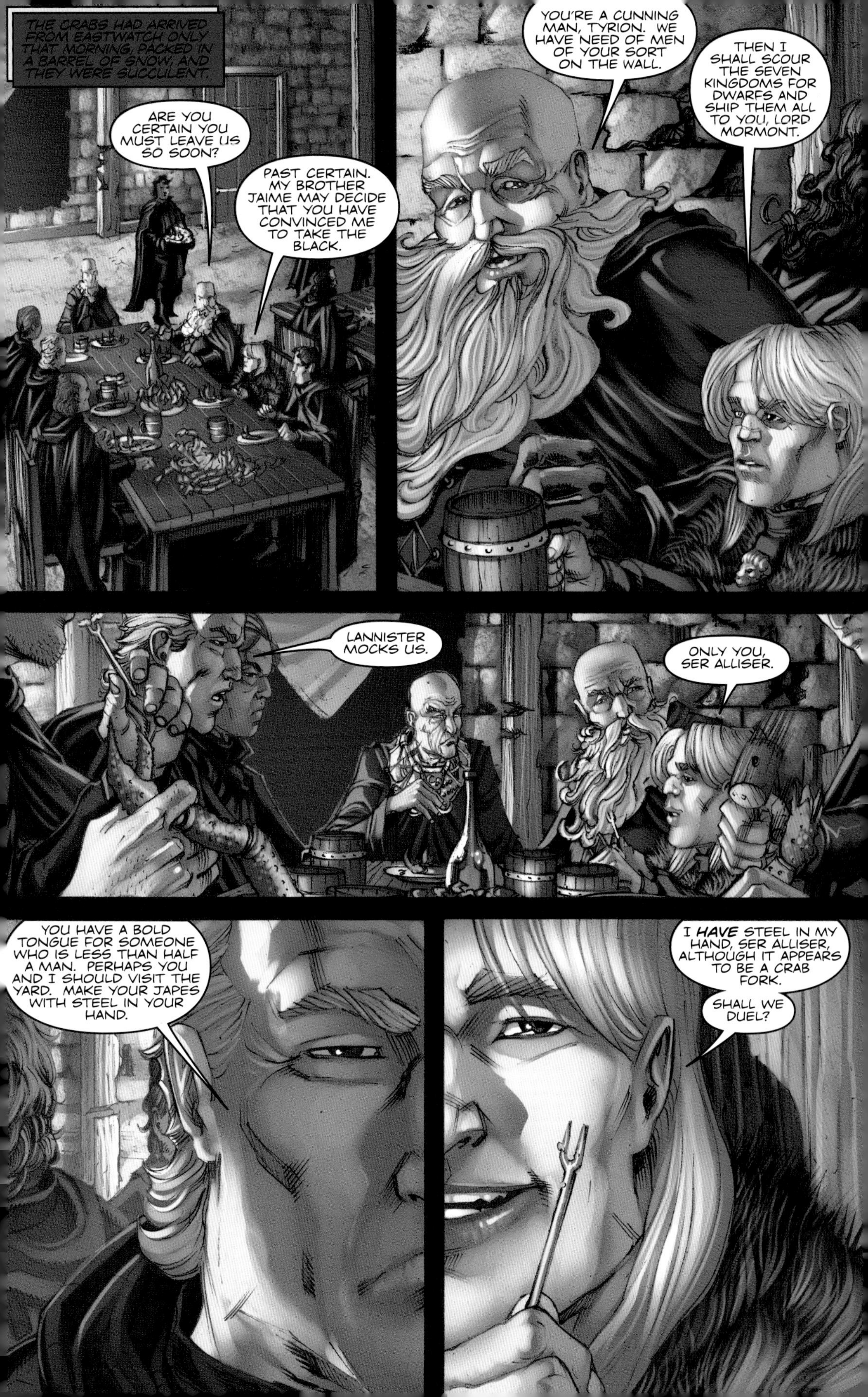
THE CRABS HAD ARRIVED FROM EASTWATCH ONLY THAT MORNING, PACKED IN A BARREL OF SNOW, AND THEY WERE SUCCULENT.
ARE YOU CERTAIN YOU MUST LEAVE US SO SOON?
PAST CERTAIN. MY BROTHER JAIME MAY DECIDE THAT YOU HAVE CONVINCED ME TO TAKE THE BLACK.
YOU'RE A CUNNING MAN, TYRION. WE HAVE NEED OF MEN OF YOUR SORT ON THE WALL.
THEN I SHALL SCOUR THE SEVEN KINGDOMS FOR DWARFS AND SHIP THEM ALL TO YOU, LORD MORMONT.
LANNISTER MOCKS US.
ONLY YOU, SER ALLISER.
YOU HAVE A BOLD TONGUE FOR SOMEONE WHO IS LESS THAN HALF A MAN. PERHAPS YOU AND I SHOULD VISIT THE YARD. MAKE YOUR JAPES WITH STEEL IN YOUR HAND.
I HAVE STEEL IN MY HAND, SER ALLISER, ALTHOUGH IT APPEARS TO BE A CRAB FORK.
SHALL WE DUEL?

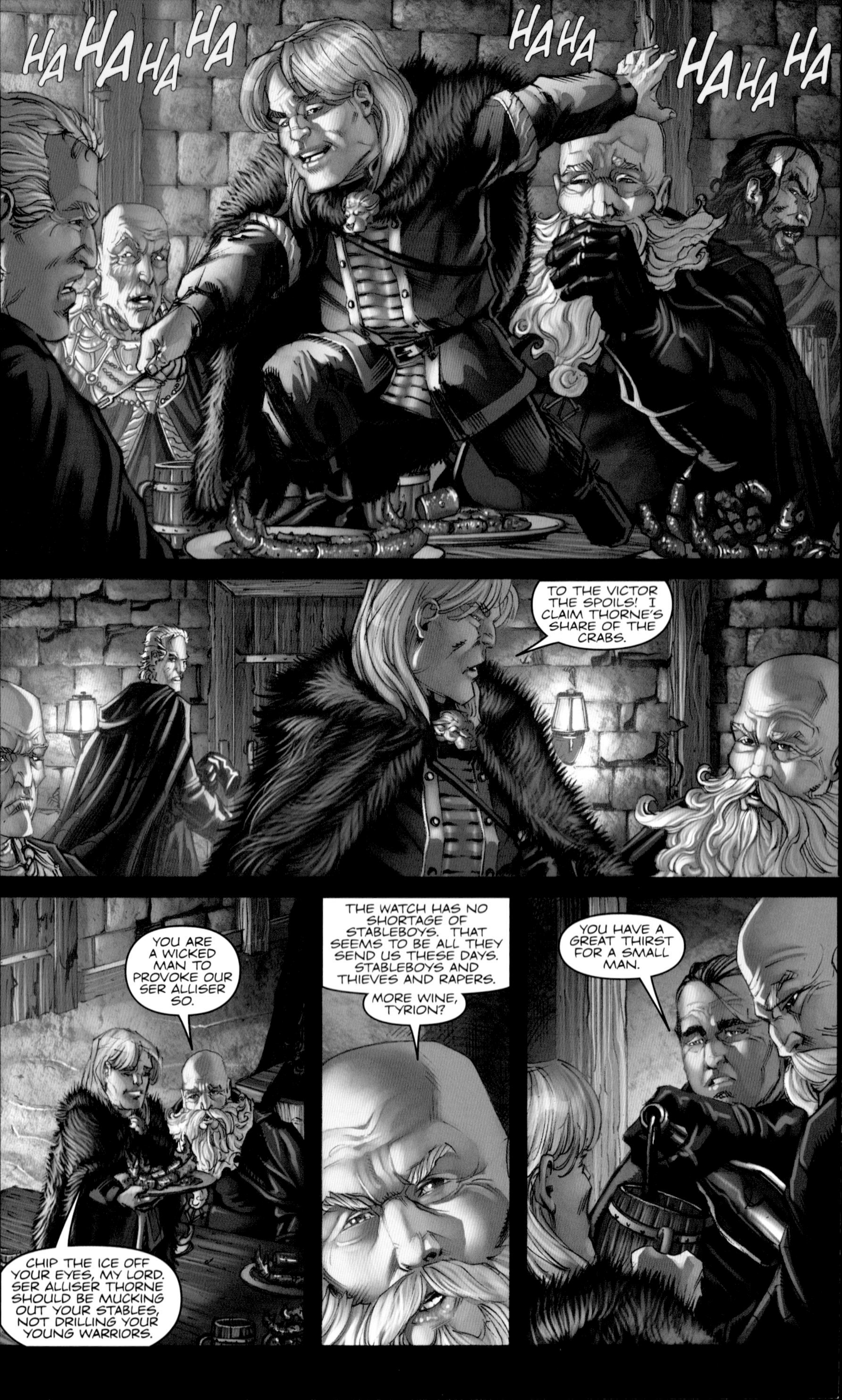
HA HA HA HA HA HA
HA HA
HA HA HA HA
TO THE VICTOR THE SPOILS! I CLAIM THORNE'S SHARE OF THE CRABS.
YOU ARE A WICKED MAN TO PROVOKE OUR SER ALLISER SO.
CHIP THE ICE OFF YOUR EYES, MY LORD. SER ALLISER THORNE SHOULD BE MUCKING OUT YOUR STABLES, NOT DRILLING YOUR YOUNG WARRIORS.
THE WATCH HAS NO SHORTAGE OF STABLEBOYS. THAT SEEMS TO BE ALL THEY SEND US THESE DAYS. STABLEBOYS AND THIEVES AND RAPERS.
MORE WINE, TYRION?
YOU HAVE A GREAT THIRST FOR A SMALL MAN.

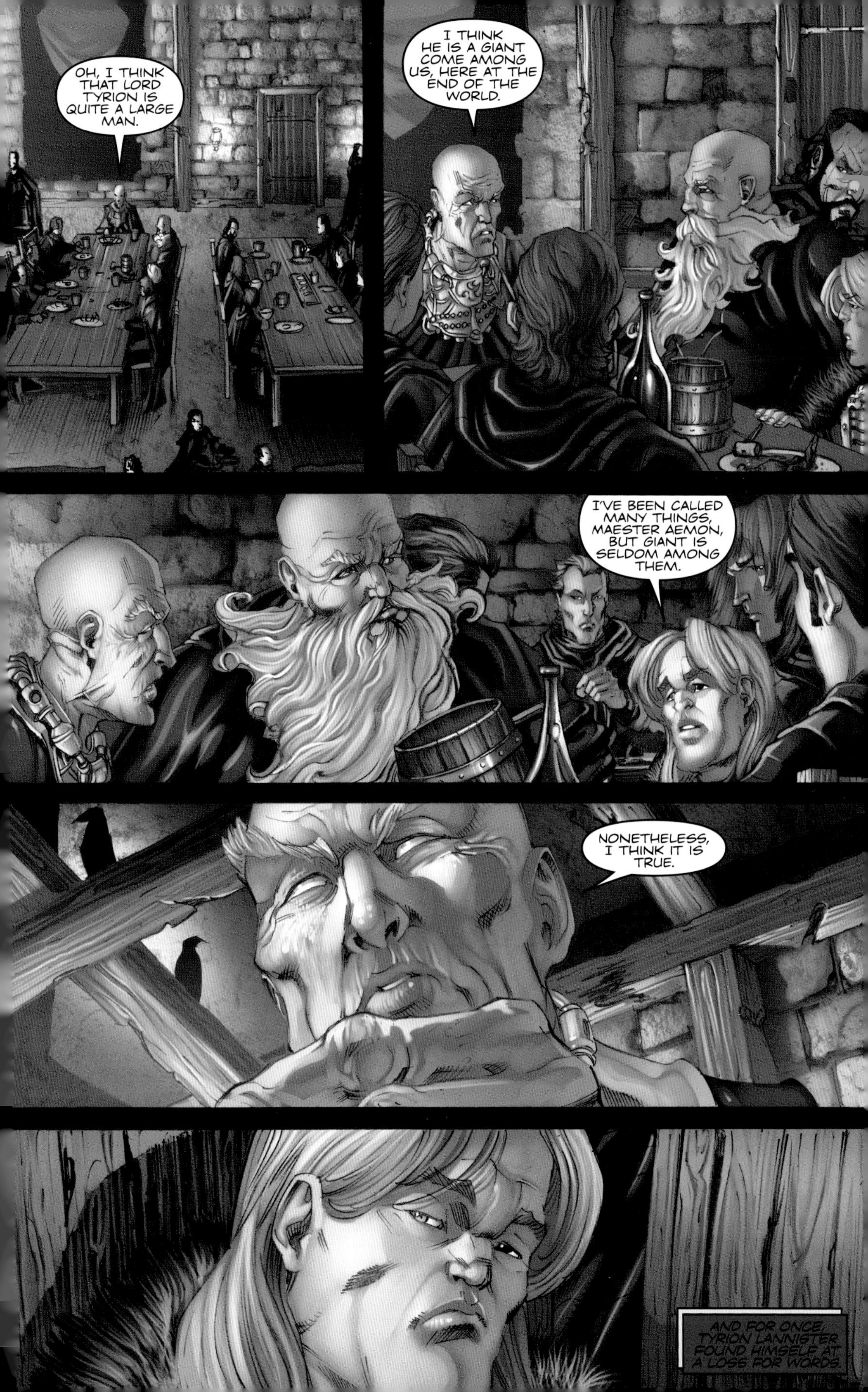
OH, I THINK THAT LORD TYRION IS QUITE A LARGE MAN.
I THINK HE IS A GIANT COME AMONG US, HERE AT THE END OF THE WORLD.
I'VE BEEN CALLED MANY THINGS, MAESTER AEMON, BUT GIANT IS SELDOM AMONG THEM.
NONETHELESS, I THINK IT IS TRUE.
AND FOR ONCE, TYRION LANNISTER FOUND HIMSELF AT A LOSS FOR WORDS.

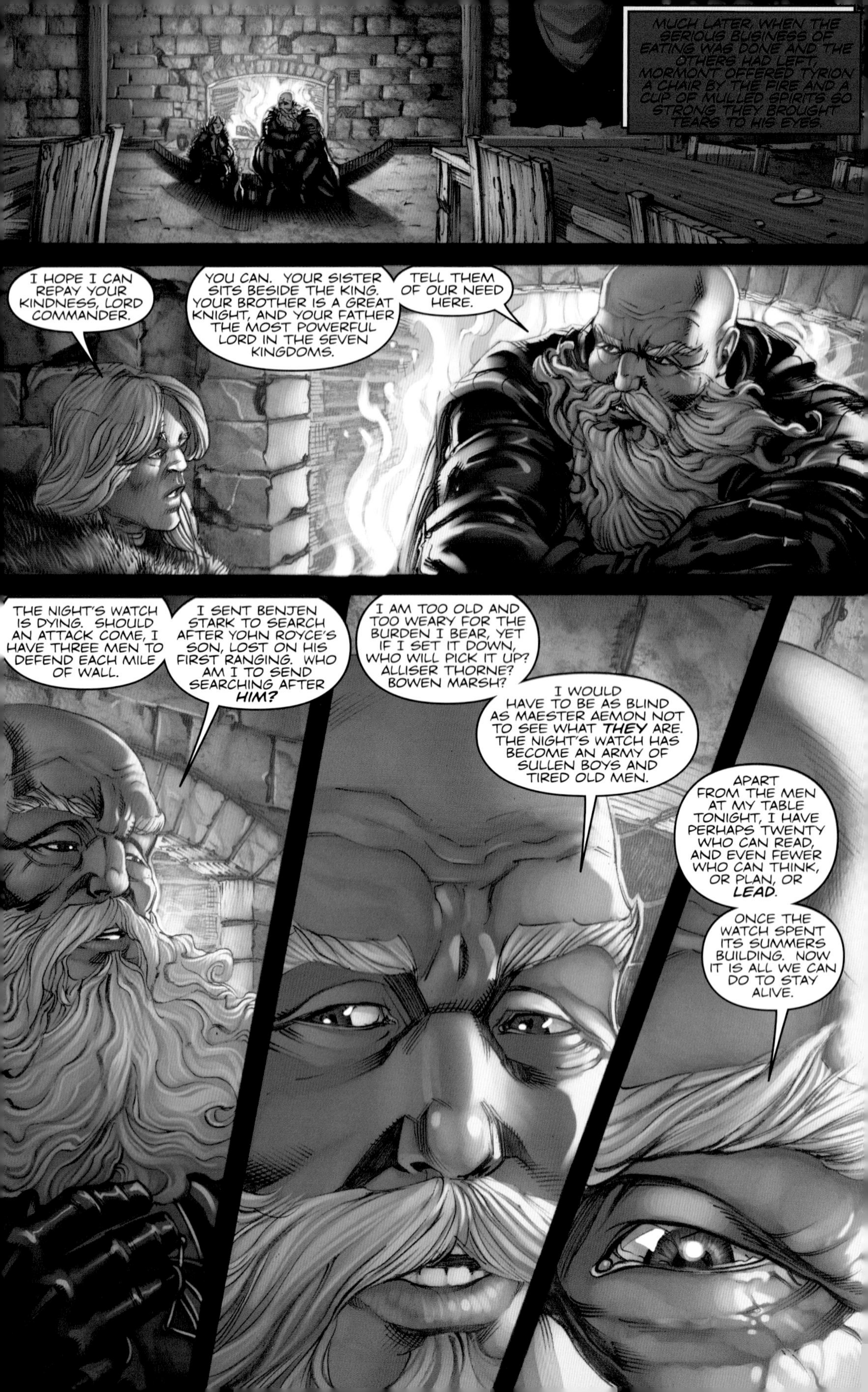
MUCH LATER, WHEN THE SERIOUS BUSINESS OF EATING WAS DONE AND THE OTHERS HAD LEFT, MORMONT OFFERED TYRION A CHAIR BY THE FIRE AND A CUP OF MULLED SPIRITS SO STRONG THEY BROUGHT TEARS TO HIS EYES.
I HOPE I CAN REPAY YOUR KINDNESS, LORD COMMANDER.
YOU CAN. YOUR SISTER SITS BESIDE THE KING. YOUR BROTHER IS A GREAT KNIGHT, AND YOUR FATHER THE MOST POWERFUL LORD IN THE SEVEN KINGDOMS.
TELL THEM OF OUR NEED HERE.
THE NIGHT'S WATCH IS DYING. SHOULD AN ATTACK COME, I HAVE THREE MEN TO DEFEND EACH MILE OF WALL.
I SENT BENJEN STARK TO SEARCH AFTER YOHN ROYCE'S SON, LOST ON HIS FIRST RANGING. WHO AM I TO SEND SEARCHING AFTER ***HIM?***
I AM TOO OLD AND TOO WEARY FOR THE BURDEN I BEAR, YET IF I SET IT DOWN, WHO WILL PICK IT UP? ALLISER THORNE? BOWEN MARSH?
I WOULD HAVE TO BE AS BLIND AS MAESTER AEMON NOT TO SEE WHAT ***THEY*** ARE. THE NIGHT'S WATCH HAS BECOME AN ARMY OF SULLEN BOYS AND TIRED OLD MEN.
APART FROM THE MEN AT MY TABLE TONIGHT, I HAVE PERHAPS TWENTY WHO CAN READ, AND EVEN FEWER WHO CAN THINK, OR PLAN, OR ***LEAD***.
ONCE THE WATCH SPENT ITS SUMMERS BUILDING. NOW IT IS ALL WE CAN DO TO STAY ALIVE.

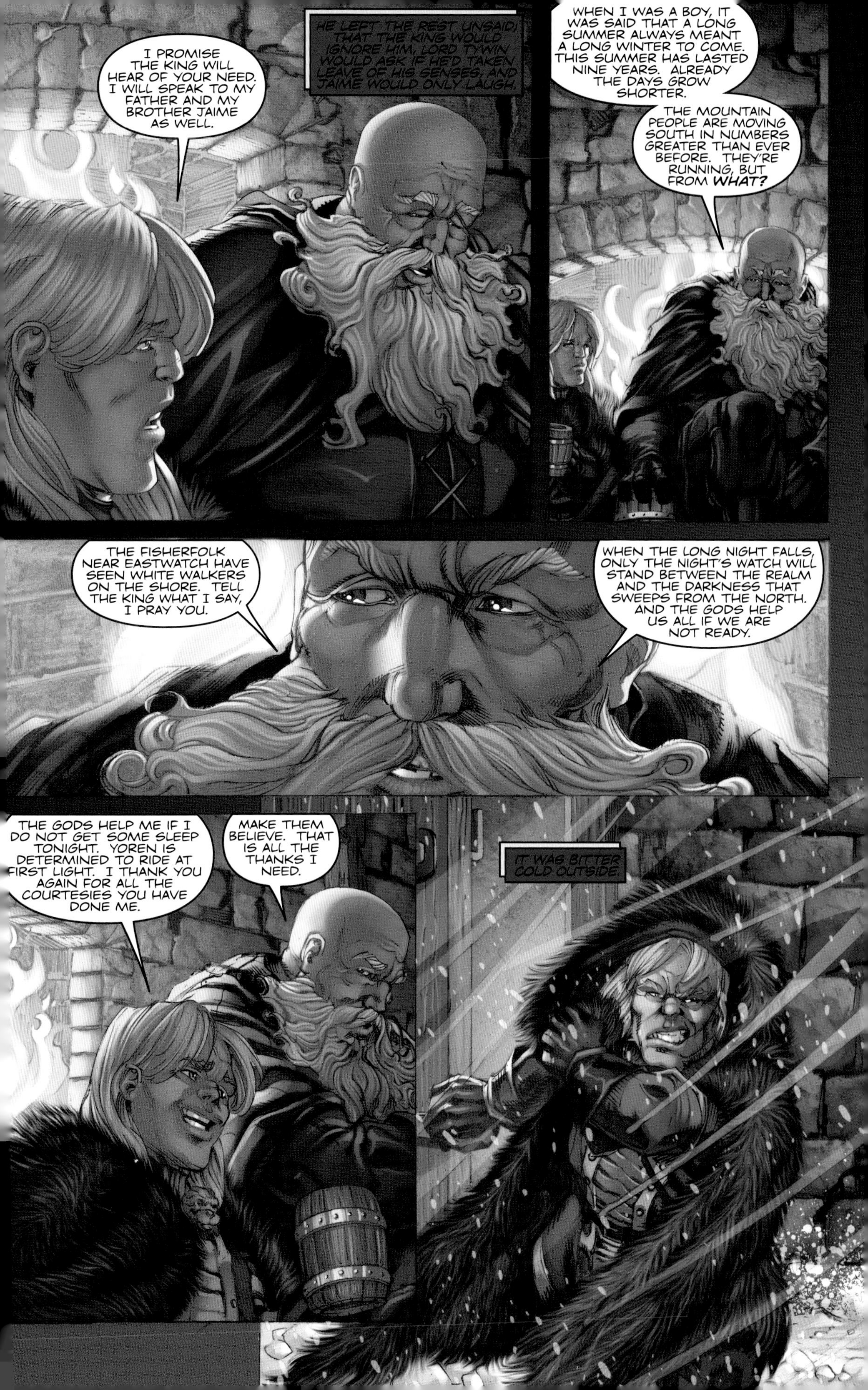
I PROMISE THE KING WILL HEAR OF YOUR NEED. I WILL SPEAK TO MY FATHER AND MY BROTHER JAIME AS WELL.
HE LEFT THE REST UNSAID: THAT THE KING WOULD IGNORE HIM, LORD TYWIN WOULD ASK IF HE'D TAKEN LEAVE OF HIS SENSES, AND JAIME WOULD ONLY LAUGH.
WHEN I WAS A BOY, IT WAS SAID THAT A LONG SUMMER ALWAYS MEANT A LONG WINTER TO COME. THIS SUMMER HAS LASTED NINE YEARS. ALREADY THE DAYS GROW SHORTER.
THE MOUNTAIN PEOPLE ARE MOVING SOUTH IN NUMBERS GREATER THAN EVER BEFORE. THEY'RE RUNNING, BUT FROM WHAT?
THE FISHERFOLK NEAR EASTWATCH HAVE SEEN WHITE WALKERS ON THE SHORE. TELL THE KING WHAT I SAY, I PRAY YOU.
WHEN THE LONG NIGHT FALLS, ONLY THE NIGHT'S WATCH WILL STAND BETWEEN THE REALM AND THE DARKNESS THAT SWEEPS FROM THE NORTH. AND THE GODS HELP US ALL IF WE ARE NOT READY.
THE GODS HELP ME IF I DO NOT GET SOME SLEEP TONIGHT. YOREN IS DETERMINED TO RIDE AT FIRST LIGHT. I THANK YOU AGAIN FOR ALL THE COURTESIES YOU HAVE DONE ME.
MAKE THEM BELIEVE. THAT IS ALL THE THANKS I NEED.
IT WAS BITTER COLD OUTSIDE.

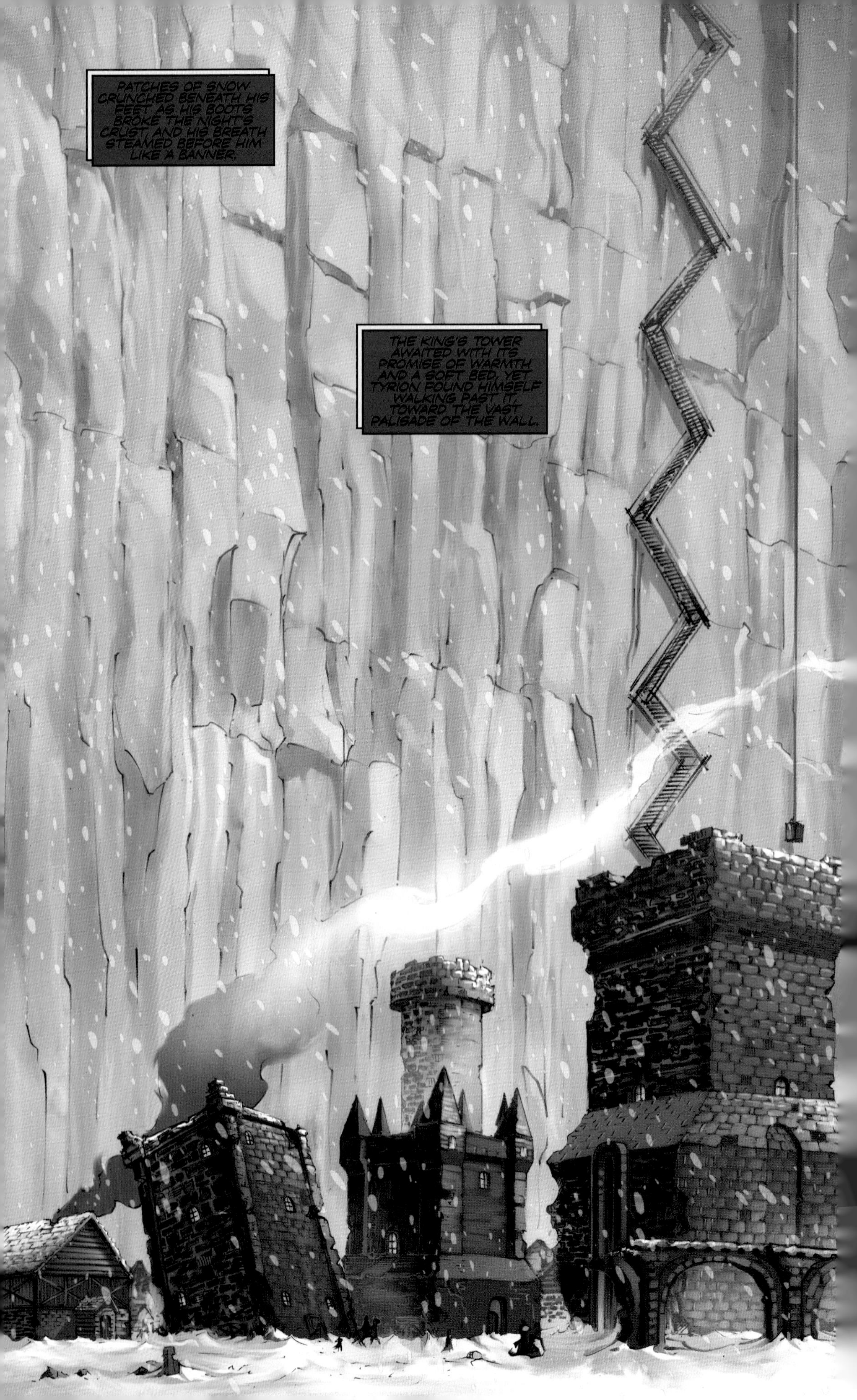
PATCHES OF SNOW CRUNCHED BENEATH HIS FEET AS HIS BOOTS BROKE THE NIGHT'S CRUST, AND HIS BREATH STEAMED BEFORE HIM LIKE A BANNER.
THE KING'S TOWER AWAITED WITH ITS PROMISE OF WARMTH AND A SOFT BED, YET TYRION FOUND HIMSELF WALKING PAST IT, TOWARD THE VAST PALISADE OF THE WALL.

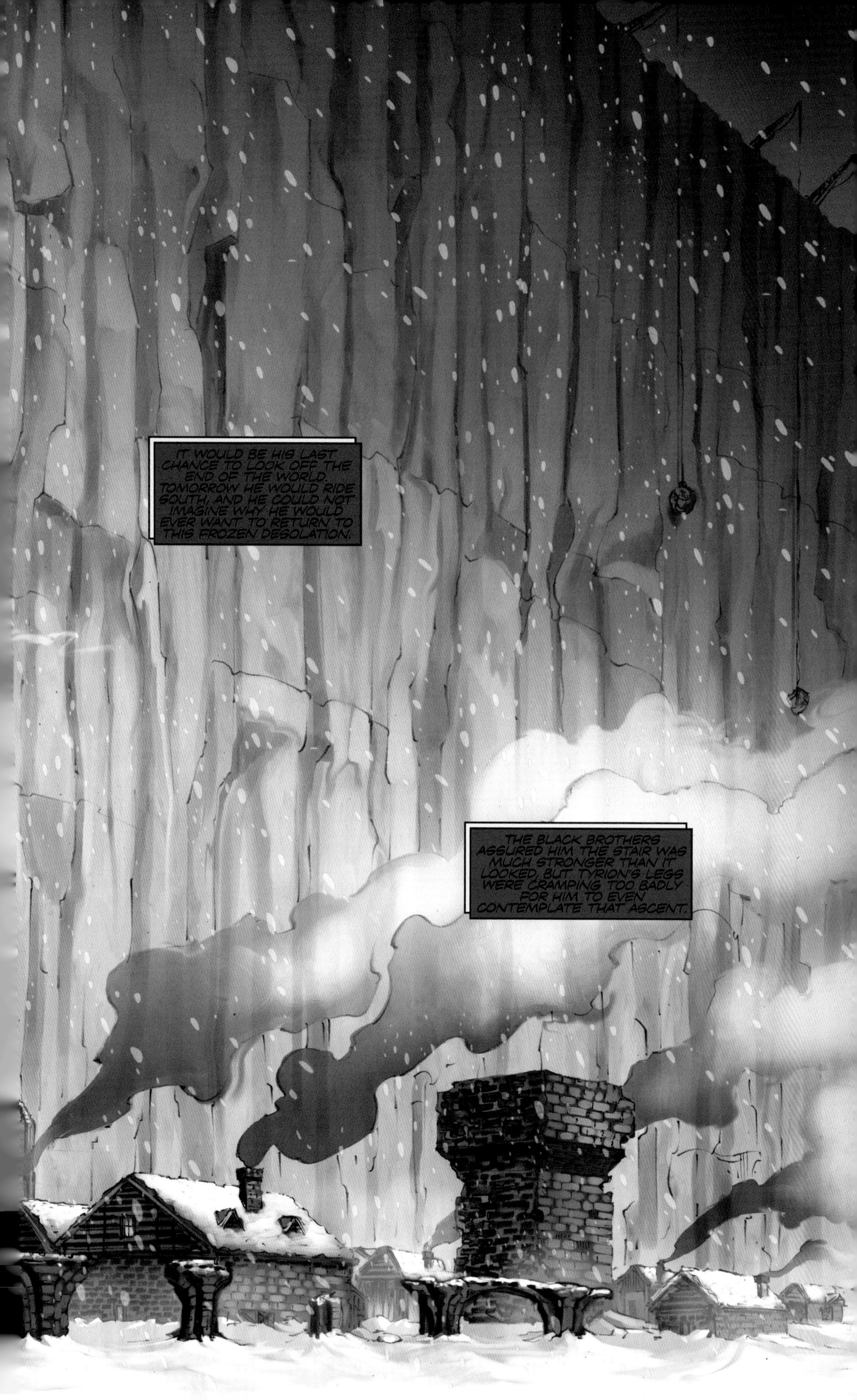
IT WOULD BE HIS LAST CHANCE TO LOOK OFF THE END OF THE WORLD. TOMORROW HE WOULD RIDE SOUTH, AND HE COULD NOT IMAGINE WHY HE WOULD EVER WANT TO RETURN TO THIS FROZEN DESOLATION.
THE BLACK BROTHERS ASSURED HIM THE STAIR WAS MUCH STRONGER THAN IT LOOKED, BUT TYRION'S LEGS WERE CRAMPING TOO BADLY FOR HIM TO EVEN CONTEMPLATE THAT ASCENT.

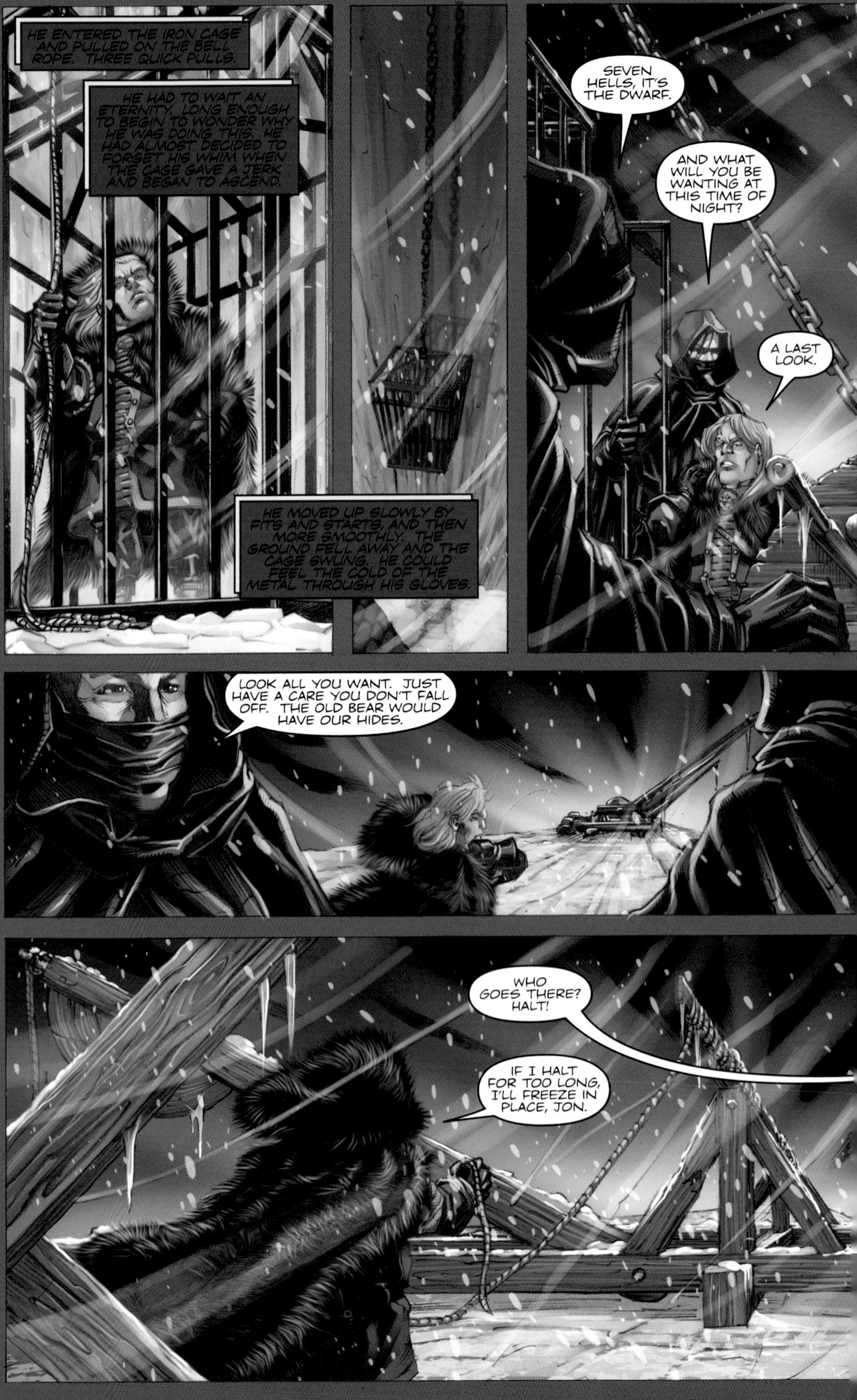
HE ENTERED THE IRON CAGE AND PULLED ON THE BELL ROPE. THREE QUICK PULLS.
HE HAD TO WAIT AN ETERNITY, LONG ENOUGH TO BEGIN TO WONDER WHY HE WAS DOING THIS. HE HAD ALMOST DECIDED TO FORGET HIS WHIM WHEN THE CAGE GAVE A JERK AND BEGAN TO ASCEND.
HE MOVED UP SLOWLY BY FITS AND STARTS, AND THEN MORE SMOOTHLY. THE GROUND FELL AWAY AND THE CAGE SWUNG. HE COULD FEEL THE COLD OF THE METAL THROUGH HIS GLOVES.
SEVEN HELLS, IT'S THE DWARF.
AND WHAT WILL YOU BE WANTING AT THIS TIME OF NIGHT?
A LAST LOOK.
LOOK ALL YOU WANT. JUST HAVE A CARE YOU DON'T FALL OFF. THE OLD BEAR WOULD HAVE OUR HIDES.
WHO GOES THERE? HALT!
IF I HALT FOR TOO LONG, I'LL FREEZE IN PLACE, JON.

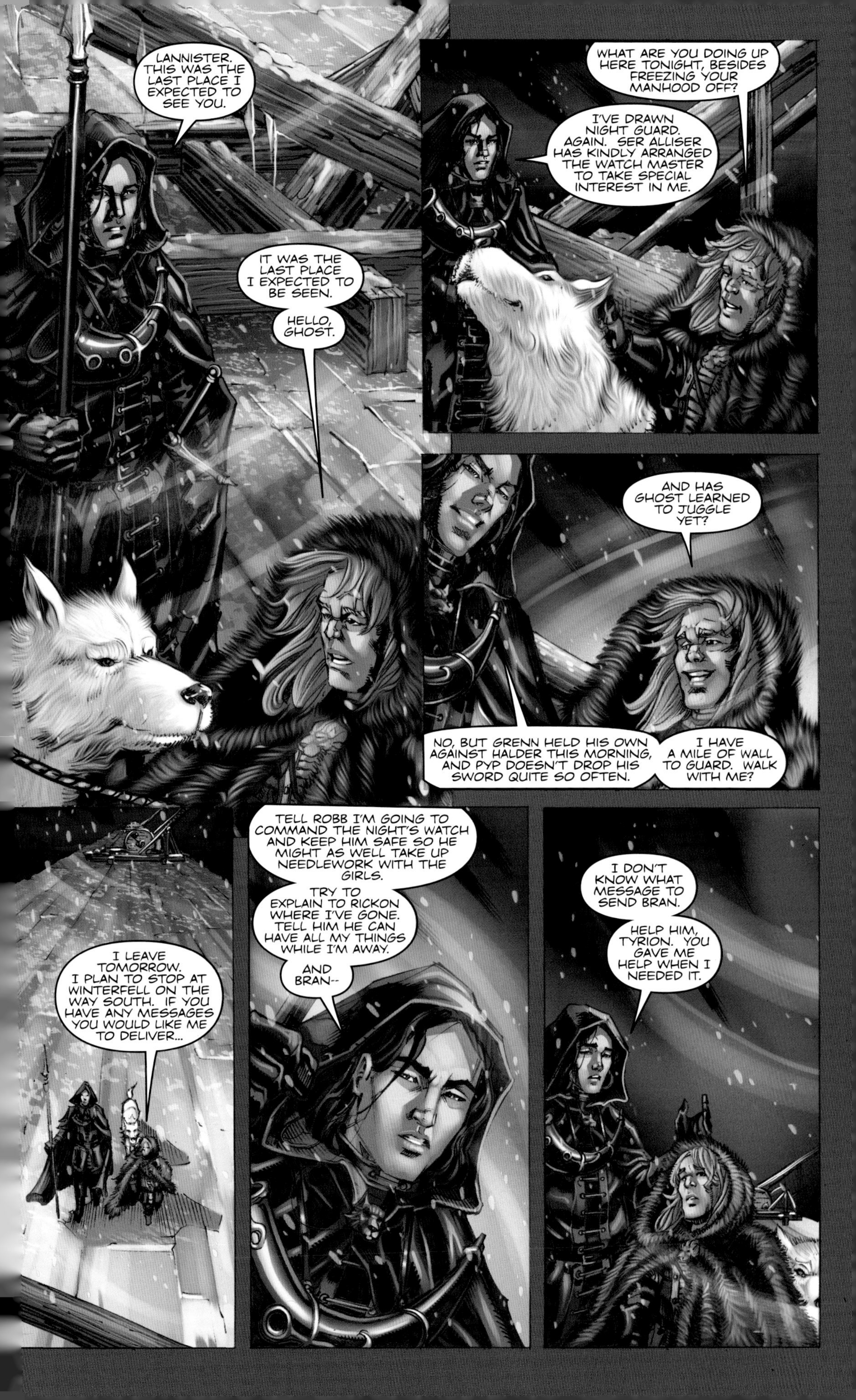
LANNISTER. THIS WAS THE LAST PLACE I EXPECTED TO SEE YOU.
IT WAS THE LAST PLACE I EXPECTED TO BE SEEN.
HELLO, GHOST.
WHAT ARE YOU DOING UP HERE TONIGHT, BESIDES FREEZING YOUR MANHOOD OFF?
I'VE DRAWN NIGHT GUARD. AGAIN. SER ALLISER HAS KINDLY ARRANGED THE WATCH MASTER TO TAKE SPECIAL INTEREST IN ME.
AND HAS GHOST LEARNED TO JUGGLE YET?
NO, BUT GRENN HELD HIS OWN AGAINST HALDER THIS MORNING, AND PYP DOESN'T DROP HIS SWORD QUITE SO OFTEN.
I HAVE A MILE OF WALL TO GUARD. WALK WITH ME?
I LEAVE TOMORROW. I PLAN TO STOP AT WINTERFELL ON THE WAY SOUTH. IF YOU HAVE ANY MESSAGES YOU WOULD LIKE ME TO DELIVER...
TELL ROBB I'M GOING TO COMMAND THE NIGHT'S WATCH AND KEEP HIM SAFE SO HE MIGHT AS WELL TAKE UP NEEDLEWORK WITH THE GIRLS.
TRY TO EXPLAIN TO RICKON WHERE I'VE GONE. TELL HIM HE CAN HAVE ALL MY THINGS WHILE I'M AWAY.
AND BRAN--
I DON'T KNOW WHAT MESSAGE TO SEND BRAN.
HELP HIM, TYRION. YOU GAVE ME HELP WHEN I NEEDED IT.

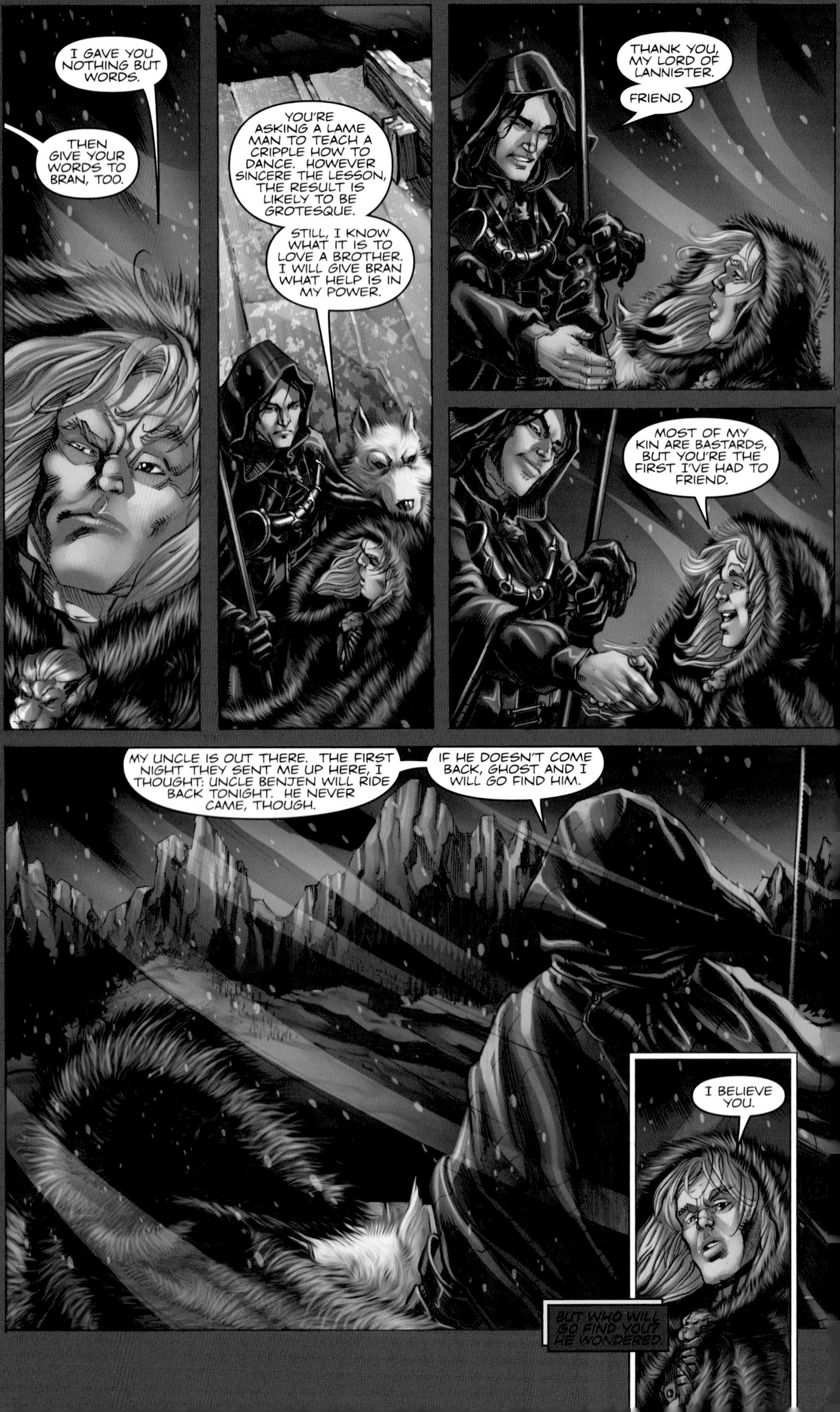
I GAVE YOU NOTHING BUT WORDS.
THEN GIVE YOUR WORDS TO BRAN, TOO.
YOU'RE ASKING A LAME MAN TO TEACH A CRIPPLE HOW TO DANCE. HOWEVER SINCERE THE LESSON, THE RESULT IS LIKELY TO BE GROTESQUE.
STILL, I KNOW WHAT IT IS TO LOVE A BROTHER. I WILL GIVE BRAN WHAT HELP IS IN MY POWER.
THANK YOU, MY LORD OF LANNISTER.
FRIEND.
MOST OF MY KIN ARE BASTARDS, BUT YOU'RE THE FIRST I'VE HAD TO FRIEND.
MY UNCLE IS OUT THERE. THE FIRST NIGHT THEY SENT ME UP HERE, I THOUGHT: UNCLE BENJEN WILL RIDE BACK TONIGHT. HE NEVER CAME, THOUGH.
IF HE DOESN'T COME BACK, GHOST AND I WILL GO FIND HIM.
I BELIEVE YOU.
BUT WHO WILL GO FIND YOU? HE WONDERED.

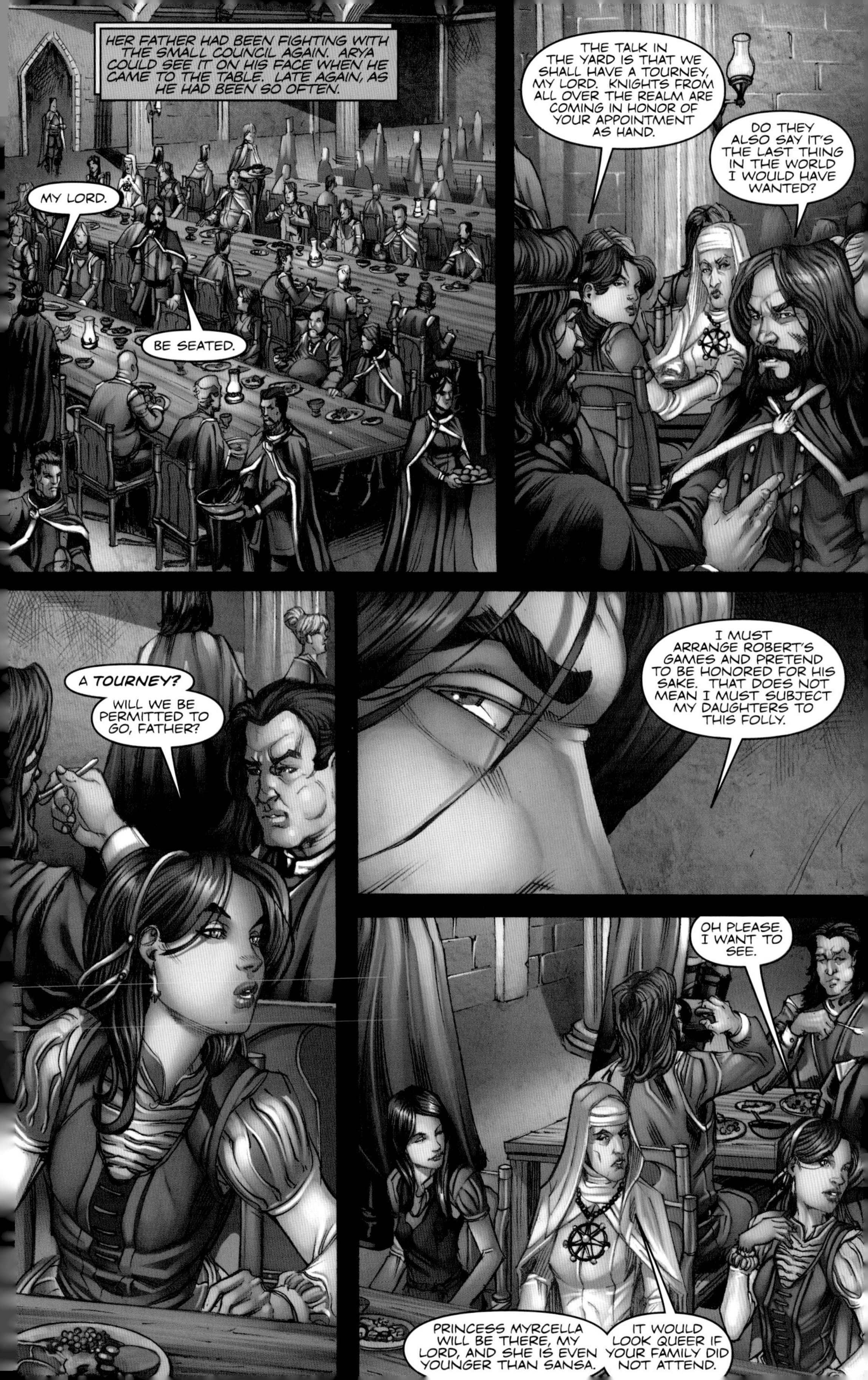
HER FATHER HAD BEEN FIGHTING WITH THE SMALL COUNCIL AGAIN. ARYA COULD SEE IT ON HIS FACE WHEN HE CAME TO THE TABLE. LATE AGAIN, AS HE HAD BEEN SO OFTEN.
MY LORD.
BE SEATED.
THE TALK IN THE YARD IS THAT WE SHALL HAVE A TOURNEY, MY LORD. KNIGHTS FROM ALL OVER THE REALM ARE COMING IN HONOR OF YOUR APPOINTMENT AS HAND.
DO THEY ALSO SAY IT'S THE LAST THING IN THE WORLD I WOULD HAVE WANTED?
A *TOURNEY?* WILL WE BE PERMITTED TO GO, FATHER?
I MUST ARRANGE ROBERT'S GAMES AND PRETEND TO BE HONORED FOR HIS SAKE. THAT DOES NOT MEAN I MUST SUBJECT MY DAUGHTERS TO THIS FOLLY.
OH PLEASE. I WANT TO SEE.
PRINCESS MYRCELLA WILL BE THERE, MY LORD, AND SHE IS EVEN YOUNGER THAN SANSA.
IT WOULD LOOK QUEER IF YOUR FAMILY DID NOT ATTEND.

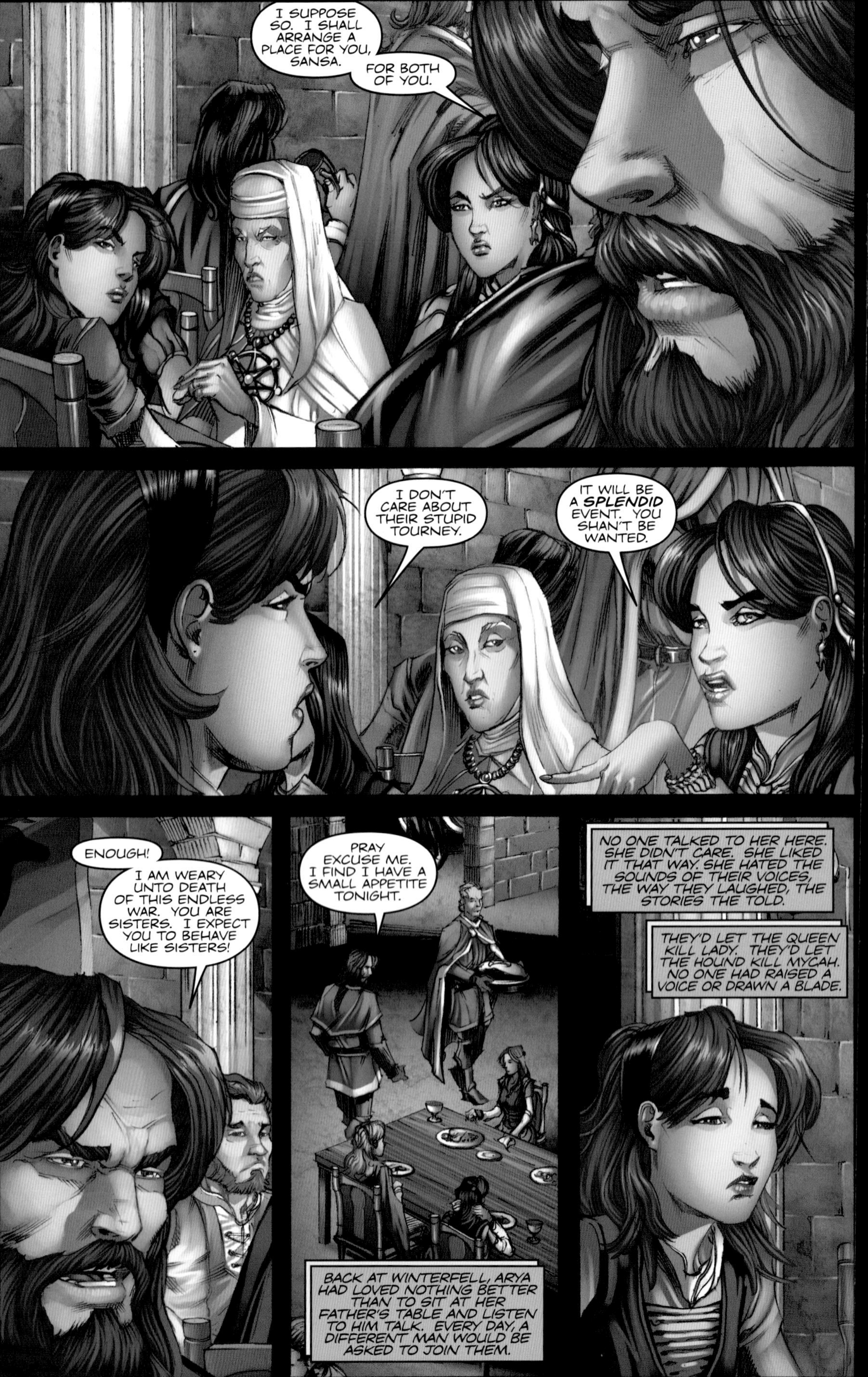
I SUPPOSE SO. I SHALL ARRANGE A PLACE FOR YOU, SANSA.
FOR BOTH OF YOU.
I DON'T CARE ABOUT THEIR STUPID TOURNEY.
IT WILL BE A **SPLENDID** EVENT. YOU SHAN'T BE WANTED.
ENOUGH!
I AM WEARY UNTO DEATH OF THIS ENDLESS WAR. YOU ARE SISTERS. I EXPECT YOU TO BEHAVE LIKE SISTERS!
PRAY EXCUSE ME. I FIND I HAVE A SMALL APPETITE TONIGHT.
BACK AT WINTERFELL, ARYA HAD LOVED NOTHING BETTER THAN TO SIT AT HER FATHER'S TABLE AND LISTEN TO HIM TALK. EVERY DAY, A DIFFERENT MAN WOULD BE ASKED TO JOIN THEM.
NO ONE TALKED TO HER HERE. SHE DIDN'T CARE. SHE LIKED IT THAT WAY. SHE HATED THE SOUNDS OF THEIR VOICES, THE WAY THEY LAUGHED, THE STORIES THE TOLD.
THEY'D LET THE QUEEN KILL LADY. THEY'D LET THE HOUND KILL MYCAH. NO ONE HAD RAISED A VOICE OR DRAWN A BLADE.

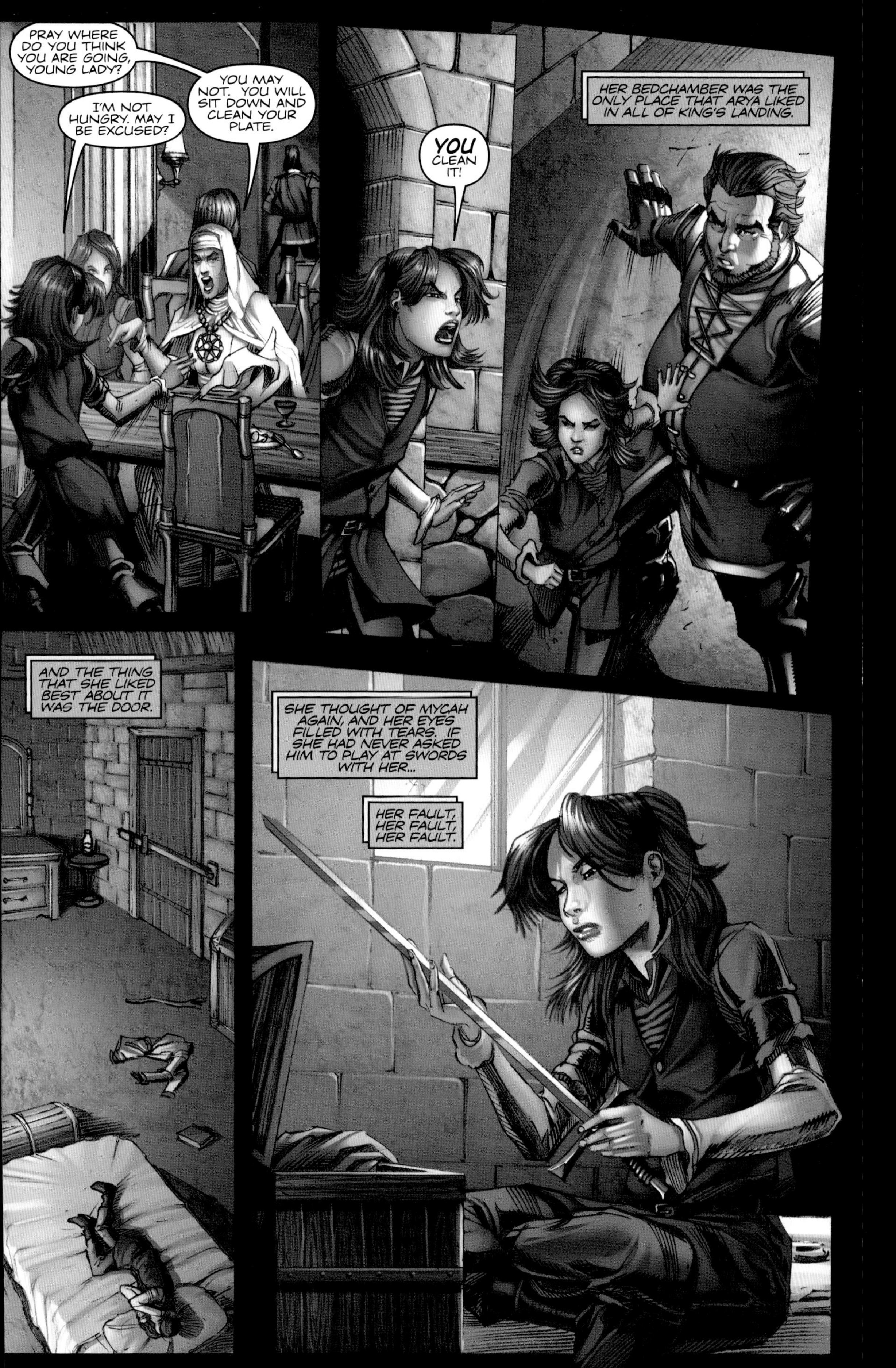
PRAY WHERE DO YOU THINK YOU ARE GOING, YOUNG LADY?
I'M NOT HUNGRY. MAY I BE EXCUSED?
YOU MAY NOT. YOU WILL SIT DOWN AND CLEAN YOUR PLATE.
YOU CLEAN IT!
HER BEDCHAMBER WAS THE ONLY PLACE THAT ARYA LIKED IN ALL OF KING'S LANDING.
AND THE THING THAT SHE LIKED BEST ABOUT IT WAS THE DOOR.
SHE THOUGHT OF MYCAH AGAIN, AND HER EYES FILLED WITH TEARS. IF SHE HAD NEVER ASKED HIM TO PLAY AT SWORDS WITH HER...
HER FAULT, HER FAULT, HER FAULT.

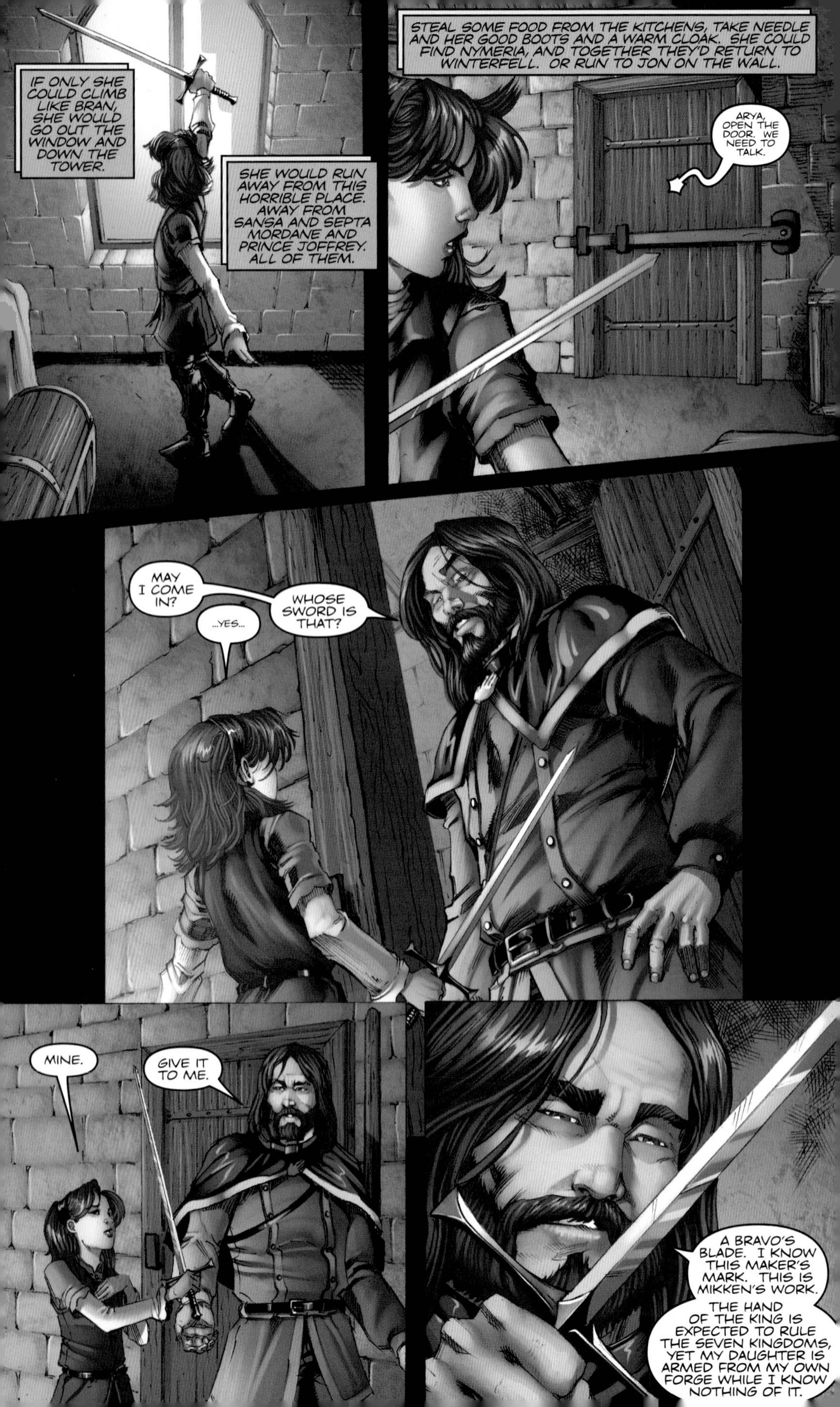
IF ONLY SHE COULD CLIMB LIKE BRAN, SHE WOULD GO OUT THE WINDOW AND DOWN THE TOWER.
SHE WOULD RUN AWAY FROM THIS HORRIBLE PLACE. AWAY FROM SANSA AND SEPTA MORDANE AND PRINCE JOFFREY. ALL OF THEM.
STEAL SOME FOOD FROM THE KITCHENS, TAKE NEEDLE AND HER GOOD BOOTS AND A WARM CLOAK. SHE COULD FIND NYMERIA, AND TOGETHER THEY'D RETURN TO WINTERFELL. OR RUN TO JON ON THE WALL.
ARYA, OPEN THE DOOR. WE NEED TO TALK.
MAY I COME IN?
...YES...
WHOSE SWORD IS THAT?
MINE.
GIVE IT TO ME.
A BRAVO'S BLADE. I KNOW THIS MAKER'S MARK. THIS IS MIKKEN'S WORK.
THE HAND OF THE KING IS EXPECTED TO RULE THE SEVEN KINGDOMS, YET MY DAUGHTER IS ARMED FROM MY OWN FORGE WHILE I KNOW NOTHING OF IT.

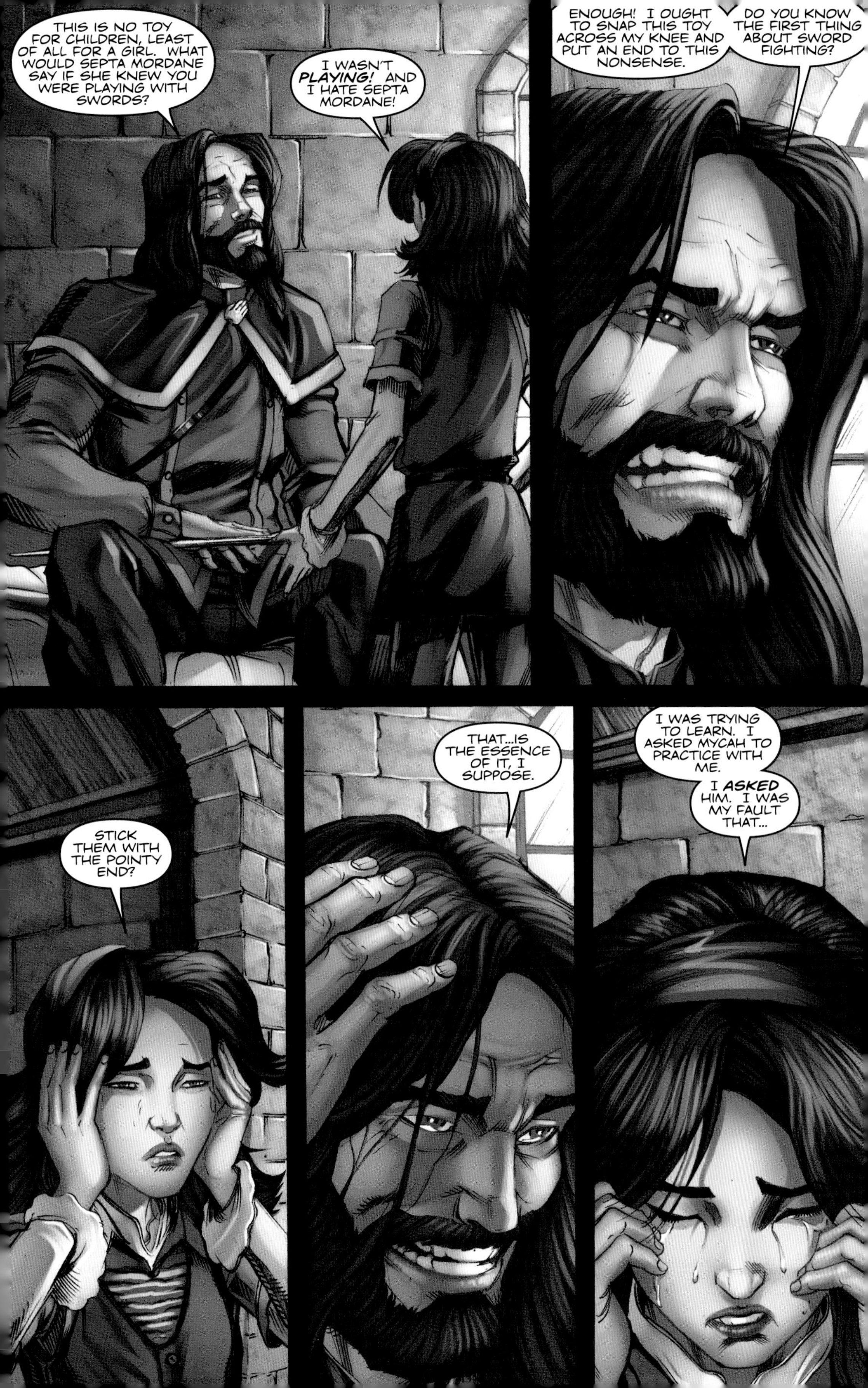
THIS IS NO TOY FOR CHILDREN, LEAST OF ALL FOR A GIRL. WHAT WOULD SEPTA MORDANE SAY IF SHE KNEW YOU WERE PLAYING WITH SWORDS?
I WASN'T *PLAYING!* AND I HATE SEPTA MORDANE!
ENOUGH! I OUGHT TO SNAP THIS TOY ACROSS MY KNEE AND PUT AN END TO THIS NONSENSE.
DO YOU KNOW THE FIRST THING ABOUT SWORD FIGHTING?
STICK THEM WITH THE POINTY END?
THAT...IS THE ESSENCE OF IT, I SUPPOSE.
I WAS TRYING TO LEARN. I ASKED MYCAH TO PRACTICE WITH ME.
I **ASKED** HIM. I WAS MY FAULT THAT...

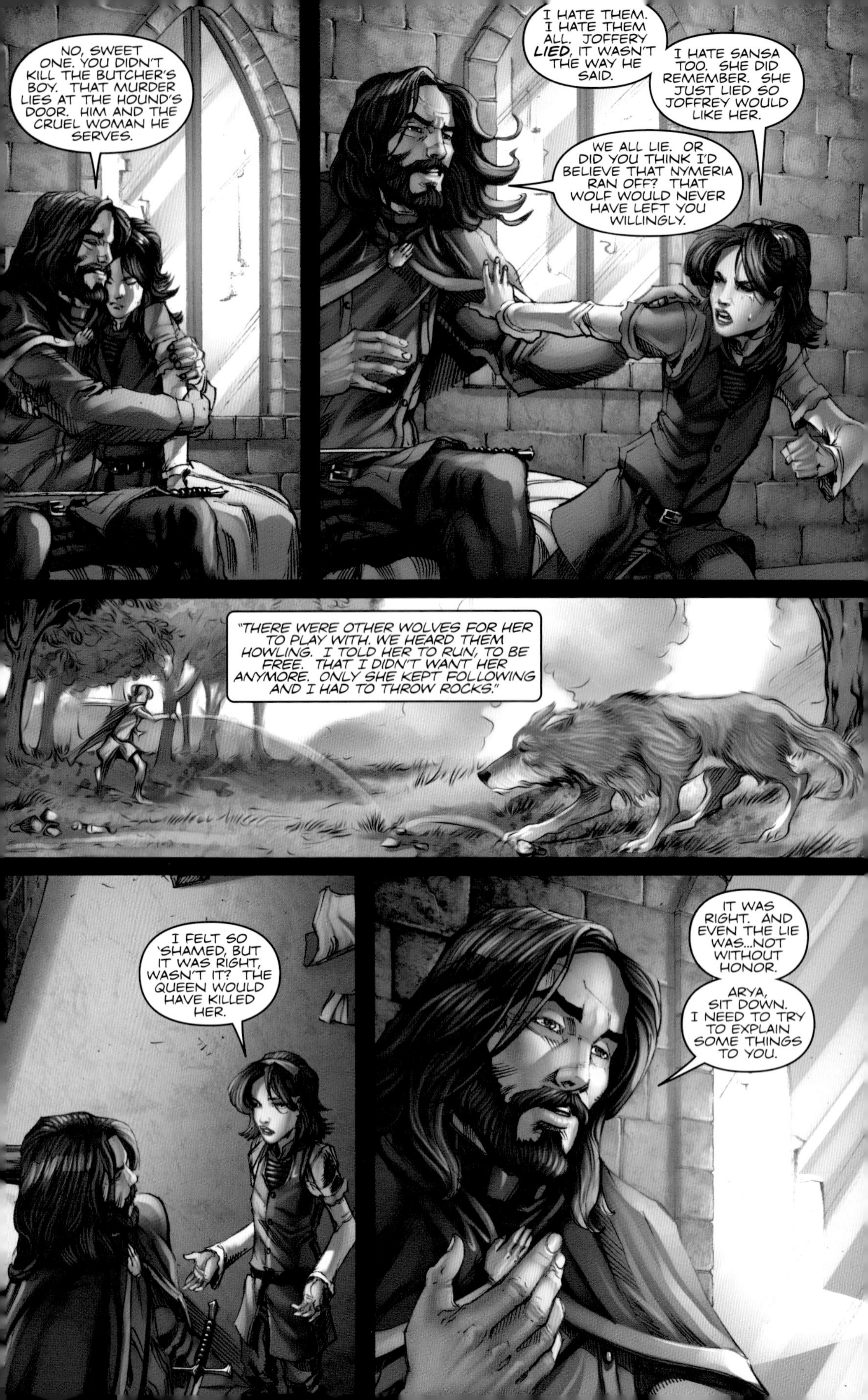
NO, SWEET ONE. YOU DIDN'T KILL THE BUTCHER'S BOY. THAT MURDER LIES AT THE HOUND'S DOOR. HIM AND THE CRUEL WOMAN HE SERVES.
I HATE THEM. I HATE THEM ALL. JOFFERY LIED, IT WASN'T THE WAY HE SAID.
I HATE SANSA TOO. SHE DID REMEMBER. SHE JUST LIED SO JOFFREY WOULD LIKE HER.
WE ALL LIE. OR DID YOU THINK I'D BELIEVE THAT NYMERIA RAN OFF? THAT WOLF WOULD NEVER HAVE LEFT YOU WILLINGLY.
"THERE WERE OTHER WOLVES FOR HER TO PLAY WITH. WE HEARD THEM HOWLING. I TOLD HER TO RUN, TO BE FREE. THAT I DIDN'T WANT HER ANYMORE. ONLY SHE KEPT FOLLOWING AND I HAD TO THROW ROCKS."
I FELT SO 'SHAMED, BUT IT WAS RIGHT, WASN'T IT? THE QUEEN WOULD HAVE KILLED HER.
IT WAS RIGHT. AND EVEN THE LIE WAS...NOT WITHOUT HONOR.
ARYA, SIT DOWN. I NEED TO TRY TO EXPLAIN SOME THINGS TO YOU.

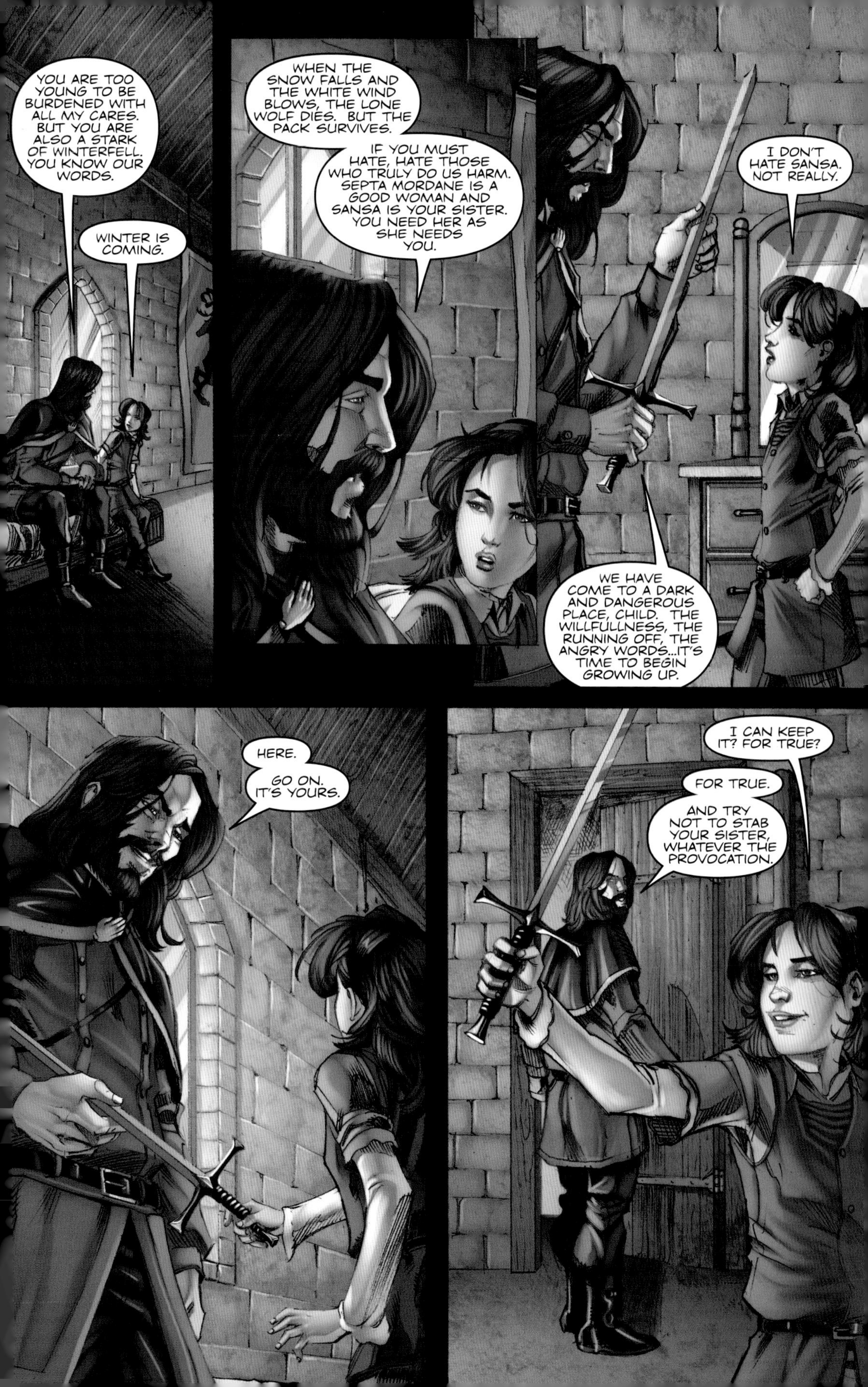
YOU ARE TOO YOUNG TO BE BURDENED WITH ALL MY CARES. BUT YOU ARE ALSO A STARK OF WINTERFELL. YOU KNOW OUR WORDS.
WINTER IS COMING.
WHEN THE SNOW FALLS AND THE WHITE WIND BLOWS, THE LONE WOLF DIES. BUT THE PACK SURVIVES.
IF YOU MUST HATE, HATE THOSE WHO TRULY DO US HARM. SEPTA MORDANE IS A GOOD WOMAN AND SANSA IS YOUR SISTER. YOU NEED HER AS SHE NEEDS YOU.
I DON'T HATE SANSA. NOT REALLY.
WE HAVE COME TO A DARK AND DANGEROUS PLACE, CHILD. THE WILLFULLNESS, THE RUNNING OFF, THE ANGRY WORDS...IT'S TIME TO BEGIN GROWING UP.
HERE.
GO ON. IT'S YOURS.
I CAN KEEP IT? FOR TRUE?
FOR TRUE.
AND TRY NOT TO STAB YOUR SISTER, WHATEVER THE PROVOCATION.

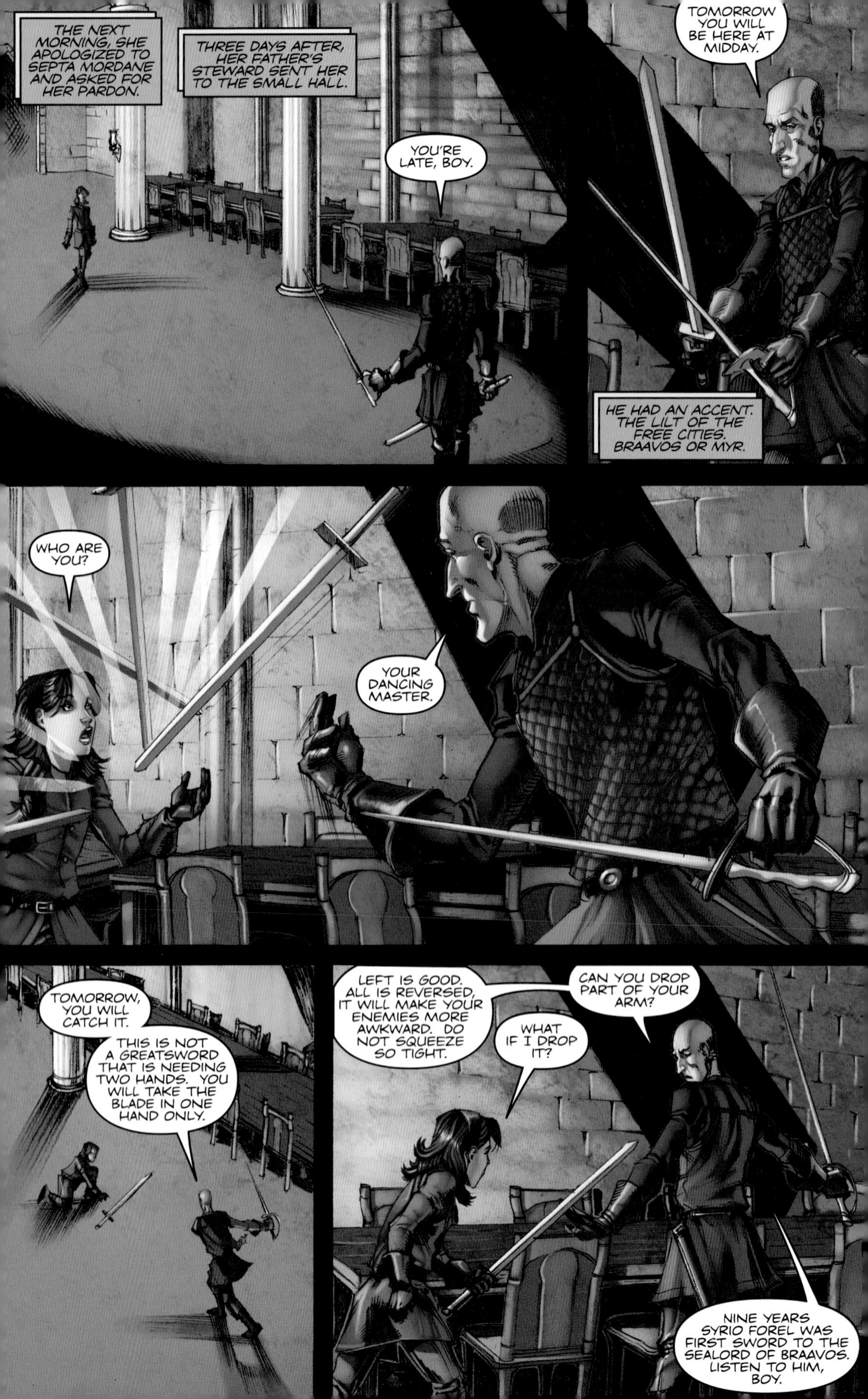
THE NEXT MORNING, SHE APOLOGIZED TO SEPTA MORDANE AND ASKED FOR HER PARDON.
THREE DAYS AFTER, HER FATHER'S STEWARD SENT HER TO THE SMALL HALL.
YOU'RE LATE, BOY.
TOMORROW YOU WILL BE HERE AT MIDDAY.
HE HAD AN ACCENT. THE LILT OF THE FREE CITIES. BRAAVOS OR MYR.
WHO ARE YOU?
YOUR DANCING MASTER.
TOMORROW, YOU WILL CATCH IT.
THIS IS NOT A GREATSWORD THAT IS NEEDING TWO HANDS. YOU WILL TAKE THE BLADE IN ONE HAND ONLY.
WHAT IF I DROP IT?
CAN YOU DROP PART OF YOUR ARM?
LEFT IS GOOD. ALL IS REVERSED, IT WILL MAKE YOUR ENEMIES MORE AWKWARD. DO NOT SQUEEZE SO TIGHT.
NINE YEARS SYRIO FOREL WAS FIRST SWORD TO THE SEALORD OF BRAAVOS. LISTEN TO HIM, BOY.

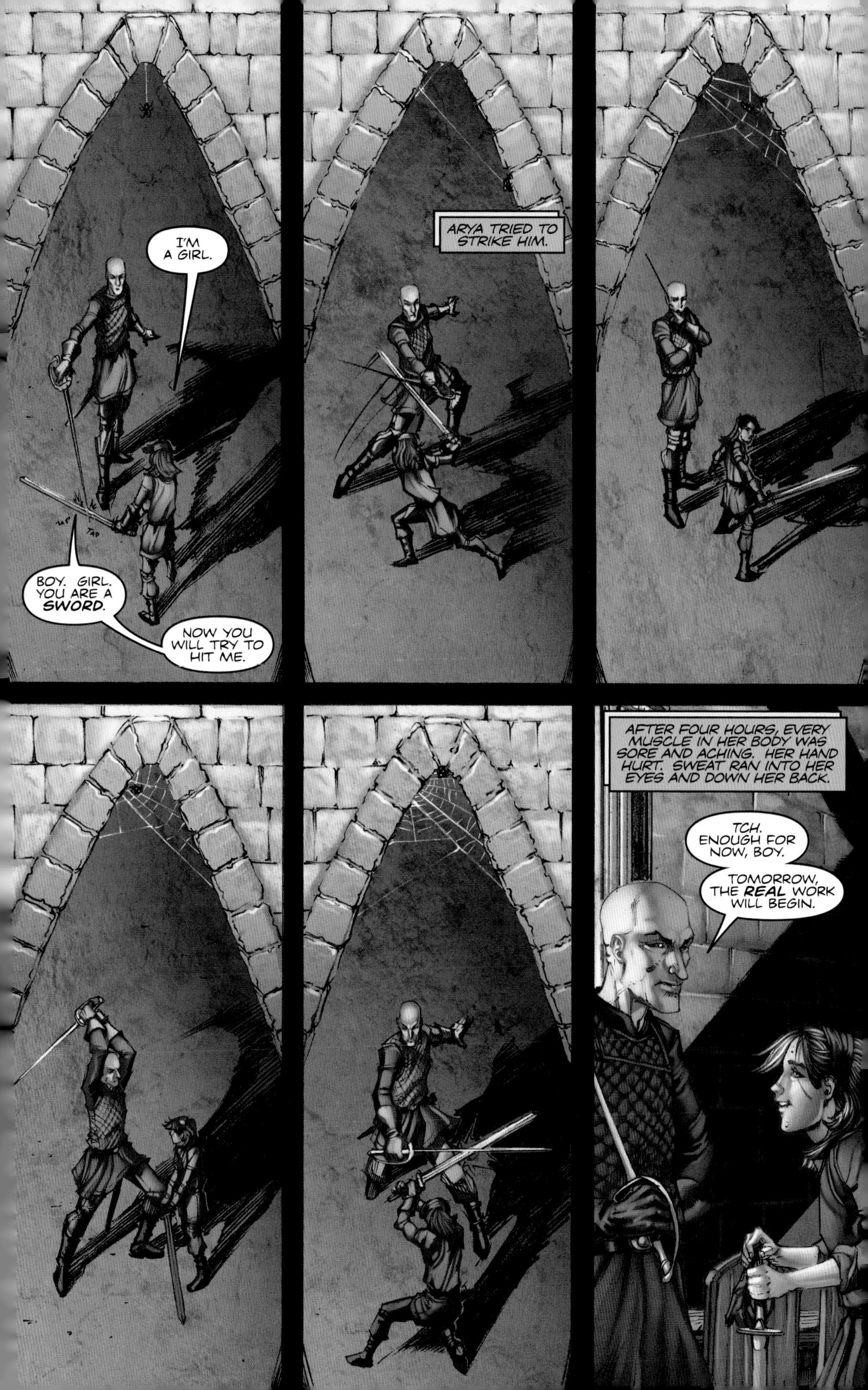
I'M A GIRL.
BOY. GIRL. YOU ARE A SWORD.
NOW YOU WILL TRY TO HIT ME.
ARYA TRIED TO STRIKE HIM.
AFTER FOUR HOURS, EVERY MUSCLE IN HER BODY WAS SORE AND ACHING. HER HAND HURT. SWEAT RAN INTO HER EYES AND DOWN HER BACK.
TCH. ENOUGH FOR NOW, BOY.
TOMORROW, THE REAL WORK WILL BEGIN.

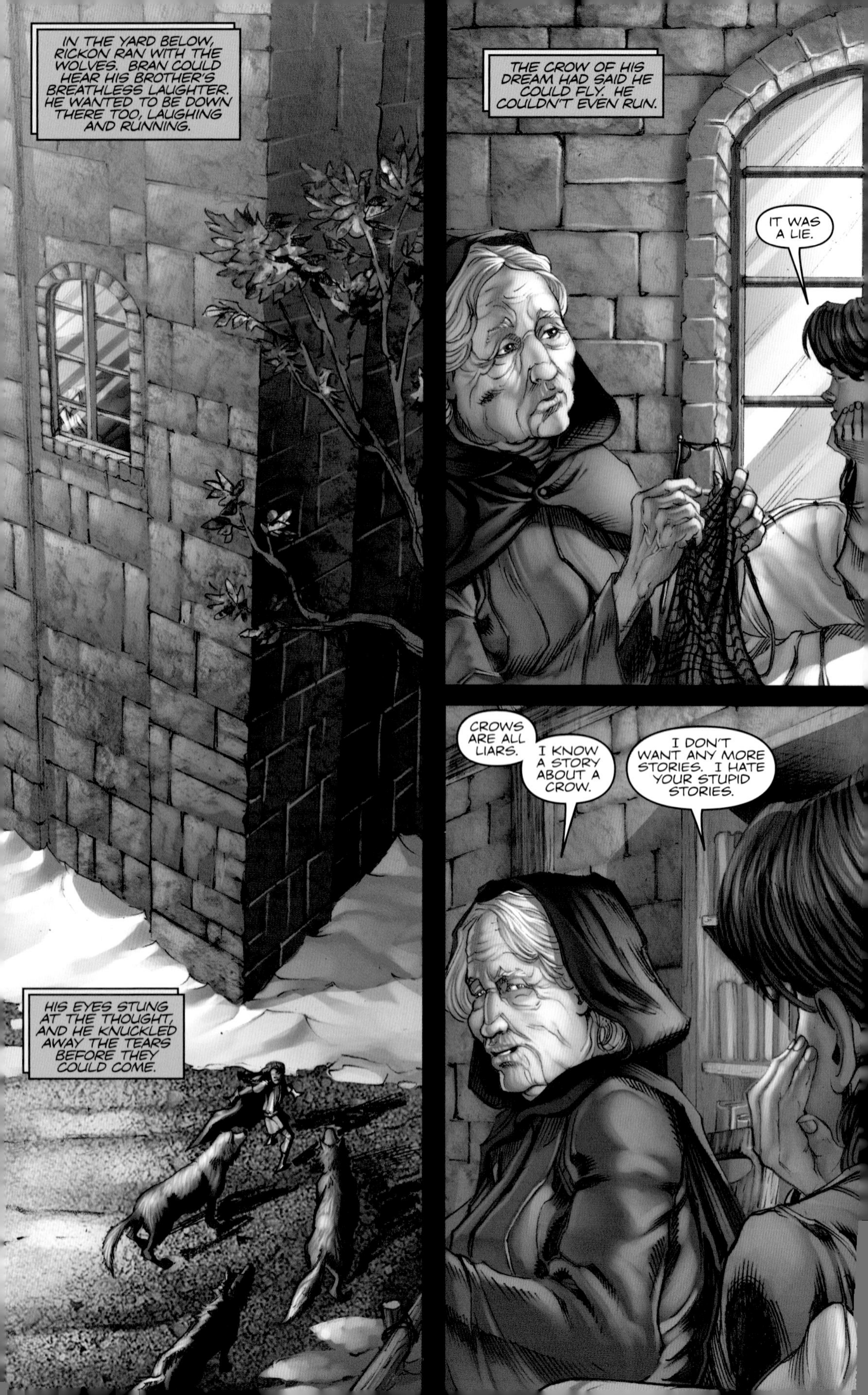
IN THE YARD BELOW, RICKON RAN WITH THE WOLVES. BRAN COULD HEAR HIS BROTHER'S BREATHLESS LAUGHTER. HE WANTED TO BE DOWN THERE TOO, LAUGHING AND RUNNING.
HIS EYES STUNG AT THE THOUGHT, AND HE KNUCKLED AWAY THE TEARS BEFORE THEY COULD COME.
THE CROW OF HIS DREAM HAD SAID HE COULD FLY. HE COULDN'T EVEN RUN.
IT WAS A LIE.
CROWS ARE ALL LIARS.
I KNOW A STORY ABOUT A CROW.
I DON'T WANT ANY MORE STORIES. I HATE YOUR STUPID STORIES.

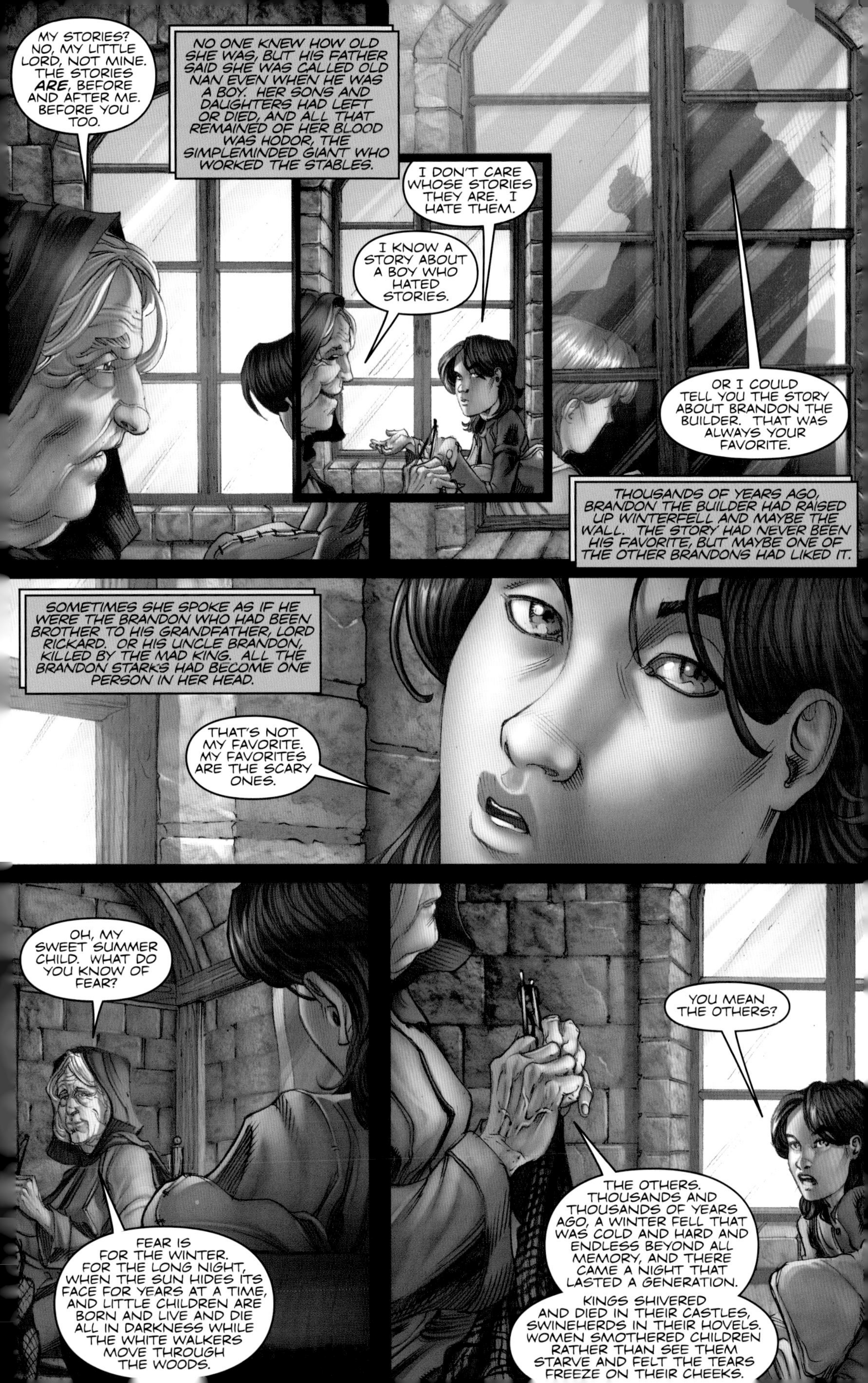
MY STORIES? NO, MY LITTLE LORD, NOT MINE. THE STORIES ARE, BEFORE AND AFTER ME. BEFORE YOU TOO.
NO ONE KNEW HOW OLD SHE WAS, BUT HIS FATHER SAID SHE WAS CALLED OLD NAN EVEN WHEN HE WAS A BOY. HER SONS AND DAUGHTERS HAD LEFT OR DIED, AND ALL THAT REMAINED OF HER BLOOD WAS HODOR, THE SIMPLEMINDED GIANT WHO WORKED THE STABLES.
I DON'T CARE WHOSE STORIES THEY ARE. I HATE THEM.
I KNOW A STORY ABOUT A BOY WHO HATED STORIES.
OR I COULD TELL YOU THE STORY ABOUT BRANDON THE BUILDER. THAT WAS ALWAYS YOUR FAVORITE.
THOUSANDS OF YEARS AGO, BRANDON THE BUILDER HAD RAISED UP WINTERFELL AND MAYBE THE WALL. THE STORY HAD NEVER BEEN HIS FAVORITE, BUT MAYBE ONE OF THE OTHER BRANDONS HAD LIKED IT.
SOMETIMES SHE SPOKE AS IF HE WERE THE BRANDON WHO HAD BEEN BROTHER TO HIS GRANDFATHER, LORD RICKARD. OR HIS UNCLE BRANDON, KILLED BY THE MAD KING. ALL THE BRANDON STARKS HAD BECOME ONE PERSON IN HER HEAD.
THAT'S NOT MY FAVORITE. MY FAVORITES ARE THE SCARY ONES.
OH, MY SWEET SUMMER CHILD. WHAT DO YOU KNOW OF FEAR?
FEAR IS FOR THE WINTER. FOR THE LONG NIGHT, WHEN THE SUN HIDES ITS FACE FOR YEARS AT A TIME, AND LITTLE CHILDREN ARE BORN AND LIVE AND DIE ALL IN DARKNESS WHILE THE WHITE WALKERS MOVE THROUGH THE WOODS.
YOU MEAN THE OTHERS?
THE OTHERS. THOUSANDS AND THOUSANDS OF YEARS AGO, A WINTER FELL THAT WAS COLD AND HARD AND ENDLESS BEYOND ALL MEMORY, AND THERE CAME A NIGHT THAT LASTED A GENERATION.
KINGS SHIVERED AND DIED IN THEIR CASTLES, SWINEHERDS IN THEIR HOVELS. WOMEN SMOTHERED CHILDREN RATHER THAN SEE THEM STARVE AND FELT THE TEARS FREEZE ON THEIR CHEEKS.

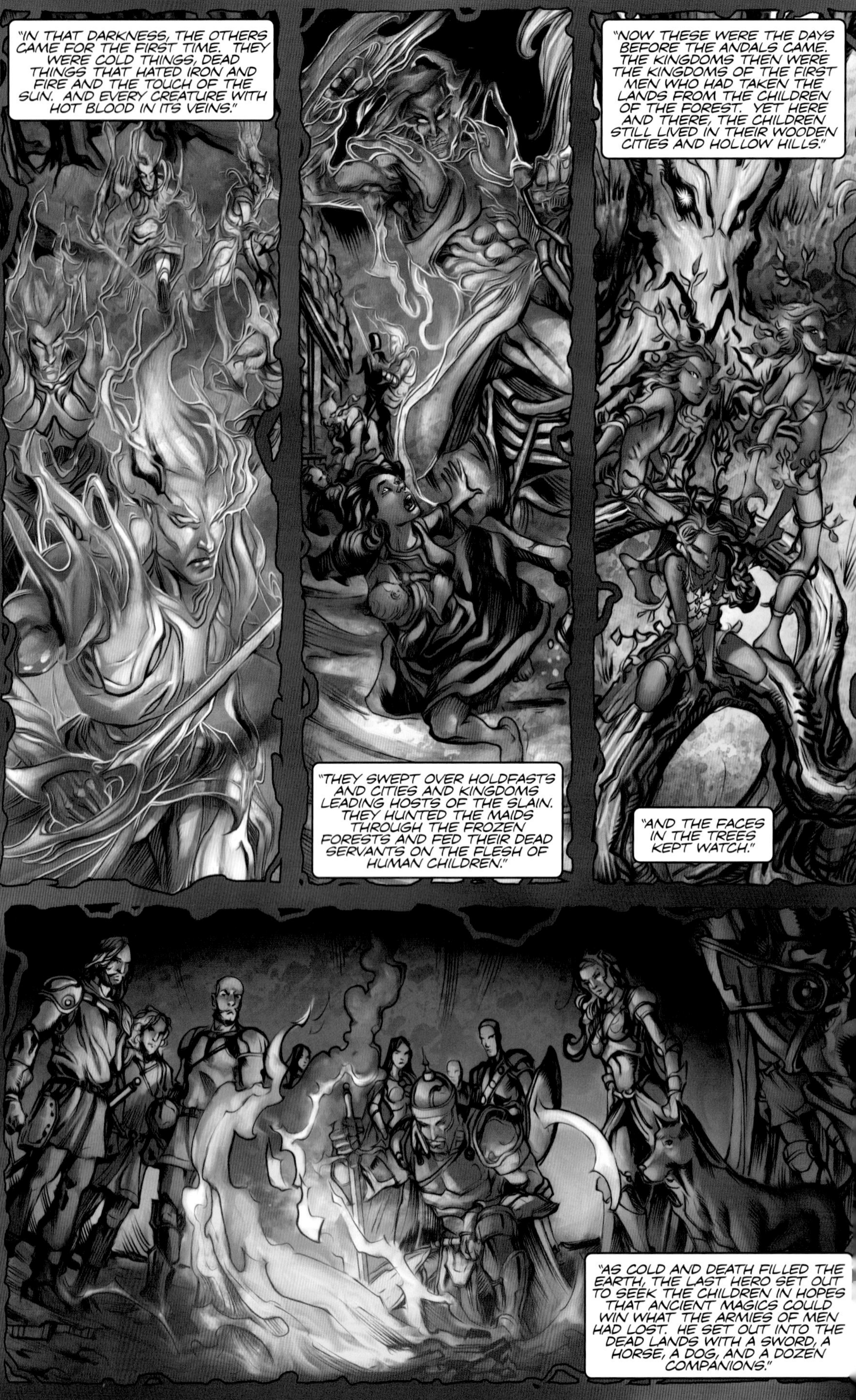
"IN THAT DARKNESS, THE OTHERS CAME FOR THE FIRST TIME. THEY WERE COLD THINGS, DEAD THINGS THAT HATED IRON AND FIRE AND THE TOUCH OF THE SUN. AND EVERY CREATURE WITH HOT BLOOD IN ITS VEINS."
"THEY SWEPT OVER HOLDFASTS AND CITIES AND KINGDOMS LEADING HOSTS OF THE SLAIN. THEY HUNTED THE MAIDS THROUGH THE FROZEN FORESTS AND FED THEIR DEAD SERVANTS ON THE FLESH OF HUMAN CHILDREN."
"NOW THESE WERE THE DAYS BEFORE THE ANDALS CAME. THE KINGDOMS THEN WERE THE KINGDOMS OF THE FIRST MEN WHO HAD TAKEN THE LANDS FROM THE CHILDREN OF THE FOREST. YET HERE AND THERE, THE CHILDREN STILL LIVED IN THEIR WOODEN CITIES AND HOLLOW HILLS."
"AND THE FACES IN THE TREES KEPT WATCH."
"AS COLD AND DEATH FILLED THE EARTH, THE LAST HERO SET OUT TO SEEK THE CHILDREN IN HOPES THAT ANCIENT MAGICS COULD WIN WHAT THE ARMIES OF MEN HAD LOST. HE SET OUT INTO THE DEAD LANDS WITH A SWORD, A HORSE, A DOG, AND A DOZEN COMPANIONS."

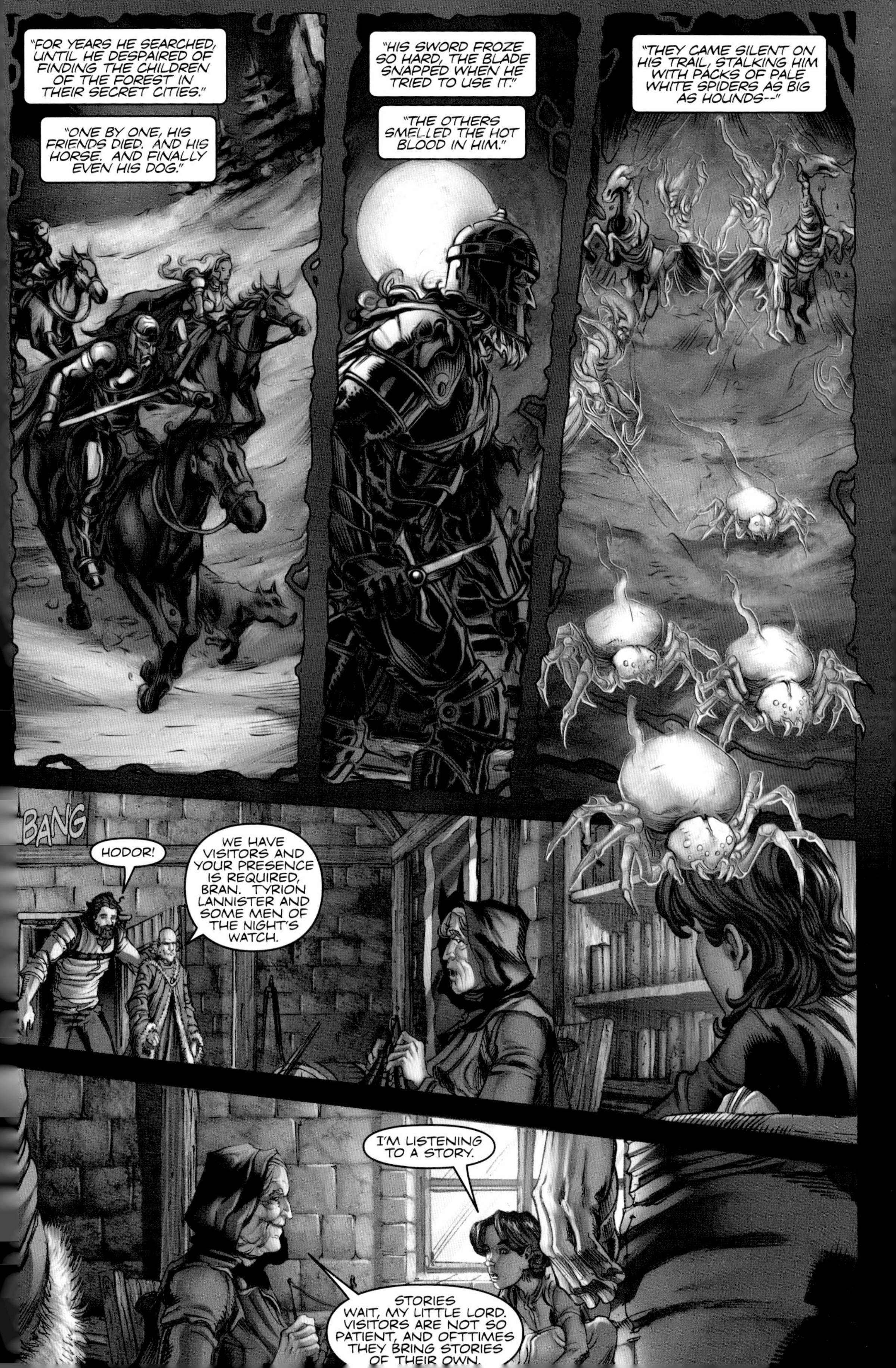
"FOR YEARS HE SEARCHED, UNTIL HE DESPAIRED OF FINDING THE CHILDREN OF THE FOREST IN THEIR SECRET CITIES."
"ONE BY ONE, HIS FRIENDS DIED. AND HIS HORSE. AND FINALLY EVEN HIS DOG."
"HIS SWORD FROZE SO HARD, THE BLADE SNAPPED WHEN HE TRIED TO USE IT."
"THE OTHERS SMELLED THE HOT BLOOD IN HIM."
"THEY CAME SILENT ON HIS TRAIL, STALKING HIM WITH PACKS OF PALE WHITE SPIDERS AS BIG AS HOUNDS--"
BANG
HODOR!
WE HAVE VISITORS AND YOUR PRESENCE IS REQUIRED, BRAN. TYRION LANNISTER AND SOME MEN OF THE NIGHT'S WATCH.
I'M LISTENING TO A STORY.
STORIES WAIT, MY LITTLE LORD. VISITORS ARE NOT SO PATIENT, AND OFTTIMES THEY BRING STORIES OF THEIR OWN.

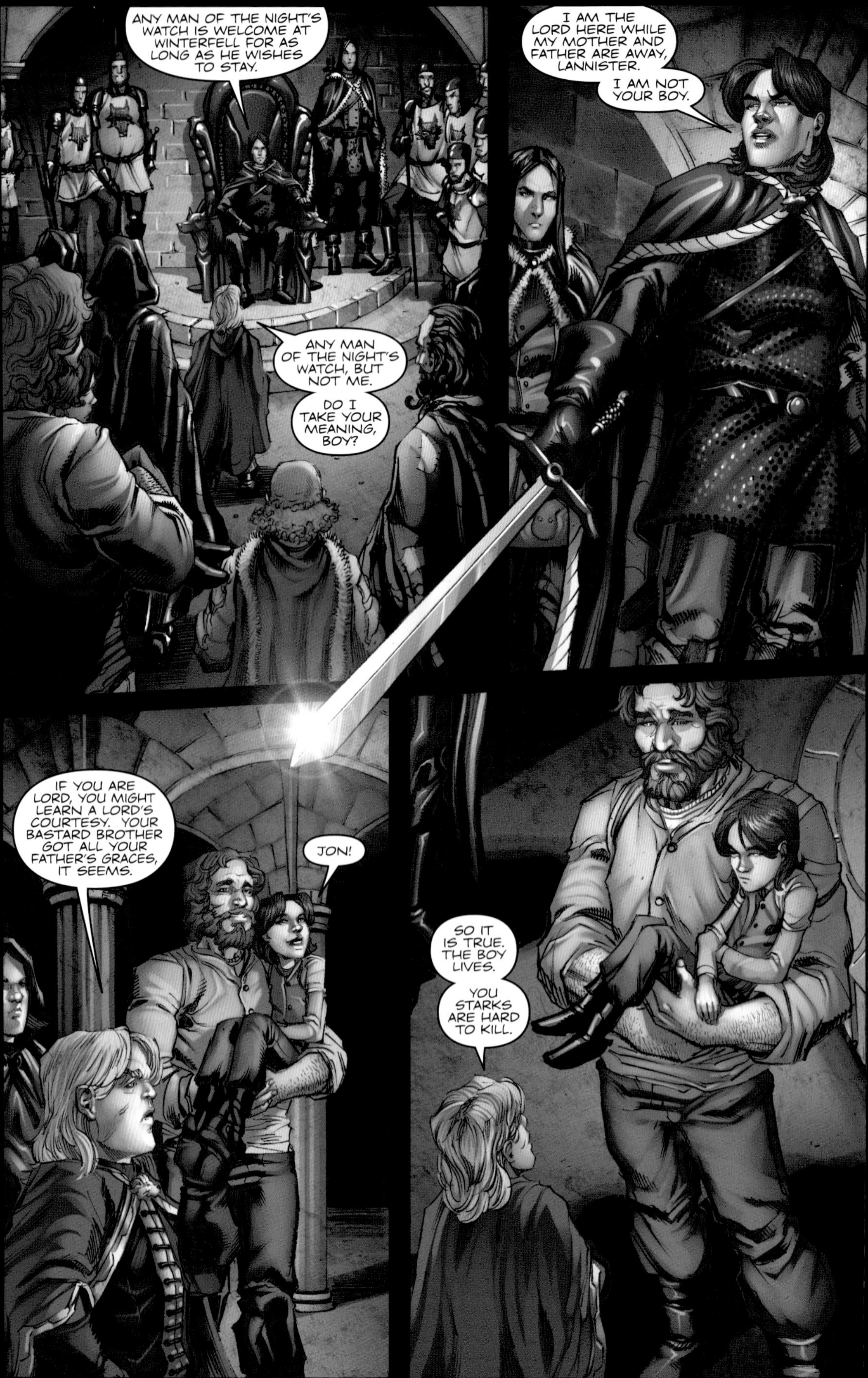
ANY MAN OF THE NIGHT'S WATCH IS WELCOME AT WINTERFELL FOR AS LONG AS HE WISHES TO STAY.
ANY MAN OF THE NIGHT'S WATCH, BUT NOT ME.
DO I TAKE YOUR MEANING, BOY?
I AM THE LORD HERE WHILE MY MOTHER AND FATHER ARE AWAY, LANNISTER.
I AM NOT YOUR BOY.
IF YOU ARE LORD, YOU MIGHT LEARN A LORD'S COURTESY. YOUR BASTARD BROTHER GOT ALL YOUR FATHER'S GRACES, IT SEEMS.
JON!
SO IT IS TRUE. THE BOY LIVES.
YOU STARKS ARE HARD TO KILL.

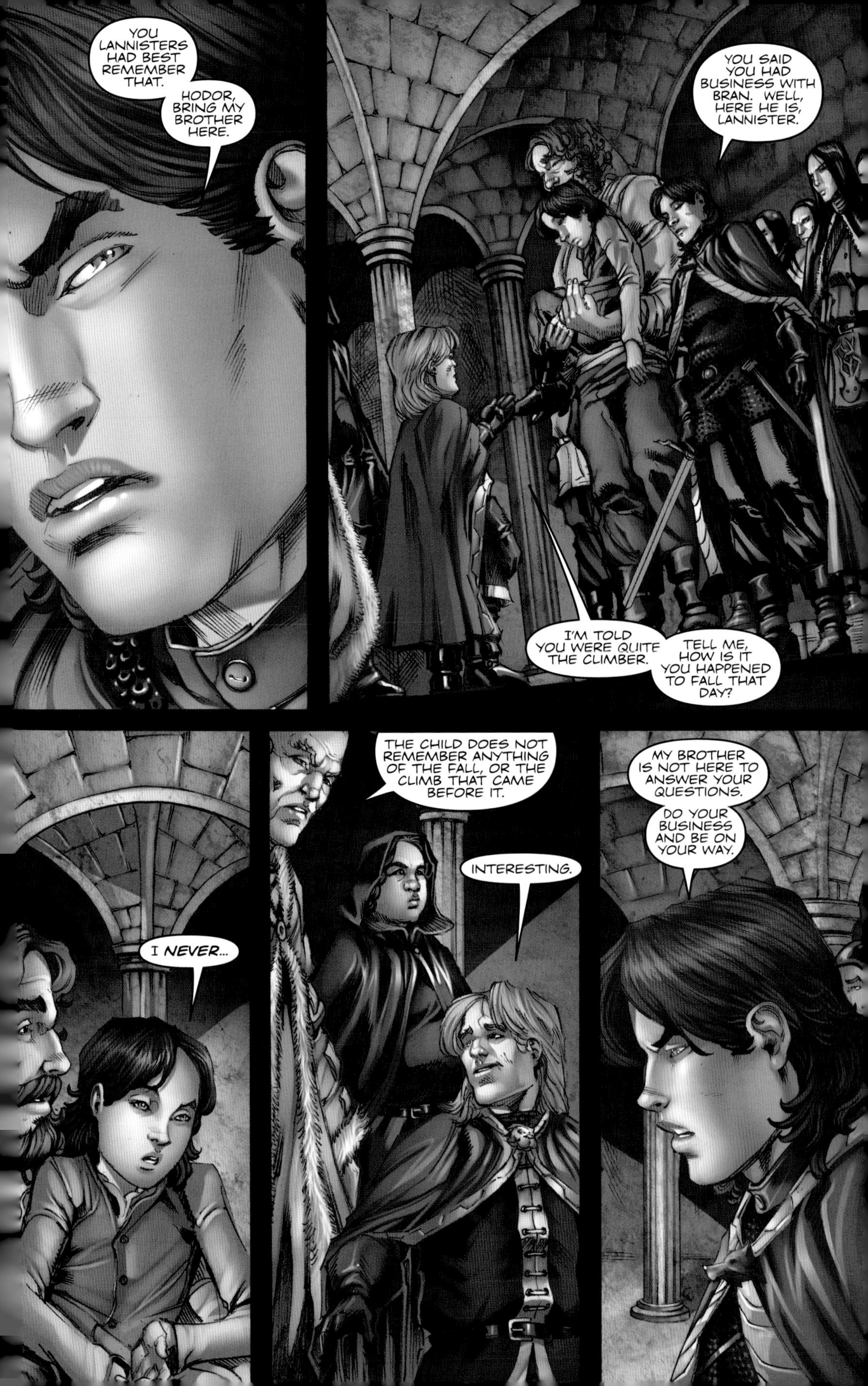
YOU LANNISTERS HAD BEST REMEMBER THAT.
HODOR, BRING MY BROTHER HERE.
YOU SAID YOU HAD BUSINESS WITH BRAN. WELL, HERE HE IS, LANNISTER.
I'M TOLD YOU WERE QUITE THE CLIMBER.
TELL ME, HOW IS IT YOU HAPPENED TO FALL THAT DAY?
I NEVER...
THE CHILD DOES NOT REMEMBER ANYTHING OF THE FALL, OR THE CLIMB THAT CAME BEFORE IT.
INTERESTING.
MY BROTHER IS NOT HERE TO ANSWER YOUR QUESTIONS.
DO YOUR BUSINESS AND BE ON YOUR WAY.

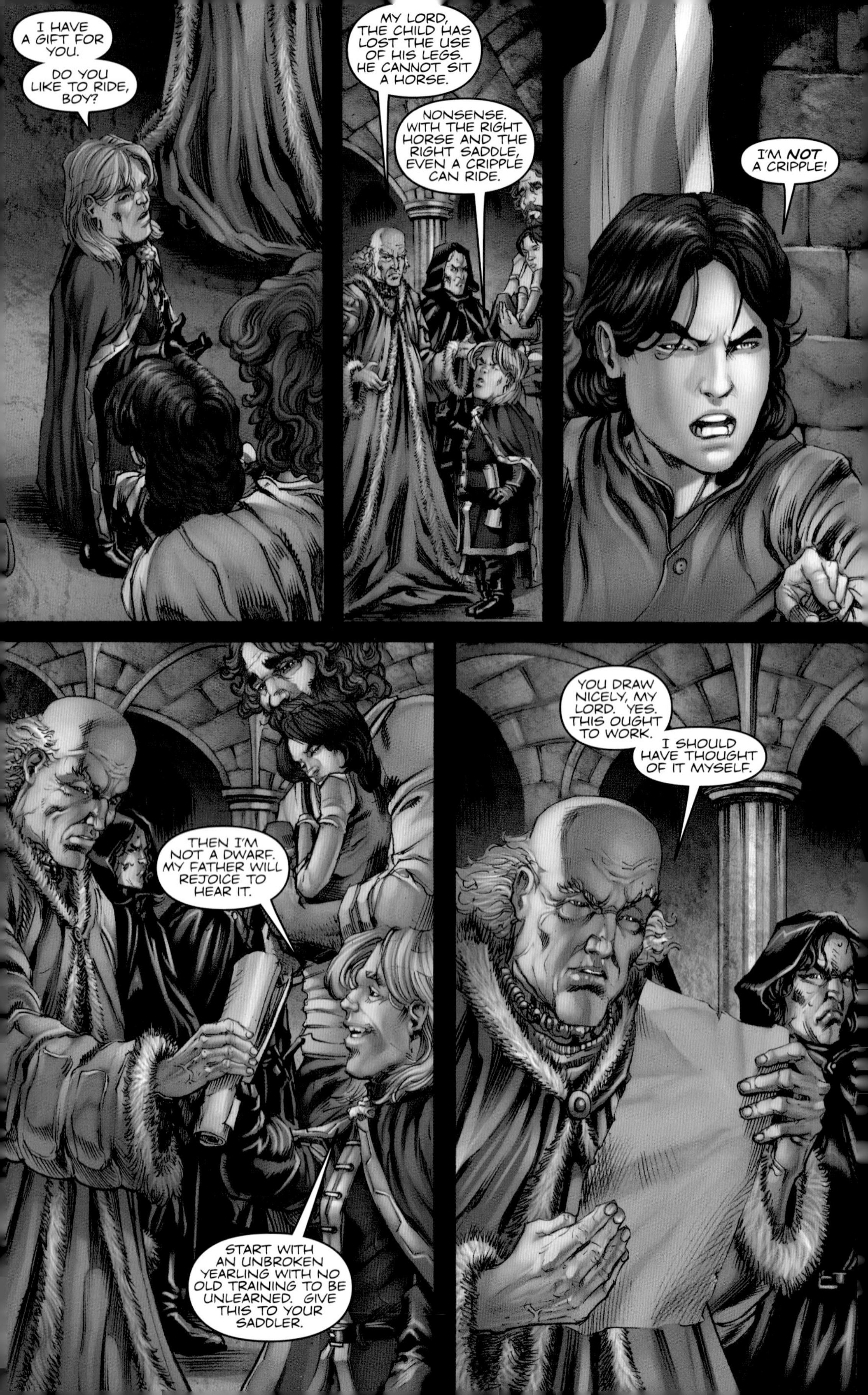
I HAVE A GIFT FOR YOU.
DO YOU LIKE TO RIDE, BOY?
MY LORD, THE CHILD HAS LOST THE USE OF HIS LEGS. HE CANNOT SIT A HORSE.
NONSENSE. WITH THE RIGHT HORSE AND THE RIGHT SADDLE, EVEN A CRIPPLE CAN RIDE.
I'M *NOT* A CRIPPLE!
THEN I'M NOT A DWARF. MY FATHER WILL REJOICE TO HEAR IT.
START WITH AN UNBROKEN YEARLING WITH NO OLD TRAINING TO BE UNLEARNED. GIVE THIS TO YOUR SADDLER.
YOU DRAW NICELY, MY LORD. YES. THIS OUGHT TO WORK.
I SHOULD HAVE THOUGHT OF IT MYSELF.

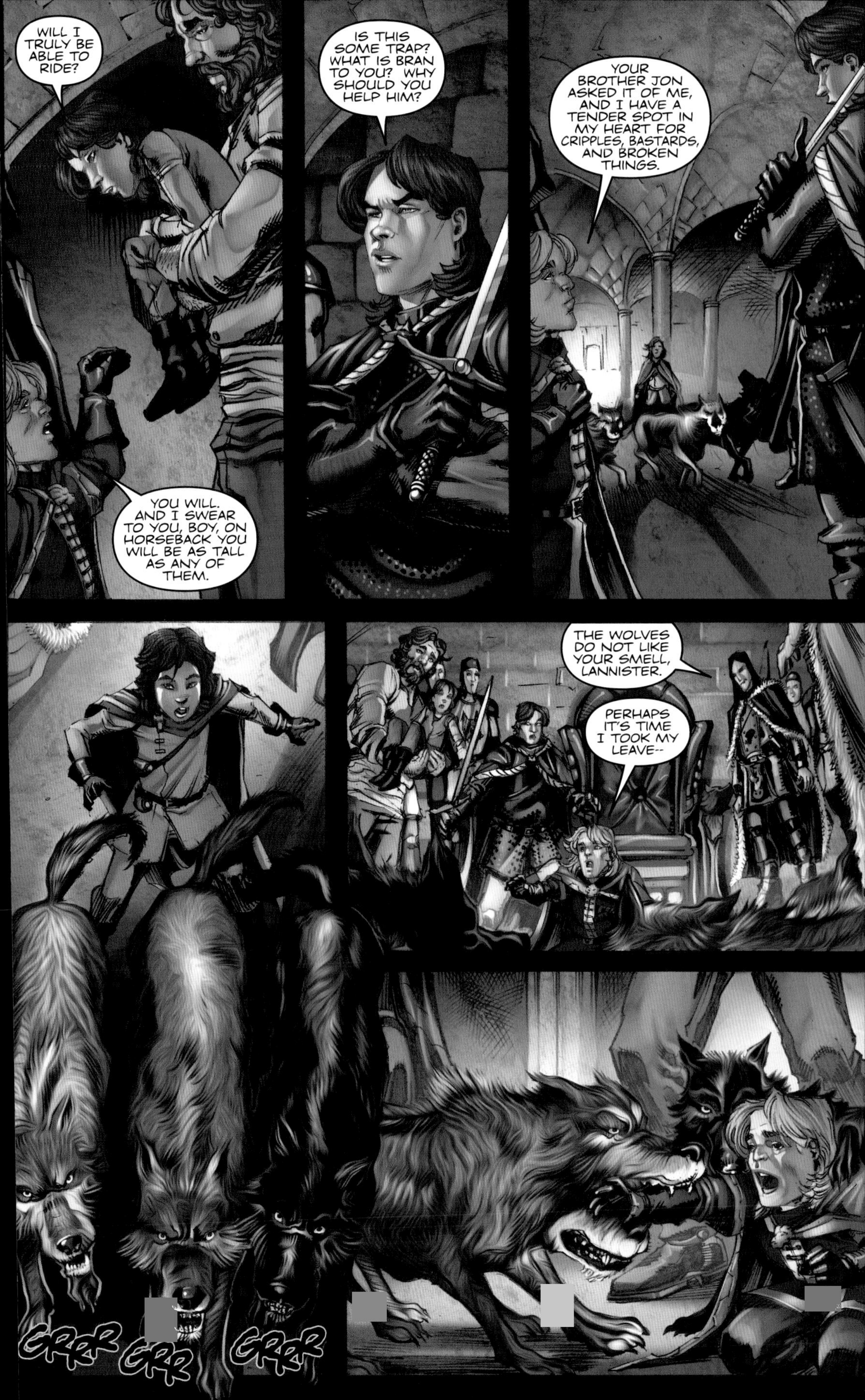
WILL I TRULY BE ABLE TO RIDE?
YOU WILL. AND I SWEAR TO YOU, BOY, ON HORSEBACK YOU WILL BE AS TALL AS ANY OF THEM.
IS THIS SOME TRAP? WHAT IS BRAN TO YOU? WHY SHOULD YOU HELP HIM?
YOUR BROTHER JON ASKED IT OF ME, AND I HAVE A TENDER SPOT IN MY HEART FOR CRIPPLES, BASTARDS, AND BROKEN THINGS.
THE WOLVES DO NOT LIKE YOUR SMELL, LANNISTER.
PERHAPS IT'S TIME I TOOK MY LEAVE--
GRRR
GRR
GRRR

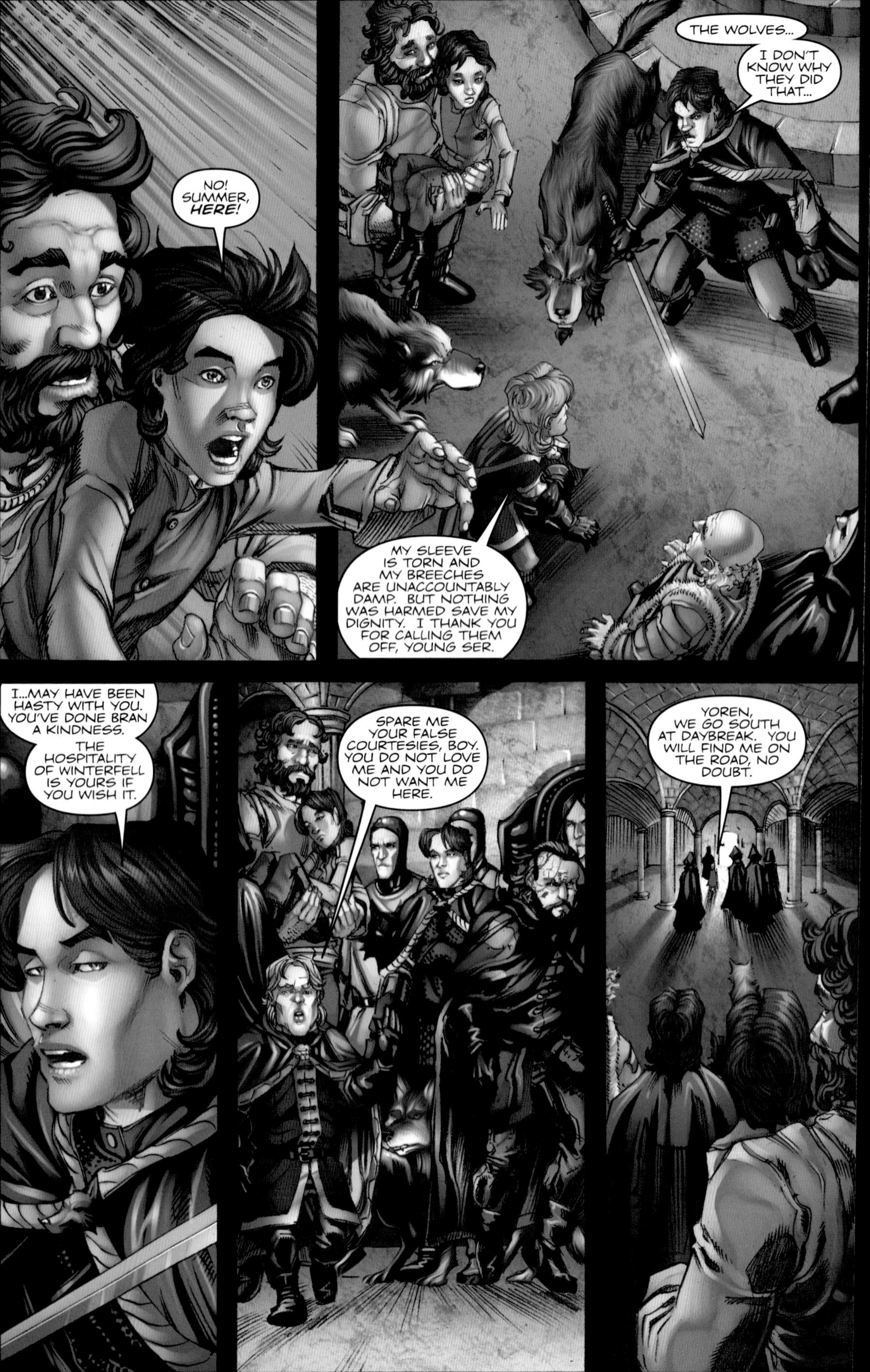
NO! SUMMER, HERE!
THE WOLVES... I DON'T KNOW WHY THEY DID THAT...
MY SLEEVE IS TORN AND MY BREECHES ARE UNACCOUNTABLY DAMP. BUT NOTHING WAS HARMED SAVE MY DIGNITY. I THANK YOU FOR CALLING THEM OFF, YOUNG SER.
I...MAY HAVE BEEN HASTY WITH YOU. YOU'VE DONE BRAN A KINDNESS.
THE HOSPITALITY OF WINTERFELL IS YOURS IF YOU WISH IT.
SPARE ME YOUR FALSE COURTESIES, BOY. YOU DO NOT LOVE ME AND YOU DO NOT WANT ME HERE.
YOREN, WE GO SOUTH AT DAYBREAK. YOU WILL FIND ME ON THE ROAD, NO DOUBT.

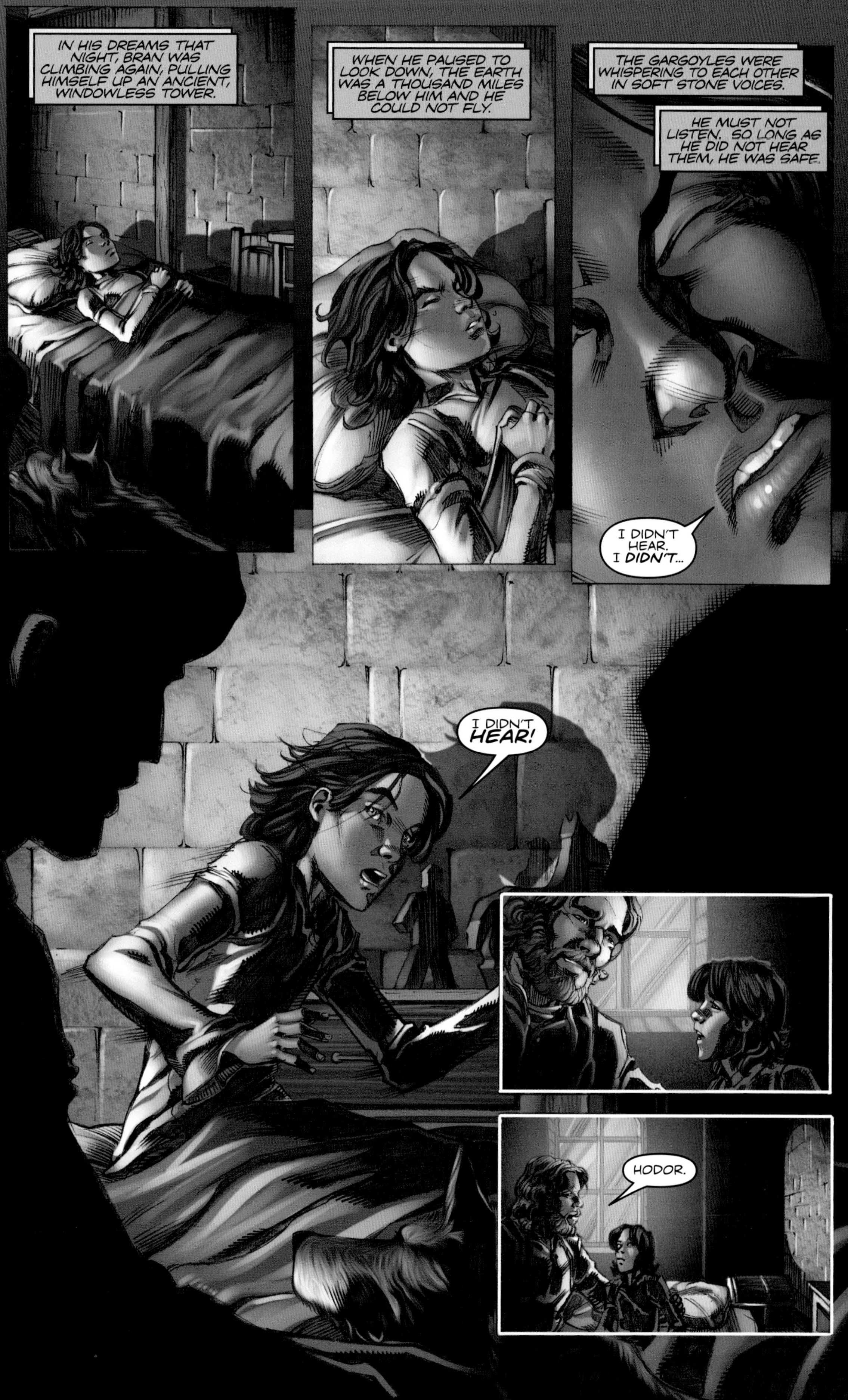
IN HIS DREAMS THAT NIGHT, BRAN WAS CLIMBING AGAIN, PULLING HIMSELF UP AN ANCIENT, WINDOWLESS TOWER.
WHEN HE PAUSED TO LOOK DOWN, THE EARTH WAS A THOUSAND MILES BELOW HIM AND HE COULD NOT FLY.
THE GARGOYLES WERE WHISPERING TO EACH OTHER IN SOFT STONE VOICES.
HE MUST NOT LISTEN. SO LONG AS HE DID NOT HEAR THEM, HE WAS SAFE.
I DIDN'T HEAR. I DIDN'T...
I DIDN'T HEAR!
HODOR.

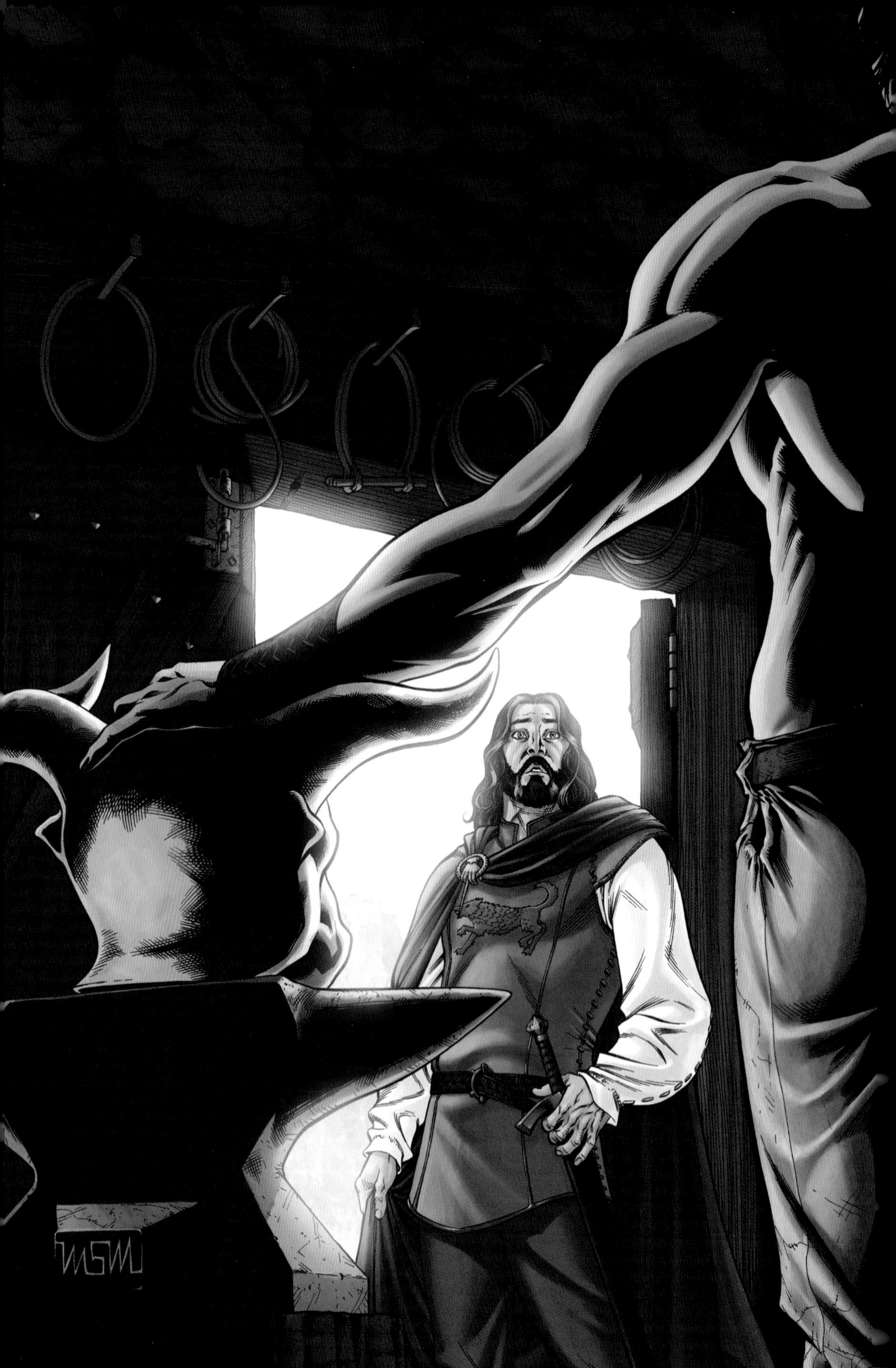

ISSUE #8

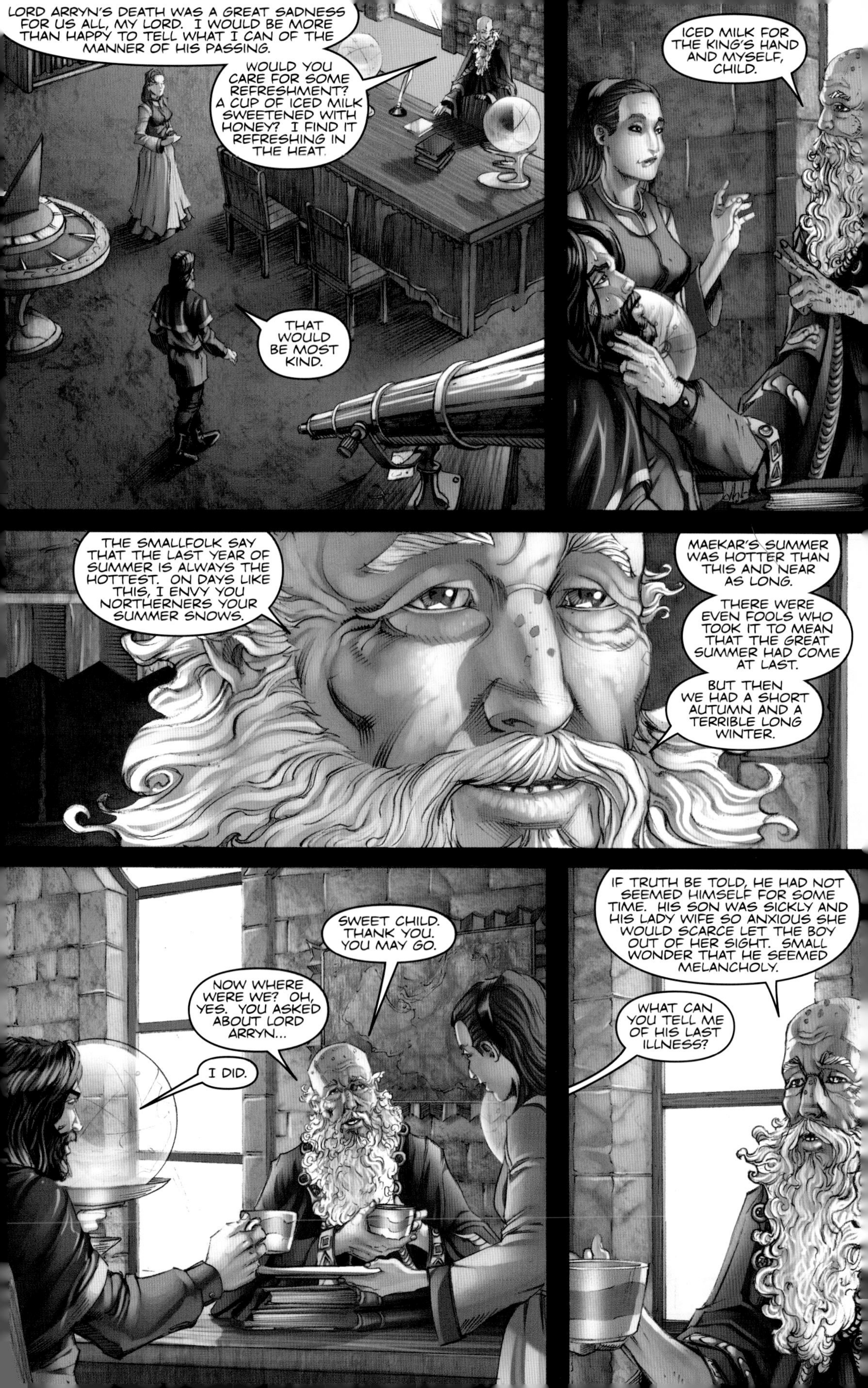
LORD ARRYN'S DEATH WAS A GREAT SADNESS FOR US ALL, MY LORD. I WOULD BE MORE THAN HAPPY TO TELL WHAT I CAN OF THE MANNER OF HIS PASSING.
WOULD YOU CARE FOR SOME REFRESHMENT? A CUP OF ICED MILK SWEETENED WITH HONEY? I FIND IT REFRESHING IN THE HEAT.
THAT WOULD BE MOST KIND.
ICED MILK FOR THE KING'S HAND AND MYSELF, CHILD.
THE SMALLFOLK SAY THAT THE LAST YEAR OF SUMMER IS ALWAYS THE HOTTEST. ON DAYS LIKE THIS, I ENVY YOU NORTHERNERS YOUR SUMMER SNOWS.
MAEKAR'S SUMMER WAS HOTTER THAN THIS AND NEAR AS LONG.
THERE WERE EVEN FOOLS WHO TOOK IT TO MEAN THAT THE GREAT SUMMER HAD COME AT LAST.
BUT THEN WE HAD A SHORT AUTUMN AND A TERRIBLE LONG WINTER.
SWEET CHILD. THANK YOU. YOU MAY GO.
NOW WHERE WERE WE? OH, YES. YOU ASKED ABOUT LORD ARRYN...
I DID.
IF TRUTH BE TOLD, HE HAD NOT SEEMED HIMSELF FOR SOME TIME. HIS SON WAS SICKLY AND HIS LADY WIFE SO ANXIOUS SHE WOULD SCARCE LET THE BOY OUT OF HER SIGHT. SMALL WONDER THAT HE SEEMED MELANCHOLY.
WHAT CAN YOU TELL ME OF HIS LAST ILLNESS?

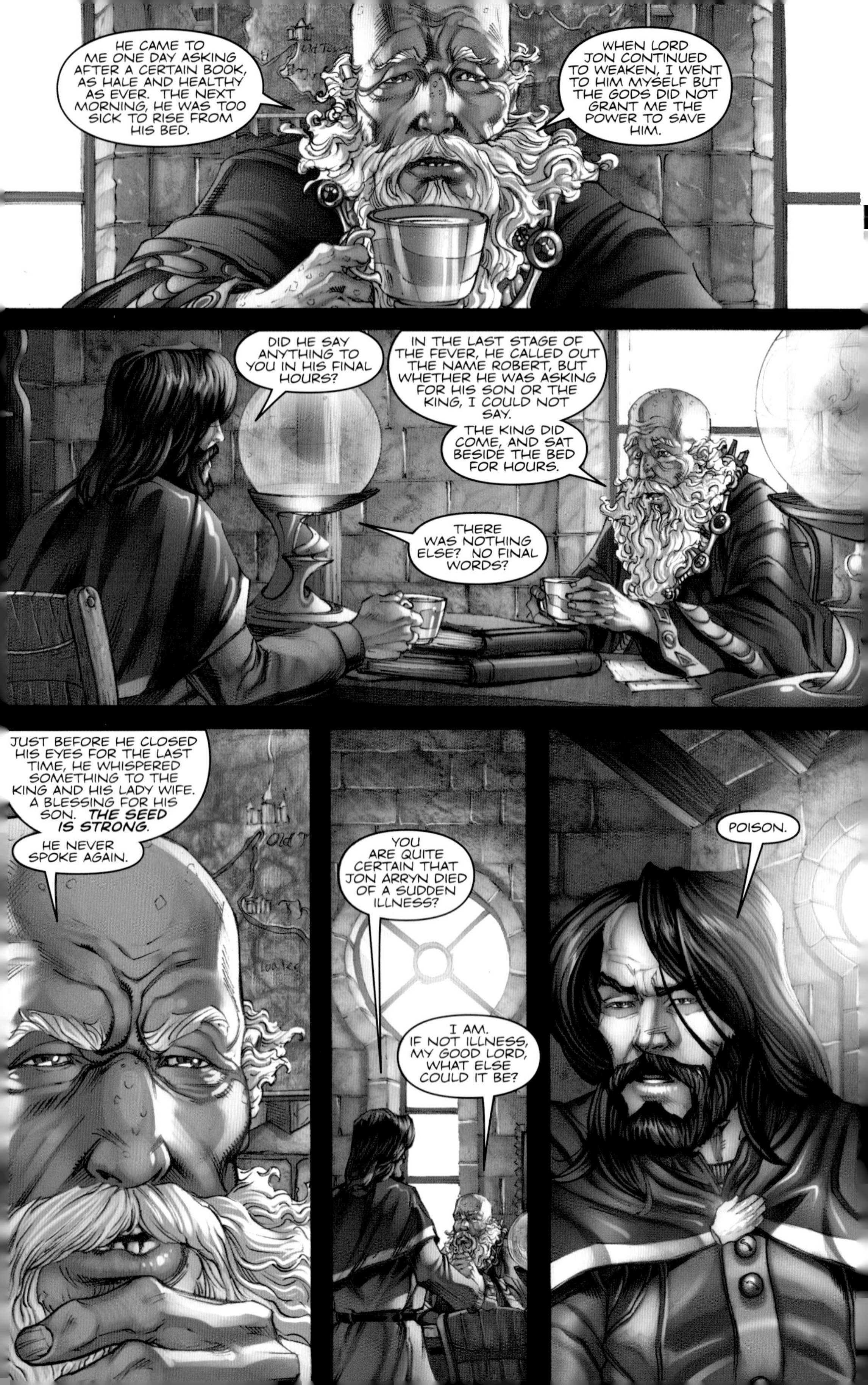
HE CAME TO ME ONE DAY ASKING AFTER A CERTAIN BOOK, AS HALE AND HEALTHY AS EVER. THE NEXT MORNING, HE WAS TOO SICK TO RISE FROM HIS BED.
WHEN LORD JON CONTINUED TO WEAKEN, I WENT TO HIM MYSELF BUT THE GODS DID NOT GRANT ME THE POWER TO SAVE HIM.
DID HE SAY ANYTHING TO YOU IN HIS FINAL HOURS?
IN THE LAST STAGE OF THE FEVER, HE CALLED OUT THE NAME ROBERT, BUT WHETHER HE WAS ASKING FOR HIS SON OR THE KING, I COULD NOT SAY.
THE KING DID COME, AND SAT BESIDE THE BED FOR HOURS.
THERE WAS NOTHING ELSE? NO FINAL WORDS?
JUST BEFORE HE CLOSED HIS EYES FOR THE LAST TIME, HE WHISPERED SOMETHING TO THE KING AND HIS LADY WIFE. A BLESSING FOR HIS SON. ***THE SEED IS STRONG***.
HE NEVER SPOKE AGAIN.
YOU ARE QUITE CERTAIN THAT JON ARRYN DIED OF A SUDDEN ILLNESS?
I AM. IF NOT ILLNESS, MY GOOD LORD, WHAT ELSE COULD IT BE?
POISON.

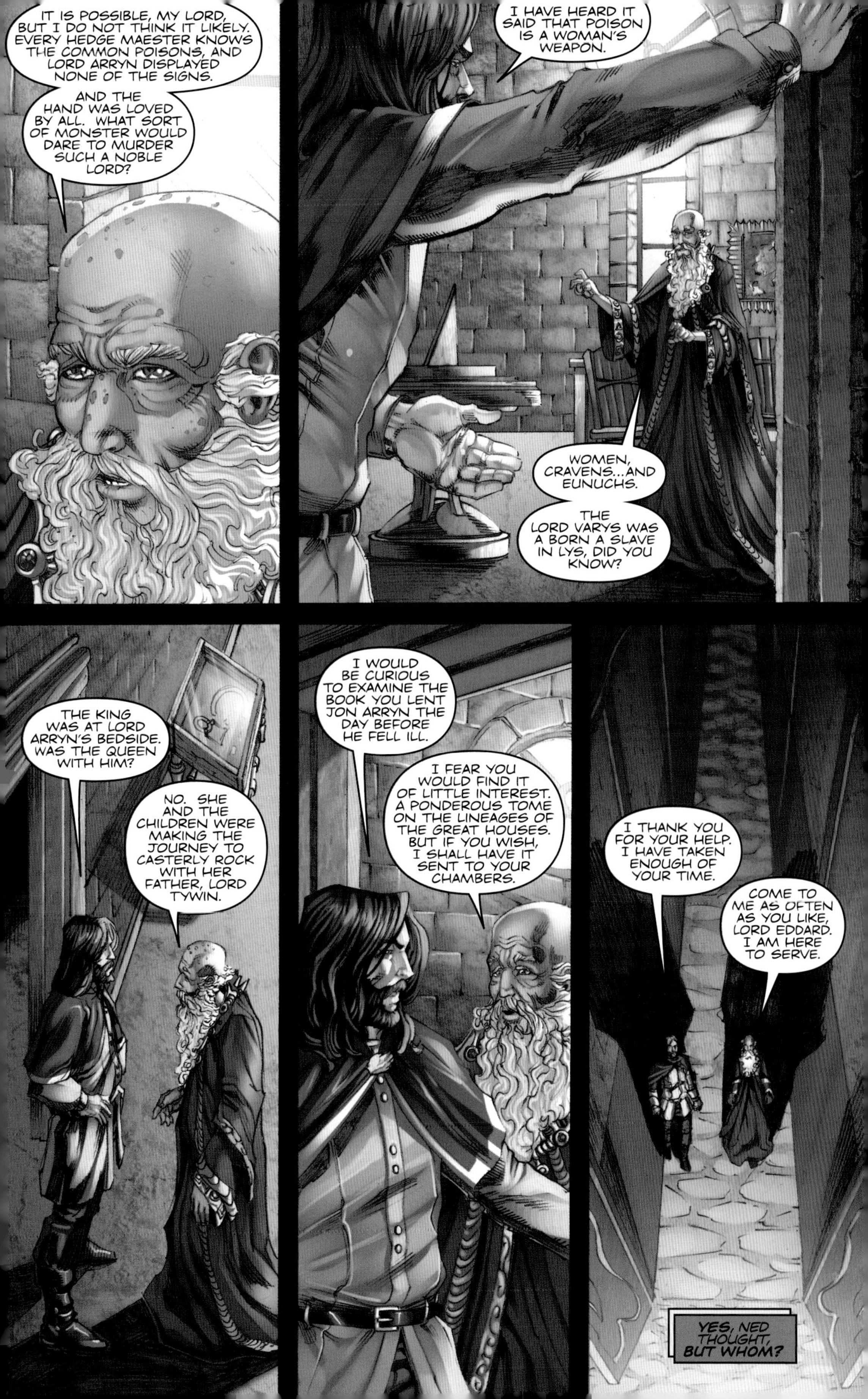
IT IS POSSIBLE, MY LORD, BUT I DO NOT THINK IT LIKELY. EVERY HEDGE MAESTER KNOWS THE COMMON POISONS, AND LORD ARRYN DISPLAYED NONE OF THE SIGNS.
AND THE HAND WAS LOVED BY ALL. WHAT SORT OF MONSTER WOULD DARE TO MURDER SUCH A NOBLE LORD?
I HAVE HEARD IT SAID THAT POISON IS A WOMAN'S WEAPON.
WOMEN, CRAVENS...AND EUNUCHS.
THE LORD VARYS WAS A BORN A SLAVE IN LYS, DID YOU KNOW?
THE KING WAS AT LORD ARRYN'S BEDSIDE. WAS THE QUEEN WITH HIM?
NO. SHE AND THE CHILDREN WERE MAKING THE JOURNEY TO CASTERLY ROCK WITH HER FATHER, LORD TYWIN.
I WOULD BE CURIOUS TO EXAMINE THE BOOK YOU LENT JON ARRYN THE DAY BEFORE HE FELL ILL.
I FEAR YOU WOULD FIND IT OF LITTLE INTEREST. A PONDEROUS TOME ON THE LINEAGES OF THE GREAT HOUSES. BUT IF YOU WISH, I SHALL HAVE IT SENT TO YOUR CHAMBERS.
I THANK YOU FOR YOUR HELP. I HAVE TAKEN ENOUGH OF YOUR TIME.
COME TO ME AS OFTEN AS YOU LIKE, LORD EDDARD. I AM HERE TO SERVE.
YES, NED THOUGHT, BUT WHOM?

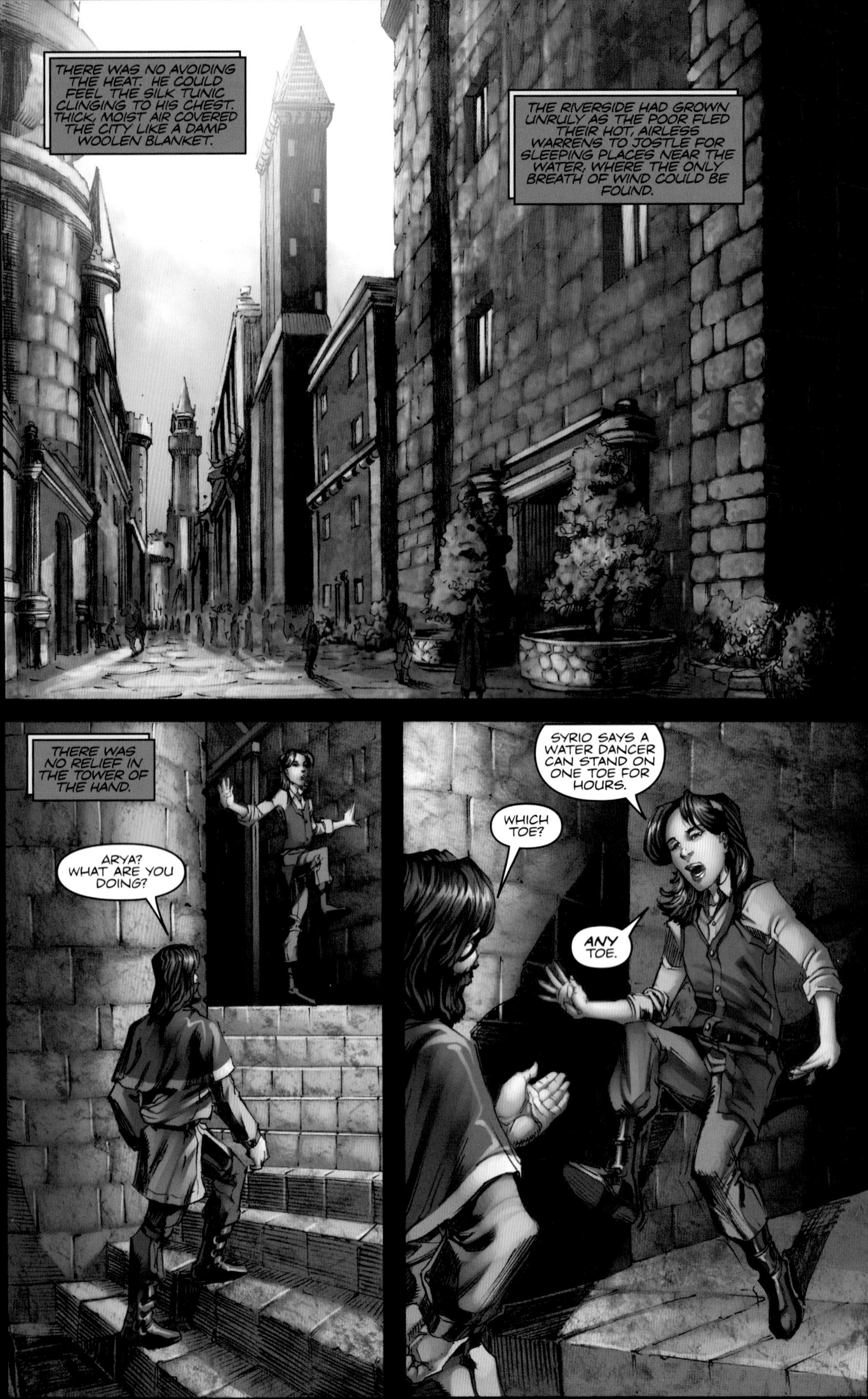
THERE WAS NO AVOIDING THE HEAT. HE COULD FEEL THE SILK TUNIC CLINGING TO HIS CHEST. THICK, MOIST AIR COVERED THE CITY LIKE A DAMP WOOLEN BLANKET.
THE RIVERSIDE HAD GROWN UNRULY AS THE POOR FLED THEIR HOT, AIRLESS WARRENS TO JOSTLE FOR SLEEPING PLACES NEAR THE WATER, WHERE THE ONLY BREATH OF WIND COULD BE FOUND.
THERE WAS NO RELIEF IN THE TOWER OF THE HAND.
ARYA? WHAT ARE YOU DOING?
SYRIO SAYS A WATER DANCER CAN STAND ON ONE TOE FOR HOURS.
WHICH TOE?
ANY TOE.

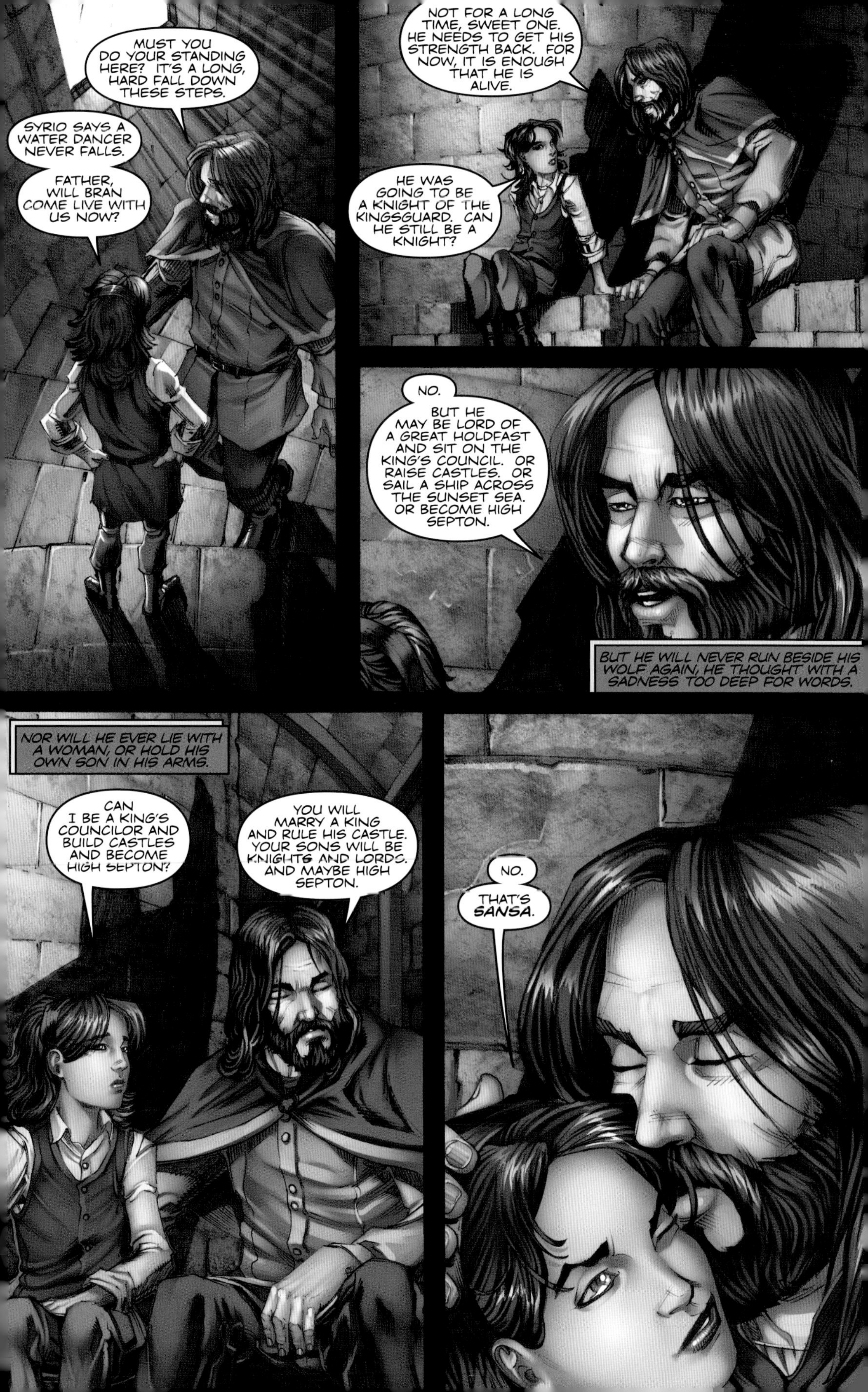
MUST YOU DO YOUR STANDING HERE? IT'S A LONG, HARD FALL DOWN THESE STEPS.
SYRIO SAYS A WATER DANCER NEVER FALLS.
FATHER, WILL BRAN COME LIVE WITH US NOW?
NOT FOR A LONG TIME, SWEET ONE. HE NEEDS TO GET HIS STRENGTH BACK. FOR NOW, IT IS ENOUGH THAT HE IS ALIVE.
HE WAS GOING TO BE A KNIGHT OF THE KINGSGUARD. CAN HE STILL BE A KNIGHT?
NO.
BUT HE MAY BE LORD OF A GREAT HOLDFAST AND SIT ON THE KING'S COUNCIL. OR RAISE CASTLES. OR SAIL A SHIP ACROSS THE SUNSET SEA. OR BECOME HIGH SEPTON.
BUT HE WILL NEVER RUN BESIDE HIS WOLF AGAIN, HE THOUGHT WITH A SADNESS TOO DEEP FOR WORDS.
NOR WILL HE EVER LIE WITH A WOMAN, OR HOLD HIS OWN SON IN HIS ARMS.
CAN I BE A KING'S COUNCILOR AND BUILD CASTLES AND BECOME HIGH SEPTON?
YOU WILL MARRY A KING AND RULE HIS CASTLE. YOUR SONS WILL BE KNIGHTS AND LORDS. AND MAYBE HIGH SEPTON.
NO.
THAT'S SANSA.

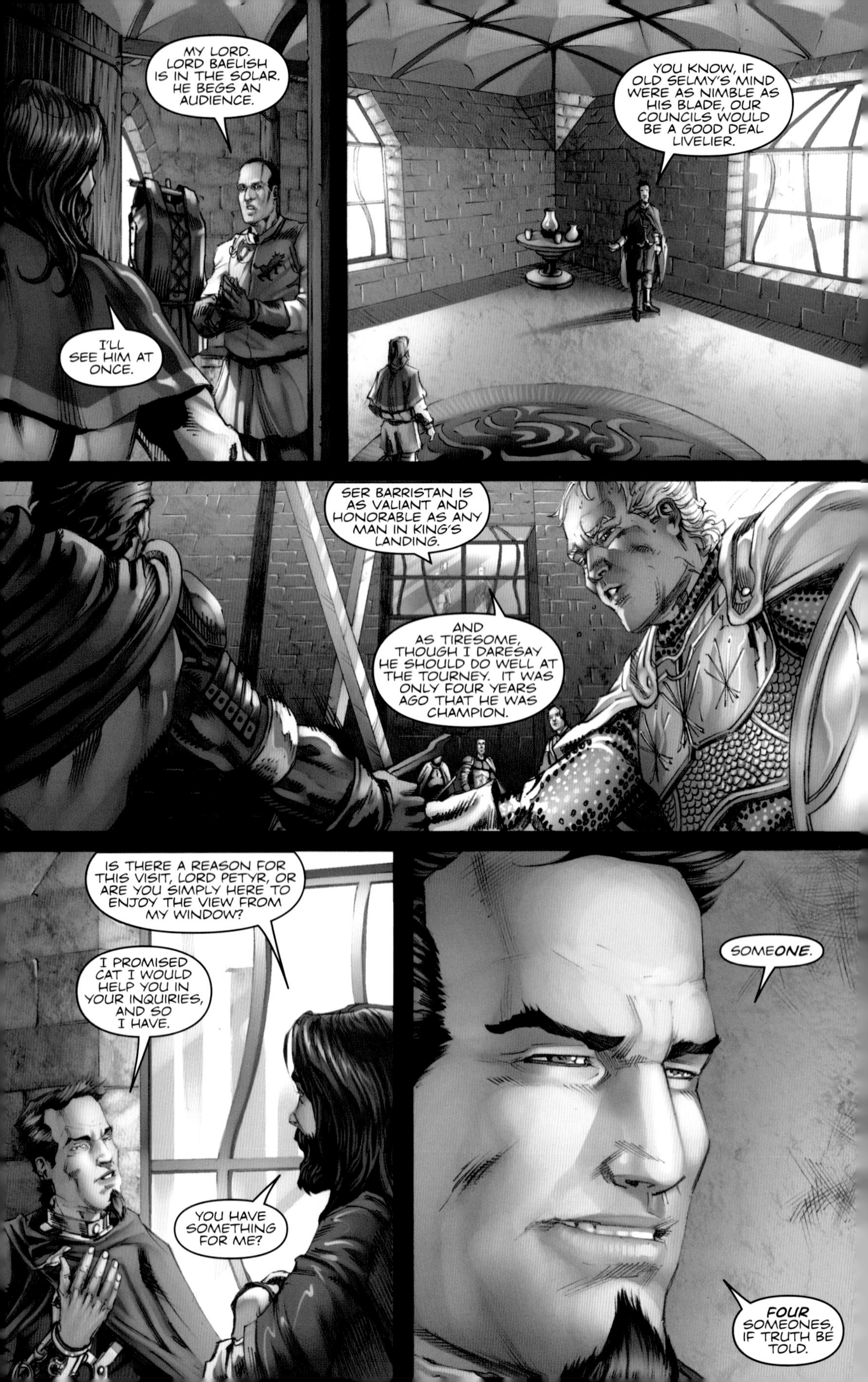
MY LORD. LORD BAELISH IS IN THE SOLAR. HE BEGS AN AUDIENCE.
I'LL SEE HIM AT ONCE.
YOU KNOW, IF OLD SELMY'S MIND WERE AS NIMBLE AS HIS BLADE, OUR COUNCILS WOULD BE A GOOD DEAL LIVELIER.
SER BARRISTAN IS AS VALIANT AND HONORABLE AS ANY MAN IN KING'S LANDING.
AND AS TIRESOME, THOUGH I DARESAY HE SHOULD DO WELL AT THE TOURNEY. IT WAS ONLY FOUR YEARS AGO THAT HE WAS CHAMPION.
IS THERE A REASON FOR THIS VISIT, LORD PETYR, OR ARE YOU SIMPLY HERE TO ENJOY THE VIEW FROM MY WINDOW?
I PROMISED CAT I WOULD HELP YOU IN YOUR INQUIRIES, AND SO I HAVE.
YOU HAVE SOMETHING FOR ME?
SOME*ONE*.
FOUR SOMEONES, IF TRUTH BE TOLD.

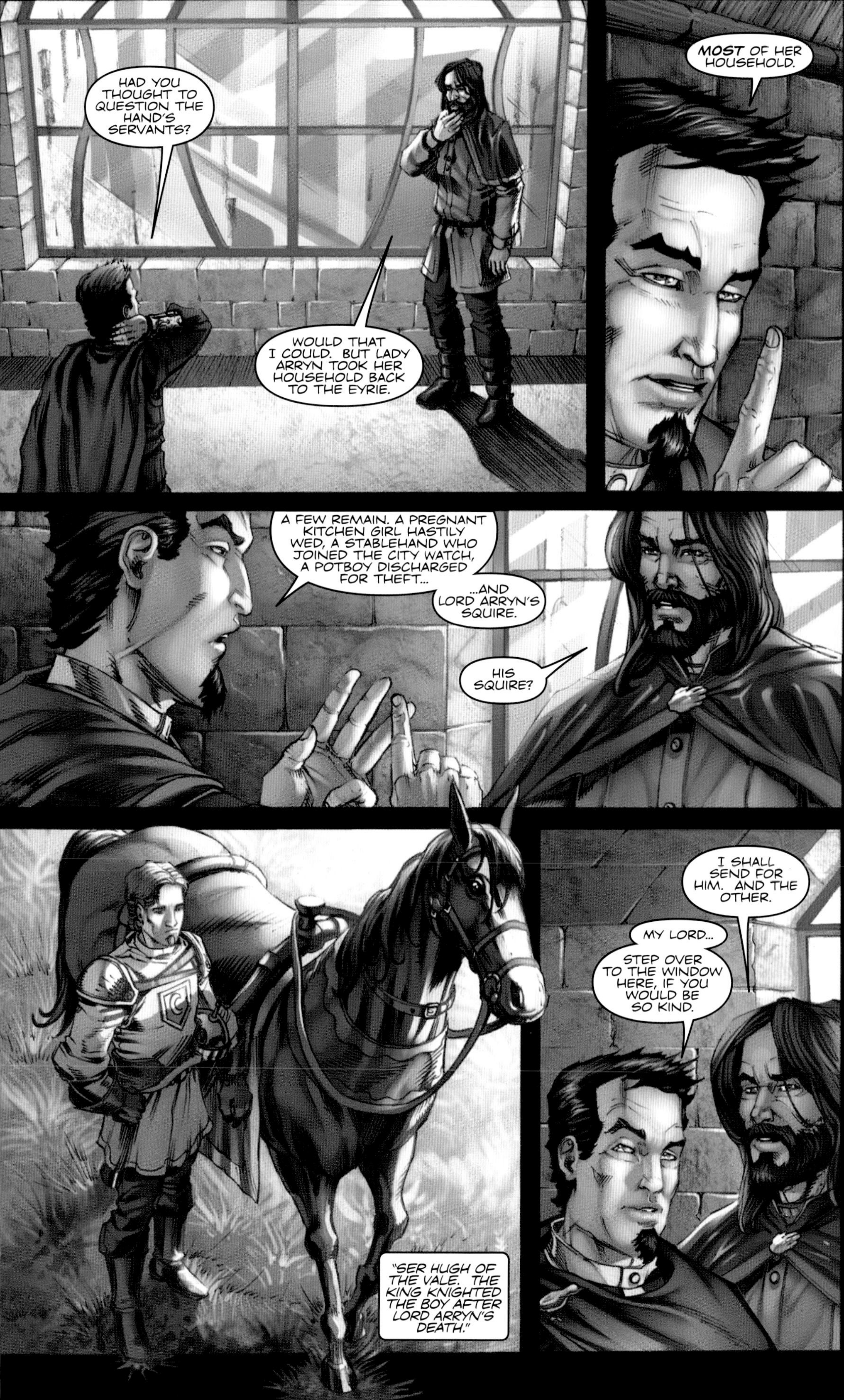
HAD YOU THOUGHT TO QUESTION THE HAND'S SERVANTS?
WOULD THAT I COULD. BUT LADY ARRYN TOOK HER HOUSEHOLD BACK TO THE EYRIE.
MOST OF HER HOUSEHOLD.
A FEW REMAIN. A PREGNANT KITCHEN GIRL HASTILY WED, A STABLEHAND WHO JOINED THE CITY WATCH, A POTBOY DISCHARGED FOR THEFT...
...AND LORD ARRYN'S SQUIRE.
HIS SQUIRE?
"SER HUGH OF THE VALE. THE KING KNIGHTED THE BOY AFTER LORD ARRYN'S DEATH."
I SHALL SEND FOR HIM. AND THE OTHER.
MY LORD...
STEP OVER TO THE WINDOW HERE, IF YOU WOULD BE SO KIND.

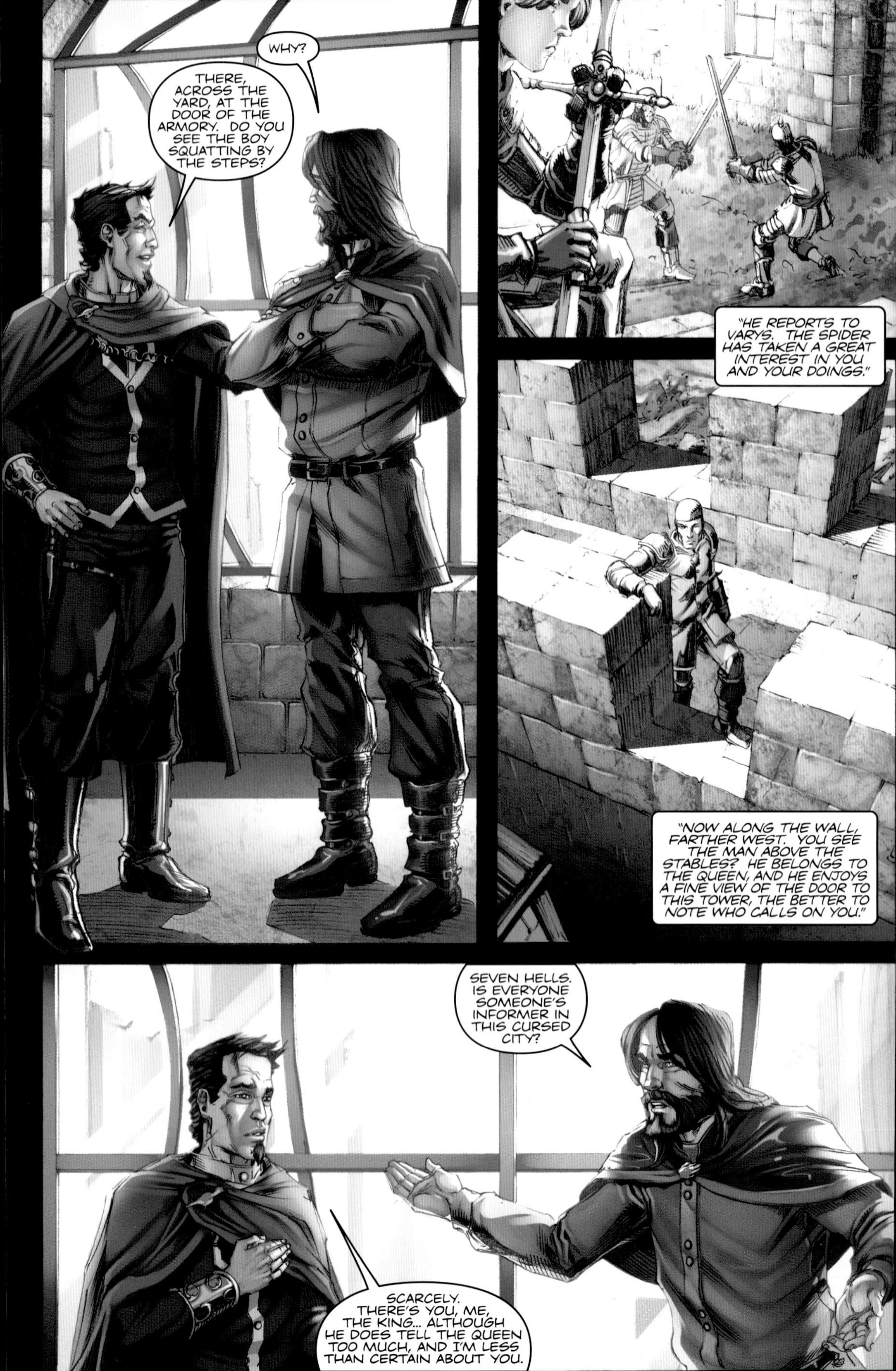
THERE, ACROSS THE YARD, AT THE DOOR OF THE ARMORY. DO YOU SEE THE BOY SQUATTING BY THE STEPS?
WHY?
"HE REPORTS TO VARYS. THE SPIDER HAS TAKEN A GREAT INTEREST IN YOU AND YOUR DOINGS."
"NOW ALONG THE WALL, FARTHER WEST. YOU SEE THE MAN ABOVE THE STABLES? HE BELONGS TO THE QUEEN, AND HE ENJOYS A FINE VIEW OF THE DOOR TO THIS TOWER, THE BETTER TO NOTE WHO CALLS ON YOU."
SEVEN HELLS. IS EVERYONE SOMEONE'S INFORMER IN THIS CURSED CITY?
SCARCELY. THERE'S YOU, ME, THE KING... ALTHOUGH HE DOES TELL THE QUEEN TOO MUCH, AND I'M LESS THAN CERTAIN ABOUT YOU.

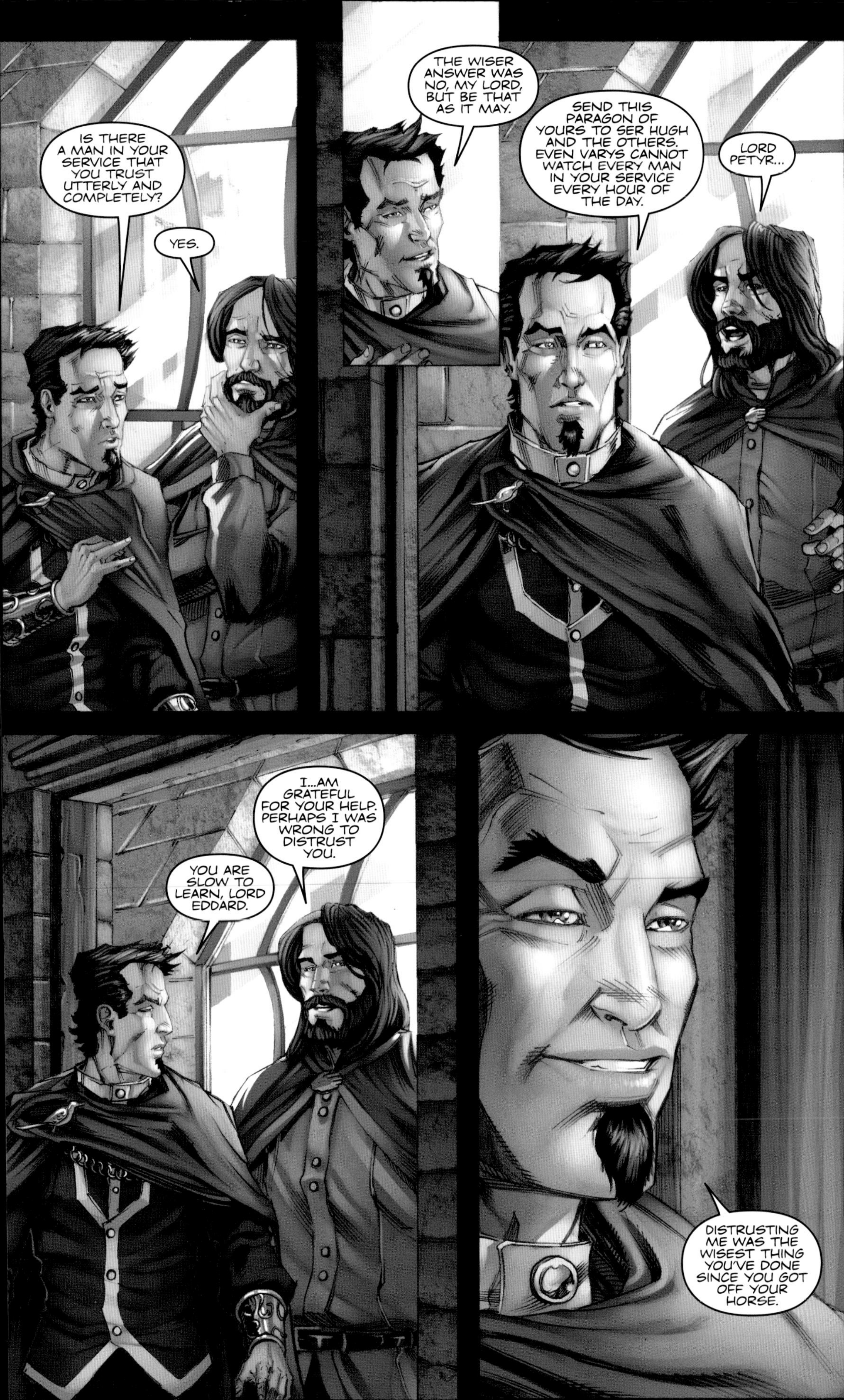
IS THERE A MAN IN YOUR SERVICE THAT YOU TRUST UTTERLY AND COMPLETELY?
YES.
THE WISER ANSWER WAS NO, MY LORD, BUT BE THAT AS IT MAY.
SEND THIS PARAGON OF YOURS TO SER HUGH AND THE OTHERS. EVEN VARYS CANNOT WATCH EVERY MAN IN YOUR SERVICE EVERY HOUR OF THE DAY.
LORD PETYR...
I...AM GRATEFUL FOR YOUR HELP. PERHAPS I WAS WRONG TO DISTRUST YOU.
YOU ARE SLOW TO LEARN, LORD EDDARD.
DISTRUSTING ME WAS THE WISEST THING YOU'VE DONE SINCE YOU GOT OFF YOUR HORSE.

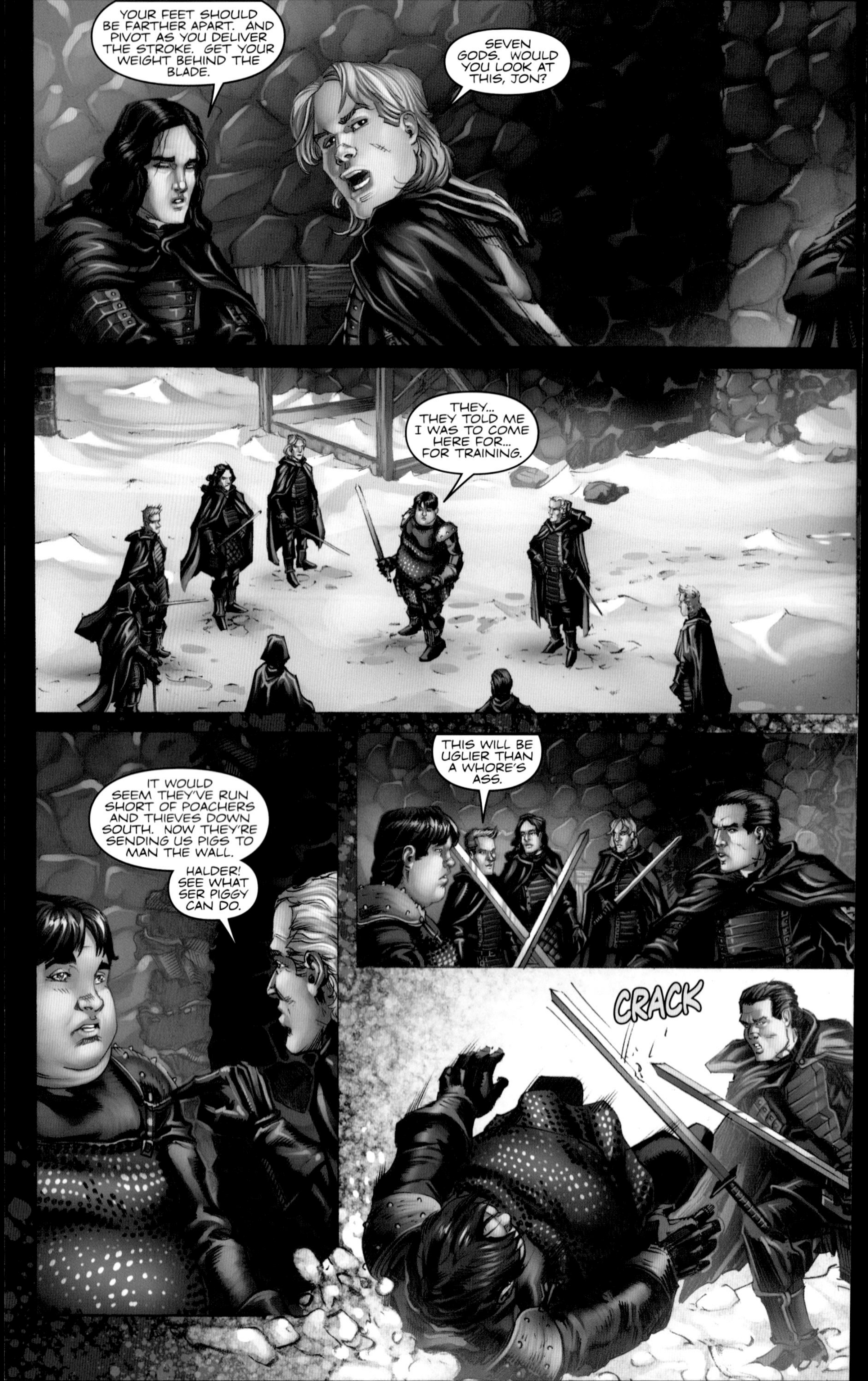
YOUR FEET SHOULD BE FARTHER APART. AND PIVOT AS YOU DELIVER THE STROKE. GET YOUR WEIGHT BEHIND THE BLADE.
SEVEN GODS. WOULD YOU LOOK AT THIS, JON?
THEY... THEY TOLD ME I WAS TO COME HERE FOR... FOR TRAINING.
IT WOULD SEEM THEY'VE RUN SHORT OF POACHERS AND THIEVES DOWN SOUTH. NOW THEY'RE SENDING US PIGS TO MAN THE WALL.
HALDER! SEE WHAT SER PIGGY CAN DO.
THIS WILL BE UGLIER THAN A WHORE'S ASS.
CRACK

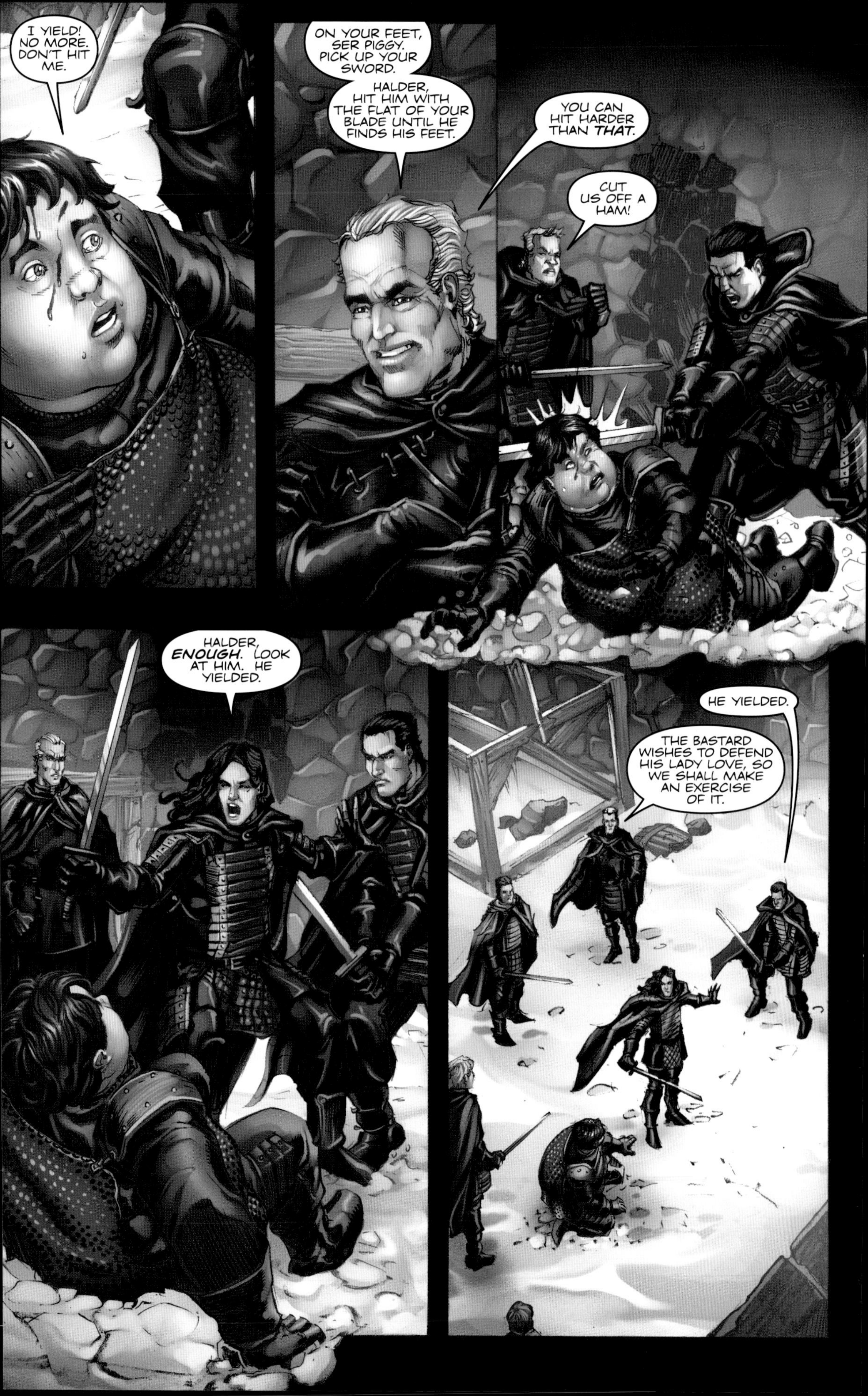
I YIELD! NO MORE. DON'T HIT ME.
ON YOUR FEET, SER PIGGY. PICK UP YOUR SWORD.
HALDER, HIT HIM WITH THE FLAT OF YOUR BLADE UNTIL HE FINDS HIS FEET.
YOU CAN HIT HARDER THAN THAT.
CUT US OFF A HAM!
HALDER, ENOUGH. LOOK AT HIM. HE YIELDED.
HE YIELDED.
THE BASTARD WISHES TO DEFEND HIS LADY LOVE, SO WE SHALL MAKE AN EXERCISE OF IT.

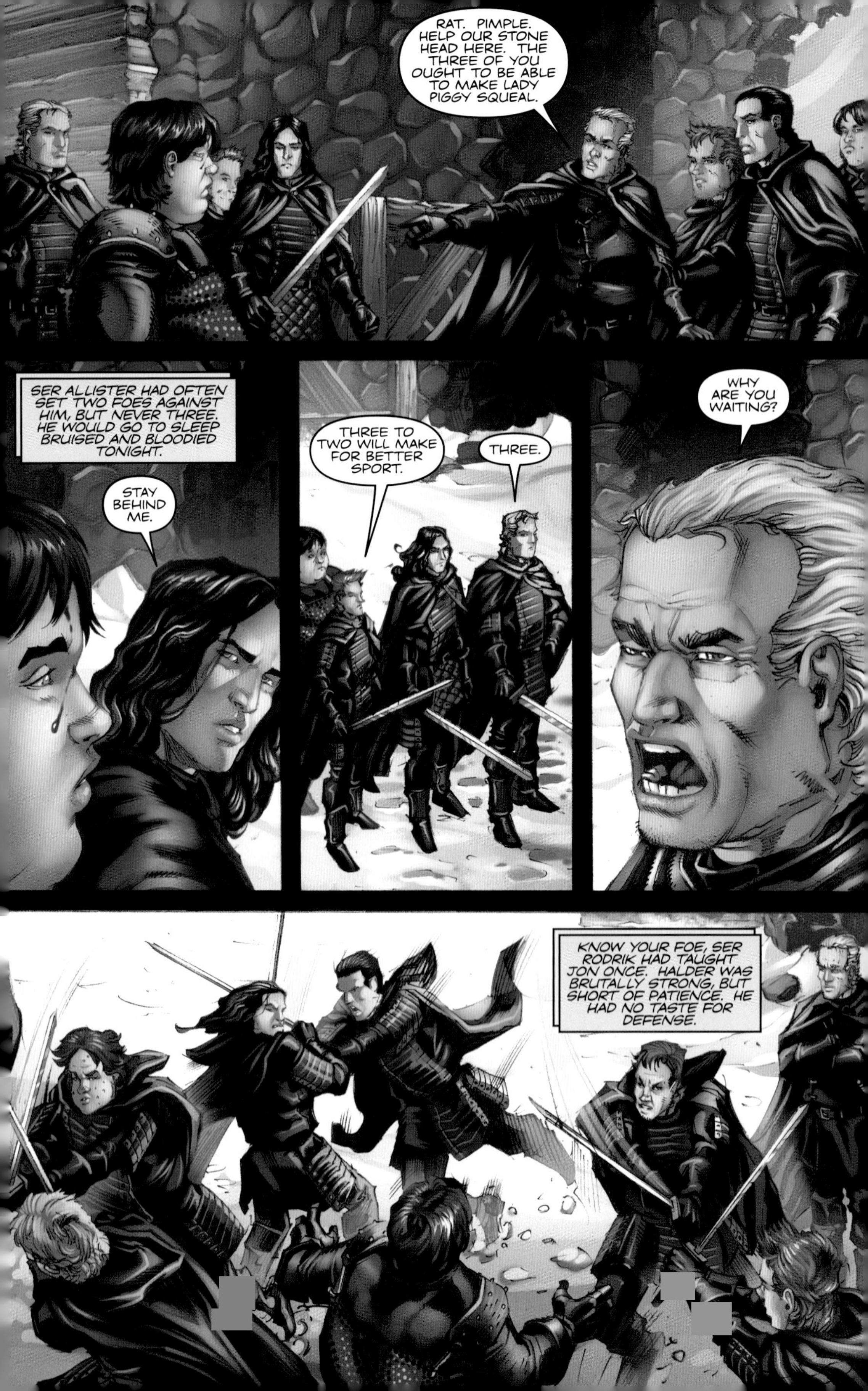
RAT. PIMPLE. HELP OUR STONE HEAD HERE. THE THREE OF YOU OUGHT TO BE ABLE TO MAKE LADY PIGGY SQUEAL.
SER ALLISTER HAD OFTEN SET TWO FOES AGAINST HIM, BUT NEVER THREE. HE WOULD GO TO SLEEP BRUISED AND BLOODIED TONIGHT.
STAY BEHIND ME.
THREE TO TWO WILL MAKE FOR BETTER SPORT.
THREE.
WHY ARE YOU WAITING?
KNOW YOUR FOE, SER RODRIK HAD TAUGHT JON ONCE. HALDER WAS BRUTALLY STRONG, BUT SHORT OF PATIENCE. HE HAD NO TASTE FOR DEFENSE.

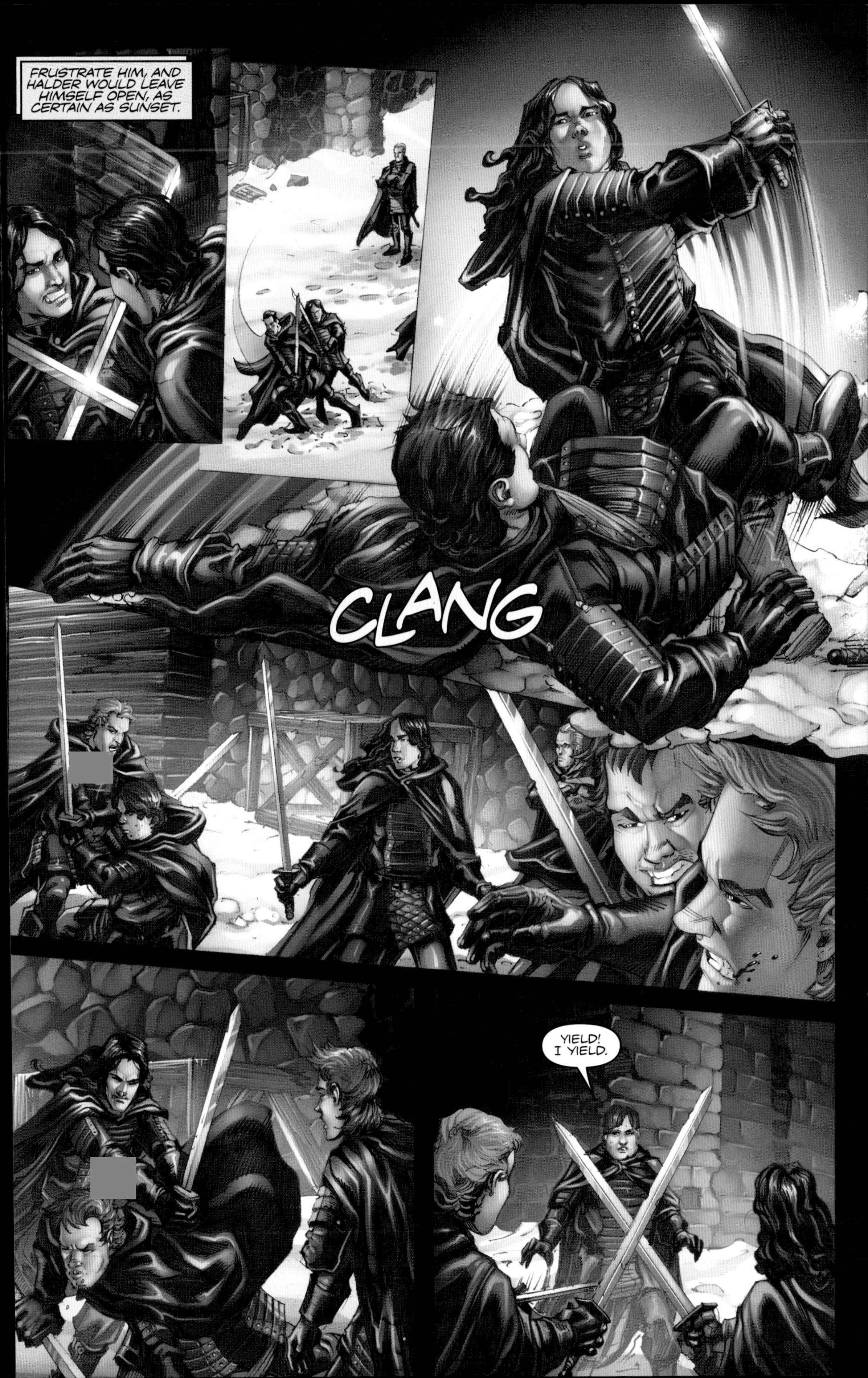
FRUSTRATE HIM, AND HALDER WOULD LEAVE HIMSELF OPEN, AS CERTAIN AS SUNSET.
CLANG
YIELD! I YIELD.

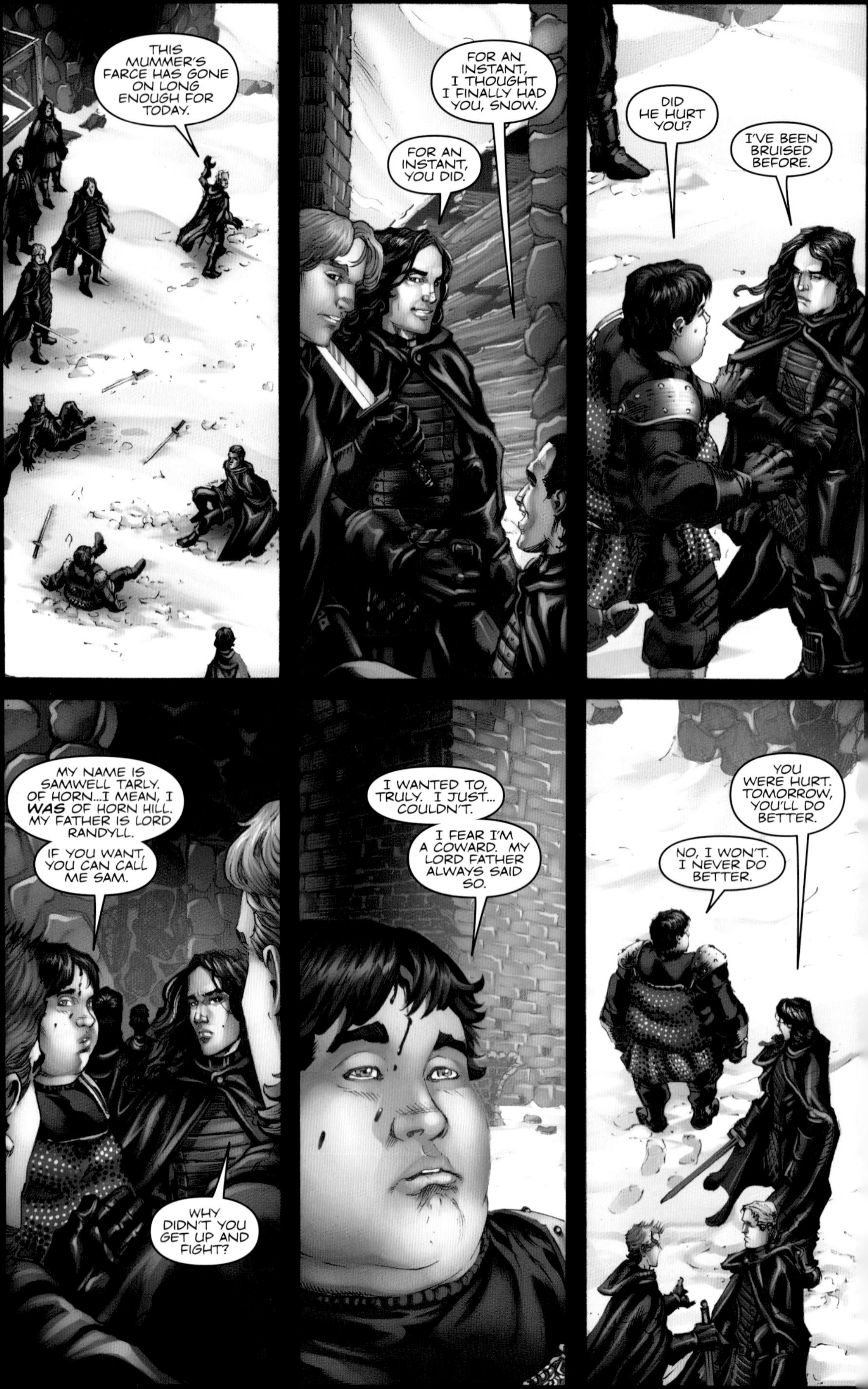
THIS MUMMER'S FARCE HAS GONE ON LONG ENOUGH FOR TODAY.
FOR AN INSTANT, I THOUGHT I FINALLY HAD YOU, SNOW.
FOR AN INSTANT, YOU DID.
DID HE HURT YOU?
I'VE BEEN BRUISED BEFORE.
MY NAME IS SAMWELL TARLY. OF HORN...I MEAN, I WAS OF HORN HILL. MY FATHER IS LORD RANDYLL.
IF YOU WANT, YOU CAN CALL ME SAM.
WHY DIDN'T YOU GET UP AND FIGHT?
I WANTED TO, TRULY. I JUST... COULDN'T.
I FEAR I'M A COWARD. MY LORD FATHER ALWAYS SAID SO.
YOU WERE HURT. TOMORROW, YOU'LL DO BETTER.
NO, I WON'T. I NEVER DO BETTER.

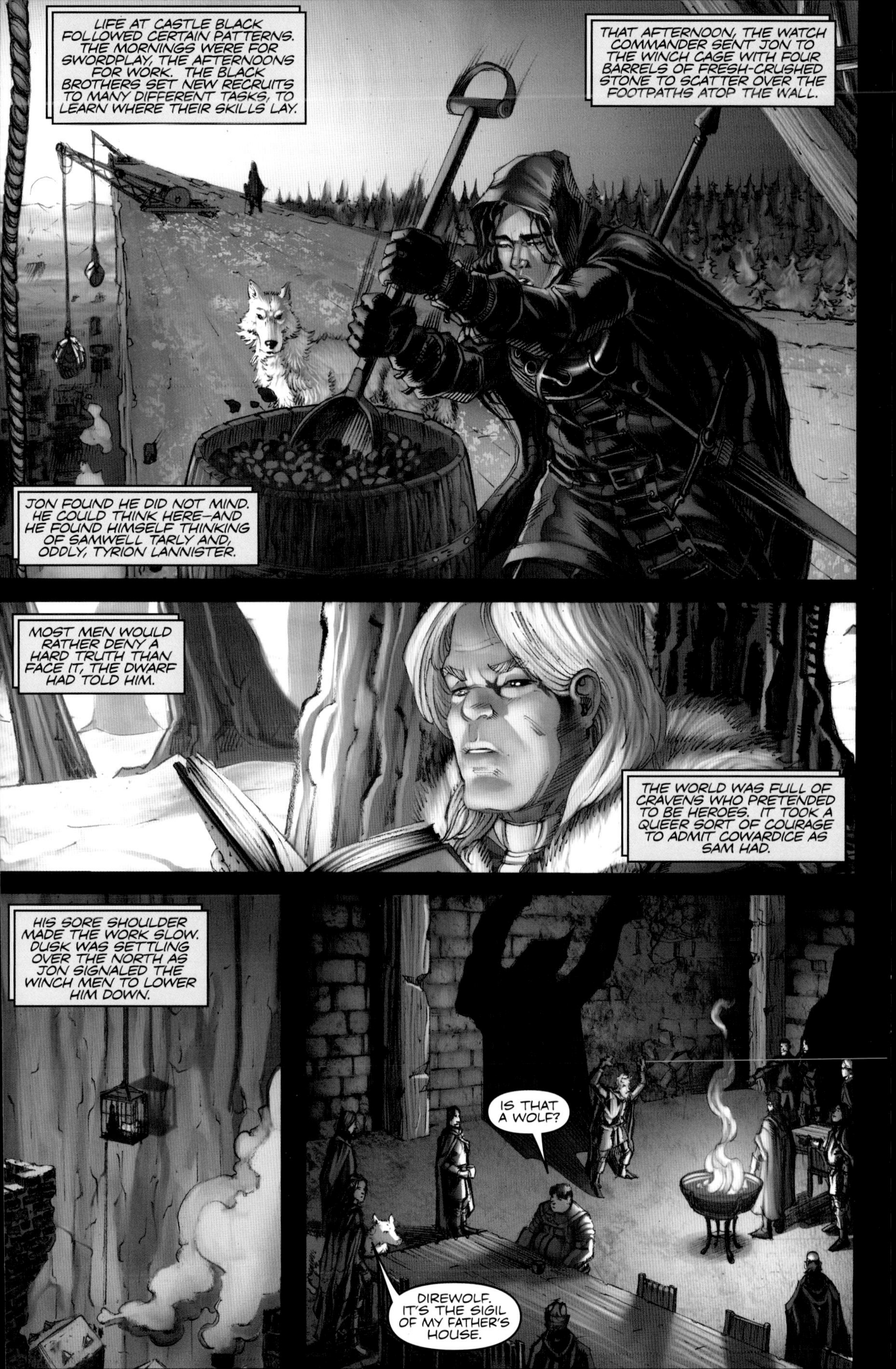

LIFE AT CASTLE BLACK FOLLOWED CERTAIN PATTERNS. THE MORNINGS WERE FOR SWORDPLAY, THE AFTERNOONS FOR WORK. THE BLACK BROTHERS SET NEW RECRUITS TO MANY DIFFERENT TASKS, TO LEARN WHERE THEIR SKILLS LAY.
THAT AFTERNOON, THE WATCH COMMANDER SENT JON TO THE WINCH CAGE WITH FOUR BARRELS OF FRESH-CRUSHED STONE TO SCATTER OVER THE FOOTPATHS ATOP THE WALL.
JON FOUND HE DID NOT MIND. HE COULD THINK HERE—AND HE FOUND HIMSELF THINKING OF SAMWELL TARLY AND, ODDLY, TYRION LANNISTER.
MOST MEN WOULD RATHER DENY A HARD TRUTH THAN FACE IT, THE DWARF HAD TOLD HIM.
THE WORLD WAS FULL OF CRAVENS WHO PRETENDED TO BE HEROES. IT TOOK A QUEER SORT OF COURAGE TO ADMIT COWARDICE AS SAM HAD.
HIS SORE SHOULDER MADE THE WORK SLOW. DUSK WAS SETTLING OVER THE NORTH AS JON SIGNALED THE WINCH MEN TO LOWER HIM DOWN.
IS THAT A WOLF?
DIREWOLF. IT'S THE SIGIL OF MY FATHER'S HOUSE.

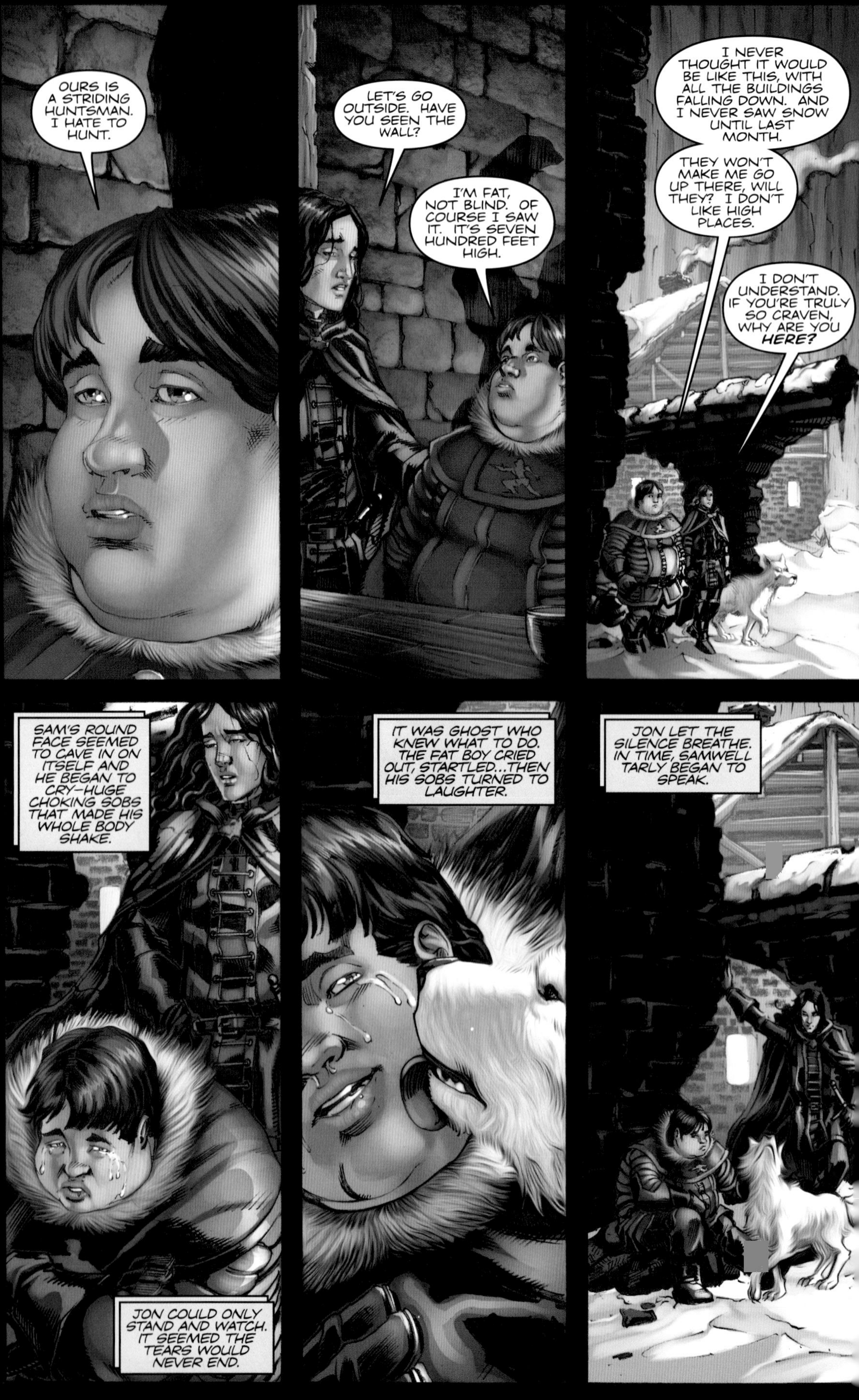
OURS IS A STRIDING HUNTSMAN. I HATE TO HUNT.
LET'S GO OUTSIDE. HAVE YOU SEEN THE WALL?
I'M FAT, NOT BLIND. OF COURSE I SAW IT. IT'S SEVEN HUNDRED FEET HIGH.
I NEVER THOUGHT IT WOULD BE LIKE THIS, WITH ALL THE BUILDINGS FALLING DOWN. AND I NEVER SAW SNOW UNTIL LAST MONTH.
THEY WON'T MAKE ME GO UP THERE, WILL THEY? I DON'T LIKE HIGH PLACES.
I DON'T UNDERSTAND. IF YOU'RE TRULY SO CRAVEN, WHY ARE YOU *HERE?*
SAM'S ROUND FACE SEEMED TO CAVE IN ON ITSELF AND HE BEGAN TO CRY—HUGE CHOKING SOBS THAT MADE HIS WHOLE BODY SHAKE.
JON COULD ONLY STAND AND WATCH. IT SEEMED THE TEARS WOULD NEVER END.
IT WAS GHOST WHO KNEW WHAT TO DO. THE FAT BOY CRIED OUT, STARTLED...THEN HIS SOBS TURNED TO LAUGHTER.
JON LET THE SILENCE BREATHE. IN TIME, SAMWELL TARLY BEGAN TO SPEAK.

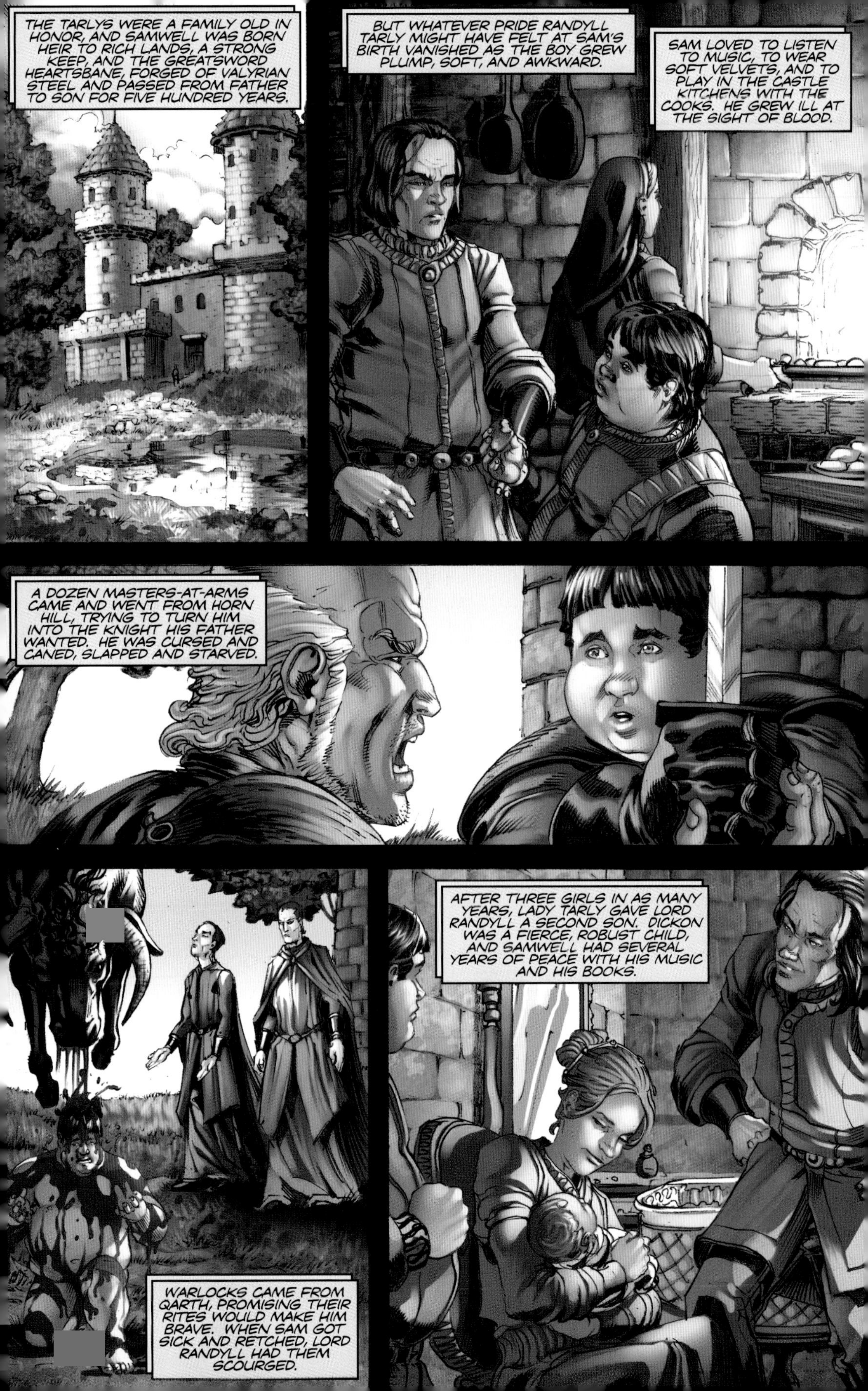
THE TARLYS WERE A FAMILY OLD IN HONOR, AND SAMWELL WAS BORN HEIR TO RICH LANDS, A STRONG KEEP, AND THE GREATSWORD HEARTSBANE, FORGED OF VALYRIAN STEEL AND PASSED FROM FATHER TO SON FOR FIVE HUNDRED YEARS.
BUT WHATEVER PRIDE RANDYLL TARLY MIGHT HAVE FELT AT SAM'S BIRTH VANISHED AS THE BOY GREW PLUMP, SOFT, AND AWKWARD.
SAM LOVED TO LISTEN TO MUSIC, TO WEAR SOFT VELVETS, AND TO PLAY IN THE CASTLE KITCHENS WITH THE COOKS. HE GREW ILL AT THE SIGHT OF BLOOD.
A DOZEN MASTERS-AT-ARMS CAME AND WENT FROM HORN HILL, TRYING TO TURN HIM INTO THE KNIGHT HIS FATHER WANTED. HE WAS CURSED AND CANED, SLAPPED AND STARVED.
WARLOCKS CAME FROM QARTH, PROMISING THEIR RITES WOULD MAKE HIM BRAVE. WHEN SAM GOT SICK AND RETCHED, LORD RANDYLL HAD THEM SCOURGED.
AFTER THREE GIRLS IN AS MANY YEARS, LADY TARLY GAVE LORD RANDYLL A SECOND SON. DICKON WAS A FIERCE, ROBUST CHILD, AND SAMWELL HAD SEVERAL YEARS OF PEACE WITH HIS MUSIC AND HIS BOOKS.

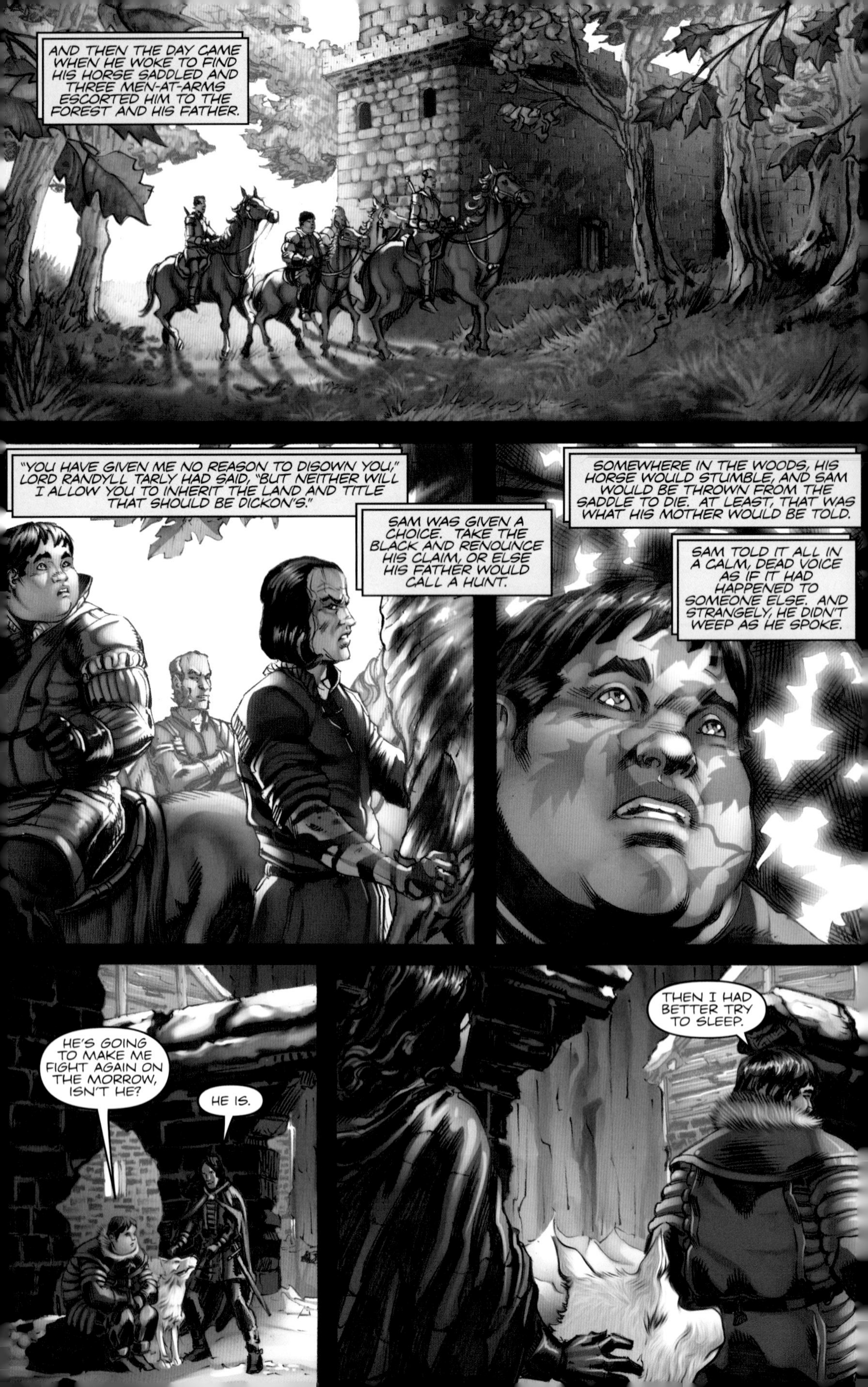
AND THEN THE DAY CAME WHEN HE WOKE TO FIND HIS HORSE SADDLED AND THREE MEN-AT-ARMS ESCORTED HIM TO THE FOREST AND HIS FATHER.
"YOU HAVE GIVEN ME NO REASON TO DISOWN YOU," LORD RANDYLL TARLY HAD SAID, "BUT NEITHER WILL I ALLOW YOU TO INHERIT THE LAND AND TITLE THAT SHOULD BE DICKON'S."
SAM WAS GIVEN A CHOICE. TAKE THE BLACK AND RENOUNCE HIS CLAIM, OR ELSE HIS FATHER WOULD CALL A HUNT.
SOMEWHERE IN THE WOODS, HIS HORSE WOULD STUMBLE, AND SAM WOULD BE THROWN FROM THE SADDLE TO DIE. AT LEAST, THAT WAS WHAT HIS MOTHER WOULD BE TOLD.
SAM TOLD IT ALL IN A CALM, DEAD VOICE AS IF IT HAD HAPPENED TO SOMEONE ELSE. AND STRANGELY, HE DIDN'T WEEP AS HE SPOKE.
HE'S GOING TO MAKE ME FIGHT AGAIN ON THE MORROW, ISN'T HE?
HE IS.
THEN I HAD BETTER TRY TO SLEEP.

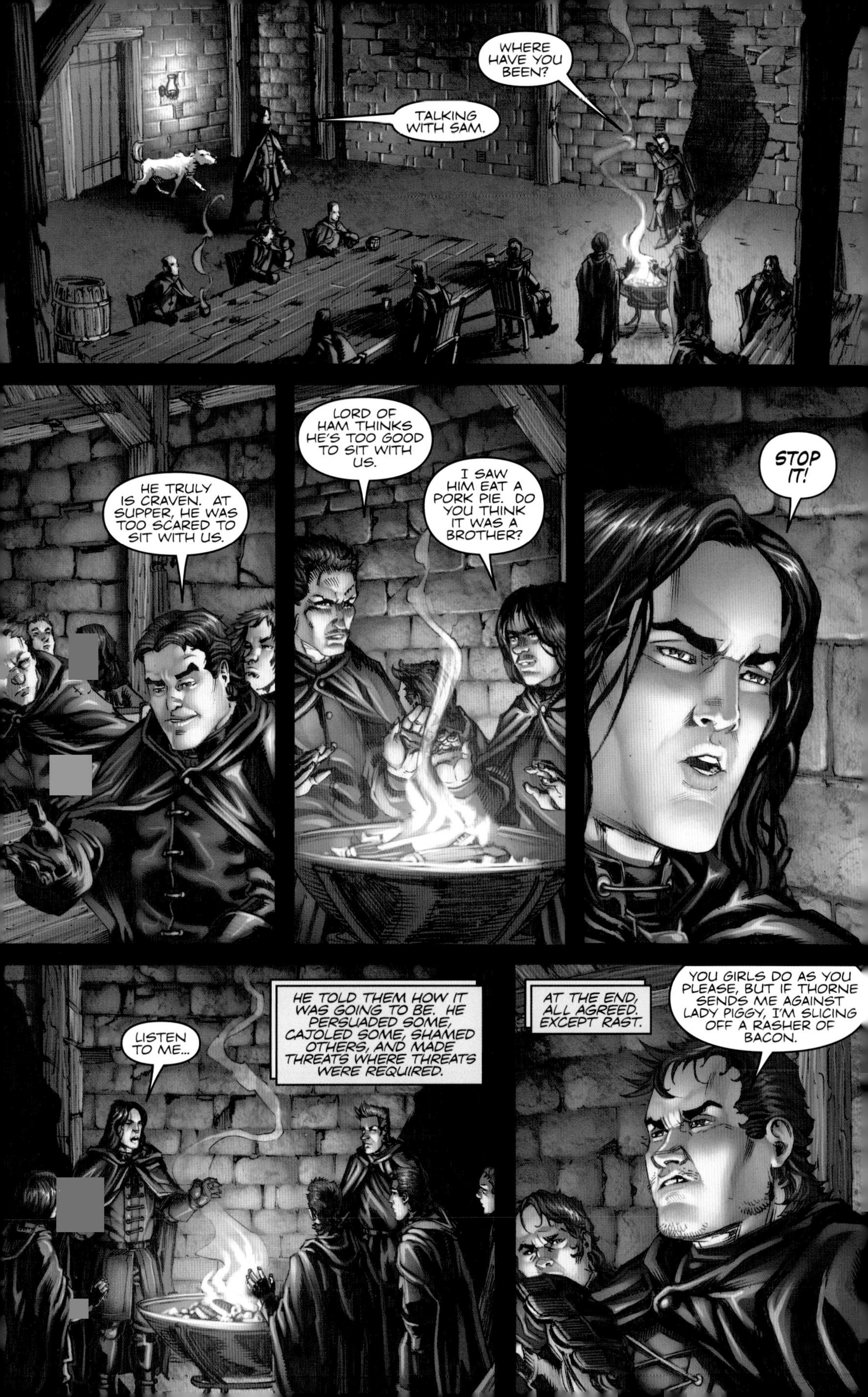
WHERE HAVE YOU BEEN?
TALKING WITH SAM.
HE TRULY IS CRAVEN. AT SUPPER, HE WAS TOO SCARED TO SIT WITH US.
LORD OF HAM THINKS HE'S TOO GOOD TO SIT WITH US.
I SAW HIM EAT A PORK PIE. DO YOU THINK IT WAS A BROTHER?
STOP IT!
LISTEN TO ME...
HE TOLD THEM HOW IT WAS GOING TO BE. HE PERSUADED SOME, CAJOLED SOME, SHAMED OTHERS, AND MADE THREATS WHERE THREATS WERE REQUIRED.
AT THE END, ALL AGREED. EXCEPT RAST.
YOU GIRLS DO AS YOU PLEASE, BUT IF THORNE SENDS ME AGAINST LADY PIGGY, I'M SLICING OFF A RASHER OF BACON.

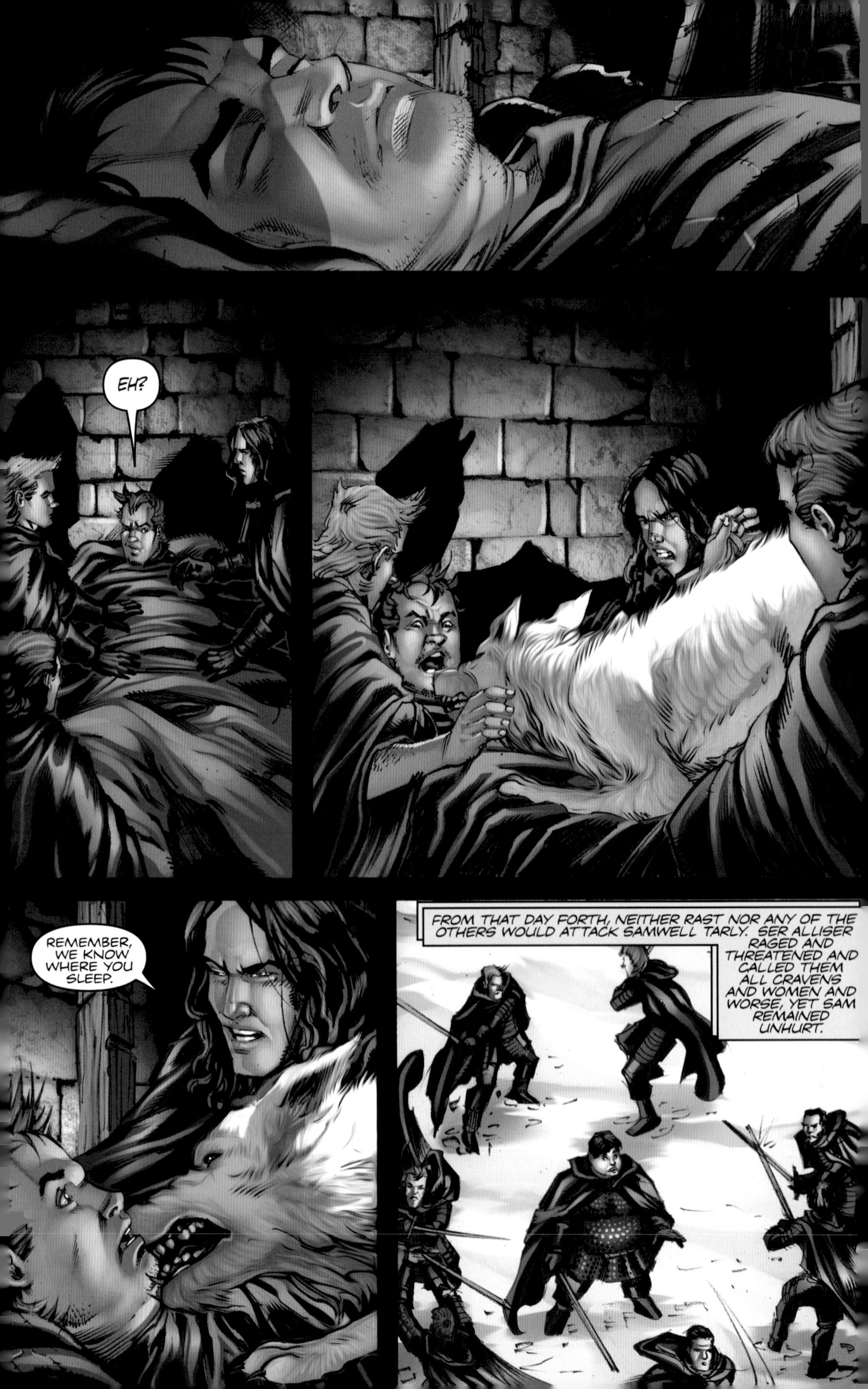
EH?
REMEMBER, WE KNOW WHERE YOU SLEEP.
FROM THAT DAY FORTH, NEITHER RAST NOR ANY OF THE OTHERS WOULD ATTACK SAMWELL TARLY. SER ALLISER RAGED AND THREATENED AND CALLED THEM ALL CRAVENS AND WOMEN AND WORSE, YET SAM REMAINED UNHURT.

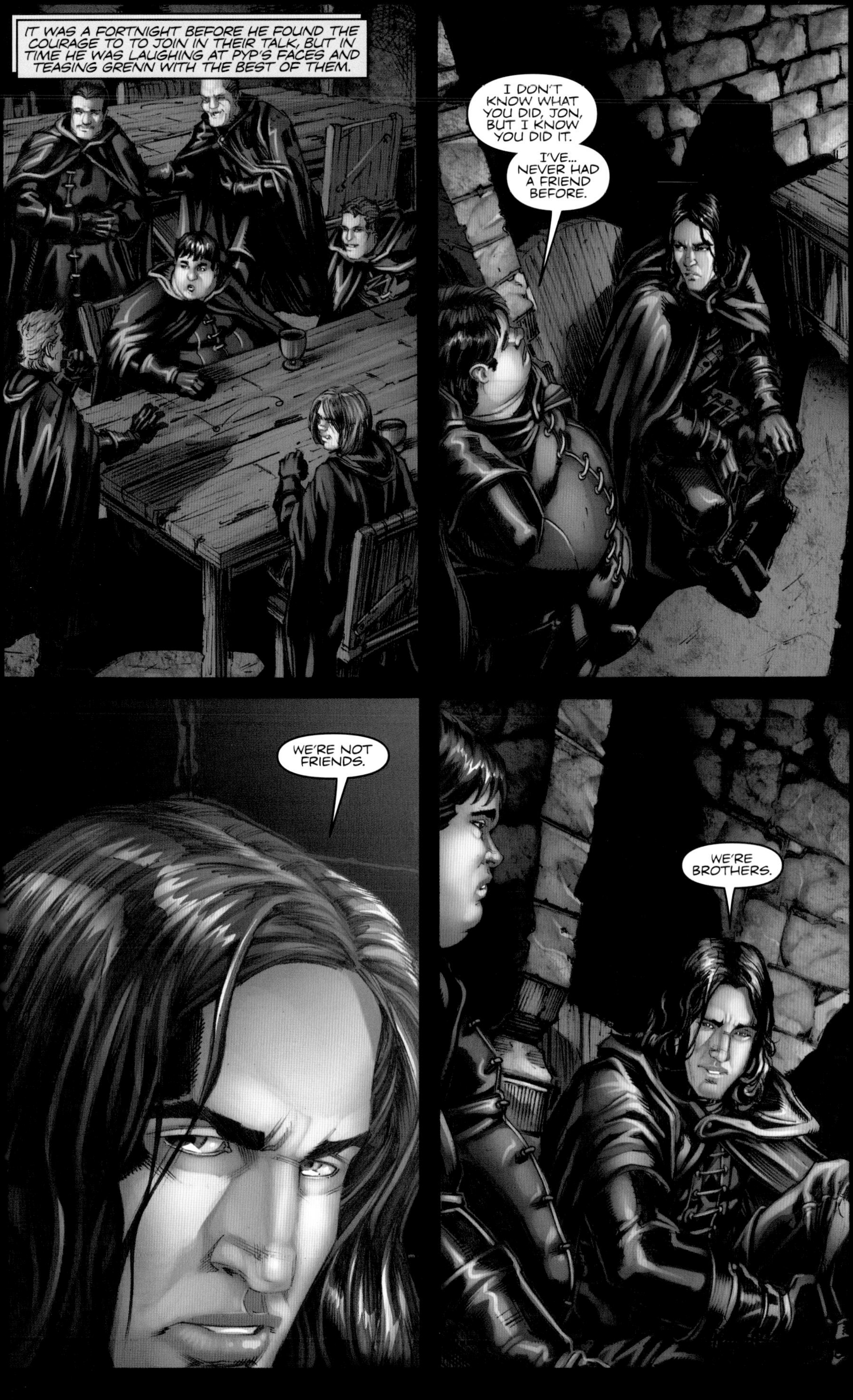
IT WAS A FORTNIGHT BEFORE HE FOUND THE COURAGE TO TO JOIN IN THEIR TALK, BUT IN TIME HE WAS LAUGHING AT PYP'S FACES AND TEASING GRENN WITH THE BEST OF THEM.
I DON'T KNOW WHAT YOU DID, JON, BUT I KNOW YOU DID IT.
I'VE... NEVER HAD A FRIEND BEFORE.
WE'RE NOT FRIENDS.
WE'RE BROTHERS.

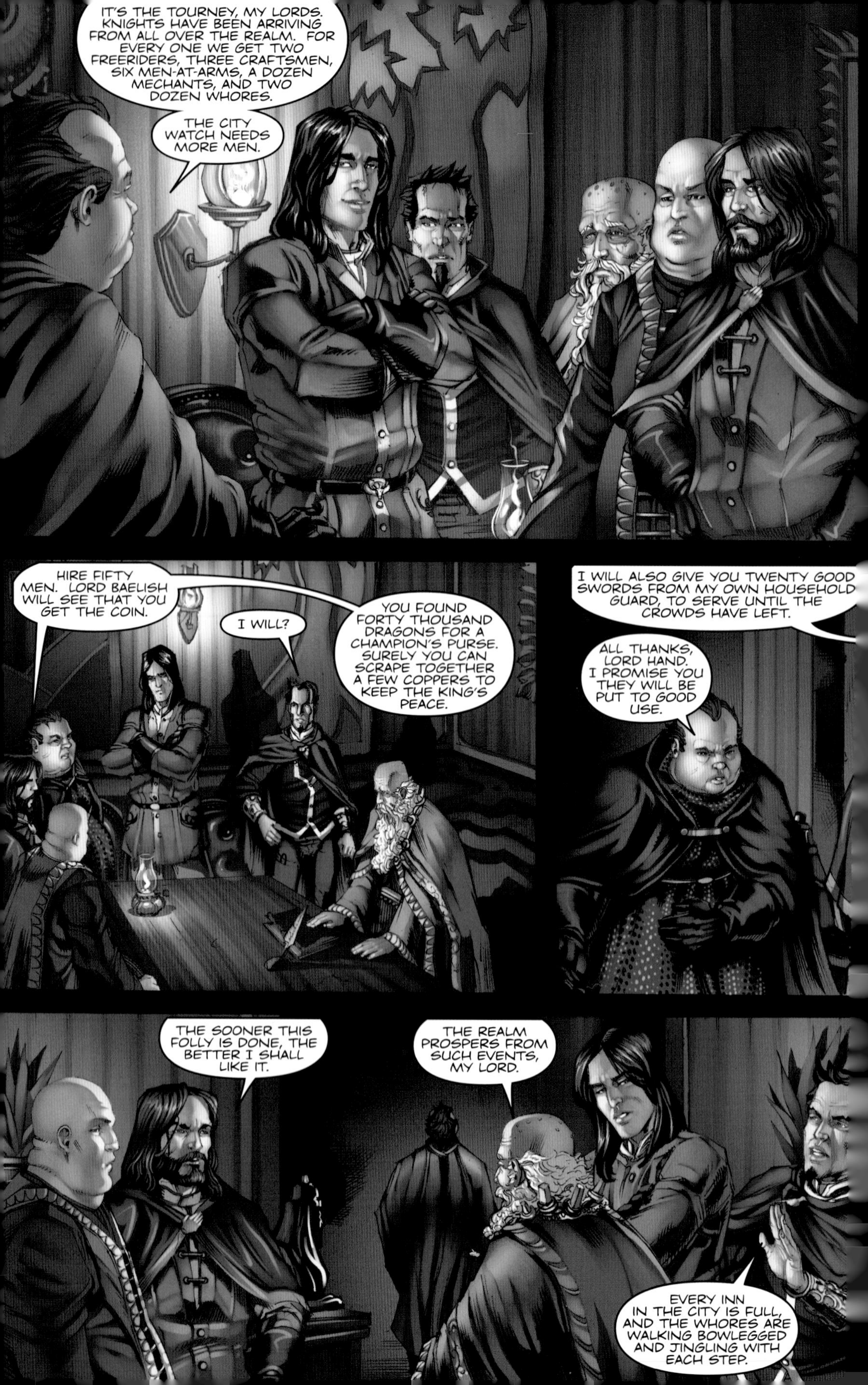
IT'S THE TOURNEY, MY LORDS. KNIGHTS HAVE BEEN ARRIVING FROM ALL OVER THE REALM. FOR EVERY ONE WE GET TWO FREERIDERS, THREE CRAFTSMEN, SIX MEN-AT-ARMS, A DOZEN MECHANTS, AND TWO DOZEN WHORES.
THE CITY WATCH NEEDS MORE MEN.
HIRE FIFTY MEN. LORD BAELISH WILL SEE THAT YOU GET THE COIN.
I WILL?
YOU FOUND FORTY THOUSAND DRAGONS FOR A CHAMPION'S PURSE. SURELY YOU CAN SCRAPE TOGETHER A FEW COPPERS TO KEEP THE KING'S PEACE.
I WILL ALSO GIVE YOU TWENTY GOOD SWORDS FROM MY OWN HOUSEHOLD GUARD, TO SERVE UNTIL THE CROWDS HAVE LEFT.
ALL THANKS, LORD HAND. I PROMISE YOU THEY WILL BE PUT TO GOOD USE.
THE SOONER THIS FOLLY IS DONE, THE BETTER I SHALL LIKE IT.
THE REALM PROSPERS FROM SUCH EVENTS, MY LORD.
EVERY INN IN THE CITY IS FULL, AND THE WHORES ARE WALKING BOWLEGGED AND JINGLING WITH EACH STEP.

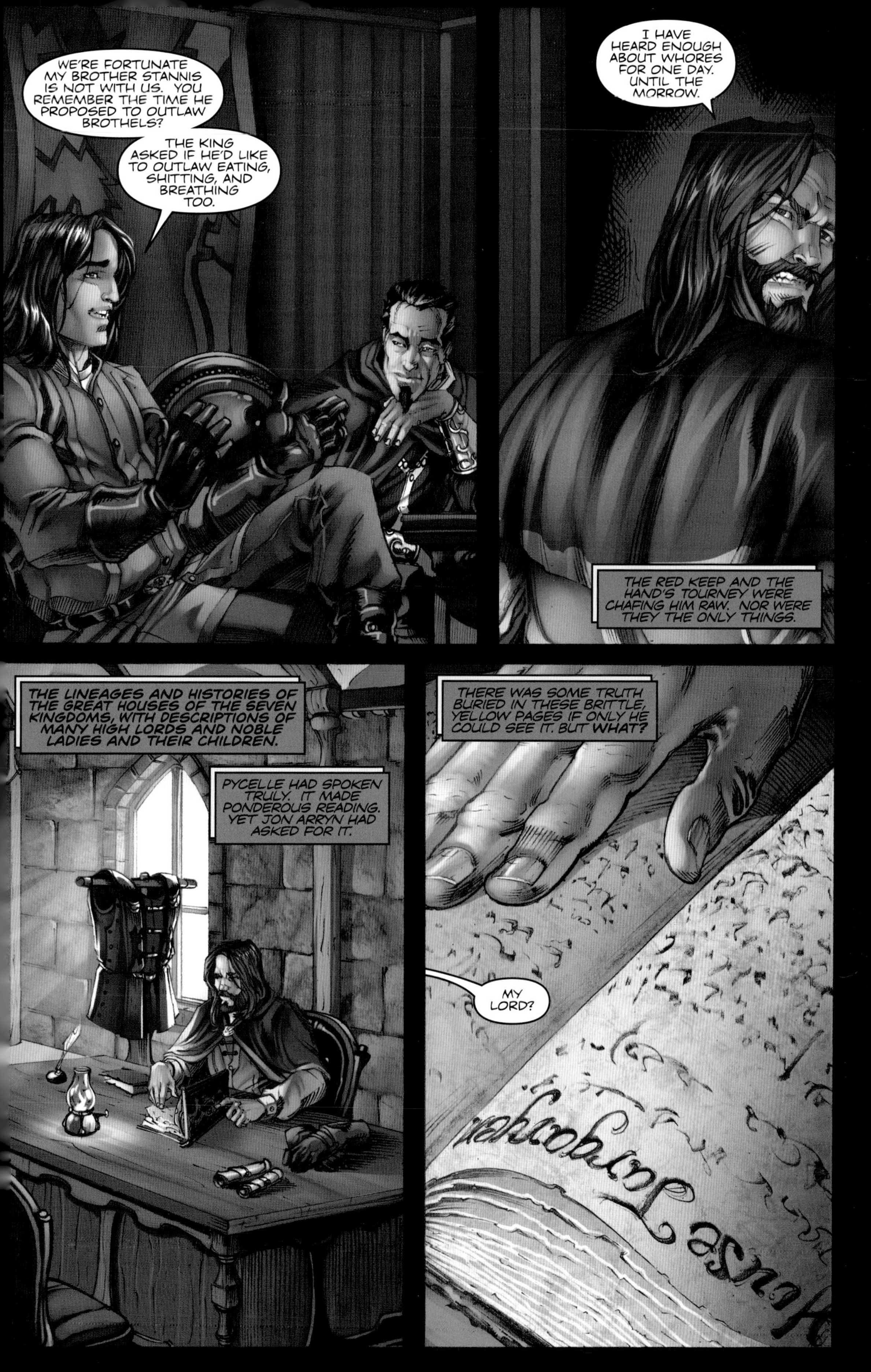
WE'RE FORTUNATE MY BROTHER STANNIS IS NOT WITH US. YOU REMEMBER THE TIME HE PROPOSED TO OUTLAW BROTHELS?
THE KING ASKED IF HE'D LIKE TO OUTLAW EATING, SHITTING, AND BREATHING TOO.
I HAVE HEARD ENOUGH ABOUT WHORES FOR ONE DAY. UNTIL THE MORROW.
THE RED KEEP AND THE HAND'S TOURNEY WERE CHAFING HIM RAW. NOR WERE THEY THE ONLY THINGS.
THE LINEAGES AND HISTORIES OF THE GREAT HOUSES OF THE SEVEN KINGDOMS, WITH DESCRIPTIONS OF MANY HIGH LORDS AND NOBLE LADIES AND THEIR CHILDREN.
PYCELLE HAD SPOKEN TRULY. IT MADE PONDEROUS READING. YET JON ARRYN HAD ASKED FOR IT.
THERE WAS SOME TRUTH BURIED IN THESE BRITTLE, YELLOW PAGES IF ONLY HE COULD SEE IT. BUT WHAT?
MY LORD?

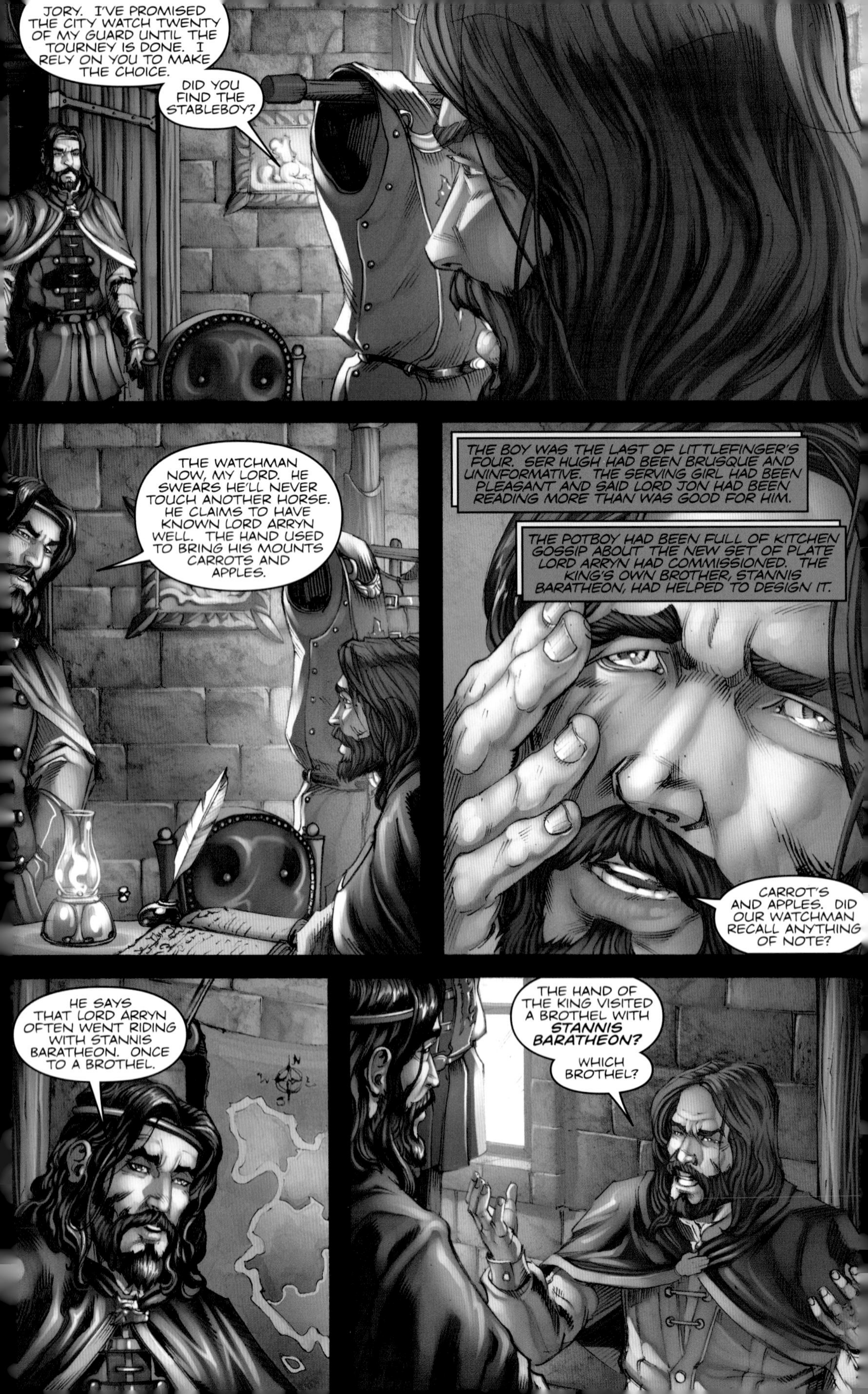
JORY. I'VE PROMISED THE CITY WATCH TWENTY OF MY GUARD UNTIL THE TOURNEY IS DONE. I RELY ON YOU TO MAKE THE CHOICE.
DID YOU FIND THE STABLEBOY?
THE WATCHMAN NOW, MY LORD. HE SWEARS HE'LL NEVER TOUCH ANOTHER HORSE. HE CLAIMS TO HAVE KNOWN LORD ARRYN WELL. THE HAND USED TO BRING HIS MOUNTS CARROTS AND APPLES.
THE BOY WAS THE LAST OF LITTLEFINGER'S FOUR. SER HUGH HAD BEEN BRUSQUE AND UNINFORMATIVE. THE SERVING GIRL HAD BEEN PLEASANT AND SAID LORD JON HAD BEEN READING MORE THAN WAS GOOD FOR HIM.
THE POTBOY HAD BEEN FULL OF KITCHEN GOSSIP ABOUT THE NEW SET OF PLATE LORD ARRYN HAD COMMISSIONED. THE KING'S OWN BROTHER, STANNIS BARATHEON, HAD HELPED TO DESIGN IT.
CARROT'S AND APPLES. DID OUR WATCHMAN RECALL ANYTHING OF NOTE?
HE SAYS THAT LORD ARRYN OFTEN WENT RIDING WITH STANNIS BARATHEON. ONCE TO A BROTHEL.
THE HAND OF THE KING VISITED A BROTHEL WITH ***STANNIS BARATHEON?***
WHICH BROTHEL?

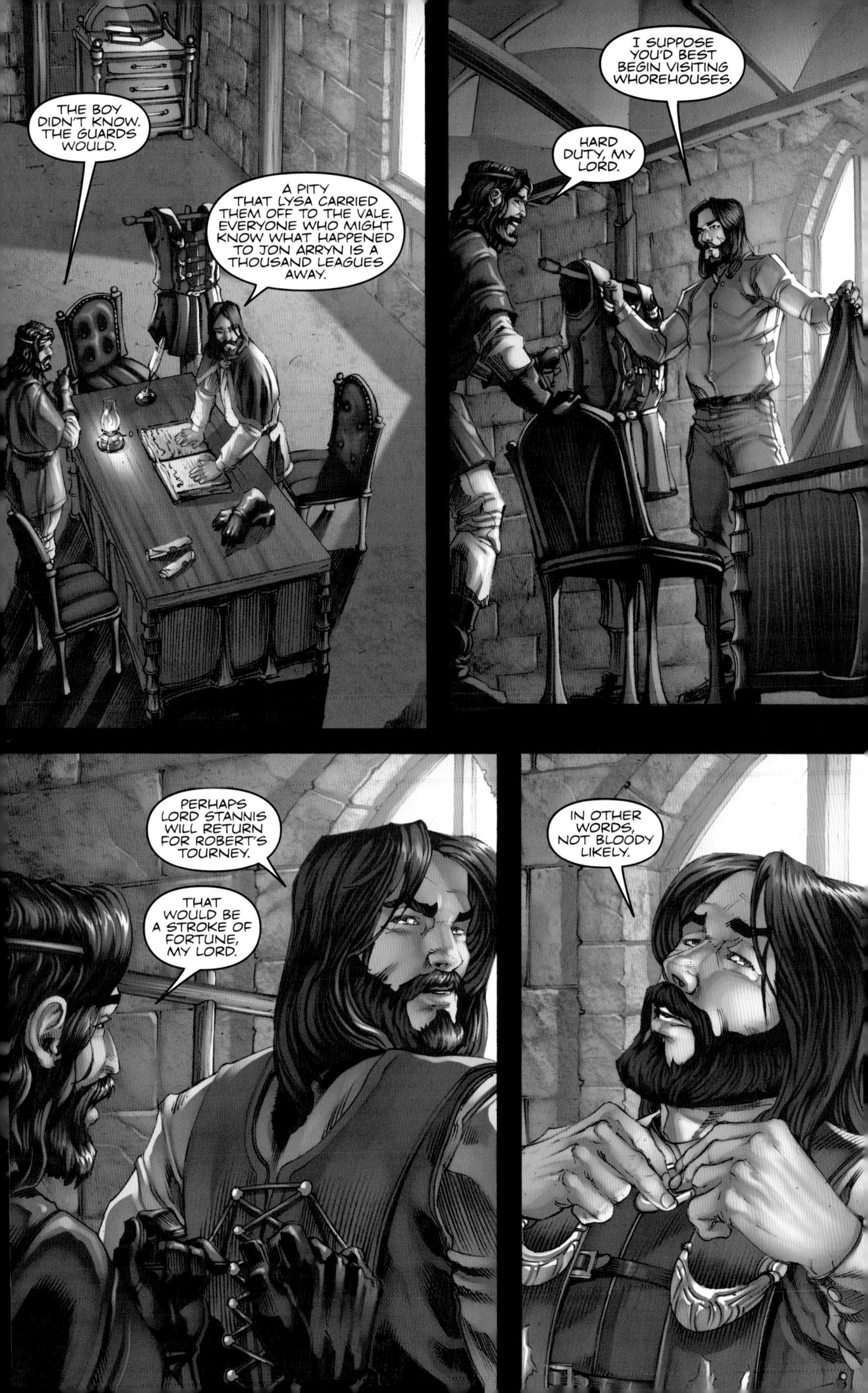
THE BOY DIDN'T KNOW. THE GUARDS WOULD.
A PITY THAT LYSA CARRIED THEM OFF TO THE VALE. EVERYONE WHO MIGHT KNOW WHAT HAPPENED TO JON ARRYN IS A THOUSAND LEAGUES AWAY.
I SUPPOSE YOU'D BEST BEGIN VISITING WHOREHOUSES.
HARD DUTY, MY LORD.
PERHAPS LORD STANNIS WILL RETURN FOR ROBERT'S TOURNEY.
THAT WOULD BE A STROKE OF FORTUNE, MY LORD.
IN OTHER WORDS, NOT BLOODY LIKELY.

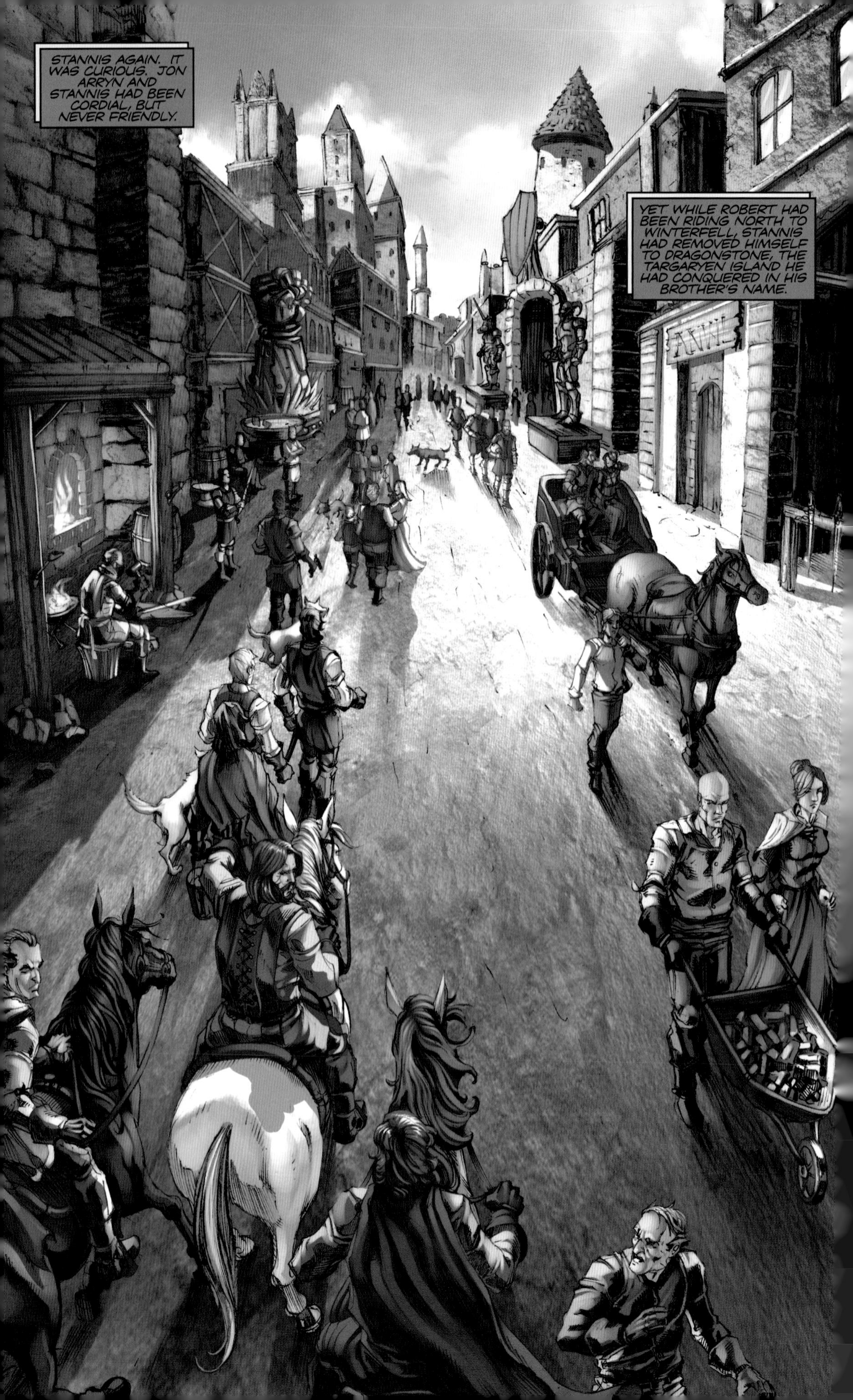
STANNIS AGAIN. IT WAS CURIOUS. JON ARRYN AND STANNIS HAD BEEN CORDIAL, BUT NEVER FRIENDLY.
YET WHILE ROBERT HAD BEEN RIDING NORTH TO WINTERFELL, STANNIS HAD REMOVED HIMSELF TO DRAGONSTONE, THE TARGARYEN ISLAND HE HAD CONQUERED IN HIS BROTHER'S NAME.

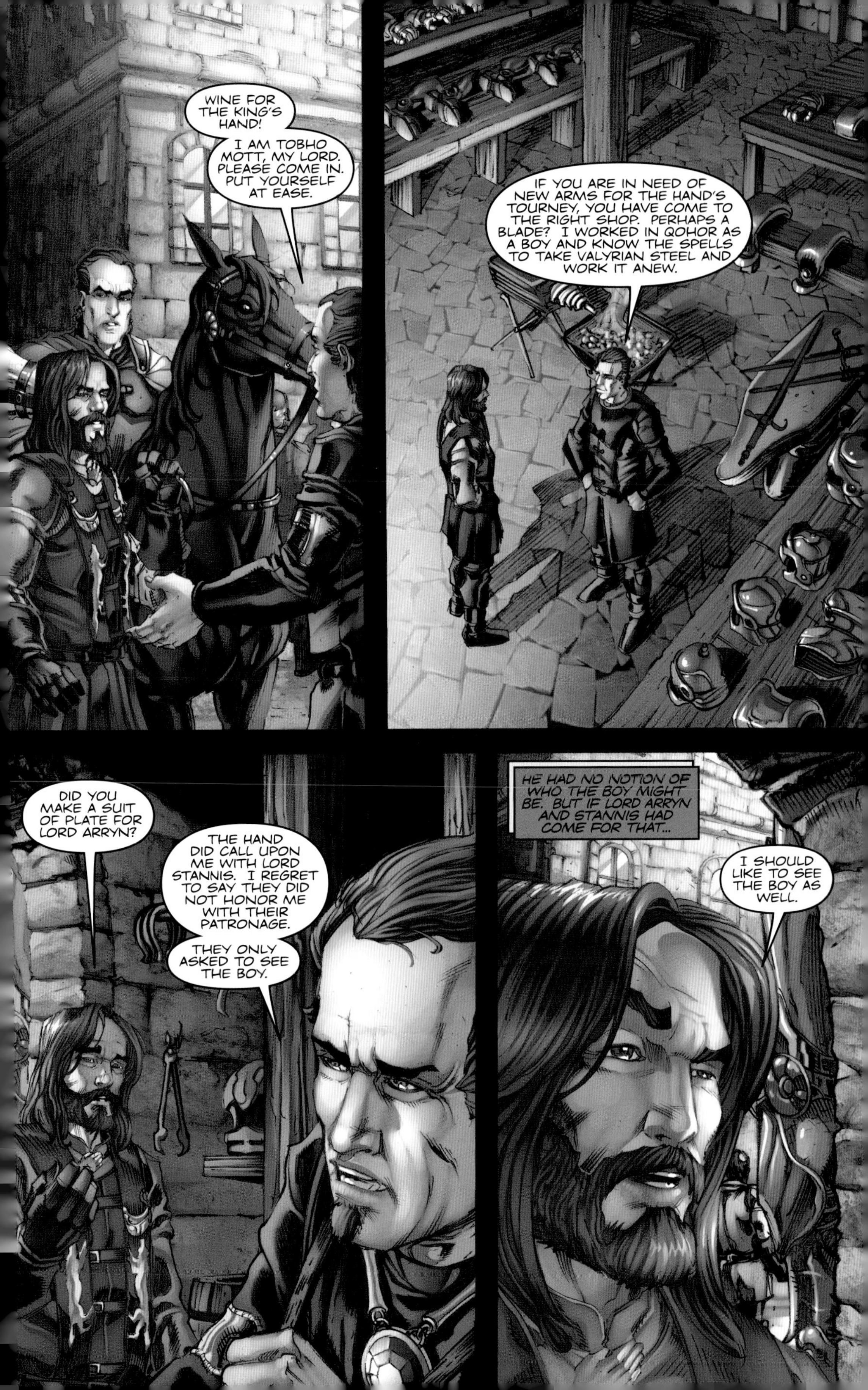
WINE FOR THE KING'S HAND!
I AM TOBHO MOTT, MY LORD. PLEASE COME IN. PUT YOURSELF AT EASE.
IF YOU ARE IN NEED OF NEW ARMS FOR THE HAND'S TOURNEY, YOU HAVE COME TO THE RIGHT SHOP. PERHAPS A BLADE? I WORKED IN QOHOR AS A BOY AND KNOW THE SPELLS TO TAKE VALYRIAN STEEL AND WORK IT ANEW.
DID YOU MAKE A SUIT OF PLATE FOR LORD ARRYN?
THE HAND DID CALL UPON ME WITH LORD STANNIS. I REGRET TO SAY THEY DID NOT HONOR ME WITH THEIR PATRONAGE.
THEY ONLY ASKED TO SEE THE BOY.
HE HAD NO NOTION OF WHO THE BOY MIGHT BE. BUT IF LORD ARRYN AND STANNIS HAD COME FOR THAT...
I SHOULD LIKE TO SEE THE BOY AS WELL.

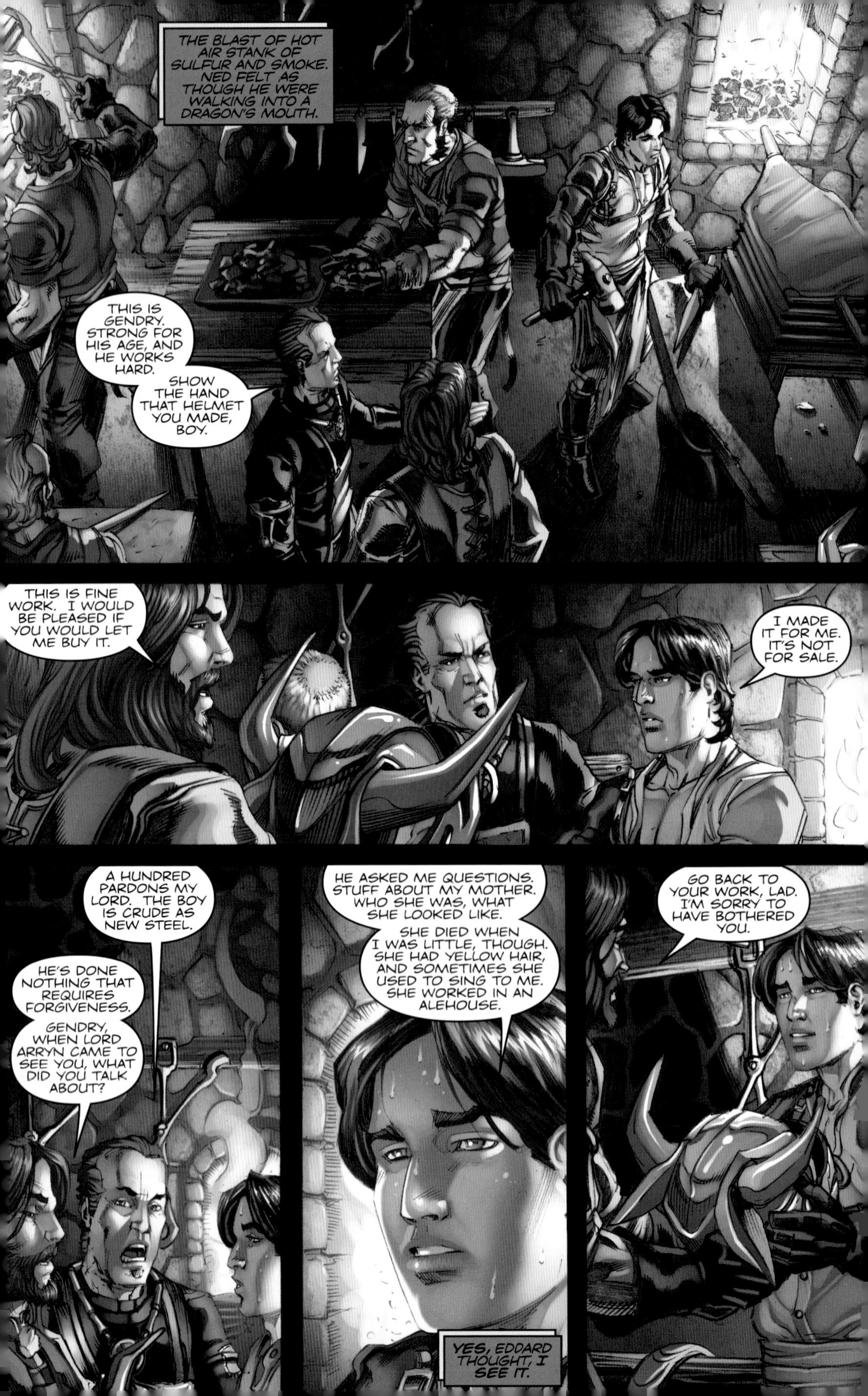
THE BLAST OF HOT AIR STANK OF SULFUR AND SMOKE. NED FELT AS THOUGH HE WERE WALKING INTO A DRAGON'S MOUTH.
THIS IS GENDRY. STRONG FOR HIS AGE, AND HE WORKS HARD.
SHOW THE HAND THAT HELMET YOU MADE, BOY.
THIS IS FINE WORK. I WOULD BE PLEASED IF YOU WOULD LET ME BUY IT.
I MADE IT FOR ME. IT'S NOT FOR SALE.
A HUNDRED PARDONS MY LORD. THE BOY IS CRUDE AS NEW STEEL.
HE'S DONE NOTHING THAT REQUIRES FORGIVENESS.
GENDRY, WHEN LORD ARRYN CAME TO SEE YOU, WHAT DID YOU TALK ABOUT?
HE ASKED ME QUESTIONS. STUFF ABOUT MY MOTHER. WHO SHE WAS, WHAT SHE LOOKED LIKE.
SHE DIED WHEN I WAS LITTLE, THOUGH. SHE HAD YELLOW HAIR, AND SOMETIMES SHE USED TO SING TO ME. SHE WORKED IN AN ALEHOUSE.
YES, EDDARD THOUGHT, I SEE IT.
GO BACK TO YOUR WORK, LAD. I'M SORRY TO HAVE BOTHERED YOU.

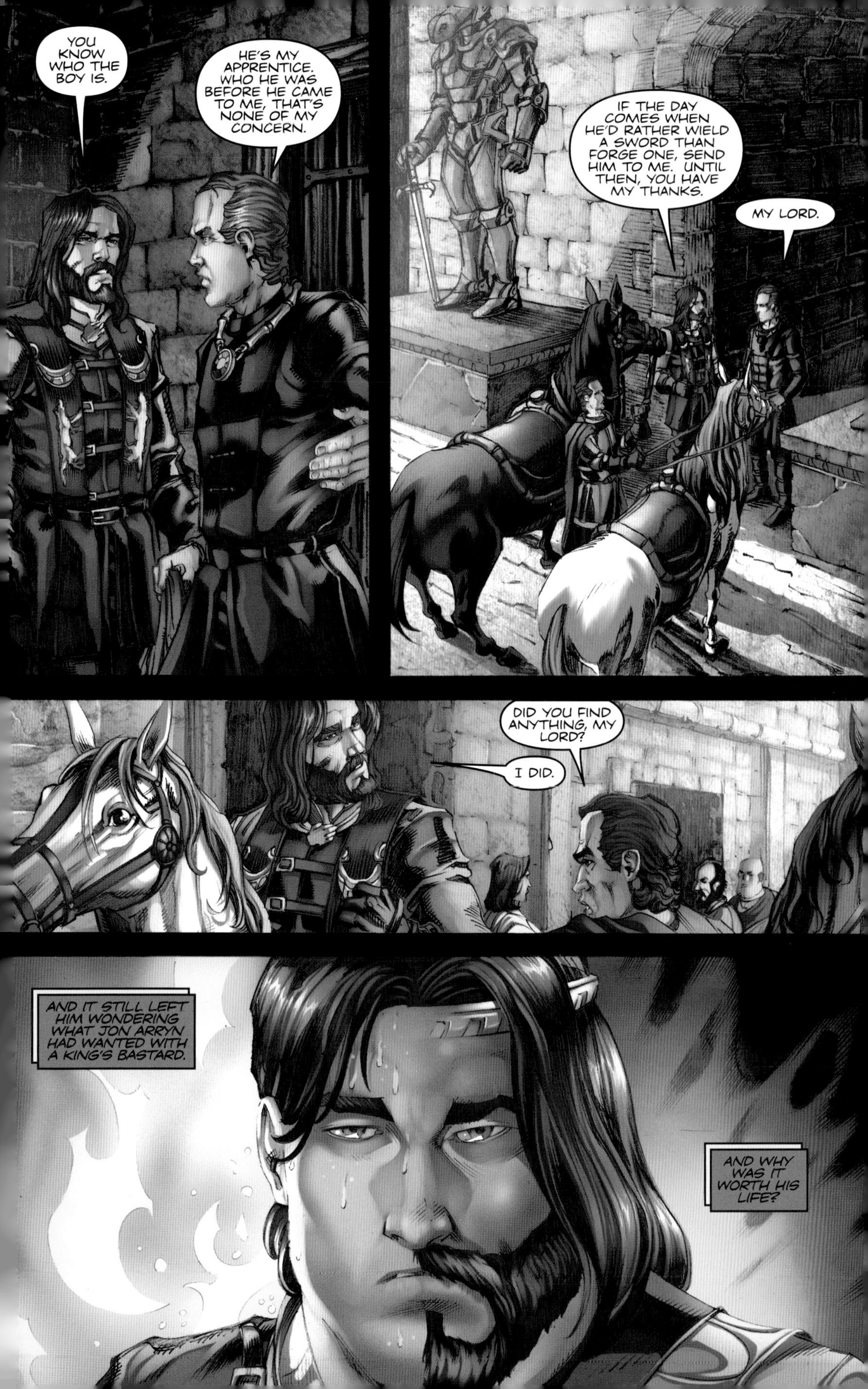
YOU KNOW WHO THE BOY IS.
HE'S MY APPRENTICE. WHO HE WAS BEFORE HE CAME TO ME, THAT'S NONE OF MY CONCERN.
IF THE DAY COMES WHEN HE'D RATHER WIELD A SWORD THAN FORGE ONE, SEND HIM TO ME. UNTIL THEN, YOU HAVE MY THANKS.
MY LORD.
DID YOU FIND ANYTHING, MY LORD?
I DID.
AND IT STILL LEFT HIM WONDERING WHAT JON ARRYN HAD WANTED WITH A KING'S BASTARD.
AND WHY WAS IT WORTH HIS LIFE?

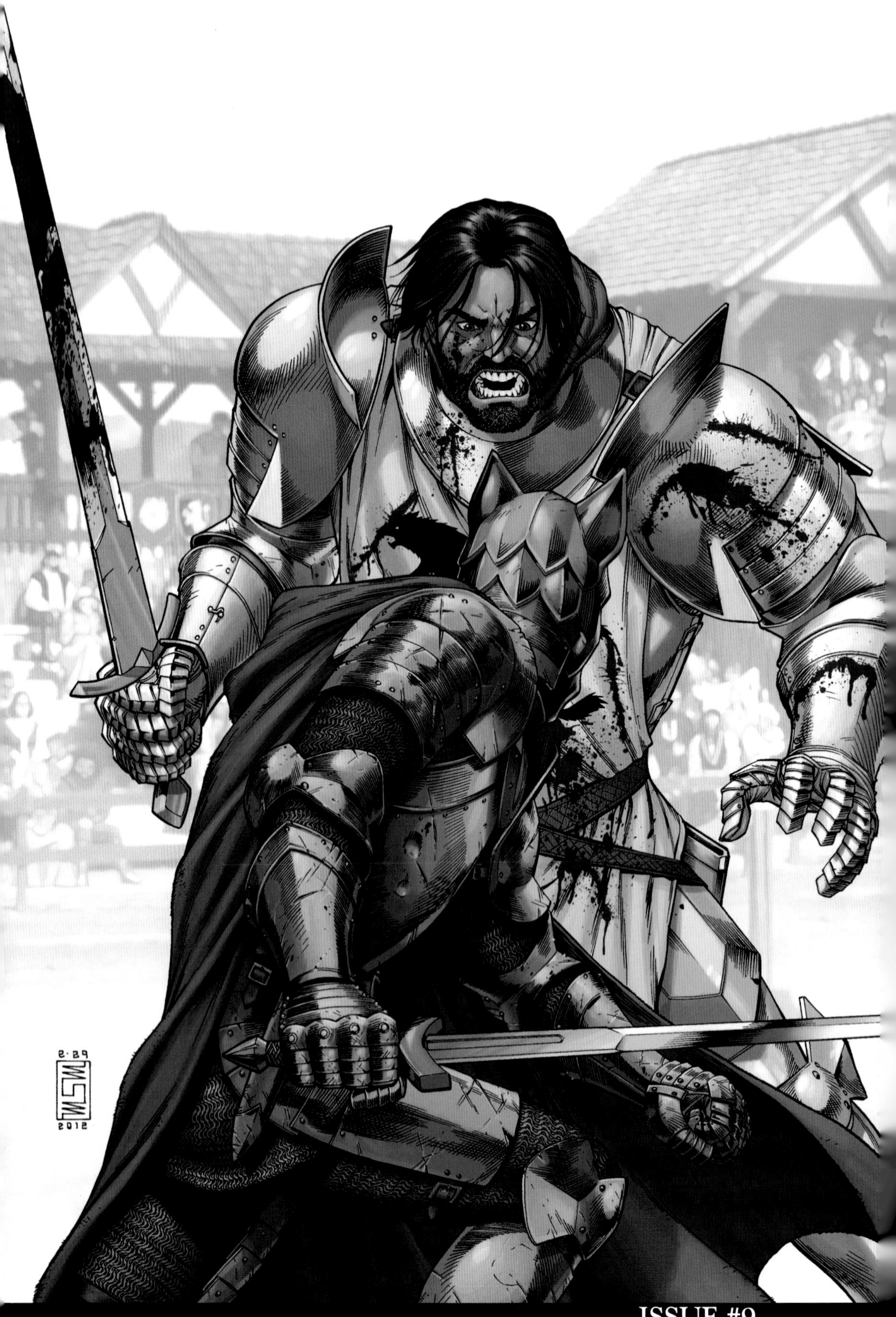

ISSUE #9

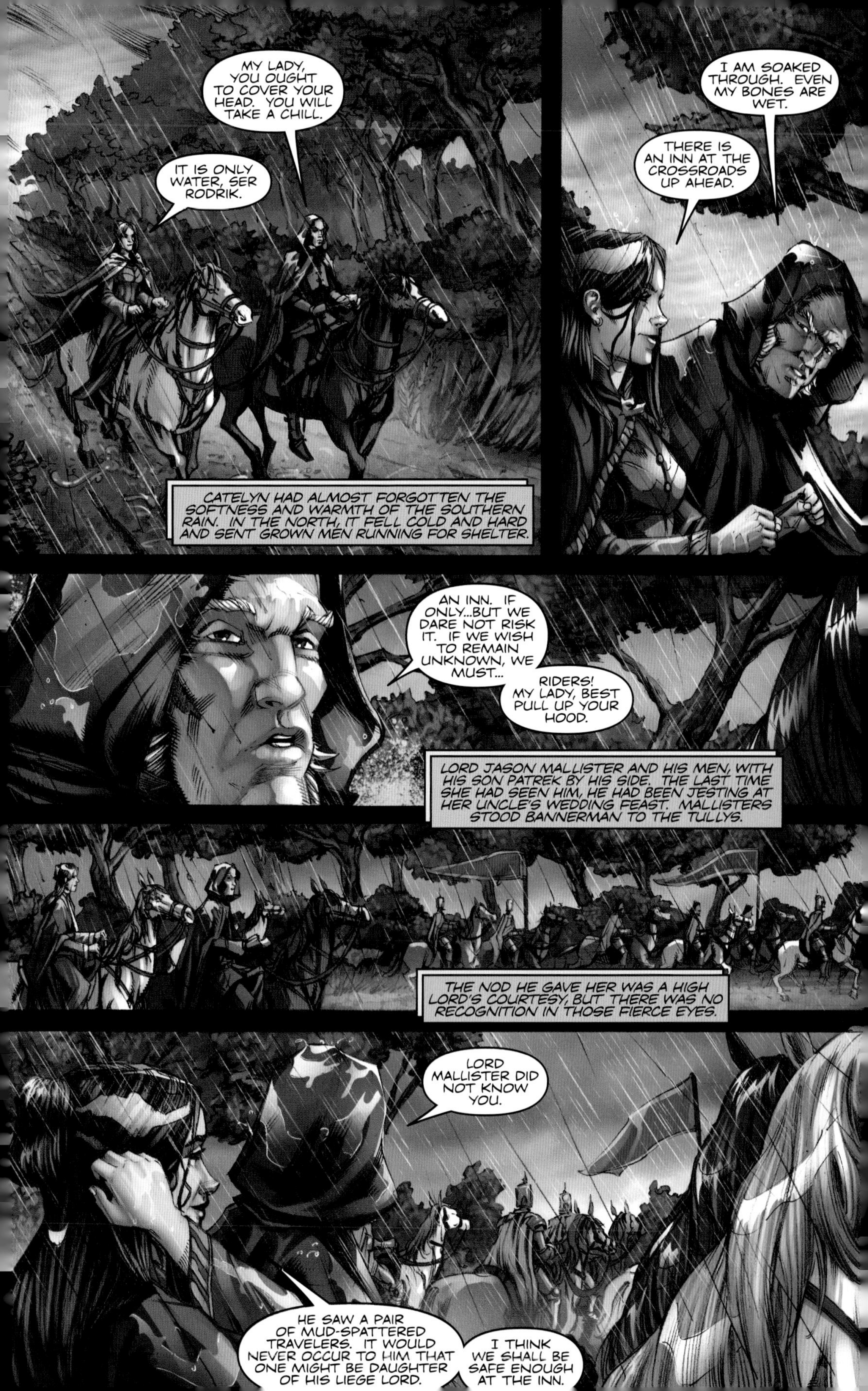
MY LADY, YOU OUGHT TO COVER YOUR HEAD. YOU WILL TAKE A CHILL.
IT IS ONLY WATER, SER RODRIK.
CATELYN HAD ALMOST FORGOTTEN THE SOFTNESS AND WARMTH OF THE SOUTHERN RAIN. IN THE NORTH, IT FELL COLD AND HARD AND SENT GROWN MEN RUNNING FOR SHELTER.
I AM SOAKED THROUGH. EVEN MY BONES ARE WET.
THERE IS AN INN AT THE CROSSROADS UP AHEAD.
AN INN. IF ONLY...BUT WE DARE NOT RISK IT. IF WE WISH TO REMAIN UNKNOWN, WE MUST...
RIDERS! MY LADY, BEST PULL UP YOUR HOOD.
LORD JASON MALLISTER AND HIS MEN, WITH HIS SON PATREK BY HIS SIDE. THE LAST TIME SHE HAD SEEN HIM, HE HAD BEEN JESTING AT HER UNCLE'S WEDDING FEAST. MALLISTERS STOOD BANNERMAN TO THE TULLYS.
THE NOD HE GAVE HER WAS A HIGH LORD'S COURTESY, BUT THERE WAS NO RECOGNITION IN THOSE FIERCE EYES.
LORD MALLISTER DID NOT KNOW YOU.
HE SAW A PAIR OF MUD-SPATTERED TRAVELERS. IT WOULD NEVER OCCUR TO HIM THAT ONE MIGHT BE DAUGHTER OF HIS LIEGE LORD.
I THINK WE SHALL BE SAFE ENOUGH AT THE INN.

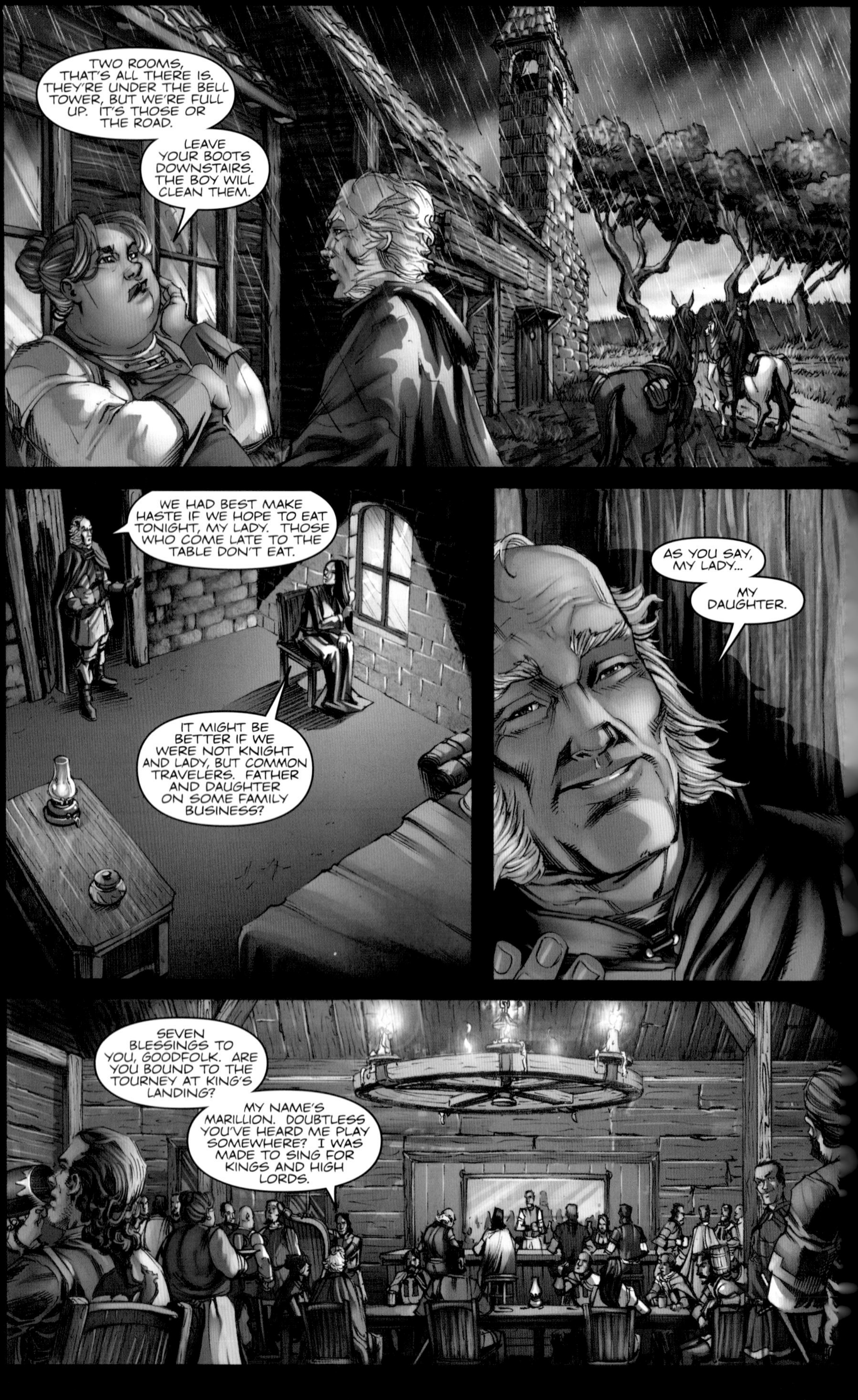
TWO ROOMS, THAT'S ALL THERE IS. THEY'RE UNDER THE BELL TOWER, BUT WE'RE FULL UP. IT'S THOSE OR THE ROAD.
LEAVE YOUR BOOTS DOWNSTAIRS. THE BOY WILL CLEAN THEM.
WE HAD BEST MAKE HASTE IF WE HOPE TO EAT TONIGHT, MY LADY. THOSE WHO COME LATE TO THE TABLE DON'T EAT.
IT MIGHT BE BETTER IF WE WERE NOT KNIGHT AND LADY, BUT COMMON TRAVELERS. FATHER AND DAUGHTER ON SOME FAMILY BUSINESS?
AS YOU SAY, MY LADY...
MY DAUGHTER.
SEVEN BLESSINGS TO YOU, GOODFOLK. ARE YOU BOUND TO THE TOURNEY AT KING'S LANDING?
MY NAME'S MARILLION. DOUBTLESS YOU'VE HEARD ME PLAY SOMEWHERE? I WAS MADE TO SING FOR KINGS AND HIGH LORDS.

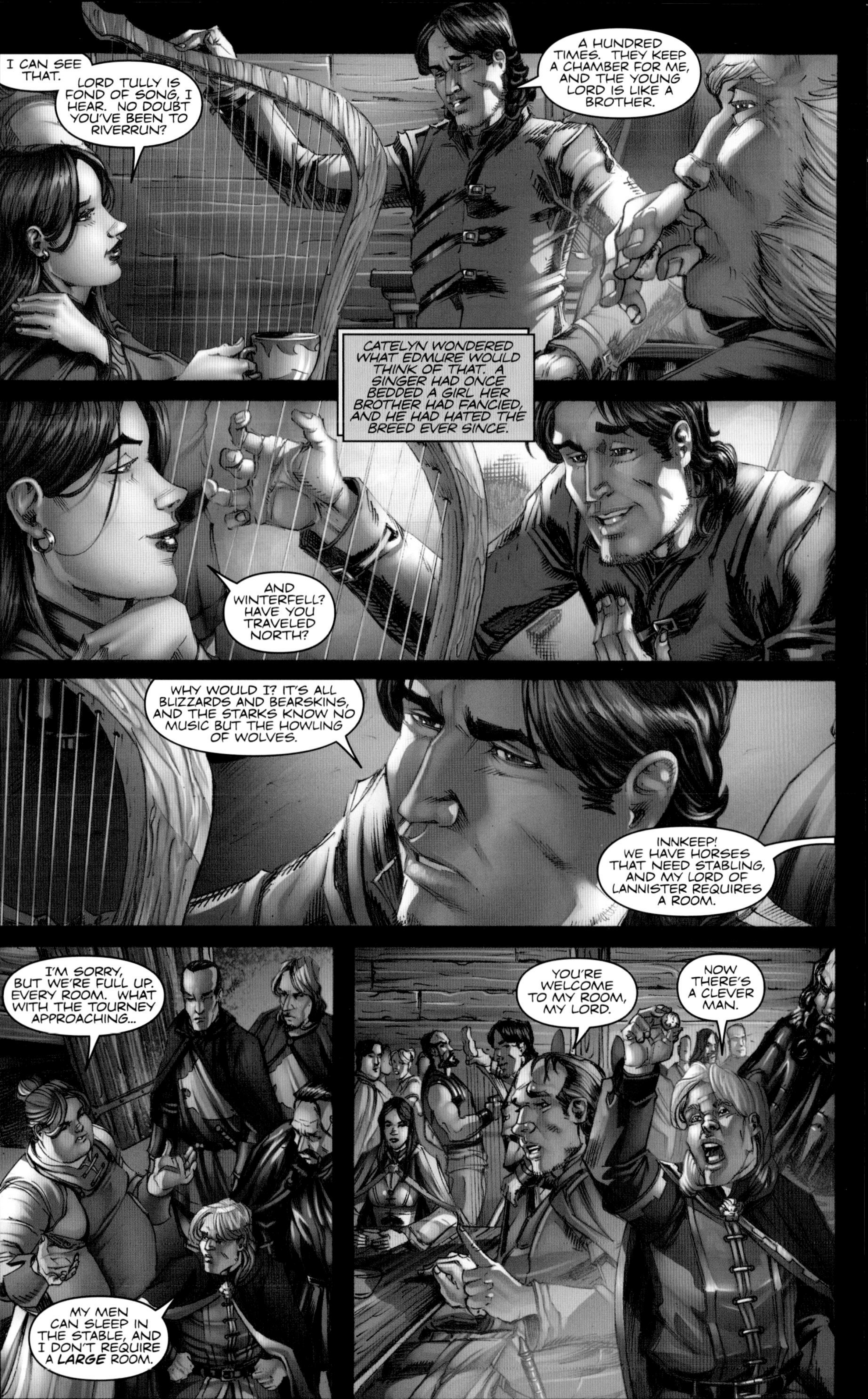

I CAN SEE THAT.
LORD TULLY IS FOND OF SONG, I HEAR. NO DOUBT YOU'VE BEEN TO RIVERRUN?
A HUNDRED TIMES. THEY KEEP A CHAMBER FOR ME, AND THE YOUNG LORD IS LIKE A BROTHER.
CATELYN WONDERED WHAT EDMURE WOULD THINK OF THAT. A SINGER HAD ONCE BEDDED A GIRL HER BROTHER HAD FANCIED, AND HE HAD HATED THE BREED EVER SINCE.
AND WINTERFELL? HAVE YOU TRAVELED NORTH?
WHY WOULD I? IT'S ALL BLIZZARDS AND BEARSKINS, AND THE STARKS KNOW NO MUSIC BUT THE HOWLING OF WOLVES.
INNKEEP! WE HAVE HORSES THAT NEED STABLING, AND MY LORD OF LANNISTER REQUIRES A ROOM.
I'M SORRY, BUT WE'RE FULL UP. EVERY ROOM. WHAT WITH THE TOURNEY APPROACHING...
MY MEN CAN SLEEP IN THE STABLE, AND I DON'T REQUIRE A LARGE ROOM.
YOU'RE WELCOME TO MY ROOM, MY LORD.
NOW THERE'S A CLEVER MAN.

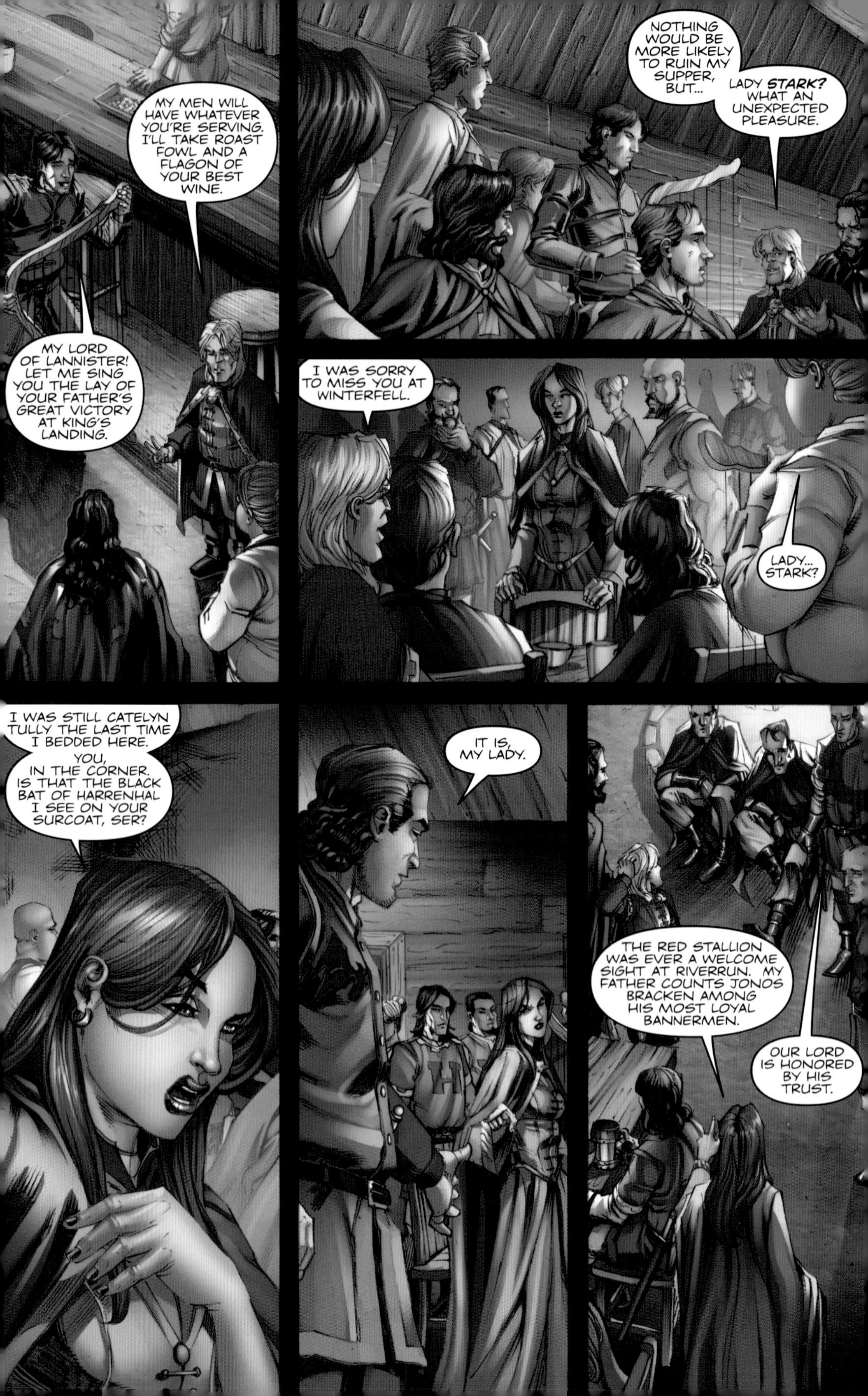
MY MEN WILL HAVE WHATEVER YOU'RE SERVING. I'LL TAKE ROAST FOWL AND A FLAGON OF YOUR BEST WINE.
MY LORD OF LANNISTER! LET ME SING YOU THE LAY OF YOUR FATHER'S GREAT VICTORY AT KING'S LANDING.
NOTHING WOULD BE MORE LIKELY TO RUIN MY SUPPER, BUT...
LADY **STARK?** WHAT AN UNEXPECTED PLEASURE.
I WAS SORRY TO MISS YOU AT WINTERFELL.
LADY... STARK?
I WAS STILL CATELYN TULLY THE LAST TIME I BEDDED HERE.
YOU, IN THE CORNER. IS THAT THE BLACK BAT OF HARRENHAL I SEE ON YOUR SURCOAT, SER?
IT IS, MY LADY.
THE RED STALLION WAS EVER A WELCOME SIGHT AT RIVERRUN. MY FATHER COUNTS JONOS BRACKEN AMONG HIS MOST LOYAL BANNERMEN.
OUR LORD IS HONORED BY HIS TRUST.

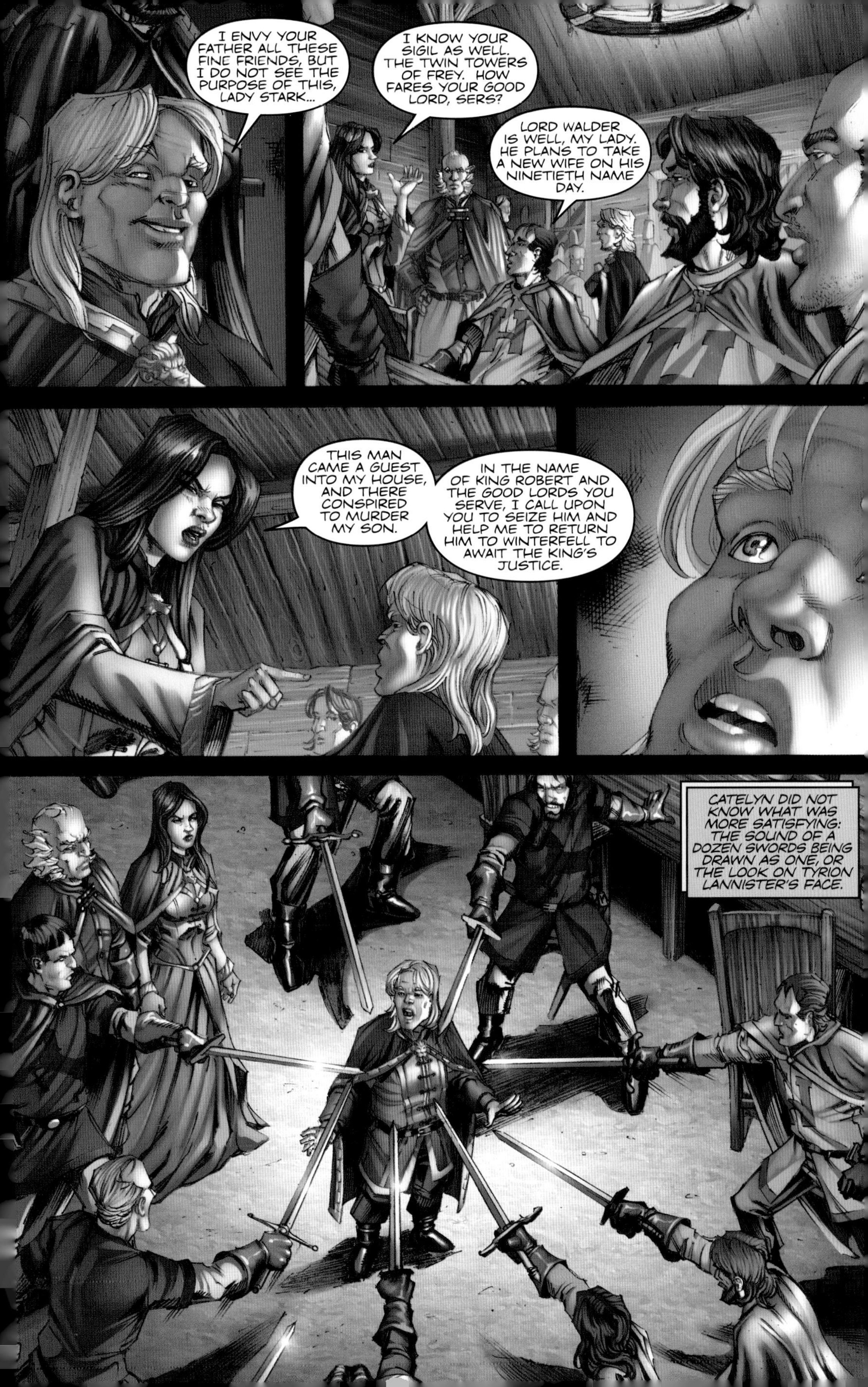
I ENVY YOUR FATHER ALL THESE FINE FRIENDS, BUT I DO NOT SEE THE PURPOSE OF THIS, LADY STARK...
I KNOW YOUR SIGIL AS WELL. THE TWIN TOWERS OF FREY. HOW FARES YOUR GOOD LORD, SERS?
LORD WALDER IS WELL, MY LADY. HE PLANS TO TAKE A NEW WIFE ON HIS NINETIETH NAME DAY.
THIS MAN CAME A GUEST INTO MY HOUSE, AND THERE CONSPIRED TO MURDER MY SON.
IN THE NAME OF KING ROBERT AND THE GOOD LORDS YOU SERVE, I CALL UPON YOU TO SEIZE HIM AND HELP ME TO RETURN HIM TO WINTERFELL TO AWAIT THE KING'S JUSTICE.
CATELYN DID NOT KNOW WHAT WAS MORE SATISFYING: THE SOUND OF A DOZEN SWORDS BEING DRAWN AS ONE, OR THE LOOK ON TYRION LANNISTER'S FACE.

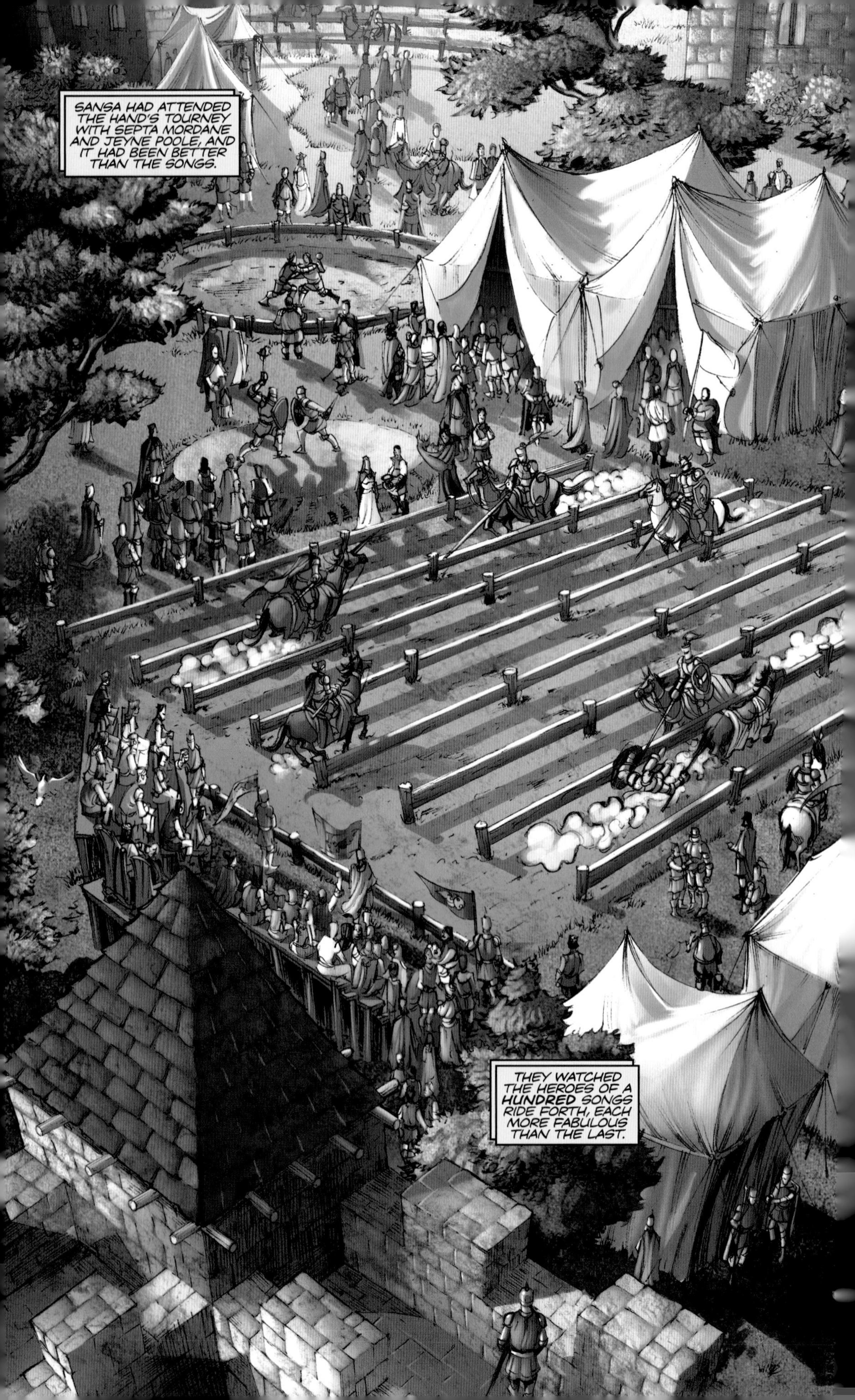
SANSA HAD ATTENDED THE HAND'S TOURNEY WITH SEPTA MORDANE AND JEYNE POOLE, AND IT HAD BEEN BETTER THAN THE SONGS.
THEY WATCHED THE HEROES OF A **HUNDRED** SONGS RIDE FORTH, EACH MORE FABULOUS THAN THE LAST.

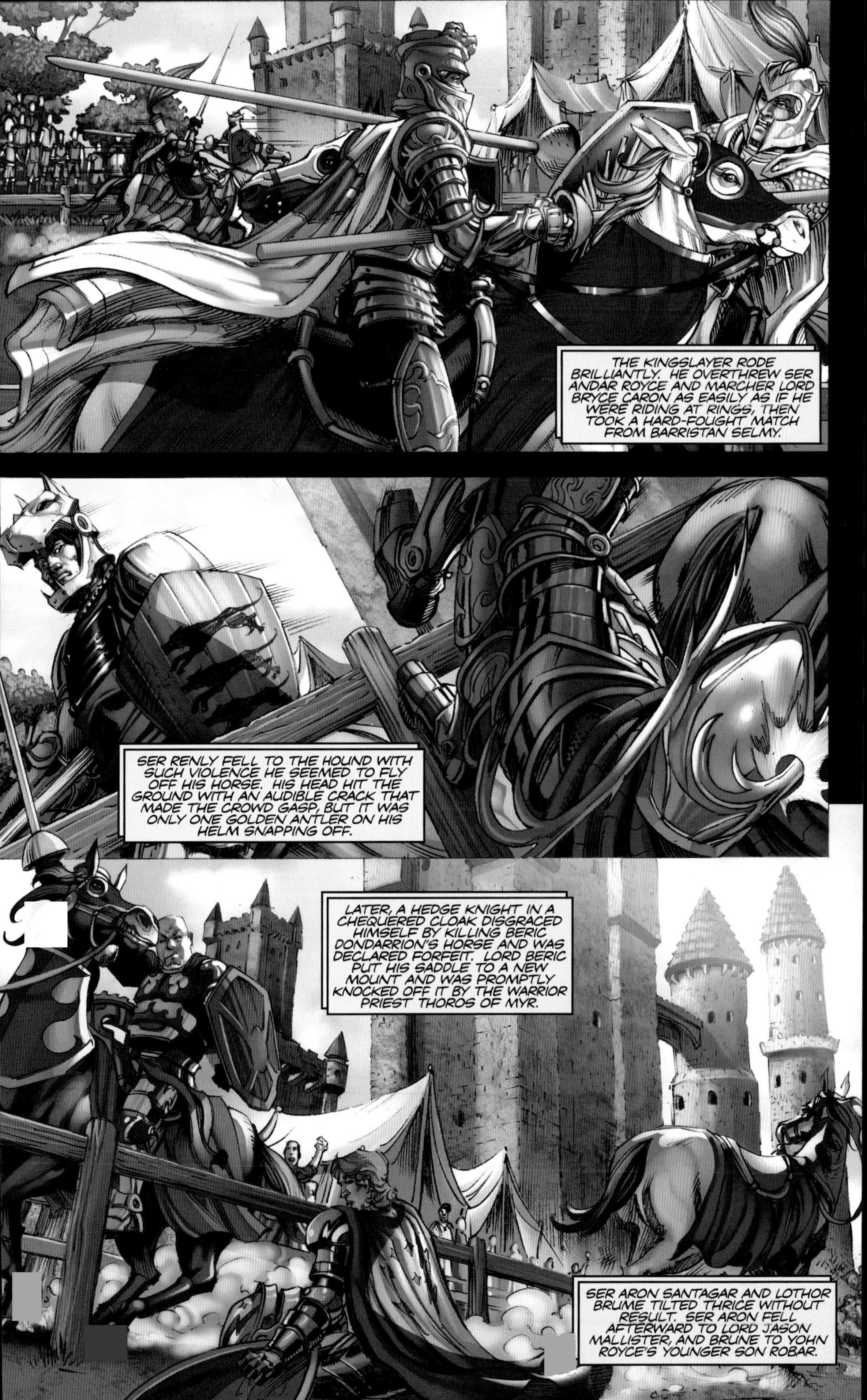
THE KINGSLAYER RODE BRILLIANTLY. HE OVERTHREW SER ANDAR ROYCE AND MARCHER LORD BRYCE CARON AS EASILY AS IF HE WERE RIDING AT RINGS, THEN TOOK A HARD-FOUGHT MATCH FROM BARRISTAN SELMY.
SER RENLY FELL TO THE HOUND WITH SUCH VIOLENCE HE SEEMED TO FLY OFF HIS HORSE. HIS HEAD HIT THE GROUND WITH AN AUDIBLE CRACK THAT MADE THE CROWD GASP, BUT IT WAS ONLY ONE GOLDEN ANTLER ON HIS HELM SNAPPING OFF.
LATER, A HEDGE KNIGHT IN A CHEQUERED CLOAK DISGRACED HIMSELF BY KILLING BERIC DONDARRION'S HORSE AND WAS DECLARED FORFEIT. LORD BERIC PUT HIS SADDLE TO A NEW MOUNT AND WAS PROMPTLY KNOCKED OFF IT BY THE WARRIOR PRIEST THOROS OF MYR.
SER ARON SANTAGAR AND LOTHOR BRUME TILTED THRICE WITHOUT RESULT. SER ARON FELL AFTERWARD TO LORD JASON MALLISTER, AND BRUNE TO YOHN ROYCE'S YOUNGER SON ROBAR.

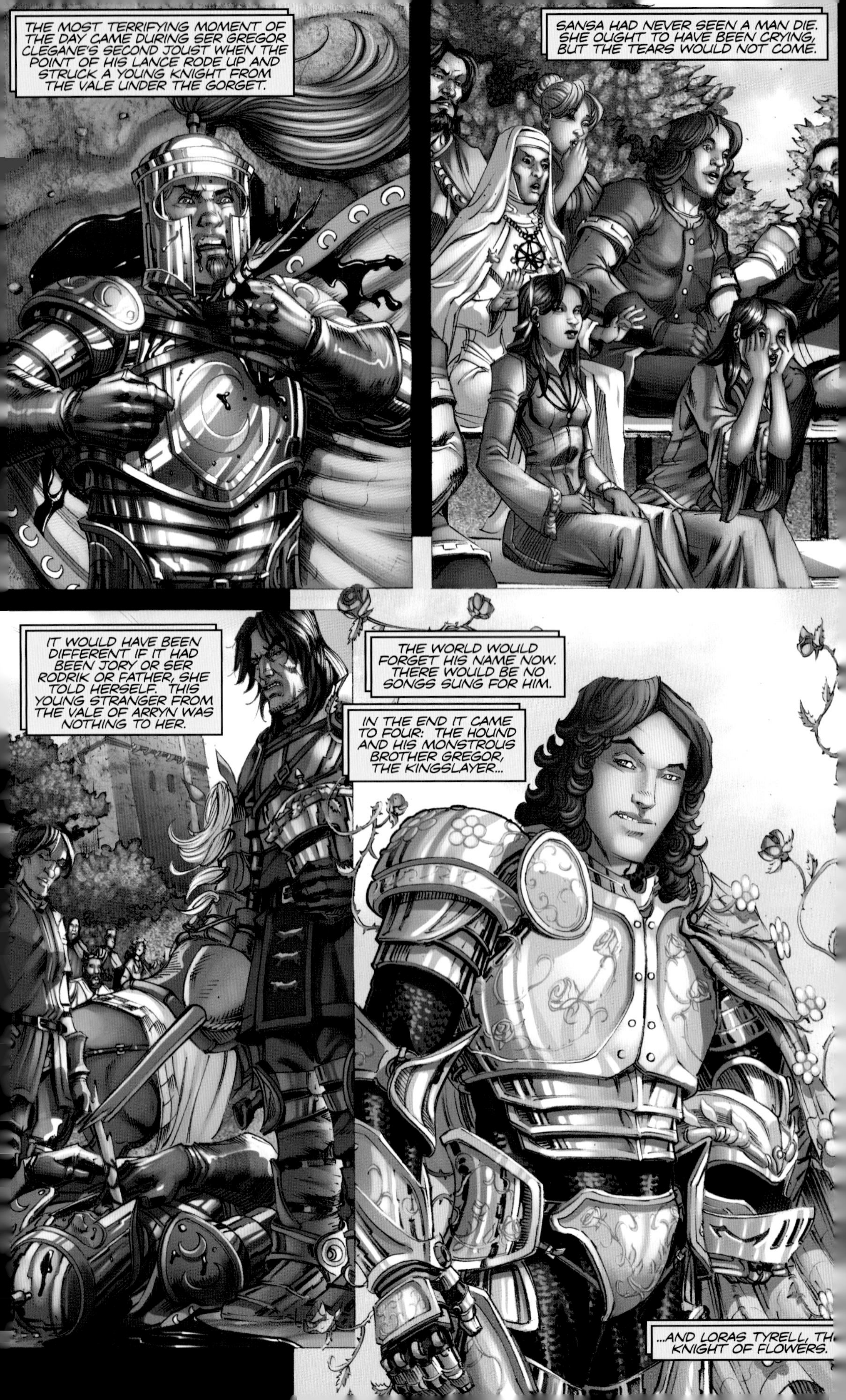
THE MOST TERRIFYING MOMENT OF THE DAY CAME DURING SER GREGOR CLEGANE'S SECOND JOUST WHEN THE POINT OF HIS LANCE RODE UP AND STRUCK A YOUNG KNIGHT FROM THE VALE UNDER THE GORGET.
SANSA HAD NEVER SEEN A MAN DIE. SHE OUGHT TO HAVE BEEN CRYING, BUT THE TEARS WOULD NOT COME.
IT WOULD HAVE BEEN DIFFERENT IF IT HAD BEEN JORY OR SER RODRIK OR FATHER, SHE TOLD HERSELF. THIS YOUNG STRANGER FROM THE VALE OF ARRYN WAS NOTHING TO HER.
THE WORLD WOULD FORGET HIS NAME NOW. THERE WOULD BE NO SONGS SUNG FOR HIM.
IN THE END IT CAME TO FOUR: THE HOUND AND HIS MONSTROUS BROTHER GREGOR, THE KINGSLAYER...
...AND LORAS TYRELL, THE KNIGHT OF FLOWERS.

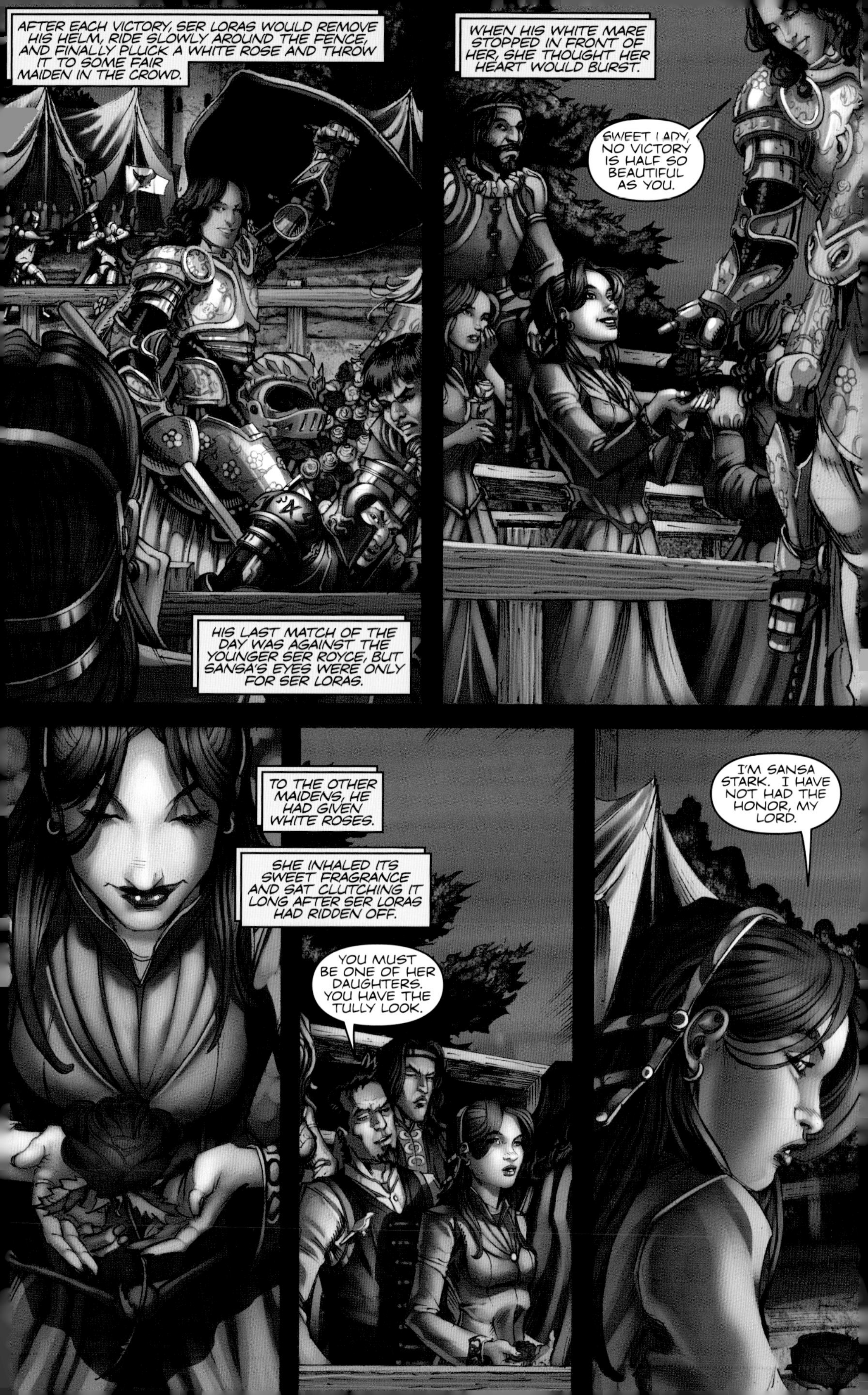
AFTER EACH VICTORY, SER LORAS WOULD REMOVE HIS HELM, RIDE SLOWLY AROUND THE FENCE, AND FINALLY PLUCK A WHITE ROSE AND THROW IT TO SOME FAIR MAIDEN IN THE CROWD.
HIS LAST MATCH OF THE DAY WAS AGAINST THE YOUNGER SER ROYCE, BUT SANSA'S EYES WERE ONLY FOR SER LORAS.
WHEN HIS WHITE MARE STOPPED IN FRONT OF HER, SHE THOUGHT HER HEART WOULD BURST.
SWEET LADY, NO VICTORY IS HALF SO BEAUTIFUL AS YOU.
TO THE OTHER MAIDENS, HE HAD GIVEN WHITE ROSES.
SHE INHALED ITS SWEET FRAGRANCE AND SAT CLUTCHING IT LONG AFTER SER LORAS HAD RIDDEN OFF.
YOU MUST BE ONE OF HER DAUGHTERS. YOU HAVE THE TULLY LOOK.
I'M SANSA STARK. I HAVE NOT HAD THE HONOR, MY LORD.

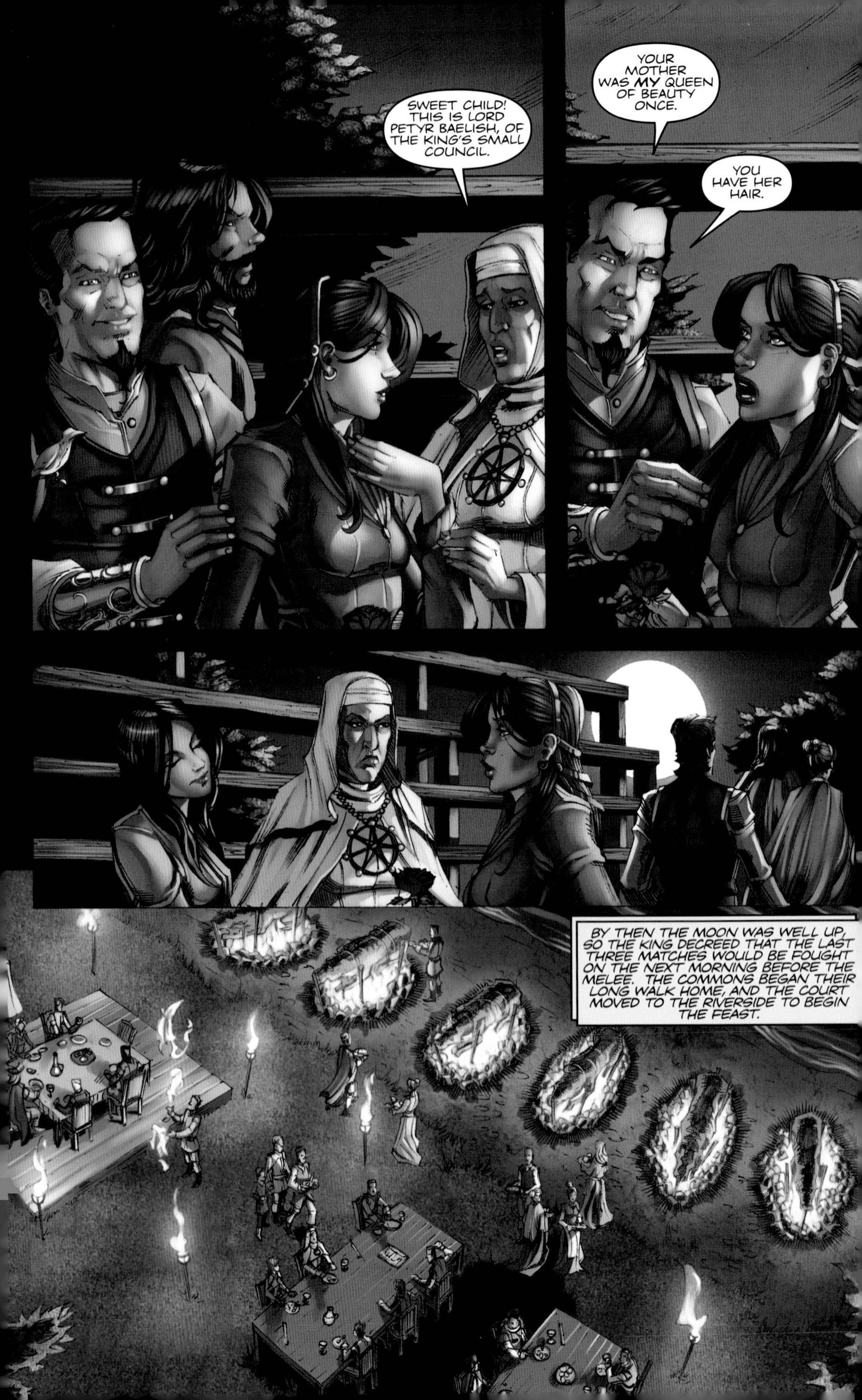
SWEET CHILD! THIS IS LORD PETYR BAELISH, OF THE KING'S SMALL COUNCIL.
YOUR MOTHER WAS **MY** QUEEN OF BEAUTY ONCE.
YOU HAVE HER HAIR.
BY THEN THE MOON WAS WELL UP, SO THE KING DECREED THAT THE LAST THREE MATCHES WOULD BE FOUGHT ON THE NEXT MORNING BEFORE THE MELEE. THE COMMONS BEGAN THEIR LONG WALK HOME, AND THE COURT MOVED TO THE RIVERSIDE TO BEGIN THE FEAST.

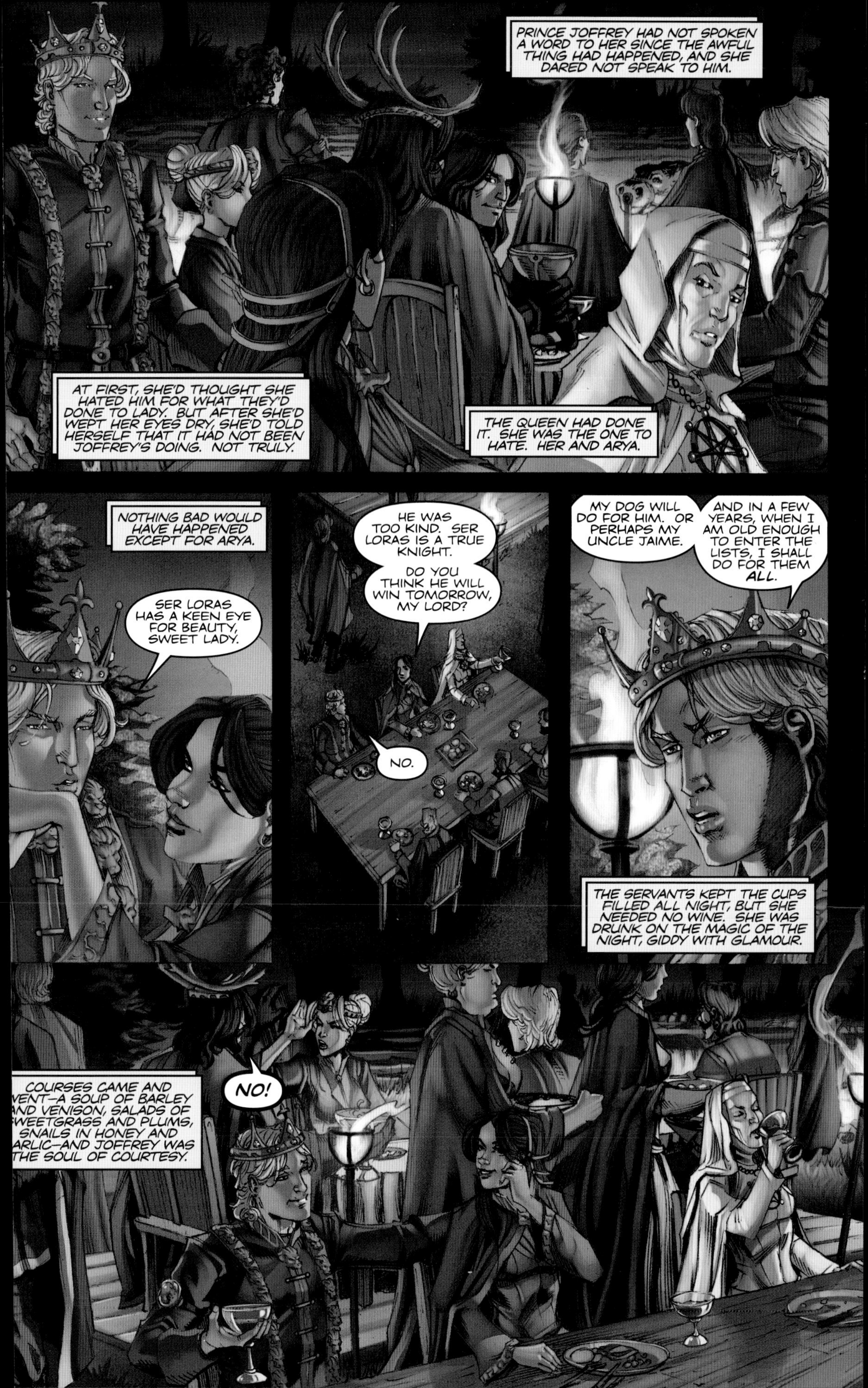
PRINCE JOFFREY HAD NOT SPOKEN A WORD TO HER SINCE THE AWFUL THING HAD HAPPENED, AND SHE DARED NOT SPEAK TO HIM.
AT FIRST, SHE'D THOUGHT SHE HATED HIM FOR WHAT THEY'D DONE TO LADY. BUT AFTER SHE'D WEPT HER EYES DRY, SHE'D TOLD HERSELF THAT IT HAD NOT BEEN JOFFREY'S DOING. NOT TRULY.
THE QUEEN HAD DONE IT. SHE WAS THE ONE TO HATE. HER AND ARYA.
NOTHING BAD WOULD HAVE HAPPENED EXCEPT FOR ARYA.
SER LORAS HAS A KEEN EYE FOR BEAUTY, SWEET LADY.
HE WAS TOO KIND. SER LORAS IS A TRUE KNIGHT.
DO YOU THINK HE WILL WIN TOMORROW, MY LORD?
NO.
MY DOG WILL DO FOR HIM. OR PERHAPS MY UNCLE JAIME.
AND IN A FEW YEARS, WHEN I AM OLD ENOUGH TO ENTER THE LISTS, I SHALL DO FOR THEM ALL.
THE SERVANTS KEPT THE CUPS FILLED ALL NIGHT, BUT SHE NEEDED NO WINE. SHE WAS DRUNK ON THE MAGIC OF THE NIGHT, GIDDY WITH GLAMOUR.
COURSES CAME AND WENT—A SOUP OF BARLEY AND VENISON, SALADS OF SWEETGRASS AND PLUMS, SNAILS IN HONEY AND GARLIC—AND JOFFREY WAS THE SOUL OF COURTESY.
NO!

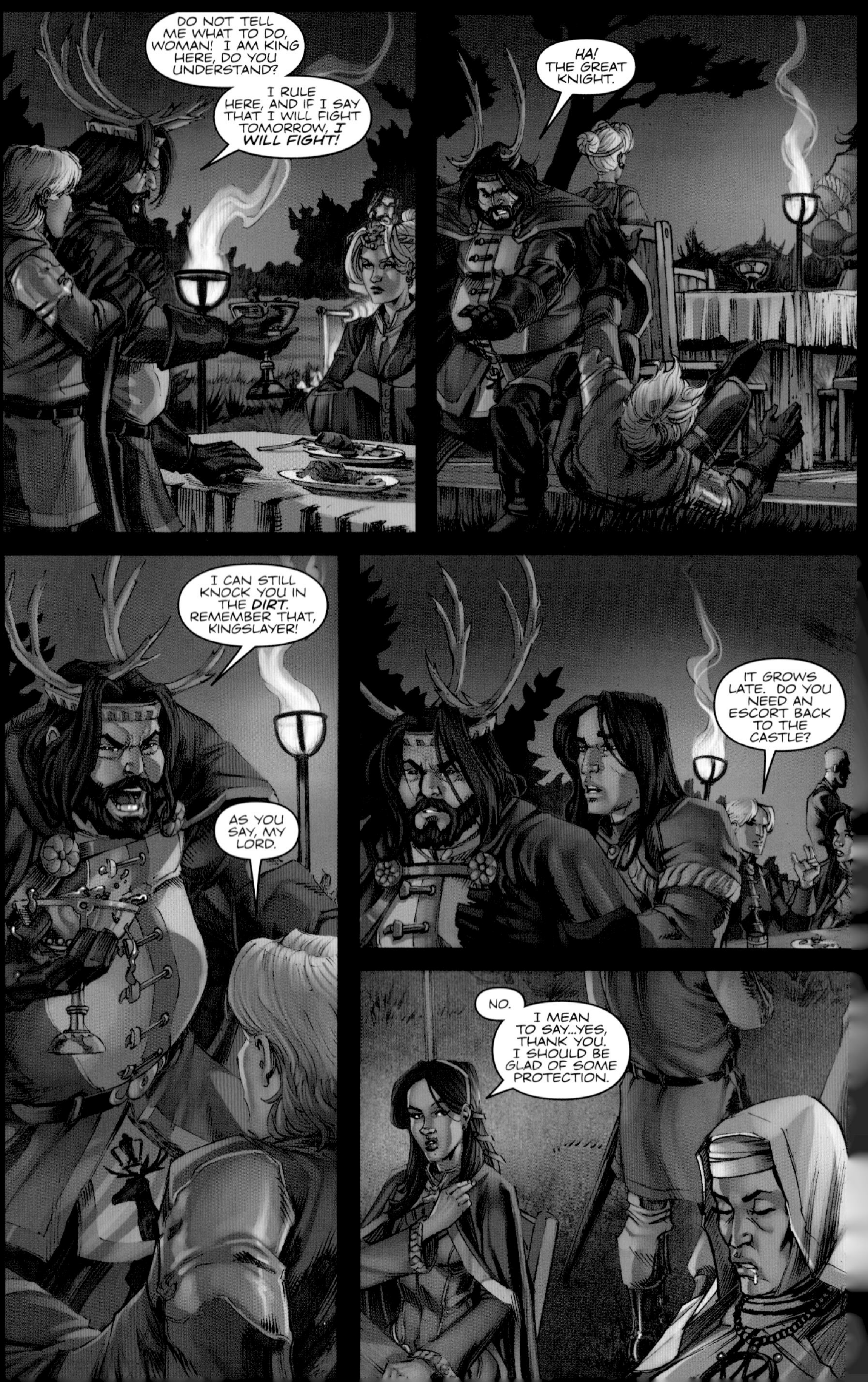
DO NOT TELL ME WHAT TO DO, WOMAN! I AM KING HERE, DO YOU UNDERSTAND?
I RULE HERE, AND IF I SAY THAT I WILL FIGHT TOMORROW, *I WILL FIGHT!*
HA! THE GREAT KNIGHT.
I CAN STILL KNOCK YOU IN THE ***DIRT***. REMEMBER THAT, KINGSLAYER!
AS YOU SAY, MY LORD.
IT GROWS LATE. DO YOU NEED AN ESCORT BACK TO THE CASTLE?
NO.
I MEAN TO SAY...YES, THANK YOU. I SHOULD BE GLAD OF SOME PROTECTION.

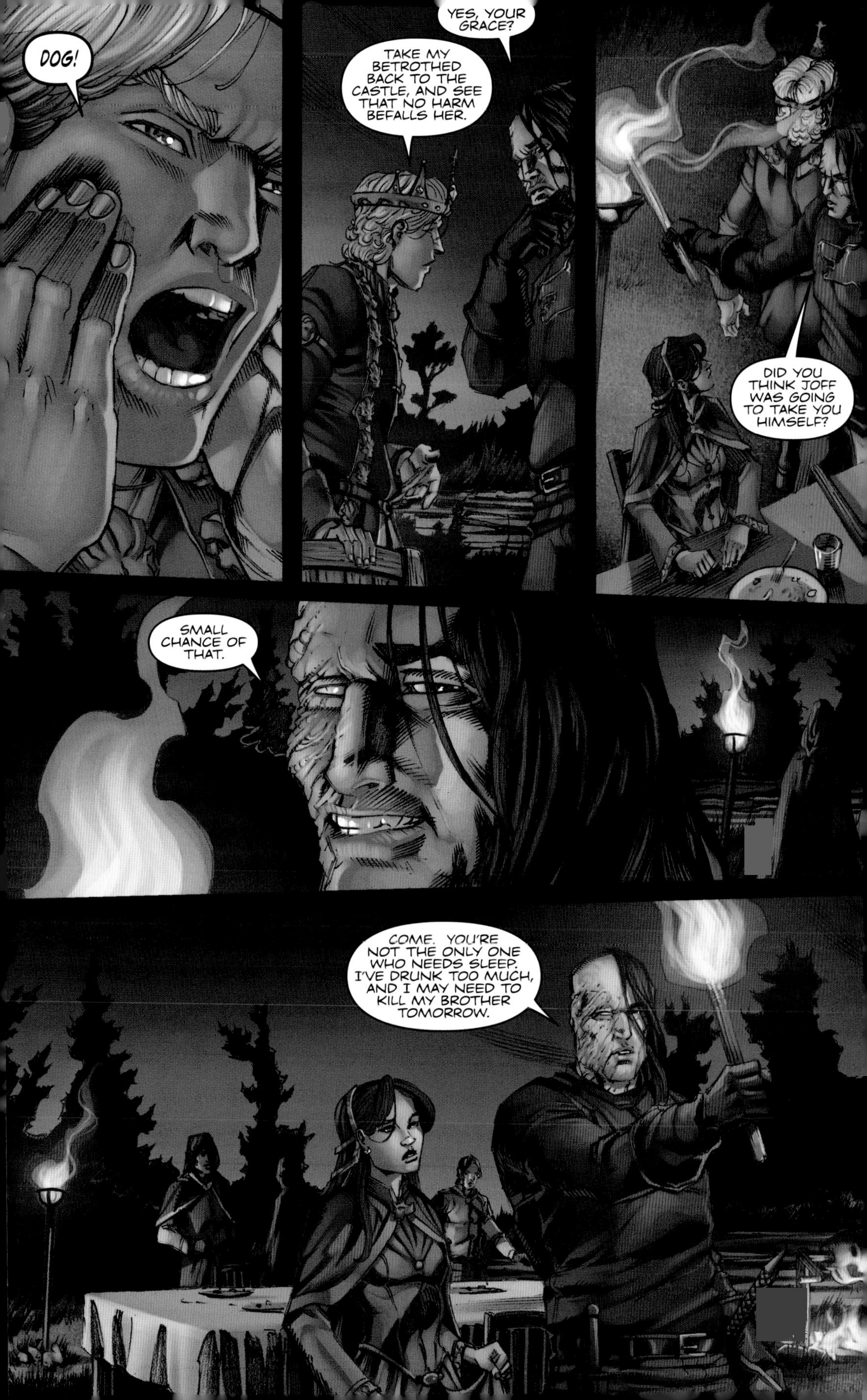

DOG!
YES, YOUR GRACE?
TAKE MY BETROTHED BACK TO THE CASTLE, AND SEE THAT NO HARM BEFALLS HER.
DID YOU THINK JOFF WAS GOING TO TAKE YOU HIMSELF?
SMALL CHANCE OF THAT.
COME. YOU'RE NOT THE ONLY ONE WHO NEEDS SLEEP. I'VE DRUNK TOO MUCH, AND I MAY NEED TO KILL MY BROTHER TOMORROW.

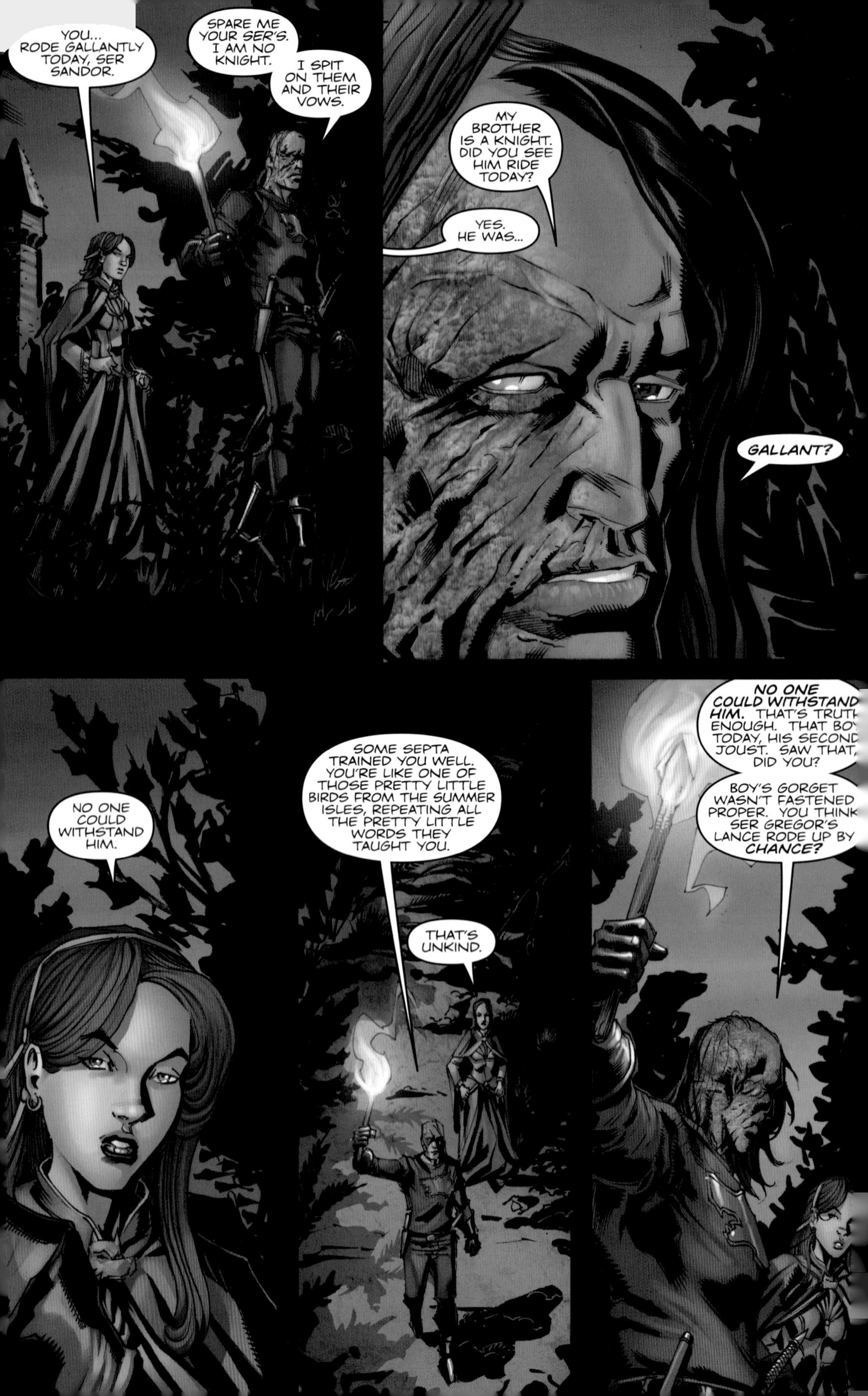
YOU... RODE GALLANTLY TODAY, SER SANDOR.
SPARE ME YOUR SER'S. I AM NO KNIGHT.
I SPIT ON THEM AND THEIR VOWS.
MY BROTHER IS A KNIGHT. DID YOU SEE HIM RIDE TODAY?
YES. HE WAS...
GALLANT?
NO ONE COULD WITHSTAND HIM.
SOME SEPTA TRAINED YOU WELL. YOU'RE LIKE ONE OF THOSE PRETTY LITTLE BIRDS FROM THE SUMMER ISLES, REPEATING ALL THE PRETTY LITTLE WORDS THEY TAUGHT YOU.
THAT'S UNKIND.
NO ONE COULD WITHSTAND HIM. THAT'S TRUTH ENOUGH. THAT BOY TODAY, HIS SECOND JOUST. SAW THAT, DID YOU?
BOY'S GORGET WASN'T FASTENED PROPER. YOU THINK SER GREGOR'S LANCE RODE UP BY CHANCE?

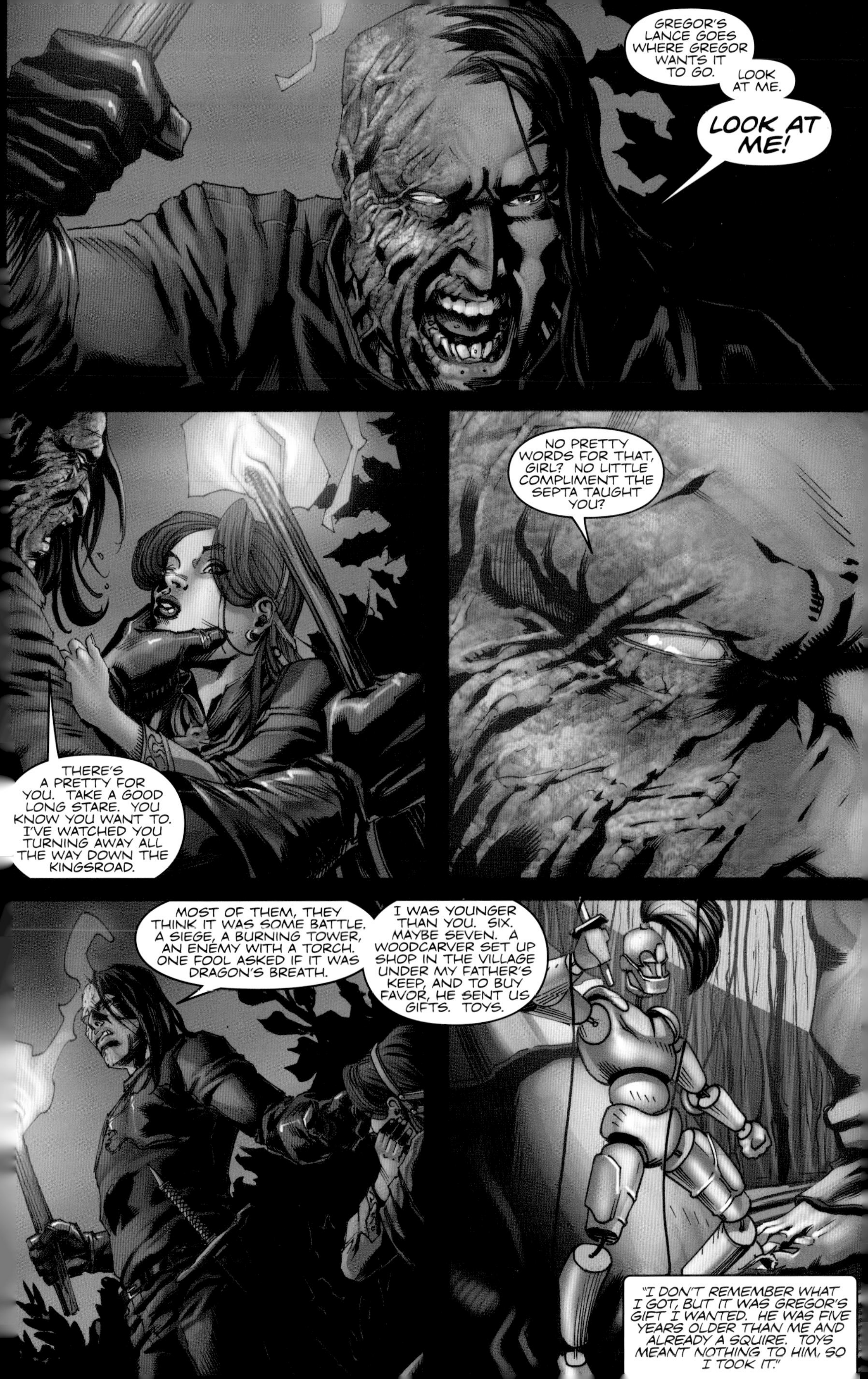
GREGOR'S LANCE GOES WHERE GREGOR WANTS IT TO GO.
LOOK AT ME.
LOOK AT ME!
THERE'S A PRETTY FOR YOU. TAKE A GOOD LONG STARE. YOU KNOW YOU WANT TO. I'VE WATCHED YOU TURNING AWAY ALL THE WAY DOWN THE KINGSROAD.
NO PRETTY WORDS FOR THAT, GIRL? NO LITTLE COMPLIMENT THE SEPTA TAUGHT YOU?
MOST OF THEM, THEY THINK IT WAS SOME BATTLE. A SIEGE, A BURNING TOWER, AN ENEMY WITH A TORCH. ONE FOOL ASKED IF IT WAS DRAGON'S BREATH.
I WAS YOUNGER THAN YOU. SIX. MAYBE SEVEN. A WOODCARVER SET UP SHOP IN THE VILLAGE UNDER MY FATHER'S KEEP, AND TO BUY FAVOR, HE SENT US GIFTS. TOYS.
"I DON'T REMEMBER WHAT I GOT, BUT IT WAS GREGOR'S GIFT I WANTED. HE WAS FIVE YEARS OLDER THAN ME AND ALREADY A SQUIRE. TOYS MEANT NOTHING TO HIM, SO I TOOK IT."

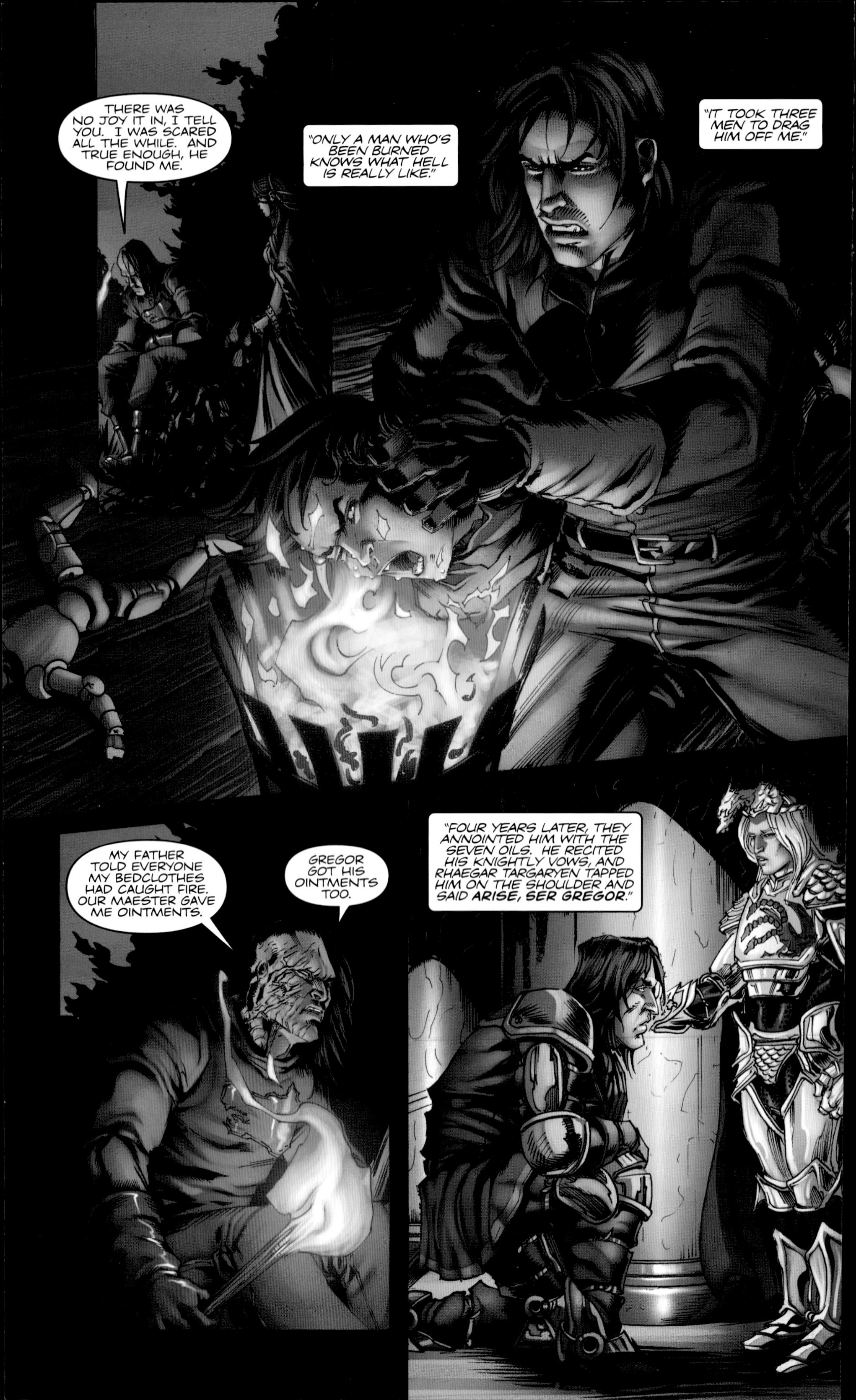
THERE WAS NO JOY IT IN, I TELL YOU. I WAS SCARED ALL THE WHILE. AND TRUE ENOUGH, HE FOUND ME.
"ONLY A MAN WHO'S BEEN BURNED KNOWS WHAT HELL IS REALLY LIKE."
"IT TOOK THREE MEN TO DRAG HIM OFF ME."
MY FATHER TOLD EVERYONE MY BEDCLOTHES HAD CAUGHT FIRE. OUR MAESTER GAVE ME OINTMENTS.
GREGOR GOT HIS OINTMENTS TOO.
"FOUR YEARS LATER, THEY ANNOINTED HIM WITH THE SEVEN OILS. HE RECITED HIS KNIGHTLY VOWS, AND RHAEGAR TARGARYEN TAPPED HIM ON THE SHOULDER AND SAID **ARISE, SER GREGOR**."

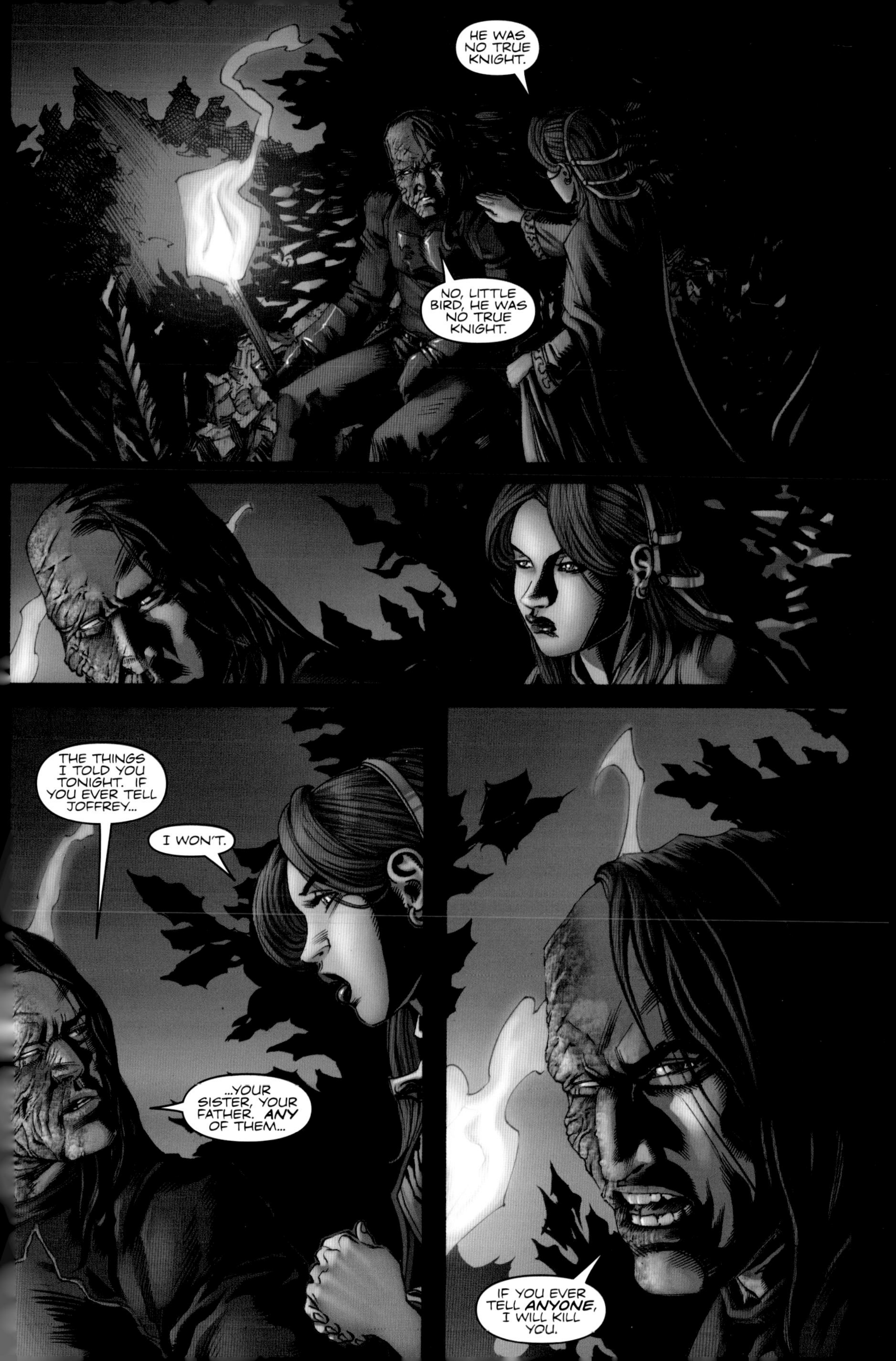
HE WAS NO TRUE KNIGHT.
NO, LITTLE BIRD, HE WAS NO TRUE KNIGHT.
THE THINGS I TOLD YOU TONIGHT. IF YOU EVER TELL JOFFREY...
I WON'T.
...YOUR SISTER, YOUR FATHER. ANY OF THEM...
IF YOU EVER TELL ANYONE, I WILL KILL YOU.

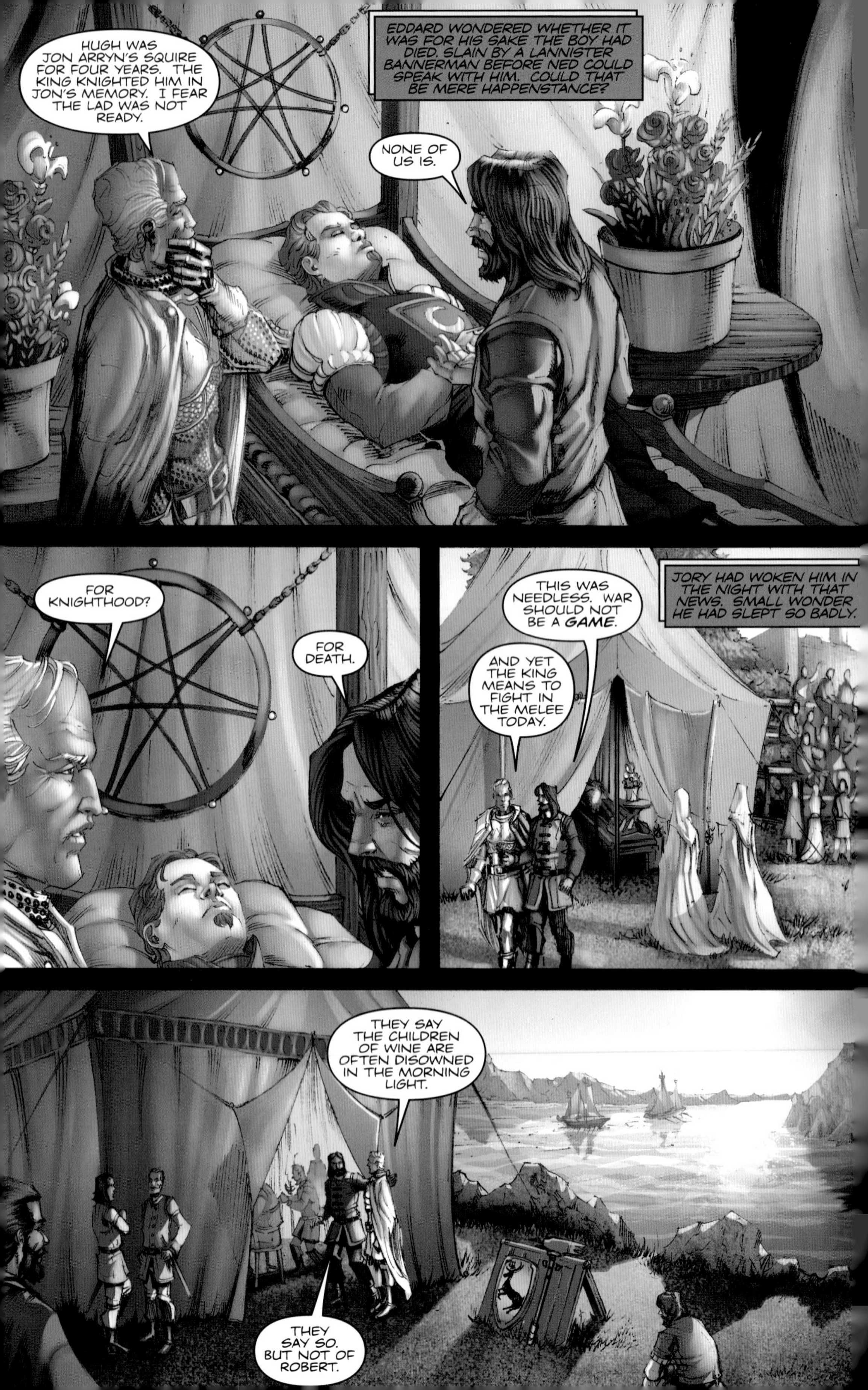
HUGH WAS JON ARRYN'S SQUIRE FOR FOUR YEARS. THE KING KNIGHTED HIM IN JON'S MEMORY. I FEAR THE LAD WAS NOT READY.
EDDARD WONDERED WHETHER IT WAS FOR HIS SAKE THE BOY HAD DIED. SLAIN BY A LANNISTER BANNERMAN BEFORE NED COULD SPEAK WITH HIM. COULD THAT BE MERE HAPPENSTANCE?
NONE OF US IS.
FOR KNIGHTHOOD?
FOR DEATH.
JORY HAD WOKEN HIM IN THE NIGHT WITH THAT NEWS. SMALL WONDER HE HAD SLEPT SO BADLY.
THIS WAS NEEDLESS. WAR SHOULD NOT BE A GAME.
AND YET THE KING MEANS TO FIGHT IN THE MELEE TODAY.
THEY SAY THE CHILDREN OF WINE ARE OFTEN DISOWNED IN THE MORNING LIGHT.
THEY SAY SO. BUT NOT OF ROBERT.

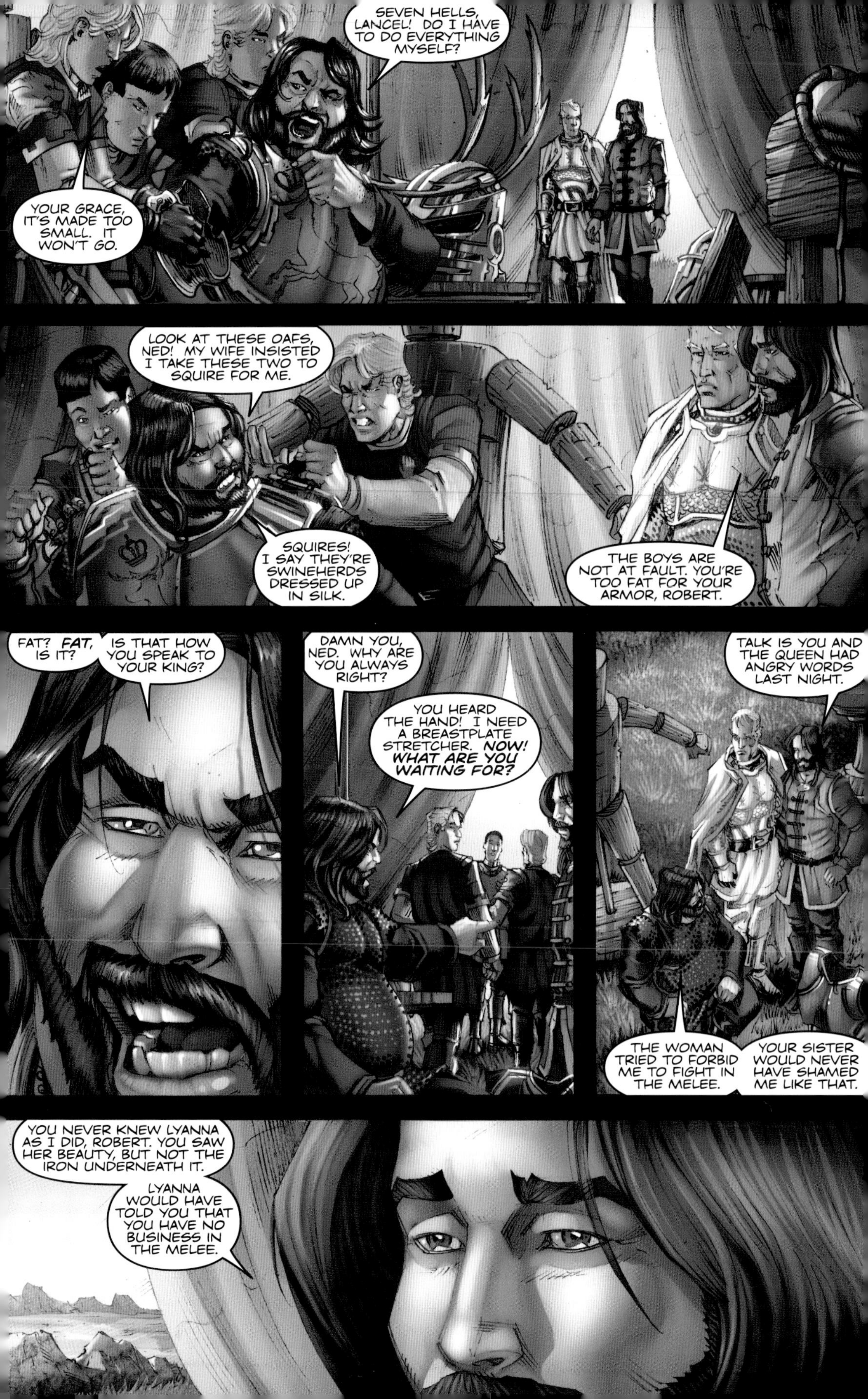
SEVEN HELLS, LANCEL! DO I HAVE TO DO EVERYTHING MYSELF?
YOUR GRACE, IT'S MADE TOO SMALL. IT WON'T GO.
LOOK AT THESE OAFS, NED! MY WIFE INSISTED I TAKE THESE TWO TO SQUIRE FOR ME.
SQUIRES! I SAY THEY'RE SWINEHERDS DRESSED UP IN SILK.
THE BOYS ARE NOT AT FAULT. YOU'RE TOO FAT FOR YOUR ARMOR, ROBERT.
FAT? FAT, IS IT?
IS THAT HOW YOU SPEAK TO YOUR KING?
DAMN YOU, NED. WHY ARE YOU ALWAYS RIGHT?
YOU HEARD THE HAND! I NEED A BREASTPLATE STRETCHER. NOW! WHAT ARE YOU WAITING FOR?
TALK IS YOU AND THE QUEEN HAD ANGRY WORDS LAST NIGHT.
THE WOMAN TRIED TO FORBID ME TO FIGHT IN THE MELEE.
YOUR SISTER WOULD NEVER HAVE SHAMED ME LIKE THAT.
YOU NEVER KNEW LYANNA AS I DID, ROBERT. YOU SAW HER BEAUTY, BUT NOT THE IRON UNDERNEATH IT.
LYANNA WOULD HAVE TOLD YOU THAT YOU HAVE NO BUSINESS IN THE MELEE.

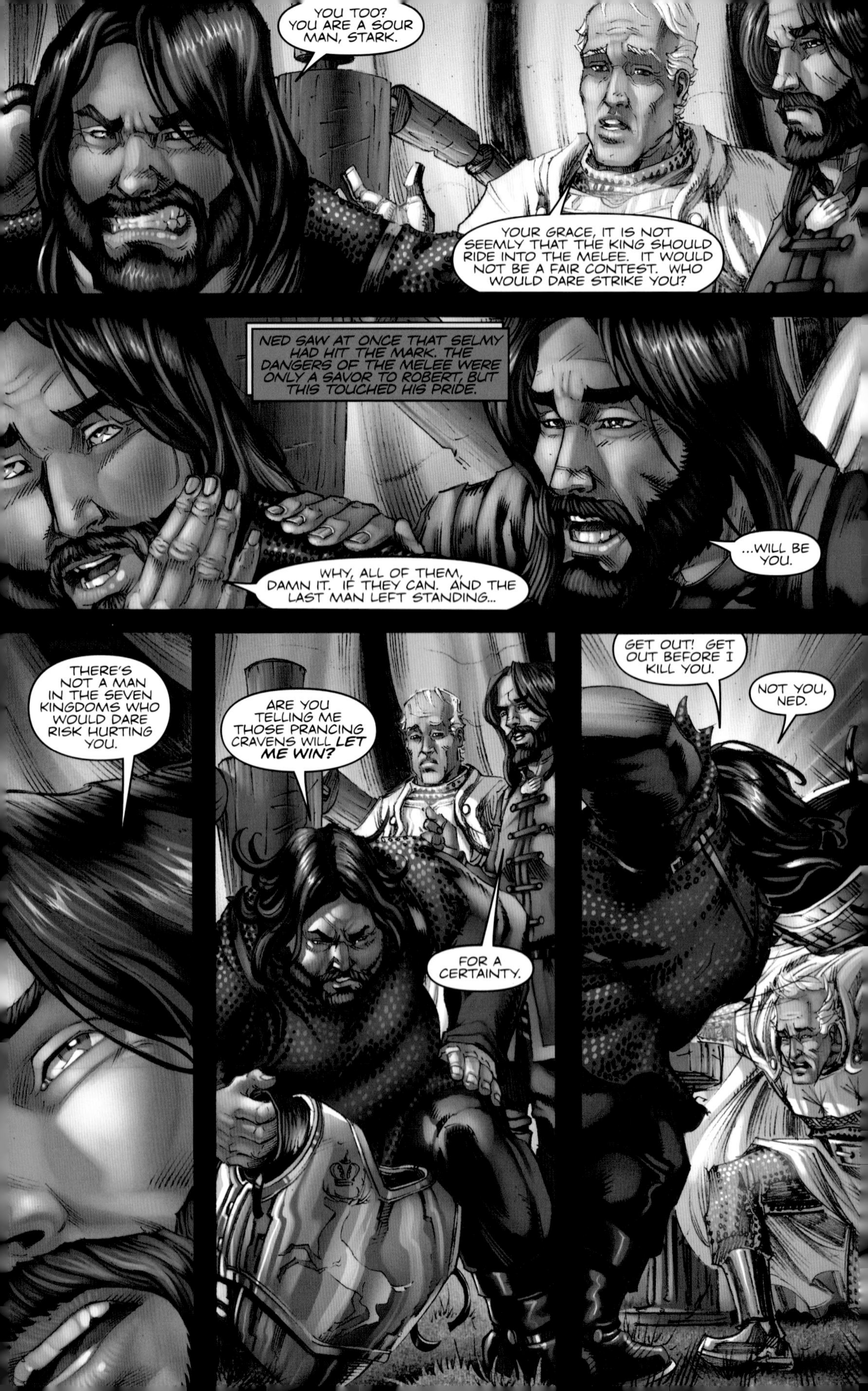
YOU TOO? YOU ARE A SOUR MAN, STARK.
YOUR GRACE, IT IS NOT SEEMLY THAT THE KING SHOULD RIDE INTO THE MELEE. IT WOULD NOT BE A FAIR CONTEST. WHO WOULD DARE STRIKE YOU?
NED SAW AT ONCE THAT SELMY HAD HIT THE MARK. THE DANGERS OF THE MELEE WERE ONLY A SAVOR TO ROBERT, BUT THIS TOUCHED HIS PRIDE.
WHY, ALL OF THEM, DAMN IT. IF THEY CAN. AND THE LAST MAN LEFT STANDING...
...WILL BE YOU.
THERE'S NOT A MAN IN THE SEVEN KINGDOMS WHO WOULD DARE RISK HURTING YOU.
ARE YOU TELLING ME THOSE PRANCING CRAVENS WILL ***LET ME WIN?***
FOR A CERTAINTY.
GET OUT! GET OUT BEFORE I KILL YOU.
NOT YOU, NED.

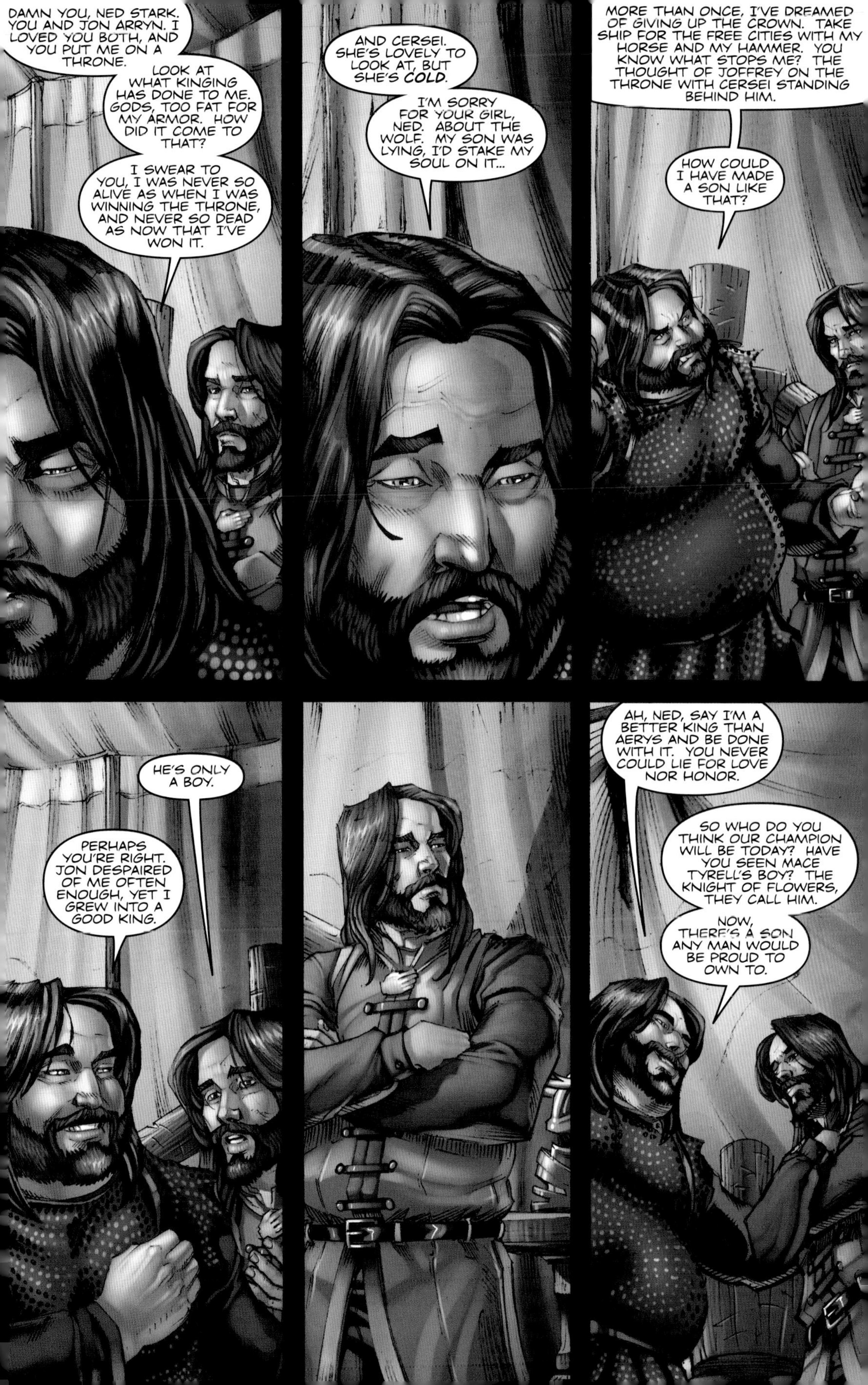
DAMN YOU, NED STARK. YOU AND JON ARRYN. I LOVED YOU BOTH, AND YOU PUT ME ON A THRONE.
LOOK AT WHAT KINGING HAS DONE TO ME. GODS, TOO FAT FOR MY ARMOR. HOW DID IT COME TO THAT?
I SWEAR TO YOU, I WAS NEVER SO ALIVE AS WHEN I WAS WINNING THE THRONE, AND NEVER SO DEAD AS NOW THAT I'VE WON IT.
AND CERSEI. SHE'S LOVELY TO LOOK AT, BUT SHE'S COLD.
I'M SORRY FOR YOUR GIRL, NED. ABOUT THE WOLF. MY SON WAS LYING, I'D STAKE MY SOUL ON IT...
MORE THAN ONCE, I'VE DREAMED OF GIVING UP THE CROWN. TAKE SHIP FOR THE FREE CITIES WITH MY HORSE AND MY HAMMER. YOU KNOW WHAT STOPS ME? THE THOUGHT OF JOFFREY ON THE THRONE WITH CERSEI STANDING BEHIND HIM.
HOW COULD I HAVE MADE A SON LIKE THAT?
HE'S ONLY A BOY.
PERHAPS YOU'RE RIGHT. JON DESPAIRED OF ME OFTEN ENOUGH, YET I GREW INTO A GOOD KING.
AH, NED, SAY I'M A BETTER KING THAN AERYS AND BE DONE WITH IT. YOU NEVER COULD LIE FOR LOVE NOR HONOR.
SO WHO DO YOU THINK OUR CHAMPION WILL BE TODAY? HAVE YOU SEEN MACE TYRELL'S BOY? THE KNIGHT OF FLOWERS, THEY CALL HIM.
NOW, THERE'S A SON ANY MAN WOULD BE PROUD TO OWN TO.

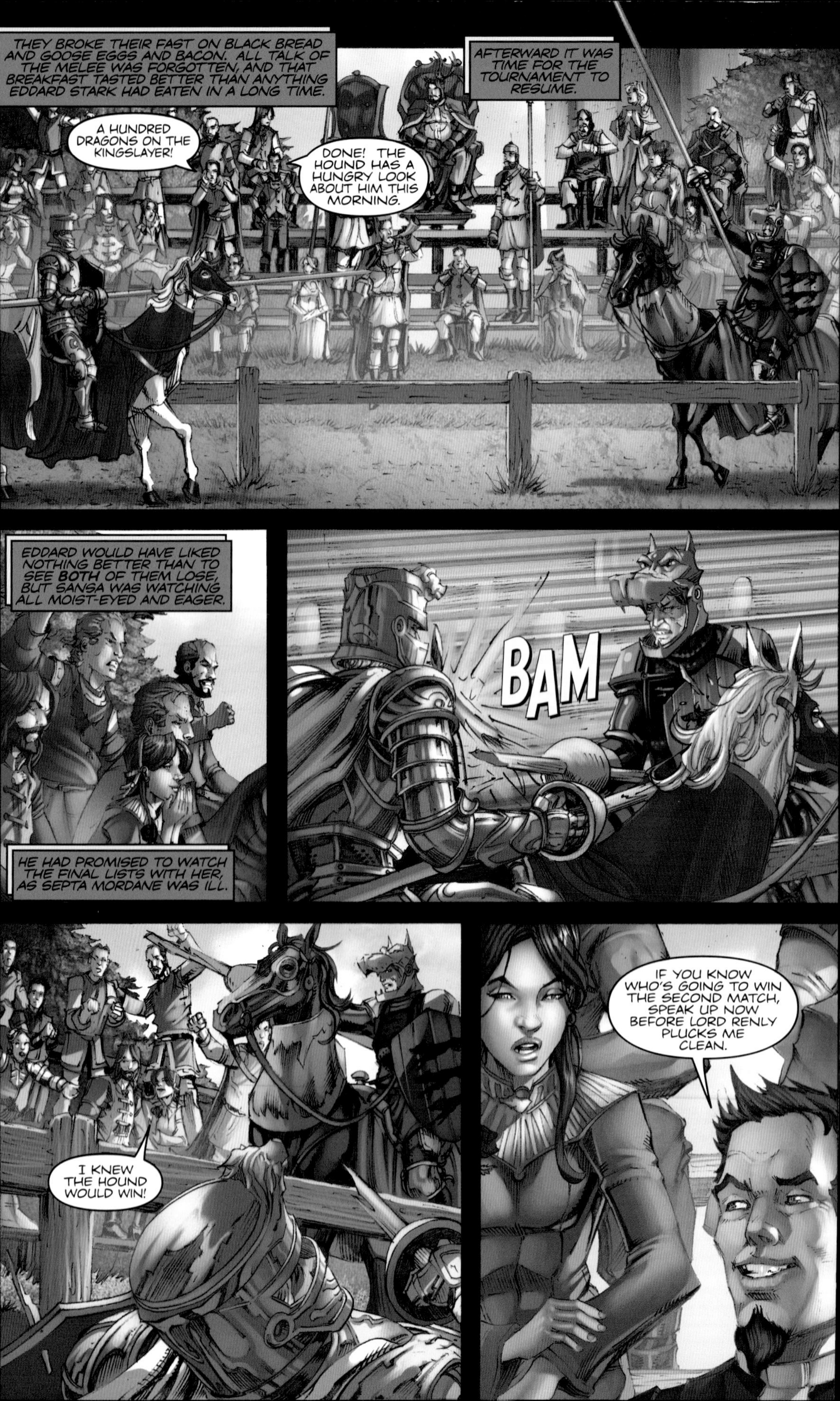
THEY BROKE THEIR FAST ON BLACK BREAD AND GOOSE EGGS AND BACON. ALL TALK OF THE MELEE WAS FORGOTTEN, AND THAT BREAKFAST TASTED BETTER THAN ANYTHING EDDARD STARK HAD EATEN IN A LONG TIME.
AFTERWARD IT WAS TIME FOR THE TOURNAMENT TO RESUME.
A HUNDRED DRAGONS ON THE KINGSLAYER!
DONE! THE HOUND HAS A HUNGRY LOOK ABOUT HIM THIS MORNING.
EDDARD WOULD HAVE LIKED NOTHING BETTER THAN TO SEE BOTH OF THEM LOSE, BUT SANSA WAS WATCHING ALL MOIST-EYED AND EAGER.
HE HAD PROMISED TO WATCH THE FINAL LISTS WITH HER, AS SEPTA MORDANE WAS ILL.
BAM
I KNEW THE HOUND WOULD WIN!
IF YOU KNOW WHO'S GOING TO WIN THE SECOND MATCH, SPEAK UP NOW BEFORE LORD RENLY PLUCKS ME CLEAN.

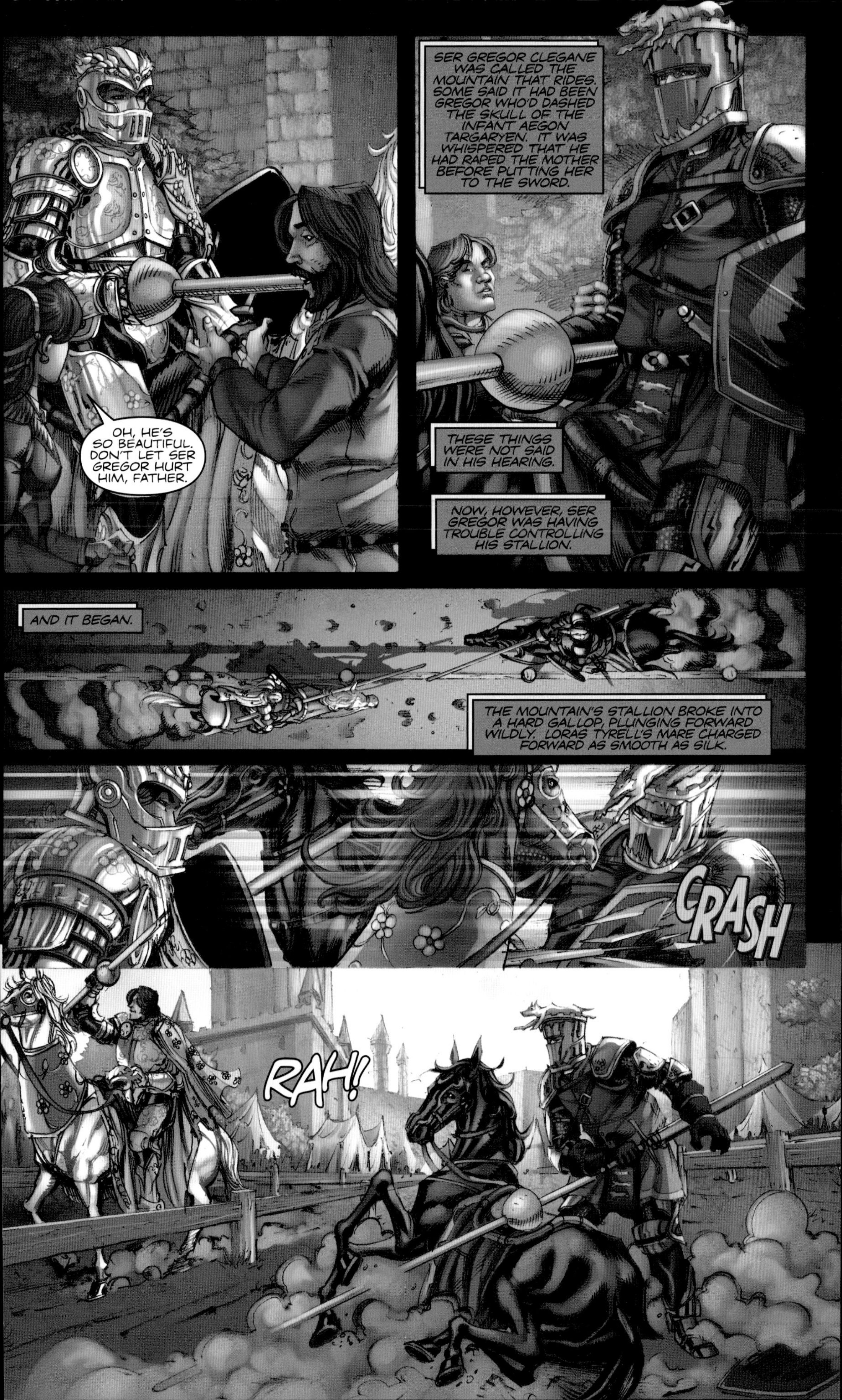
SER GREGOR CLEGANE WAS CALLED THE MOUNTAIN THAT RIDES. SOME SAID IT HAD BEEN GREGOR WHO'D DASHED THE SKULL OF THE INFANT AEGON TARGARYEN. IT WAS WHISPERED THAT HE HAD RAPED THE MOTHER BEFORE PUTTING HER TO THE SWORD.
OH, HE'S SO BEAUTIFUL. DON'T LET SER GREGOR HURT HIM, FATHER.
THESE THINGS WERE NOT SAID IN HIS HEARING.
NOW, HOWEVER, SER GREGOR WAS HAVING TROUBLE CONTROLLING HIS STALLION.
AND IT BEGAN.
THE MOUNTAIN'S STALLION BROKE INTO A HARD GALLOP, PLUNGING FORWARD WILDLY. LORAS TYRELL'S MARE CHARGED FORWARD AS SMOOTH AS SILK.
CRASH
RAH!!

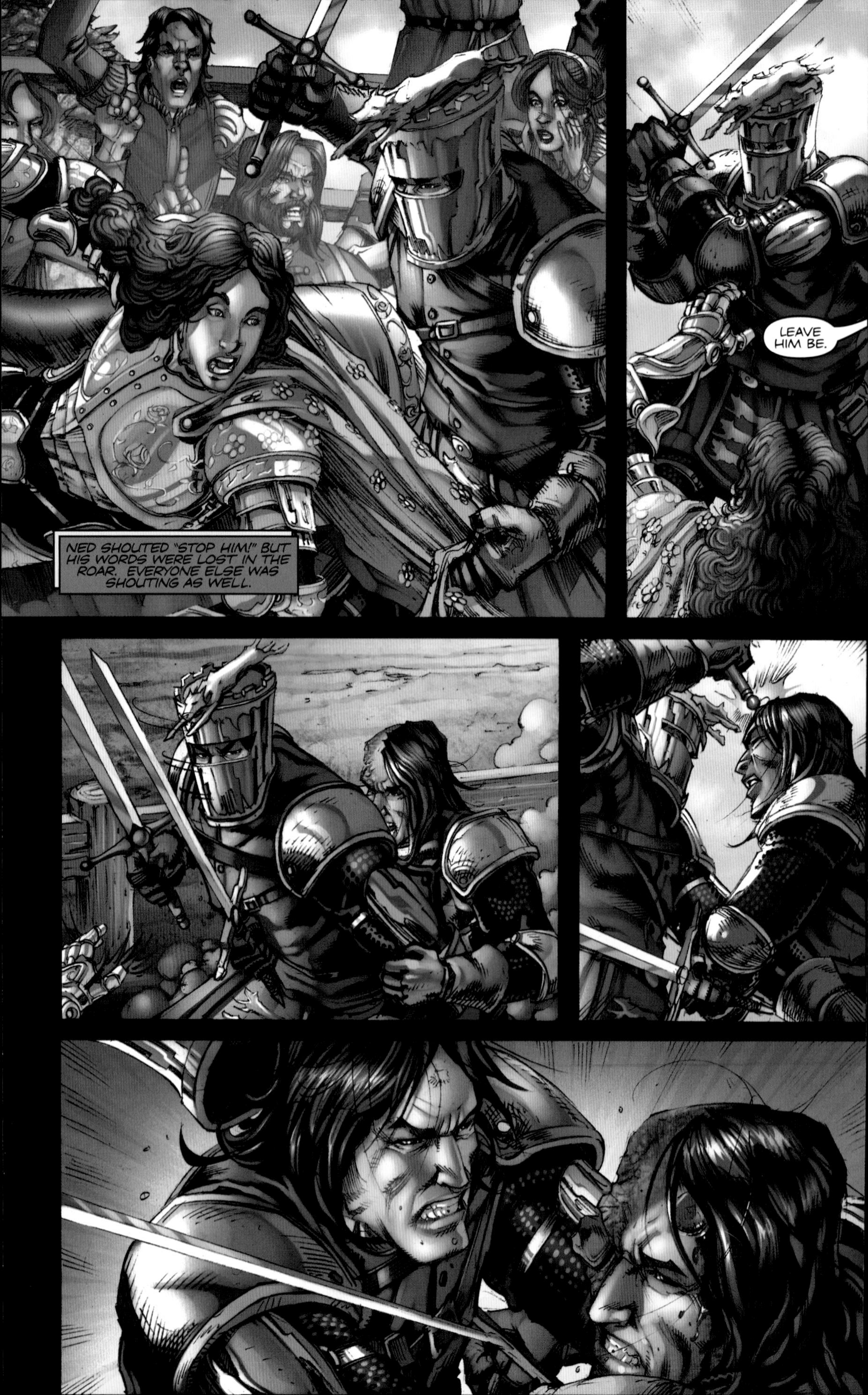
NED SHOUTED "STOP HIM!" BUT HIS WORDS WERE LOST IN THE ROAR. EVERYONE ELSE WAS SHOUTING AS WELL.
LEAVE HIM BE.

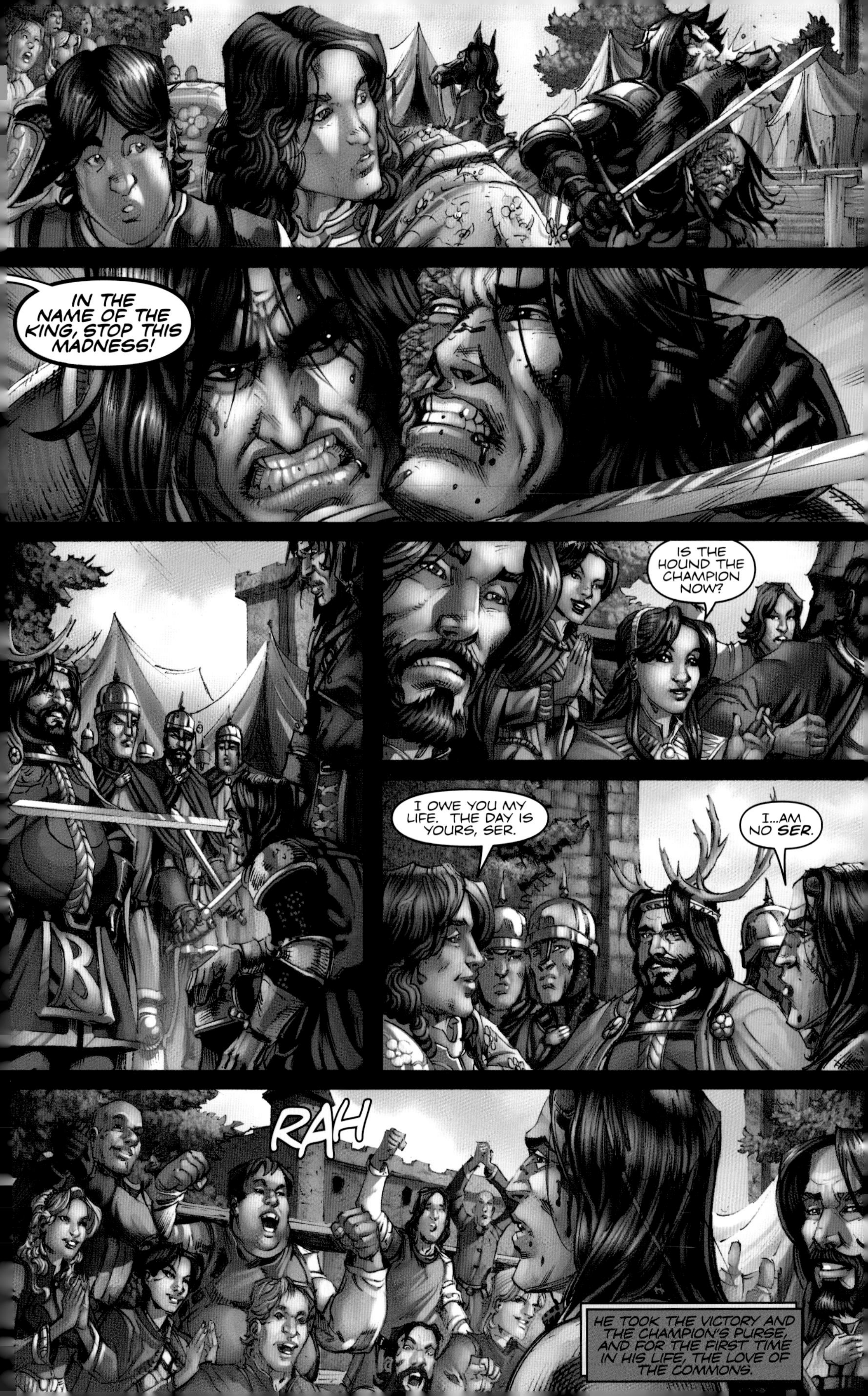
IN THE NAME OF THE KING, STOP THIS MADNESS!
IS THE HOUND THE CHAMPION NOW?
I OWE YOU MY LIFE. THE DAY IS YOURS, SER.
I...AM NO SER.
RAH
HE TOOK THE VICTORY AND THE CHAMPION'S PURSE, AND FOR THE FIRST TIME IN HIS LIFE, THE LOVE OF THE COMMONS.

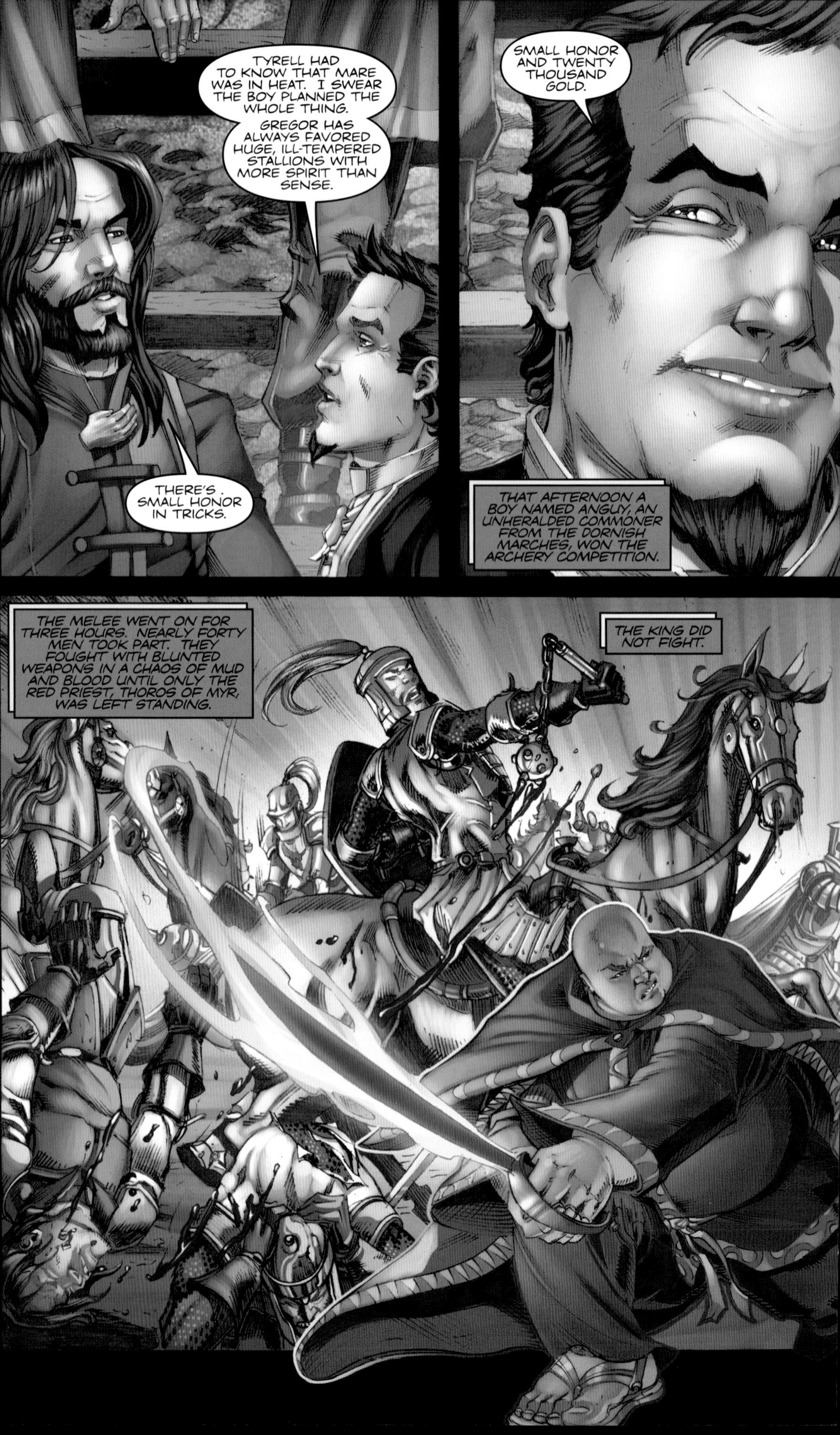
TYRELL HAD TO KNOW THAT MARE WAS IN HEAT. I SWEAR THE BOY PLANNED THE WHOLE THING.
GREGOR HAS ALWAYS FAVORED HUGE, ILL-TEMPERED STALLIONS WITH MORE SPIRIT THAN SENSE.
THERE'S SMALL HONOR IN TRICKS.
SMALL HONOR AND TWENTY THOUSAND GOLD.
THAT AFTERNOON A BOY NAMED ANGUY, AN UNHERALDED COMMONER FROM THE DORNISH MARCHES, WON THE ARCHERY COMPETITION.
THE MELEE WENT ON FOR THREE HOURS. NEARLY FORTY MEN TOOK PART. THEY FOUGHT WITH BLUNTED WEAPONS IN A CHAOS OF MUD AND BLOOD UNTIL ONLY THE RED PRIEST, THOROS OF MYR, WAS LEFT STANDING.
THE KING DID NOT FIGHT.

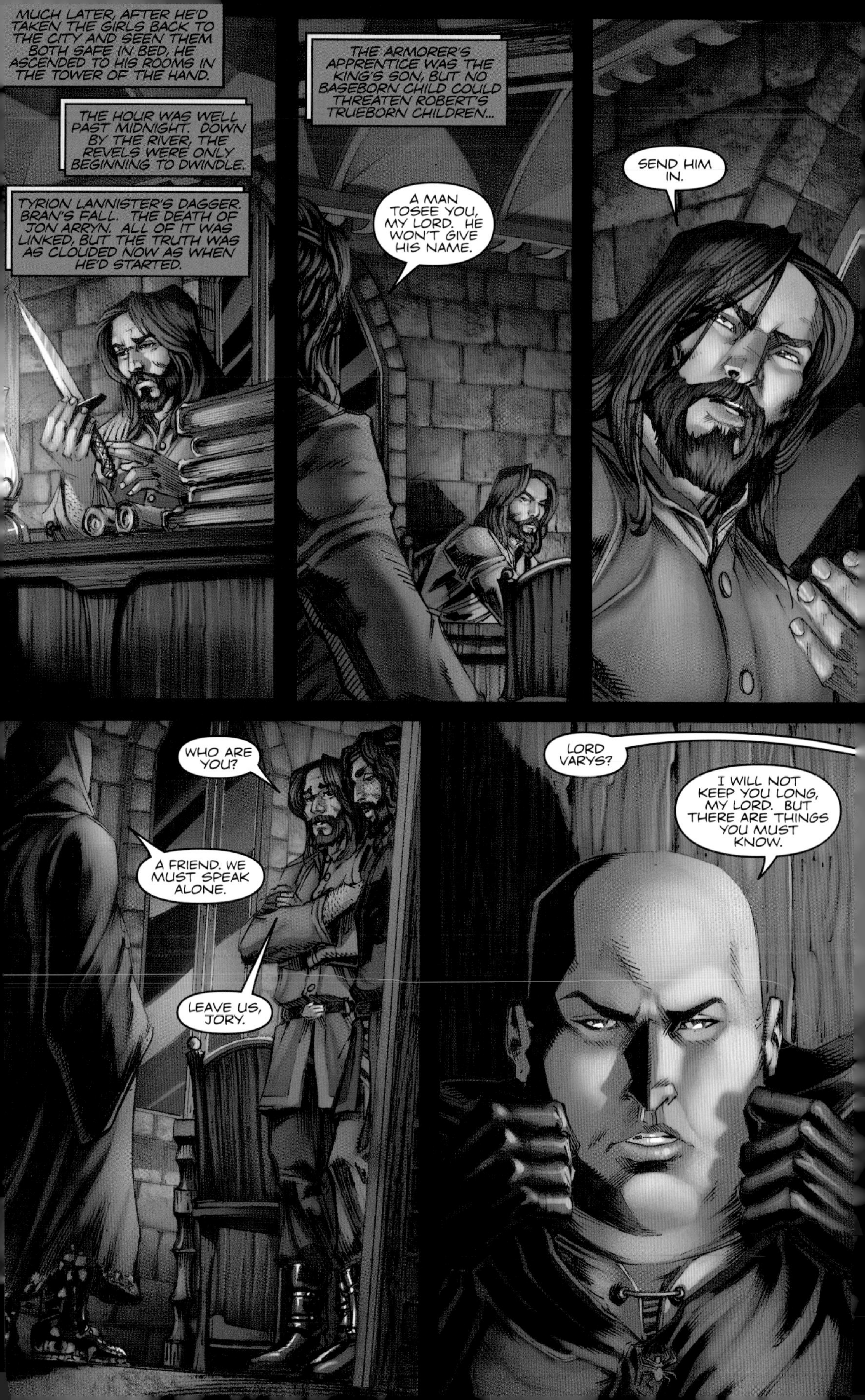
MUCH LATER, AFTER HE'D TAKEN THE GIRLS BACK TO THE CITY AND SEEN THEM BOTH SAFE IN BED, HE ASCENDED TO HIS ROOMS IN THE TOWER OF THE HAND.
THE HOUR WAS WELL PAST MIDNIGHT. DOWN BY THE RIVER, THE REVELS WERE ONLY BEGINNING TO DWINDLE.
TYRION LANNISTER'S DAGGER. BRAN'S FALL. THE DEATH OF JON ARRYN. ALL OF IT WAS LINKED, BUT THE TRUTH WAS AS CLOUDED NOW AS WHEN HE'D STARTED.
THE ARMORER'S APPRENTICE WAS THE KING'S SON, BUT NO BASEBORN CHILD COULD THREATEN ROBERT'S TRUEBORN CHILDREN...
A MAN TOSEE YOU, MY LORD. HE WON'T GIVE HIS NAME.
SEND HIM IN.
WHO ARE YOU?
A FRIEND. WE MUST SPEAK ALONE.
LEAVE US, JORY.
LORD VARYS?
I WILL NOT KEEP YOU LONG, MY LORD. BUT THERE ARE THINGS YOU MUST KNOW.

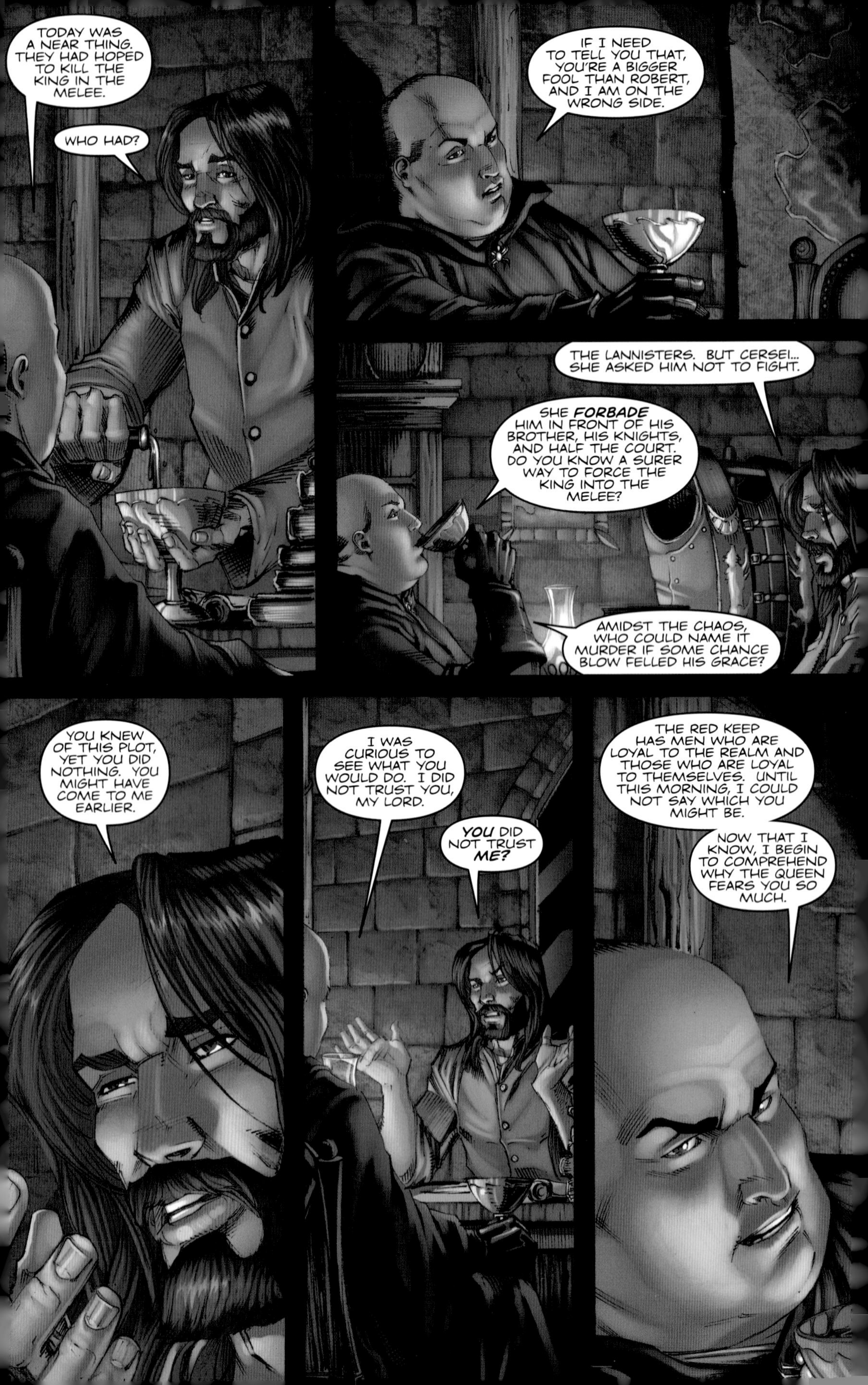
TODAY WAS A NEAR THING. THEY HAD HOPED TO KILL THE KING IN THE MELEE.
WHO HAD?
IF I NEED TO TELL YOU THAT, YOU'RE A BIGGER FOOL THAN ROBERT, AND I AM ON THE WRONG SIDE.
THE LANNISTERS. BUT CERSEI... SHE ASKED HIM NOT TO FIGHT.
SHE **FORBADE** HIM IN FRONT OF HIS BROTHER, HIS KNIGHTS, AND HALF THE COURT. DO YOU KNOW A SURER WAY TO FORCE THE KING INTO THE MELEE?
AMIDST THE CHAOS, WHO COULD NAME IT MURDER IF SOME CHANCE BLOW FELLED HIS GRACE?
YOU KNEW OF THIS PLOT, YET YOU DID NOTHING. YOU MIGHT HAVE COME TO ME EARLIER.
I WAS CURIOUS TO SEE WHAT YOU WOULD DO. I DID NOT TRUST YOU, MY LORD.
YOU DID NOT TRUST ***ME?***
THE RED KEEP HAS MEN WHO ARE LOYAL TO THE REALM AND THOSE WHO ARE LOYAL TO THEMSELVES. UNTIL THIS MORNING, I COULD NOT SAY WHICH YOU MIGHT BE.
NOW THAT I KNOW, I BEGIN TO COMPREHEND WHY THE QUEEN FEARS YOU SO MUCH.

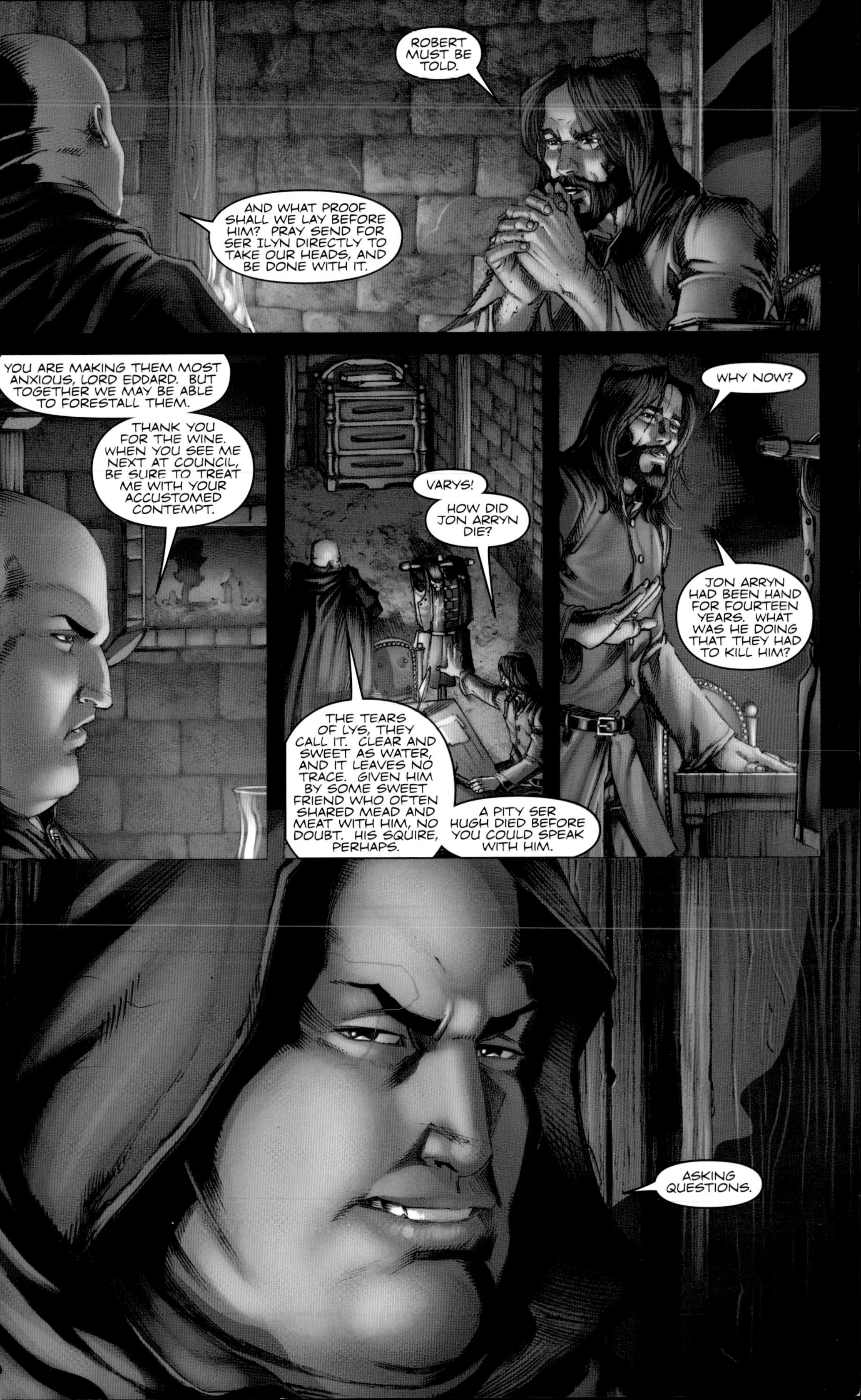
ROBERT MUST BE TOLD.
AND WHAT PROOF SHALL WE LAY BEFORE HIM? PRAY SEND FOR SER ILYN DIRECTLY TO TAKE OUR HEADS, AND BE DONE WITH IT.
YOU ARE MAKING THEM MOST ANXIOUS, LORD EDDARD. BUT TOGETHER WE MAY BE ABLE TO FORESTALL THEM.
THANK YOU FOR THE WINE. WHEN YOU SEE ME NEXT AT COUNCIL, BE SURE TO TREAT ME WITH YOUR ACCUSTOMED CONTEMPT.
VARYS!
HOW DID JON ARRYN DIE?
THE TEARS OF LYS, THEY CALL IT. CLEAR AND SWEET AS WATER, AND IT LEAVES NO TRACE. GIVEN HIM BY SOME SWEET FRIEND WHO OFTEN SHARED MEAD AND MEAT WITH HIM, NO DOUBT. HIS SQUIRE, PERHAPS.
A PITY SER HUGH DIED BEFORE YOU COULD SPEAK WITH HIM.
WHY NOW?
JON ARRYN HAD BEEN HAND FOR FOURTEEN YEARS. WHAT WAS HE DOING THAT THEY HAD TO KILL HIM?
ASKING QUESTIONS.

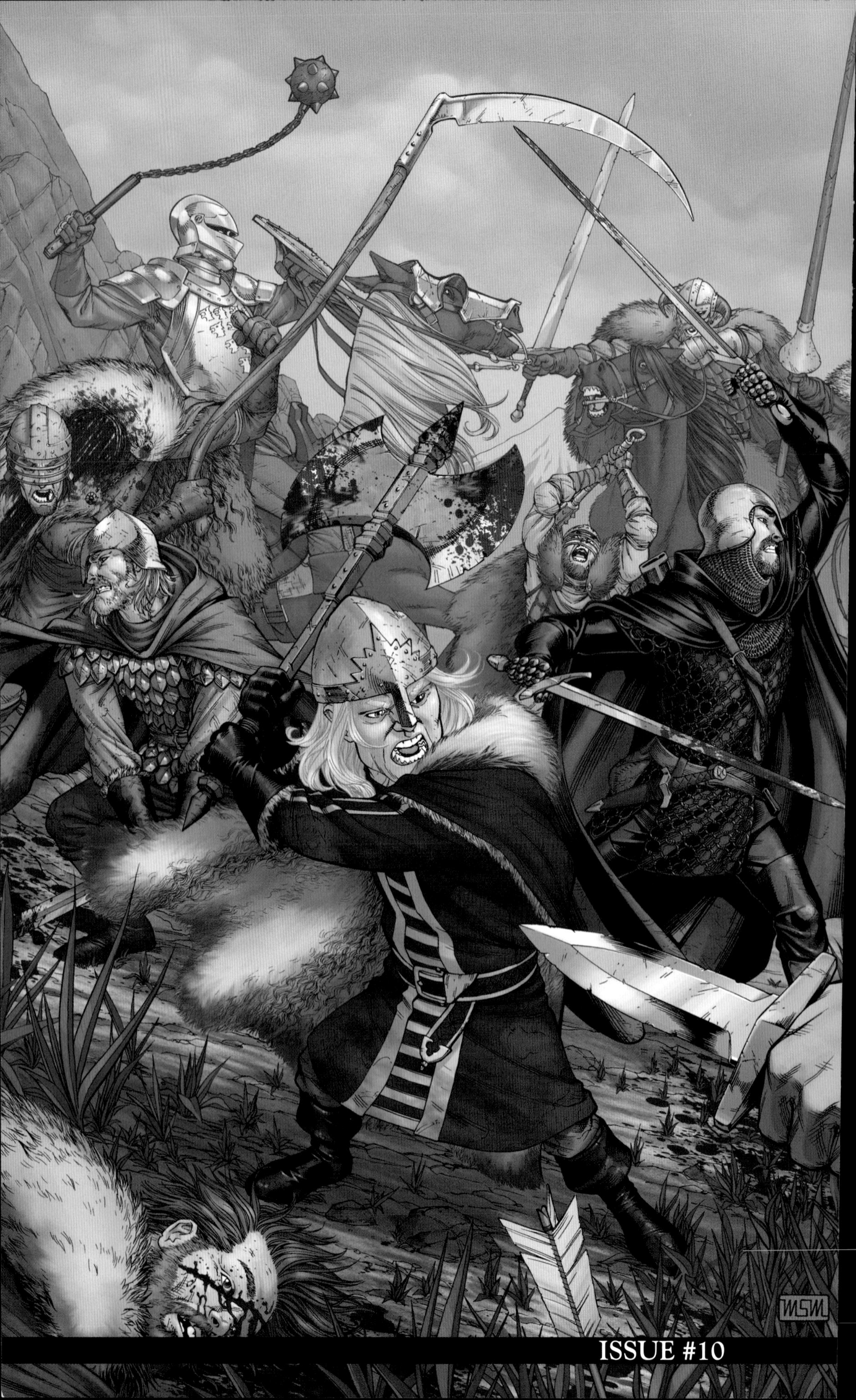
ISSUE #10

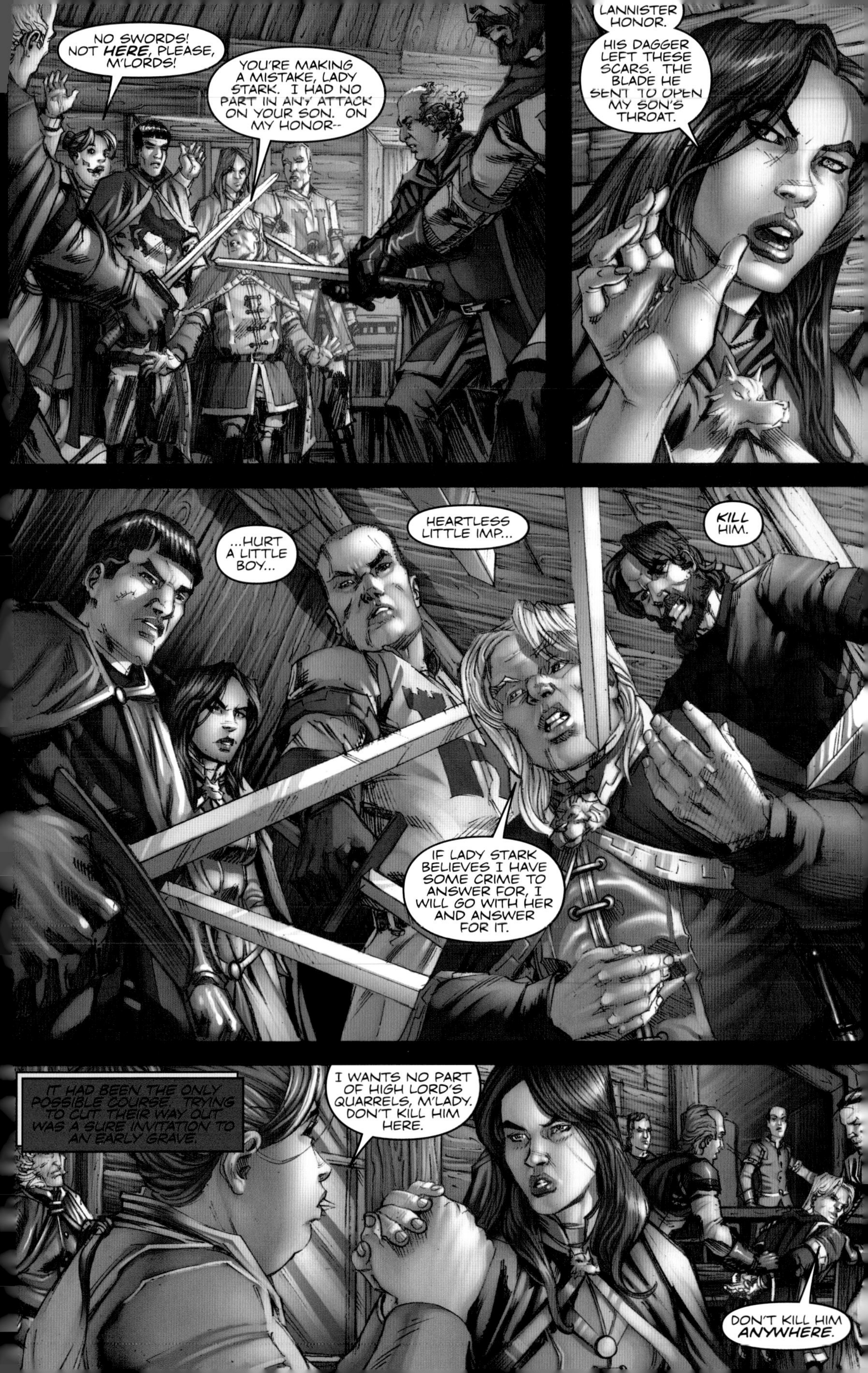
NO SWORDS! NOT HERE, PLEASE, M'LORDS!
YOU'RE MAKING A MISTAKE, LADY STARK. I HAD NO PART IN ANY ATTACK ON YOUR SON. ON MY HONOR--
LANNISTER HONOR.
HIS DAGGER LEFT THESE SCARS. THE BLADE HE SENT TO OPEN MY SON'S THROAT.
...HURT A LITTLE BOY...
HEARTLESS LITTLE IMP...
KILL HIM.
IF LADY STARK BELIEVES I HAVE SOME CRIME TO ANSWER FOR, I WILL GO WITH HER AND ANSWER FOR IT.
IT HAD BEEN THE ONLY POSSIBLE COURSE. TRYING TO CUT THEIR WAY OUT WAS A SURE INVITATION TO AN EARLY GRAVE.
I WANTS NO PART OF HIGH LORD'S QUARRELS, M'LADY. DON'T KILL HIM HERE.
DON'T KILL HIM ANYWHERE.

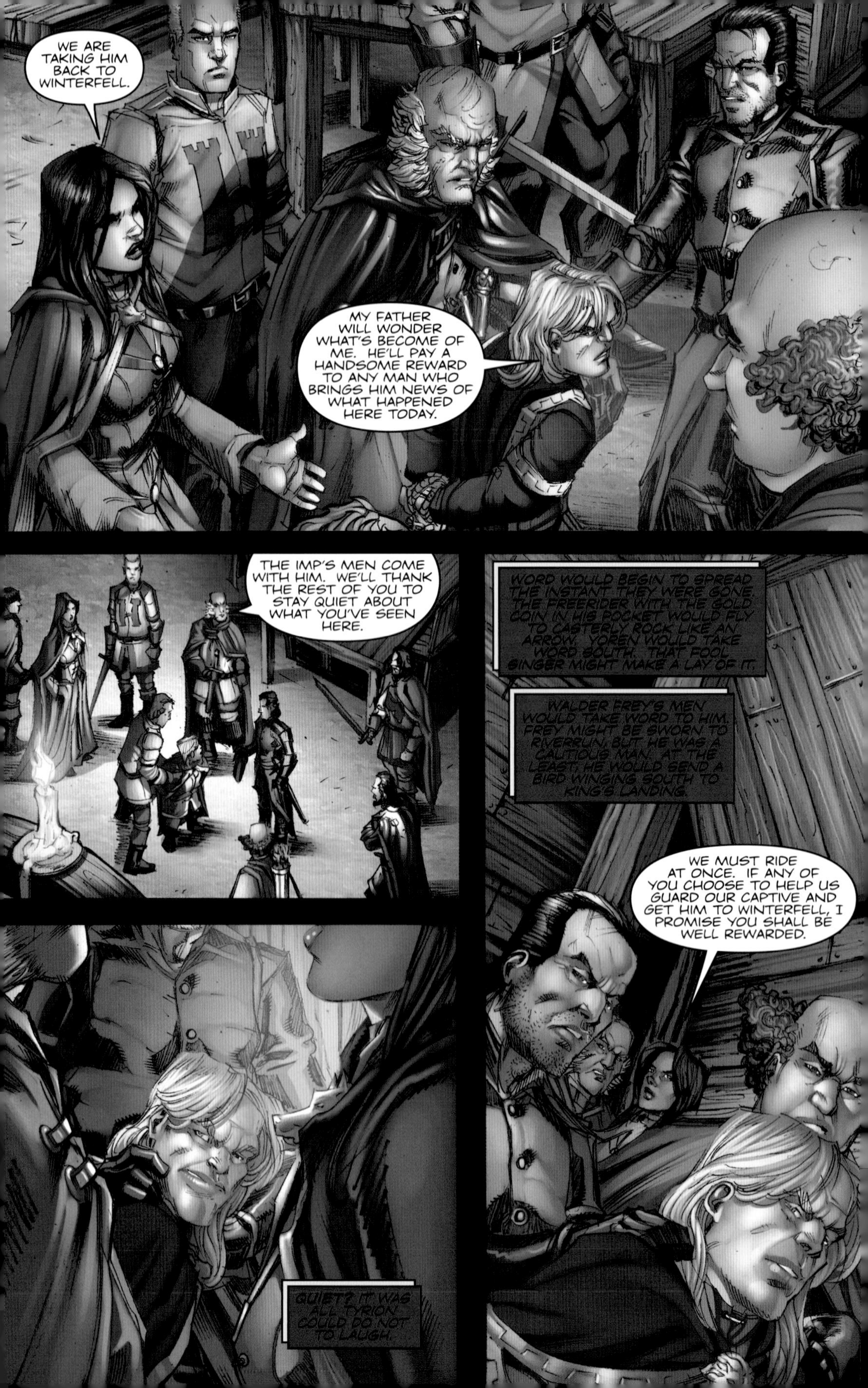
WE ARE TAKING HIM BACK TO WINTERFELL.
MY FATHER WILL WONDER WHAT'S BECOME OF ME. HE'LL PAY A HANDSOME REWARD TO ANY MAN WHO BRINGS HIM NEWS OF WHAT HAPPENED HERE TODAY.
THE IMP'S MEN COME WITH HIM. WE'LL THANK THE REST OF YOU TO STAY QUIET ABOUT WHAT YOU'VE SEEN HERE.
QUIET? IT WAS ALL TYRION COULD DO NOT TO LAUGH.
WORD WOULD BEGIN TO SPREAD THE INSTANT THEY WERE GONE. THE FREERIDER WITH THE GOLD COIN IN HIS POCKET WOULD FLY TO CASTERLY ROCK LIKE AN ARROW. YOREN WOULD TAKE WORD SOUTH. THAT FOOL SINGER MIGHT MAKE A LAY OF IT.
WALDER FREY'S MEN WOULD TAKE WORD TO HIM. FREY MIGHT BE SWORN TO RIVERRUN, BUT HE WAS A CAUTIOUS MAN. AT THE LEAST, HE WOULD SEND A BIRD WINGING SOUTH TO KING'S LANDING.
WE MUST RIDE AT ONCE. IF ANY OF YOU CHOOSE TO HELP US GUARD OUR CAPTIVE AND GET HIM TO WINTERFELL, I PROMISE YOU SHALL BE WELL REWARDED.

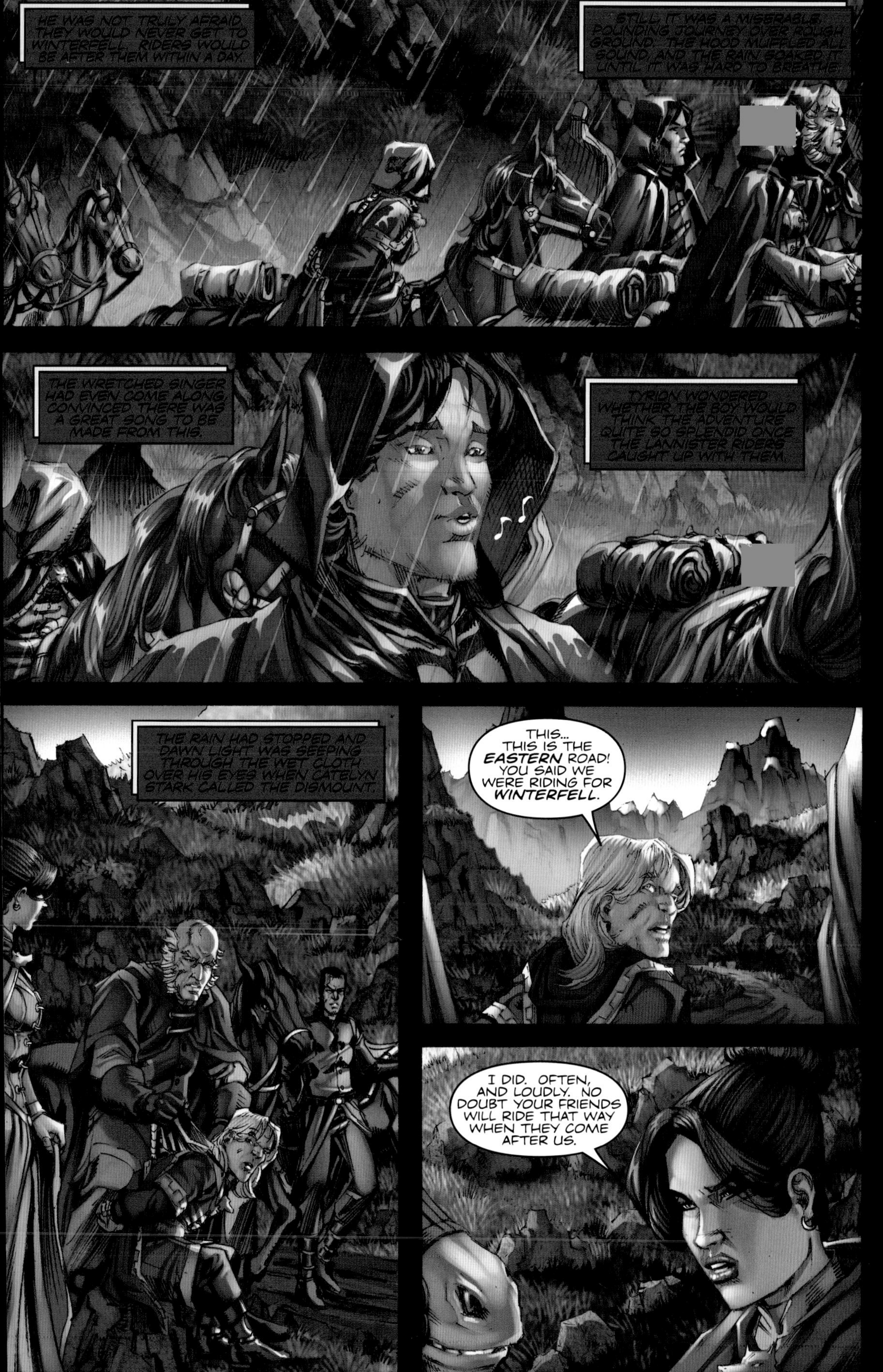
HE WAS NOT TRULY AFRAID THEY WOULD NEVER GET TO WINTERFELL. RIDERS WOULD BE AFTER THEM WITHIN A DAY.
STILL, IT WAS A MISERABLE POUNDING JOURNEY OVER ROUGH GROUND. THE HOOD MUFFLED ALL SOUND, AND THE RAIN SOAKED IT UNTIL IT WAS HARD TO BREATHE.
THE WRETCHED SINGER HAD EVEN COME ALONG, CONVINCED THERE WAS A GREAT SONG TO BE MADE FROM THIS.
TYRION WONDERED WHETHER THE BOY WOULD THINK THE ADVENTURE QUITE SO SPLENDID ONCE THE LANNISTER RIDERS CAUGHT UP WITH THEM.
THE RAIN HAD STOPPED AND DAWN LIGHT WAS SEEPING THROUGH THE WET CLOTH OVER HIS EYES WHEN CATELYN STARK CALLED THE DISMOUNT.
THIS... THIS IS THE **EASTERN** ROAD! YOU SAID WE WERE RIDING FOR **WINTERFELL**.
I DID. OFTEN, AND LOUDLY. NO DOUBT YOUR FRIENDS WILL RIDE THAT WAY WHEN THEY COME AFTER US.

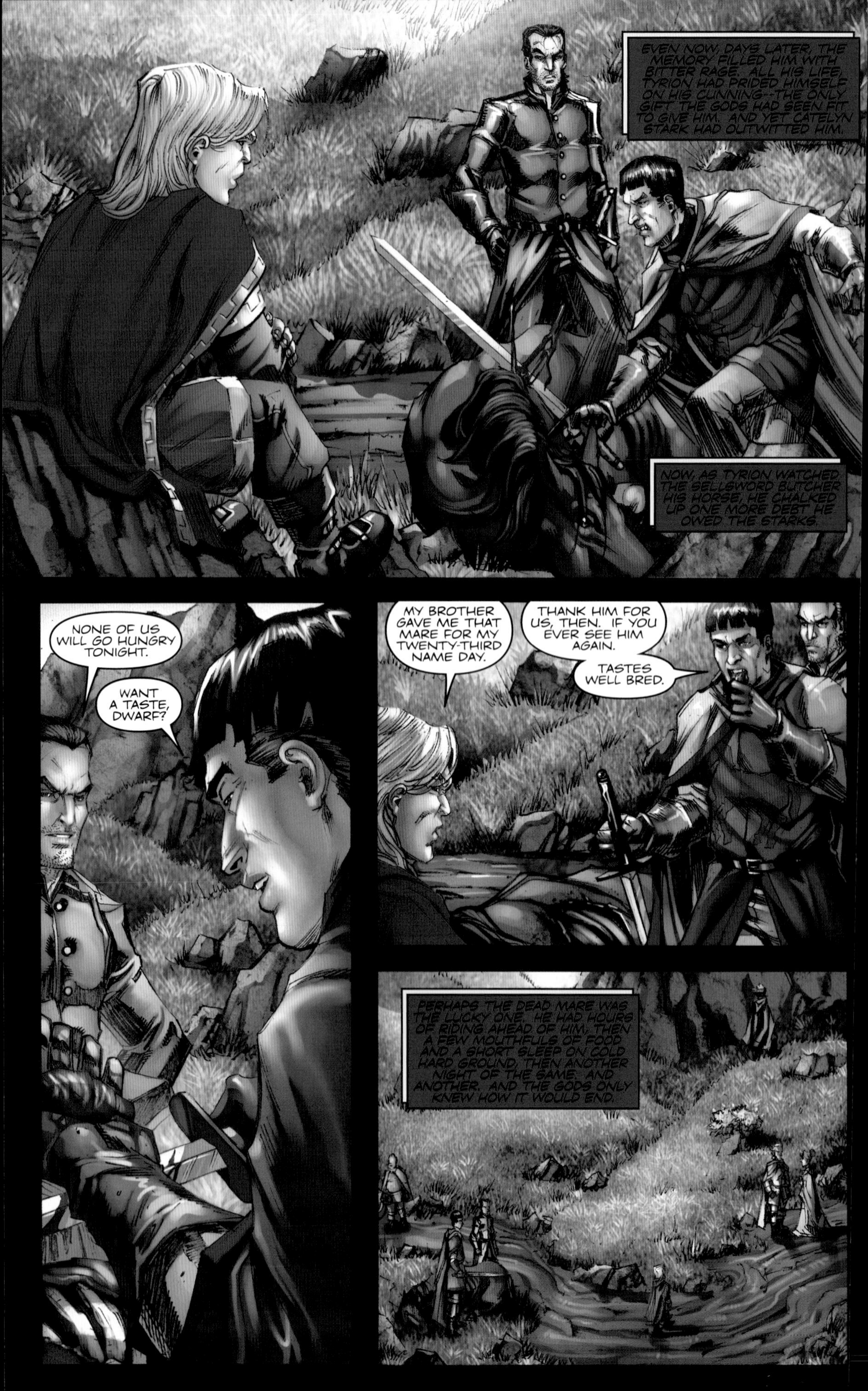
EVEN NOW, DAYS LATER, THE MEMORY FILLED HIM WITH BITTER RAGE. ALL HIS LIFE, TYRION HAD PRIDED HIMSELF ON HIS CUNNING--THE ONLY GIFT THE GODS HAD SEEN FIT TO GIVE HIM. AND YET CATELYN STARK HAD OUTWITTED HIM.
NOW, AS TYRION WATCHED THE SELLSWORD BUTCHER HIS HORSE, HE CHALKED UP ONE MORE DEBT HE OWED THE STARKS.
NONE OF US WILL GO HUNGRY TONIGHT.
WANT A TASTE, DWARF?
MY BROTHER GAVE ME THAT MARE FOR MY TWENTY-THIRD NAME DAY.
THANK HIM FOR US, THEN. IF YOU EVER SEE HIM AGAIN.
TASTES WELL BRED.
PERHAPS THE DEAD MARE WAS THE LUCKY ONE. HE HAD HOURS OF RIDING AHEAD OF HIM, THEN A FEW MOUTHFULS OF FOOD AND A SHORT SLEEP ON COLD HARD GROUND, THEN ANOTHER NIGHT OF THE SAME. AND ANOTHER. AND THE GODS ONLY KNEW HOW IT WOULD END.

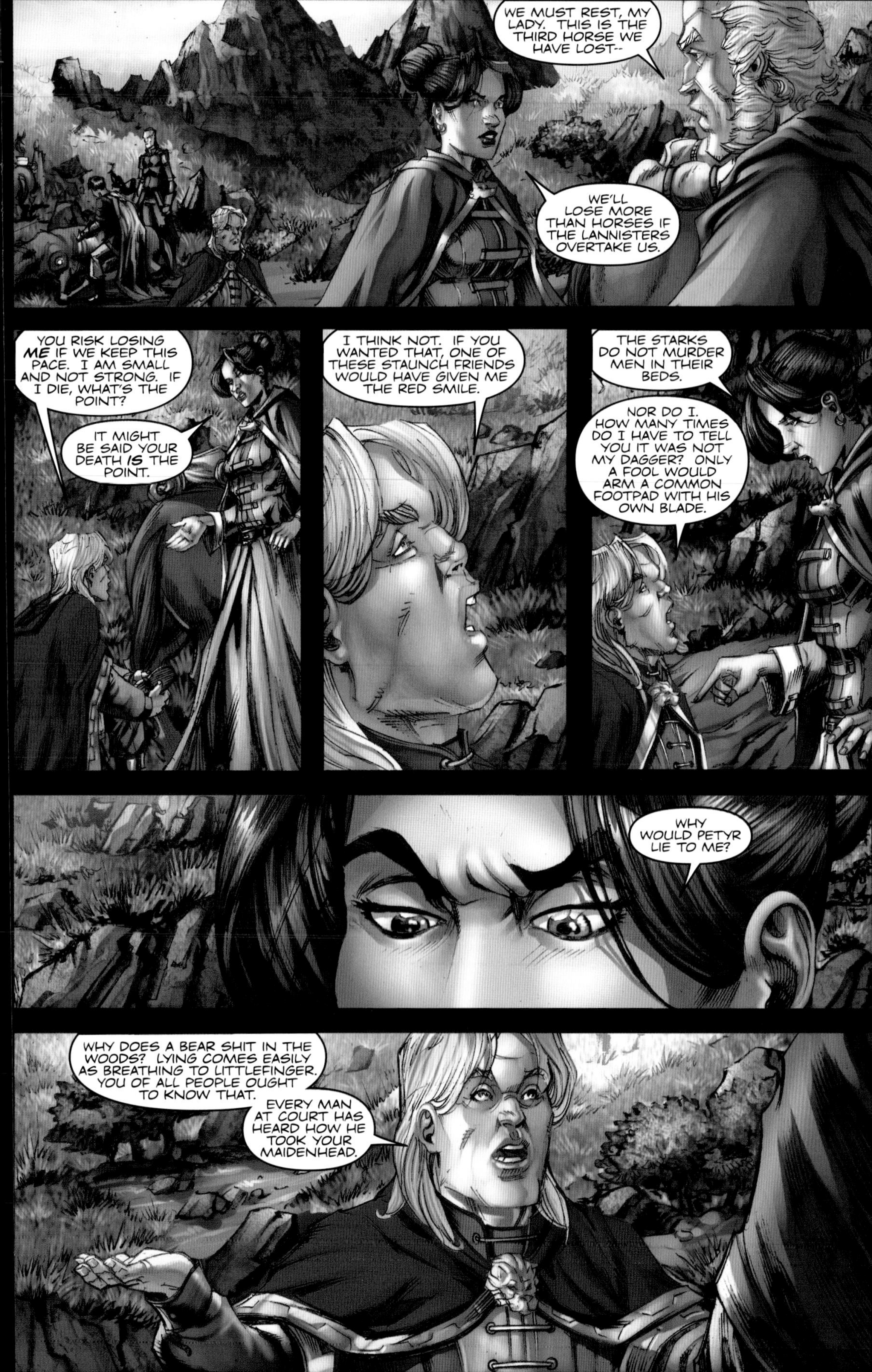

WE MUST REST, MY LADY. THIS IS THE THIRD HORSE WE HAVE LOST--
WE'LL LOSE MORE THAN HORSES IF THE LANNISTERS OVERTAKE US.
YOU RISK LOSING ME IF WE KEEP THIS PACE. I AM SMALL AND NOT STRONG. IF I DIE, WHAT'S THE POINT?
IT MIGHT BE SAID YOUR DEATH IS THE POINT.
I THINK NOT. IF YOU WANTED THAT, ONE OF THESE STAUNCH FRIENDS WOULD HAVE GIVEN ME THE RED SMILE.
THE STARKS DO NOT MURDER MEN IN THEIR BEDS.
NOR DO I. HOW MANY TIMES DO I HAVE TO TELL YOU IT WAS NOT MY DAGGER? ONLY A FOOL WOULD ARM A COMMON FOOTPAD WITH HIS OWN BLADE.
WHY WOULD PETYR LIE TO ME?
WHY DOES A BEAR SHIT IN THE WOODS? LYING COMES EASILY AS BREATHING TO LITTLEFINGER. YOU OF ALL PEOPLE OUGHT TO KNOW THAT.
EVERY MAN AT COURT HAS HEARD HOW HE TOOK YOUR MAIDENHEAD.

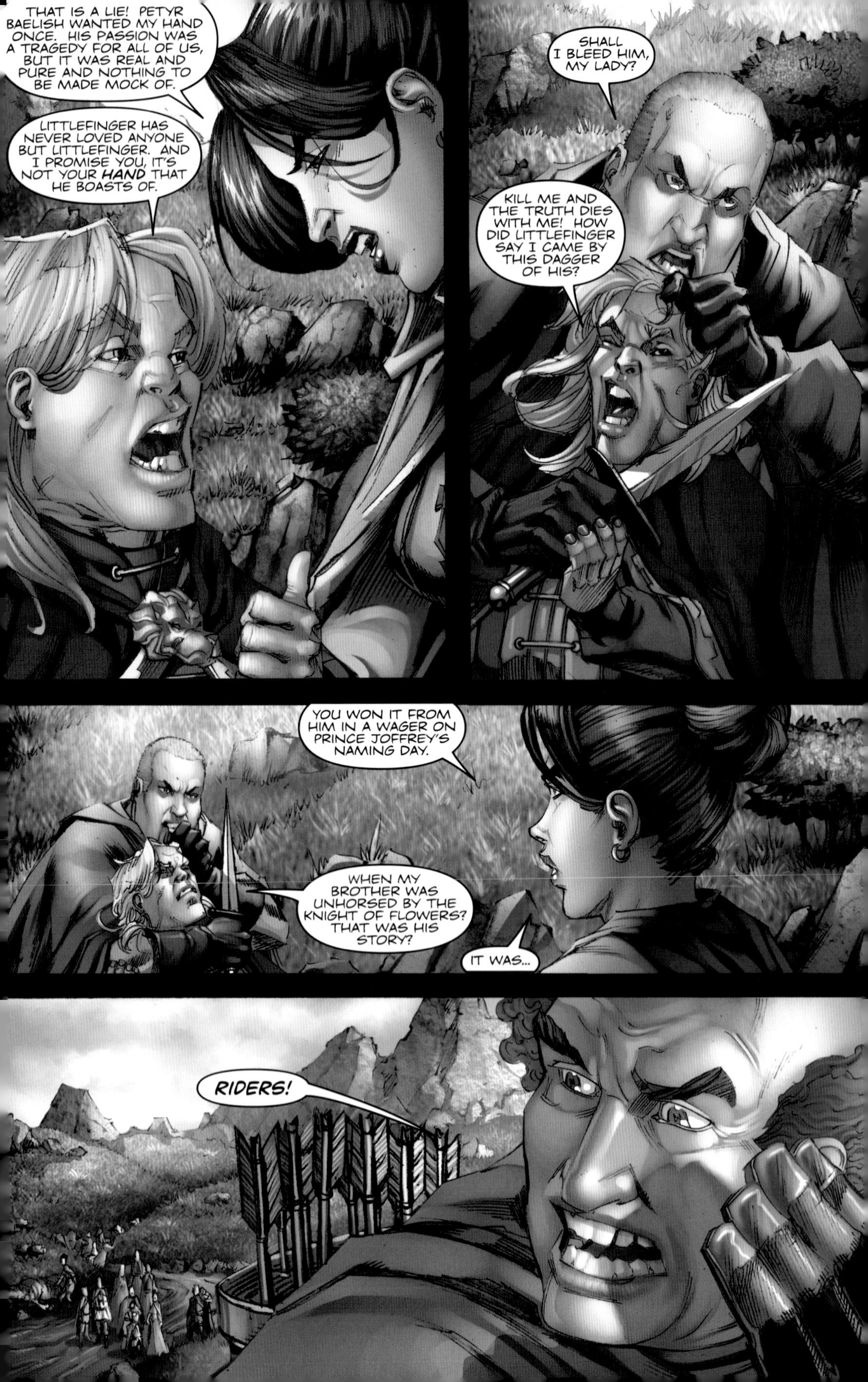
THAT IS A LIE! PETYR BAELISH WANTED MY HAND ONCE. HIS PASSION WAS A TRAGEDY FOR ALL OF US, BUT IT WAS REAL AND PURE AND NOTHING TO BE MADE MOCK OF.
LITTLEFINGER HAS NEVER LOVED ANYONE BUT LITTLEFINGER. AND I PROMISE YOU, IT'S NOT YOUR **HAND** THAT HE BOASTS OF.
SHALL I BLEED HIM, MY LADY?
KILL ME AND THE TRUTH DIES WITH ME! HOW DID LITTLEFINGER SAY I CAME BY THIS DAGGER OF HIS?
YOU WON IT FROM HIM IN A WAGER ON PRINCE JOFFREY'S NAMING DAY.
WHEN MY BROTHER WAS UNHORSED BY THE KNIGHT OF FLOWERS? THAT WAS HIS STORY?
IT WAS...
RIDERS!

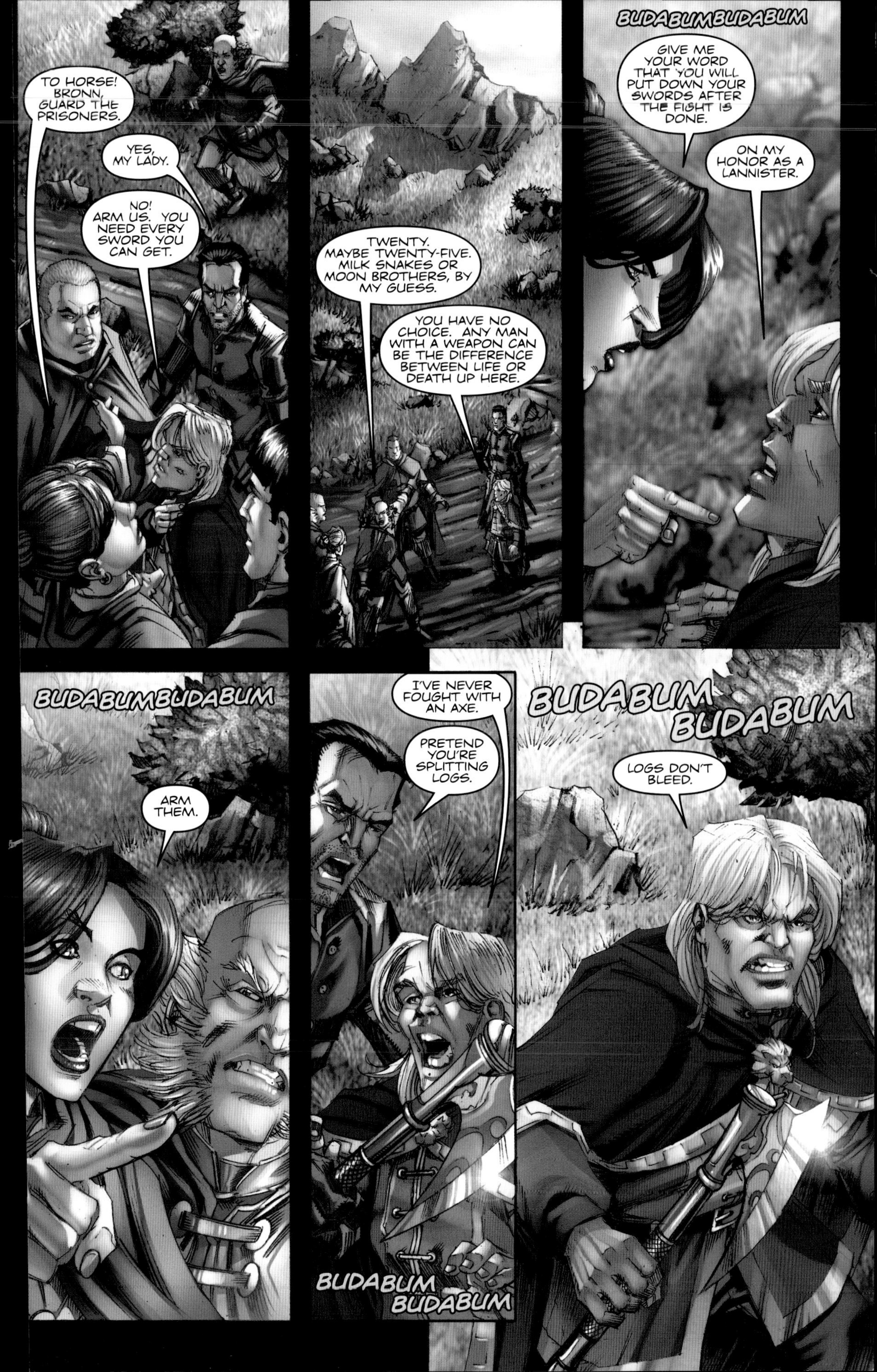
TO HORSE! BRONN, GUARD THE PRISONERS.
YES, MY LADY.
NO! ARM US. YOU NEED EVERY SWORD YOU CAN GET.
TWENTY. MAYBE TWENTY-FIVE. MILK SNAKES OR MOON BROTHERS, BY MY GUESS.
YOU HAVE NO CHOICE. ANY MAN WITH A WEAPON CAN BE THE DIFFERENCE BETWEEN LIFE OR DEATH UP HERE.
BUDABUMBUDABUM
GIVE ME YOUR WORD THAT YOU WILL PUT DOWN YOUR SWORDS AFTER THE FIGHT IS DONE.
ON MY HONOR AS A LANNISTER.
BUDABUMBUDABUM
ARM THEM.
I'VE NEVER FOUGHT WITH AN AXE.
PRETEND YOU'RE SPLITTING LOGS.
BUDABUM BUDABUM
BUDABUM BUDABUM
LOGS DON'T BLEED.

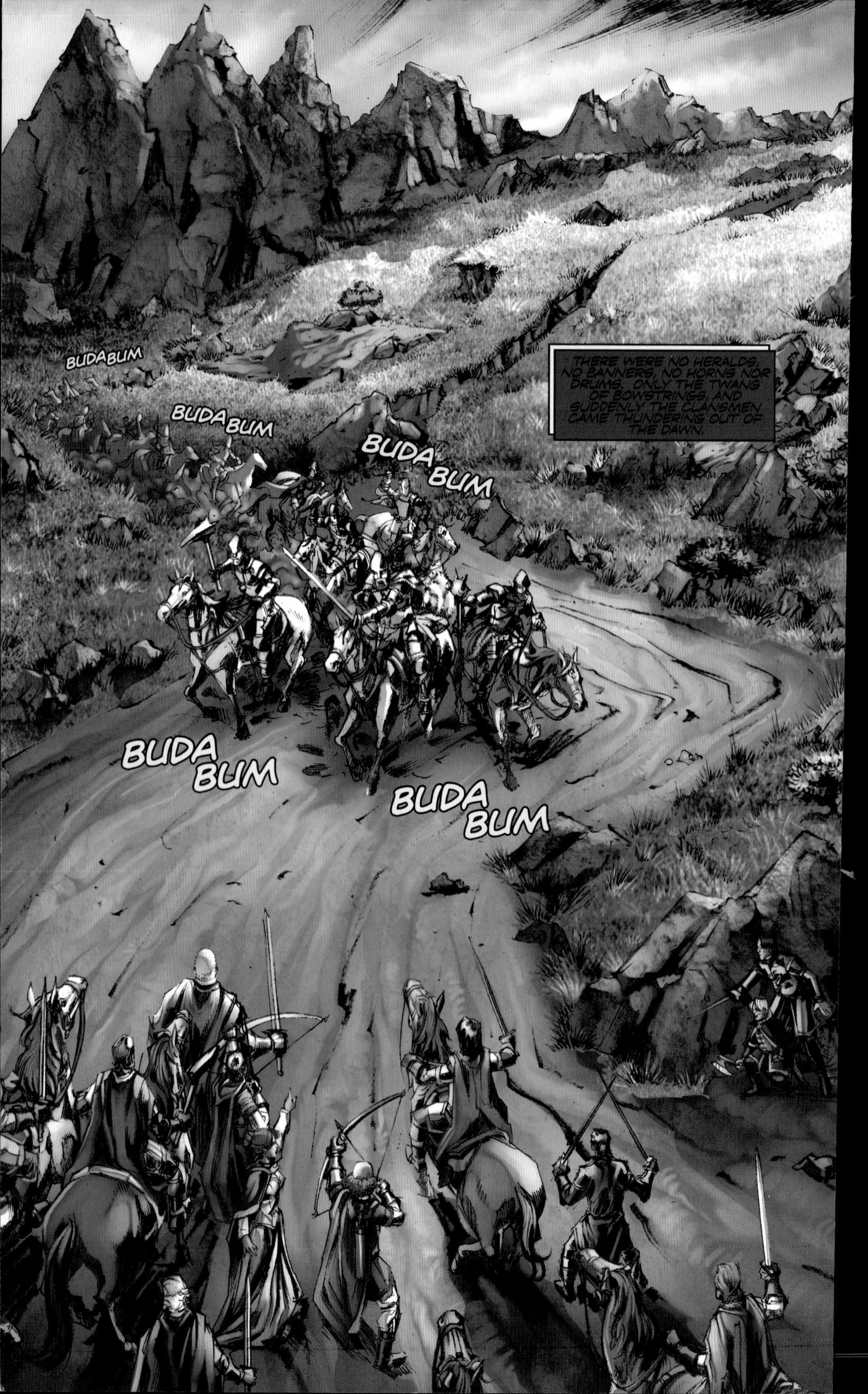
THERE WERE NO HERALDS, NO BANNERS, NO HORNS NOR DRUMS. ONLY THE TWANG OF BOWSTRINGS, AND SUDDENLY THE CLANSMEN CAME THUNDERING OUT OF THE DAWN.
BUDABUM
BUDABUM
BUDA BUM
BUDA BUM
BUDA BUM

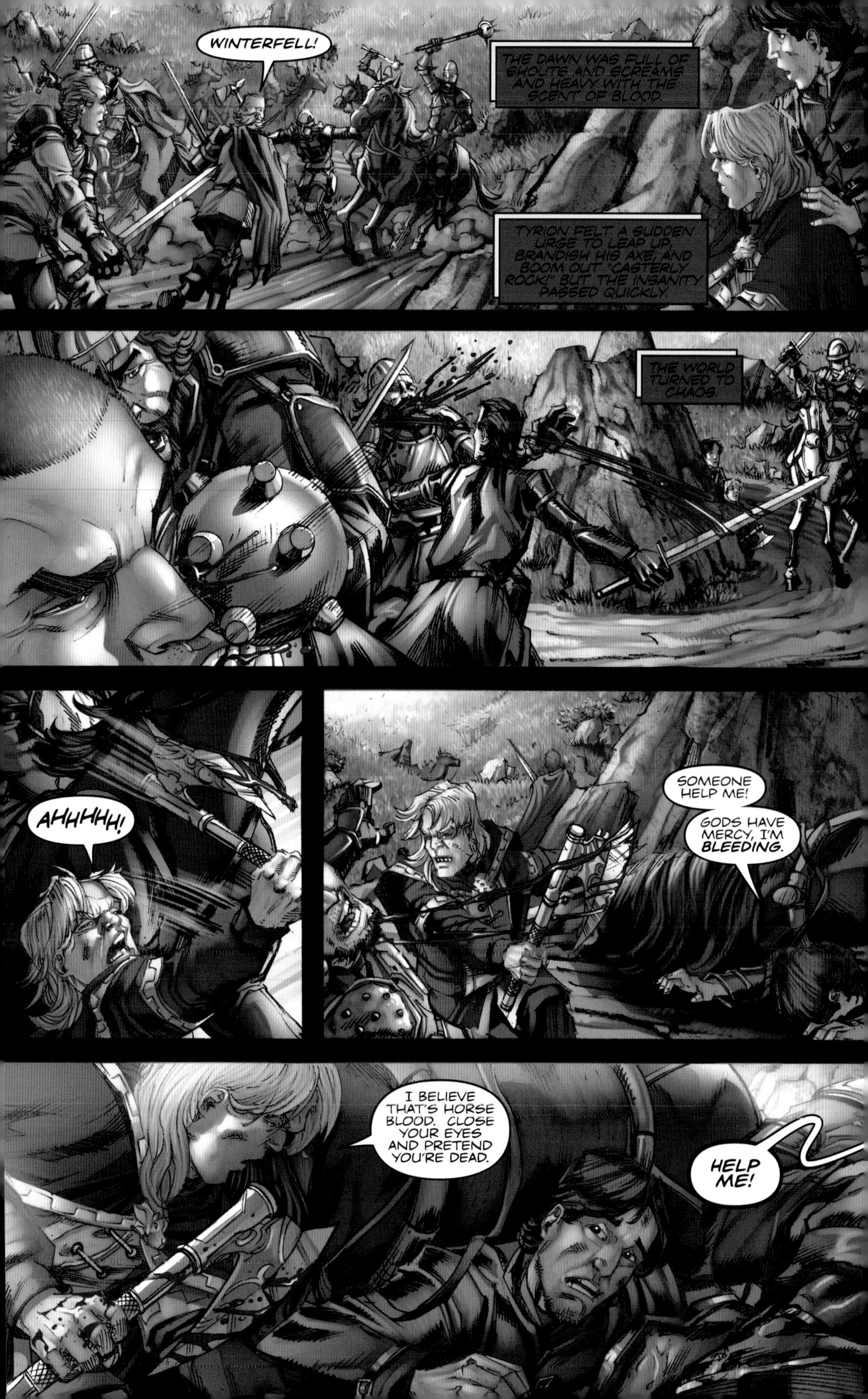

WINTERFELL!
THE DAWN WAS FULL OF SHOUTS AND SCREAMS AND HEAVY WITH THE SCENT OF BLOOD.
TYRION FELT A SUDDEN URGE TO LEAP UP, BRANDISH HIS AXE, AND BOOM OUT "CASTERLY ROCK!" BUT THE INSANITY PASSED QUICKLY.
THE WORLD TURNED TO CHAOS.
AHHHHH!
SOMEONE HELP ME!
GODS HAVE MERCY, I'M BLEEDING.
I BELIEVE THAT'S HORSE BLOOD. CLOSE YOUR EYES AND PRETEND YOU'RE DEAD.
HELP ME!

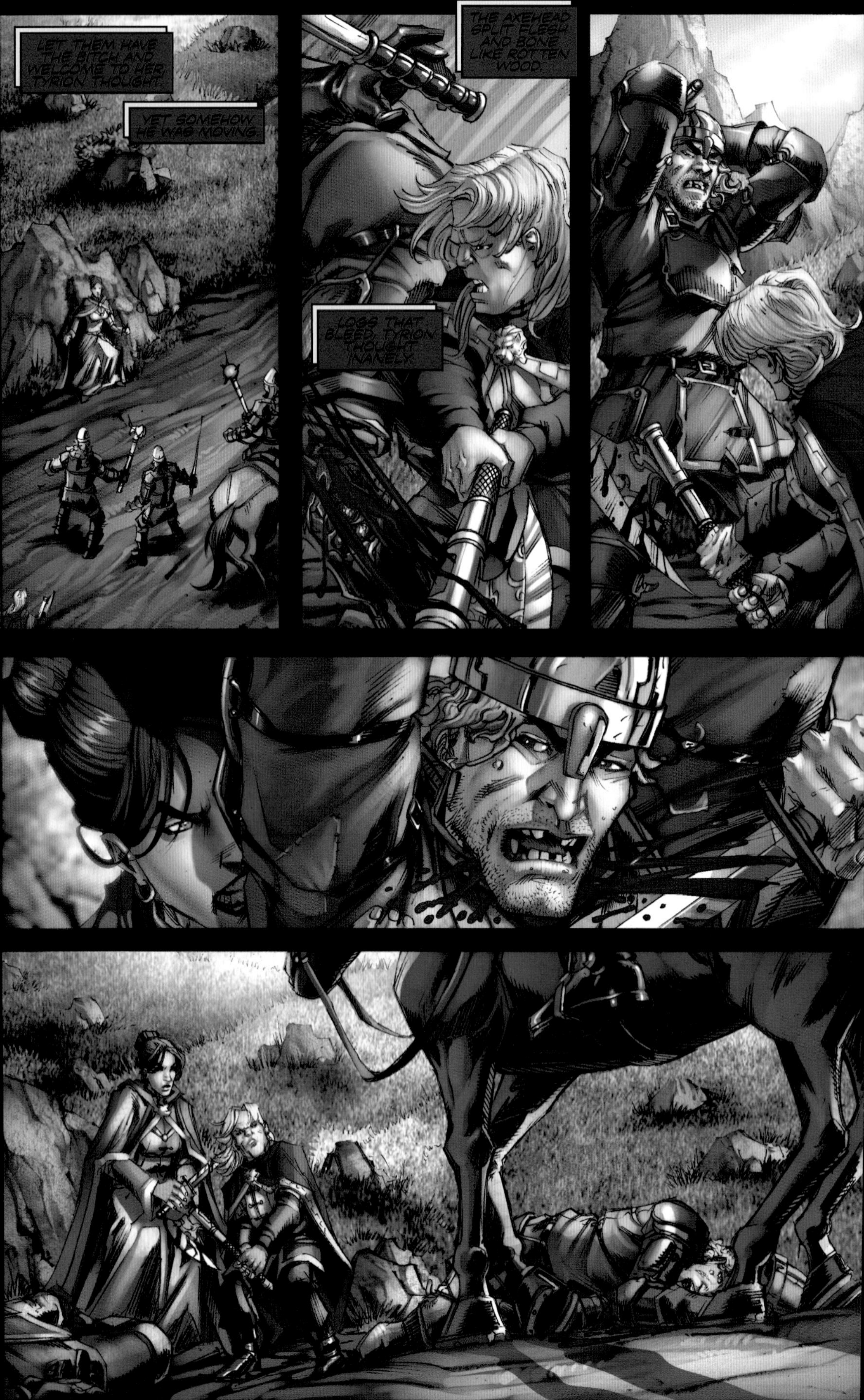
LET THEM HAVE THE BITCH AND WELCOME TO HER, TYRION THOUGHT.
YET SOMEHOW HE WAS MOVING.
THE AXEHEAD SPLIT FLESH AND BONE LIKE ROTTEN WOOD.
LOGS THAT BLEED, TYRION THOUGHT INANELY.

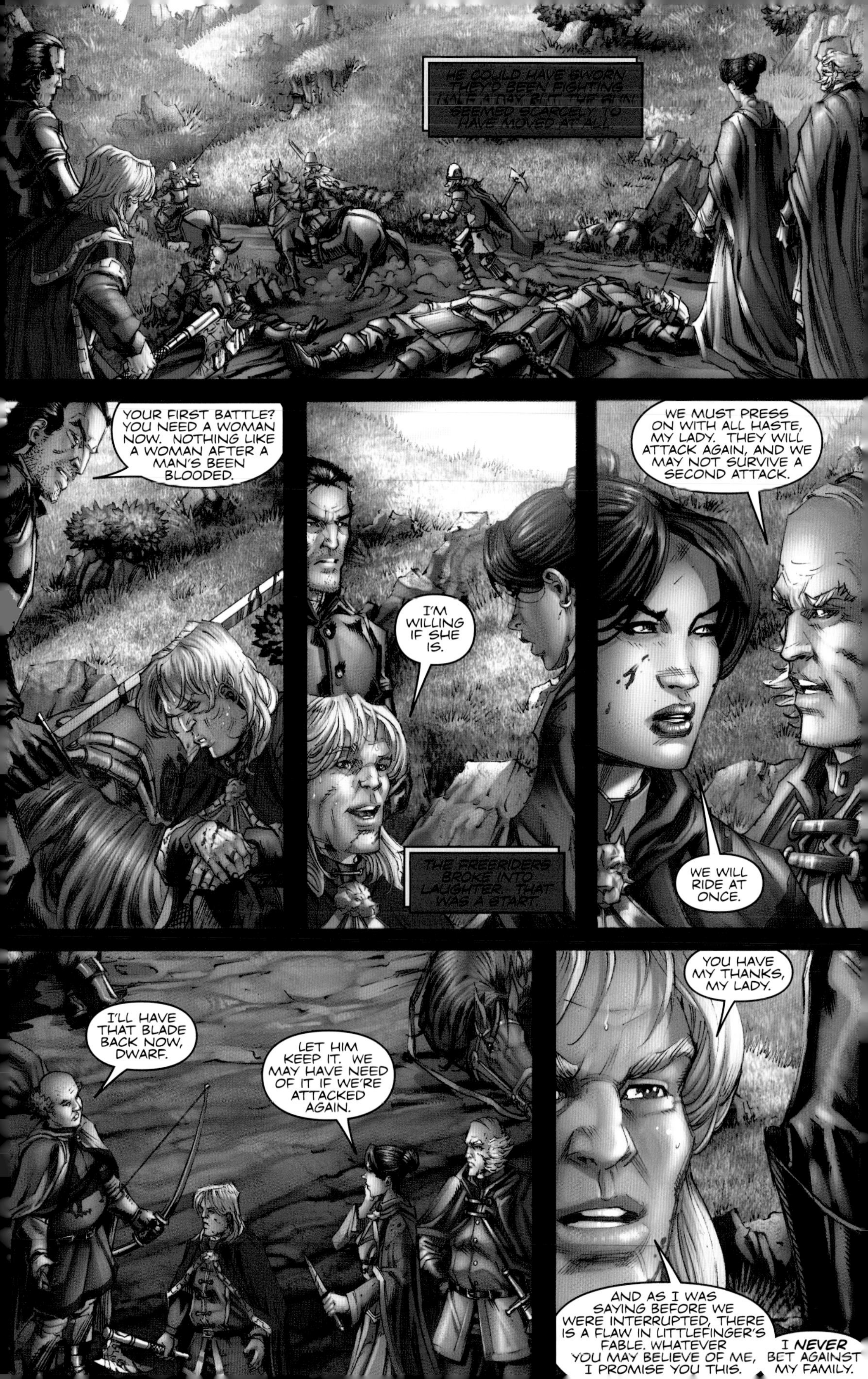
HE COULD HAVE SWORN THEY'D BEEN FIGHTING HALF A DAY BUT THE SUN SEEMED SCARCELY TO HAVE MOVED AT ALL.
YOUR FIRST BATTLE? YOU NEED A WOMAN NOW. NOTHING LIKE A WOMAN AFTER A MAN'S BEEN BLOODED.
I'M WILLING IF SHE IS.
THE FREERIDERS BROKE INTO LAUGHTER. THAT WAS A START.
WE MUST PRESS ON WITH ALL HASTE, MY LADY. THEY WILL ATTACK AGAIN, AND WE MAY NOT SURVIVE A SECOND ATTACK.
WE WILL RIDE AT ONCE.
I'LL HAVE THAT BLADE BACK NOW, DWARF.
LET HIM KEEP IT. WE MAY HAVE NEED OF IT IF WE'RE ATTACKED AGAIN.
YOU HAVE MY THANKS, MY LADY.
AND AS I WAS SAYING BEFORE WE WERE INTERRUPTED, THERE IS A FLAW IN LITTLEFINGER'S FABLE. WHATEVER YOU MAY BELIEVE OF ME, I PROMISE YOU THIS.
I **NEVER** BET AGAINST MY FAMILY.

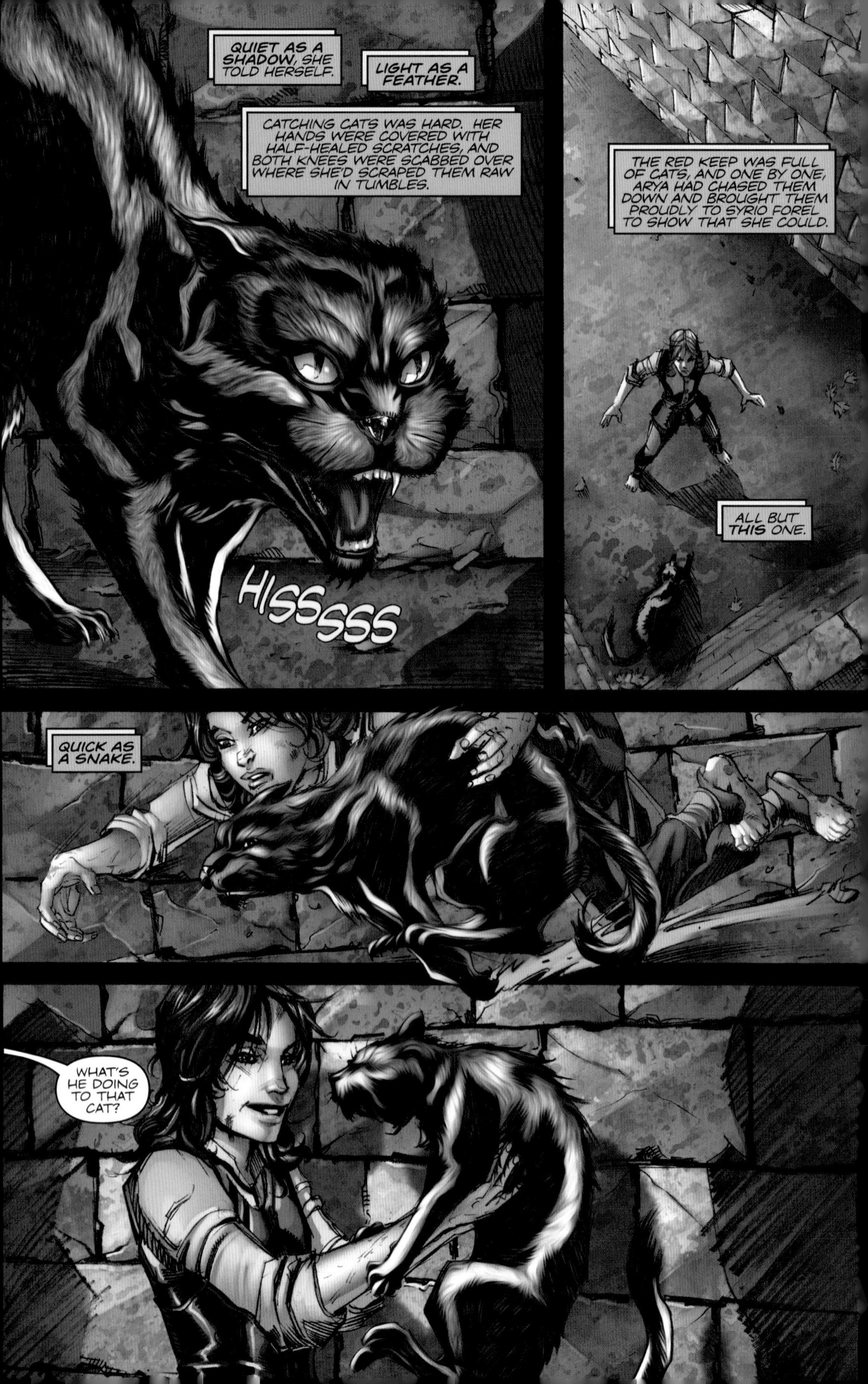
QUIET AS A SHADOW, SHE TOLD HERSELF.
LIGHT AS A FEATHER.
CATCHING CATS WAS HARD. HER HANDS WERE COVERED WITH HALF-HEALED SCRATCHES, AND BOTH KNEES WERE SCABBED OVER WHERE SHE'D SCRAPED THEM RAW IN TUMBLES.
HISSSSS
THE RED KEEP WAS FULL OF CATS, AND ONE BY ONE, ARYA HAD CHASED THEM DOWN AND BROUGHT THEM PROUDLY TO SYRIO FOREL TO SHOW THAT SHE COULD.
ALL BUT THIS ONE.
QUICK AS A SNAKE.
WHAT'S HE DOING TO THAT CAT?

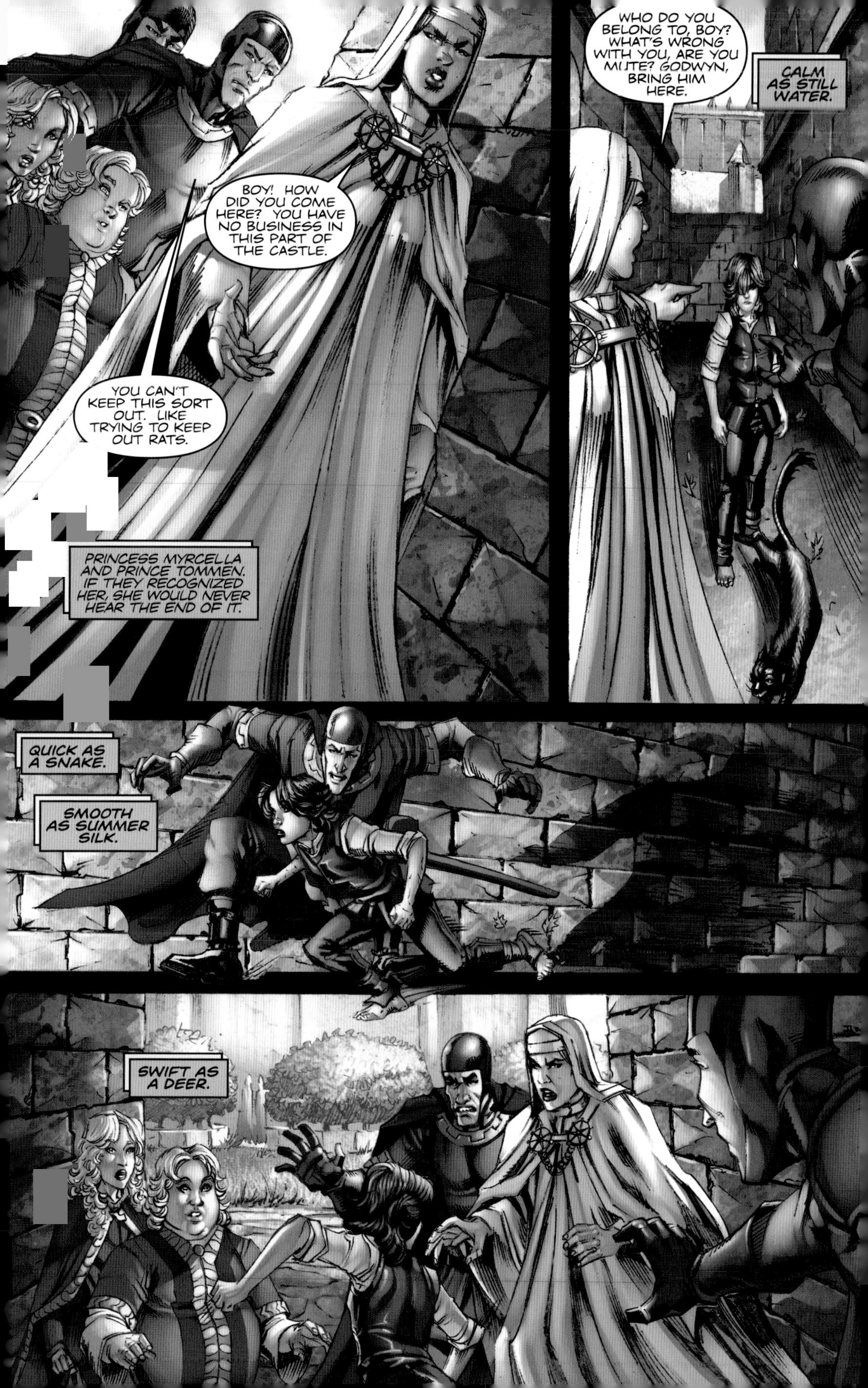
BOY! HOW DID YOU COME HERE? YOU HAVE NO BUSINESS IN THIS PART OF THE CASTLE.
YOU CAN'T KEEP THIS SORT OUT. LIKE TRYING TO KEEP OUT RATS.
PRINCESS MYRCELLA AND PRINCE TOMMEN. IF THEY RECOGNIZED HER, SHE WOULD NEVER HEAR THE END OF IT.
WHO DO YOU BELONG TO, BOY? WHAT'S WRONG WITH YOU, ARE YOU MUTE? GODWYN, BRING HIM HERE.
CALM AS STILL WATER.
QUICK AS A SNAKE.
SMOOTH AS SUMMER SILK.
SWIFT AS A DEER.

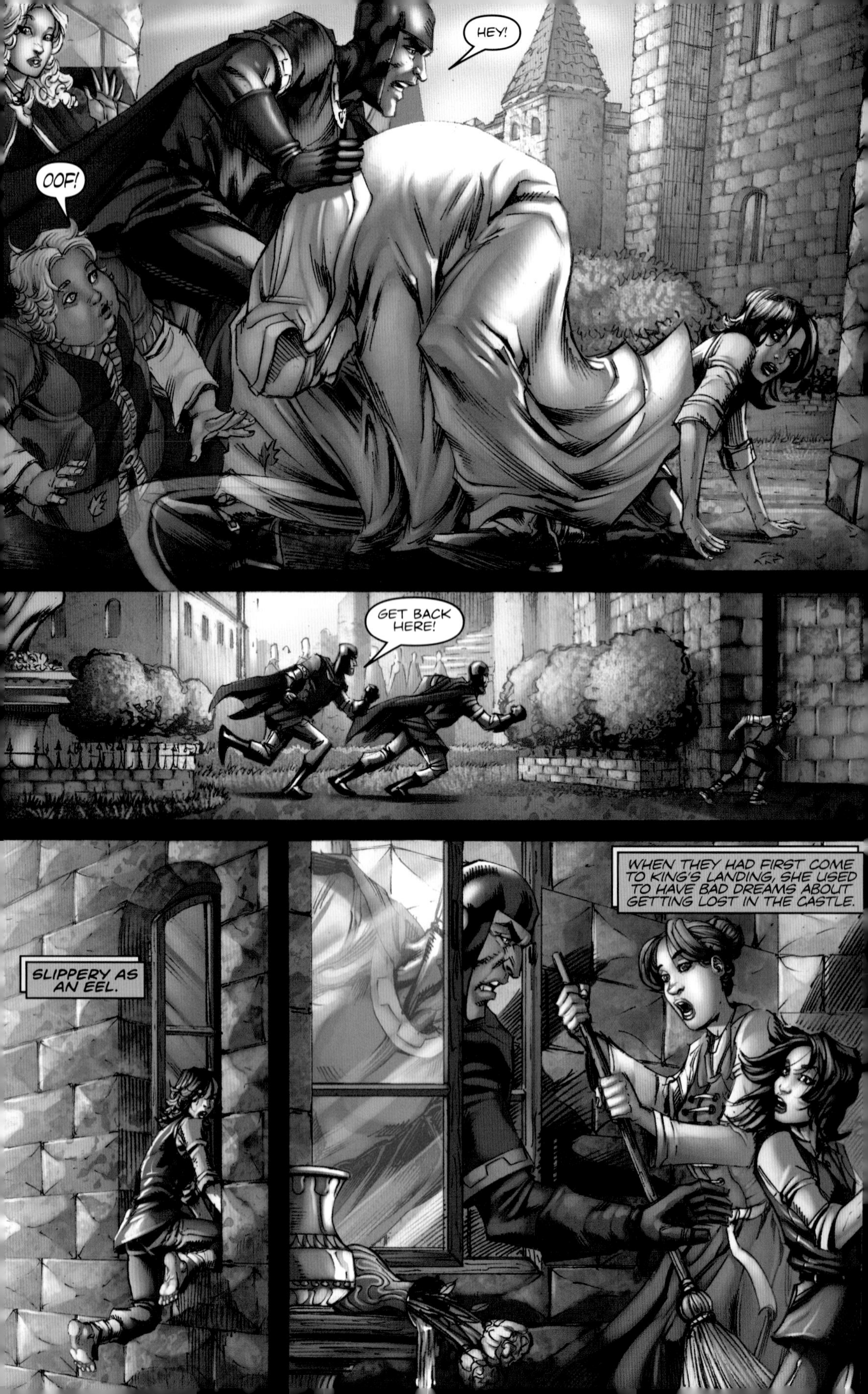
HEY!
OOF!
GET BACK HERE!
SLIPPERY AS AN EEL.
WHEN THEY HAD FIRST COME TO KING'S LANDING, SHE USED TO HAVE BAD DREAMS ABOUT GETTING LOST IN THE CASTLE.

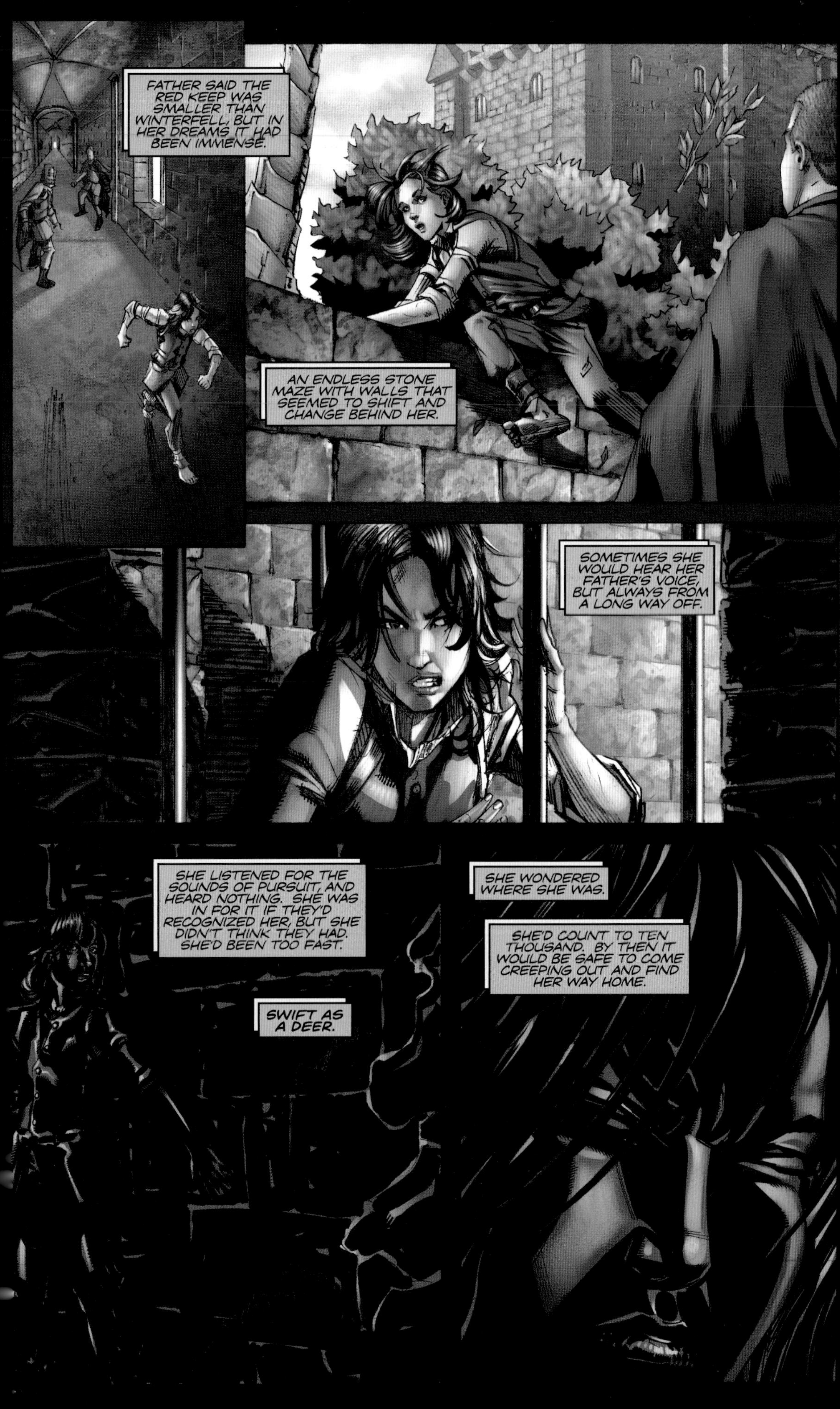
FATHER SAID THE RED KEEP WAS SMALLER THAN WINTERFELL, BUT IN HER DREAMS IT HAD BEEN IMMENSE.
AN ENDLESS STONE MAZE WITH WALLS THAT SEEMED TO SHIFT AND CHANGE BEHIND HER.
SOMETIMES SHE WOULD HEAR HER FATHER'S VOICE, BUT ALWAYS FROM A LONG WAY OFF.
SHE LISTENED FOR THE SOUNDS OF PURSUIT, AND HEARD NOTHING. SHE WAS IN FOR IT IF THEY'D RECOGNIZED HER, BUT SHE DIDN'T THINK THEY HAD. SHE'D BEEN TOO FAST.
SWIFT AS A DEER.
SHE WONDERED WHERE SHE WAS.
SHE'D COUNT TO TEN THOUSAND. BY THEN IT WOULD BE SAFE TO COME CREEPING OUT AND FIND HER WAY HOME.

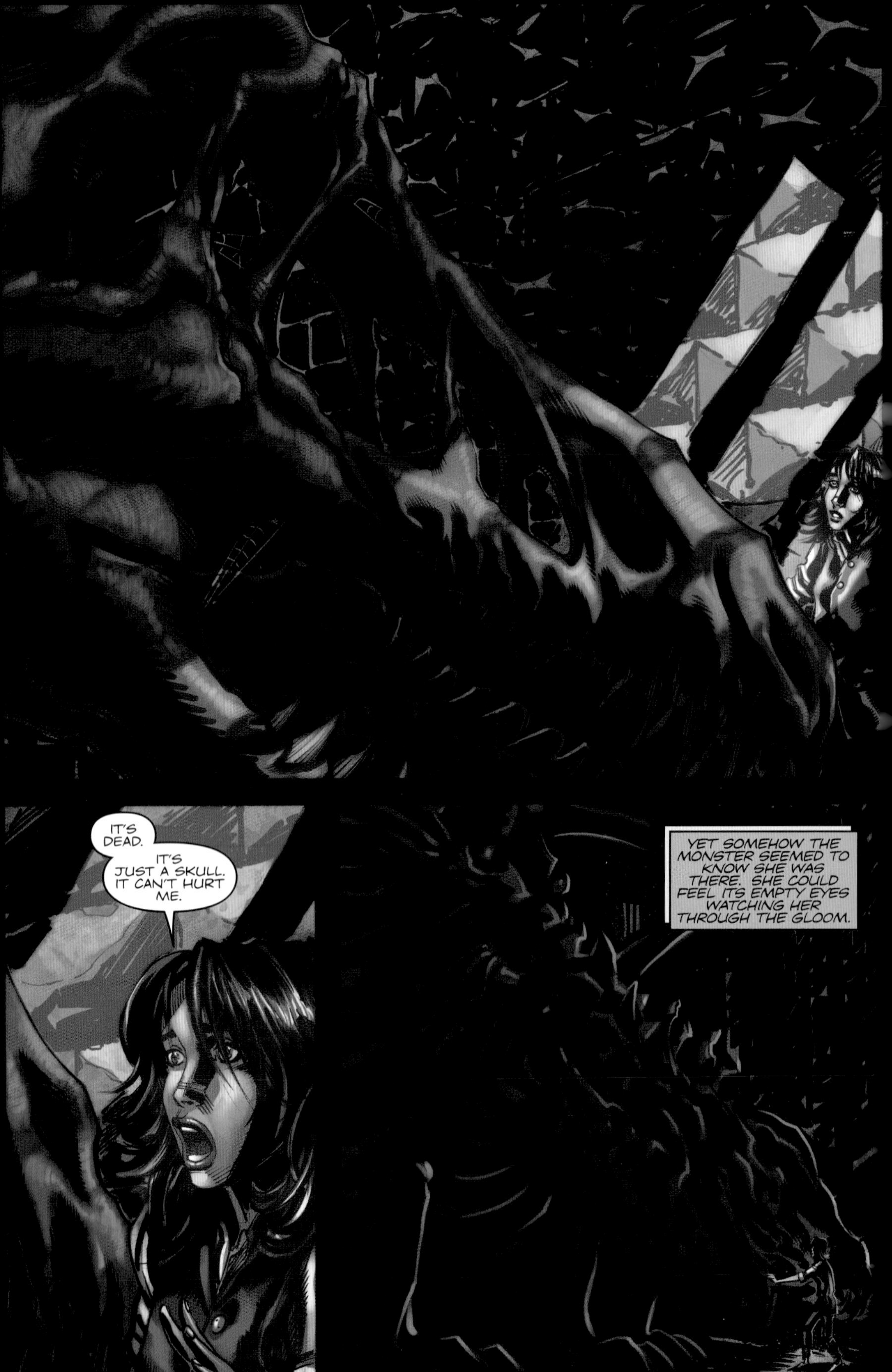
IT'S DEAD.
IT'S JUST A SKULL. IT CAN'T HURT ME.
YET SOMEHOW THE MONSTER SEEMED TO KNOW SHE WAS THERE. SHE COULD FEEL ITS EMPTY EYES WATCHING HER THROUGH THE GLOOM.

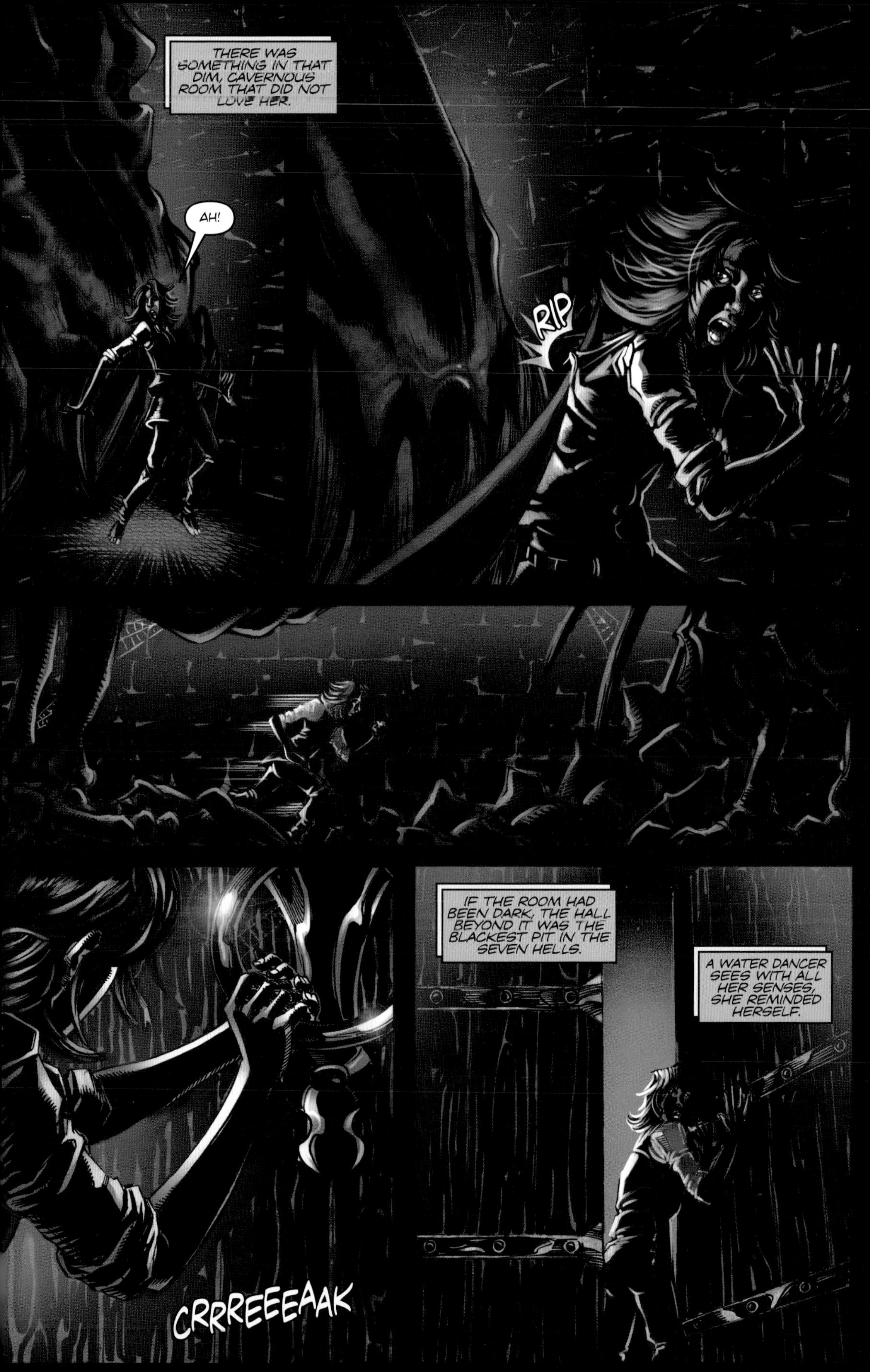
THERE WAS SOMETHING IN THAT DIM, CAVERNOUS ROOM THAT DID NOT LOVE HER.
AH!
RIP
CRRREEEEAAK
IF THE ROOM HAD BEEN DARK, THE HALL BEYOND IT WAS THE BLACKEST PIT IN THE SEVEN HELLS.
A WATER DANCER SEES WITH ALL HER SENSES, SHE REMINDED HERSELF.

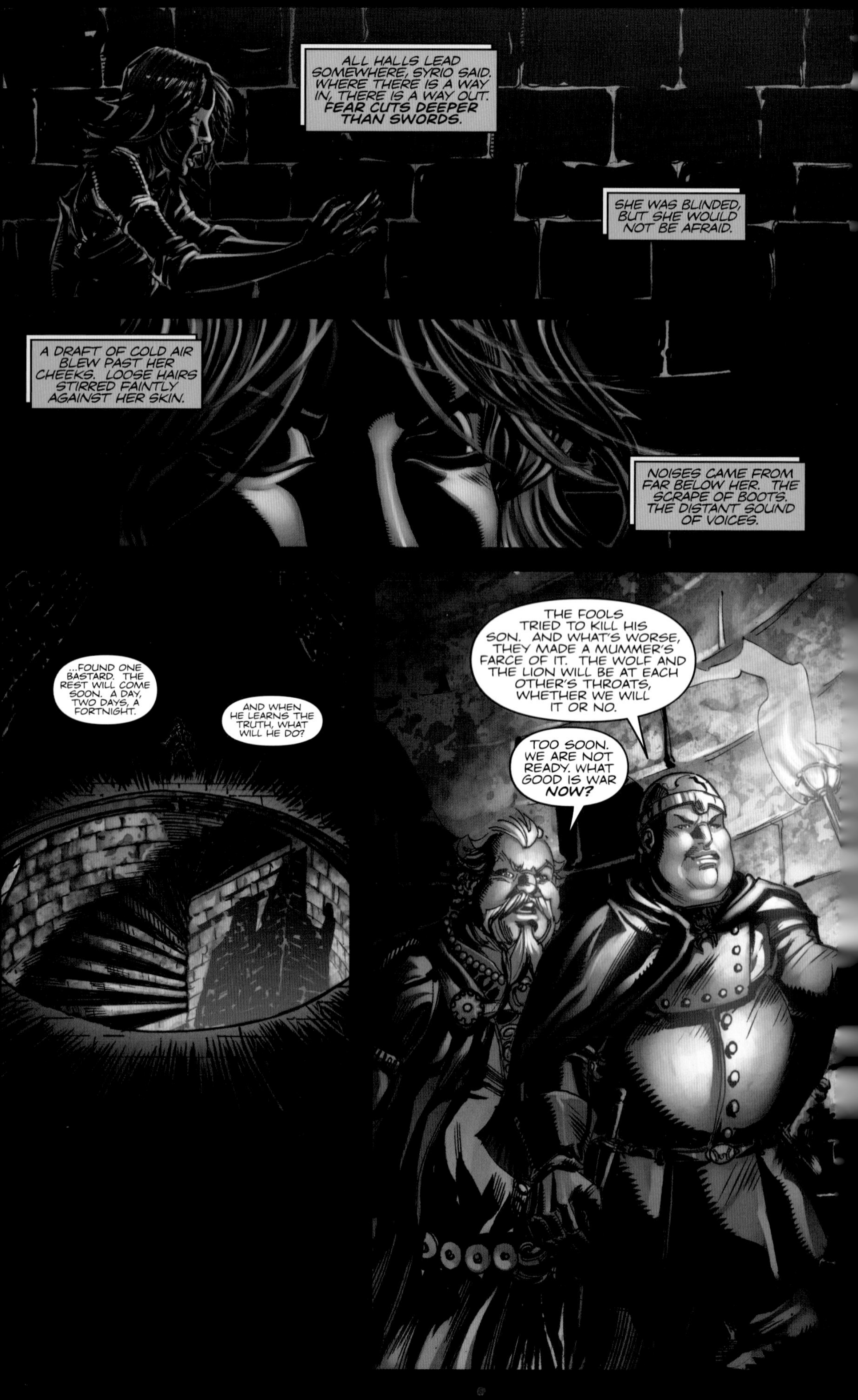
ALL HALLS LEAD SOMEWHERE, SYRIO SAID. WHERE THERE IS A WAY IN, THERE IS A WAY OUT. FEAR CUTS DEEPER THAN SWORDS.
SHE WAS BLINDED, BUT SHE WOULD NOT BE AFRAID.
A DRAFT OF COLD AIR BLEW PAST HER CHEEKS. LOOSE HAIRS STIRRED FAINTLY AGAINST HER SKIN.
NOISES CAME FROM FAR BELOW HER. THE SCRAPE OF BOOTS. THE DISTANT SOUND OF VOICES.
...FOUND ONE BASTARD. THE REST WILL COME SOON. A DAY, TWO DAYS, A FORTNIGHT.
AND WHEN HE LEARNS THE TRUTH, WHAT WILL HE DO?
THE FOOLS TRIED TO KILL HIS SON. AND WHAT'S WORSE, THEY MADE A MUMMER'S FARCE OF IT. THE WOLF AND THE LION WILL BE AT EACH OTHER'S THROATS, WHETHER WE WILL IT OR NO.
TOO SOON. WE ARE NOT READY. WHAT GOOD IS WAR NOW?

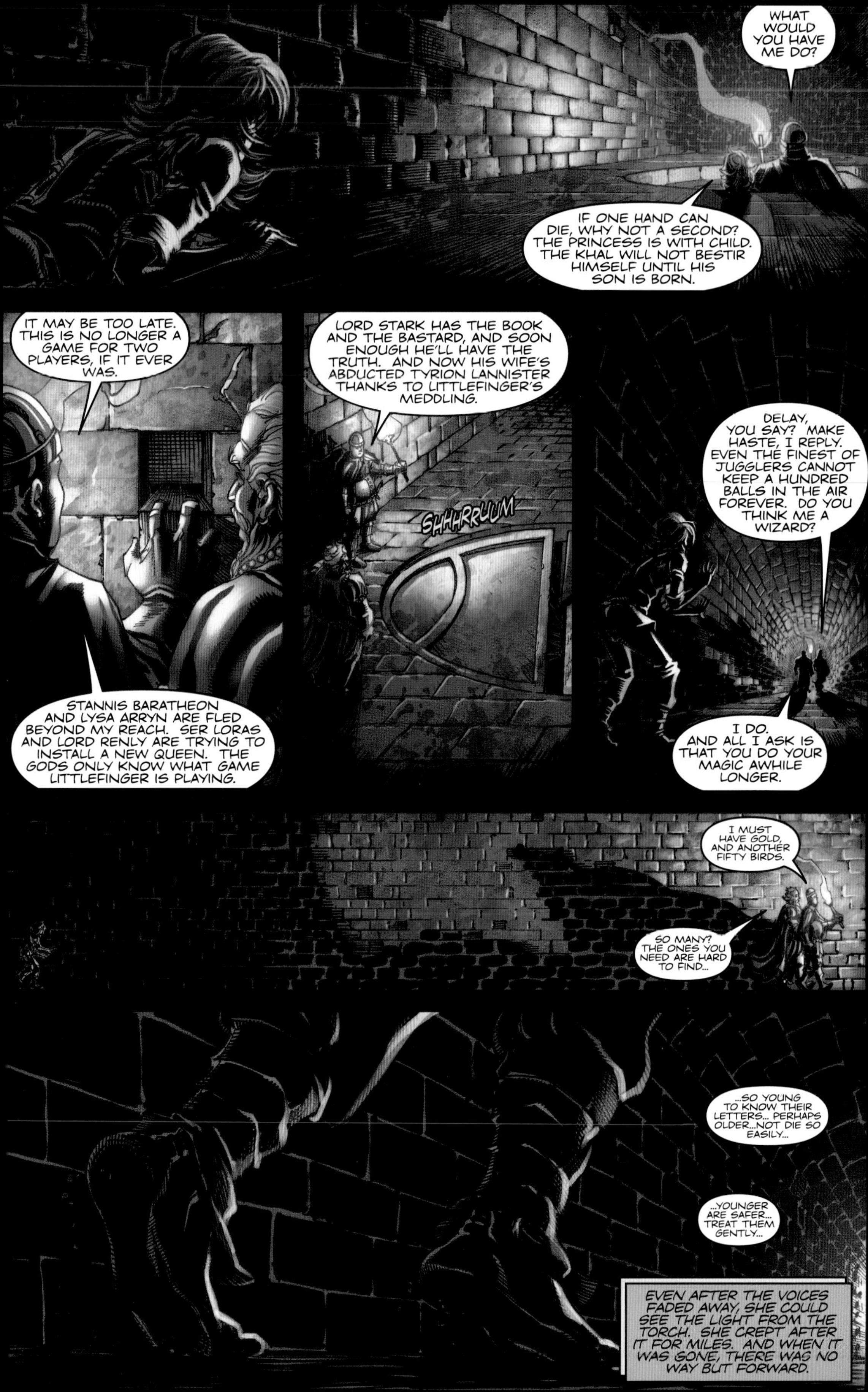
WHAT WOULD YOU HAVE ME DO?
IF ONE HAND CAN DIE, WHY NOT A SECOND? THE PRINCESS IS WITH CHILD. THE KHAL WILL NOT BESTIR HIMSELF UNTIL HIS SON IS BORN.
IT MAY BE TOO LATE. THIS IS NO LONGER A GAME FOR TWO PLAYERS, IF IT EVER WAS.
STANNIS BARATHEON AND LYSA ARRYN ARE FLED BEYOND MY REACH. SER LORAS AND LORD RENLY ARE TRYING TO INSTALL A NEW QUEEN. THE GODS ONLY KNOW WHAT GAME LITTLEFINGER IS PLAYING.
LORD STARK HAS THE BOOK AND THE BASTARD, AND SOON ENOUGH HE'LL HAVE THE TRUTH. AND NOW HIS WIFE'S ABDUCTED TYRION LANNISTER THANKS TO LITTLEFINGER'S MEDDLING.
SHHHRRUUM
DELAY, YOU SAY? MAKE HASTE, I REPLY. EVEN THE FINEST OF JUGGLERS CANNOT KEEP A HUNDRED BALLS IN THE AIR FOREVER. DO YOU THINK ME A WIZARD?
I DO. AND ALL I ASK IS THAT YOU DO YOUR MAGIC AWHILE LONGER.
I MUST HAVE GOLD, AND ANOTHER FIFTY BIRDS.
SO MANY? THE ONES YOU NEED ARE HARD TO FIND...
...SO YOUNG TO KNOW THEIR LETTERS... PERHAPS OLDER...NOT DIE SO EASILY...
...YOUNGER ARE SAFER... TREAT THEM GENTLY...
EVEN AFTER THE VOICES FADED AWAY, SHE COULD SEE THE LIGHT FROM THE TORCH. SHE CREPT AFTER IT FOR MILES. AND WHEN IT WAS GONE, THERE WAS NO WAY BUT FORWARD.

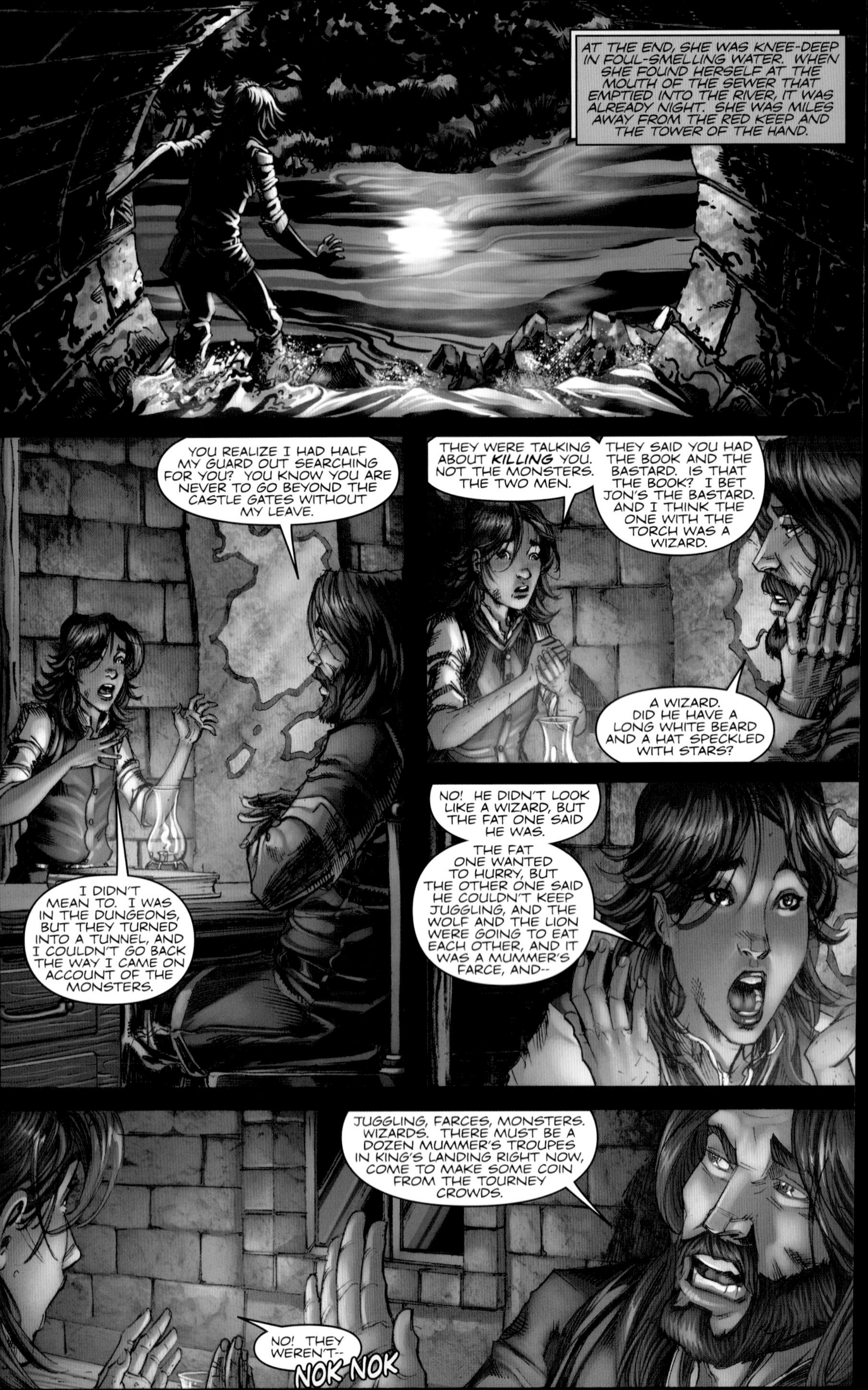
AT THE END, SHE WAS KNEE-DEEP IN FOUL-SMELLING WATER. WHEN SHE FOUND HERSELF AT THE MOUTH OF THE SEWER THAT EMPTIED INTO THE RIVER, IT WAS ALREADY NIGHT. SHE WAS MILES AWAY FROM THE RED KEEP AND THE TOWER OF THE HAND.
YOU REALIZE I HAD HALF MY GUARD OUT SEARCHING FOR YOU? YOU KNOW YOU ARE NEVER TO GO BEYOND THE CASTLE GATES WITHOUT MY LEAVE.
I DIDN'T MEAN TO. I WAS IN THE DUNGEONS, BUT THEY TURNED INTO A TUNNEL, AND I COULDN'T GO BACK THE WAY I CAME ON ACCOUNT OF THE MONSTERS.
THEY WERE TALKING ABOUT *KILLING* YOU. NOT THE MONSTERS. THE TWO MEN.
THEY SAID YOU HAD THE BOOK AND THE BASTARD. IS THAT THE BOOK? I BET JON'S THE BASTARD. AND I THINK THE ONE WITH THE TORCH WAS A WIZARD.
A WIZARD. DID HE HAVE A LONG WHITE BEARD AND A HAT SPECKLED WITH STARS?
NO! HE DIDN'T LOOK LIKE A WIZARD, BUT THE FAT ONE SAID HE WAS.
THE FAT ONE WANTED TO HURRY, BUT THE OTHER ONE SAID HE COULDN'T KEEP JUGGLING, AND THE WOLF AND THE LION WERE GOING TO EAT EACH OTHER, AND IT WAS A MUMMER'S FARCE, AND--
JUGGLING, FARCES, MONSTERS. WIZARDS. THERE MUST BE A DOZEN MUMMER'S TROUPES IN KING'S LANDING RIGHT NOW, COME TO MAKE SOME COIN FROM THE TOURNEY CROWDS.
NO! THEY WEREN'T--
NOK NOK

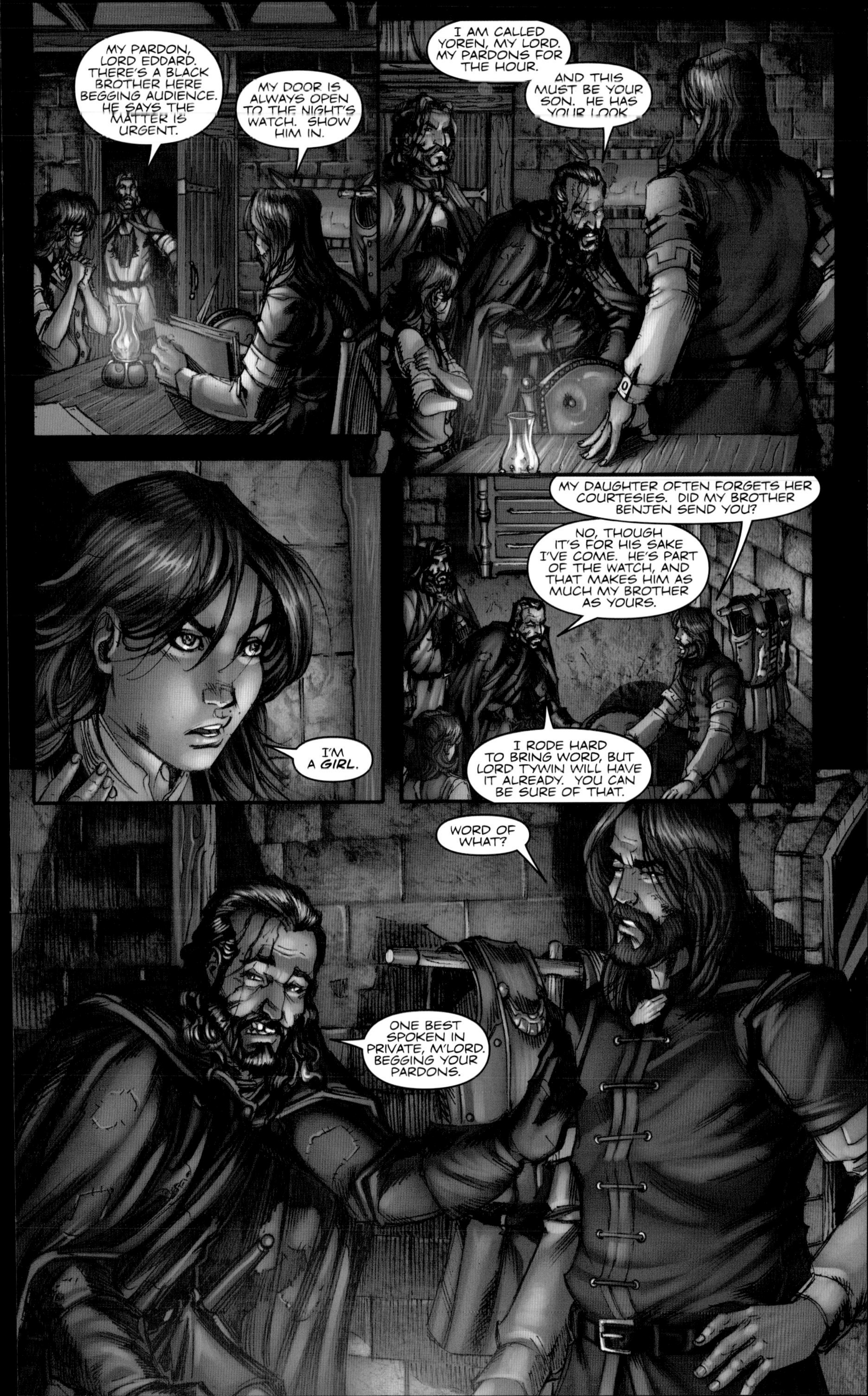
MY PARDON, LORD EDDARD. THERE'S A BLACK BROTHER HERE BEGGING AUDIENCE. HE SAYS THE MATTER IS URGENT.
MY DOOR IS ALWAYS OPEN TO THE NIGHT'S WATCH. SHOW HIM IN.
I AM CALLED YOREN, MY LORD. MY PARDONS FOR THE HOUR.
AND THIS MUST BE YOUR SON. HE HAS YOUR LOOK.
I'M A GIRL.
MY DAUGHTER OFTEN FORGETS HER COURTESIES. DID MY BROTHER BENJEN SEND YOU?
NO, THOUGH IT'S FOR HIS SAKE I'VE COME. HE'S PART OF THE WATCH, AND THAT MAKES HIM AS MUCH MY BROTHER AS YOURS.
I RODE HARD TO BRING WORD, BUT LORD TYWIN WILL HAVE IT ALREADY. YOU CAN BE SURE OF THAT.
WORD OF WHAT?
ONE BEST SPOKEN IN PRIVATE, M'LORD. BEGGING YOUR PARDONS.

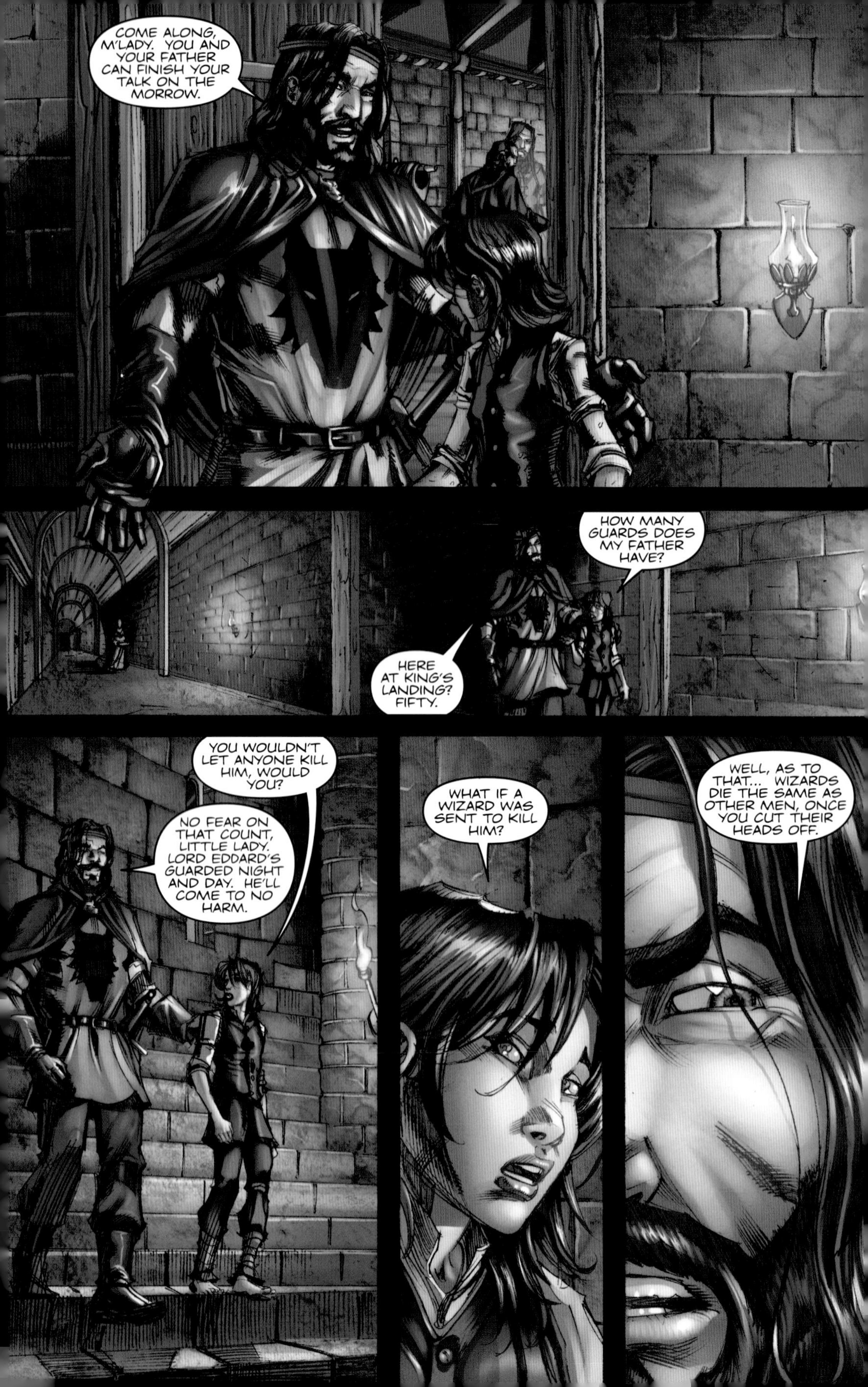
COME ALONG, M'LADY. YOU AND YOUR FATHER CAN FINISH YOUR TALK ON THE MORROW.
HOW MANY GUARDS DOES MY FATHER HAVE?
HERE AT KING'S LANDING? FIFTY.
YOU WOULDN'T LET ANYONE KILL HIM, WOULD YOU?
NO FEAR ON THAT COUNT, LITTLE LADY. LORD EDDARD'S GUARDED NIGHT AND DAY. HE'LL COME TO NO HARM.
WHAT IF A WIZARD WAS SENT TO KILL HIM?
WELL, AS TO THAT... WIZARDS DIE THE SAME AS OTHER MEN, ONCE YOU CUT THEIR HEADS OFF.

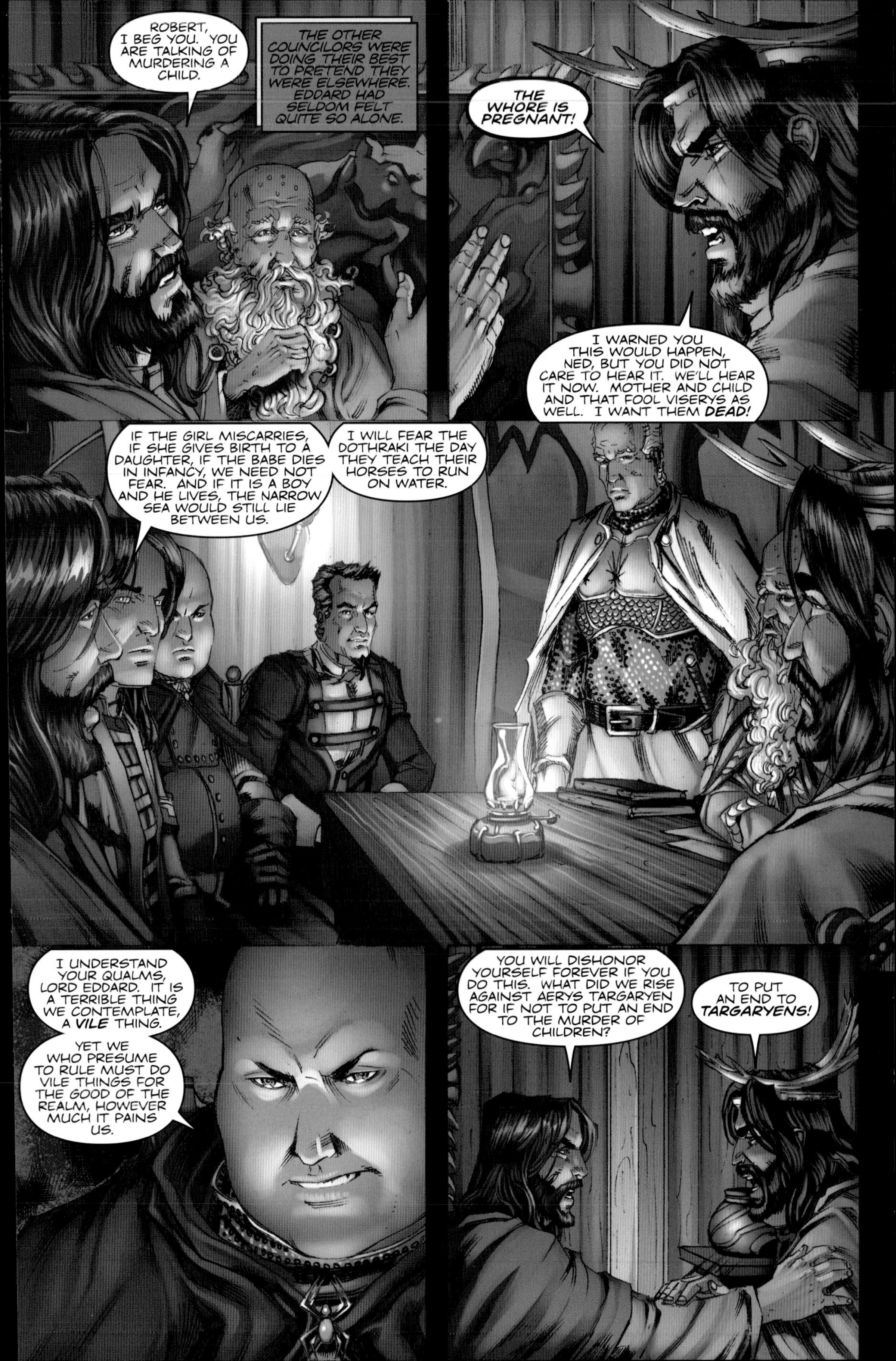
ROBERT, I BEG YOU. YOU ARE TALKING OF MURDERING A CHILD.
THE OTHER COUNCILORS WERE DOING THEIR BEST TO PRETEND THEY WERE ELSEWHERE. EDDARD HAD SELDOM FELT QUITE SO ALONE.
THE WHORE IS PREGNANT!
I WARNED YOU THIS WOULD HAPPEN, NED, BUT YOU DID NOT CARE TO HEAR IT. WE'LL HEAR IT NOW. MOTHER AND CHILD AND THAT FOOL VISERYS AS WELL. I WANT THEM DEAD!
IF THE GIRL MISCARRIES, IF SHE GIVES BIRTH TO A DAUGHTER, IF THE BABE DIES IN INFANCY, WE NEED NOT FEAR. AND IF IT IS A BOY AND HE LIVES, THE NARROW SEA WOULD STILL LIE BETWEEN US.
I WILL FEAR THE DOTHRAKI THE DAY THEY TEACH THEIR HORSES TO RUN ON WATER.
I UNDERSTAND YOUR QUALMS, LORD EDDARD. IT IS A TERRIBLE THING WE CONTEMPLATE, A VILE THING.
YET WE WHO PRESUME TO RULE MUST DO VILE THINGS FOR THE GOOD OF THE REALM, HOWEVER MUCH IT PAINS US.
YOU WILL DISHONOR YOURSELF FOREVER IF YOU DO THIS. WHAT DID WE RISE AGAINST AERYS TARGARYEN FOR IF NOT TO PUT AN END TO THE MURDER OF CHILDREN?
TO PUT AN END TO TARGARYENS!

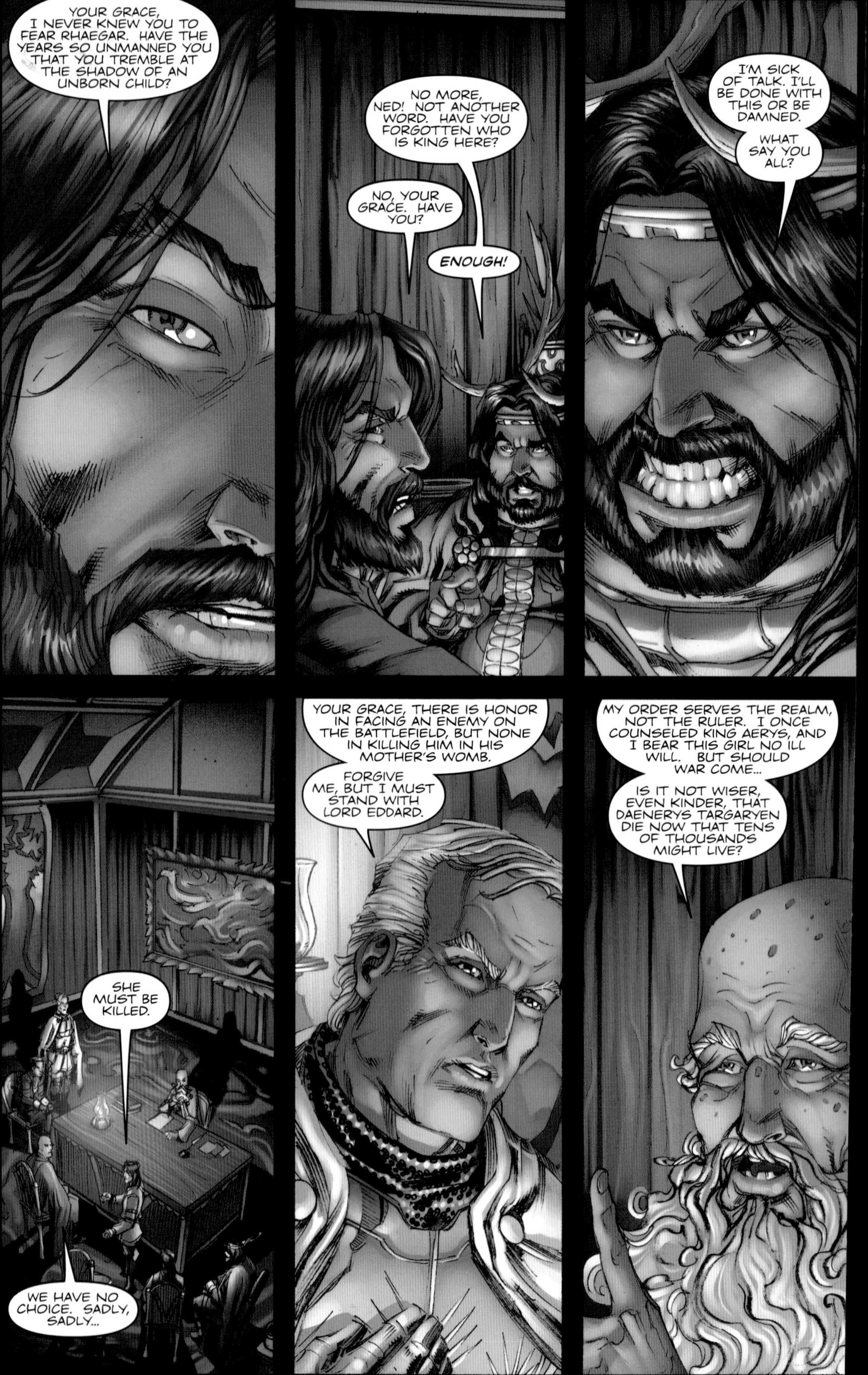
YOUR GRACE, I NEVER KNEW YOU TO FEAR RHAEGAR. HAVE THE YEARS SO UNMANNED YOU THAT YOU TREMBLE AT THE SHADOW OF AN UNBORN CHILD?
NO MORE, NED! NOT ANOTHER WORD. HAVE YOU FORGOTTEN WHO IS KING HERE?
NO, YOUR GRACE. HAVE YOU?
ENOUGH!
I'M SICK OF TALK. I'LL BE DONE WITH THIS OR BE DAMNED.
WHAT SAY YOU ALL?
SHE MUST BE KILLED.
WE HAVE NO CHOICE. SADLY, SADLY...
YOUR GRACE, THERE IS HONOR IN FACING AN ENEMY ON THE BATTLEFIELD, BUT NONE IN KILLING HIM IN HIS MOTHER'S WOMB.
FORGIVE ME, BUT I MUST STAND WITH LORD EDDARD.
MY ORDER SERVES THE REALM, NOT THE RULER. I ONCE COUNSELED KING AERYS, AND I BEAR THIS GIRL NO ILL WILL. BUT SHOULD WAR COME...
IS IT NOT WISER, EVEN KINDER, THAT DAENERYS TARGARYEN DIE NOW THAT TENS OF THOUSANDS MIGHT LIVE?

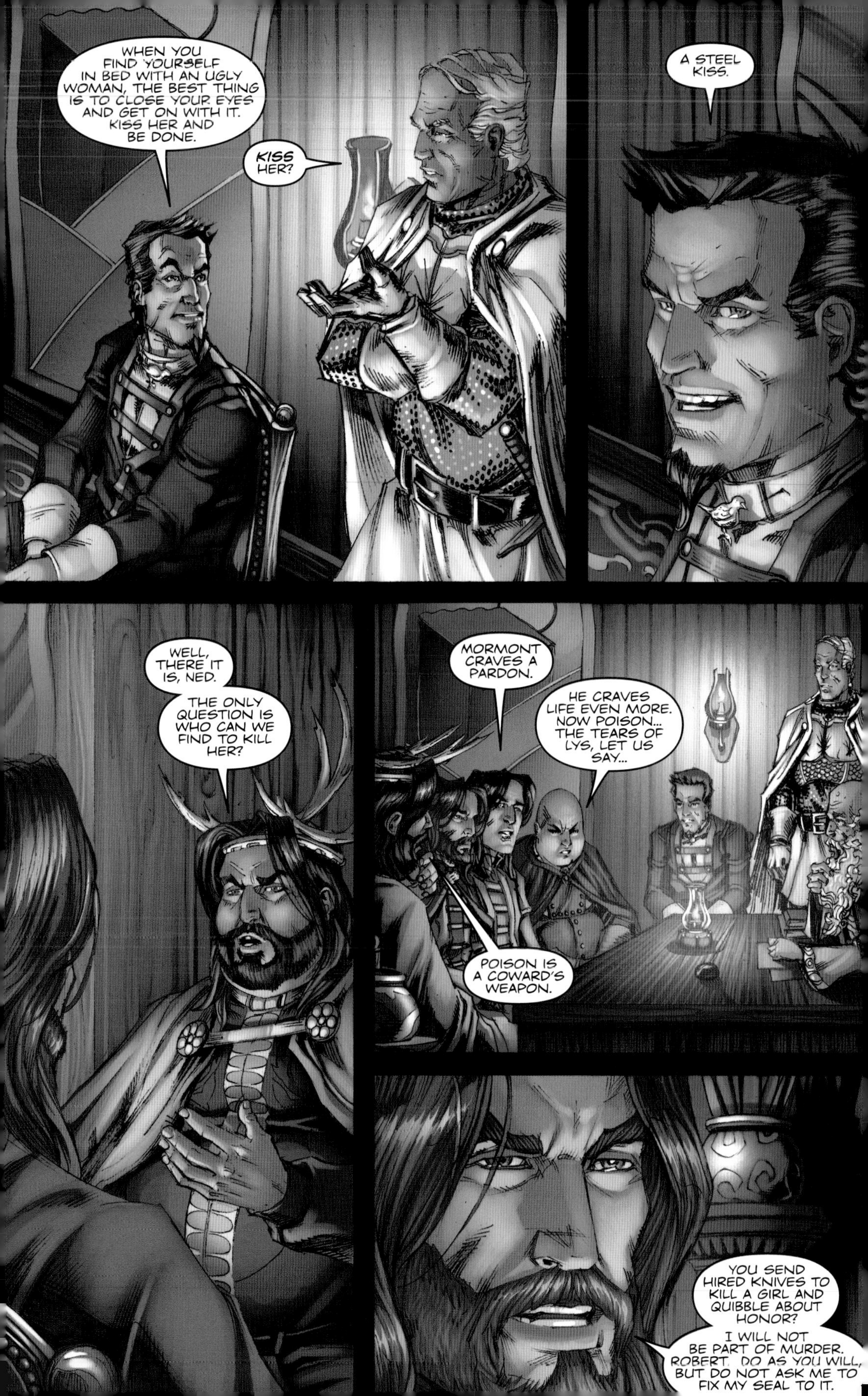
WHEN YOU FIND YOURSELF IN BED WITH AN UGLY WOMAN, THE BEST THING IS TO CLOSE YOUR EYES AND GET ON WITH IT. KISS HER AND BE DONE.
KISS HER?
A STEEL KISS.
WELL, THERE IT IS, NED.
THE ONLY QUESTION IS WHO CAN WE FIND TO KILL HER?
MORMONT CRAVES A PARDON.
HE CRAVES LIFE EVEN MORE. NOW POISON... THE TEARS OF LYS, LET US SAY...
POISON IS A COWARD'S WEAPON.
YOU SEND HIRED KNIVES TO KILL A GIRL AND QUIBBLE ABOUT HONOR?
I WILL NOT BE PART OF MURDER. ROBERT. DO AS YOU WILL, BUT DO NOT ASK ME TO FIX MY SEAL TO IT.

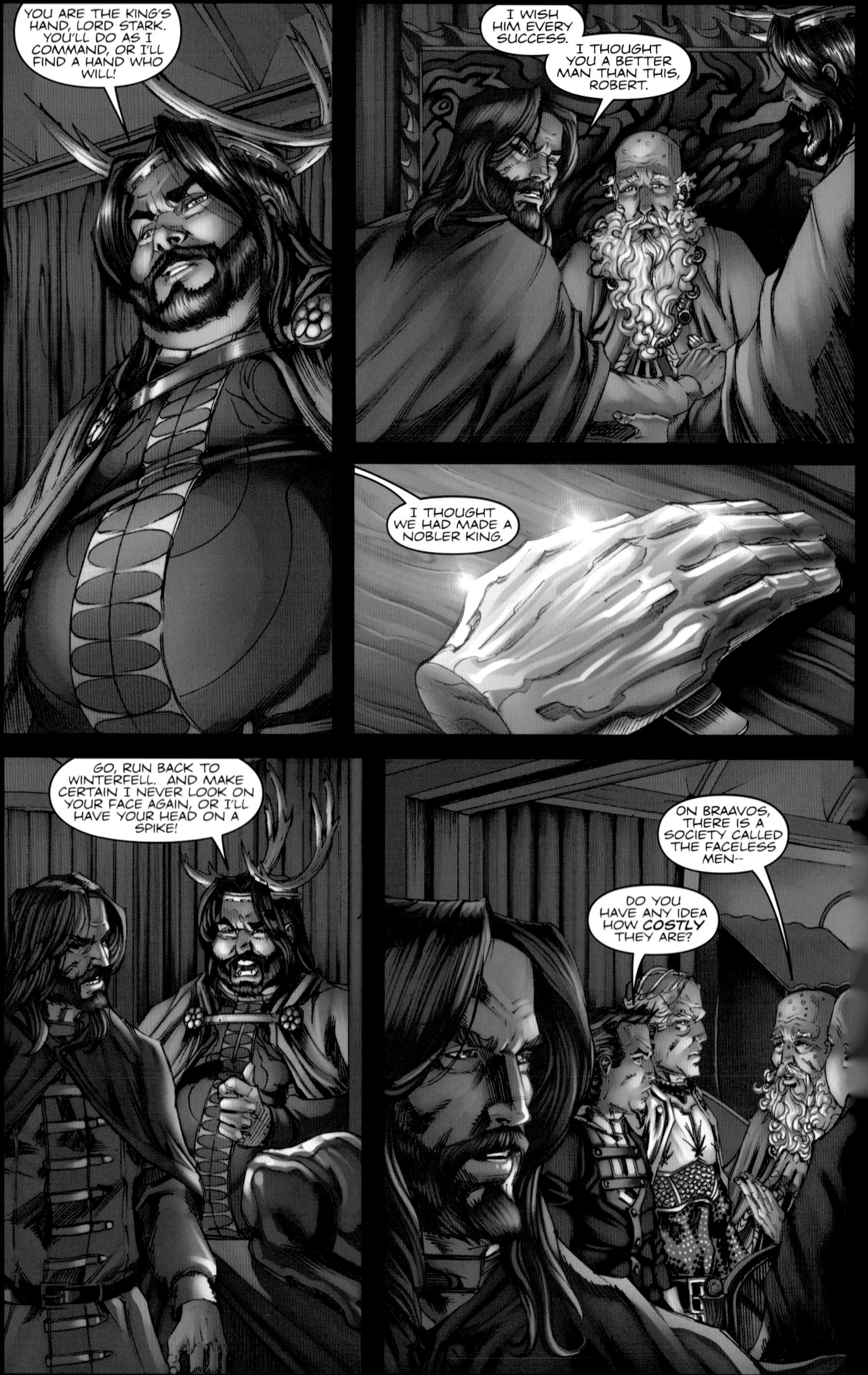

YOU ARE THE KING'S HAND, LORD STARK. YOU'LL DO AS I COMMAND, OR I'LL FIND A HAND WHO WILL!
I WISH HIM EVERY SUCCESS.
I THOUGHT YOU A BETTER MAN THAN THIS, ROBERT.
I THOUGHT WE HAD MADE A NOBLER KING.
GO, RUN BACK TO WINTERFELL. AND MAKE CERTAIN I NEVER LOOK ON YOUR FACE AGAIN, OR I'LL HAVE YOUR HEAD ON A SPIKE!
ON BRAAVOS, THERE IS A SOCIETY CALLED THE FACELESS MEN--
DO YOU HAVE ANY IDEA HOW **COSTLY** THEY ARE?

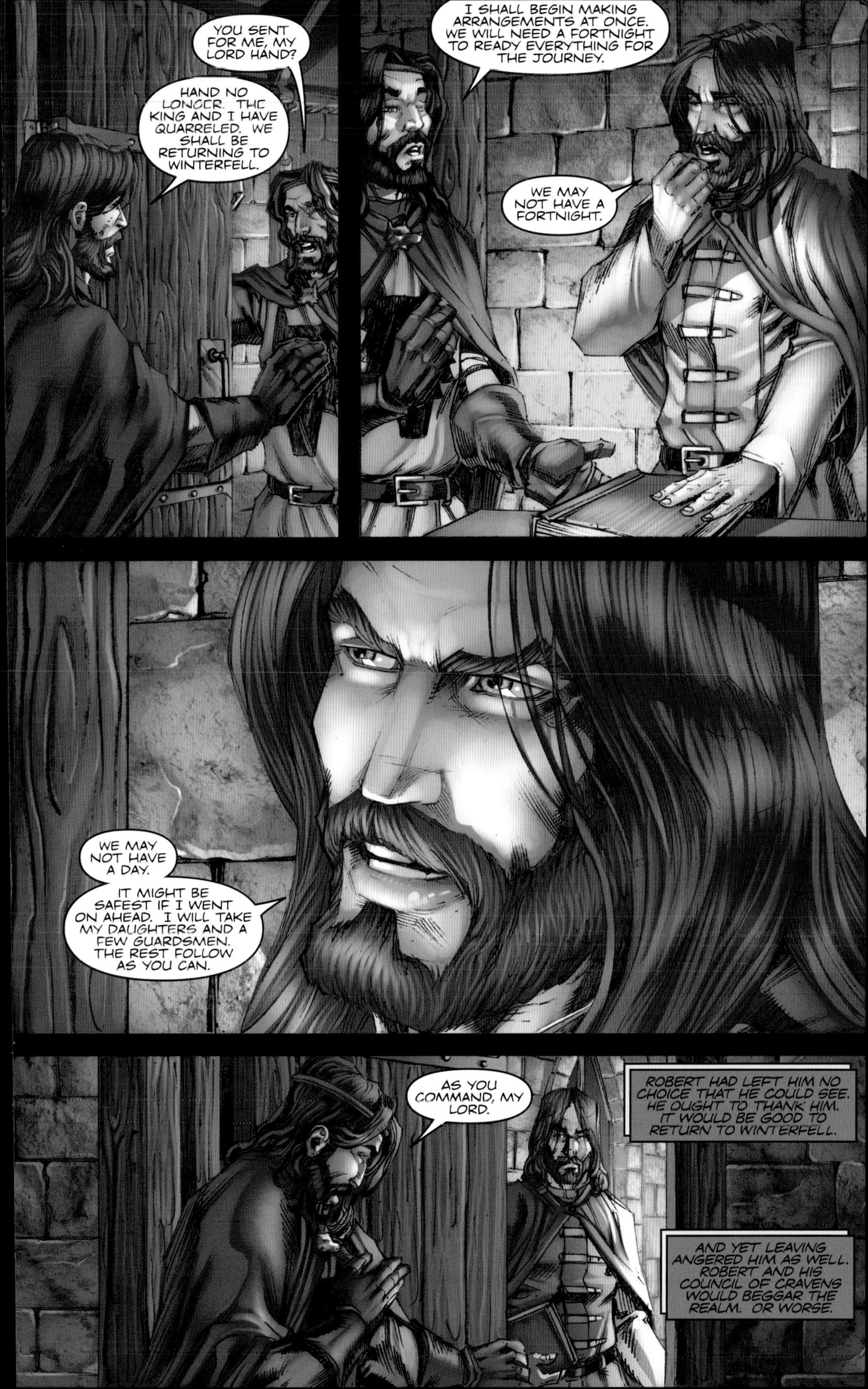

YOU SENT FOR ME, MY LORD HAND?
HAND NO LONGER. THE KING AND I HAVE QUARRELED. WE SHALL BE RETURNING TO WINTERFELL.
I SHALL BEGIN MAKING ARRANGEMENTS AT ONCE. WE WILL NEED A FORTNIGHT TO READY EVERYTHING FOR THE JOURNEY.
WE MAY NOT HAVE A FORTNIGHT.
WE MAY NOT HAVE A DAY.
IT MIGHT BE SAFEST IF I WENT ON AHEAD. I WILL TAKE MY DAUGHTERS AND A FEW GUARDSMEN. THE REST FOLLOW AS YOU CAN.
AS YOU COMMAND, MY LORD.
ROBERT HAD LEFT HIM NO CHOICE THAT HE COULD SEE. HE OUGHT TO THANK HIM. IT WOULD BE GOOD TO RETURN TO WINTERFELL.
AND YET LEAVING ANGERED HIM AS WELL. ROBERT AND HIS COUNCIL OF CRAVENS WOULD BEGGAR THE REALM. OR WORSE.

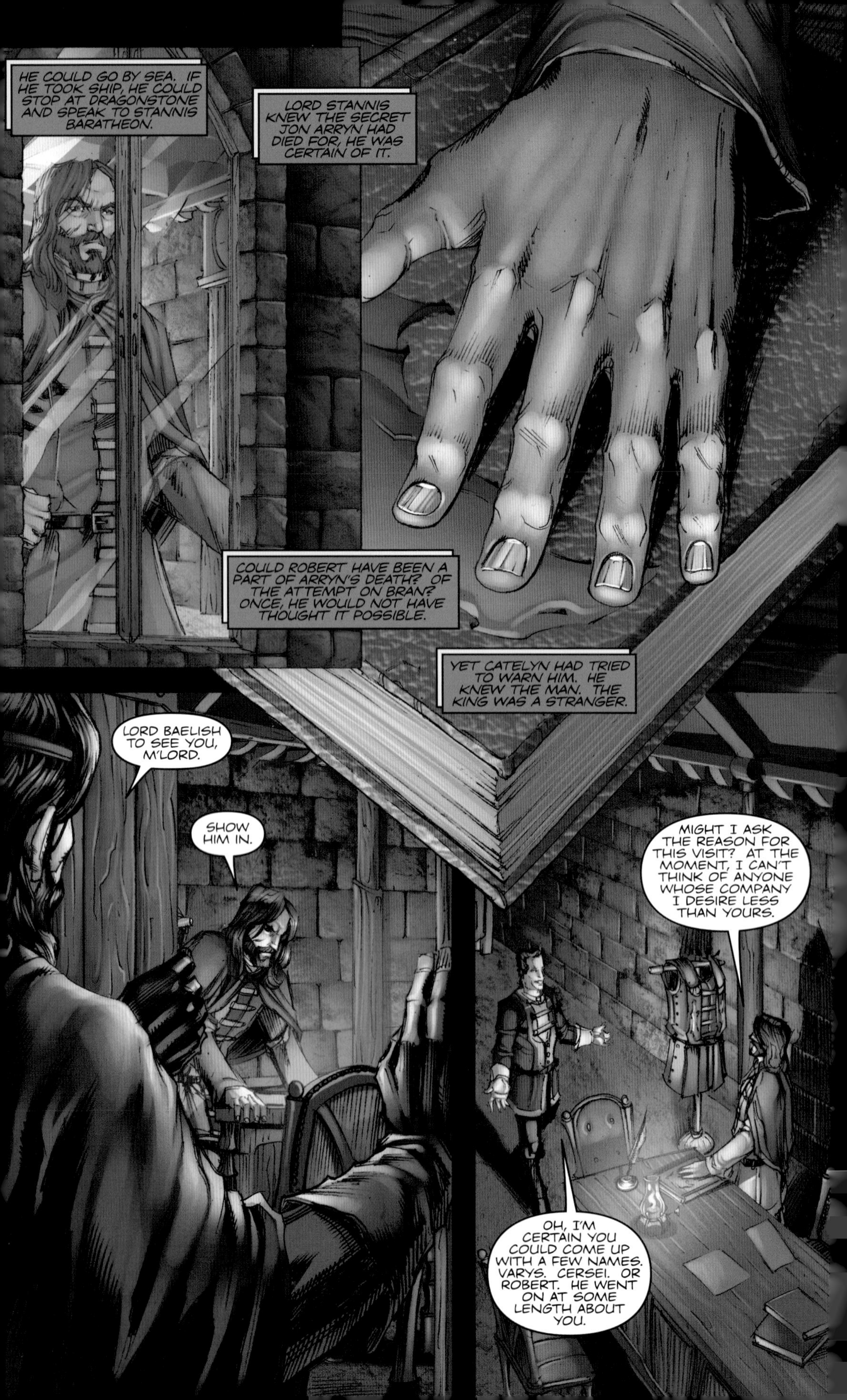
HE COULD GO BY SEA. IF HE TOOK SHIP, HE COULD STOP AT DRAGONSTONE AND SPEAK TO STANNIS BARATHEON.
LORD STANNIS KNEW THE SECRET JON ARRYN HAD DIED FOR, HE WAS CERTAIN OF IT.
COULD ROBERT HAVE BEEN A PART OF ARRYN'S DEATH? OF THE ATTEMPT ON BRAN? ONCE, HE WOULD NOT HAVE THOUGHT IT POSSIBLE.
YET CATELYN HAD TRIED TO WARN HIM. HE KNEW THE MAN. THE KING WAS A STRANGER.
LORD BAELISH TO SEE YOU, M'LORD.
SHOW HIM IN.
MIGHT I ASK THE REASON FOR THIS VISIT? AT THE MOMENT, I CAN'T THINK OF ANYONE WHOSE COMPANY I DESIRE LESS THAN YOURS.
OH, I'M CERTAIN YOU COULD COME UP WITH A FEW NAMES. VARYS. CERSEI. OR ROBERT. HE WENT ON AT SOME LENGTH ABOUT YOU.

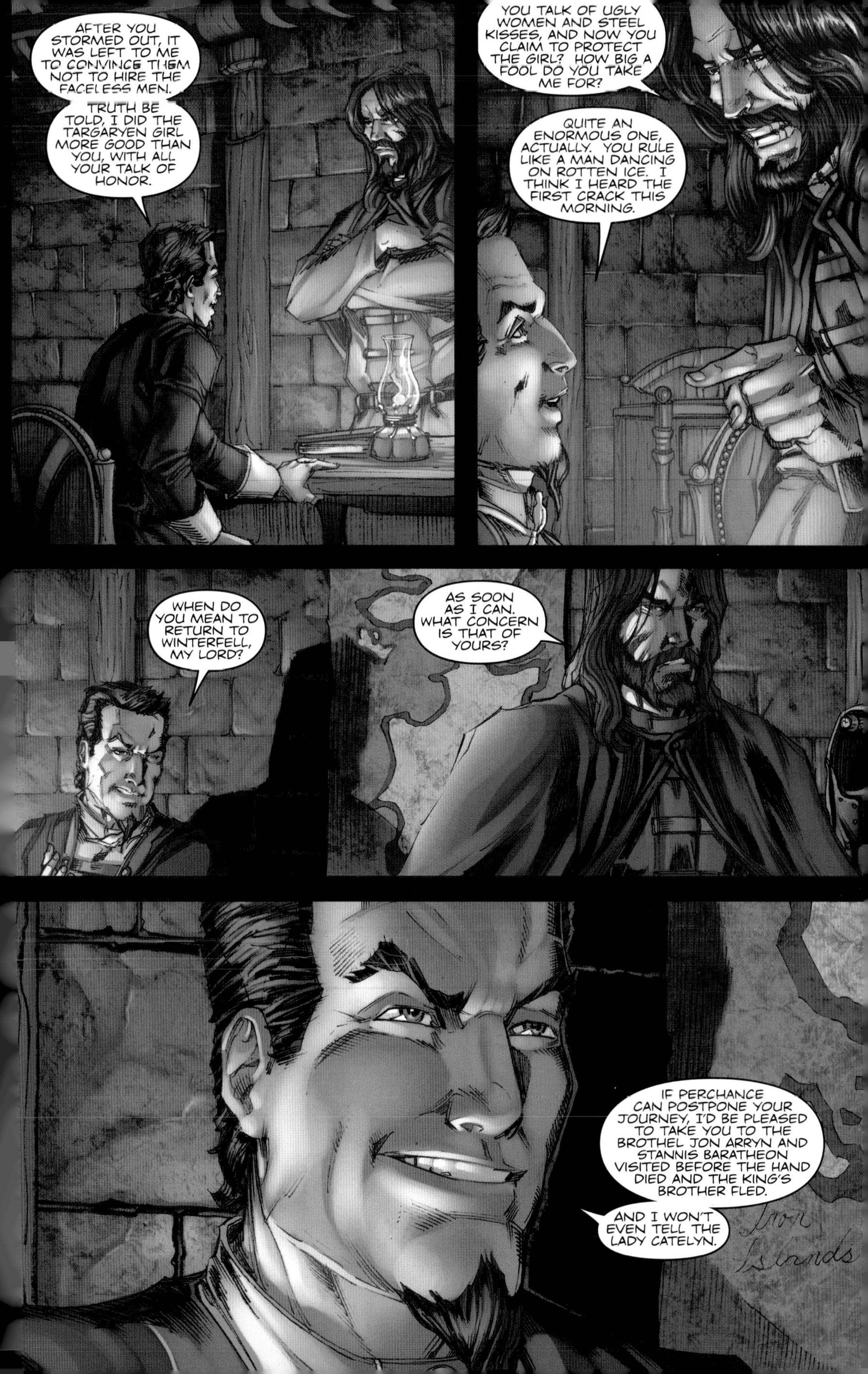
AFTER YOU STORMED OUT, IT WAS LEFT TO ME TO CONVINCE THEM NOT TO HIRE THE FACELESS MEN.
TRUTH BE TOLD, I DID THE TARGARYEN GIRL MORE GOOD THAN YOU, WITH ALL YOUR TALK OF HONOR.
YOU TALK OF UGLY WOMEN AND STEEL KISSES, AND NOW YOU CLAIM TO PROTECT THE GIRL? HOW BIG A FOOL DO YOU TAKE ME FOR?
QUITE AN ENORMOUS ONE, ACTUALLY. YOU RULE LIKE A MAN DANCING ON ROTTEN ICE. I THINK I HEARD THE FIRST CRACK THIS MORNING.
WHEN DO YOU MEAN TO RETURN TO WINTERFELL, MY LORD?
AS SOON AS I CAN. WHAT CONCERN IS THAT OF YOURS?
IF PERCHANCE CAN POSTPONE YOUR JOURNEY, I'D BE PLEASED TO TAKE YOU TO THE BROTHEL JON ARRYN AND STANNIS BARATHEON VISITED BEFORE THE HAND DIED AND THE KING'S BROTHER FLED.
AND I WON'T EVEN TELL THE LADY CATELYN.
Iron Islands

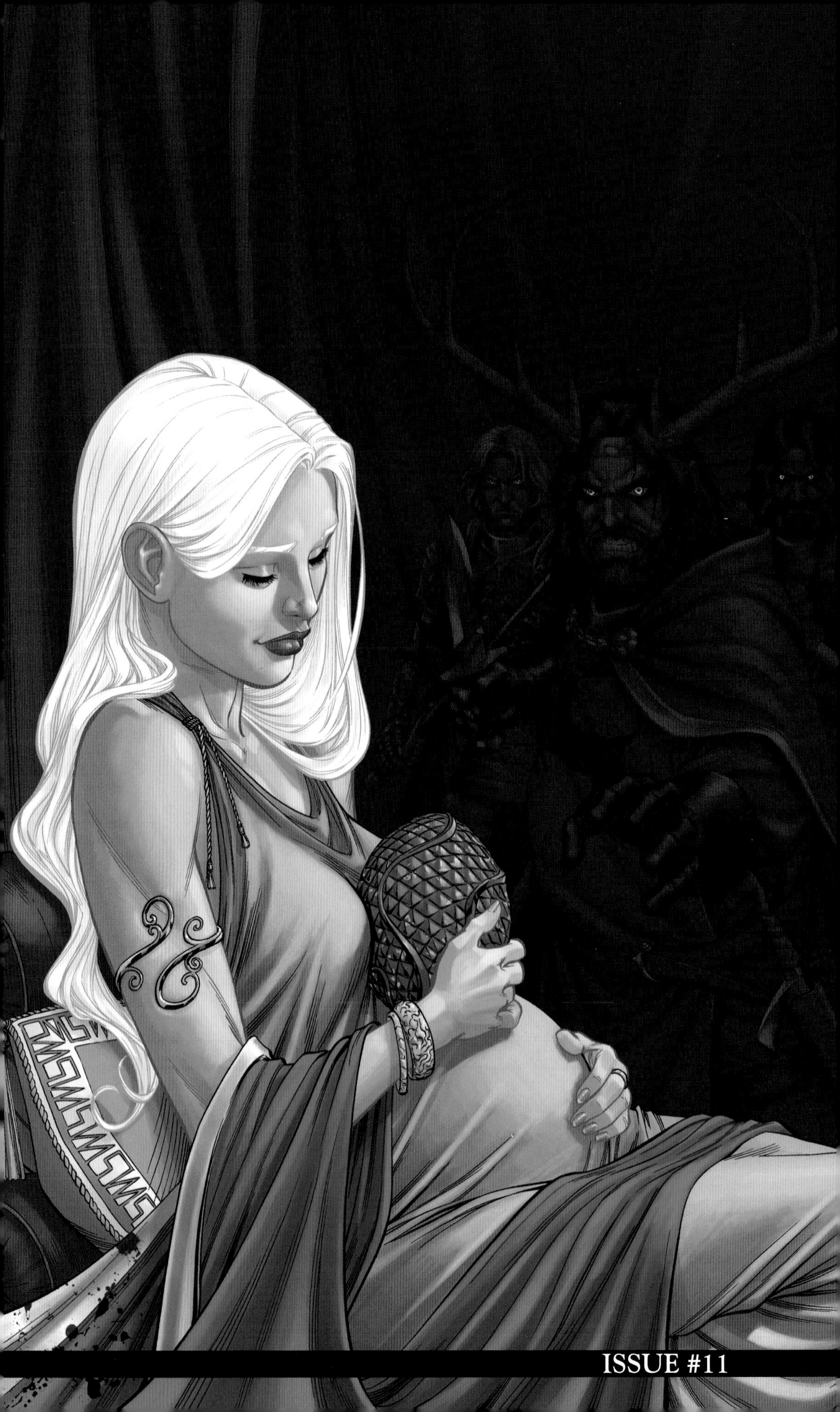

ISSUE #11

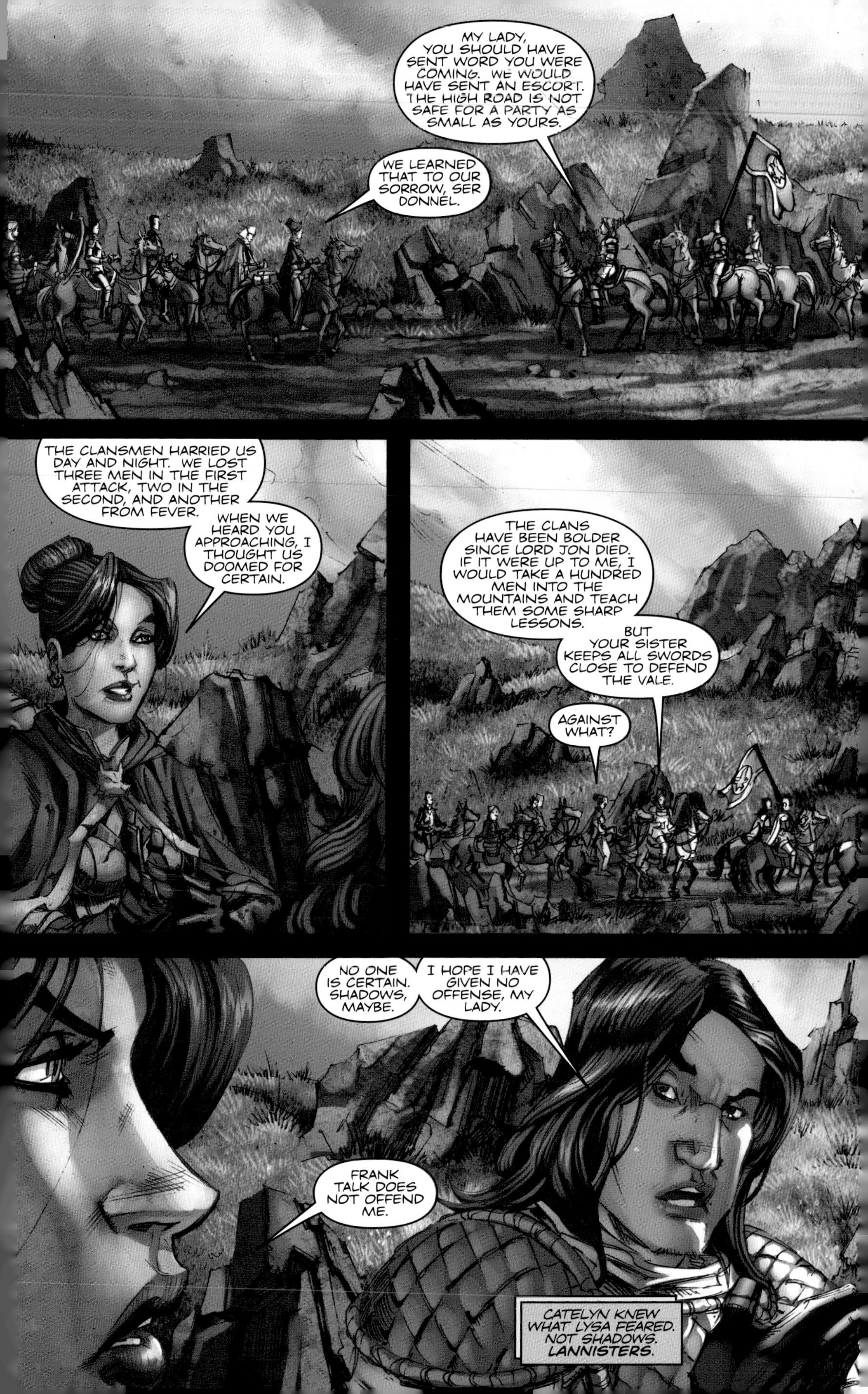
MY LADY, YOU SHOULD HAVE SENT WORD YOU WERE COMING. WE WOULD HAVE SENT AN ESCORT. THE HIGH ROAD IS NOT SAFE FOR A PARTY AS SMALL AS YOURS.
WE LEARNED THAT TO OUR SORROW, SER DONNEL.
THE CLANSMEN HARRIED US DAY AND NIGHT. WE LOST THREE MEN IN THE FIRST ATTACK, TWO IN THE SECOND, AND ANOTHER FROM FEVER.
WHEN WE HEARD YOU APPROACHING, I THOUGHT US DOOMED FOR CERTAIN.
THE CLANS HAVE BEEN BOLDER SINCE LORD JON DIED. IF IT WERE UP TO ME, I WOULD TAKE A HUNDRED MEN INTO THE MOUNTAINS AND TEACH THEM SOME SHARP LESSONS.
BUT YOUR SISTER KEEPS ALL SWORDS CLOSE TO DEFEND THE VALE.
AGAINST WHAT?
NO ONE IS CERTAIN. SHADOWS, MAYBE.
I HOPE I HAVE GIVEN NO OFFENSE, MY LADY.
FRANK TALK DOES NOT OFFEND ME.
CATELYN KNEW WHAT LYSA FEARED. NOT SHADOWS. LANNISTERS.

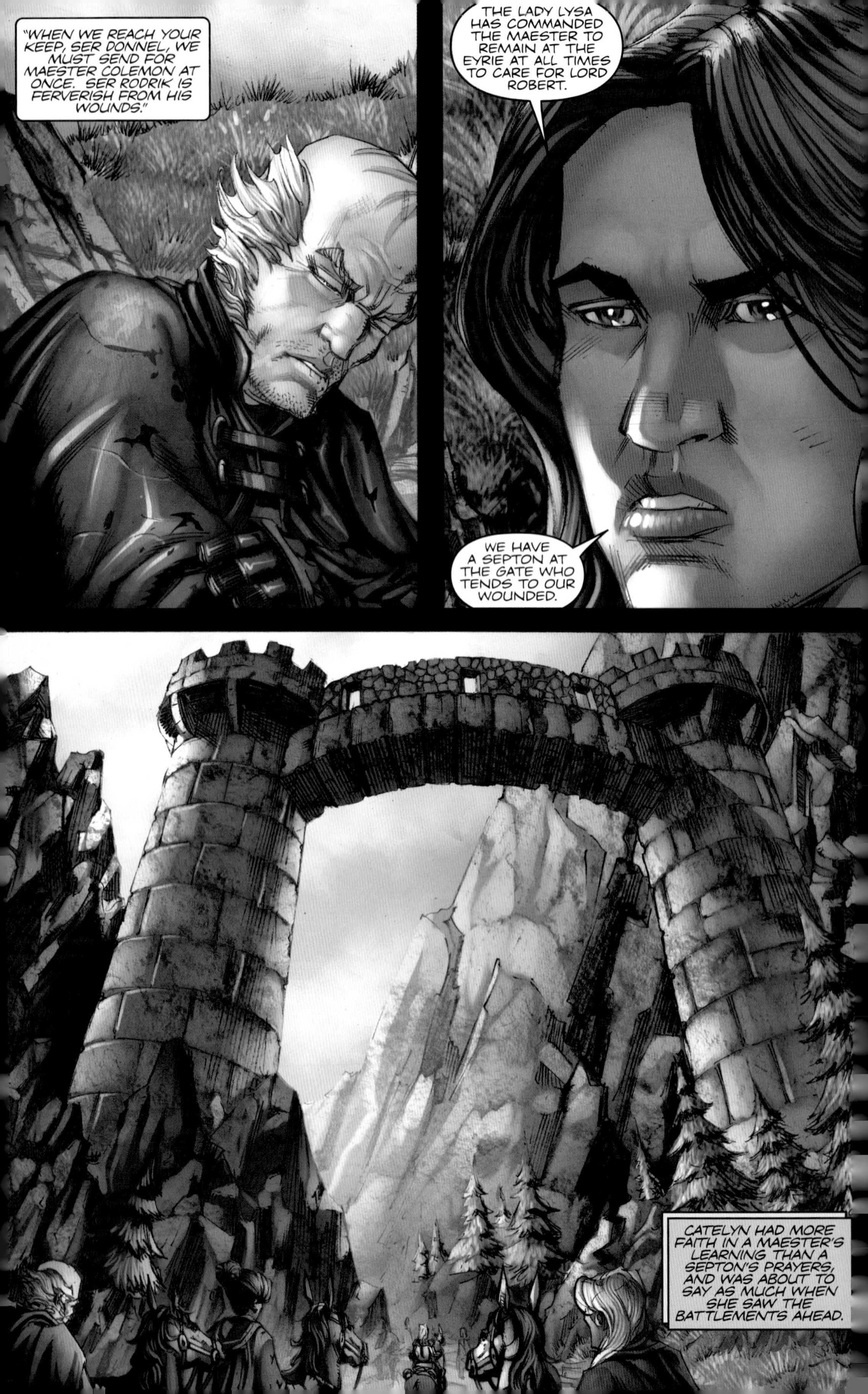
"WHEN WE REACH YOUR KEEP, SER DONNEL, WE MUST SEND FOR MAESTER COLEMON AT ONCE. SER RODRIK IS FERVERISH FROM HIS WOUNDS."
THE LADY LYSA HAS COMMANDED THE MAESTER TO REMAIN AT THE EYRIE AT ALL TIMES TO CARE FOR LORD ROBERT.
WE HAVE A SEPTON AT THE GATE WHO TENDS TO OUR WOUNDED.
CATELYN HAD MORE FAITH IN A MAESTER'S LEARNING THAN A SEPTON'S PRAYERS, AND WAS ABOUT TO SAY AS MUCH WHEN SHE SAW THE BATTLEMENTS AHEAD.

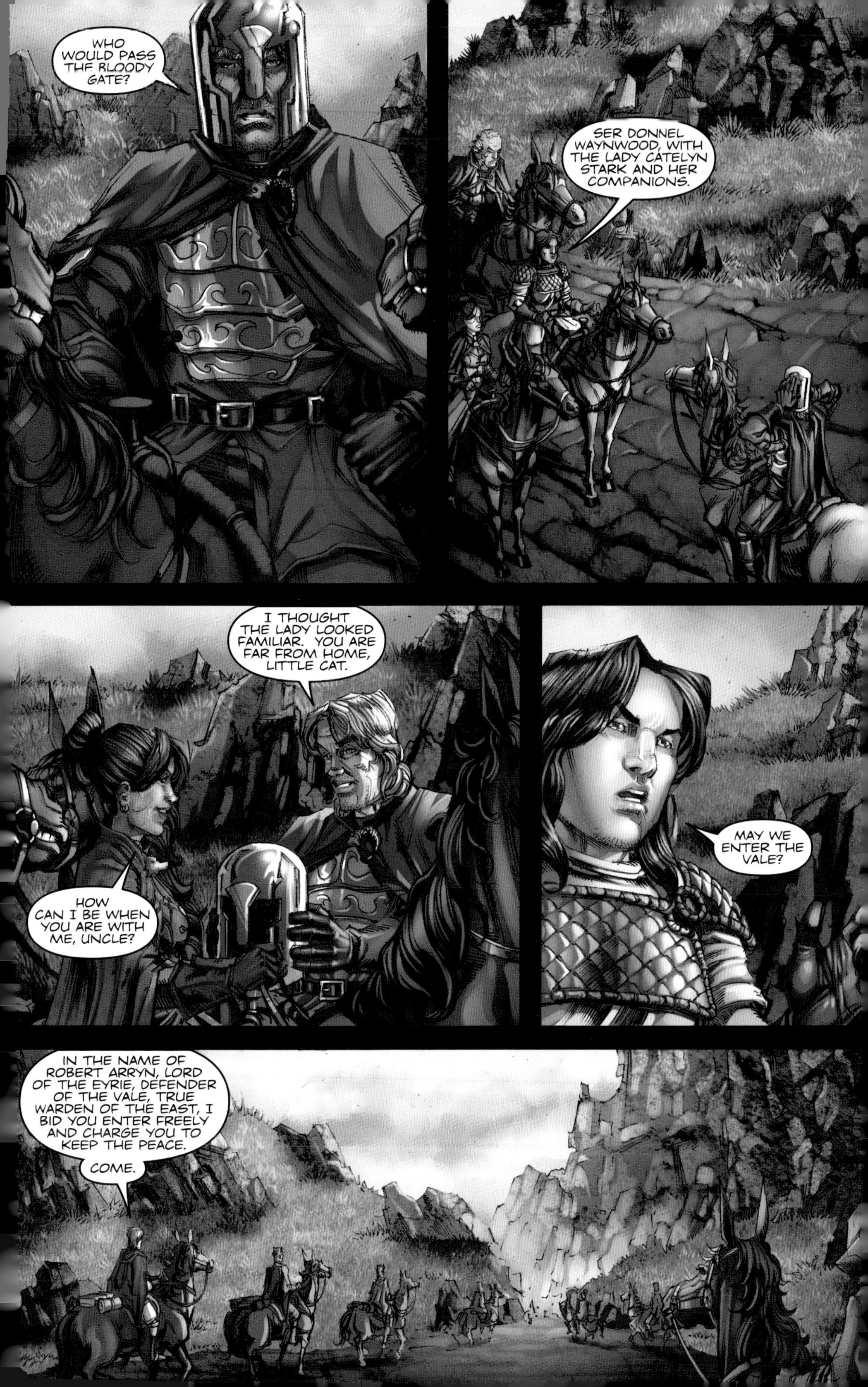
WHO WOULD PASS THE BLOODY GATE?
SER DONNEL WAYNWOOD, WITH THE LADY CATELYN STARK AND HER COMPANIONS.
I THOUGHT THE LADY LOOKED FAMILIAR. YOU ARE FAR FROM HOME, LITTLE CAT.
HOW CAN I BE WHEN YOU ARE WITH ME, UNCLE?
MAY WE ENTER THE VALE?
IN THE NAME OF ROBERT ARRYN, LORD OF THE EYRIE, DEFENDER OF THE VALE, TRUE WARDEN OF THE EAST, I BID YOU ENTER FREELY AND CHARGE YOU TO KEEP THE PEACE.
COME.

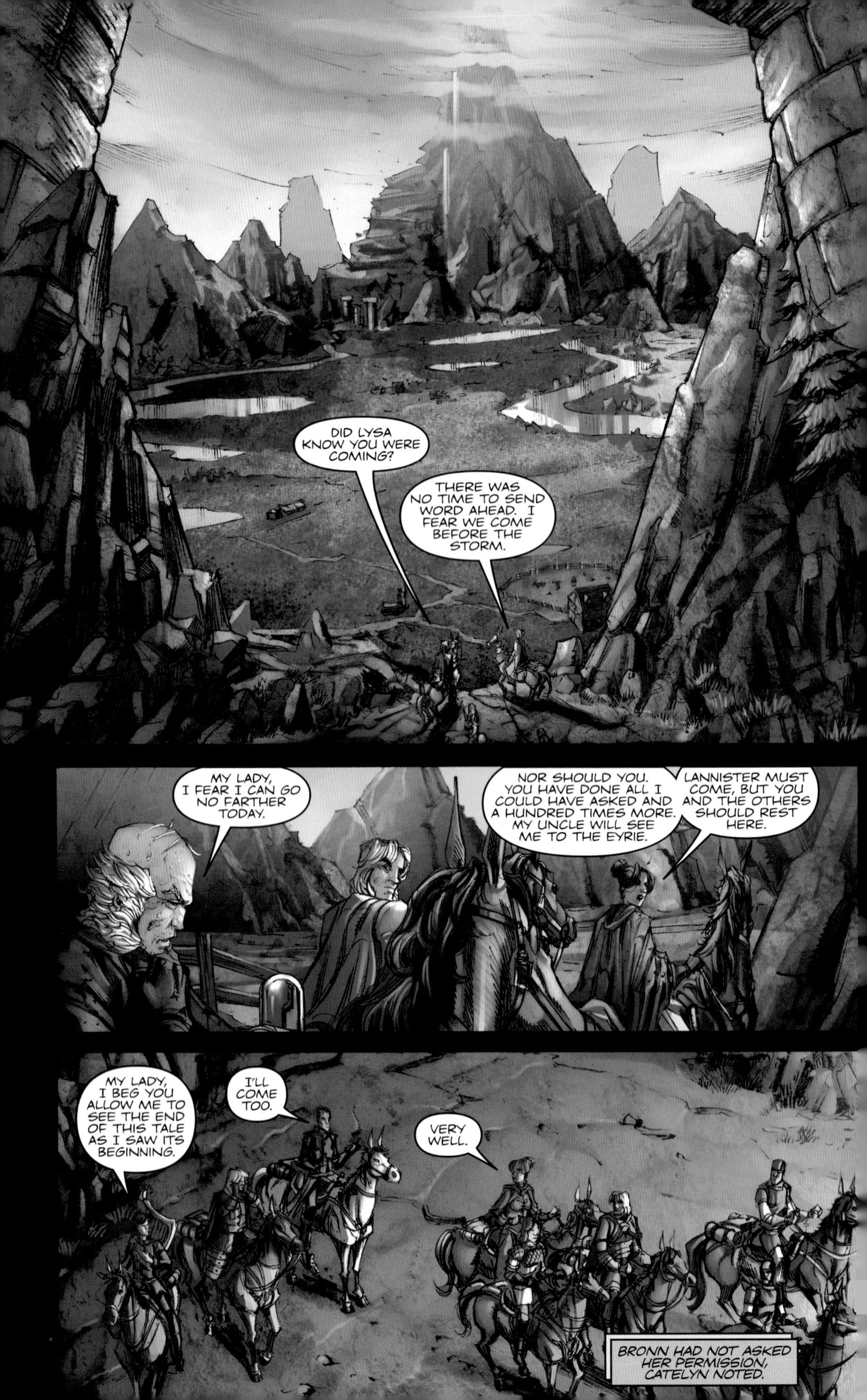
DID LYSA KNOW YOU WERE COMING?
THERE WAS NO TIME TO SEND WORD AHEAD. I FEAR WE COME BEFORE THE STORM.
MY LADY, I FEAR I CAN GO NO FARTHER TODAY.
NOR SHOULD YOU. YOU HAVE DONE ALL I COULD HAVE ASKED AND A HUNDRED TIMES MORE. MY UNCLE WILL SEE ME TO THE EYRIE.
LANNISTER MUST COME, BUT YOU AND THE OTHERS SHOULD REST HERE.
MY LADY, I BEG YOU ALLOW ME TO SEE THE END OF THIS TALE AS I SAW ITS BEGINNING.
I'LL COME TOO.
VERY WELL.
BRONN HAD NOT ASKED HER PERMISSION, CATELYN NOTED.

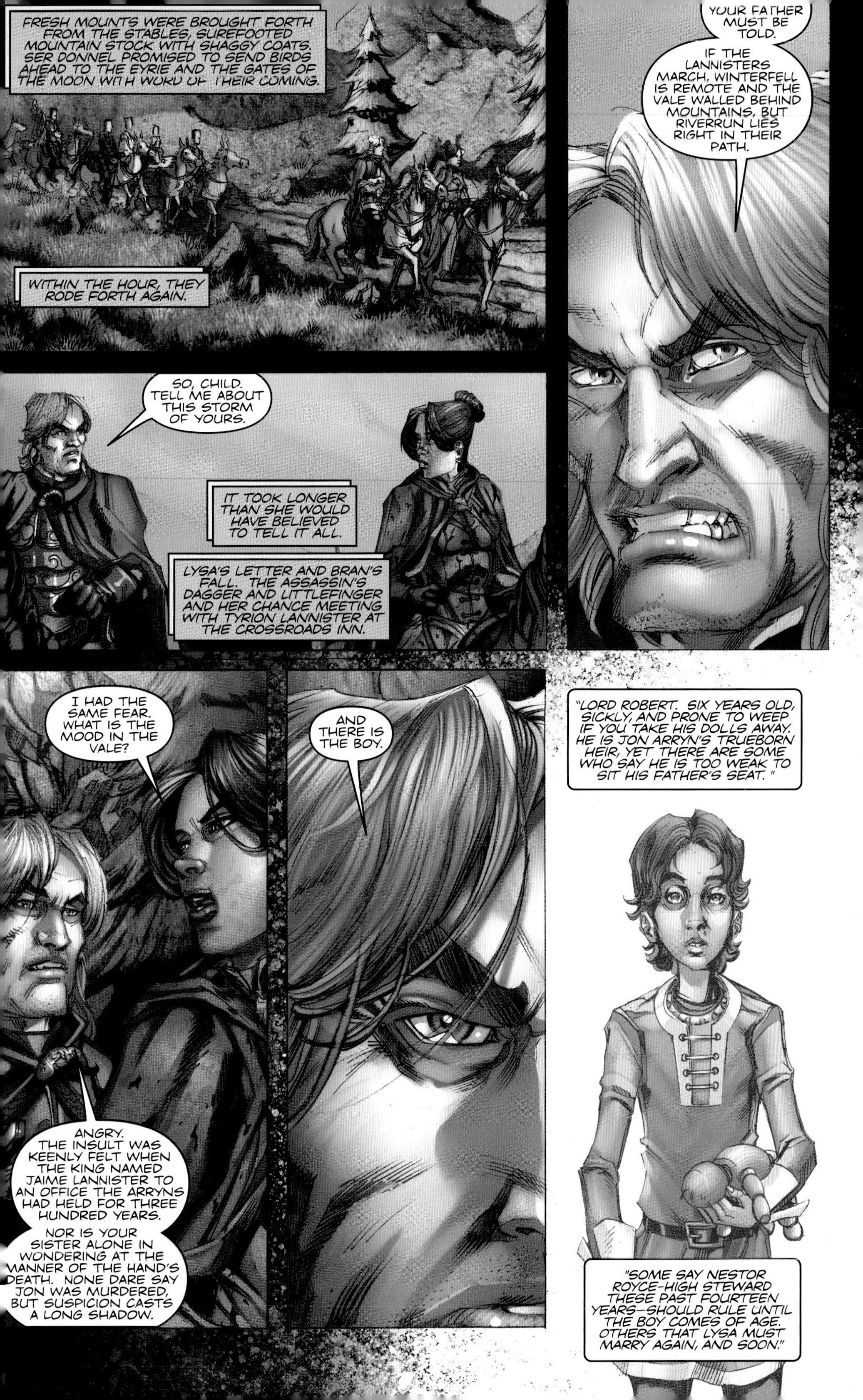
FRESH MOUNTS WERE BROUGHT FORTH FROM THE STABLES, SUREFOOTED MOUNTAIN STOCK WITH SHAGGY COATS. SER DONNEL PROMISED TO SEND BIRDS AHEAD TO THE EYRIE AND THE GATES OF THE MOON WITH WORD OF THEIR COMING.
WITHIN THE HOUR, THEY RODE FORTH AGAIN.
SO, CHILD. TELL ME ABOUT THIS STORM OF YOURS.
IT TOOK LONGER THAN SHE WOULD HAVE BELIEVED TO TELL IT ALL.
LYSA'S LETTER AND BRAN'S FALL. THE ASSASSIN'S DAGGER AND LITTLEFINGER AND HER CHANCE MEETING WITH TYRION LANNISTER AT THE CROSSROADS INN.
YOUR FATHER MUST BE TOLD.
IF THE LANNISTERS MARCH, WINTERFELL IS REMOTE AND THE VALE WALLED BEHIND MOUNTAINS, BUT RIVERRUN LIES RIGHT IN THEIR PATH.
I HAD THE SAME FEAR. WHAT IS THE MOOD IN THE VALE?
ANGRY. THE INSULT WAS KEENLY FELT WHEN THE KING NAMED JAIME LANNISTER TO AN OFFICE THE ARRYNS HAD HELD FOR THREE HUNDRED YEARS.
NOR IS YOUR SISTER ALONE IN WONDERING AT THE MANNER OF THE HAND'S DEATH. NONE DARE SAY JON WAS MURDERED, BUT SUSPICION CASTS A LONG SHADOW.
AND THERE IS THE BOY.
"LORD ROBERT. SIX YEARS OLD, SICKLY, AND PRONE TO WEEP IF YOU TAKE HIS DOLLS AWAY. HE IS JON ARRYN'S TRUEBORN HEIR, YET THERE ARE SOME WHO SAY HE IS TOO WEAK TO SIT HIS FATHER'S SEAT."
"SOME SAY NESTOR ROYCE—HIGH STEWARD THESE PAST FOURTEEN YEARS—SHOULD RULE UNTIL THE BOY COMES OF AGE. OTHERS THAT LYSA MUST MARRY AGAIN, AND SOON."

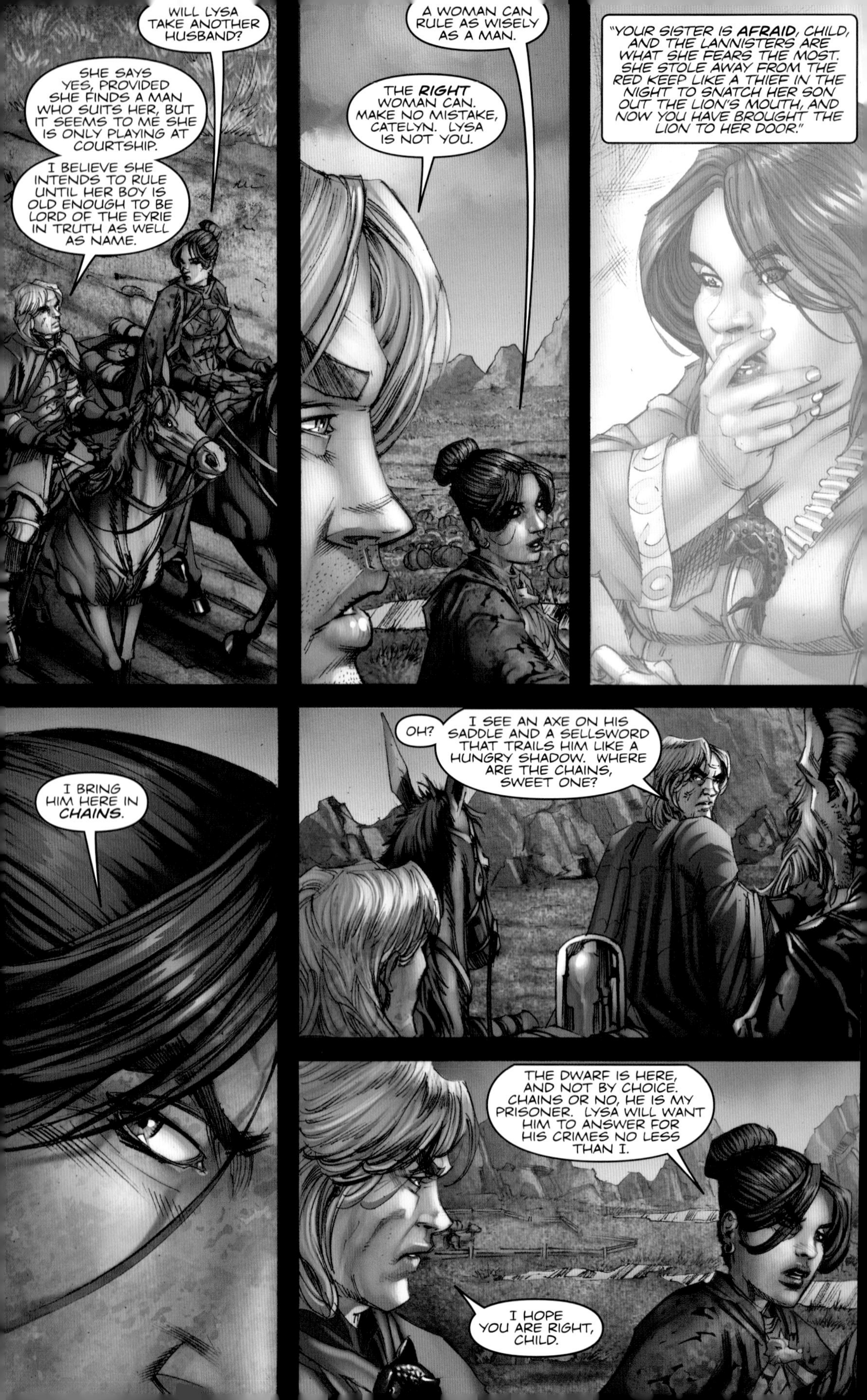
WILL LYSA TAKE ANOTHER HUSBAND?
SHE SAYS YES, PROVIDED SHE FINDS A MAN WHO SUITS HER, BUT IT SEEMS TO ME SHE IS ONLY PLAYING AT COURTSHIP.
I BELIEVE SHE INTENDS TO RULE UNTIL HER BOY IS OLD ENOUGH TO BE LORD OF THE EYRIE IN TRUTH AS WELL AS NAME.
A WOMAN CAN RULE AS WISELY AS A MAN.
THE RIGHT WOMAN CAN. MAKE NO MISTAKE, CATELYN. LYSA IS NOT YOU.
"YOUR SISTER IS AFRAID, CHILD, AND THE LANNISTERS ARE WHAT SHE FEARS THE MOST. SHE STOLE AWAY FROM THE RED KEEP LIKE A THIEF IN THE NIGHT TO SNATCH HER SON OUT THE LION'S MOUTH, AND NOW YOU HAVE BROUGHT THE LION TO HER DOOR."
I BRING HIM HERE IN CHAINS.
OH?
I SEE AN AXE ON HIS SADDLE AND A SELLSWORD THAT TRAILS HIM LIKE A HUNGRY SHADOW. WHERE ARE THE CHAINS, SWEET ONE?
THE DWARF IS HERE, AND NOT BY CHOICE. CHAINS OR NO, HE IS MY PRISONER. LYSA WILL WANT HIM TO ANSWER FOR HIS CRIMES NO LESS THAN I.
I HOPE YOU ARE RIGHT, CHILD.

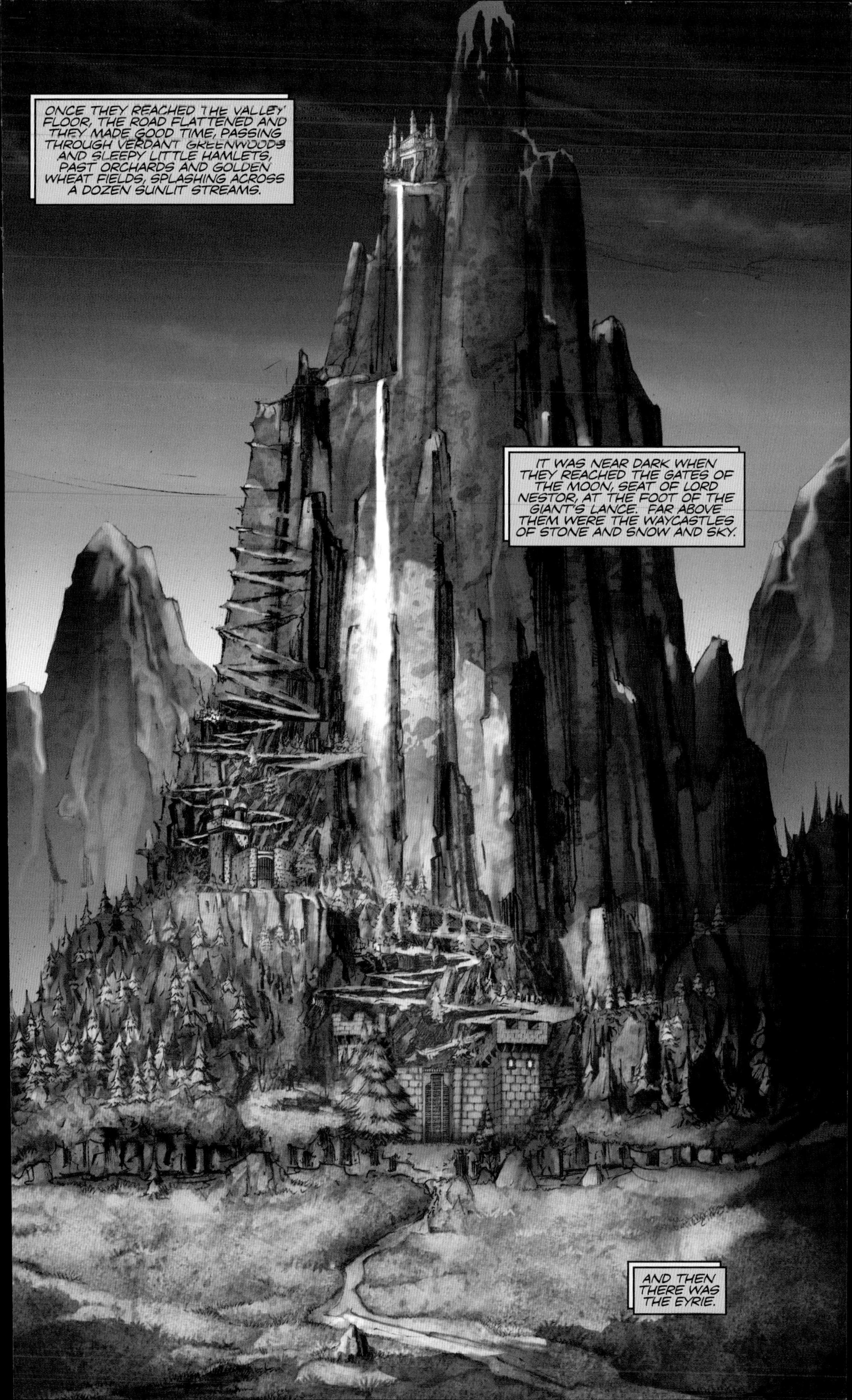
ONCE THEY REACHED THE VALLEY FLOOR, THE ROAD FLATTENED AND THEY MADE GOOD TIME, PASSING THROUGH VERDANT GREENWOODS AND SLEEPY LITTLE HAMLETS, PAST ORCHARDS AND GOLDEN WHEAT FIELDS, SPLASHING ACROSS A DOZEN SUNLIT STREAMS.
IT WAS NEAR DARK WHEN THEY REACHED THE GATES OF THE MOON, SEAT OF LORD NESTOR, AT THE FOOT OF THE GIANT'S LANCE. FAR ABOVE THEM WERE THE WAYCASTLES OF STONE AND SNOW AND SKY.
AND THEN THERE WAS THE EYRIE.

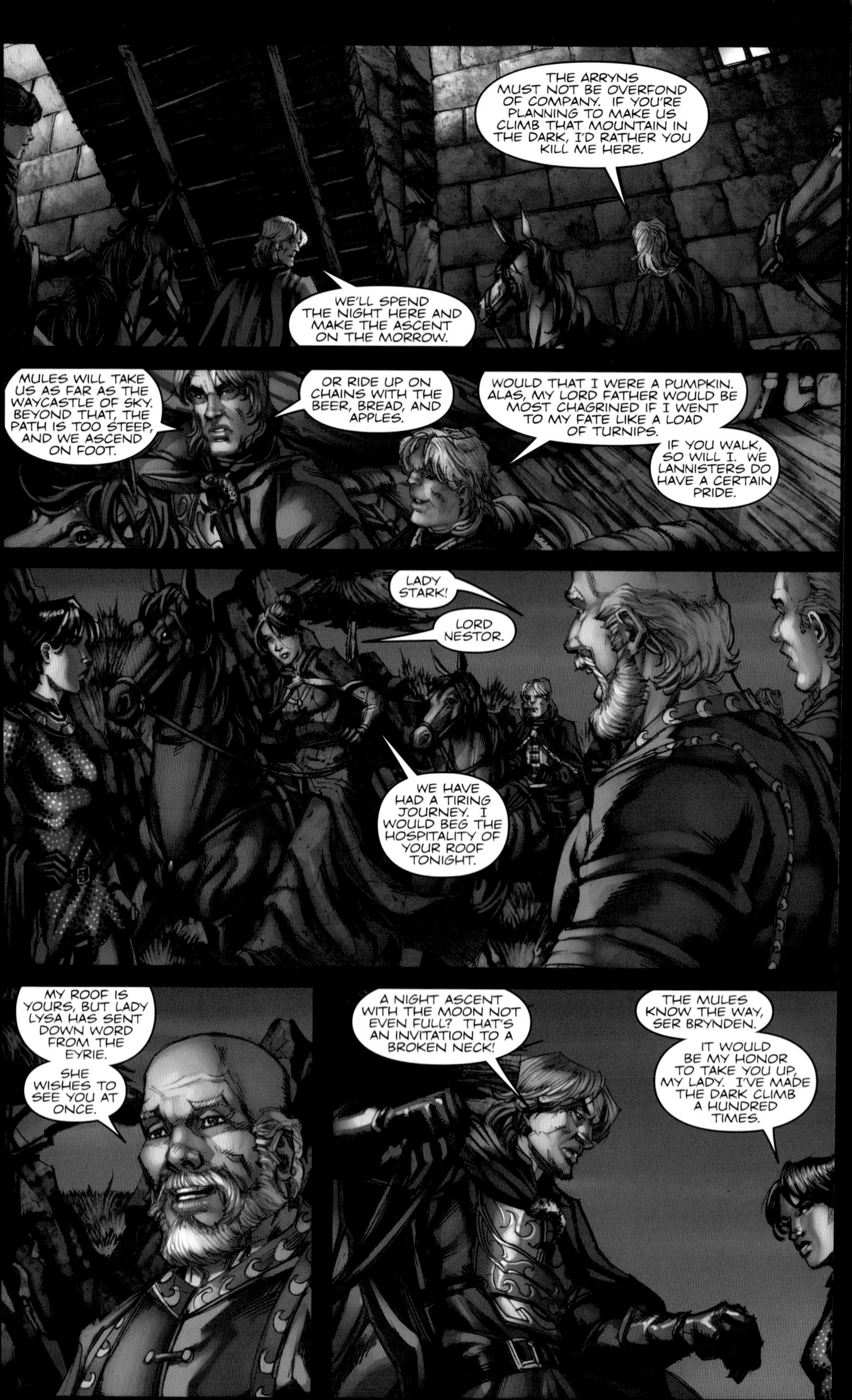
THE ARRYNS MUST NOT BE OVERFOND OF COMPANY. IF YOU'RE PLANNING TO MAKE US CLIMB THAT MOUNTAIN IN THE DARK, I'D RATHER YOU KILL ME HERE.
WE'LL SPEND THE NIGHT HERE AND MAKE THE ASCENT ON THE MORROW.
MULES WILL TAKE US AS FAR AS THE WAYCASTLE OF SKY. BEYOND THAT, THE PATH IS TOO STEEP, AND WE ASCEND ON FOOT.
OR RIDE UP ON CHAINS WITH THE BEER, BREAD, AND APPLES.
WOULD THAT I WERE A PUMPKIN. ALAS, MY LORD FATHER WOULD BE MOST CHAGRINED IF I WENT TO MY FATE LIKE A LOAD OF TURNIPS.
IF YOU WALK, SO WILL I. WE LANNISTERS DO HAVE A CERTAIN PRIDE.
LADY STARK!
LORD NESTOR.
WE HAVE HAD A TIRING JOURNEY. I WOULD BEG THE HOSPITALITY OF YOUR ROOF TONIGHT.
MY ROOF IS YOURS, BUT LADY LYSA HAS SENT DOWN WORD FROM THE EYRIE.
SHE WISHES TO SEE YOU AT ONCE.
A NIGHT ASCENT WITH THE MOON NOT EVEN FULL? THAT'S AN INVITATION TO A BROKEN NECK!
THE MULES KNOW THE WAY, SER BRYNDEN.
IT WOULD BE MY HONOR TO TAKE YOU UP, MY LADY. I'VE MADE THE DARK CLIMB A HUNDRED TIMES.

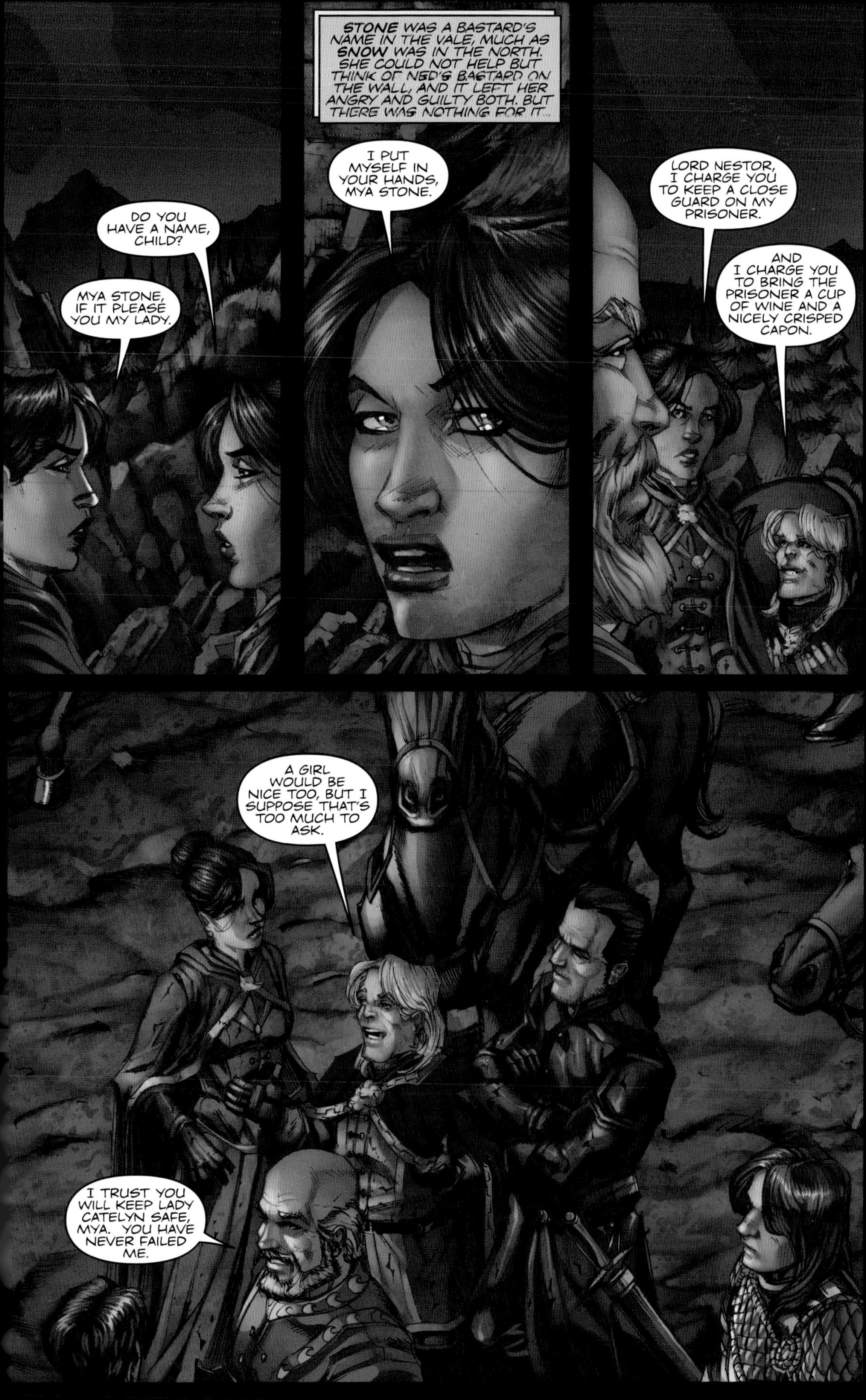
DO YOU HAVE A NAME, CHILD?
MYA STONE, IF IT PLEASE YOU MY LADY.
STONE WAS A BASTARD'S NAME IN THE VALE, MUCH AS SNOW WAS IN THE NORTH. SHE COULD NOT HELP BUT THINK OF NED'S BASTARD ON THE WALL, AND IT LEFT HER ANGRY AND GUILTY BOTH. BUT THERE WAS NOTHING FOR IT...
I PUT MYSELF IN YOUR HANDS, MYA STONE.
LORD NESTOR, I CHARGE YOU TO KEEP A CLOSE GUARD ON MY PRISONER.
AND I CHARGE YOU TO BRING THE PRISONER A CUP OF WINE AND A NICELY CRISPED CAPON.
A GIRL WOULD BE NICE TOO, BUT I SUPPOSE THAT'S TOO MUCH TO ASK.
I TRUST YOU WILL KEEP LADY CATELYN SAFE, MYA. YOU HAVE NEVER FAILED ME.

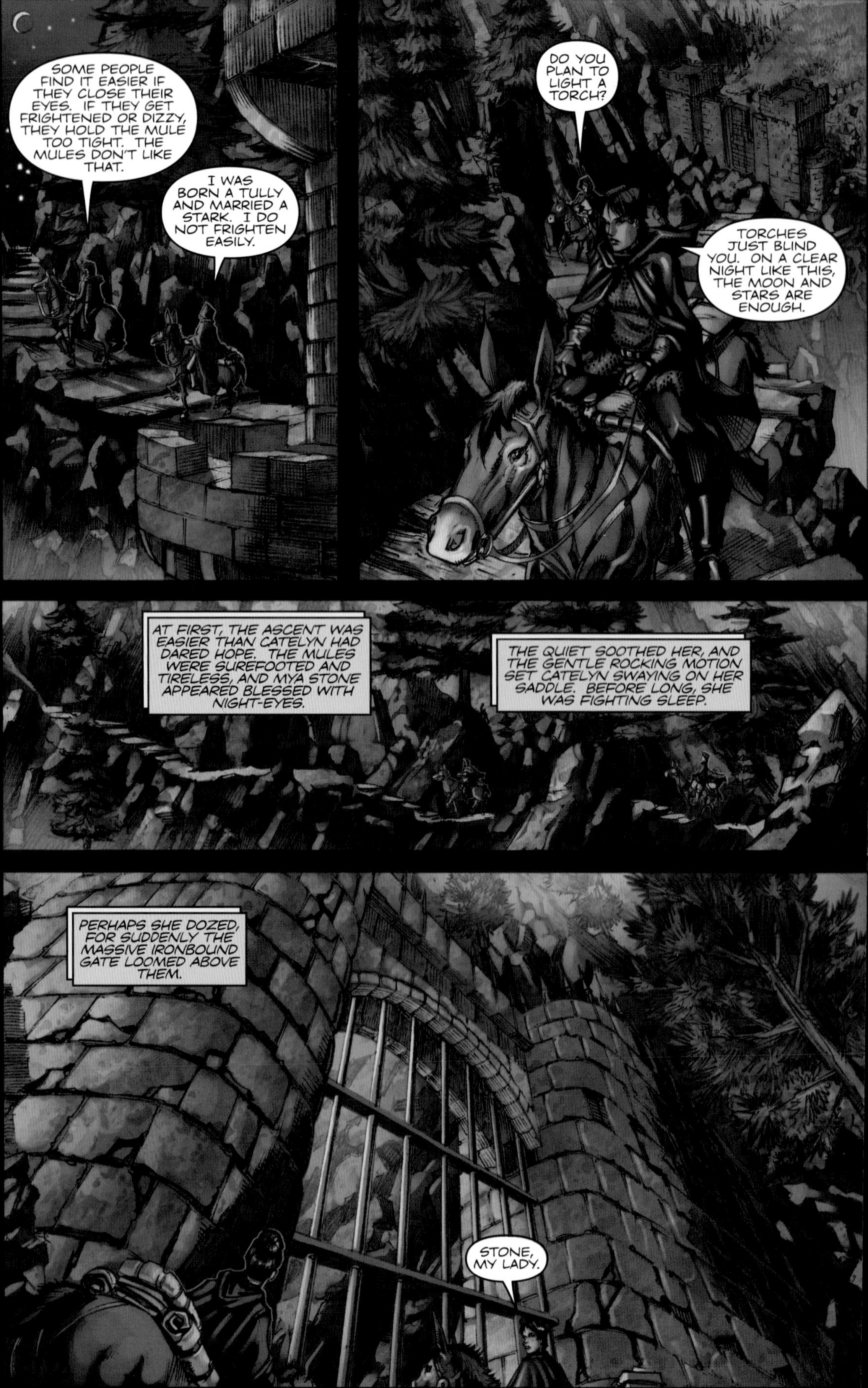

SOME PEOPLE FIND IT EASIER IF THEY CLOSE THEIR EYES. IF THEY GET FRIGHTENED OR DIZZY, THEY HOLD THE MULE TOO TIGHT. THE MULES DON'T LIKE THAT.
I WAS BORN A TULLY AND MARRIED A STARK. I DO NOT FRIGHTEN EASILY.
DO YOU PLAN TO LIGHT A TORCH?
TORCHES JUST BLIND YOU. ON A CLEAR NIGHT LIKE THIS, THE MOON AND STARS ARE ENOUGH.
AT FIRST, THE ASCENT WAS EASIER THAN CATELYN HAD DARED HOPE. THE MULES WERE SUREFOOTED AND TIRELESS, AND MYA STONE APPEARED BLESSED WITH NIGHT-EYES.
THE QUIET SOOTHED HER, AND THE GENTLE ROCKING MOTION SET CATELYN SWAYING ON HER SADDLE. BEFORE LONG, SHE WAS FIGHTING SLEEP.
PERHAPS SHE DOZED, FOR SUDDENLY THE MASSIVE IRONBOUND GATE LOOMED ABOVE THEM.
STONE, MY LADY.

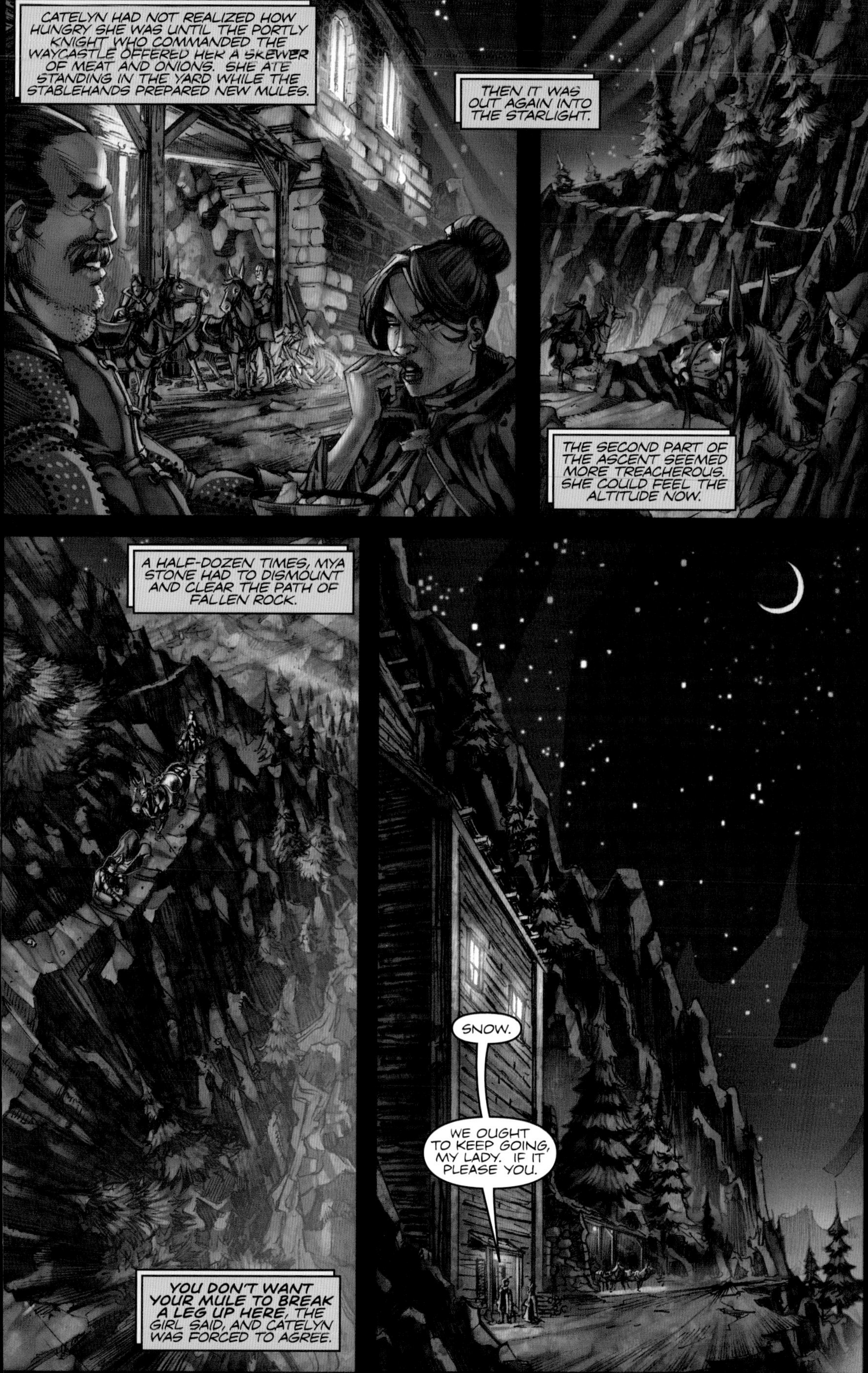
CATELYN HAD NOT REALIZED HOW HUNGRY SHE WAS UNTIL THE PORTLY KNIGHT WHO COMMANDED THE WAYCASTLE OFFERED HER A SKEWER OF MEAT AND ONIONS. SHE ATE STANDING IN THE YARD WHILE THE STABLEHANDS PREPARED NEW MULES.
THEN IT WAS OUT AGAIN INTO THE STARLIGHT.
THE SECOND PART OF THE ASCENT SEEMED MORE TREACHEROUS. SHE COULD FEEL THE ALTITUDE NOW.
A HALF-DOZEN TIMES, MYA STONE HAD TO DISMOUNT AND CLEAR THE PATH OF FALLEN ROCK.
YOU DON'T WANT YOUR MULE TO BREAK A LEG UP HERE, THE GIRL SAID, AND CATELYN WAS FORCED TO AGREE.
SNOW.
WE OUGHT TO KEEP GOING, MY LADY. IF IT PLEASE YOU.

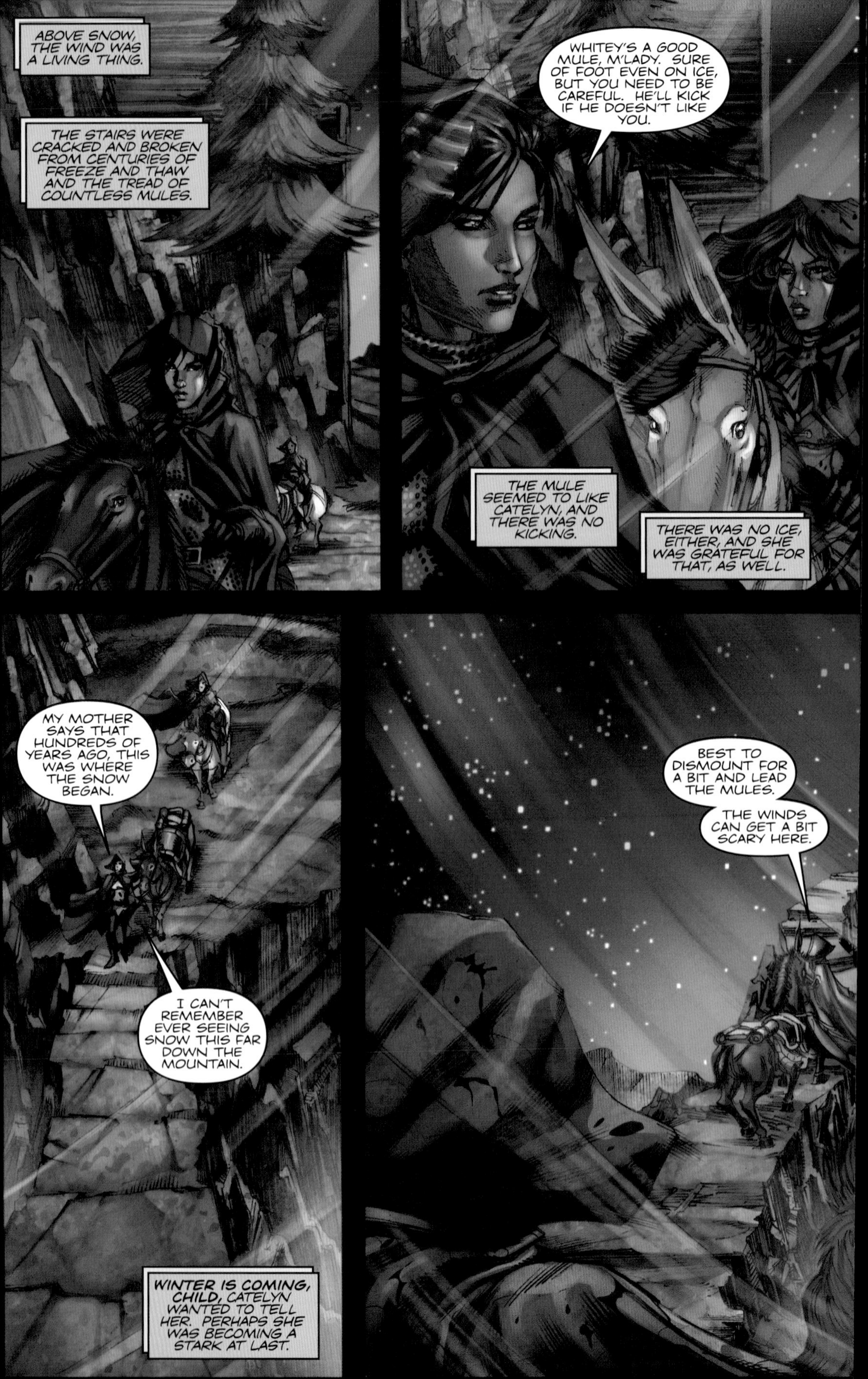
ABOVE SNOW, THE WIND WAS A LIVING THING.
THE STAIRS WERE CRACKED AND BROKEN FROM CENTURIES OF FREEZE AND THAW AND THE TREAD OF COUNTLESS MULES.
WHITEY'S A GOOD MULE, M'LADY. SURE OF FOOT EVEN ON ICE, BUT YOU NEED TO BE CAREFUL. HE'LL KICK IF HE DOESN'T LIKE YOU.
THE MULE SEEMED TO LIKE CATELYN, AND THERE WAS NO KICKING.
THERE WAS NO ICE, EITHER, AND SHE WAS GRATEFUL FOR THAT, AS WELL.
MY MOTHER SAYS THAT HUNDREDS OF YEARS AGO, THIS WAS WHERE THE SNOW BEGAN.
I CAN'T REMEMBER EVER SEEING SNOW THIS FAR DOWN THE MOUNTAIN.
WINTER IS COMING, CHILD, CATELYN WANTED TO TELL HER. PERHAPS SHE WAS BECOMING A STARK AT LAST.
BEST TO DISMOUNT FOR A BIT AND LEAD THE MULES.
THE WINDS CAN GET A BIT SCARY HERE.

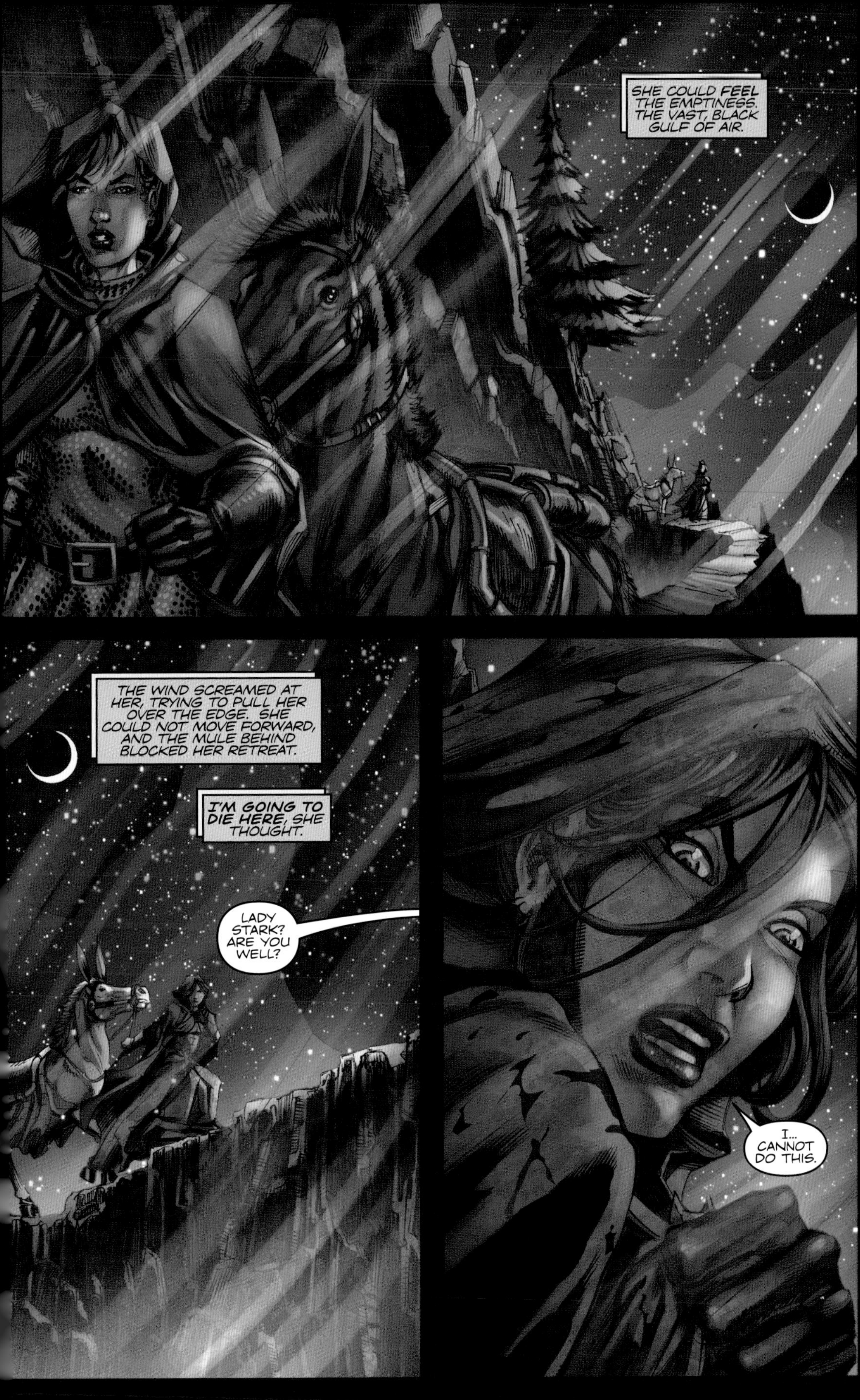
SHE COULD FEEL THE EMPTINESS. THE VAST, BLACK GULF OF AIR.
THE WIND SCREAMED AT HER, TRYING TO PULL HER OVER THE EDGE. SHE COULD NOT MOVE FORWARD, AND THE MULE BEHIND BLOCKED HER RETREAT.
I'M GOING TO DIE HERE, SHE THOUGHT.
LADY STARK? ARE YOU WELL?
I... CANNOT DO THIS.

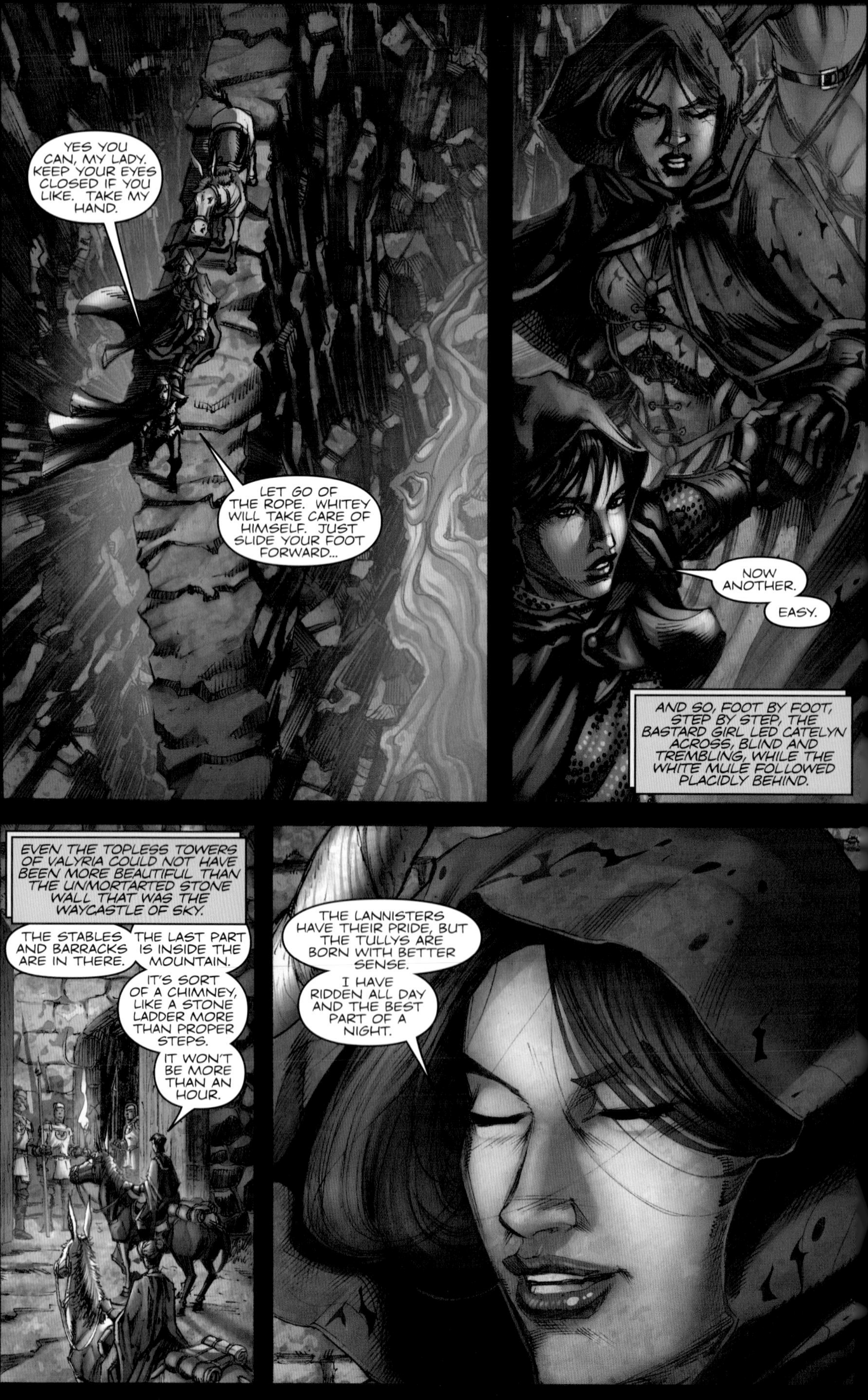
YES YOU CAN, MY LADY. KEEP YOUR EYES CLOSED IF YOU LIKE. TAKE MY HAND.
LET GO OF THE ROPE. WHITEY WILL TAKE CARE OF HIMSELF. JUST SLIDE YOUR FOOT FORWARD...
NOW ANOTHER.
EASY.
AND SO, FOOT BY FOOT, STEP BY STEP, THE BASTARD GIRL LED CATELYN ACROSS, BLIND AND TREMBLING, WHILE THE WHITE MULE FOLLOWED PLACIDLY BEHIND.
EVEN THE TOPLESS TOWERS OF VALYRIA COULD NOT HAVE BEEN MORE BEAUTIFUL THAN THE UNMORTARTED STONE WALL THAT WAS THE WAYCASTLE OF SKY.
THE STABLES AND BARRACKS ARE IN THERE.
THE LAST PART IS INSIDE THE MOUNTAIN.
IT'S SORT OF A CHIMNEY, LIKE A STONE LADDER MORE THAN PROPER STEPS.
IT WON'T BE MORE THAN AN HOUR.
THE LANNISTERS HAVE THEIR PRIDE, BUT THE TULLYS ARE BORN WITH BETTER SENSE.
I HAVE RIDDEN ALL DAY AND THE BEST PART OF A NIGHT.

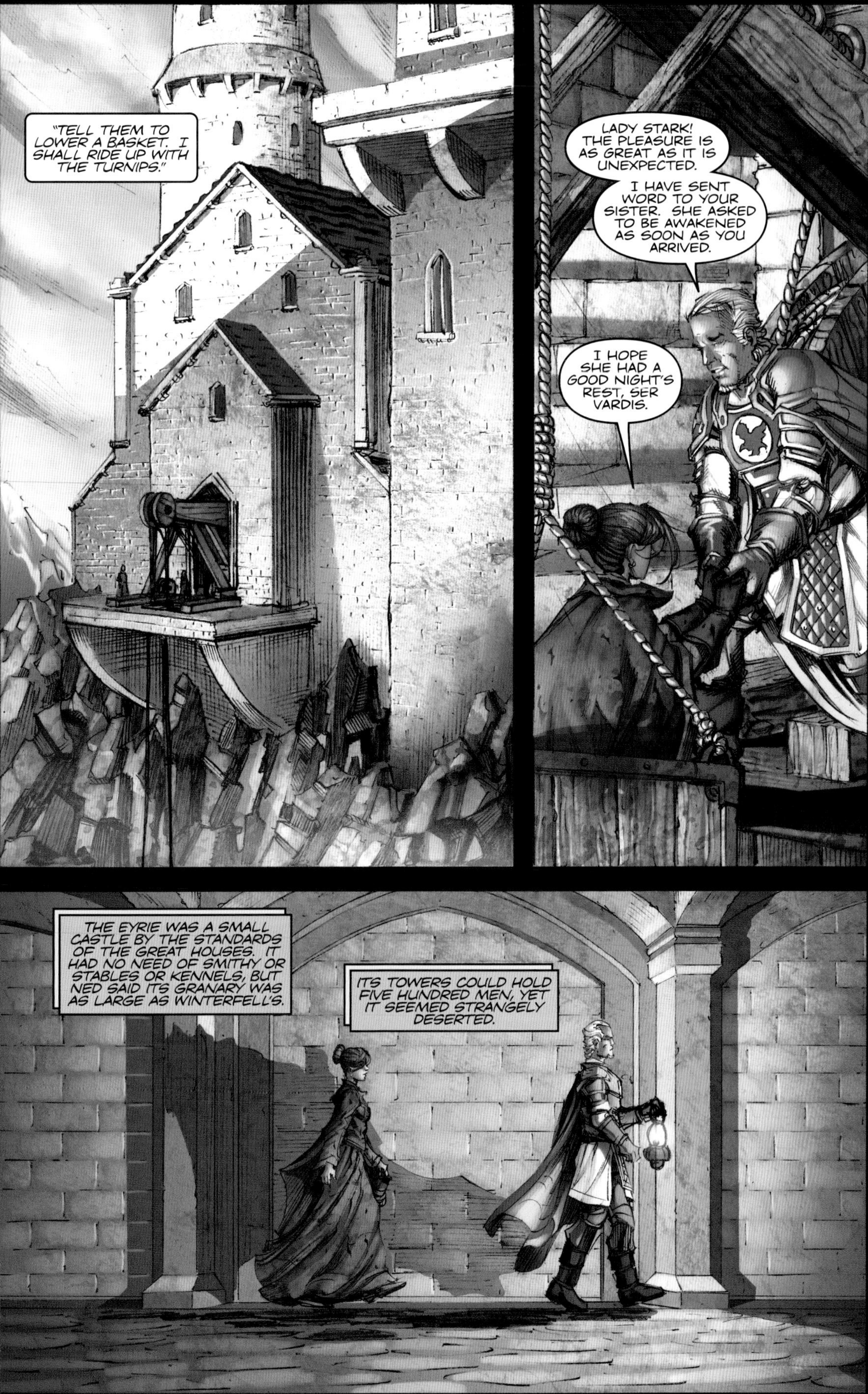
"TELL THEM TO LOWER A BASKET. I SHALL RIDE UP WITH THE TURNIPS."
LADY STARK! THE PLEASURE IS AS GREAT AS IT IS UNEXPECTED.
I HAVE SENT WORD TO YOUR SISTER. SHE ASKED TO BE AWAKENED AS SOON AS YOU ARRIVED.
I HOPE SHE HAD A GOOD NIGHT'S REST, SER VARDIS.
THE EYRIE WAS A SMALL CASTLE BY THE STANDARDS OF THE GREAT HOUSES. IT HAD NO NEED OF SMITHY OR STABLES OR KENNELS, BUT NED SAID ITS GRANARY WAS AS LARGE AS WINTERFELL'S.
ITS TOWERS COULD HOLD FIVE HUNDRED MEN, YET IT SEEMED STRANGELY DESERTED.

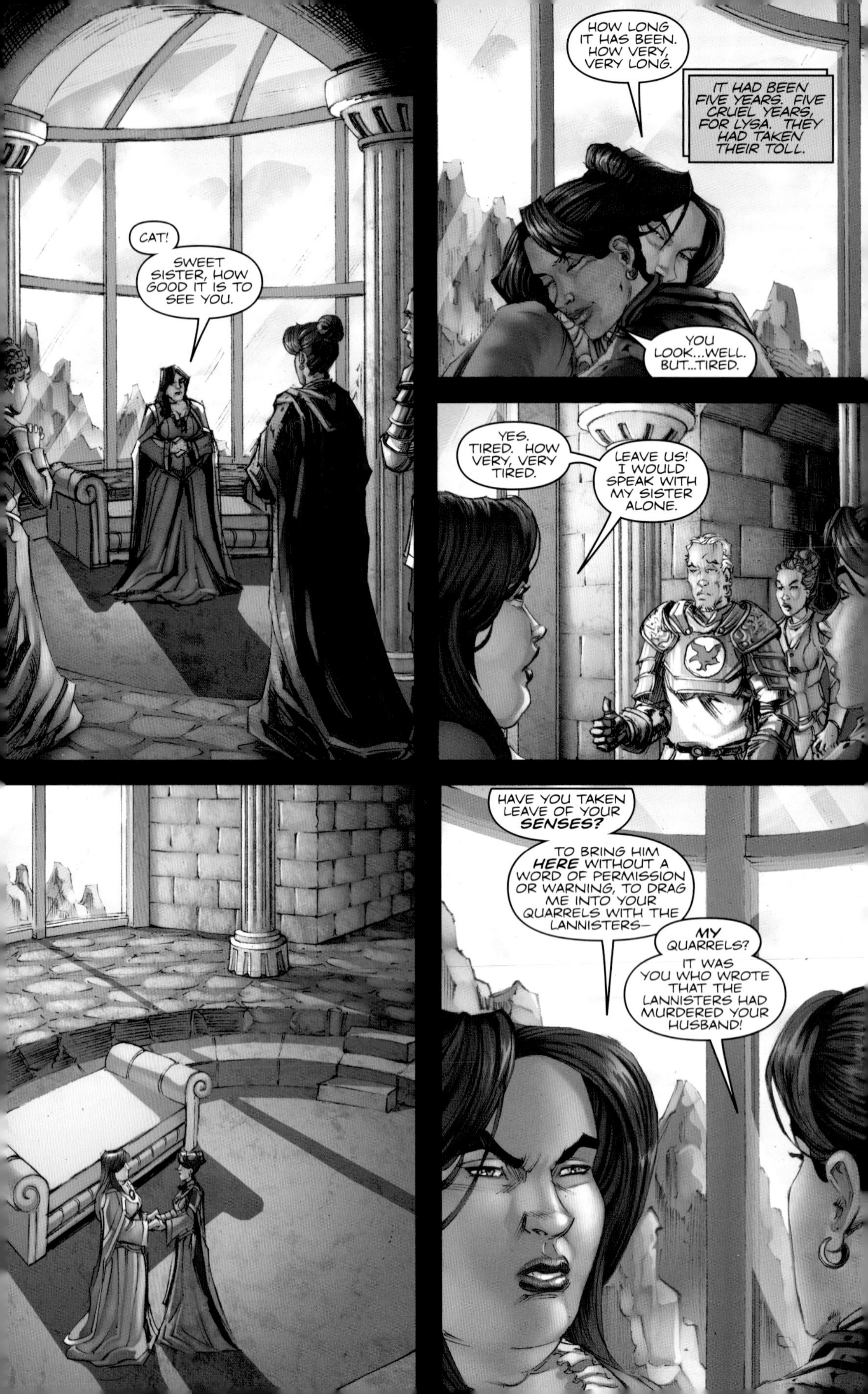
CAT!
SWEET SISTER, HOW GOOD IT IS TO SEE YOU.
HOW LONG IT HAS BEEN. HOW VERY, VERY LONG.
IT HAD BEEN FIVE YEARS. FIVE CRUEL YEARS, FOR LYSA. THEY HAD TAKEN THEIR TOLL.
YOU LOOK...WELL. BUT...TIRED.
YES. TIRED. HOW VERY, VERY TIRED.
LEAVE US! I WOULD SPEAK WITH MY SISTER ALONE.
HAVE YOU TAKEN LEAVE OF YOUR SENSES?
TO BRING HIM HERE WITHOUT A WORD OF PERMISSION OR WARNING, TO DRAG ME INTO YOUR QUARRELS WITH THE LANNISTERS–
MY QUARRELS?
IT WAS YOU WHO WROTE THAT THE LANNISTERS HAD MURDERED YOUR HUSBAND!

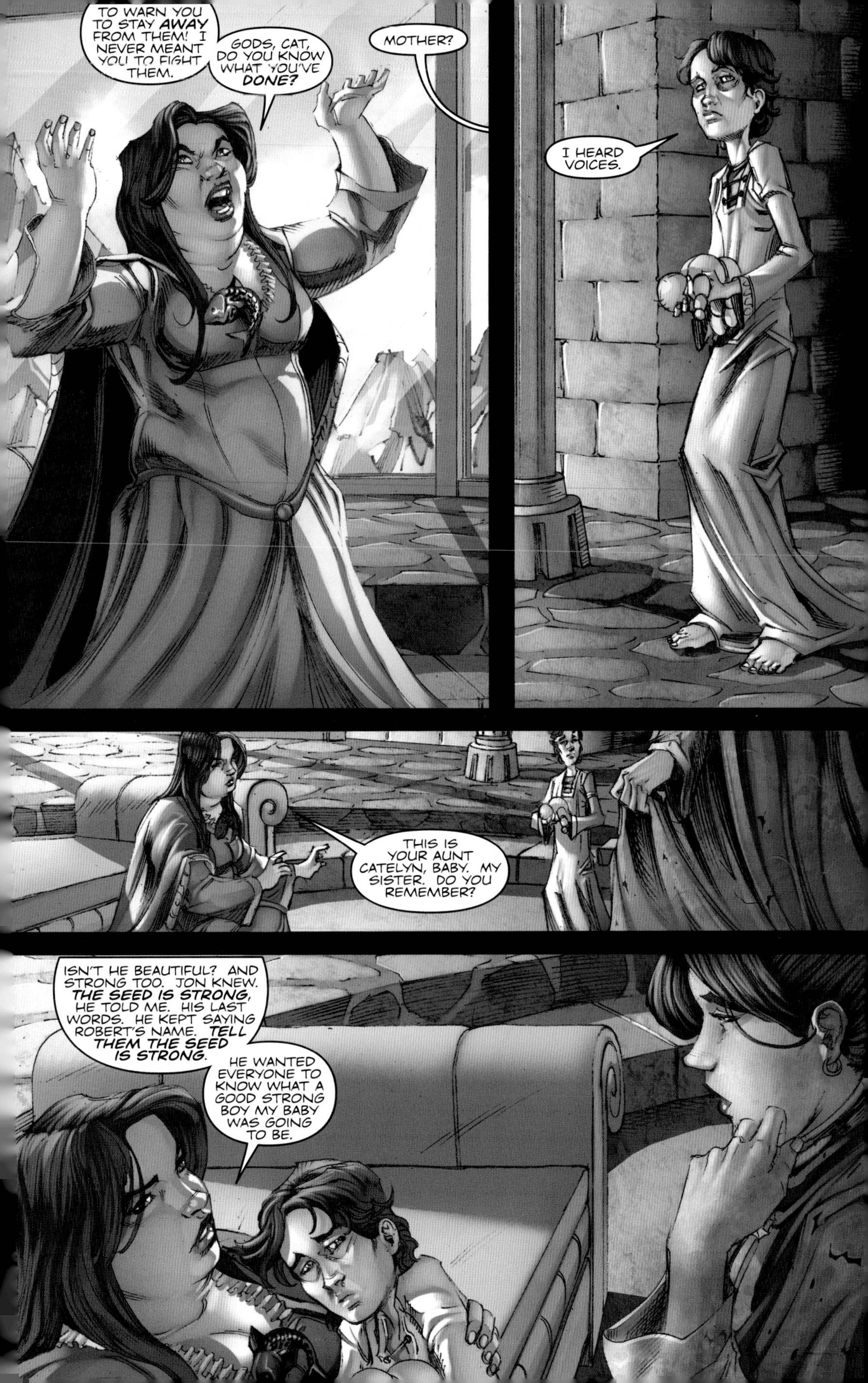

TO WARN YOU TO STAY **AWAY** FROM THEM! I NEVER MEANT YOU TO FIGHT THEM.
GODS, CAT, DO YOU KNOW WHAT YOU'VE **DONE?**
MOTHER?
I HEARD VOICES.
THIS IS YOUR AUNT CATELYN, BABY. MY SISTER. DO YOU REMEMBER?
ISN'T HE BEAUTIFUL? AND STRONG TOO. JON KNEW. ***THE SEED IS STRONG,*** HE TOLD ME. HIS LAST WORDS. HE KEPT SAYING ROBERT'S NAME. ***TELL THEM THE SEED IS STRONG.***
HE WANTED EVERYONE TO KNOW WHAT A GOOD STRONG BOY MY BABY WAS GOING TO BE.

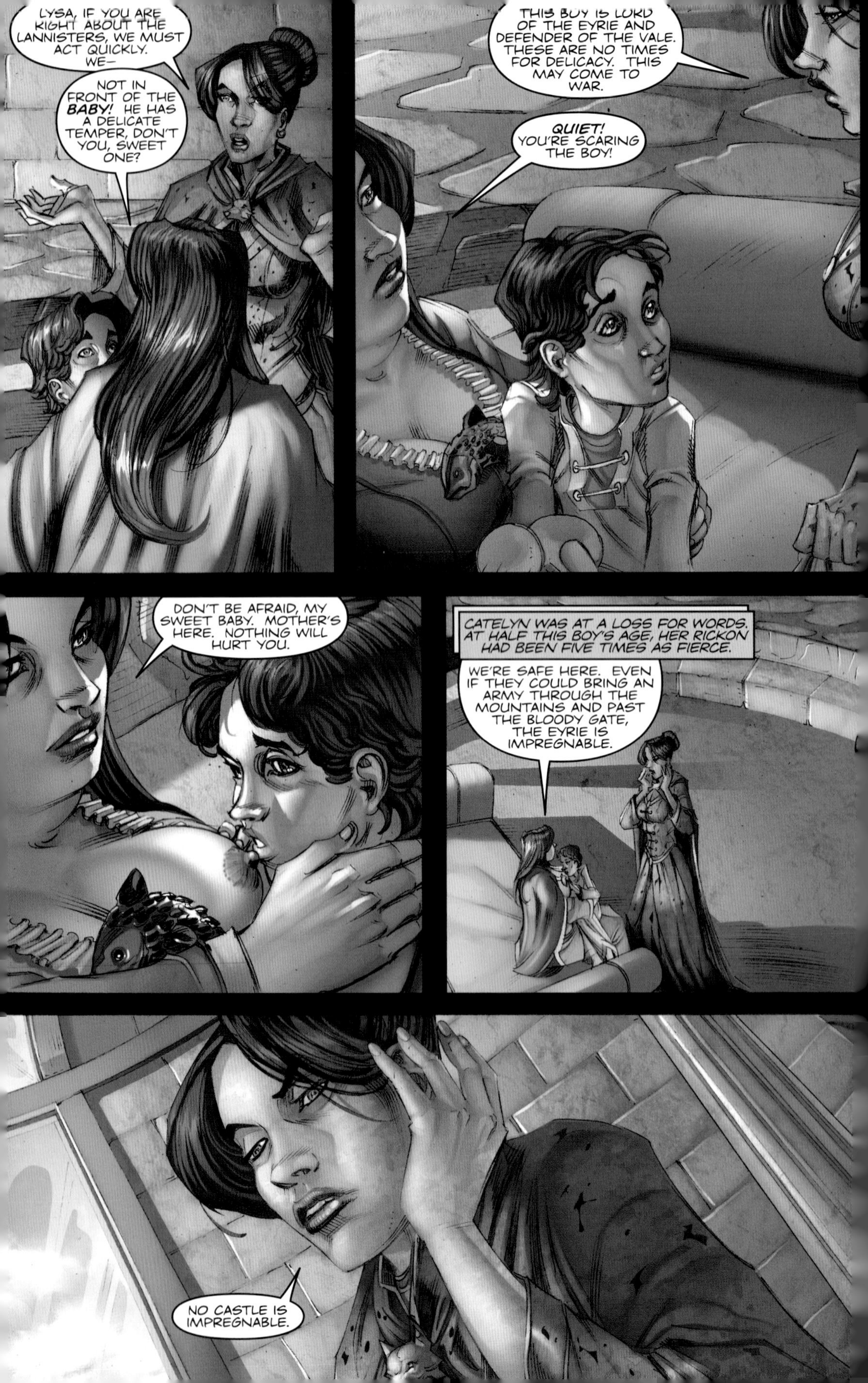
LYSA, IF YOU ARE RIGHT ABOUT THE LANNISTERS, WE MUST ACT QUICKLY. WE–
NOT IN FRONT OF THE *BABY!* HE HAS A DELICATE TEMPER, DON'T YOU, SWEET ONE?
THIS BOY IS LORD OF THE EYRIE AND DEFENDER OF THE VALE. THESE ARE NO TIMES FOR DELICACY. THIS MAY COME TO WAR.
QUIET! YOU'RE SCARING THE BOY!
DON'T BE AFRAID, MY SWEET BABY. MOTHER'S HERE. NOTHING WILL HURT YOU.
CATELYN WAS AT A LOSS FOR WORDS. AT HALF THIS BOY'S AGE, HER RICKON HAD BEEN FIVE TIMES AS FIERCE.
WE'RE SAFE HERE. EVEN IF THEY COULD BRING AN ARMY THROUGH THE MOUNTAINS AND PAST THE BLOODY GATE, THE EYRIE IS IMPREGNABLE.
NO CASTLE IS IMPREGNABLE.

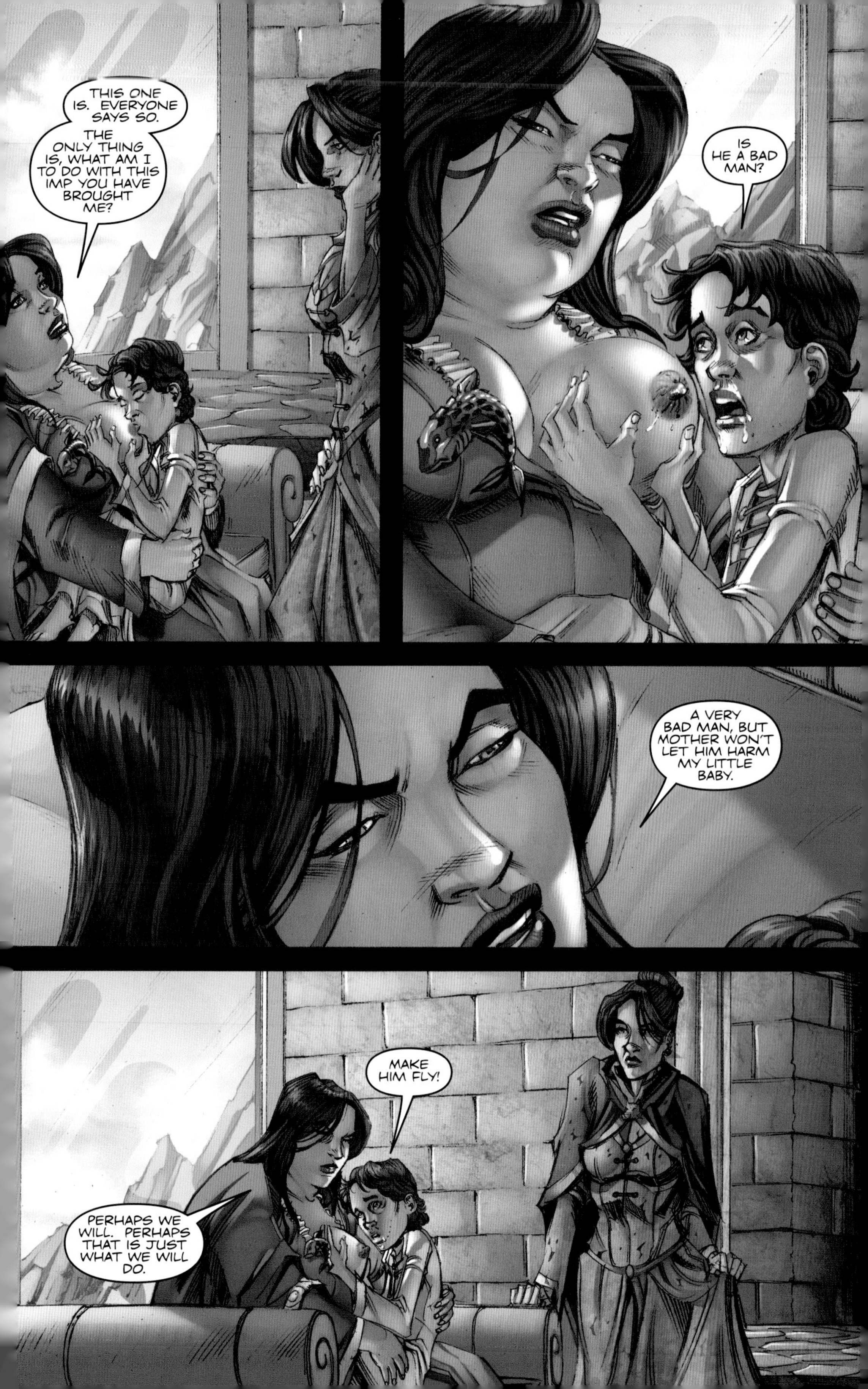
THIS ONE IS. EVERYONE SAYS SO.
THE ONLY THING IS, WHAT AM I TO DO WITH THIS IMP YOU HAVE BROUGHT ME?
IS HE A BAD MAN?
A VERY BAD MAN, BUT MOTHER WON'T LET HIM HARM MY LITTLE BABY.
MAKE HIM FLY!
PERHAPS WE WILL. PERHAPS THAT IS JUST WHAT WE WILL DO.

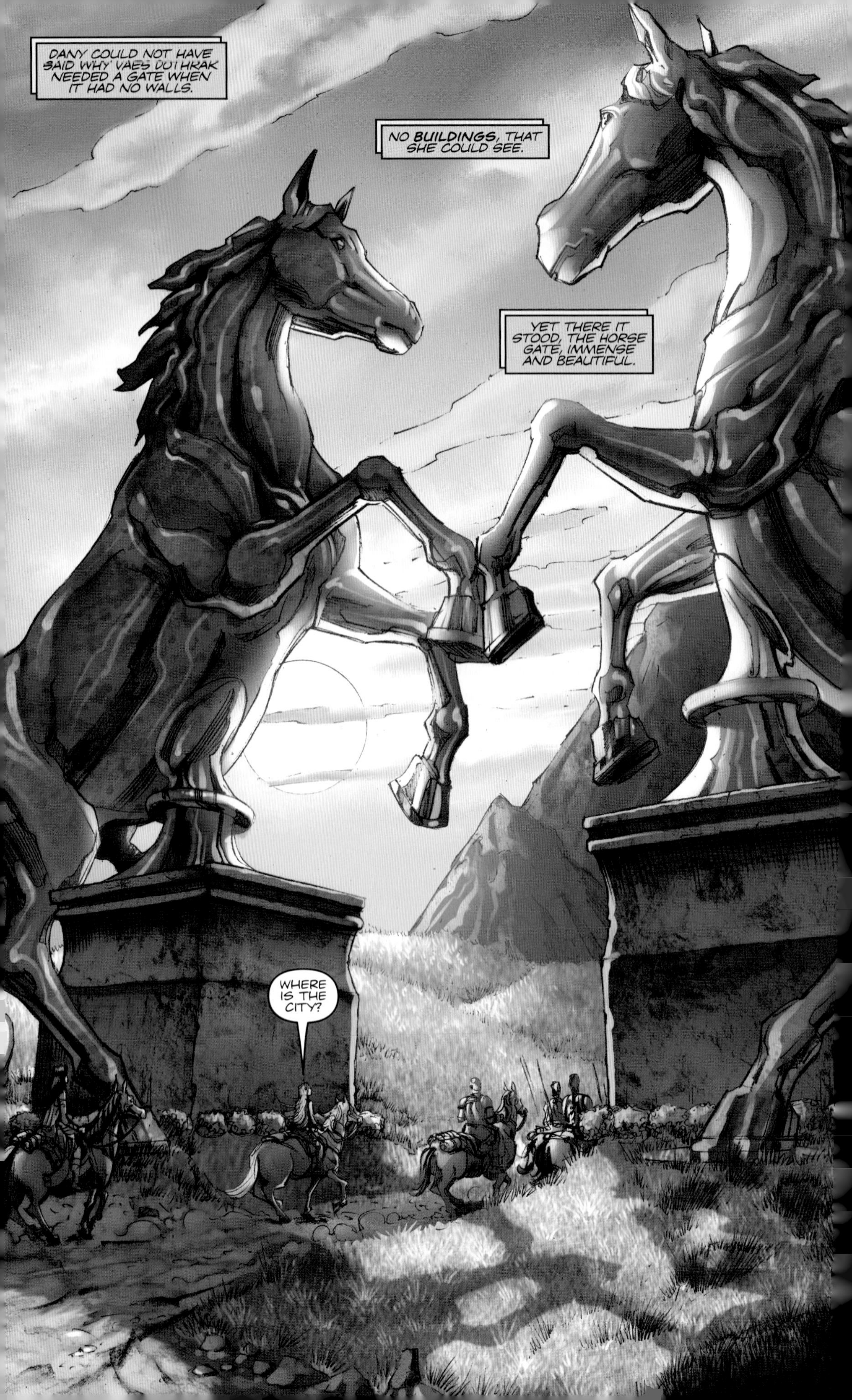
DANY COULD NOT HAVE SAID WHY VAES DOTHRAK NEEDED A GATE WHEN IT HAD NO WALLS.
NO BUILDINGS, THAT SHE COULD SEE.
YET THERE IT STOOD, THE HORSE GATE, IMMENSE AND BEAUTIFUL.
WHERE IS THE CITY?

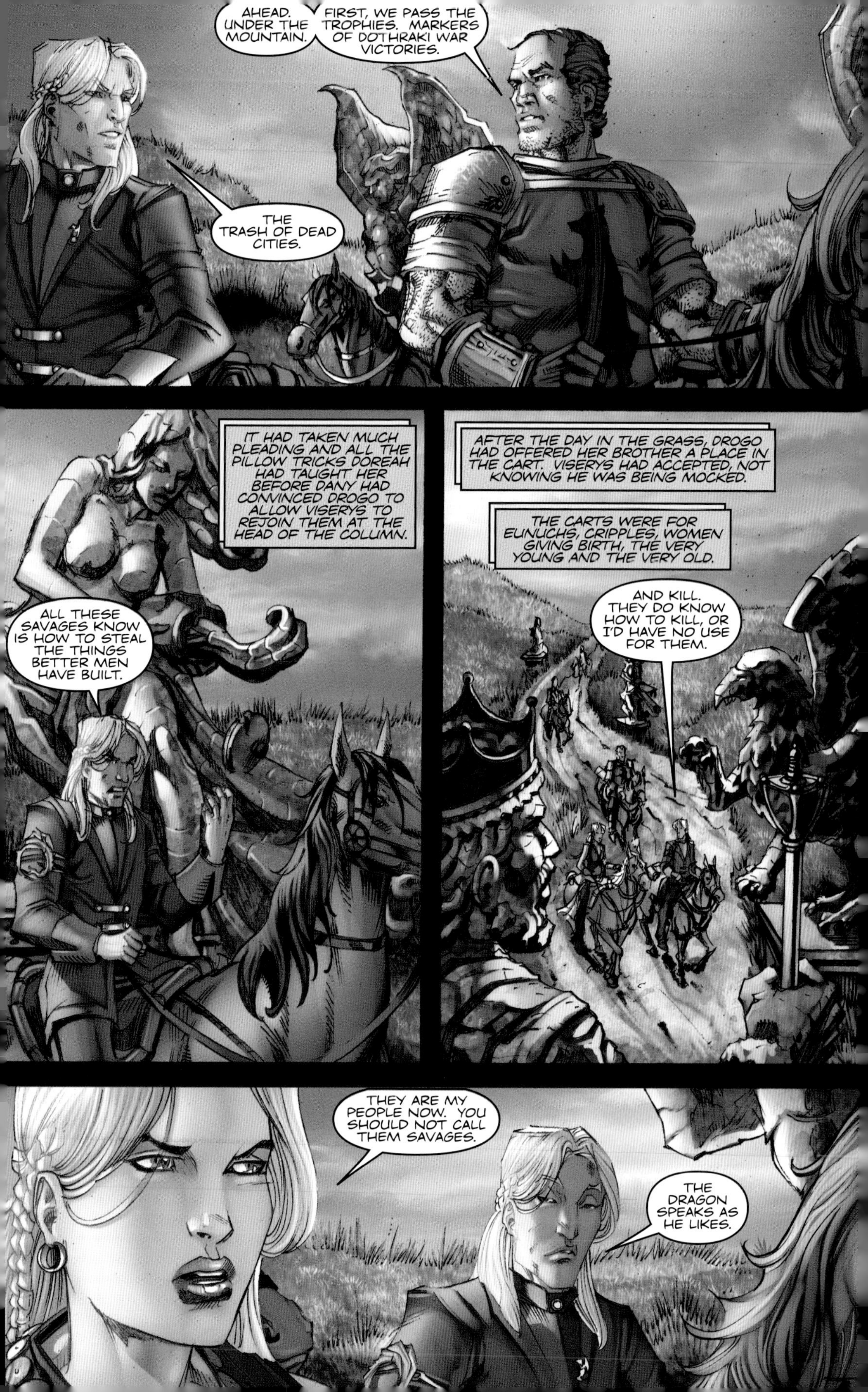
AHEAD. UNDER THE MOUNTAIN.
FIRST, WE PASS THE TROPHIES. MARKERS OF DOTHRAKI WAR VICTORIES.
THE TRASH OF DEAD CITIES.
IT HAD TAKEN MUCH PLEADING AND ALL THE PILLOW TRICKS DOREAH HAD TAUGHT HER BEFORE DANY HAD CONVINCED DROGO TO ALLOW VISERYS TO REJOIN THEM AT THE HEAD OF THE COLUMN.
ALL THESE SAVAGES KNOW IS HOW TO STEAL THE THINGS BETTER MEN HAVE BUILT.
AFTER THE DAY IN THE GRASS, DROGO HAD OFFERED HER BROTHER A PLACE IN THE CART. VISERYS HAD ACCEPTED, NOT KNOWING HE WAS BEING MOCKED.
THE CARTS WERE FOR EUNUCHS, CRIPPLES, WOMEN GIVING BIRTH, THE VERY YOUNG AND THE VERY OLD.
AND KILL. THEY DO KNOW HOW TO KILL, OR I'D HAVE NO USE FOR THEM.
THEY ARE MY PEOPLE NOW. YOU SHOULD NOT CALL THEM SAVAGES.
THE DRAGON SPEAKS AS HE LIKES.

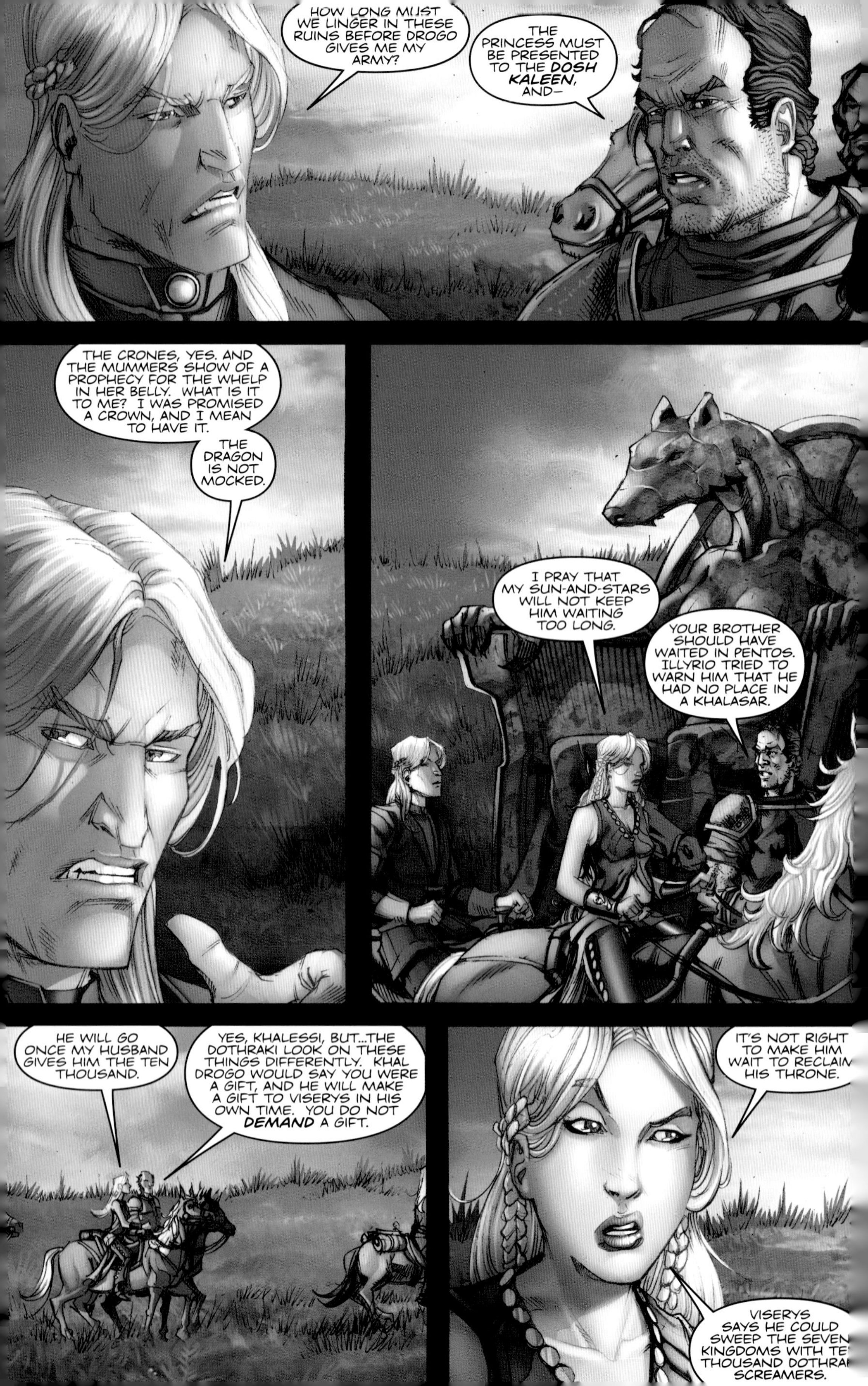
HOW LONG MUST WE LINGER IN THESE RUINS BEFORE DROGO GIVES ME MY ARMY?
THE PRINCESS MUST BE PRESENTED TO THE **DOSH KALEEN**, AND–
THE CRONES, YES. AND THE MUMMERS SHOW OF A PROPHECY FOR THE WHELP IN HER BELLY. WHAT IS IT TO ME? I WAS PROMISED A CROWN, AND I MEAN TO HAVE IT.
THE DRAGON IS NOT MOCKED.
I PRAY THAT MY SUN-AND-STARS WILL NOT KEEP HIM WAITING TOO LONG.
YOUR BROTHER SHOULD HAVE WAITED IN PENTOS. ILLYRIO TRIED TO WARN HIM THAT HE HAD NO PLACE IN A KHALASAR.
HE WILL GO ONCE MY HUSBAND GIVES HIM THE TEN THOUSAND.
YES, KHALESSI, BUT...THE DOTHRAKI LOOK ON THESE THINGS DIFFERENTLY. KHAL DROGO WOULD SAY YOU WERE A GIFT, AND HE WILL MAKE A GIFT TO VISERYS IN HIS OWN TIME. YOU DO NOT **DEMAND** A GIFT.
IT'S NOT RIGHT TO MAKE HIM WAIT TO RECLAIM HIS THRONE.
VISERYS SAYS HE COULD SWEEP THE SEVEN KINGDOMS WITH TEN THOUSAND DOTHRAKI SCREAMERS.

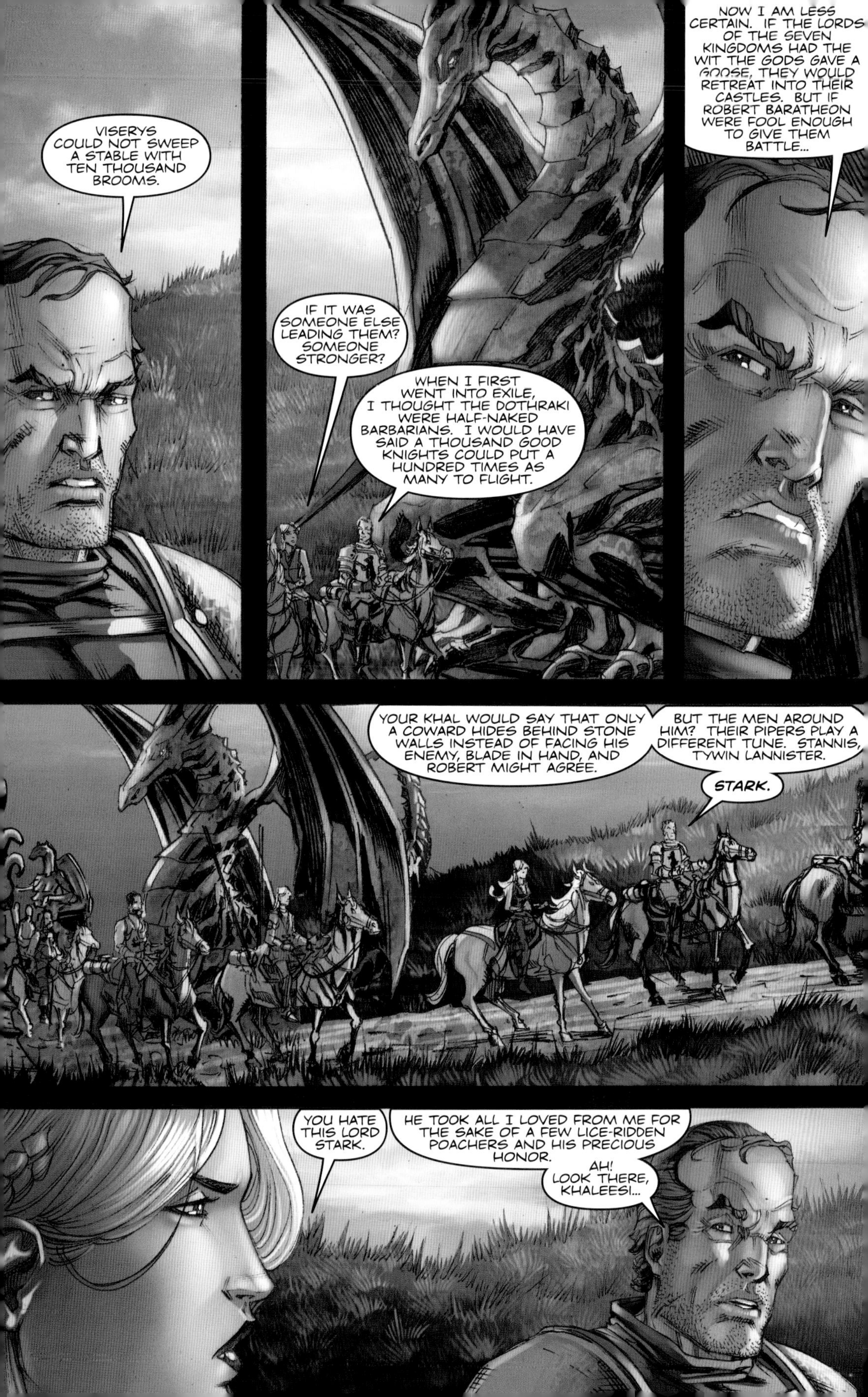
VISERYS COULD NOT SWEEP A STABLE WITH TEN THOUSAND BROOMS.
IF IT WAS SOMEONE ELSE LEADING THEM? SOMEONE STRONGER?
WHEN I FIRST WENT INTO EXILE, I THOUGHT THE DOTHRAKI WERE HALF-NAKED BARBARIANS. I WOULD HAVE SAID A THOUSAND GOOD KNIGHTS COULD PUT A HUNDRED TIMES AS MANY TO FLIGHT.
NOW I AM LESS CERTAIN. IF THE LORDS OF THE SEVEN KINGDOMS HAD THE WIT THE GODS GAVE A GOOSE, THEY WOULD RETREAT INTO THEIR CASTLES. BUT IF ROBERT BARATHEON WERE FOOL ENOUGH TO GIVE THEM BATTLE...
YOUR KHAL WOULD SAY THAT ONLY A COWARD HIDES BEHIND STONE WALLS INSTEAD OF FACING HIS ENEMY, BLADE IN HAND, AND ROBERT MIGHT AGREE.
BUT THE MEN AROUND HIM? THEIR PIPERS PLAY A DIFFERENT TUNE. STANNIS, TYWIN LANNISTER.
STARK.
YOU HATE THIS LORD STARK.
HE TOOK ALL I LOVED FROM ME FOR THE SAKE OF A FEW LICE-RIDDEN POACHERS AND HIS PRECIOUS HONOR.
AH! LOOK THERE, KHALEESI...

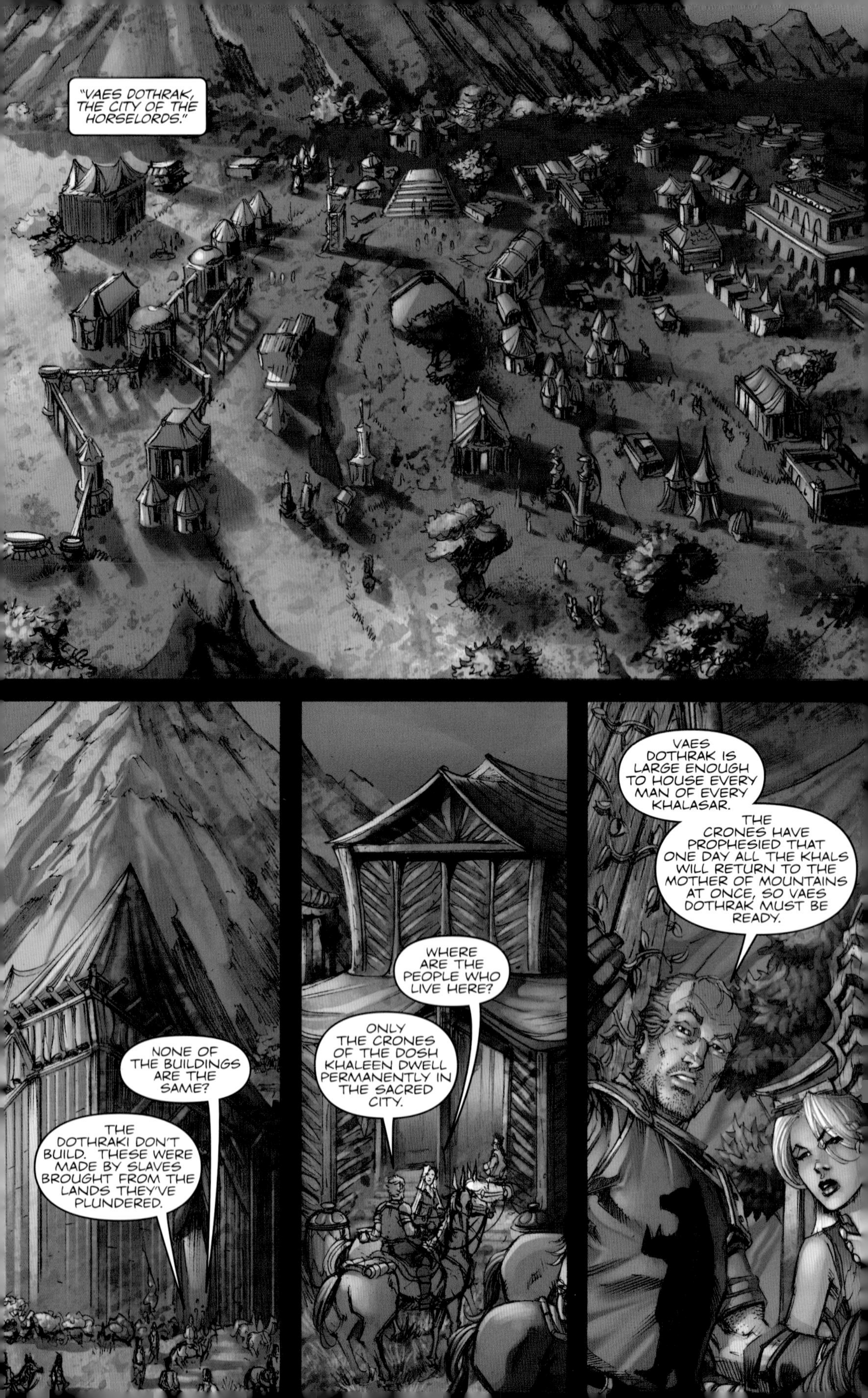
"VAES DOTHRAK, THE CITY OF THE HORSELORDS."
NONE OF THE BUILDINGS ARE THE SAME?
THE DOTHRAKI DON'T BUILD. THESE WERE MADE BY SLAVES BROUGHT FROM THE LANDS THEY'VE PLUNDERED.
WHERE ARE THE PEOPLE WHO LIVE HERE?
ONLY THE CRONES OF THE DOSH KHALEEN DWELL PERMANENTLY IN THE SACRED CITY.
VAES DOTHRAK IS LARGE ENOUGH TO HOUSE EVERY MAN OF EVERY KHALASAR.
THE CRONES HAVE PROPHESIED THAT ONE DAY ALL THE KHALS WILL RETURN TO THE MOTHER OF MOUNTAINS AT ONCE, SO VAES DOTHRAK MUST BE READY.

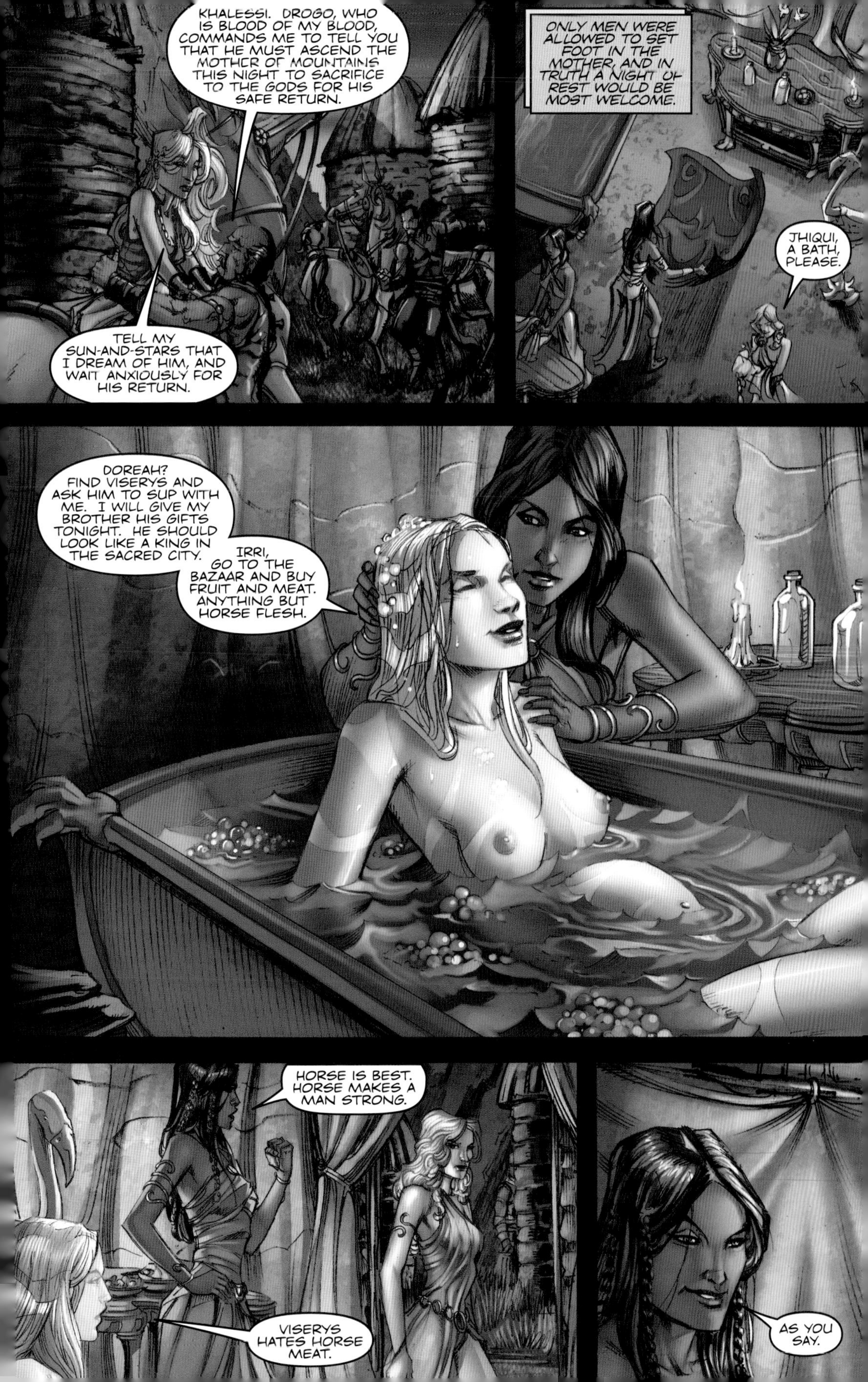
KHALESSI. DROGO, WHO IS BLOOD OF MY BLOOD, COMMANDS ME TO TELL YOU THAT HE MUST ASCEND THE MOTHER OF MOUNTAINS THIS NIGHT TO SACRIFICE TO THE GODS FOR HIS SAFE RETURN.
TELL MY SUN-AND-STARS THAT I DREAM OF HIM, AND WAIT ANXIOUSLY FOR HIS RETURN.
ONLY MEN WERE ALLOWED TO SET FOOT IN THE MOTHER, AND IN TRUTH A NIGHT OF REST WOULD BE MOST WELCOME.
JHIQUI, A BATH, PLEASE.
DOREAH? FIND VISERYS AND ASK HIM TO SUP WITH ME. I WILL GIVE MY BROTHER HIS GIFTS TONIGHT. HE SHOULD LOOK LIKE A KING IN THE SACRED CITY.
IRRI, GO TO THE BAZAAR AND BUY FRUIT AND MEAT. ANYTHING BUT HORSE FLESH.
HORSE IS BEST. HORSE MAKES A MAN STRONG.
VISERYS HATES HORSE MEAT.
AS YOU SAY.

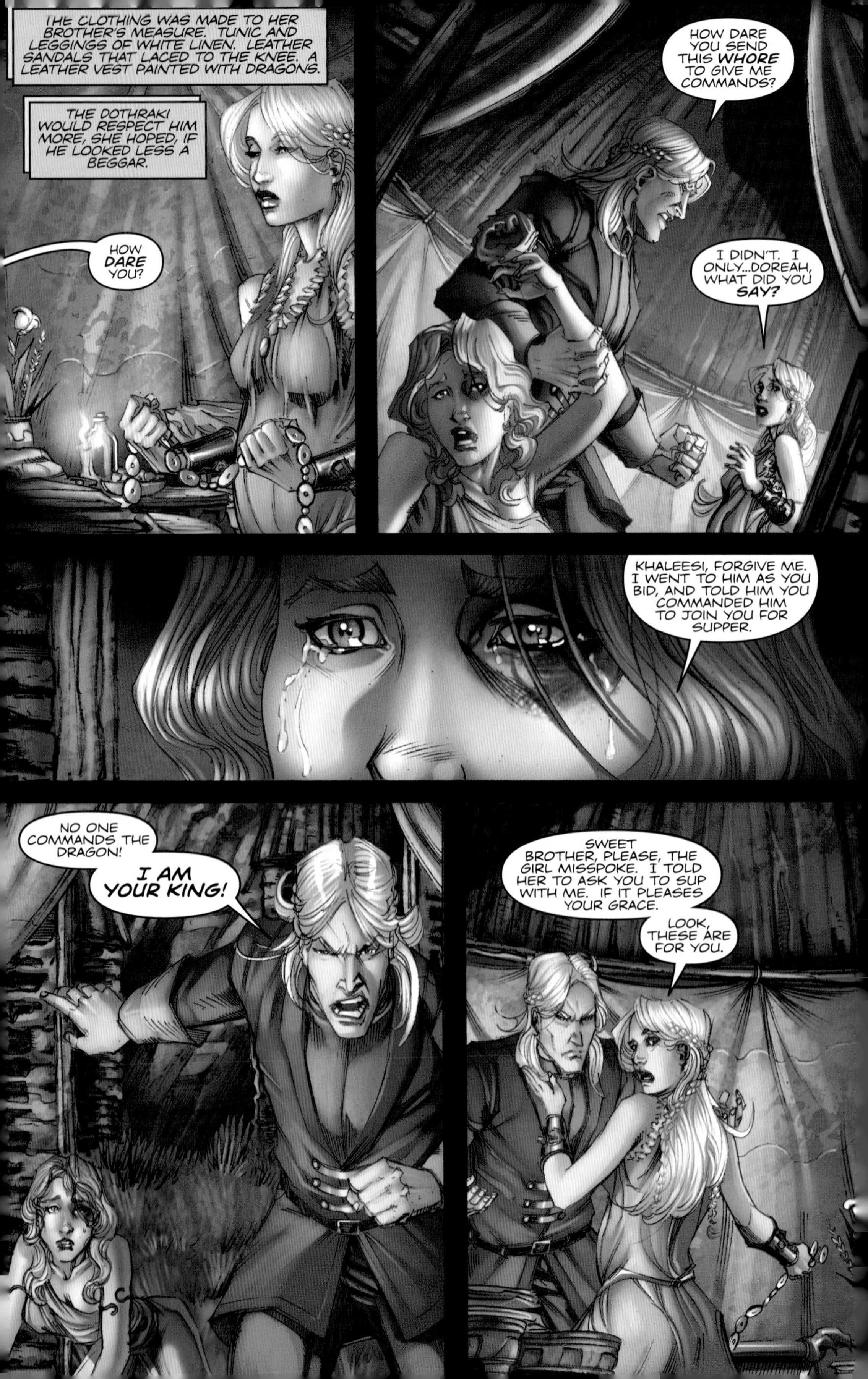
THE CLOTHING WAS MADE TO HER BROTHER'S MEASURE. TUNIC AND LEGGINGS OF WHITE LINEN. LEATHER SANDALS THAT LACED TO THE KNEE. A LEATHER VEST PAINTED WITH DRAGONS.
THE DOTHRAKI WOULD RESPECT HIM MORE, SHE HOPED, IF HE LOOKED LESS A BEGGAR.
HOW **DARE** YOU?
HOW DARE YOU SEND THIS **WHORE** TO GIVE ME COMMANDS?
I DIDN'T. I ONLY...DOREAH, WHAT DID YOU **SAY?**
KHALEESI, FORGIVE ME. I WENT TO HIM AS YOU BID, AND TOLD HIM YOU COMMANDED HIM TO JOIN YOU FOR SUPPER.
NO ONE COMMANDS THE DRAGON! **I AM YOUR KING!**
SWEET BROTHER, PLEASE, THE GIRL MISSPOKE. I TOLD HER TO ASK YOU TO SUP WITH ME. IF IT PLEASES YOUR GRACE.
LOOK, THESE ARE FOR YOU.

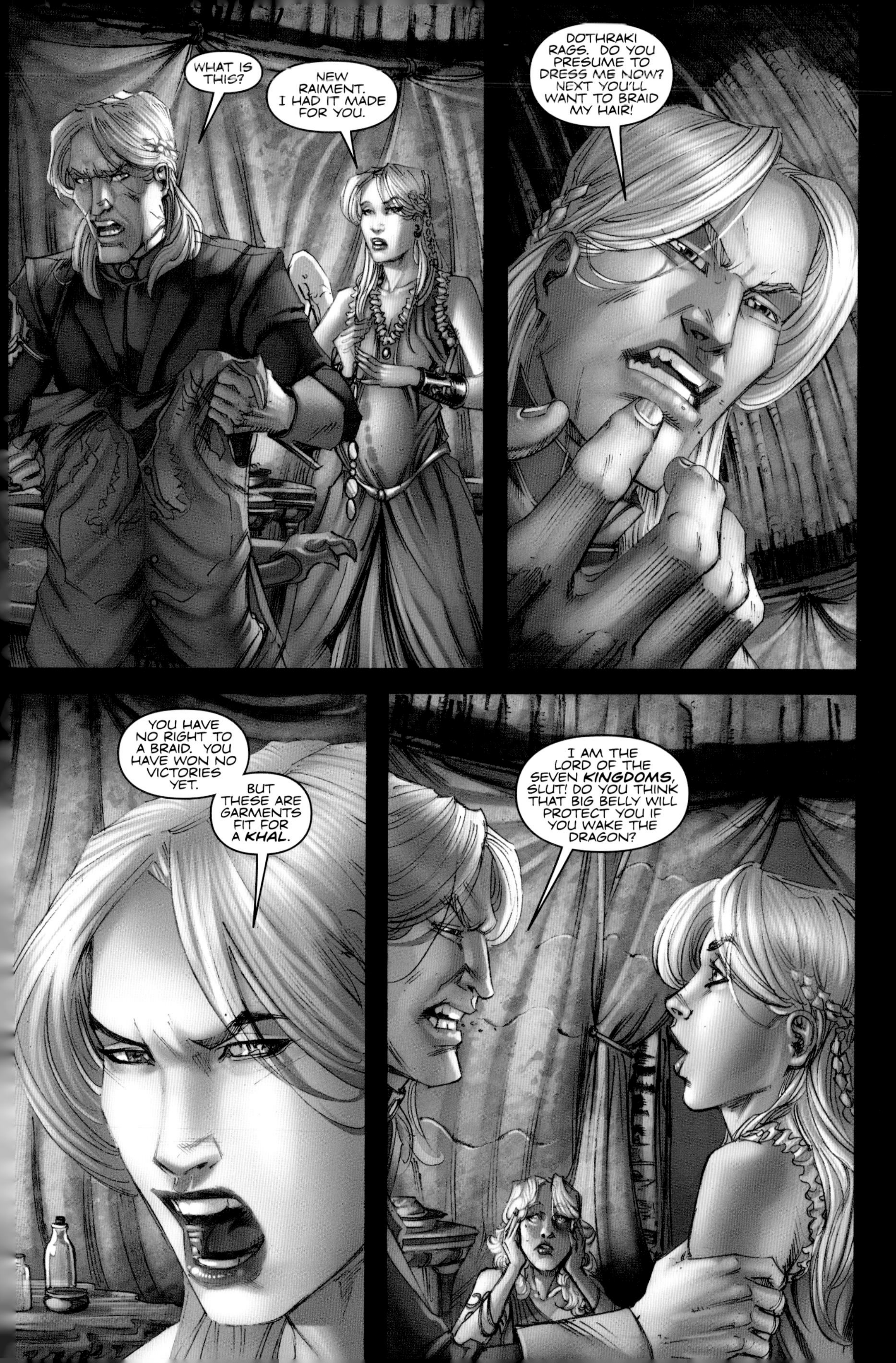
WHAT IS THIS?
NEW RAIMENT. I HAD IT MADE FOR YOU.
DOTHRAKI RAGS. DO YOU PRESUME TO DRESS ME NOW? NEXT YOU'LL WANT TO BRAID MY HAIR!
YOU HAVE NO RIGHT TO A BRAID. YOU HAVE WON NO VICTORIES YET.
BUT THESE ARE GARMENTS FIT FOR A **KHAL**.
I AM THE LORD OF THE SEVEN **KINGDOMS**, SLUT! DO YOU THINK THAT BIG BELLY WILL PROTECT YOU IF YOU WAKE THE DRAGON?

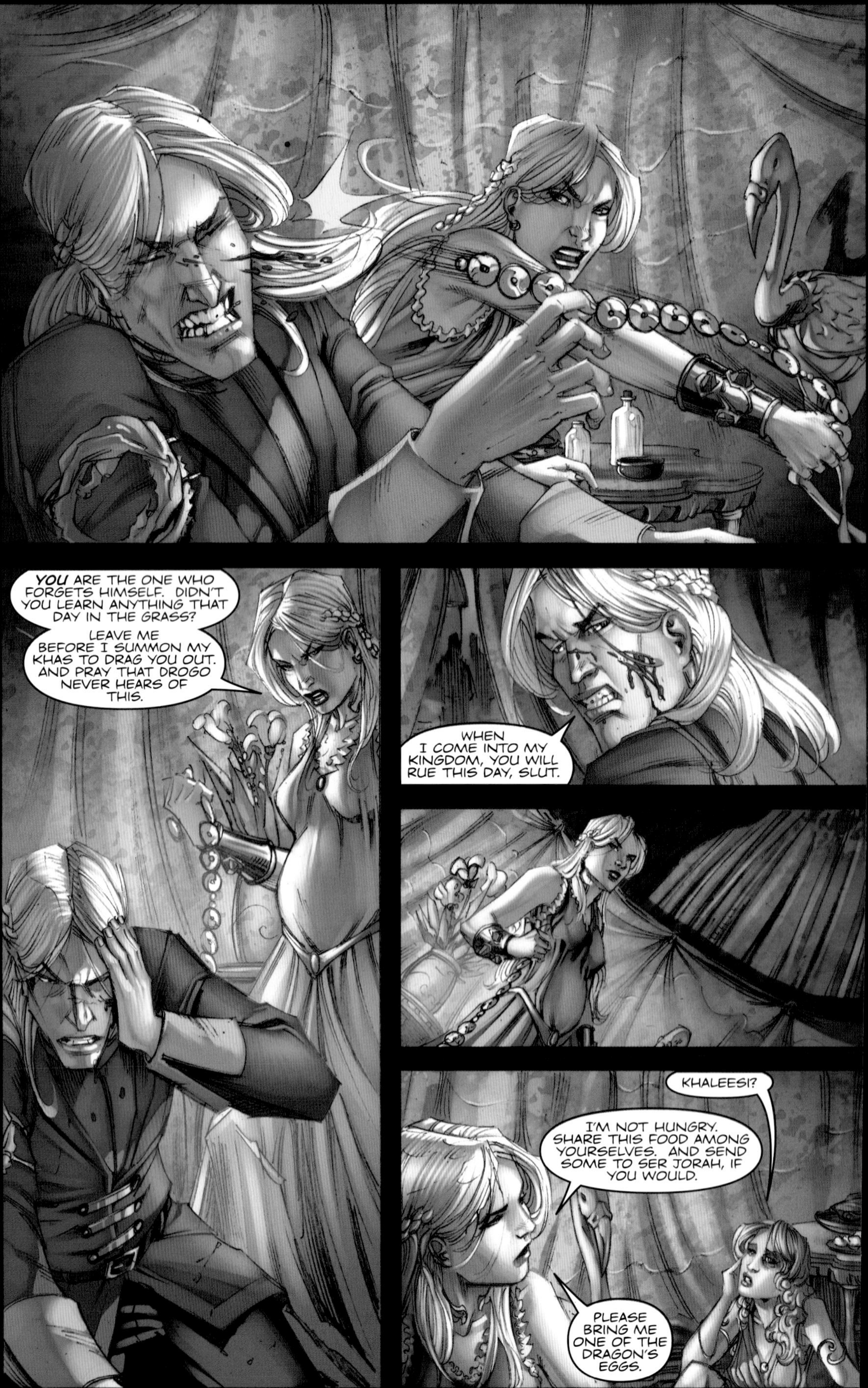

YOU ARE THE ONE WHO FORGETS HIMSELF. DIDN'T YOU LEARN ANYTHING THAT DAY IN THE GRASS?
LEAVE ME BEFORE I SUMMON MY KHAS TO DRAG YOU OUT. AND PRAY THAT DROGO NEVER HEARS OF THIS.
WHEN I COME INTO MY KINGDOM, YOU WILL RUE THIS DAY, SLUT.
KHALEESI?
I'M NOT HUNGRY. SHARE THIS FOOD AMONG YOURSELVES. AND SEND SOME TO SER JORAH, IF YOU WOULD.
PLEASE BRING ME ONE OF THE DRAGON'S EGGS.

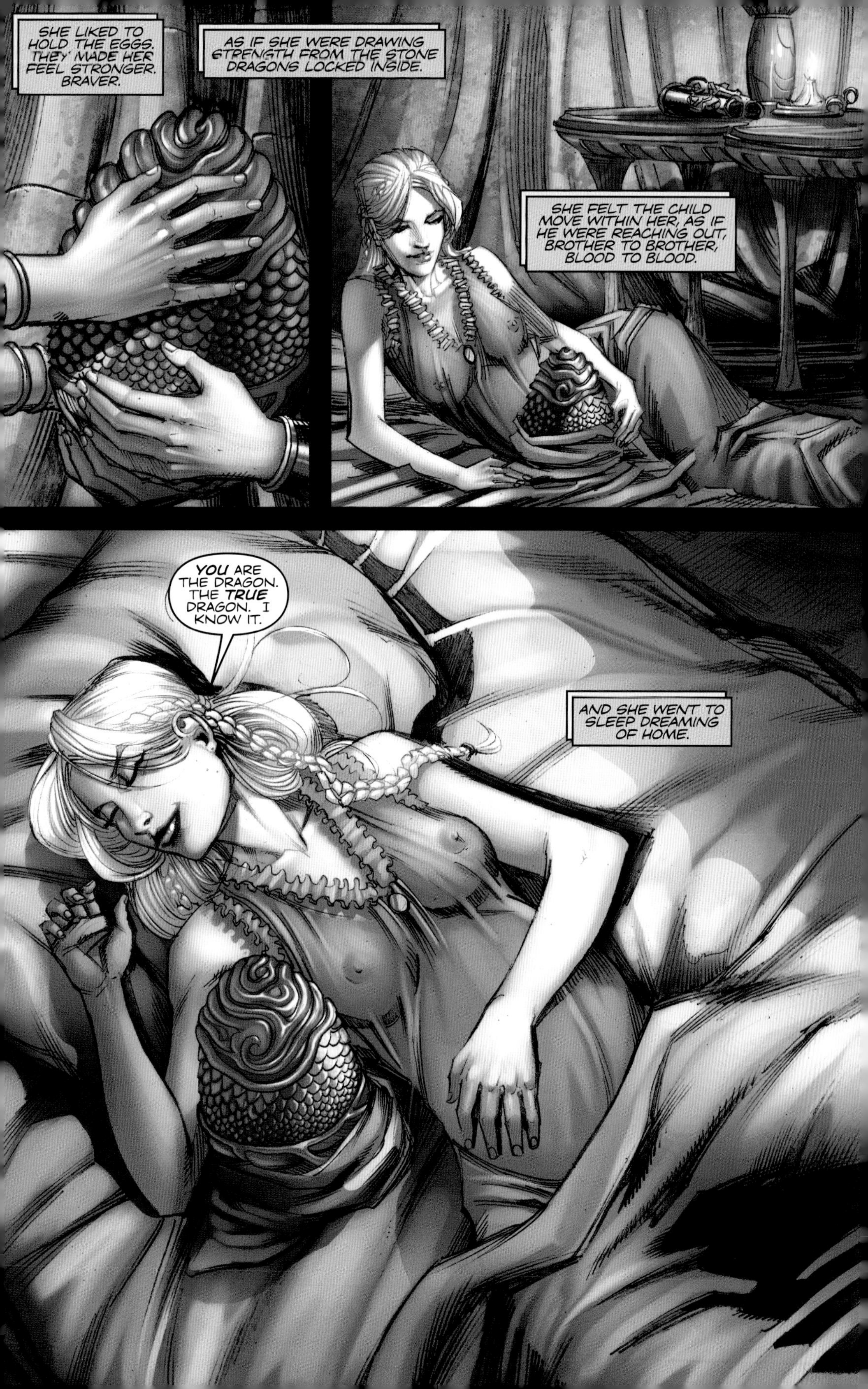

SHE LIKED TO HOLD THE EGGS. THEY MADE HER FEEL STRONGER. BRAVER.
AS IF SHE WERE DRAWING STRENGTH FROM THE STONE DRAGONS LOCKED INSIDE.
SHE FELT THE CHILD MOVE WITHIN HER, AS IF HE WERE REACHING OUT, BROTHER TO BROTHER, BLOOD TO BLOOD.
YOU ARE THE DRAGON. THE TRUE DRAGON. I KNOW IT.
AND SHE WENT TO SLEEP DREAMING OF HOME.

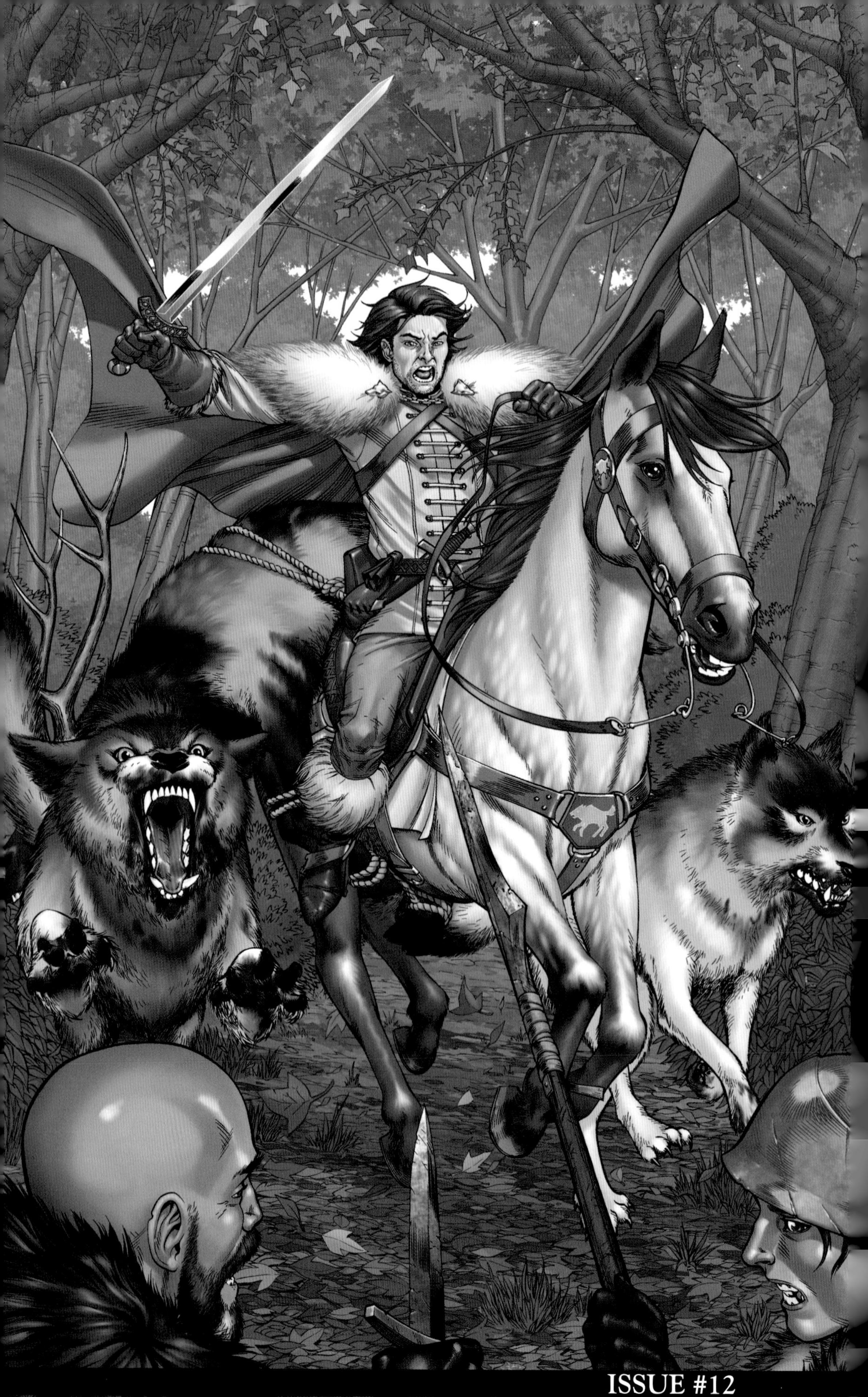

ISSUE #12

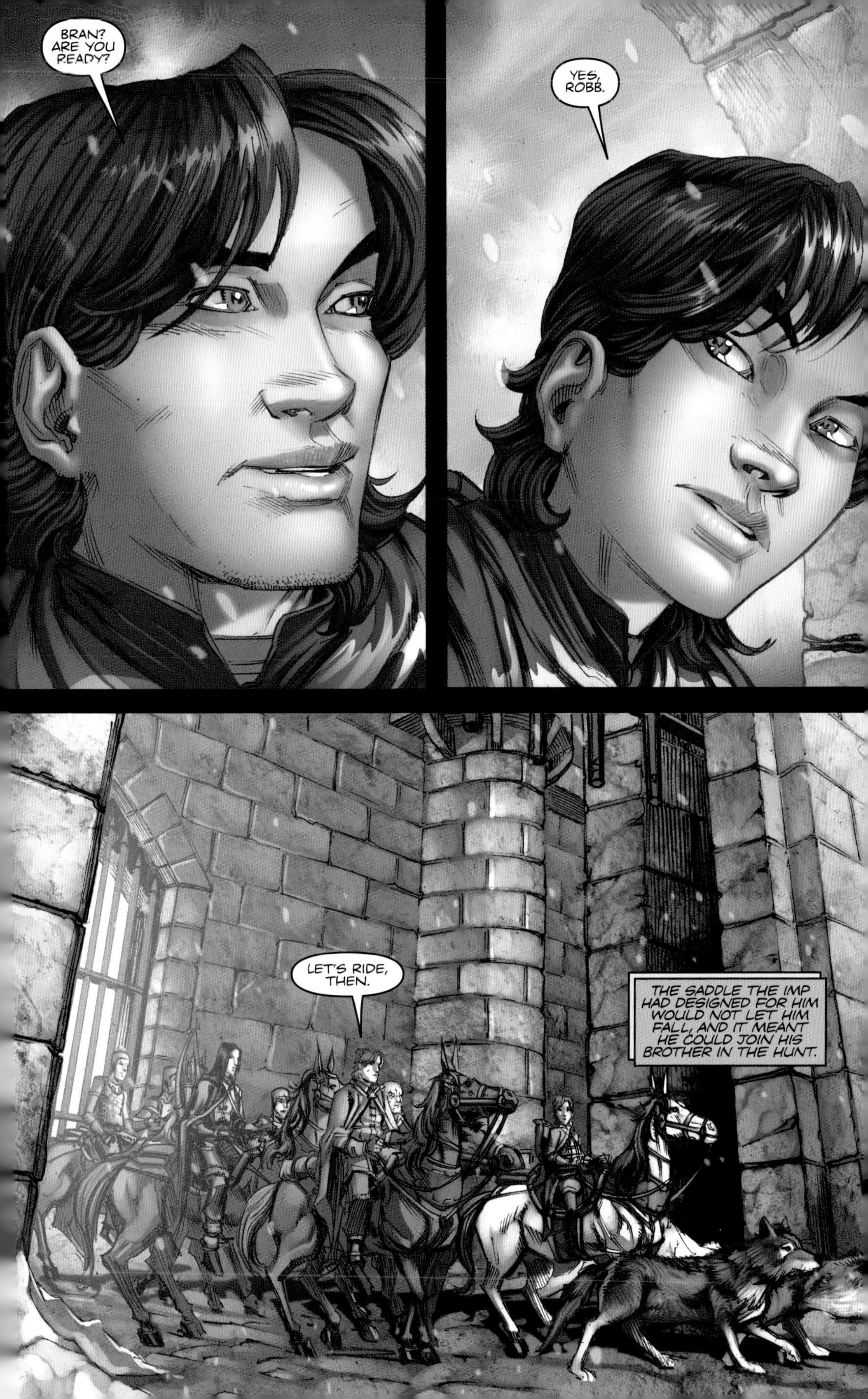
BRAN? ARE YOU READY?
YES, ROBB.
LET'S RIDE, THEN.
THE SADDLE THE IMP HAD DESIGNED FOR HIM WOULD NOT LET HIM FALL, AND IT MEANT HE COULD JOIN HIS BROTHER IN THE HUNT.

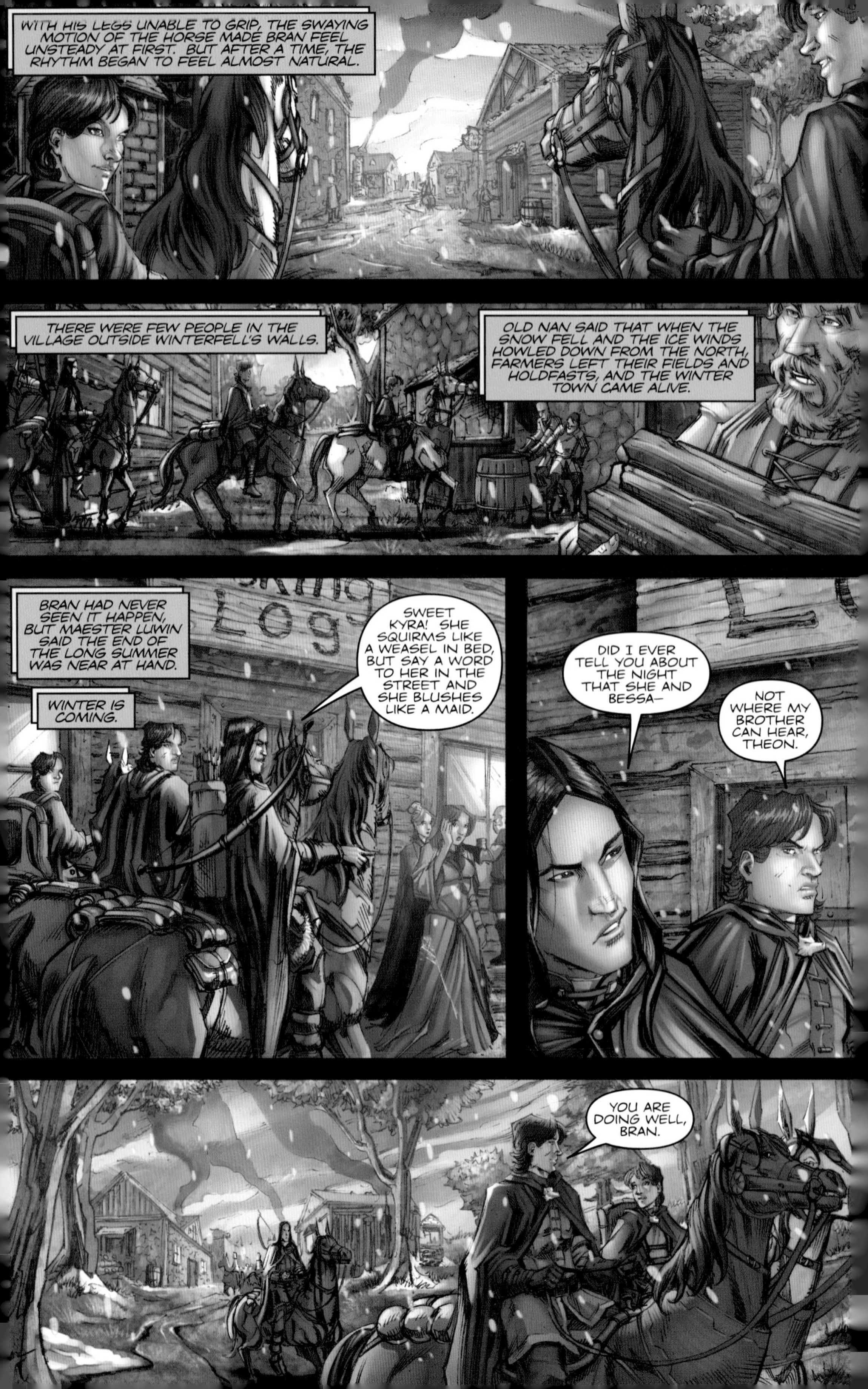
WITH HIS LEGS UNABLE TO GRIP, THE SWAYING MOTION OF THE HORSE MADE BRAN FEEL UNSTEADY AT FIRST. BUT AFTER A TIME, THE RHYTHM BEGAN TO FEEL ALMOST NATURAL.
THERE WERE FEW PEOPLE IN THE VILLAGE OUTSIDE WINTERFELL'S WALLS.
OLD NAN SAID THAT WHEN THE SNOW FELL AND THE ICE WINDS HOWLED DOWN FROM THE NORTH, FARMERS LEFT THEIR FIELDS AND HOLDFASTS, AND THE WINTER TOWN CAME ALIVE.
BRAN HAD NEVER SEEN IT HAPPEN, BUT MAESTER LUWIN SAID THE END OF THE LONG SUMMER WAS NEAR AT HAND.
WINTER IS COMING.
Log
SWEET KYRA! SHE SQUIRMS LIKE A WEASEL IN BED, BUT SAY A WORD TO HER IN THE STREET AND SHE BLUSHES LIKE A MAID.
DID I EVER TELL YOU ABOUT THE NIGHT THAT SHE AND BESSA—
NOT WHERE MY BROTHER CAN HEAR, THEON.
YOU ARE DOING WELL, BRAN.

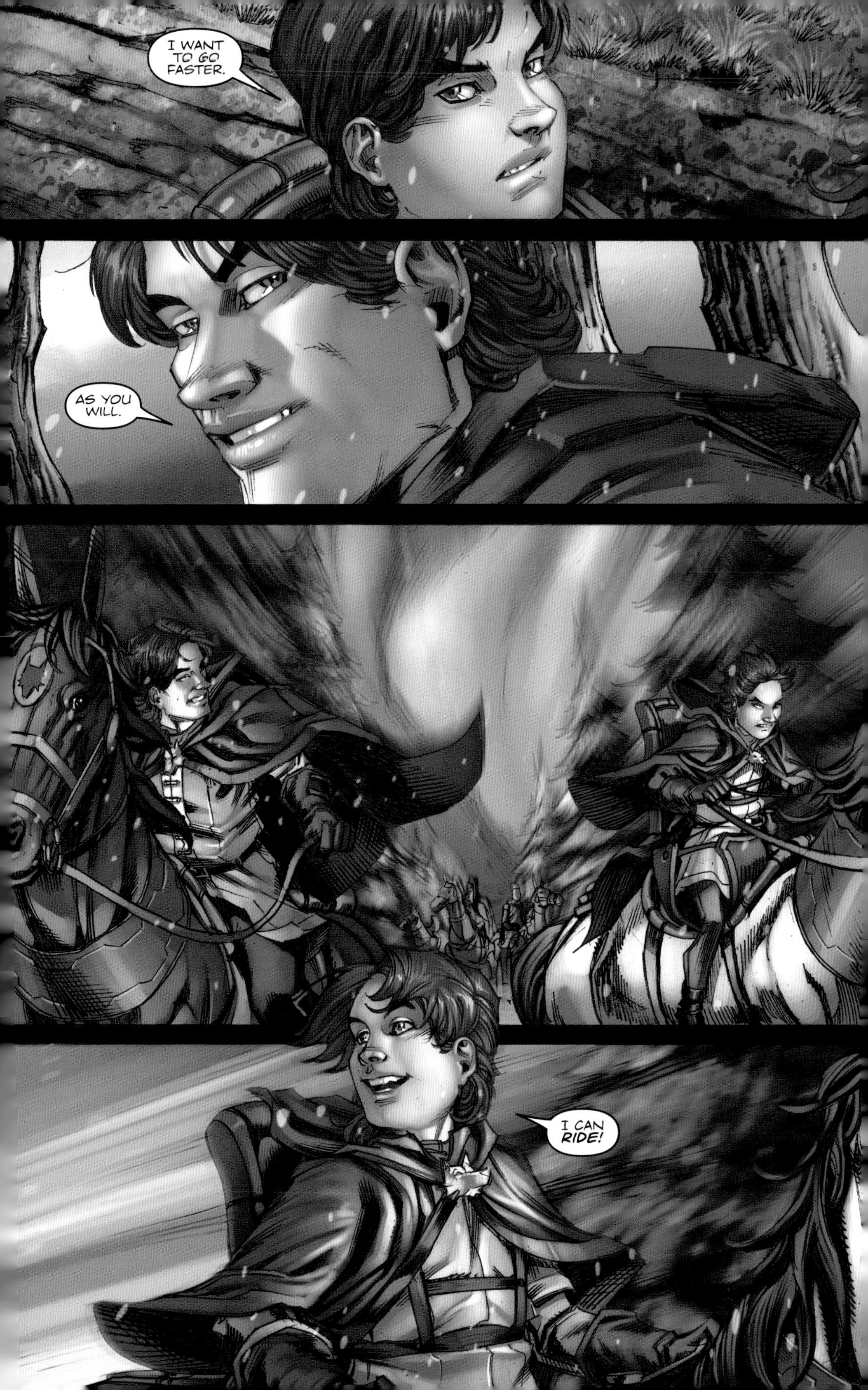
I WANT TO GO FASTER.
AS YOU WILL.
I CAN *RIDE!*

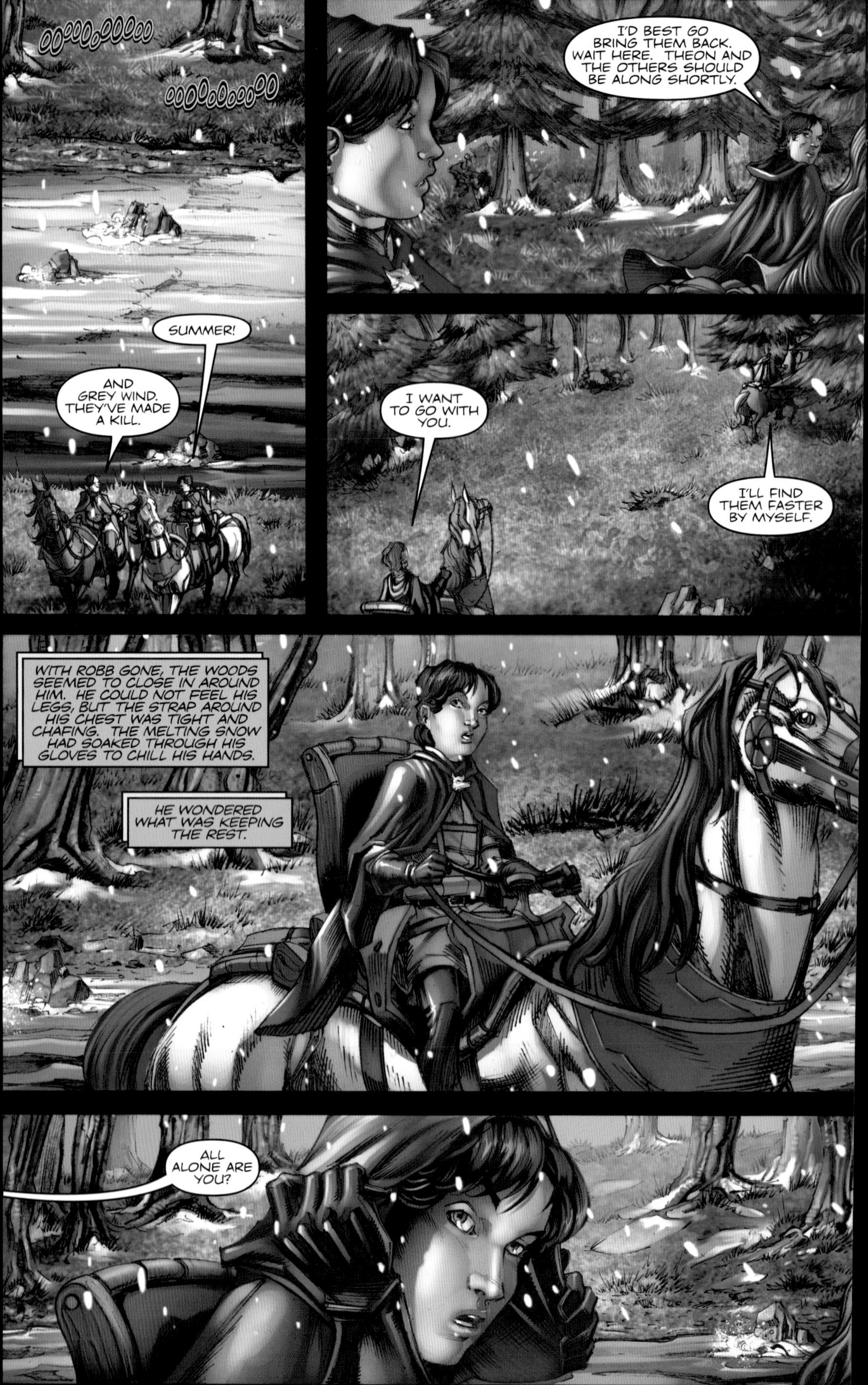
OOOOOOOOOO
OOOOOOOOOOO
I'D BEST GO BRING THEM BACK. WAIT HERE. THEON AND THE OTHERS SHOULD BE ALONG SHORTLY.
SUMMER!
AND GREY WIND. THEY'VE MADE A KILL.
I WANT TO GO WITH YOU.
I'LL FIND THEM FASTER BY MYSELF.
WITH ROBB GONE, THE WOODS SEEMED TO CLOSE IN AROUND HIM. HE COULD NOT FEEL HIS LEGS, BUT THE STRAP AROUND HIS CHEST WAS TIGHT AND CHAFING. THE MELTING SNOW HAD SOAKED THROUGH HIS GLOVES TO CHILL HIS HANDS.
HE WONDERED WHAT WAS KEEPING THE REST.
ALL ALONE ARE YOU?

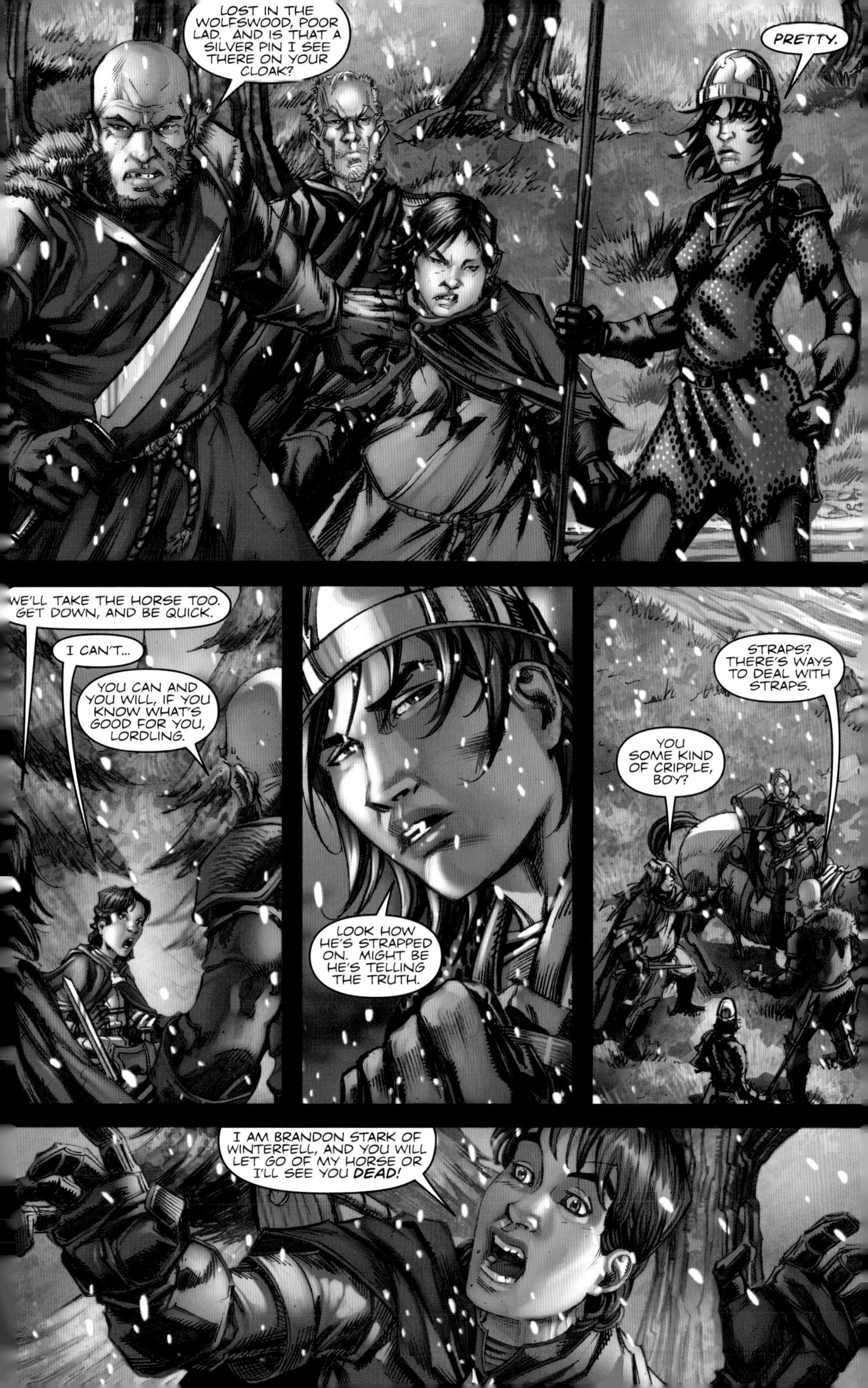
LOST IN THE WOLFSWOOD, POOR LAD. AND IS THAT A SILVER PIN I SEE THERE ON YOUR CLOAK?
PRETTY.
WE'LL TAKE THE HORSE TOO. GET DOWN, AND BE QUICK.
I CAN'T...
YOU CAN AND YOU WILL, IF YOU KNOW WHAT'S GOOD FOR YOU, LORDLING.
LOOK HOW HE'S STRAPPED ON. MIGHT BE HE'S TELLING THE TRUTH.
STRAPS? THERE'S WAYS TO DEAL WITH STRAPS.
YOU SOME KIND OF CRIPPLE, BOY?
I AM BRANDON STARK OF WINTERFELL, AND YOU WILL LET GO OF MY HORSE OR I'LL SEE YOU DEAD!

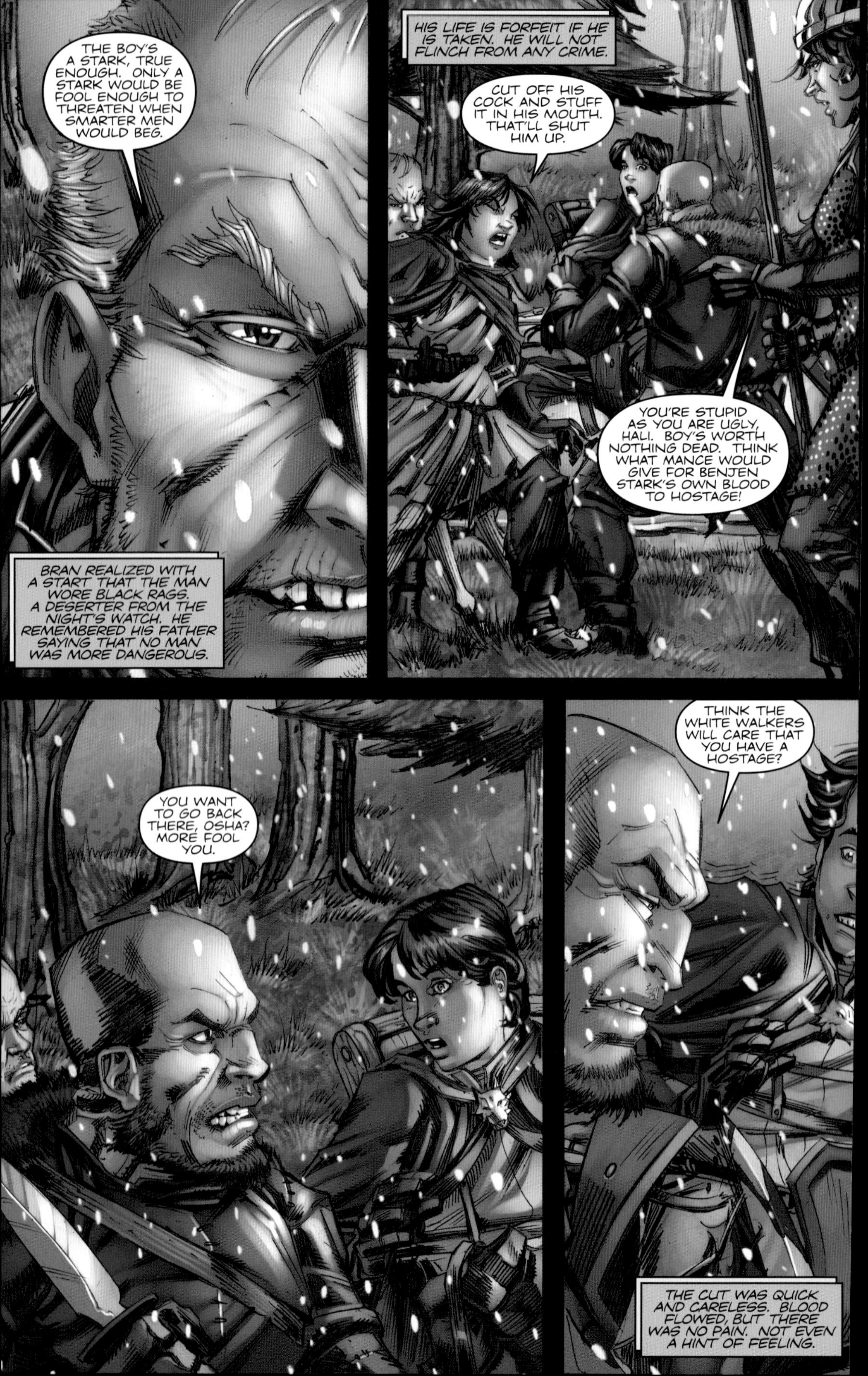
THE BOY'S A STARK, TRUE ENOUGH. ONLY A STARK WOULD BE FOOL ENOUGH TO THREATEN WHEN SMARTER MEN WOULD BEG.
BRAN REALIZED WITH A START THAT THE MAN WORE BLACK RAGS. A DESERTER FROM THE NIGHT'S WATCH. HE REMEMBERED HIS FATHER SAYING THAT NO MAN WAS MORE DANGEROUS.
HIS LIFE IS FORFEIT IF HE IS TAKEN. HE WILL NOT FLINCH FROM ANY CRIME.
CUT OFF HIS COCK AND STUFF IT IN HIS MOUTH. THAT'LL SHUT HIM UP.
YOU'RE STUPID AS YOU ARE UGLY, HALI. BOY'S WORTH NOTHING DEAD. THINK WHAT MANCE WOULD GIVE FOR BENJEN STARK'S OWN BLOOD TO HOSTAGE!
YOU WANT TO GO BACK THERE, OSHA? MORE FOOL YOU.
THINK THE WHITE WALKERS WILL CARE THAT YOU HAVE A HOSTAGE?
THE CUT WAS QUICK AND CARELESS. BLOOD FLOWED, BUT THERE WAS NO PAIN. NOT EVEN A HINT OF FEELING.

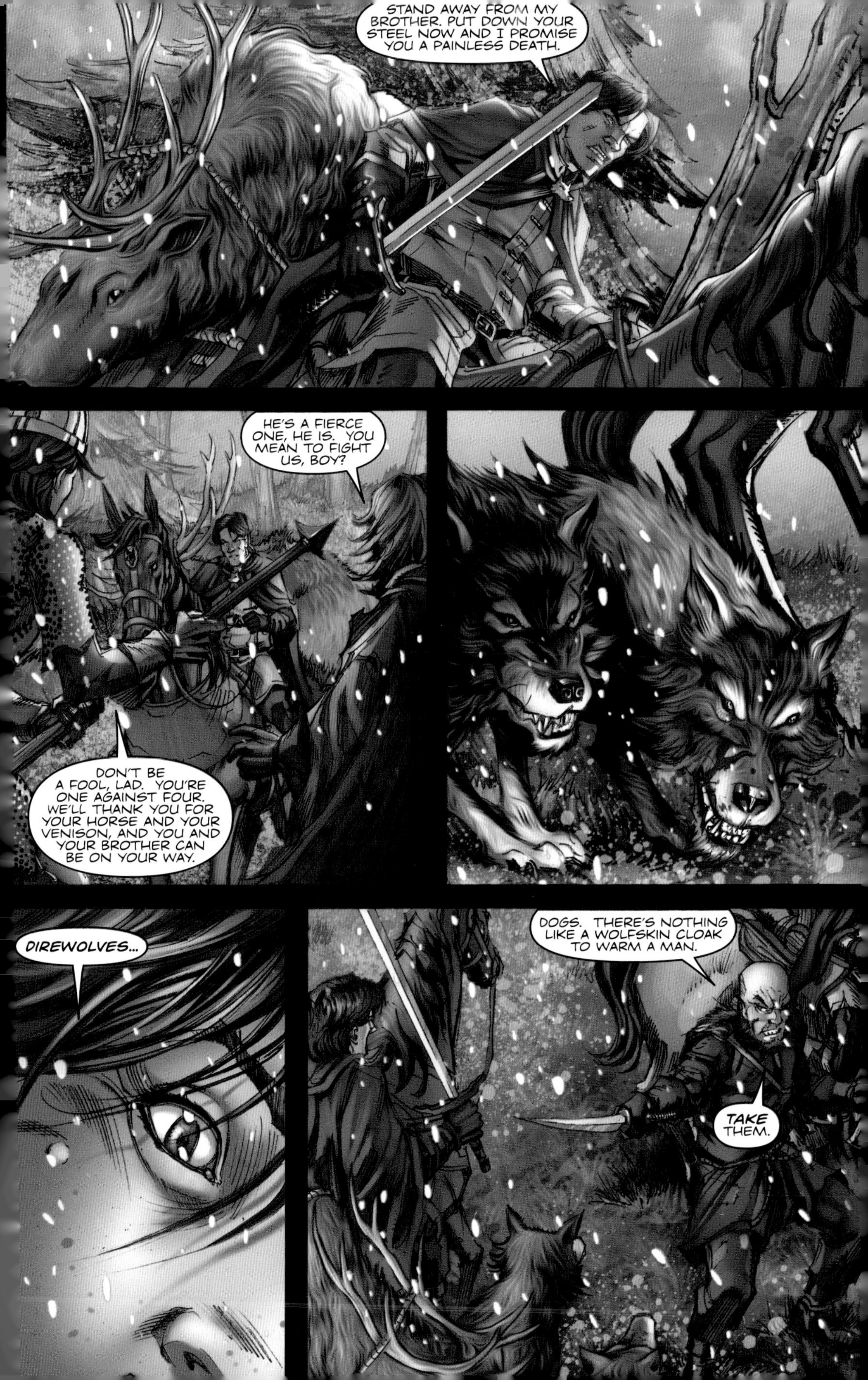
STAND AWAY FROM MY BROTHER. PUT DOWN YOUR STEEL NOW AND I PROMISE YOU A PAINLESS DEATH.
HE'S A FIERCE ONE, HE IS. YOU MEAN TO FIGHT US, BOY?
DON'T BE A FOOL, LAD. YOU'RE ONE AGAINST FOUR. WE'LL THANK YOU FOR YOUR HORSE AND YOUR VENISON, AND YOU AND YOUR BROTHER CAN BE ON YOUR WAY.
DIREWOLVES...
DOGS. THERE'S NOTHING LIKE A WOLFSKIN CLOAK TO WARM A MAN.
TAKE THEM.

WINTERFELL!

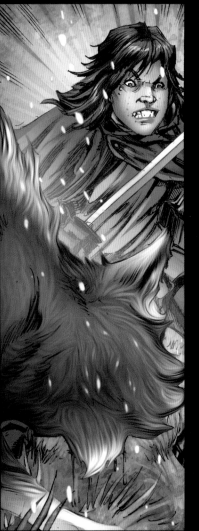

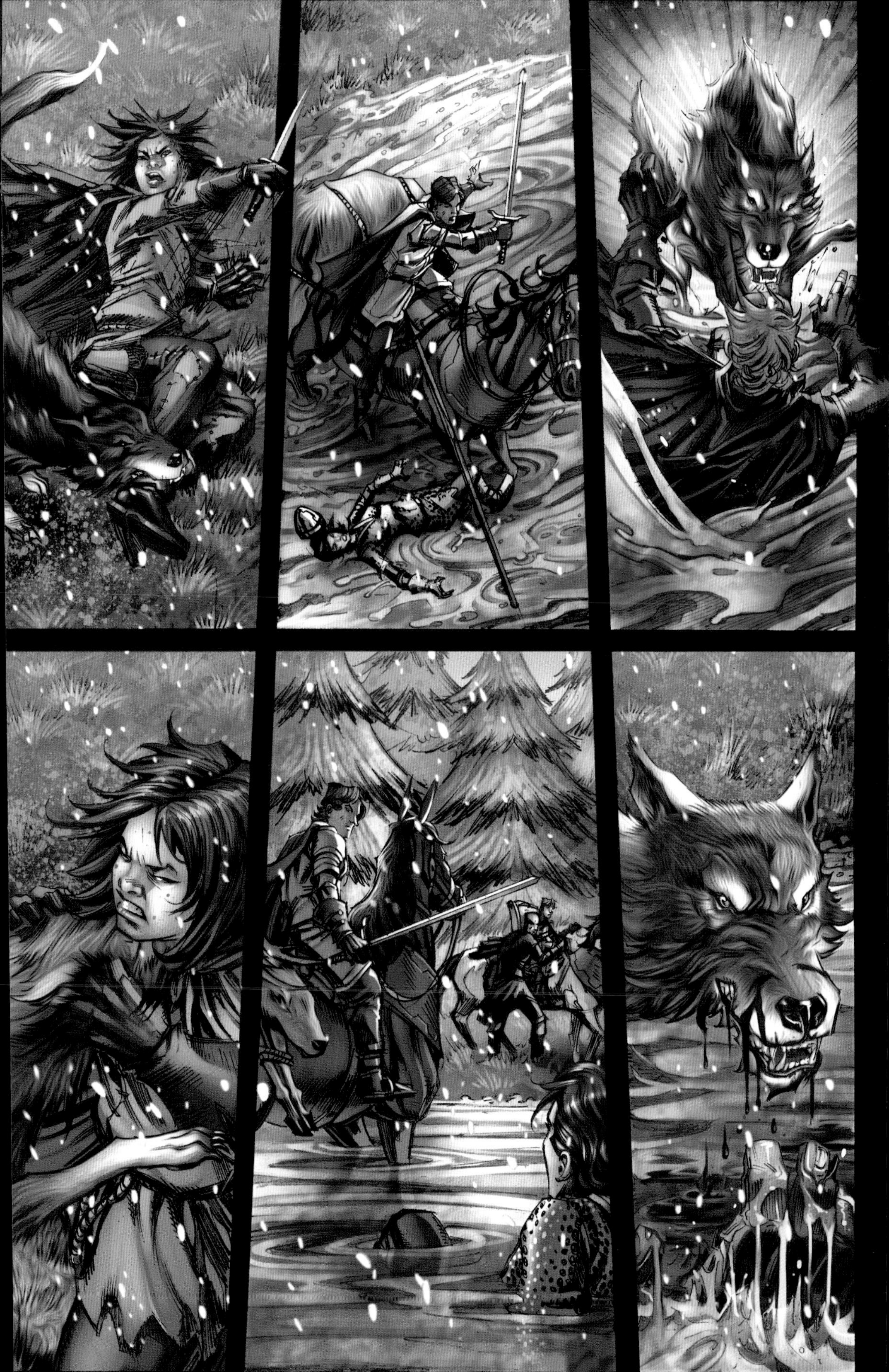

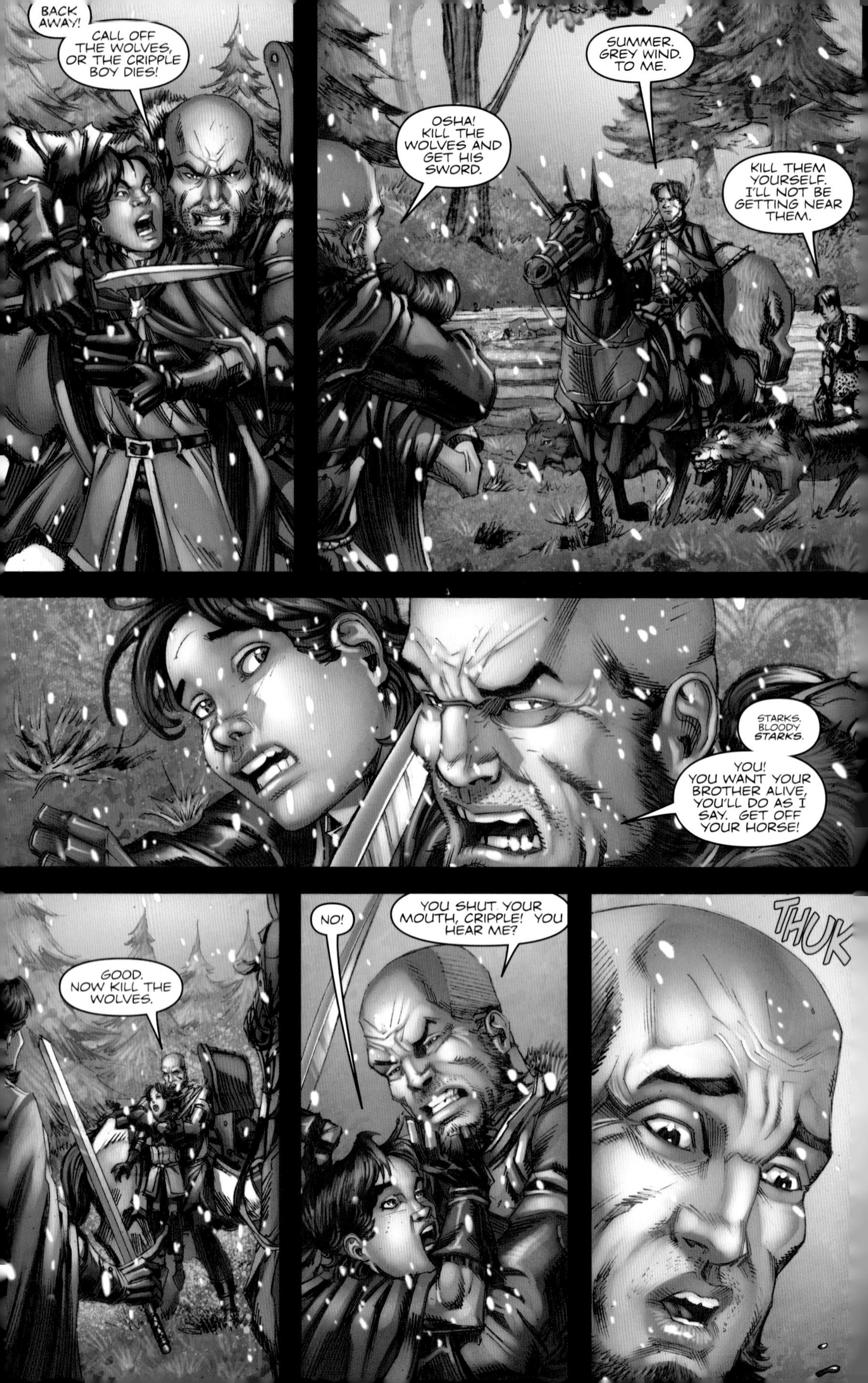

BACK AWAY!
CALL OFF THE WOLVES, OR THE CRIPPLE BOY DIES!
OSHA! KILL THE WOLVES AND GET HIS SWORD.
SUMMER. GREY WIND. TO ME.
KILL THEM YOURSELF. I'LL NOT BE GETTING NEAR THEM.
STARKS. BLOODY STARKS.
YOU! YOU WANT YOUR BROTHER ALIVE, YOU'LL DO AS I SAY. GET OFF YOUR HORSE!
GOOD. NOW KILL THE WOLVES.
NO!
YOU SHUT YOUR MOUTH, CRIPPLE! YOU HEAR ME?
THUK

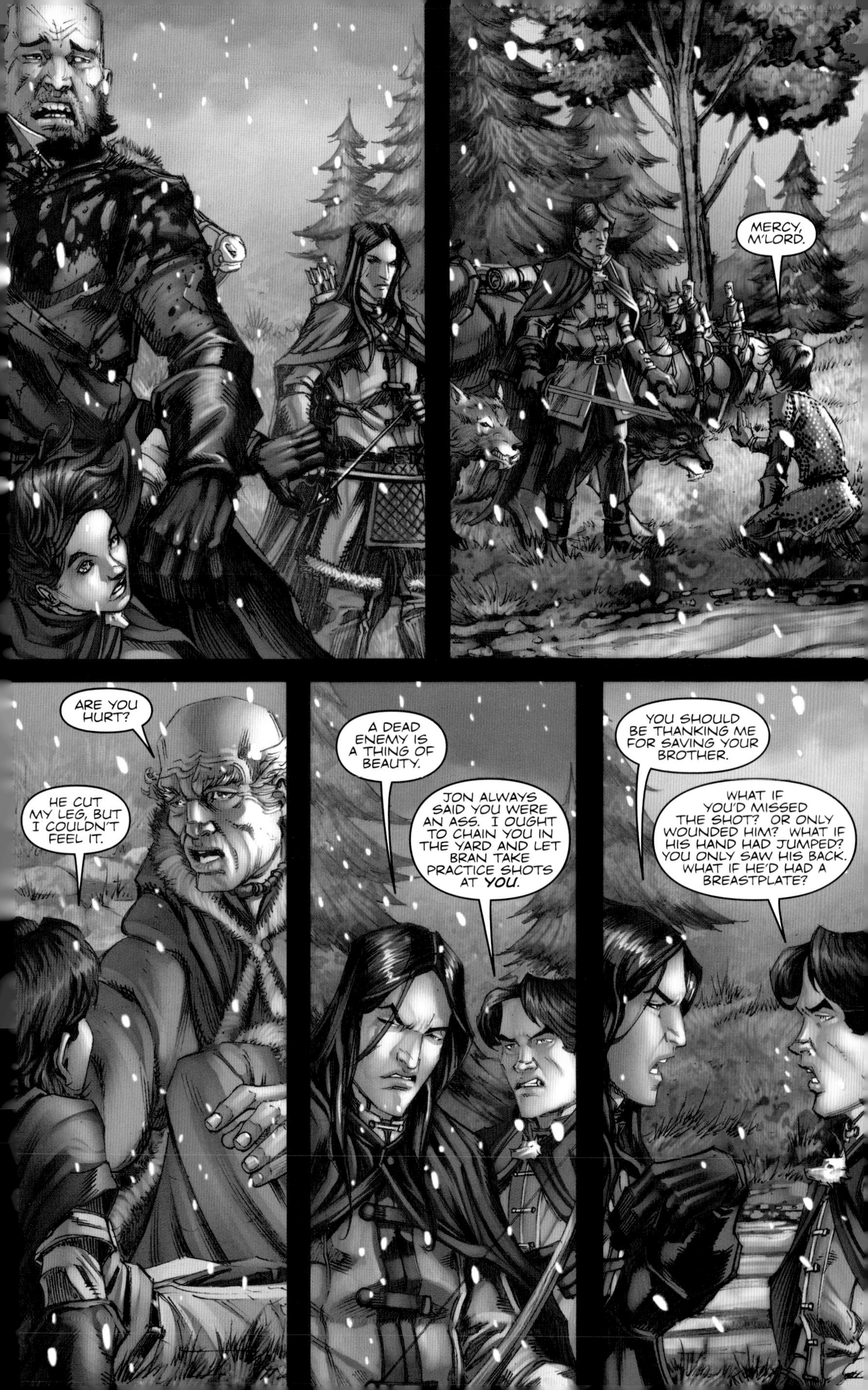
MERCY, M'LORD.
ARE YOU HURT?
HE CUT MY LEG, BUT I COULDN'T FEEL IT.
A DEAD ENEMY IS A THING OF BEAUTY.
JON ALWAYS SAID YOU WERE AN ASS. I OUGHT TO CHAIN YOU IN THE YARD AND LET BRAN TAKE PRACTICE SHOTS AT *YOU*.
YOU SHOULD BE THANKING ME FOR SAVING YOUR BROTHER.
WHAT IF YOU'D MISSED THE SHOT? OR ONLY WOUNDED HIM? WHAT IF HIS HAND HAD JUMPED? YOU ONLY SAW HIS BACK. WHAT IF HE'D HAD A BREASTPLATE?

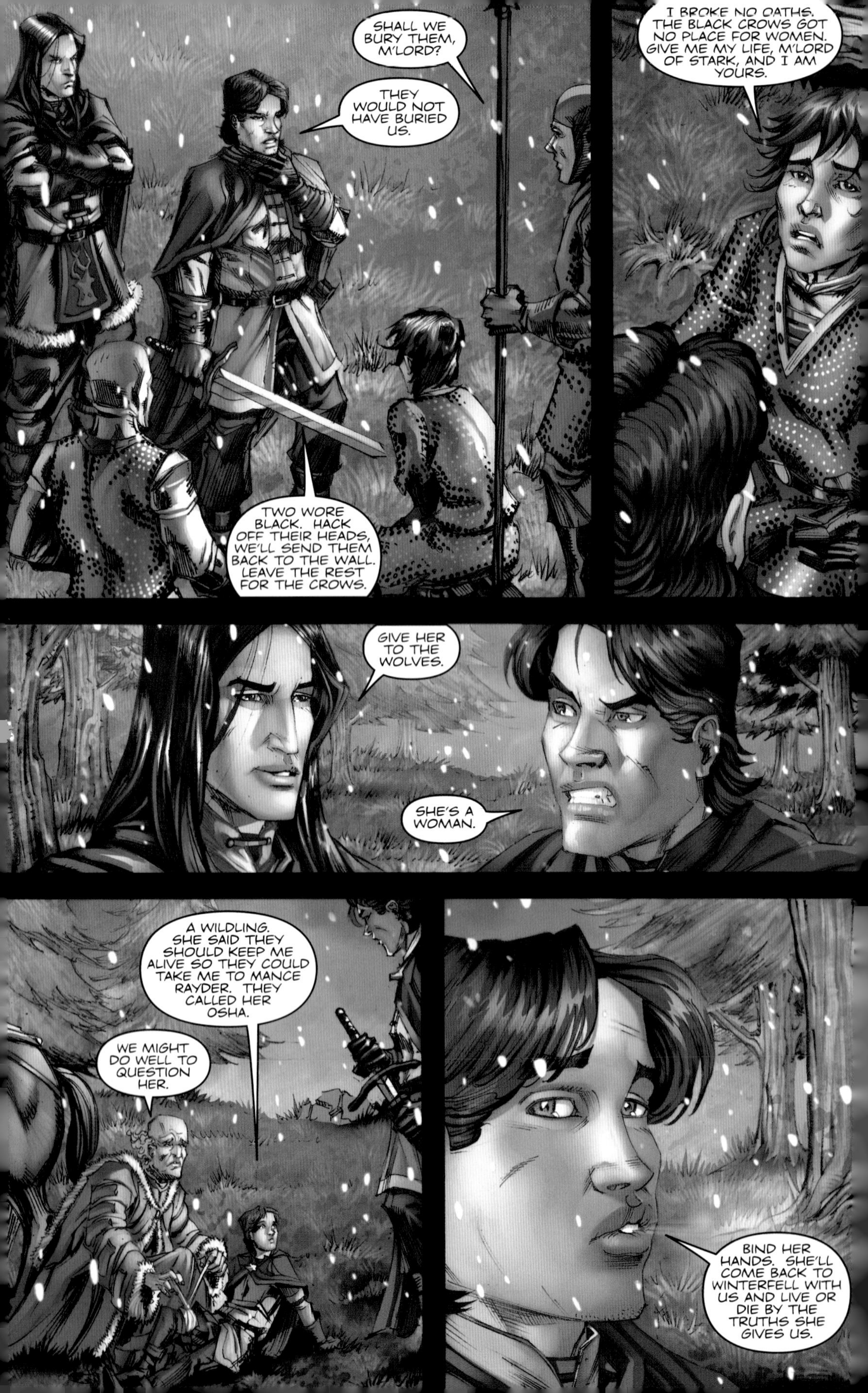
SHALL WE BURY THEM, M'LORD?
THEY WOULD NOT HAVE BURIED US.
TWO WORE BLACK. HACK OFF THEIR HEADS, WE'LL SEND THEM BACK TO THE WALL. LEAVE THE REST FOR THE CROWS.
I BROKE NO OATHS. THE BLACK CROWS GOT NO PLACE FOR WOMEN. GIVE ME MY LIFE, M'LORD OF STARK, AND I AM YOURS.
GIVE HER TO THE WOLVES.
SHE'S A WOMAN.
A WILDLING. SHE SAID THEY SHOULD KEEP ME ALIVE SO THEY COULD TAKE ME TO MANCE RAYDER. THEY CALLED HER OSHA.
WE MIGHT DO WELL TO QUESTION HER.
BIND HER HANDS. SHE'LL COME BACK TO WINTERFELL WITH US AND LIVE OR DIE BY THE TRUTHS SHE GIVES US.

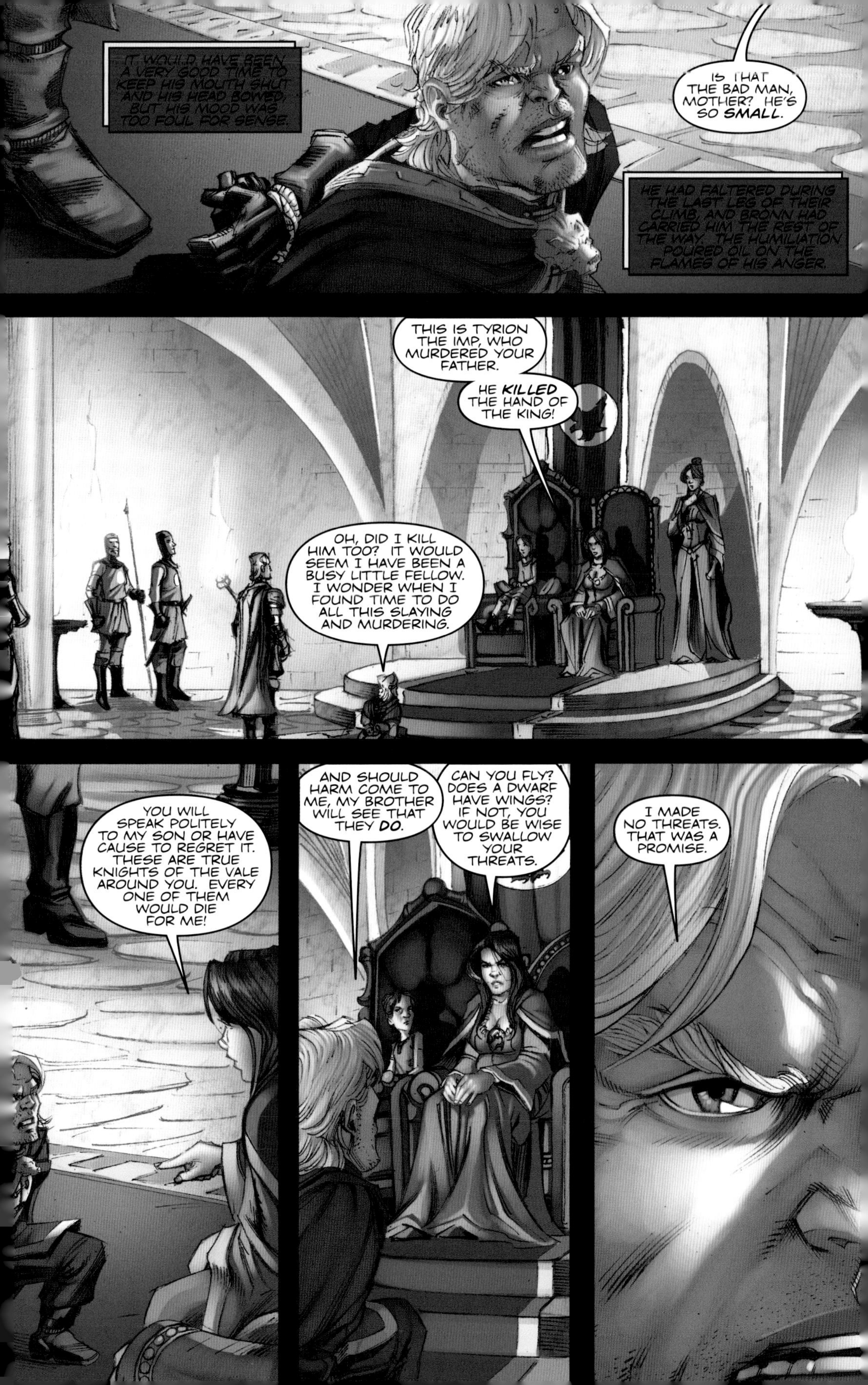
IT WOULD HAVE BEEN A VERY GOOD TIME TO KEEP HIS MOUTH SHUT AND HIS HEAD BOWED, BUT HIS MOOD WAS TOO FOUL FOR SENSE.
IS THAT THE BAD MAN, MOTHER? HE'S SO SMALL.
HE HAD FALTERED DURING THE LAST LEG OF THEIR CLIMB, AND BRONN HAD CARRIED HIM THE REST OF THE WAY. THE HUMILIATION POURED OIL ON THE FLAMES OF HIS ANGER.
THIS IS TYRION THE IMP, WHO MURDERED YOUR FATHER.
HE KILLED THE HAND OF THE KING!
OH, DID I KILL HIM TOO? IT WOULD SEEM I HAVE BEEN A BUSY LITTLE FELLOW. I WONDER WHEN I FOUND TIME TO DO ALL THIS SLAYING AND MURDERING.
YOU WILL SPEAK POLITELY TO MY SON OR HAVE CAUSE TO REGRET IT. THESE ARE TRUE KNIGHTS OF THE VALE AROUND YOU. EVERY ONE OF THEM WOULD DIE FOR ME!
AND SHOULD HARM COME TO ME, MY BROTHER WILL SEE THAT THEY DO.
CAN YOU FLY? DOES A DWARF HAVE WINGS? IF NOT, YOU WOULD BE WISE TO SWALLOW YOUR THREATS.
I MADE NO THREATS. THAT WAS A PROMISE.

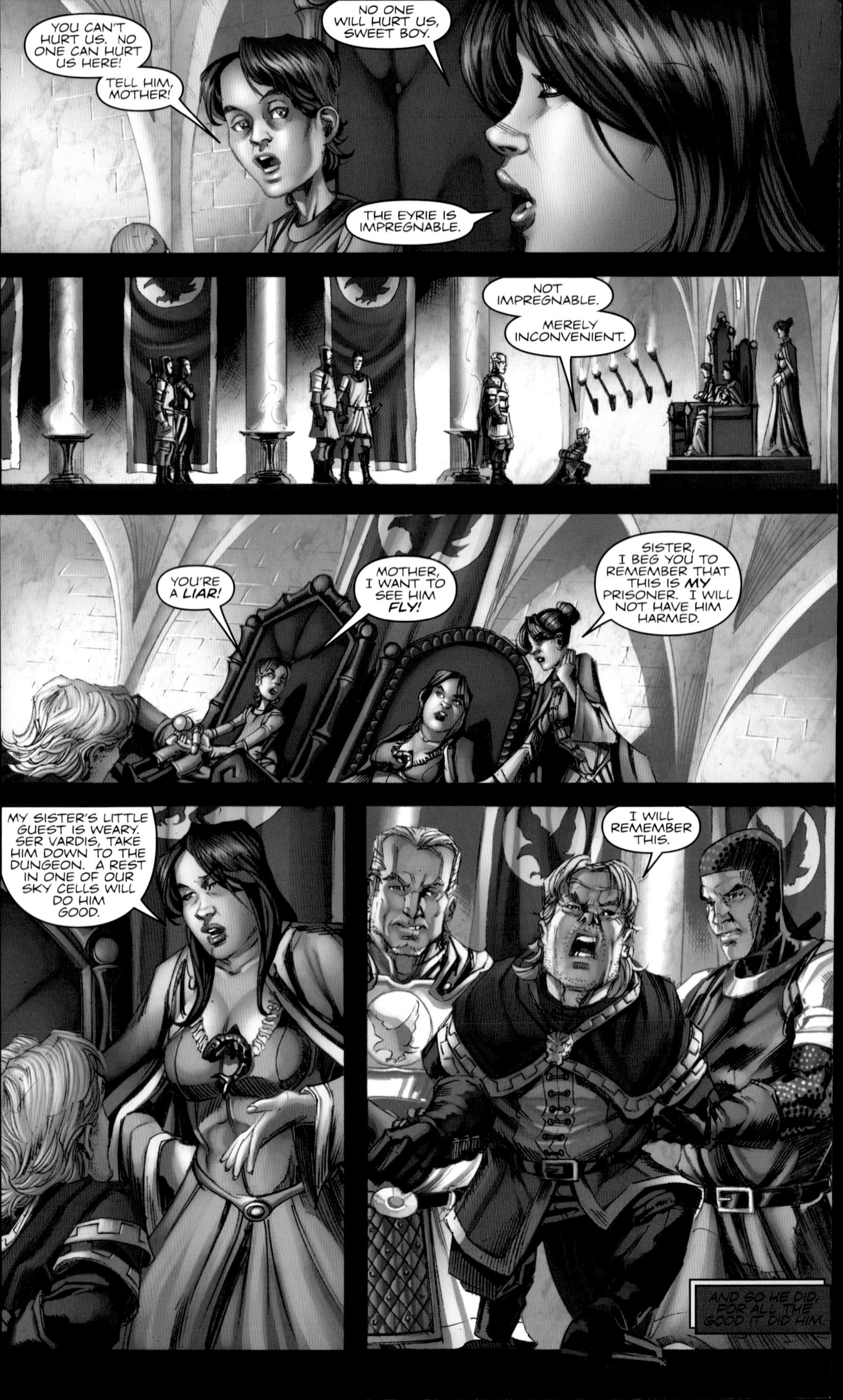
YOU CAN'T HURT US. NO ONE CAN HURT US HERE!
TELL HIM, MOTHER!
NO ONE WILL HURT US, SWEET BOY.
THE EYRIE IS IMPREGNABLE.
NOT IMPREGNABLE.
MERELY INCONVENIENT.
YOU'RE A LIAR!
MOTHER, I WANT TO SEE HIM FLY!
SISTER, I BEG YOU TO REMEMBER THAT THIS IS MY PRISONER. I WILL NOT HAVE HIM HARMED.
MY SISTER'S LITTLE GUEST IS WEARY. SER VARDIS, TAKE HIM DOWN TO THE DUNGEON. A REST IN ONE OF OUR SKY CELLS WILL DO HIM GOOD.
I WILL REMEMBER THIS.
AND SO HE DID, FOR ALL THE GOOD IT DID HIM.

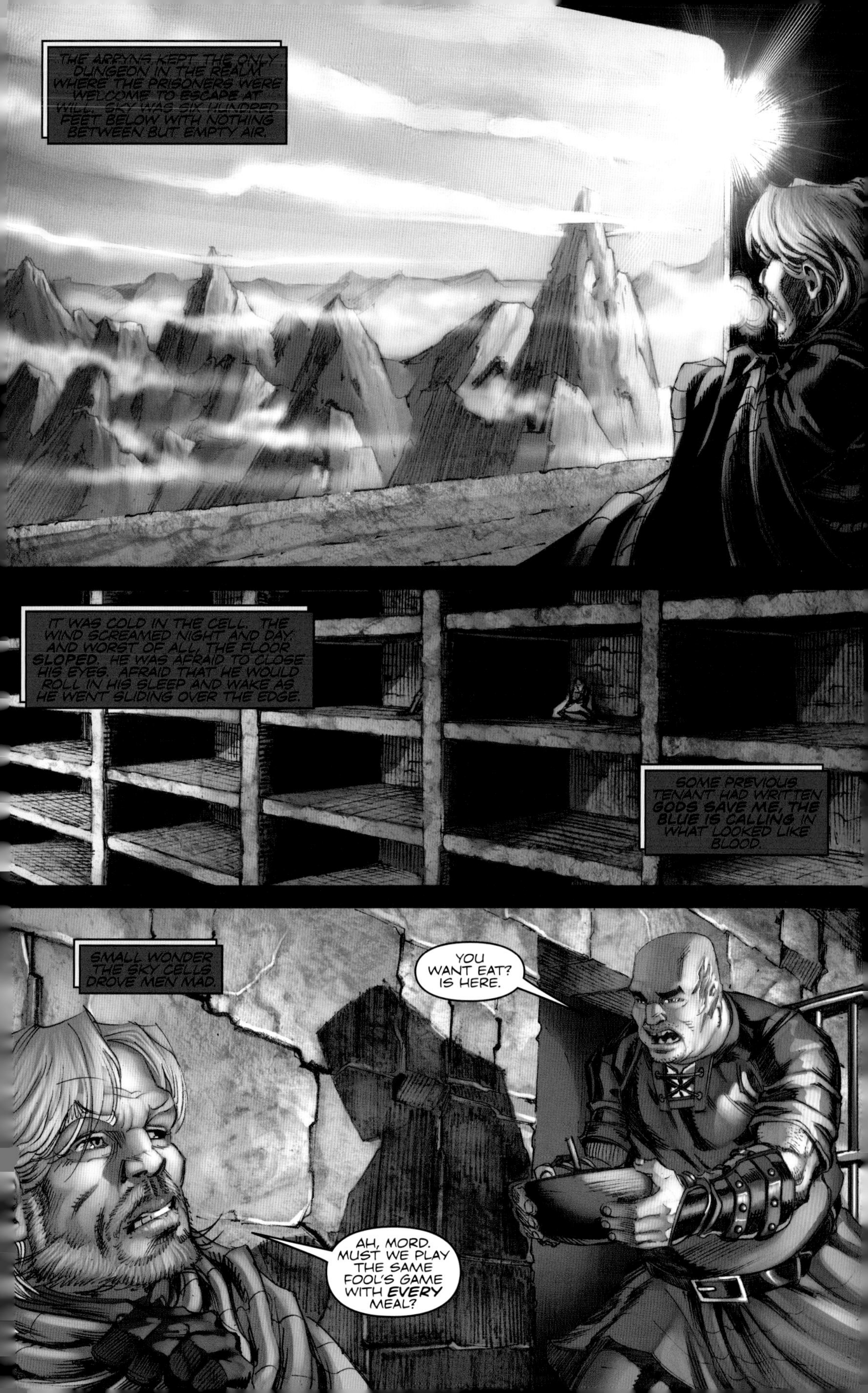
THE ARRYNS KEPT THE ONLY DUNGEON IN THE REALM WHERE THE PRISONERS WERE WELCOME TO ESCAPE AT WILL. SKY WAS SIX HUNDRED FEET BELOW WITH NOTHING BETWEEN BUT EMPTY AIR.
IT WAS COLD IN THE CELL. THE WIND SCREAMED NIGHT AND DAY. AND WORST OF ALL, THE FLOOR SLOPED. HE WAS AFRAID TO CLOSE HIS EYES. AFRAID THAT HE WOULD ROLL IN HIS SLEEP AND WAKE AS HE WENT SLIDING OVER THE EDGE.
SOME PREVIOUS TENANT HAD WRITTEN GODS SAVE ME, THE BLUE IS CALLING IN WHAT LOOKED LIKE BLOOD.
SMALL WONDER THE SKY CELLS DROVE MEN MAD.
YOU WANT EAT? IS HERE.
AH, MORD. MUST WE PLAY THE SAME FOOL'S GAME WITH EVERY MEAL?

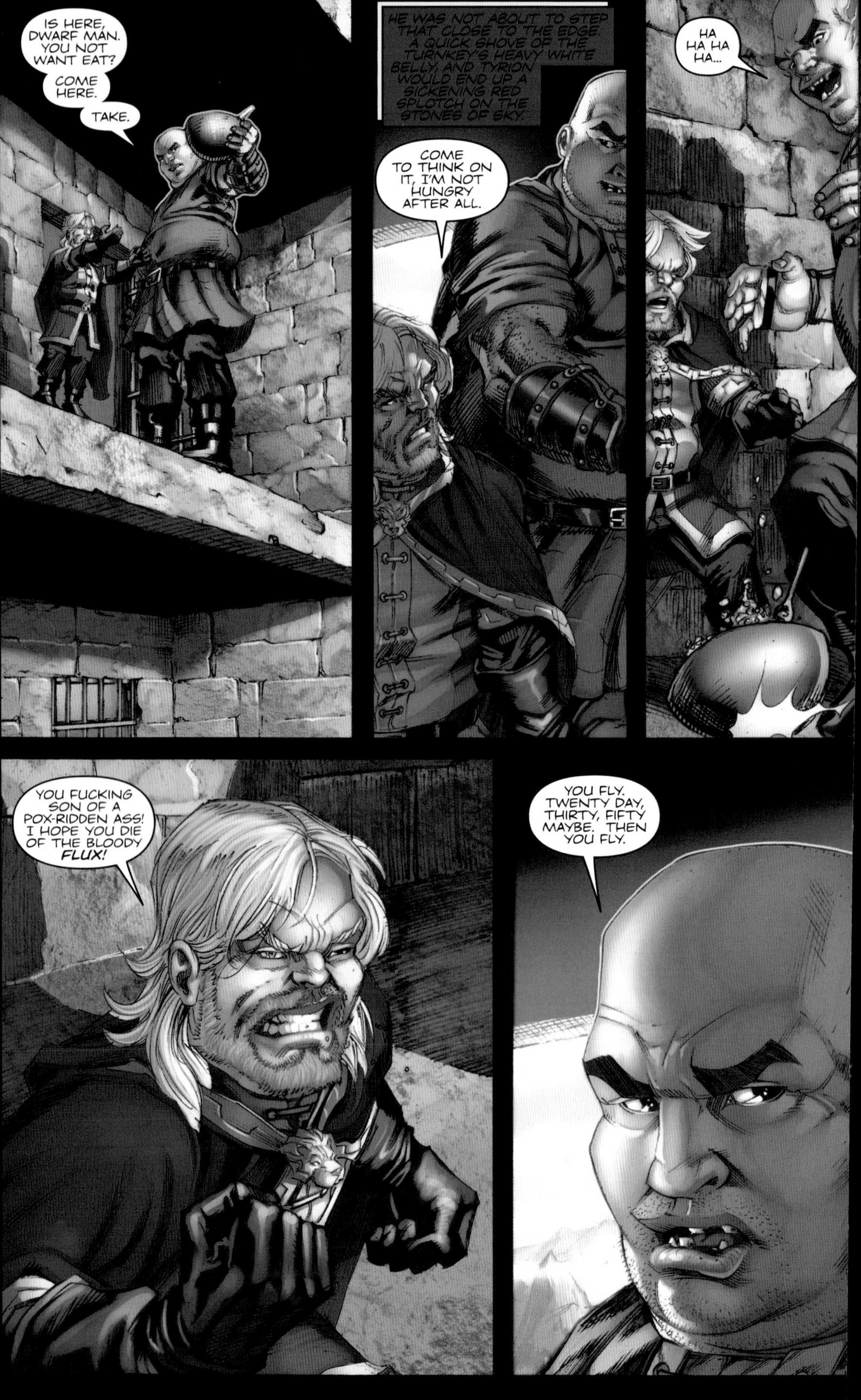
IS HERE, DWARF MAN. YOU NOT WANT EAT?
COME HERE.
TAKE.
HE WAS NOT ABOUT TO STEP THAT CLOSE TO THE EDGE. A QUICK SHOVE OF THE TURNKEY'S HEAVY WHITE BELLY, AND TYRION WOULD END UP A SICKENING RED SPLOTCH ON THE STONES OF SKY.
COME TO THINK ON IT, I'M NOT HUNGRY AFTER ALL.
HA HA HA HA...
YOU FUCKING SON OF A POX-RIDDEN ASS! I HOPE YOU DIE OF THE BLOODY FLUX!
YOU FLY. TWENTY DAY, THIRTY, FIFTY MAYBE. THEN YOU FLY.

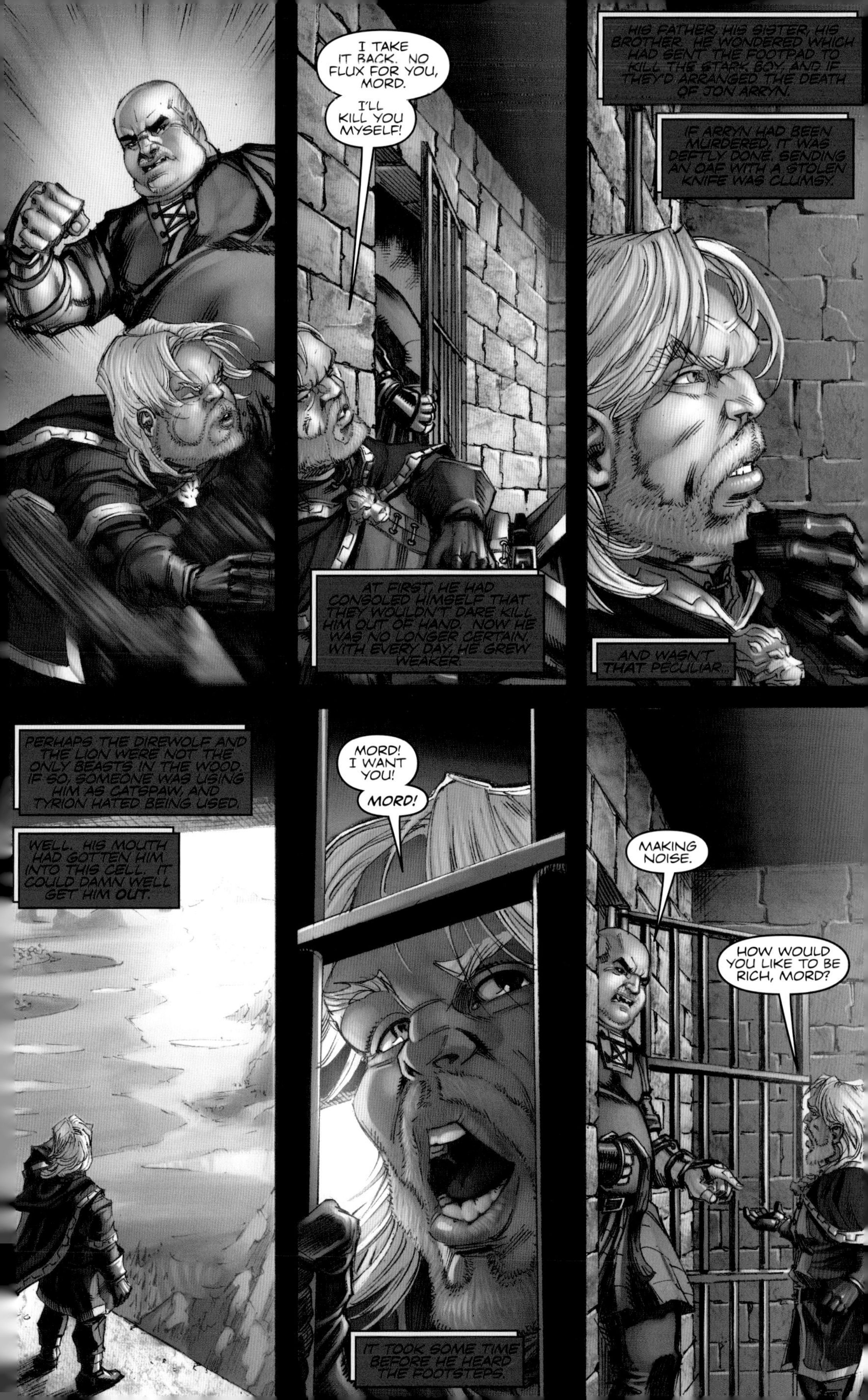
I TAKE IT BACK. NO FLUX FOR YOU, MORD.
I'LL KILL YOU MYSELF!
AT FIRST, HE HAD CONSOLED HIMSELF THAT THEY WOULDN'T DARE KILL HIM OUT OF HAND. NOW HE WAS NO LONGER CERTAIN. WITH EVERY DAY, HE GREW WEAKER.
HIS FATHER, HIS SISTER, HIS BROTHER. HE WONDERED WHICH HAD SENT THE FOOTPAD TO KILL THE STARK BOY, AND IF THEY'D ARRANGED THE DEATH OF JON ARRYN.
IF ARRYN HAD BEEN MURDERED, IT WAS DEFTLY DONE. SENDING AN OAF WITH A STOLEN KNIFE WAS CLUMSY.
AND WASN'T THAT PECULIAR...
PERHAPS THE DIREWOLF AND THE LION WERE NOT THE ONLY BEASTS IN THE WOOD. IF SO, SOMEONE WAS USING HIM AS CATSPAW, AND TYRION HATED BEING USED.
WELL. HIS MOUTH HAD GOTTEN HIM INTO THIS CELL. IT COULD DAMN WELL GET HIM OUT.
MORD! I WANT YOU!
MORD!
IT TOOK SOME TIME BEFORE HE HEARD THE FOOTSTEPS.
MAKING NOISE.
HOW WOULD YOU LIKE TO BE RICH, MORD?

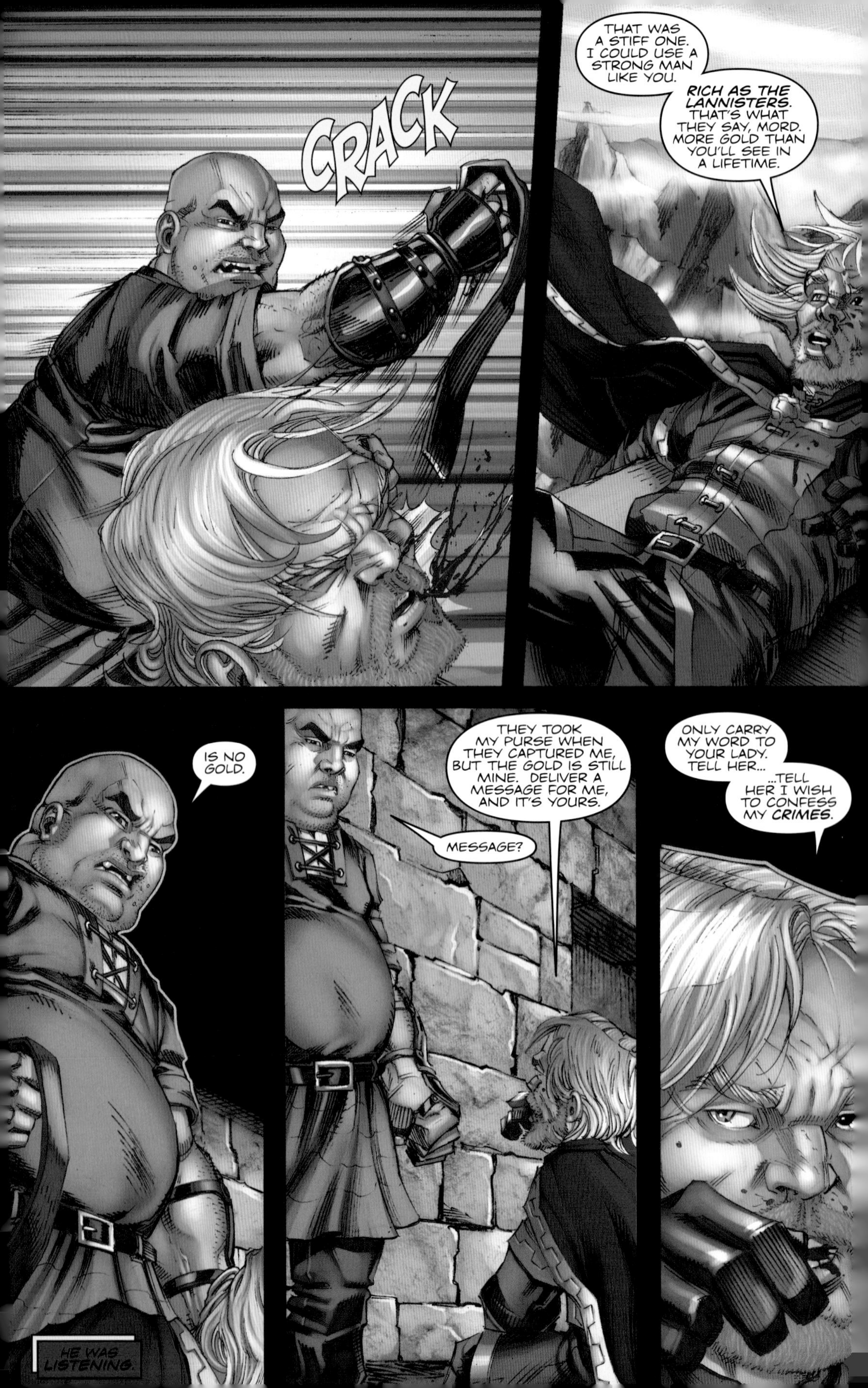
CRACK
THAT WAS A STIFF ONE. I COULD USE A STRONG MAN LIKE YOU.
RICH AS THE LANNISTERS. THAT'S WHAT THEY SAY, MORD. MORE GOLD THAN YOU'LL SEE IN A LIFETIME.
IS NO GOLD.
HE WAS LISTENING.
THEY TOOK MY PURSE WHEN THEY CAPTURED ME, BUT THE GOLD IS STILL MINE. DELIVER A MESSAGE FOR ME, AND IT'S YOURS.
MESSAGE?
ONLY CARRY MY WORD TO YOUR LADY. TELL HER...
...TELL HER I WISH TO CONFESS MY CRIMES.

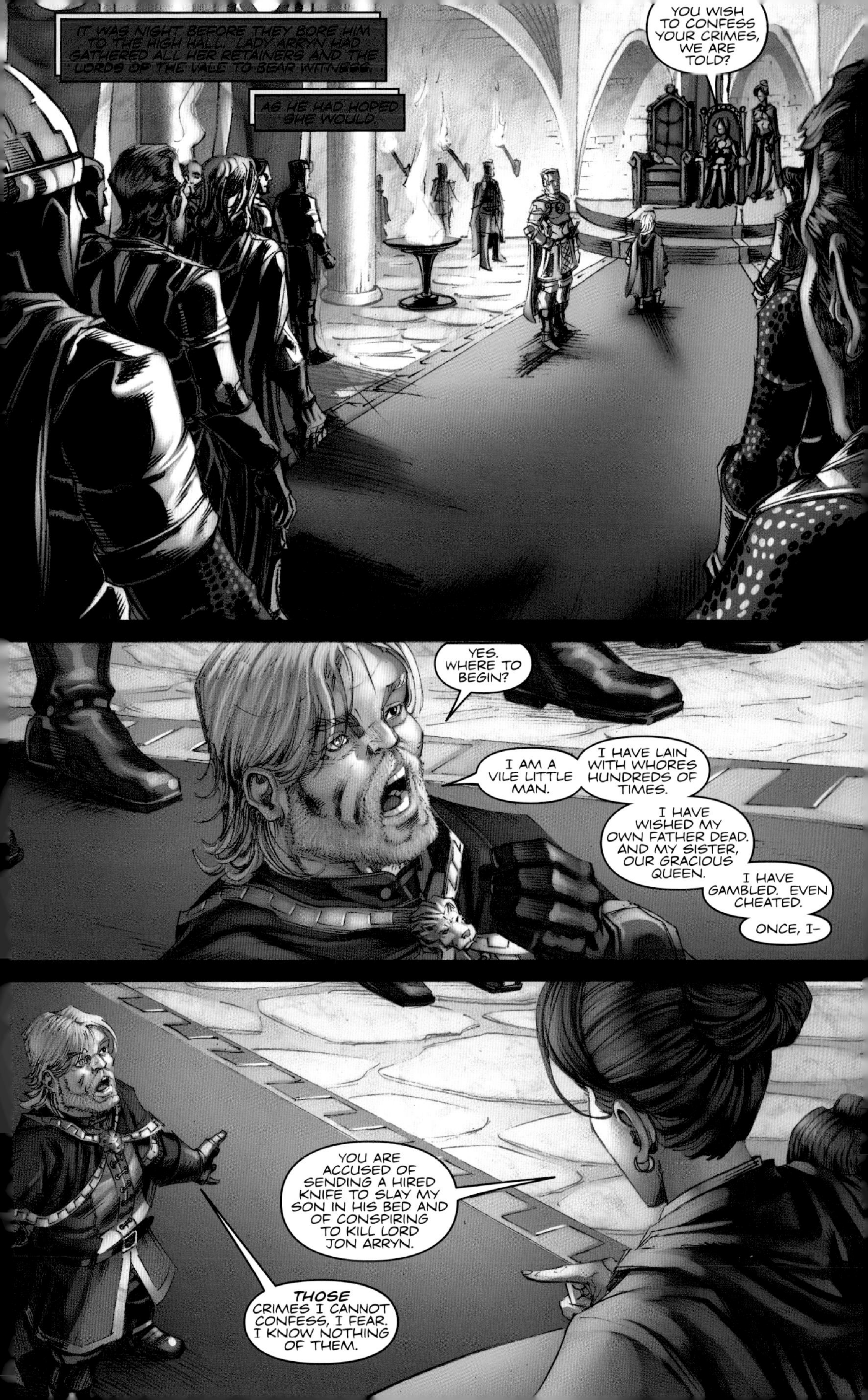
IT WAS NIGHT BEFORE THEY BORE HIM TO THE HIGH HALL. LADY ARRYN HAD GATHERED ALL HER RETAINERS AND THE LORDS OF THE VALE TO BEAR WITNESS.
AS HE HAD HOPED SHE WOULD.
YOU WISH TO CONFESS YOUR CRIMES, WE ARE TOLD?
YES. WHERE TO BEGIN?
I AM A VILE LITTLE MAN.
I HAVE LAIN WITH WHORES HUNDREDS OF TIMES.
I HAVE WISHED MY OWN FATHER DEAD. AND MY SISTER, OUR GRACIOUS QUEEN.
I HAVE GAMBLED. EVEN CHEATED.
ONCE, I–
YOU ARE ACCUSED OF SENDING A HIRED KNIFE TO SLAY MY SON IN HIS BED AND OF CONSPIRING TO KILL LORD JON ARRYN.
THOSE CRIMES I CANNOT CONFESS, I FEAR. I KNOW NOTHING OF THEM.

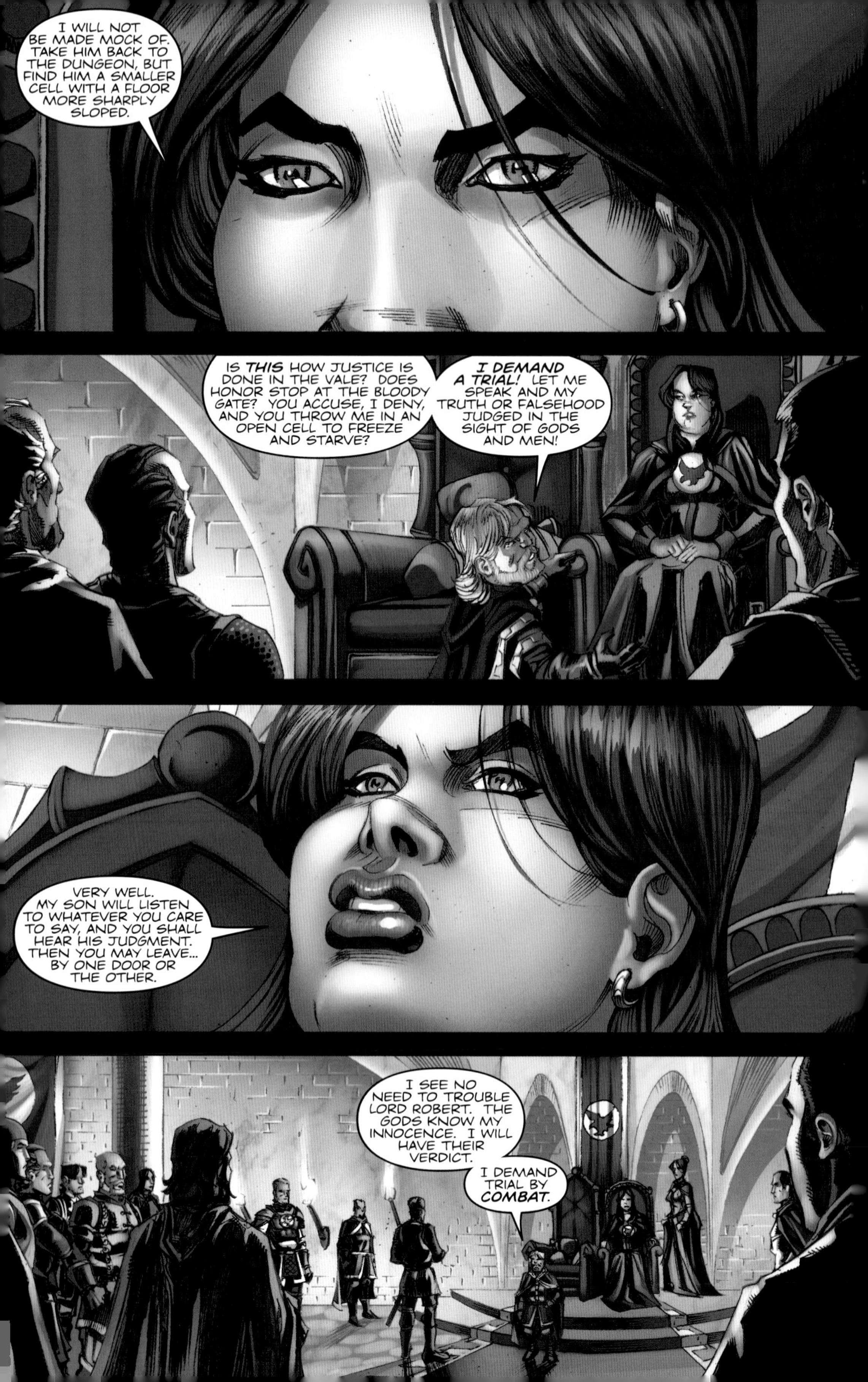
I WILL NOT BE MADE MOCK OF. TAKE HIM BACK TO THE DUNGEON, BUT FIND HIM A SMALLER CELL WITH A FLOOR MORE SHARPLY SLOPED.
IS THIS HOW JUSTICE IS DONE IN THE VALE? DOES HONOR STOP AT THE BLOODY GATE? YOU ACCUSE, I DENY, AND YOU THROW ME IN AN OPEN CELL TO FREEZE AND STARVE?
I DEMAND A TRIAL! LET ME SPEAK AND MY TRUTH OR FALSEHOOD JUDGED IN THE SIGHT OF GODS AND MEN!
VERY WELL. MY SON WILL LISTEN TO WHATEVER YOU CARE TO SAY, AND YOU SHALL HEAR HIS JUDGMENT. THEN YOU MAY LEAVE... BY ONE DOOR OR THE OTHER.
I SEE NO NEED TO TROUBLE LORD ROBERT. THE GODS KNOW MY INNOCENCE. I WILL HAVE THEIR VERDICT.
I DEMAND TRIAL BY COMBAT.

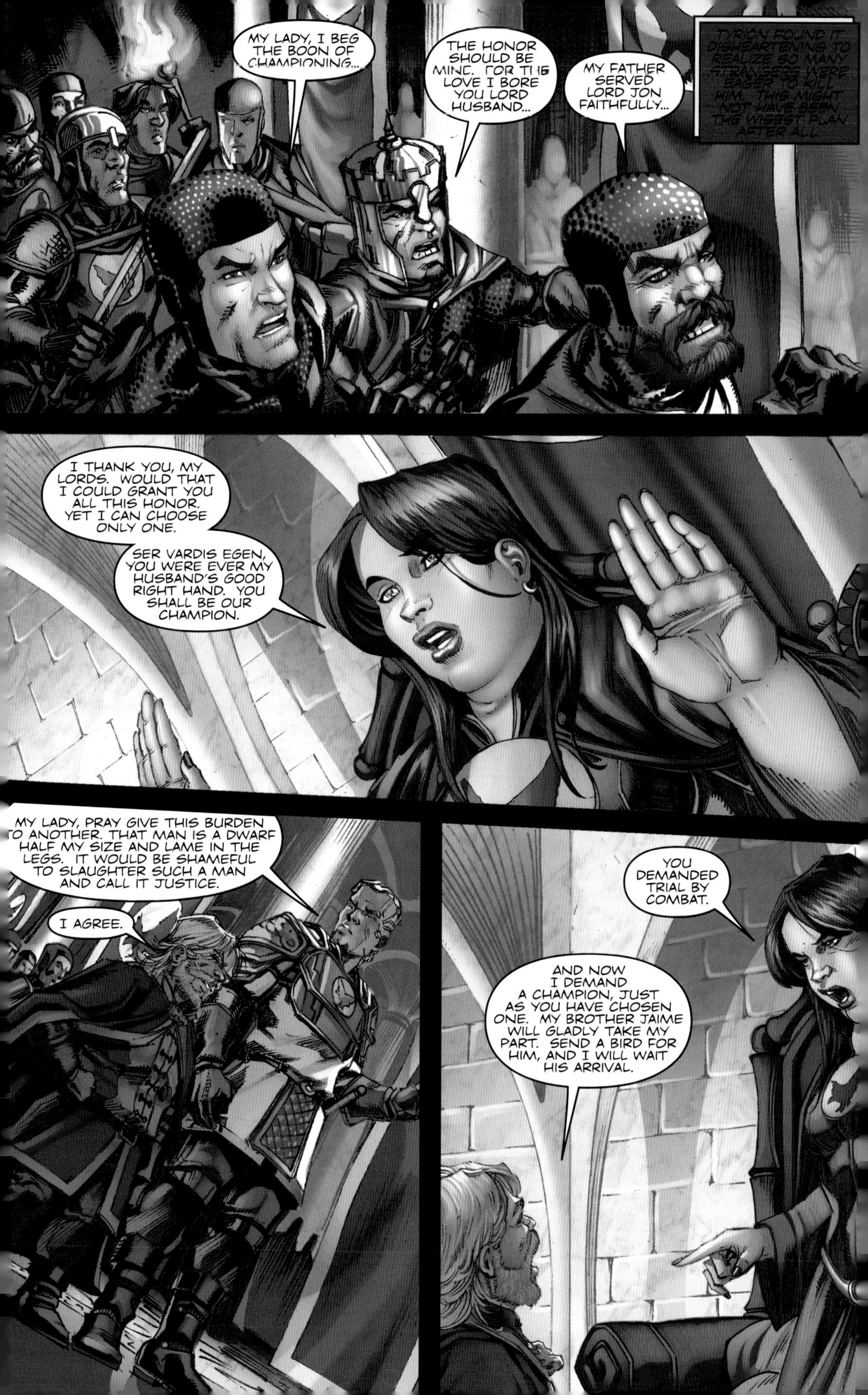
MY LADY, I BEG THE BOON OF CHAMPIONING...
THE HONOR SHOULD BE MINE. FOR THE LOVE I BORE YOU LORD HUSBAND...
MY FATHER SERVED LORD JON FAITHFULLY...
TYRION FOUND IT DISHEARTENING TO REALIZE SO MANY STRANGERS WERE EAGER TO KILL HIM. THIS MIGHT NOT HAVE BEEN THE WISEST PLAN AFTER ALL.
I THANK YOU, MY LORDS. WOULD THAT I COULD GRANT YOU ALL THIS HONOR. YET I CAN CHOOSE ONLY ONE.
SER VARDIS EGEN, YOU WERE EVER MY HUSBAND'S GOOD RIGHT HAND. YOU SHALL BE OUR CHAMPION.
MY LADY, PRAY GIVE THIS BURDEN TO ANOTHER. THAT MAN IS A DWARF HALF MY SIZE AND LAME IN THE LEGS. IT WOULD BE SHAMEFUL TO SLAUGHTER SUCH A MAN AND CALL IT JUSTICE.
I AGREE.
YOU DEMANDED TRIAL BY COMBAT.
AND NOW I DEMAND A CHAMPION, JUST AS YOU HAVE CHOSEN ONE. MY BROTHER JAIME WILL GLADLY TAKE MY PART. SEND A BIRD FOR HIM, AND I WILL WAIT HIS ARRIVAL.

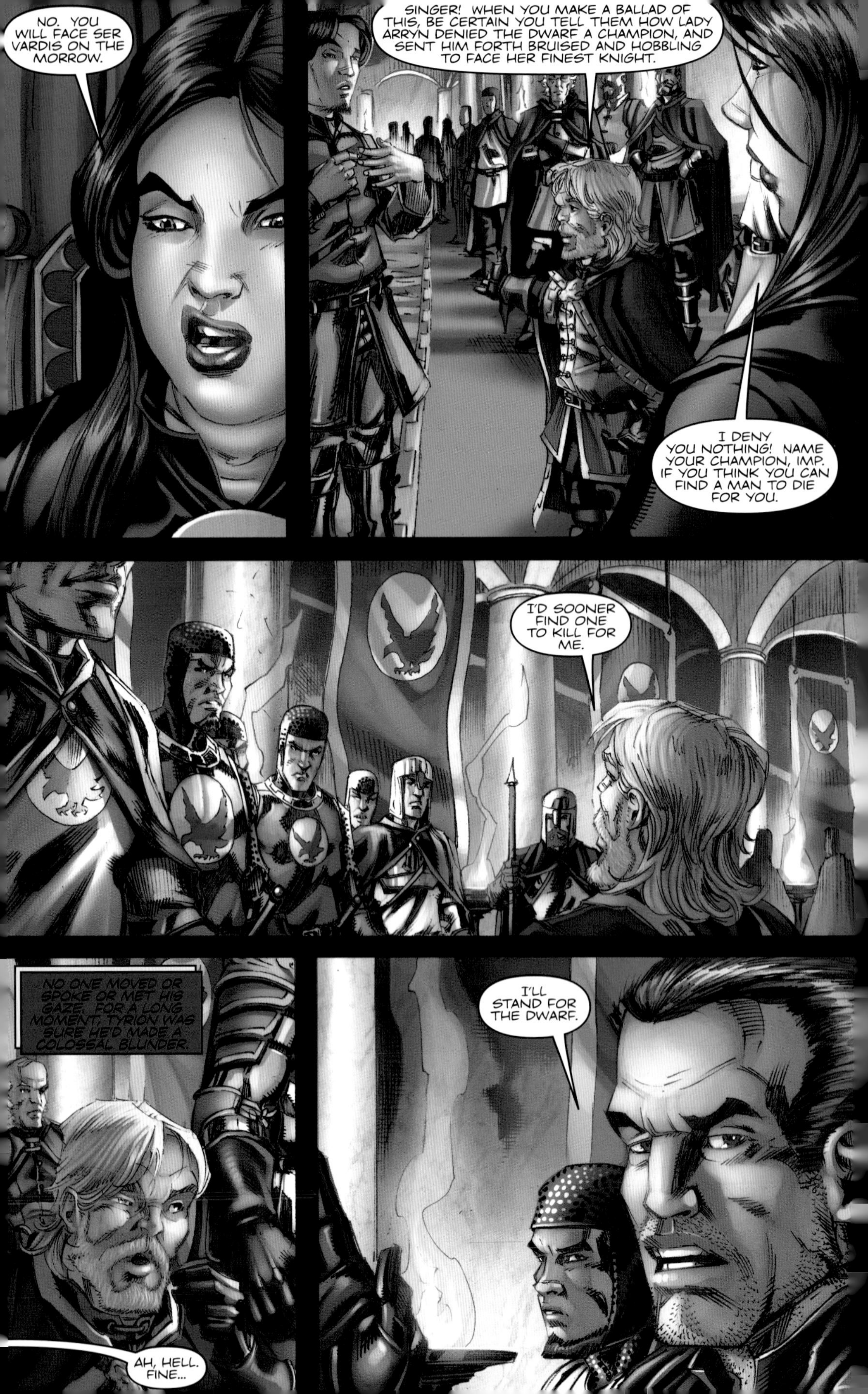
NO. YOU WILL FACE SER VARDIS ON THE MORROW.
SINGER! WHEN YOU MAKE A BALLAD OF THIS, BE CERTAIN YOU TELL THEM HOW LADY ARRYN DENIED THE DWARF A CHAMPION, AND SENT HIM FORTH BRUISED AND HOBBLING TO FACE HER FINEST KNIGHT.
I DENY YOU NOTHING! NAME YOUR CHAMPION, IMP. IF YOU THINK YOU CAN FIND A MAN TO DIE FOR YOU.
I'D SOONER FIND ONE TO KILL FOR ME.
NO ONE MOVED OR SPOKE OR MET HIS GAZE. FOR A LONG MOMENT, TYRION WAS SURE HE'D MADE A COLOSSAL BLUNDER.
AH, HELL. FINE...
I'LL STAND FOR THE DWARF.

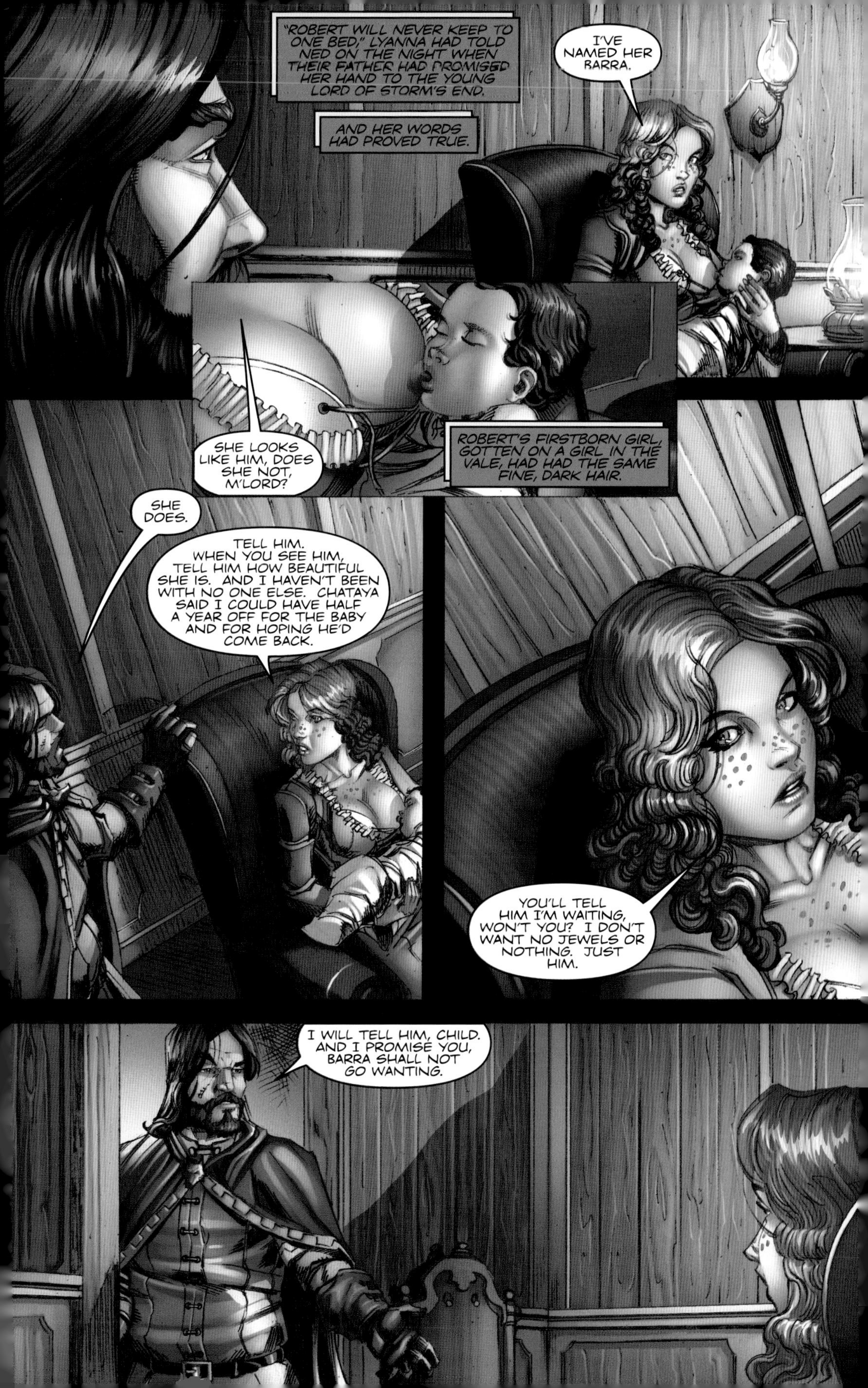
"ROBERT WILL NEVER KEEP TO ONE BED," LYANNA HAD TOLD NED ON THE NIGHT WHEN THEIR FATHER HAD PROMISED HER HAND TO THE YOUNG LORD OF STORM'S END.
AND HER WORDS HAD PROVED TRUE.
I'VE NAMED HER BARRA.
SHE LOOKS LIKE HIM, DOES SHE NOT, M'LORD?
ROBERT'S FIRSTBORN GIRL, GOTTEN ON A GIRL IN THE VALE, HAD HAD THE SAME FINE, DARK HAIR.
SHE DOES.
TELL HIM. WHEN YOU SEE HIM, TELL HIM HOW BEAUTIFUL SHE IS. AND I HAVEN'T BEEN WITH NO ONE ELSE. CHATAYA SAID I COULD HAVE HALF A YEAR OFF FOR THE BABY AND FOR HOPING HE'D COME BACK.
YOU'LL TELL HIM I'M WAITING, WON'T YOU? I DON'T WANT NO JEWELS OR NOTHING. JUST HIM.
I WILL TELL HIM, CHILD. AND I PROMISE YOU, BARRA SHALL NOT GO WANTING.

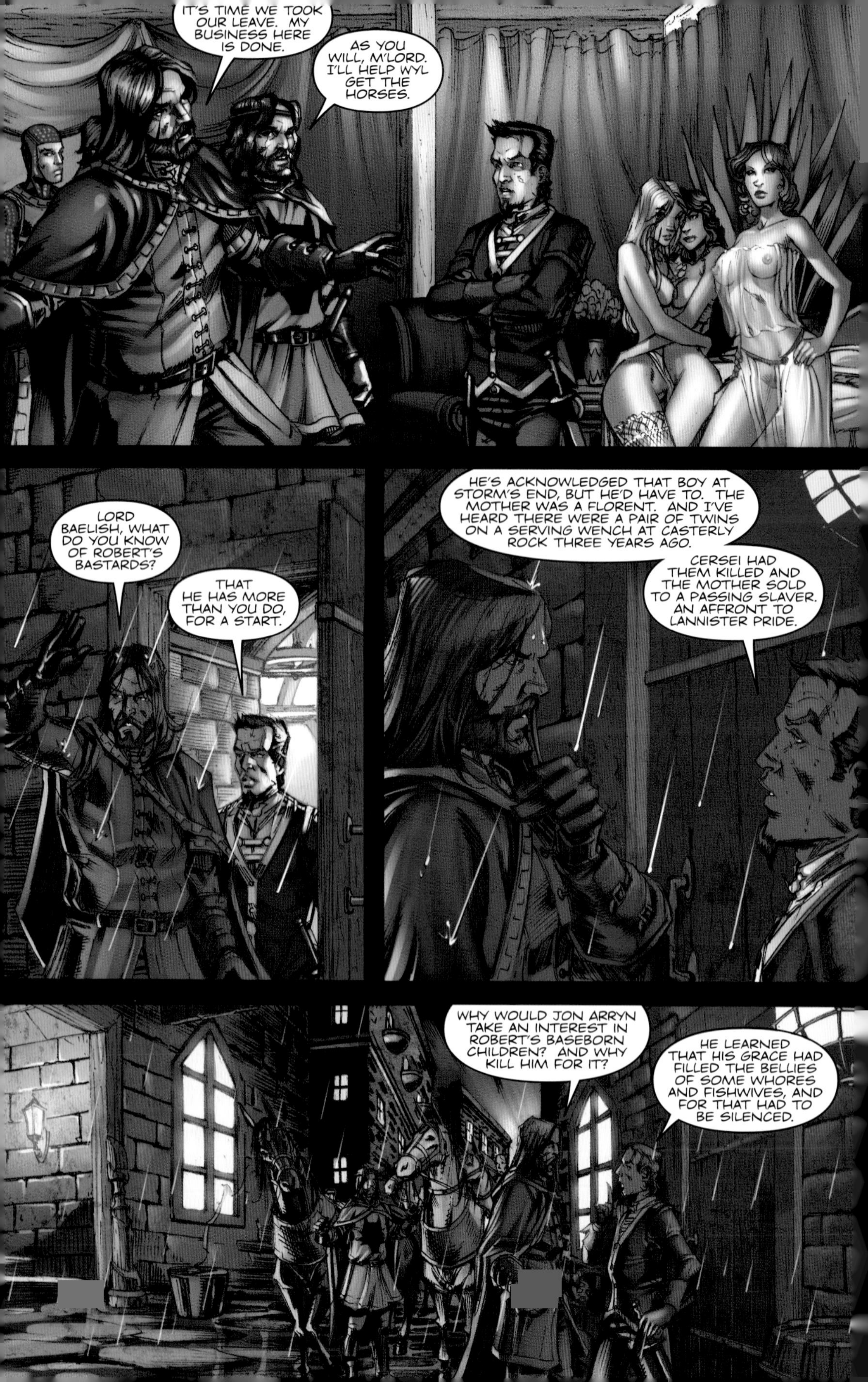
IT'S TIME WE TOOK OUR LEAVE. MY BUSINESS HERE IS DONE.
AS YOU WILL, M'LORD. I'LL HELP WYL GET THE HORSES.
LORD BAELISH, WHAT DO YOU KNOW OF ROBERT'S BASTARDS?
THAT HE HAS MORE THAN YOU DO, FOR A START.
HE'S ACKNOWLEDGED THAT BOY AT STORM'S END, BUT HE'D HAVE TO. THE MOTHER WAS A FLORENT. AND I'VE HEARD THERE WERE A PAIR OF TWINS ON A SERVING WENCH AT CASTERLY ROCK THREE YEARS AGO.
CERSEI HAD THEM KILLED AND THE MOTHER SOLD TO A PASSING SLAVER. AN AFFRONT TO LANNISTER PRIDE.
WHY WOULD JON ARRYN TAKE AN INTEREST IN ROBERT'S BASEBORN CHILDREN? AND WHY KILL HIM FOR IT?
HE LEARNED THAT HIS GRACE HAD FILLED THE BELLIES OF SOME WHORES AND FISHWIVES, AND FOR THAT HAD TO BE SILENCED.

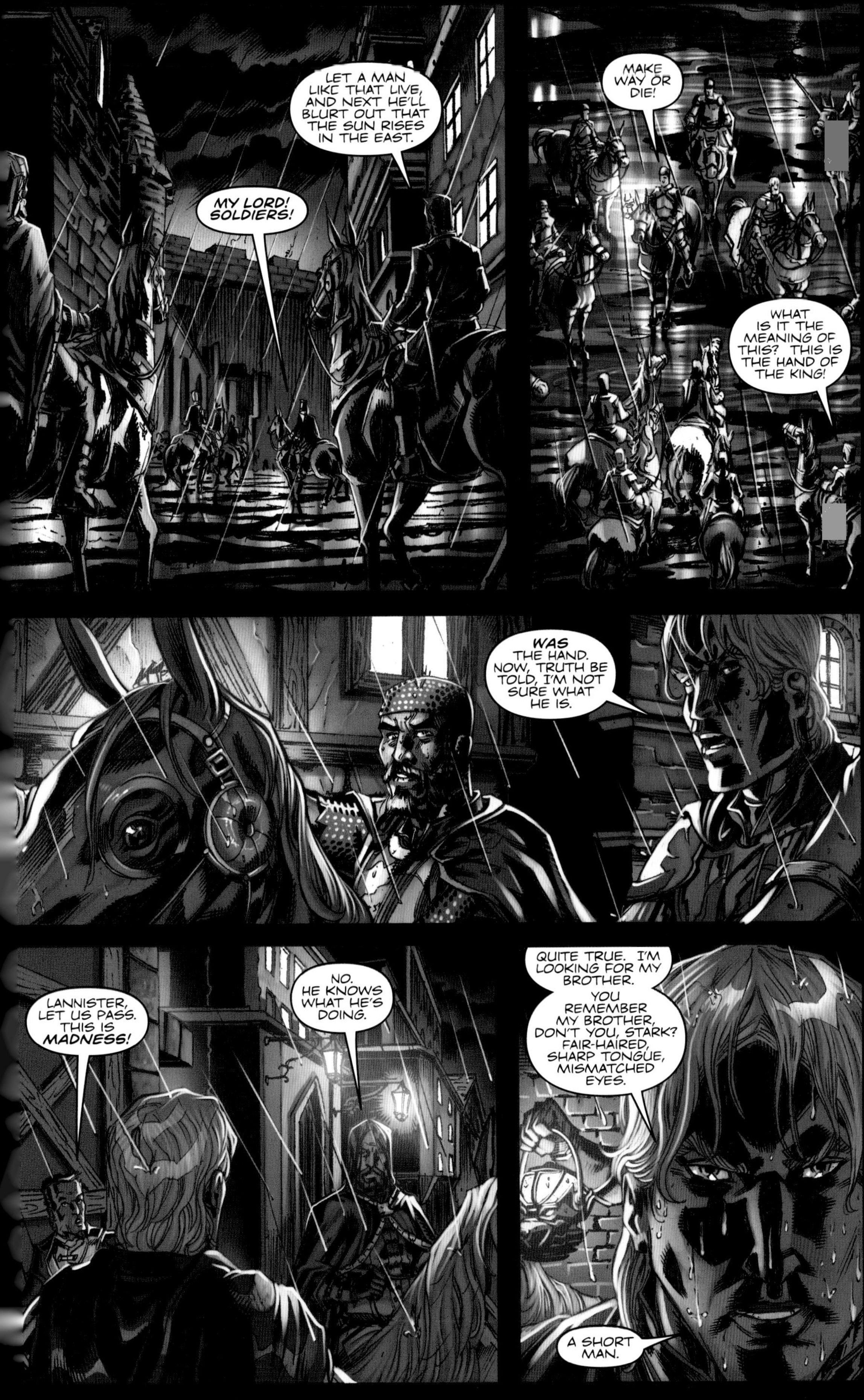
LET A MAN LIKE THAT LIVE, AND NEXT HE'LL BLURT OUT THAT THE SUN RISES IN THE EAST.
MY LORD! SOLDIERS!
MAKE WAY OR DIE!
WHAT IS IT THE MEANING OF THIS? THIS IS THE HAND OF THE KING!
WAS THE HAND. NOW, TRUTH BE TOLD, I'M NOT SURE WHAT HE IS.
LANNISTER, LET US PASS. THIS IS MADNESS!
NO. HE KNOWS WHAT HE'S DOING.
QUITE TRUE. I'M LOOKING FOR MY BROTHER.
YOU REMEMBER MY BROTHER, DON'T YOU, STARK? FAIR-HAIRED, SHARP TONGUE, MISMATCHED EYES.
A SHORT MAN.

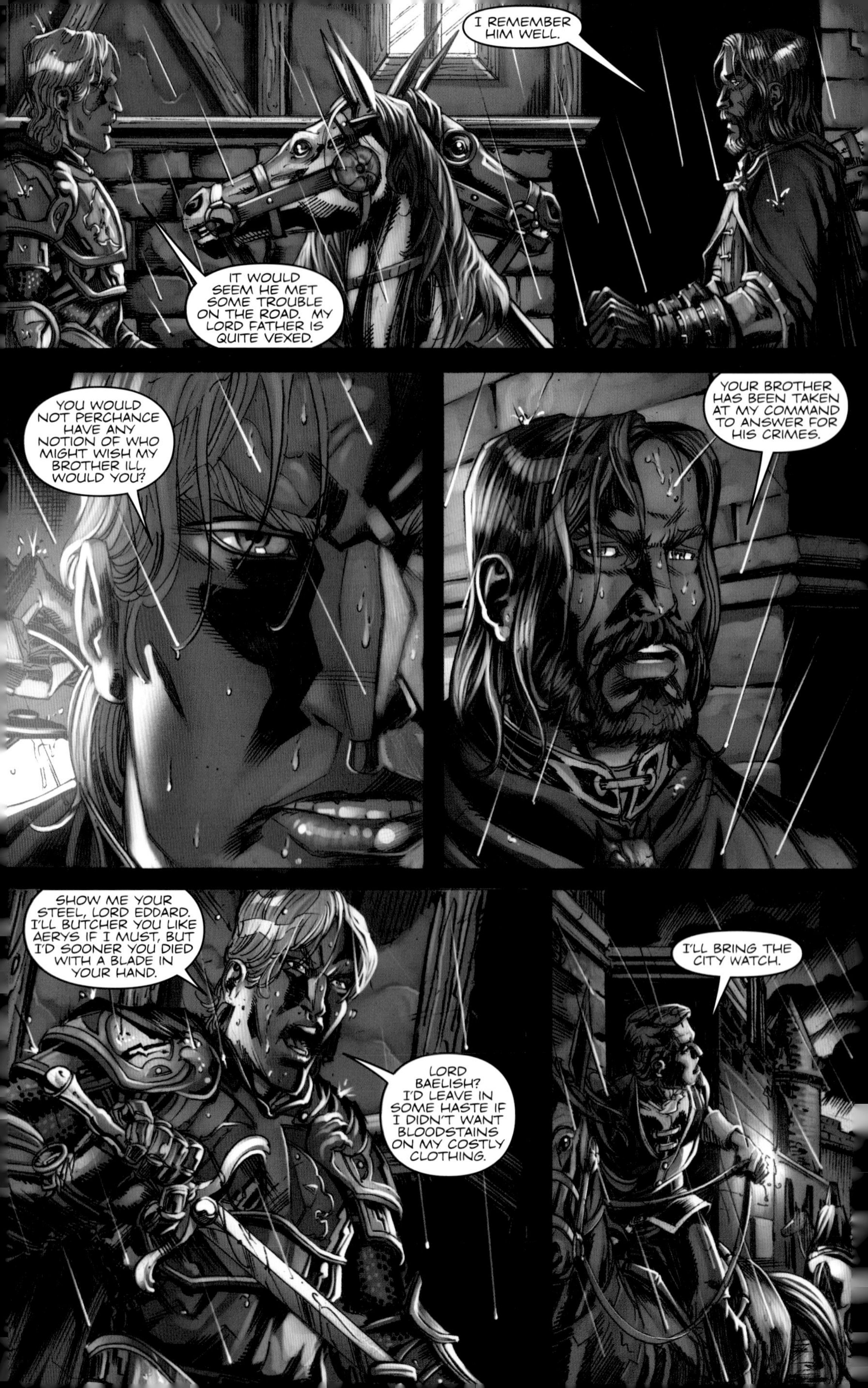
I REMEMBER HIM WELL.
IT WOULD SEEM HE MET SOME TROUBLE ON THE ROAD. MY LORD FATHER IS QUITE VEXED.
YOU WOULD NOT PERCHANCE HAVE ANY NOTION OF WHO MIGHT WISH MY BROTHER ILL, WOULD YOU?
YOUR BROTHER HAS BEEN TAKEN AT MY COMMAND TO ANSWER FOR HIS CRIMES.
SHOW ME YOUR STEEL, LORD EDDARD. I'LL BUTCHER YOU LIKE AERYS IF I MUST, BUT I'D SOONER YOU DIED WITH A BLADE IN YOUR HAND.
LORD BAELISH? I'D LEAVE IN SOME HASTE IF I DIDN'T WANT BLOODSTAINS ON MY COSTLY CLOTHING.
I'LL BRING THE CITY WATCH.

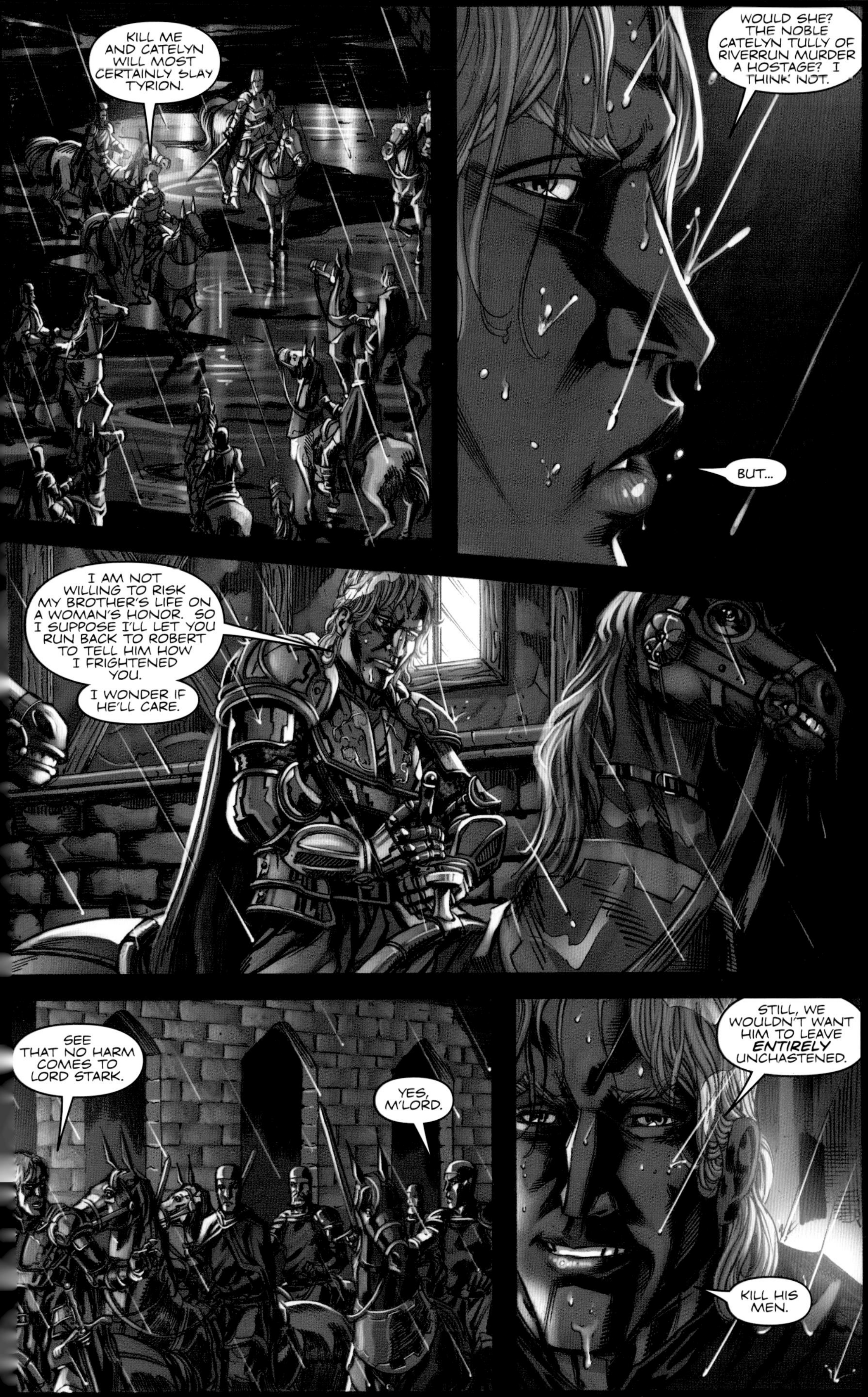
KILL ME AND CATELYN WILL MOST CERTAINLY SLAY TYRION.
WOULD SHE? THE NOBLE CATELYN TULLY OF RIVERRUN MURDER A HOSTAGE? I THINK NOT.
BUT...
I AM NOT WILLING TO RISK MY BROTHER'S LIFE ON A WOMAN'S HONOR. SO I SUPPOSE I'LL LET YOU RUN BACK TO ROBERT TO TELL HIM HOW I FRIGHTENED YOU.
I WONDER IF HE'LL CARE.
SEE THAT NO HARM COMES TO LORD STARK.
YES, M'LORD.
STILL, WE WOULDN'T WANT HIM TO LEAVE *ENTIRELY* UNCHASTENED.
KILL HIS MEN.

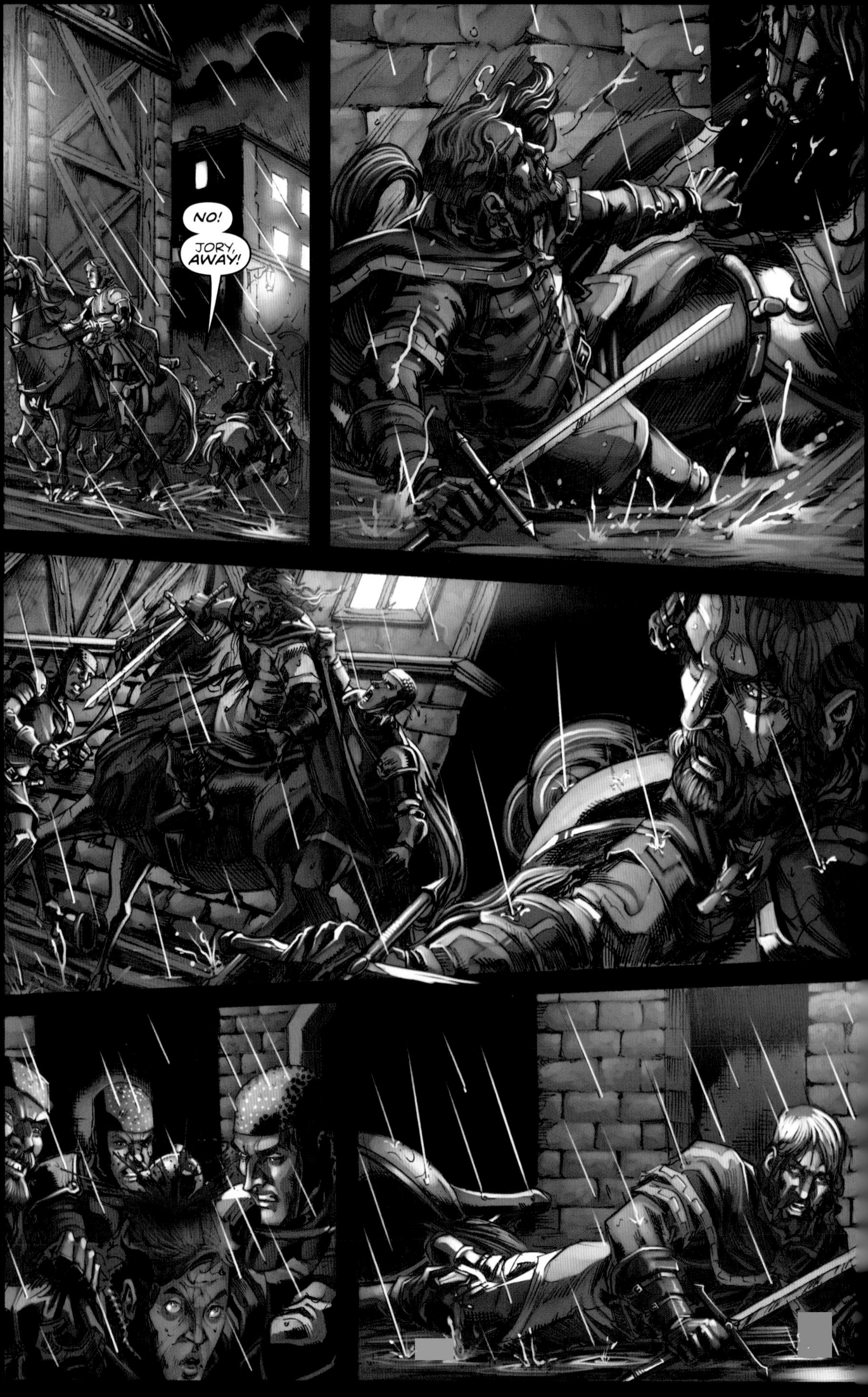
NO!
JORY, AWAY!

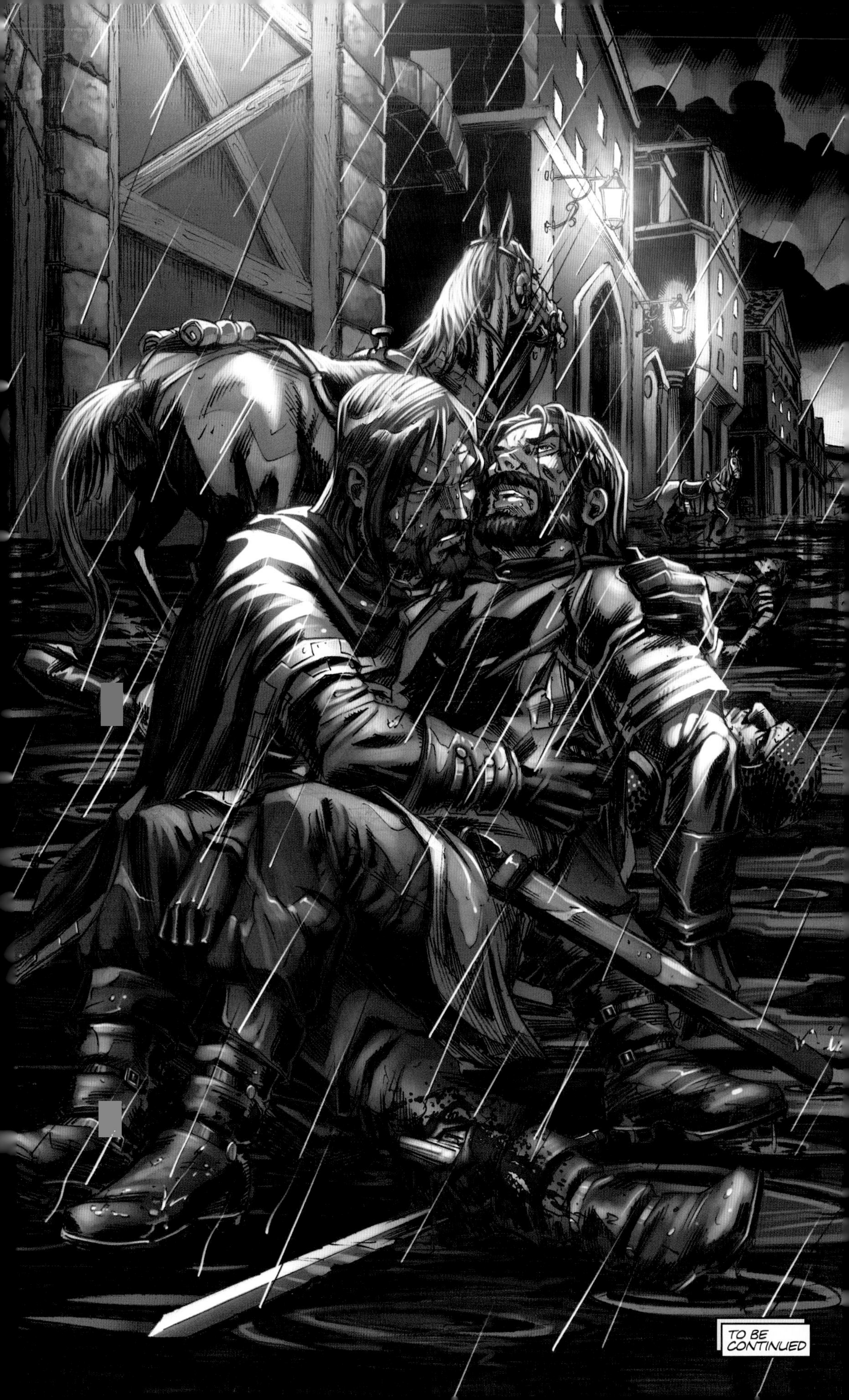
TO BE CONTINUED

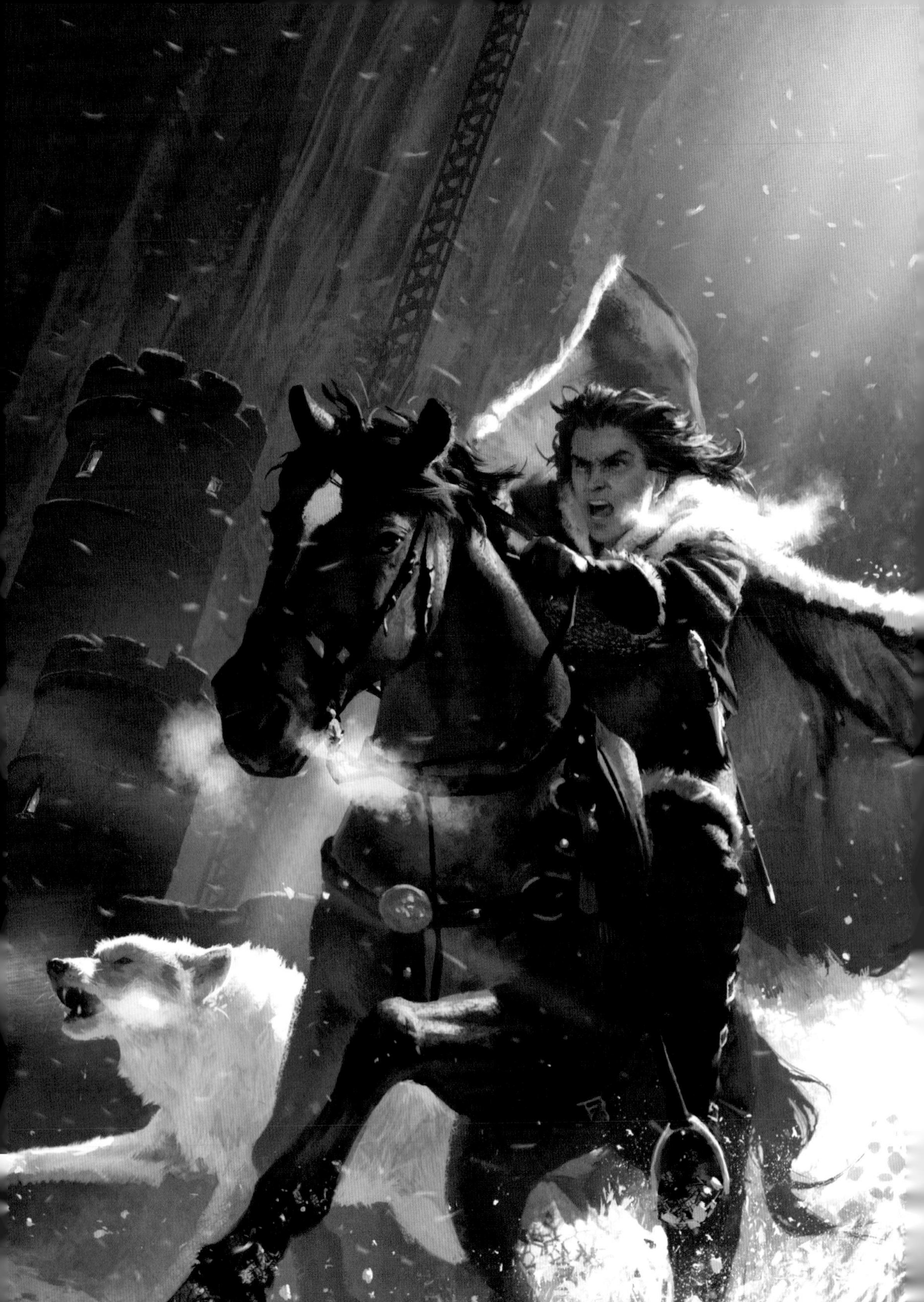

AND NOW...

HERE IS A SPECIAL, INSIDER'S LOOK AT

THE MAKING OF

A GAME OF THRONES

THE GRAPHIC NOVEL

VOLUME 2

WITH COMMENTARY BY:
ANNE GROELL (SERIES EDITOR)
TOMMY PATTERSON (ARTIST)
DANIEL ABRAHAM (ADAPTER)
JASON ULLMEYER (DYNAMITE)

THE BIRTH OF A SCENE—
The Hand's Tourney

What we are going to do this time around is to examine the process of going from text to final graphic pages for one small snippet of the book—and with commentary by various members of the creative team—so you can get a sense of how the step-by-step process works behind the scenes.

For this exercise, we will be using the first five pages of the Hand's Tourney because it is one of the things we are proudest of. It is a scene of action, pageantry, and glorious detail—and also a scene that was trickily hard to adapt given the sheer scope of what George has packed into his pages.

Here, so you can see what Daniel was up against, is the relevant passage from the novel:

SANSA

Sansa rode to the Hand's tourney with Septa Mordane and Jeyne Poole, in a litter with curtains of yellow silk so fine she could see right through them. They turned the whole world gold. Beyond the city walls, a hundred pavilions had been raised beside the river, and the common folk came out in the thousands to watch the games. The splendor of it all took Sansa's breath away; the shining armor, the great chargers caparisoned in silver and gold, the shouts of the crowd, the banners snapping in the wind...and the knights themselves, the knights most of all.

"It is better than the songs," she whispered when they found the places that her father had promised her, among the high lords and ladies. Sansa was dressed beautifully that day, in a green gown that brought out the auburn of her hair, and she knew they were looking at her and smiling.

They watched the heroes of a hundred songs ride forth, each more fabulous than the last. The seven knights of the Kingsguard took the field, all but Jaime Lannister in scaled armor the color of milk, their cloaks as white as fresh-fallen snow. Ser Jaime wore the white cloak as well, but beneath it he was shining gold from head to foot, with a lion's-head helm and a golden sword. Ser Gregor Clegane, the Mountain That Rides, thundered past them like an avalanche. Sansa remembered Lord Yohn Royce, who had guested at Winterfell two years before. "His armor is bronze, thousands and thousands of years old, engraved with magic runes that ward him against harm," she whispered to Jeyne. Septa Mordane pointed out Lord Jason Mallister, in indigo chased with silver, the wings of an eagle on his helm. He had cut down three of Rhaegar's bannermen on the Trident. The girls giggled over the warrior priest Thoros of Myr, with his flapping red robes and shaven head, until the septa told them that he had once scaled the walls of Pyke with a flaming sword in hand.

Other riders Sansa did not know; hedge knights from the Fingers and

Highgarden and the mountains of Dorne, unsung freeriders and new-made squires, the younger sons of high lords and the heirs of lesser houses. Younger men, most had done no great deeds as yet, but Sansa and Jeyne agreed that one day the Seven Kingdoms would resound to the sound of their names. Ser Balon Swann. Lord Bryce Caron of the Marches. Bronze Yohn's heir, Ser Andar Royce, and his younger brother Ser Robar, their silvered steel plate filigreed in bronze with the same ancient runes that warded their father. The twins Ser Horas and Ser Hobber, whose shields displayed the grape cluster sigil of the Redwynes, burgundy on blue. Patrek Mallister, Lord Jason's son. Six Freys of the Crossing: Ser Jared, Ser Hosteen, Ser Danwell, Ser Emmon, Ser Theo, Ser Perwyn, sons and grandsons of old Lord Walder Frey, and his bastard son Martyn Rivers as well.

Jeyne Poole confessed herself frightened by the look of Jalabhar Xho, an exile prince from the Summer Isles who wore a cape of green and scarlet feathers over skin as dark as night, but when she saw young Lord Beric Dondarrion, with his hair like red gold and his black shield slashed by lightning, she pronounced herself willing to marry him on the instant.

The Hound entered the lists as well, and so too the king's brother, handsome Lord Renly of Storm's End. Jory, Alyn, and Harwin rode for Winterfell and the north. "Jory looks a beggar among these others," Septa Mordane sniffed when he appeared. Sansa could only agree. Jory's armor was blue-grey plate without device or ornament, and a thin grey cloak hung from his shoulders like a soiled rag. Yet he acquitted himself well, unhorsing Horas Redwyne in his first joust and one of the Freys in his second. In his third match, he rode three passes at a freerider named Lothor Brune whose armor was as drab as his own. Neither man lost his seat, but Brune's lance was steadier and his blows better placed, and the king gave him the victory. Alyn and Harwin fared less well; Harwin was unhorsed in his first tilt by Ser Meryn of the Kingsguard, while Alyn fell to Ser Balon Swann.

The jousting went all day and into the dusk, the hooves of the great warhorses pounding down the lists until the field was a ragged wasteland of torn earth. A dozen times Jeyne and Sansa cried out in unison as riders crashed together, lances exploding into splinters while the commons screamed for their favorites. Jeyne covered her eyes whenever a man fell, like a frightened little girl, but Sansa was made of sterner stuff. A great lady knew how to behave at tournaments. Even Septa Mordane noted her composure and nodded in approval.

The Kingslayer rode brilliantly. He overthrew Ser Andar Royce and the Marcher Lord Bryce Caron as easily as if he were riding at rings, and then took a hard-fought match from white-haired Barristan Selmy, who had won his first two tilts against men thirty and forty years his junior.

Sandor Clegane and his immense brother, Ser Gregor the Mountain, seemed unstoppable as well, riding down one foe after the next in ferocious style. The most terrifying moment of the day came during Ser Gregor's second joust, when his lance rode up and struck a young knight from the Vale under the gorget with such force that it drove through his throat, killing him instantly. The youth fell not ten feet from where Sansa was seated. The point of Ser Gregor's lance had snapped off in his neck, and his life's blood flowed out in slow pulses, each weaker than the one before. His armor was shiny new; a bright streak of fire ran down his outstretched arm, as the steel caught the light. Then the sun went behind a cloud, and it was gone. His cloak was blue, the color of the sky on a clear summer's day, trimmed with a border of crescent moons, but as his blood seeped into it, the cloth darkened and the moons turned red, one by one.

Jeyne Poole wept so hysterically that Septa Mordane finally took her off to regain her composure, but Sansa sat with her hands folded in her lap, watching with a strange fascination. She had never seen a man die before. She ought to be crying too, she thought, but the tears would not come. Perhaps she had used up all her tears for Lady and Bran. It would be different if it had been Jory or Ser Rodrik or Father, she told herself. The young knight in the blue cloak was nothing to her, some stranger from the Vale of Arryn whose name she had forgotten as soon as she heard it. And now the world would forget his name too, Sansa realized; there would be no songs sung for him. That was sad.

After they carried off the body, a boy with a spade ran onto the field and shoveled dirt over the spot where he had fallen, to cover up the blood. Then the jousts resumed.

Ser Balon Swann also fell to Gregor, and Lord Renly to the Hound. Renly was unhorsed so violently that he seemed to fly backward off his charger, legs in the air. His head hit the ground with an audible crack that made the crowd gasp, but it was just the golden antler on his helm. One of the tines had snapped off beneath him. When Lord Renly climbed to his feet, the commons cheered wildly, for King Robert's handsome young brother was a great favorite. He handed the broken tine to his conqueror with a gracious bow. The Hound snorted and tossed the broken antler into the crowd, where the commons began to punch and claw over the little bit of gold, until Lord Renly walked out among them and restored the peace. By then Septa Mordane had returned, alone. Jeyne had been feeling ill, she explained; she had helped her back to the castle. Sansa had almost forgotten about Jeyne.

Later a hedge knight in a checkered cloak disgraced himself by killing Beric Dondarrion's horse, and was declared forfeit. Lord Beric shifted his saddle to a new mount, only to be knocked right off it by Thoros of Myr. Ser Aron Santagar and Lothor Brune tilted thrice without result; Ser Aron fell afterward to Lord Jason Mallister, and Brune to Yohn Royce's younger son, Robar.

In the end it came down to four; the Hound and his monstrous brother Gregor, Jaime Lannister the Kingslayer, and Ser Loras Tyrell, the youth they called the Knight of Flowers.

Ser Loras was the youngest son of Mace Tyrell, the Lord of Highgarden and Warden of the South. At sixteen, he was the youngest rider on the field, yet he had unhorsed three knights of the Kingsguard that morning in his first three jousts. Sansa had never seen anyone so beautiful. His plate was intricately fashioned and enameled as a bouquet of a thousand different flowers, and his snow-white stallion was draped in a blanket of red and white roses. After each victory, Ser Loras would remove his helm and ride slowly round the fence, and finally pluck a single white rose from the blanket and toss it to some fair maiden in the crowd.

His last match of the day was against the younger Royce. Ser Robar's ancestral runes proved small protection as Ser Loras split his shield and drove him from his saddle to crash with an awful clangor in the dirt. Robar lay moaning as the victor made his circuit of the field. Finally they called for a litter and carried him off to his tent, dazed and unmoving. Sansa never saw it. Her eyes were only for Ser Loras. When the white horse stopped in front of her, she thought her heart would burst.

To the other maidens he had given white roses, but the one he plucked for her was red. "Sweet lady," he said, "no victory is half so beautiful as you." Sansa took the flower timidly, struck dumb by his gallantry. His hair was a mass of lazy brown curls, his eyes like liquid gold. She inhaled the sweet fragrance of the rose and sat clutching it long after Ser Loras had ridden off.

When Sansa finally looked up, a man was standing over her, staring.

He was short, with a pointed beard and a silver streak in his hair, almost as old as her father. "You must be one of her daughters," he said to her. He had grey-green eyes that did not smile when his mouth did. "You have the Tully look."

"I'm Sansa Stark," she said, ill at ease. The man wore a heavy cloak with a fur collar, fastened with a silver mockingbird, and he had the effortless manner of a high lord, but she did not know him. "I have not had the honor, my lord."

Septa Mordane quickly took a hand. "Sweet child, this is Lord Petyr Baelish, of the king's small council."

"Your mother was *my* queen of beauty once," the man said quietly. His breath smelled of mint. "You have her hair." His fingers brushed against her cheek as he stroked one auburn lock. Quite abruptly he turned and walked away.

By then, the moon was well up and the crowd was tired, so the king decreed that the last three matches would be fought the next morning, before the melee. While the commons began their walk home, talking of the day's jousts and the matches to come on the morrow, the court moved to the riverside to begin the feast. Six monstrous huge aurochs had been roasting for hours, turning slowly on wooden spits while kitchen boys basted them with butter and herbs until the meat crackled and spit. Tables and benches had been raised outside the pavilions, piled high with sweetgrass and strawberries and fresh-baked bread.

Here is how Daniel describes the process:

> The tourney scene had a couple of aspects that were particularly challenging. First off, it's this amazing set piece. It's the Olympics of Westeros, which means all the pageantry and celebration and showmanship, and also blood and death and fear. Finding how to give the full physical scale to it meant finding places to pull back from the story and really let the art blow us away. But at the same time, there's a lot going on here. The death of Ser Hugh of the Vale is an important point in Eddard's story, and there are important character moments with Sansa and Ser Loras and Littlefinger. The narrative density of the scene is amazing.
>
> In addition, the outline we had for the issue called for a reversal from the order in the book. Where the novel has Catelyn abducting Tyrion before the tourney, we were looking at reversing that and doing the tourney first, so as to end the issue with the dramatic moment of Tyrion ringed with swords. And there was one other lovely advantage to this order that wouldn't come clear until the graphic novel came together, which is that the last scene of the previous issue (Eddard wondering why knowledge of Robert's bastard son would have been important enough to die for) would have led directly into watching Ser Hugh of the Vale dying for it. It was a lovely transition, and so it was easy to overlook all the reasons that it actually wouldn't work.

Here is Daniel's initial draft of the adaptation:

GAME OF THRONES SCRIPT
ISSUE NINE
SCRIPT BY DANIEL ABRAHAM
BASED ON ORIGINAL WORK BY GEORGE R. R. MARTIN

PAGE ONE
NOTE TO THE COLORIST: All captions from page one to twelve should be in the
color set to indicate Sansa. Please check previous issues and match.

Panel One:
A small panel. We're close in on Ser Hugh of the Vale, recently knighted former
squire of Jon Arryn. He's lying on his back, looking up at us. He's wearing full plate
and a helmet (both of them bright and new) that lets us see his face. His cloak is
sky blue, with a border of crescent moons where the blood hasn't soaked it. Where
his gorget should protect his neck, there's an open space with a splintered length of
lance in it. We're very close in on him, so we can watch him bloody and dying.

> HUGH:
> nk ahhg ahk

Panel Two:
We're pulled back a little. Ser Hugh is on the ground of a jousting field, choking
to death on his own blood. We can't see the full tourney, but we see two or three
people standing over Ser Hugh. One of them is Gregor Clegane—the Mountain That
Rides—whom we've introduced before. He is also wearing full armor and has the
remains of a shattered lance in his massive hand. Ser Hugh's lance is on the green,
abandoned. One of the horses in full armor and barding is in the background.

> HUGH:
> ah...ak...
> HUGH:...

Panel Three:
Massive panel. We've pulled back even farther, and we can see the whole tourney
laid out before us. It's gigantic. At least a dozen jousting runs, a wide stretch of
cleared ground for the melee, tents, and pavilions. Banners are snapping in the breeze.
In the background, we can see two other knights jousting. There are commoners in
massive swarms, watching by the thousands. In the foreground, Sansa is sitting with
Jeyne Poole and Septa Mordane in among the high lords and ladies watching the
games. Sansa is wearing a green gown that complements her (auburn) hair. Jeyne is
looking away, her hand to her mouth in distress. Sansa is looking on calmly.
Let's pull out the stops here.

CAP: Sansa had ridden to the Hand's tourney with Septa Mordane and Jeyne Poole,
and it had been better than the songs. They watched the heroes of a hundred songs
ride forth, each more fabulous than the last.
CAP: The most terrifying moment of the day came during Ser Gregor Clegane's
second joust, when the point of his lance rode up and struck a young knight from
the Vale under the gorget. Sansa had never seen a man die. She ought to have been
crying, but the tears would not come.
CAP: It would have been different if it had been Jory or Ser Rodrik or Father, she
told herself. This young stranger from the Vale of Arryn was nothing to her. The
world would forget his name now. There would be no songs sung for him.

PAGE TWO

NOTE ON PAGES 2 & 3: This is the highlights from the full tourney. We're seeing action shots, but in every one of them, we should also see action going on around them.

Panel One:
Jaime Lannister on a huge white warhorse. He's wearing golden armor and the while cloak of the Kingsguard and has a fresh lance in his hand. He is beautiful, but he isn't playing to the crowd.

CAP: The Kingslayer rode brilliantly. He overthrew Ser Andar Royce and Marcher Lord Bryce Caron as easily as if he were riding at rings, then took a hard-fought match from Barristan Selmy.

Panel Two:
Sandor Clegane—the Hound—jousting against Renly Barratheon. Renly is wearing a helmet with golden horns and a full suit of armor, and the Hound is knocking him off the horse.

CAP: Ser Renly fell to the Hound with such violence he seemed to fly off his horse. His head hit the ground with an audible crack that made the crowd gasp, but it was only the golden antler on his helm snapping.

Panel Three:
An image of the whole tourney grounds as seen from above, like a crane shot. The details are less important than the impression of size and extent. There should be at least a couple of jousts happening in different lanes. The crowds are huge, and all around, commoners kept apart from the royalty.

CAP: Later, a hedge knight in a checkered cloak disgraced himself by killing Beric Dondarrion's horse and was declared forfeit. Lord Beric put his saddle to a new mount and was promptly knocked off it by the warrior priest Thoros of Mount.
CAP: Ser Aron Santagar and Lothor Brume tilted thrice without result. Ser Aron fell afterward to Lord Jason Mallister, and Brune to Yohn Royce's younger son Robar.

Panel Four:
This is a panel of Ser Loras Tyrell, the Knight of Flowers. We're seeing him out of the context of the tourney, almost like a portrait. He should be looking directly at the viewer, somewhat coyly. His plate mail is elaborately enameled with flowers. His hair is long, brown, and flowing. He's beautiful, with an almost anime-like androgyny.
CAP: In the end it came to four: The Hound and his monstrous brother Gregor, the Kingslayer...
CAP:...And Loras Tyrell, the Knight of Flowers.

PAGE THREE

Panel One:
An evening scene. The moon is rising on the horizon, and the sky is twilight purple. Sansa is sitting where we saw her before, and over her shoulder we can see the jousting lane. Ser Loras Tyrell is on his horse, his hand lifted to the crowd in victory. His horse is covered in a blanket of red and white roses. Another knight, wearing bronze armor inscribed with eldrich runes (Robar Royce) is on the ground, with his squire coming to help him sit up.

CAP: After each victory, Ser Loras would remove his helm, ride slowly around the fence, and finally pluck a white rose and throw it to some fair maiden in the crowd.
CAP: His last match of the day was against the younger Ser Royce, but Sansa's eyes were only for Ser Loras.

Panel Two:
Ser Loras on his horse has stopped before Sansa. He's looking down at her gently. She's staring up at him, awestruck. It's still visibly an evening shot.

CAP: When his white mare stopped in front of her, she thought her heart would burst.
> LORAS:
> Sweet lady, no victory is half
> so beautiful as you.

Panel Three:
Close on Sansa, looking down at her cupped hands. She's holding a red rose from Ser Loras.

CAP: To the other maidens, he had given white roses.
CAP: She inhaled its sweet fragrance and sat clutching it long after he had ridden off.

Panel Four:
Sansa, in the foreground, looking out over the fields. Littlefinger is behind her, looking at her.

> LITTLEFINGER:
> You must be one of her daughters.
> You have the Tully look.

Panel Five:
Close on Sansa, turning to look over her shoulder. She's looking confused.

> SANSA:
> I'm Sansa Stark.
> I have not had the honor, my lord.

PAGE FOUR

Panel One:
Septa Mordane talking to Sansa, Littlefinger is behind them. He's smiling, but the expression doesn't reach his eyes.

> MORDANE:
> Sweet child!
> This is Lord Petyr Baelish,
> of the king's small council.

Panel Two:
Littlefinger has taken Sansa's red rose in his fingertips.

> LITTLEFINGER:
> Your mother was my queen of beauty once.

> LITTLEFINGER:
> You have her hair.

Panel Three:
A wide panel. On the left, Sansa is with Septa Mordane and Jeyne Poole, still holding the red rose. In the middle of the composition is the rising moon on the horizon. On the right, Littlefinger is walking away.

Panel Four:
Another large image. We're looking at a large noble feast at the riverside. Six huge aurochs are on spits over a fire pit. There are tables spread out, with dozens of knights and noblemen walking around. The king and Cersei are at the table of honor. A juggler is tossing a cascade of burning clubs.

CAP: By then the moon was well up, so the king decreed that the last three matches would be fought on the next morning before the melee. The commons began their long walk home, and the court moved to the riverside to begin the feast.

Eventually, Daniel and I realized that starting with the tourney and ending with Tyrion would not work, as all the knights who aid Catelyn in Tyrion's abduction were on their way to the very tourney that would follow it, and all the hand-waving to try and explain this just did not feel convincing. So, in my edit, I returned everything to its original order and recommended replacing the full page of Tyrion's abduction, which had ended the issue, with a full-page image of the tourney, since that was our biggest spectacle. And Varys's last line in the Eddard chapter did make for a very effective ending for the issue overall.

Here is the marked-up and reordered script that I returned:

PAGE SIX

NOTE TO THE COLORIST: All captions from page 6 to 17 should be in the color set to indicate Sansa. Please check previous issues and match.

Panel One:

A massive panel. On the left of the panel, we see one of the stands where the royalty sits, at enough of an angle that we can see a few of the faces. The focus of the spectators is Sansa, who is sitting with Jeyne Poole and Septa Mordane in among the high lords and ladies watching the games. Sansa is wearing a green gown that complements her (auburn) hair. Jeyne has her hand to her mouth in distress, but Sansa is looking on calmly.

Or do we want to make the massive panel the crane shot, and then put Sansa in the stands on Page Seven, panel 3? I went back and forth on this, as I think it might be hard to show both Sansa's face and what she is seeing. Maybe we would be best served making this the crane shot, and the latter the Sansa as spectator panel, facing directly into the stands.

Stretching out from the stands, we can see a vast stretch of the tourney grounds laid out before us. The whole thing is gigantic. At least a dozen jousts are happening in different lanes, with a wide stretch of cleared ground for the melee, and tons of tents and pavilions. Banners are snapping in the breeze. The crowds are huge and, all around, commoners are kept apart from the royalty.
Part of what George thought the HBO series did poorly was to give the scale of the Tourney of the Hand. So let's pull out the stops here.

CAP: Sansa had attended the Hand's tourney with Septa Mordane and Jeyne Poole, and it had been better than the songs.
CAP: They watched the heroes of a **hundred** songs ride forth, each more fabulous than the last.

I added the emphasis to downplay the repeat of "songs."

PAGE SEVEN

NOTE ON PAGES 7–9: The close-ups are the highlights from the full tourney. We're seeing action shots, but in every one of them, we should also see action going on around them, giving the sense that this is all very much a part of some larger action.

Panel One:
Jaime Lannister on a huge white warhorse. He's wearing golden armor and the white cloak of the Kingsguard and has a fresh lance in his hand. He is beautiful, but he isn't playing to the crowd.

CAP: The Kingslayer rode brilliantly. He overthrew Ser Andar Royce and Marcher Lord Bryce Caron as easily as if he were riding at rings, then took a hard-fought match from Barristan Selmy.

Panel Two:
Sandor Clegane—the Hound—jousting against Renly Barratheon. Renly is wearing a helmet with golden horns and a full suit of armor, and the Hound is knocking him off the horse.

CAP: Ser Renly fell to the Hound with such violence he seemed to fly off his horse. His head hit the ground with an audible crack that made the crowd gasp, but it was only one golden antler on his helm snapping off.

Panel Three:
An image of the whole tourney grounds as seen from above, like a crane shot. The details are less important than the impression of size and extent. Unlike in the previous panel, where we see the spectacle that Sansa sees, here we get the whole scope of the thing—all the jousting lanes, as described before, and the melee area, and the tents, and the crowds.

Again, maybe this should be Sansa, Jeyne, and the Septa seen head-on... OR we could do Page Six as: Sansa as spectator, Jaime, Renly/Hound, then Page Seven as the full-page crane shot. Weigh in, guys. Now I like this LAST idea the best!

CAP: Later, a hedge knight in a checkered cloak disgraced himself by killing Beric Dondarrion's horse and was declared forfeit. Lord Beric put his saddle to a new mount and was promptly knocked off it by the warrior priest Thoros of Mount.
CAP: Ser Aron Santagar and Lothor Brume tilted thrice without result. Ser Aron fell afterward to Lord Jason Mallister, and Brune to Yohn Royce's younger son Robar.

PAGE EIGHT

Panel One:
We're close in on Ser Hugh of the Vale, recently knighted former squire of Jon Arryn. He's lying on his back, looking up at us. He's wearing full plate and a helmet (both of them bright and new) that lets us see his face. His cloak is sky blue, with a border of crescent moons where the blood hasn't soaked it. Where his gorget should protect his neck, there's an open space with a splintered length of lance in it. We're very close in on him, so we can watch him bloody and dying.

I cut the Hugh acking bit, because it looked a little silly. I think the image can carry its own weight.

CAP: The most terrifying moment of the day came during Ser Gregor Clegane's second joust, when the point of his lance rode up and struck a young knight from the Vale under the gorget.
CAP: Sansa had never seen a man die. She ought to have been crying, but the tears would not come.

Panel Two:
We're pulled back a little. Ser Hugh is on the ground of a jousting field, choking to death on his own blood. We can't see the full tourney, but we see two or three people standing over Ser Hugh. One of them is Gregor Clegane—the Mountain That Rides—whom we've introduced before. He is also wearing full armor and has the remains of a shattered lance in his massive hand. Ser Hugh's lance is on the green, abandoned. One of the horses in full armor and barding is in the background.

No, we haven't. This is his first appearance, so let's add in the description.

CAP: It would have been different if it had been Jory or Ser Rodrik or Father, she told herself. This young stranger from the Vale of Arryn was nothing to her.
CAP: The world would forget his name now. There would be no songs sung for him.

Panel Three:
This is a panel of Ser Loras Tyrell, the Knight of Flowers. We're seeing him out of the context of the tourney, almost like a portrait. He should be looking directly at the viewer, somewhat coyly. His plate mail is elaborately enameled with flowers. His hair is long, brown, and flowing. He's beautiful, with an almost anime-like androgyny.

Ramp up the description a bit for the colorist. Hair, eyes, what the armor looks like...

CAP: In the end it came to four: The Hound and his monstrous brother Gregor, the Kingslayer...
CAP: ...And Loras Tyrell, the Knight of Flowers.

PAGE NINE

Panel One:
An evening scene. The moon is rising on the horizon, and the sky is twilight purple. Sansa is sitting where we saw her before, and over her shoulder we can see the jousting lane. Ser Loras Tyrell is on his horse, his hand lifted to the crowd in victory. His horse is covered in a blanket of red and white roses. Another knight, wearing bronze armor inscribed with eldrich runes (Robar Royce) is on the ground, with his squire coming to help him sit up.

CAP: After each victory, Ser Loras would remove his helm, ride slowly around the fence, and finally pluck a white rose and throw it to some fair maiden in the crowd.
CAP: His last match of the day was against the younger Ser Royce, but Sansa's eyes were only for Ser Loras.

Panel Two:
Ser Loras on his horse stopped before Sansa. He's looking down at her gently. She's staring up at him, awestruck. It's still visibly an evening shot.

CAP: When his white mare stopped in front of her, she thought her heart would burst.

> LORAS:
> Sweet lady, no victory is half
> so beautiful as you.

Panel Three:
Close on Sansa, looking down at her cupped hands. She's holding a red rose from Ser Loras.

CAP: To the other maidens, he had given white roses.   *Ser Loras*
CAP: She inhaled its sweet fragrance and sat clutching it long after he had ridden off.

Panel Four:
Sansa, in the foreground, looking worshipfully out over the fields. Littlefinger is behind her, looking at her.

> LITTLEFINGER:
> You must be one of her daughters.
> You have the Tully look.

Panel Five:
Close on Sansa, turning to look over her shoulder. She's looking confused.

> SANSA:
> I'm Sansa Stark.
> I have not had the honor, my lord.

Panel One:
Septa Mordane talking to Sansa. Littlefinger is behind them. He's smiling, but the expression doesn't reach his eyes.

> MORDANE:
> Sweet child!
> This is Lord Petyr Baelish,
> of the king's small council.

Panel Two:
Littlefinger has taken Sansa's red rose in his fingertips.

Or should we just have him touching her hair, which is much creepier and more intimate?

> LITTLEFINGER:
> Your mother was my queen of beauty once.

> LITTLEFINGER:
> You have her hair.

Panel Three:
A wide panel. On the left, Sansa is with Septa Mordane and Jeyne Poole, still holding the red rose. In the middle of the composition is the rising moon on the horizon. On the right, Littlefinger is walking away.

Panel Four:
Another large image. We're looking at a large noble feast at the riverside. Six huge aurochs are on spits over a fire pit. There are tables spread out, with dozens of knights and noblemen walking around. The king and Cersei are at the table of honor. A juggler is tossing a cascade of burning clubs.

CAP: By then the moon was well up, so the king decreed that the last three matches would be fought on the next morning before the melee. The commons began their long walk home, and the court moved to the riverside to begin the feast.

As you can see, we went back and forth on which image should be on the splash page, but eventually decided to do that as the big, establishing crane shot, then start focusing in more narrowly.

Daniel adds:

Once the reordering was done, and we lost the initial transition with Ser Hugh, the tourney really came into its own. We got the room for the full-page image of the whole place, which in retrospect, I think we really needed. We didn't get to focus as much on the death of Ser Hugh, but even that I don't really regret.

Like the man said, no songs will be sung for him.

And the final script took the form that you now see on the page.

Now the script goes to Tommy, who begins to work his magic. As Tommy describes it:

When drawing this book, I noticed I had to focus on getting better at expressions since the majority of what I've done so far has been conversation. So when an action scene comes along, I get superpumped and can't wait to dive into it.

As always, the only budget I have to worry about is time. I ended up taking two full months on this issue, if that tells you anything. Most pages' average people count is 10–15 per page. This scene was...well...start counting the people on the page six splash and I bet you get tired of counting and give up before you finish!

Drawing knights on horses is fun. It really is that simple. While every page had a labor-intensive crowd as backgrounds, it also had some killer action. One of the other challenges is not going too far with the laws of physics and having the scene feel like an issue of Ironman.

The splash was the most difficult, trying to show scope and action. I didn't want it to feel like a Where's Waldo poster. I also was testing out some drawing concepts based on a critique from one of my drawing buddies. The splash at the beginning of issue two had people spilling in, and while the page was nice, it didn't lead the eye. This time around I tried to gather people in groups, starting at the top and following counterclockwise and leading back to the top. I wanted it to feel like this was just a part of the tourney.

One last thing I'm proud of is page nine, panel two. I initially drew a terrible face on Sansa. As an artist, you can't see what a drawing is while you do it, so if you feel it's off, don't ignore that voice. A trick I do is to give a page a look before bed. If I feel a part is wrong, I erase it with no remorse and fix it the next day with fresh eyes. Now I think that redo is one of the best faces I've drawn. For what it's worth, I rarely use reference.

Here are the initial layouts, and what Tommy has to say about that stage in the process:

I can't state enough how all the thinking is done at the layout stage. I am trying to tell a story as clearly as possible. That is juxtaposed to the depth written into this EPIC story. Daniel, bless his heart, gets to do the first round of condensing. I can only imagine the fight in his brain about what to leave in and what to take out.

When I get the script, the hard part is done. He has clarified my course. I've gotten better at not being afraid to reduce the story even more. The neat thing about comic art is you have the whole page to view, so while a story is linear, unlike movies, you can see what just happened and what is going to happen. This allows me to avoid drawing a million people in each panel and I can zoom in on the people without losing the setting or tone. While Daniel and Anne have the final say, it took a few issues before I was able to make decisions that in my opinion help the book. As the issues have moved along, I am investing myself in the process in a way that only I can. The readers should feel themselves drawn in deeper as we progress, not just because of the story but also as the result of our execution as a creative team.

Daniel and I had only one comment on the layout, which was:

6: We're wondering about the complete top-down view of the tourney. We worry that by putting the angle directly above, it makes the whole look almost like a modern sports arena. So we'd recommend keeping the point of view high in the air but changing the angle at which we're looking at it to something more like forty-five to thirty degrees and making the whole thing look like a really big, violent Ren Faire. And when doing the lists, remember that the horses need to gallop out both ends. As shown, a few of them would be running into poles at the end of their run.

And that is it. We are SO excited to see your tourney in detail!

Tommy's initial pencils looked like this:

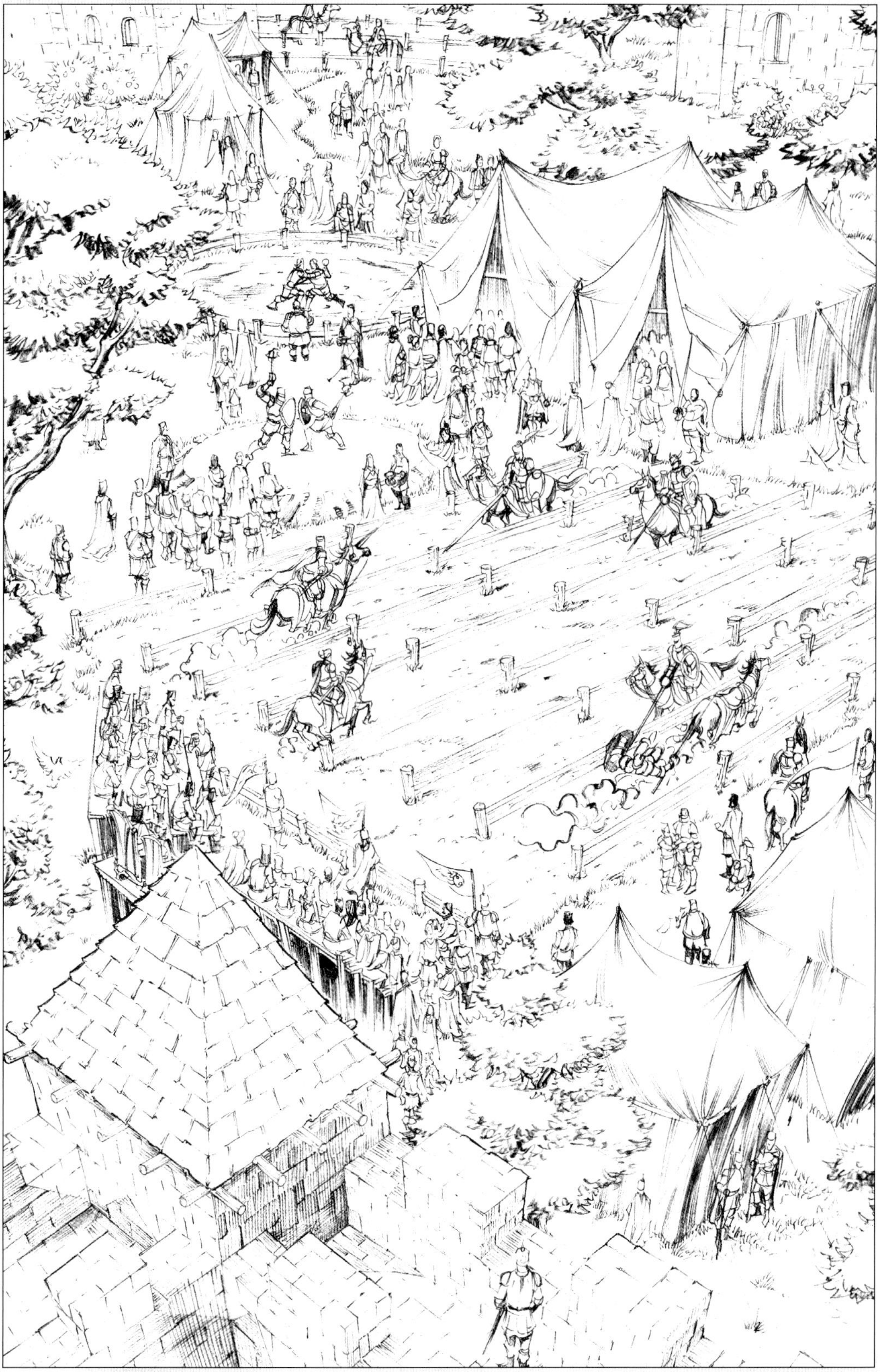

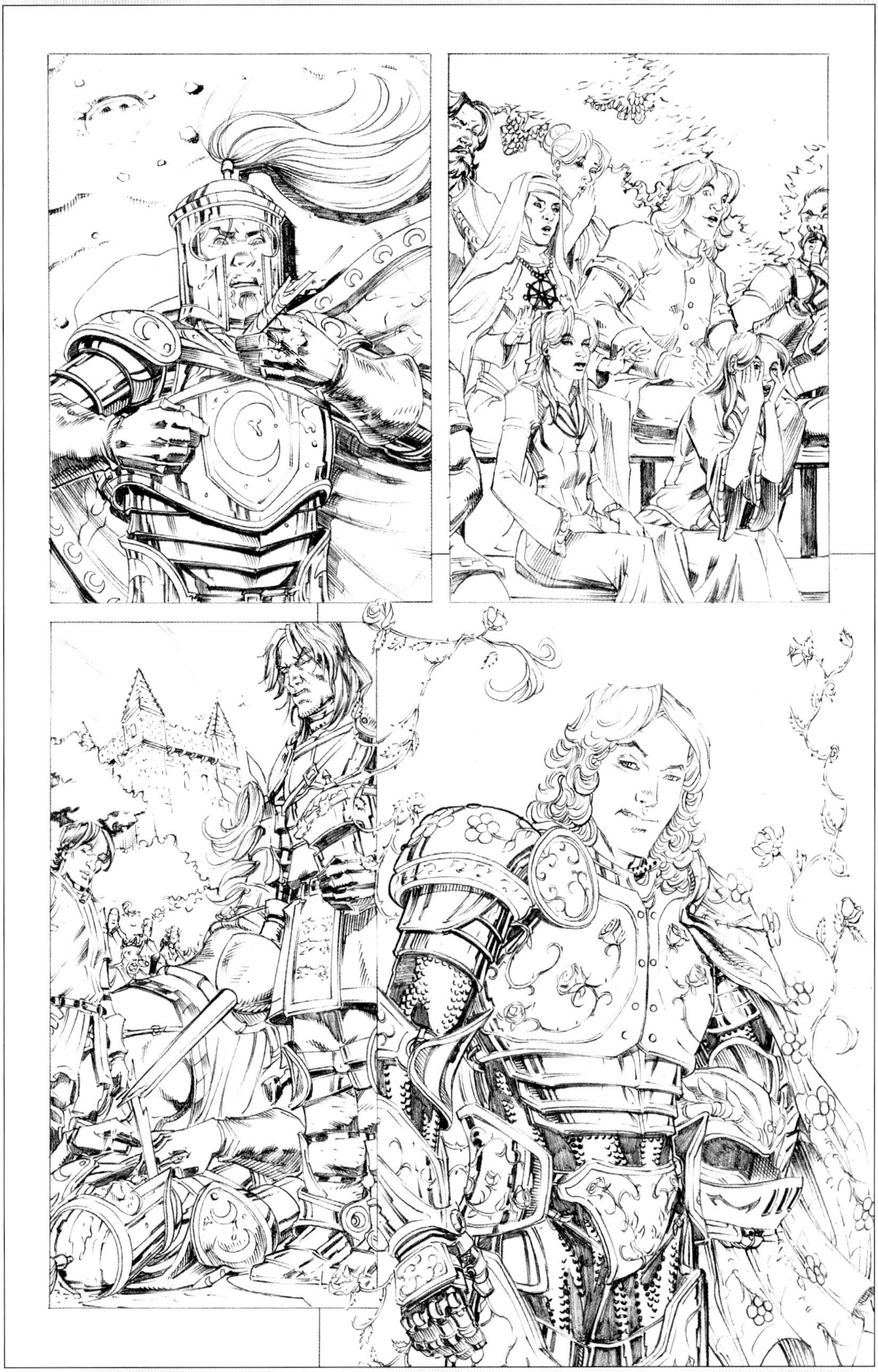

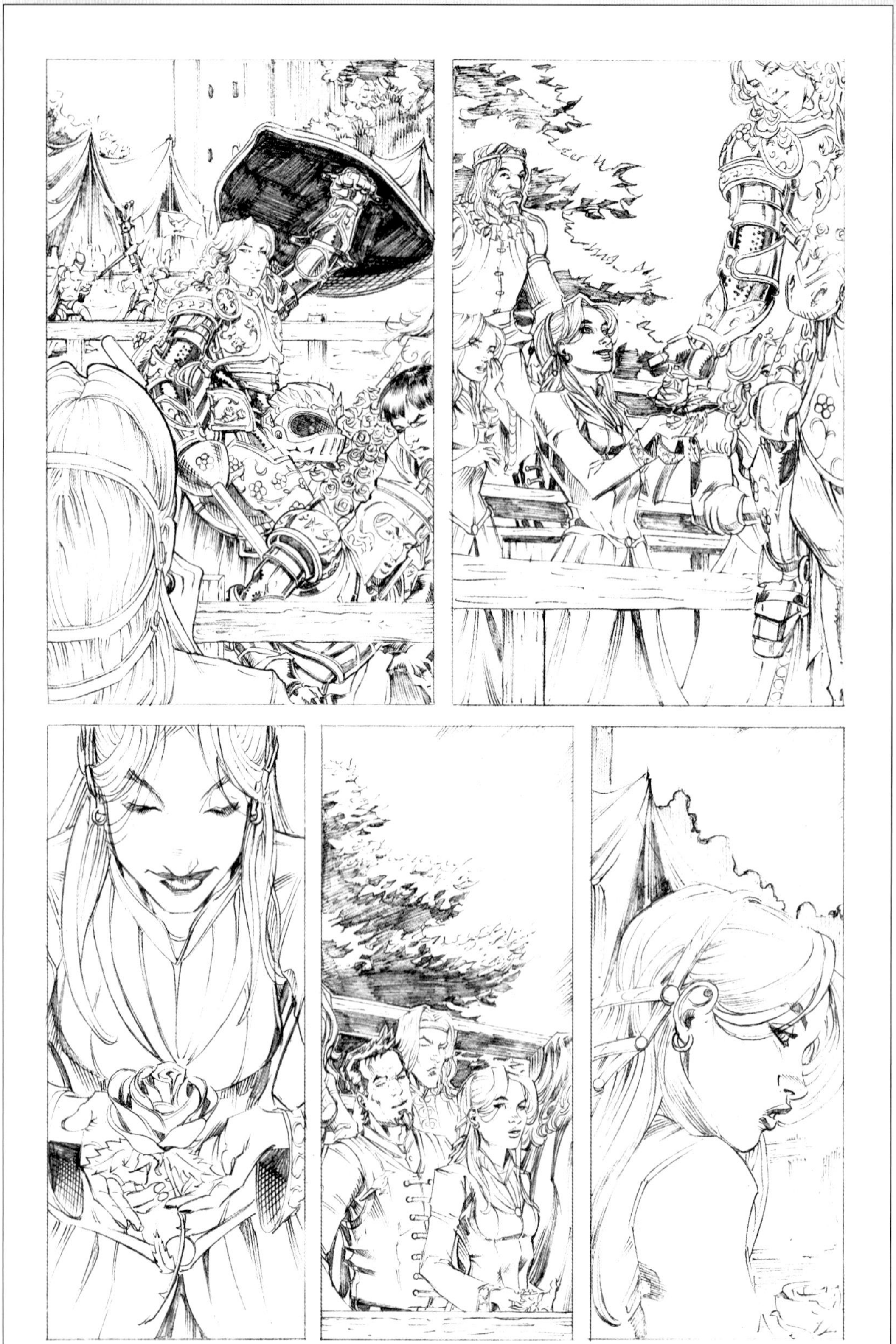

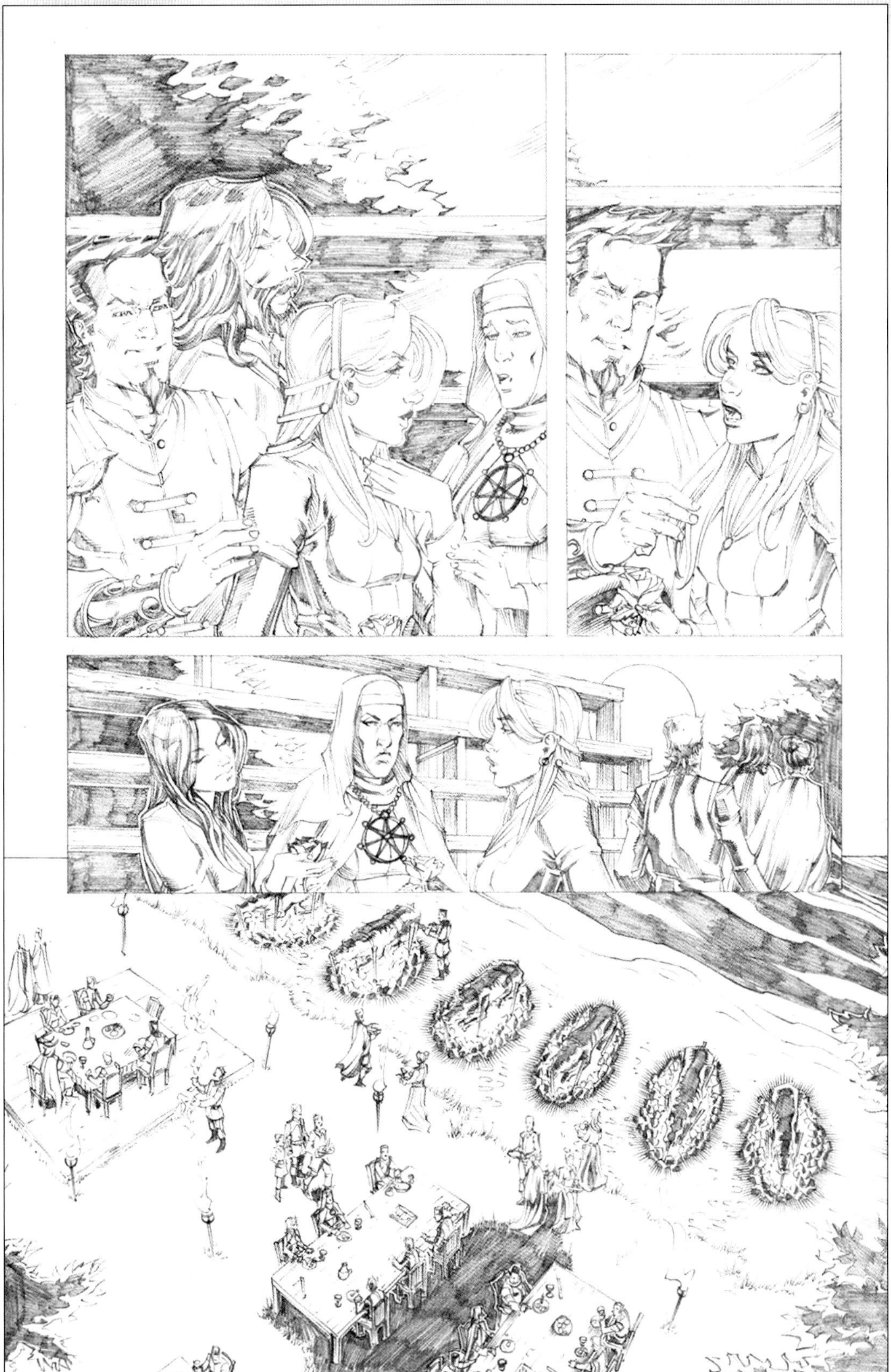

And Tommy says:

Because the layouts are where the thinking is done, the final pencils, on pages like this, are all about keeping the pencil moving. The willpower to draw crowds is draining. If you keep the pencil moving, it'll take care of itself if you've solved problems in the layout stage.

Save for comments of "Gorgeous, gorgeous, gorgeous!" our only issues were to remove the checkers from Beric Dondarrion's cloak in panel 7.3 and move the rose from Jeyne to Sansa in panel 10.3.

Here are the two corrected panels:

With the two panels corrected, Jason Ullmeyer and Joe Rybandt at Dynamite now take the reins, coordinating the talented Ivan Nunes and Marshall Dillon in colors and letters respectively. Here is how Jason describes the process:

> Once we get the final pencils, our Editor, Joe Rybandt, comes in and reviews the final pages, lets me know if they are good to format for the colorist and letterer, and advises Marshall and Dillon to look for the pages.
>
> Once the line art is approved, I get the hi-res files and, in cases like Tommy's art, where we are going straight from pencils to colors, I darken and clean up the line work if/when necessary. Luckily for me, Tommy's pages are pretty clean, so other than darkening up the lines a bit and brightening up some of the whites where necessary, there is not a ton to do. Then, once that is done, I make sure that all pages are sized/proportioned properly so that Ivan and Marshall are working on proper, print-size files. This way, when we get in the final letters and colors, there will be little to no alignment corrections to be made when assembling the final book. This helps us cut out some time on the back end of production.

Mostly, Marshall and Ivan make our jobs very easy, and there is usually little correcting on the letters-and-colors end. The initial letter files come in on the pencils—which I find makes it easier to concentrate on the new additions without the distraction of color. (It also means that Ivan is still busy working his magic.)

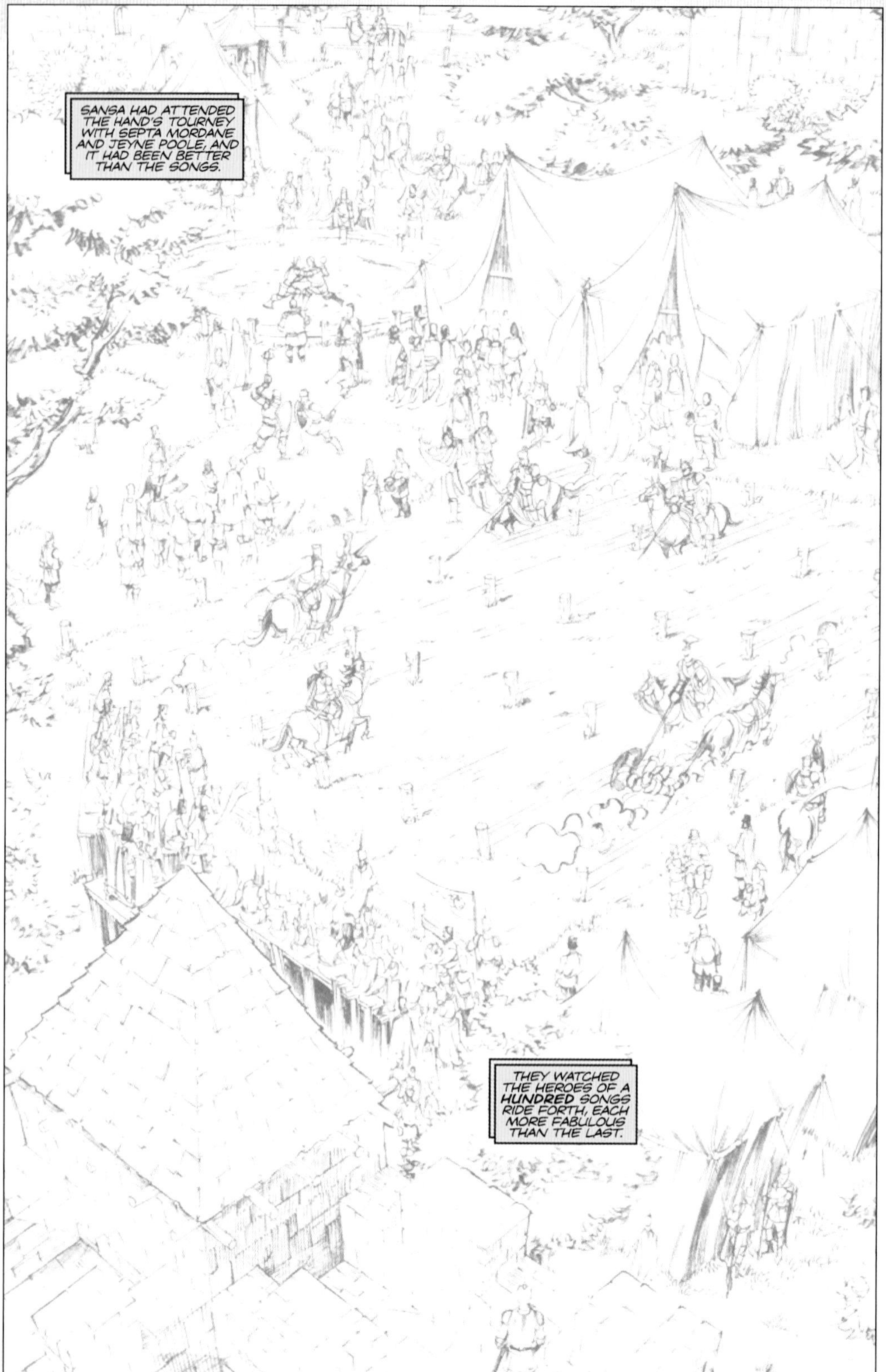
SANSA HAD ATTENDED THE HAND'S TOURNEY WITH SEPTA MORDANE AND JEYNE POOLE, AND IT HAD BEEN BETTER THAN THE SONGS.
THEY WATCHED THE HEROES OF A **HUNDRED** SONGS RIDE FORTH, EACH MORE FABULOUS THAN THE LAST.

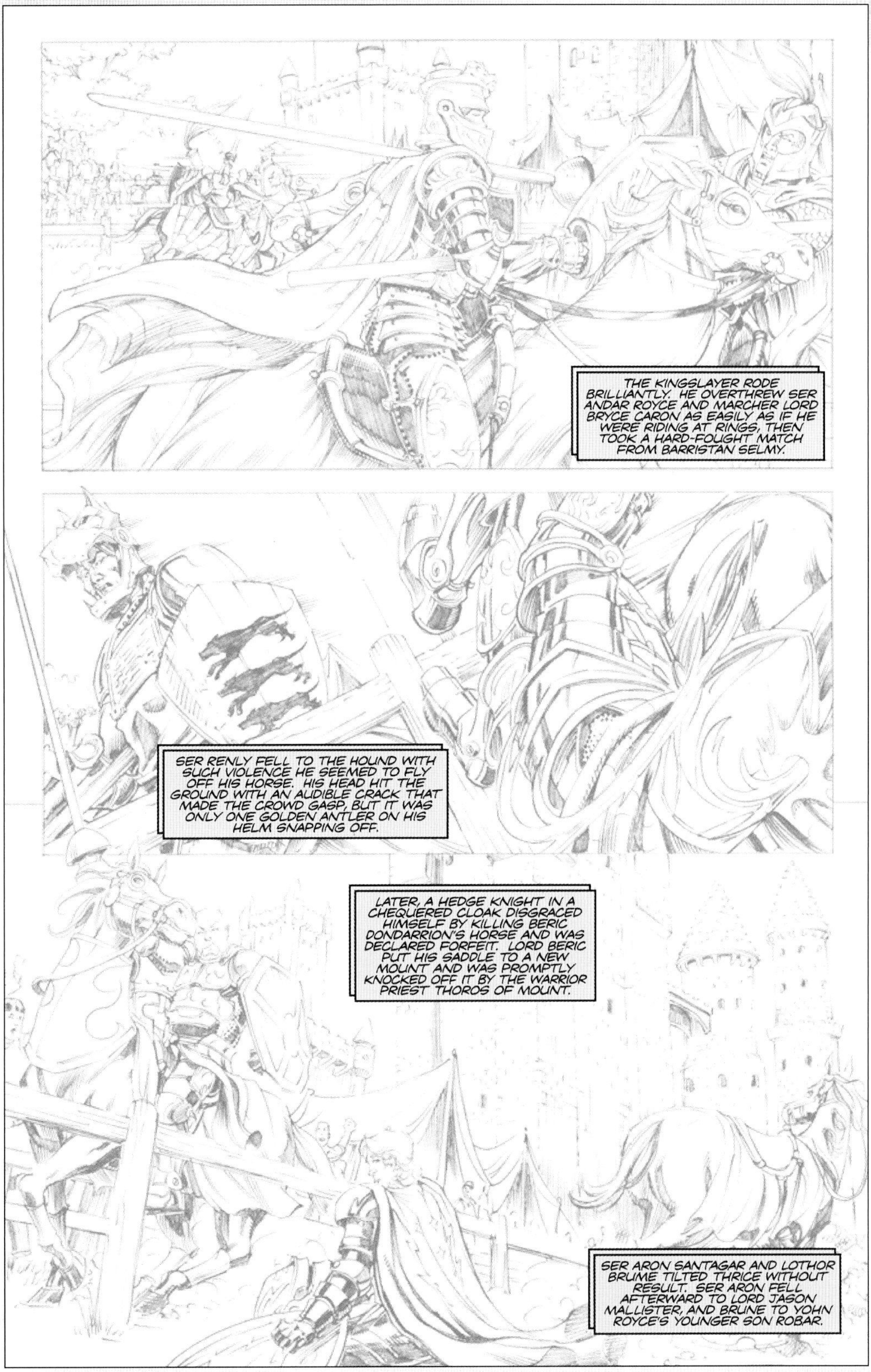
THE KINGSLAYER RODE BRILLIANTLY. HE OVERTHREW SER ANDAR ROYCE AND MARCHER LORD BRYCE CARON AS EASILY AS IF HE WERE RIDING AT RINGS, THEN TOOK A HARD-FOUGHT MATCH FROM BARRISTAN SELMY.
SER RENLY FELL TO THE HOUND WITH SUCH VIOLENCE HE SEEMED TO FLY OFF HIS HORSE. HIS HEAD HIT THE GROUND WITH AN AUDIBLE CRACK THAT MADE THE CROWD GASP, BUT IT WAS ONLY ONE GOLDEN ANTLER ON HIS HELM SNAPPING OFF.
LATER, A HEDGE KNIGHT IN A CHEQUERED CLOAK DISGRACED HIMSELF BY KILLING BERIC DONDARRION'S HORSE AND WAS DECLARED FORFEIT. LORD BERIC PUT HIS SADDLE TO A NEW MOUNT AND WAS PROMPTLY KNOCKED OFF IT BY THE WARRIOR PRIEST THOROS OF MOUNT.
SER ARON SANTAGAR AND LOTHOR BRUME TILTED THRICE WITHOUT RESULT. SER ARON FELL AFTERWARD TO LORD JASON MALLISTER, AND BRUNE TO YOHN ROYCE'S YOUNGER SON ROBAR.

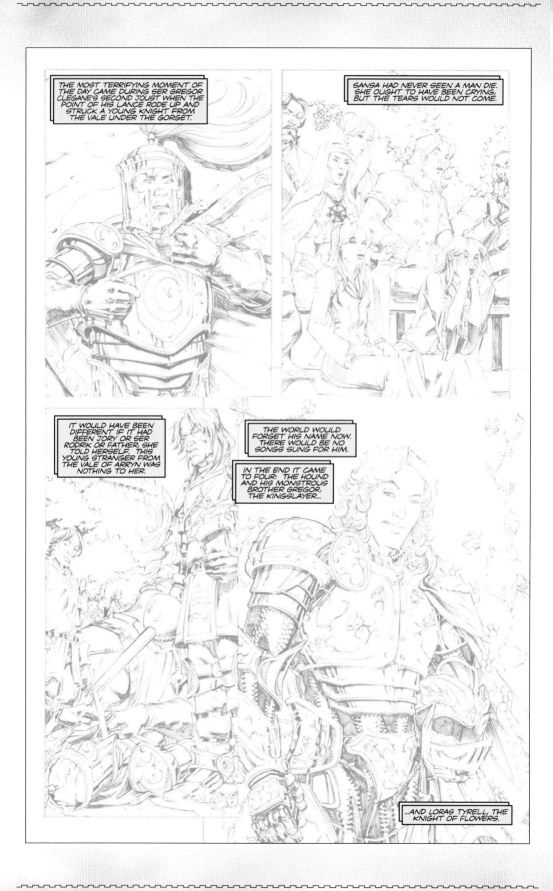

THE MOST TERRIFYING MOMENT OF THE DAY CAME DURING SER GREGOR CLEGANE'S SECOND JOUST WHEN THE POINT OF HIS LANCE RODE UP AND STRUCK A YOUNG KNIGHT FROM THE VALE UNDER THE GORGET.

SANSA HAD NEVER SEEN A MAN DIE. SHE OUGHT TO HAVE BEEN CRYING, BUT THE TEARS WOULD NOT COME.

IT WOULD HAVE BEEN DIFFERENT IF IT HAD BEEN JORY OR SER RODRIK OR FATHER, SHE TOLD HERSELF. THIS YOUNG STRANGER FROM THE VALE OF ARRYN WAS NOTHING TO HER.

THE WORLD WOULD FORGET HIS NAME NOW. THERE WOULD BE NO SONGS SUNG FOR HIM.

IN THE END IT CAME TO FOUR: THE HOUND AND HIS MONSTROUS BROTHER GREGOR, THE KINGSLAYER...

...AND LORAS TYRELL, THE KNIGHT OF FLOWERS.

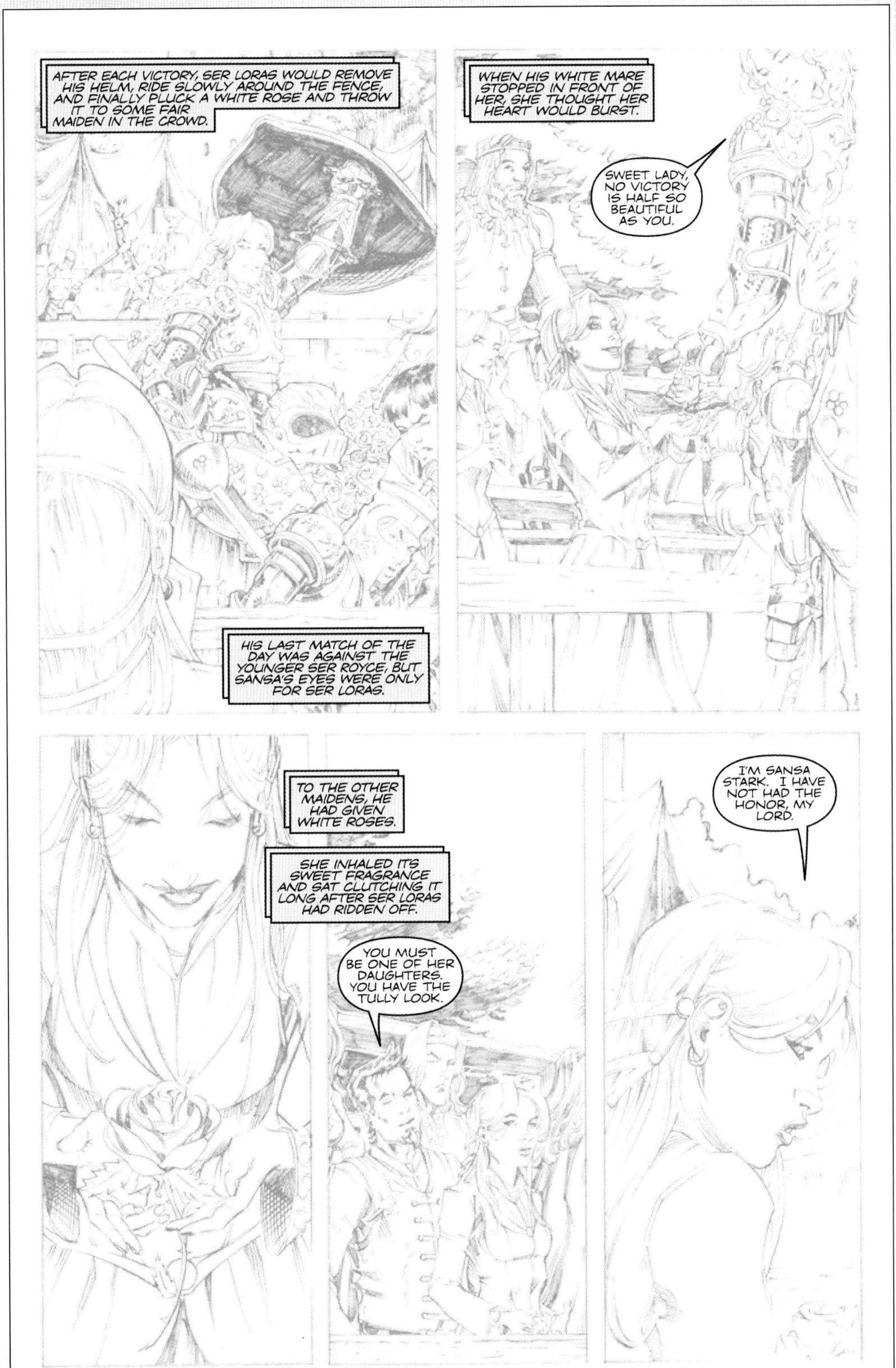
AFTER EACH VICTORY, SER LORAS WOULD REMOVE HIS HELM, RIDE SLOWLY AROUND THE FENCE, AND FINALLY PLUCK A WHITE ROSE AND THROW IT TO SOME FAIR MAIDEN IN THE CROWD.
HIS LAST MATCH OF THE DAY WAS AGAINST THE YOUNGER SER ROYCE, BUT SANSA'S EYES WERE ONLY FOR SER LORAS.
WHEN HIS WHITE MARE STOPPED IN FRONT OF HER, SHE THOUGHT HER HEART WOULD BURST.
SWEET LADY, NO VICTORY IS HALF SO BEAUTIFUL AS YOU.
TO THE OTHER MAIDENS, HE HAD GIVEN WHITE ROSES.
SHE INHALED ITS SWEET FRAGRANCE AND SAT CLUTCHING IT LONG AFTER SER LORAS HAD RIDDEN OFF.
YOU MUST BE ONE OF HER DAUGHTERS. YOU HAVE THE TULLY LOOK.
I'M SANSA STARK. I HAVE NOT HAD THE HONOR, MY LORD.

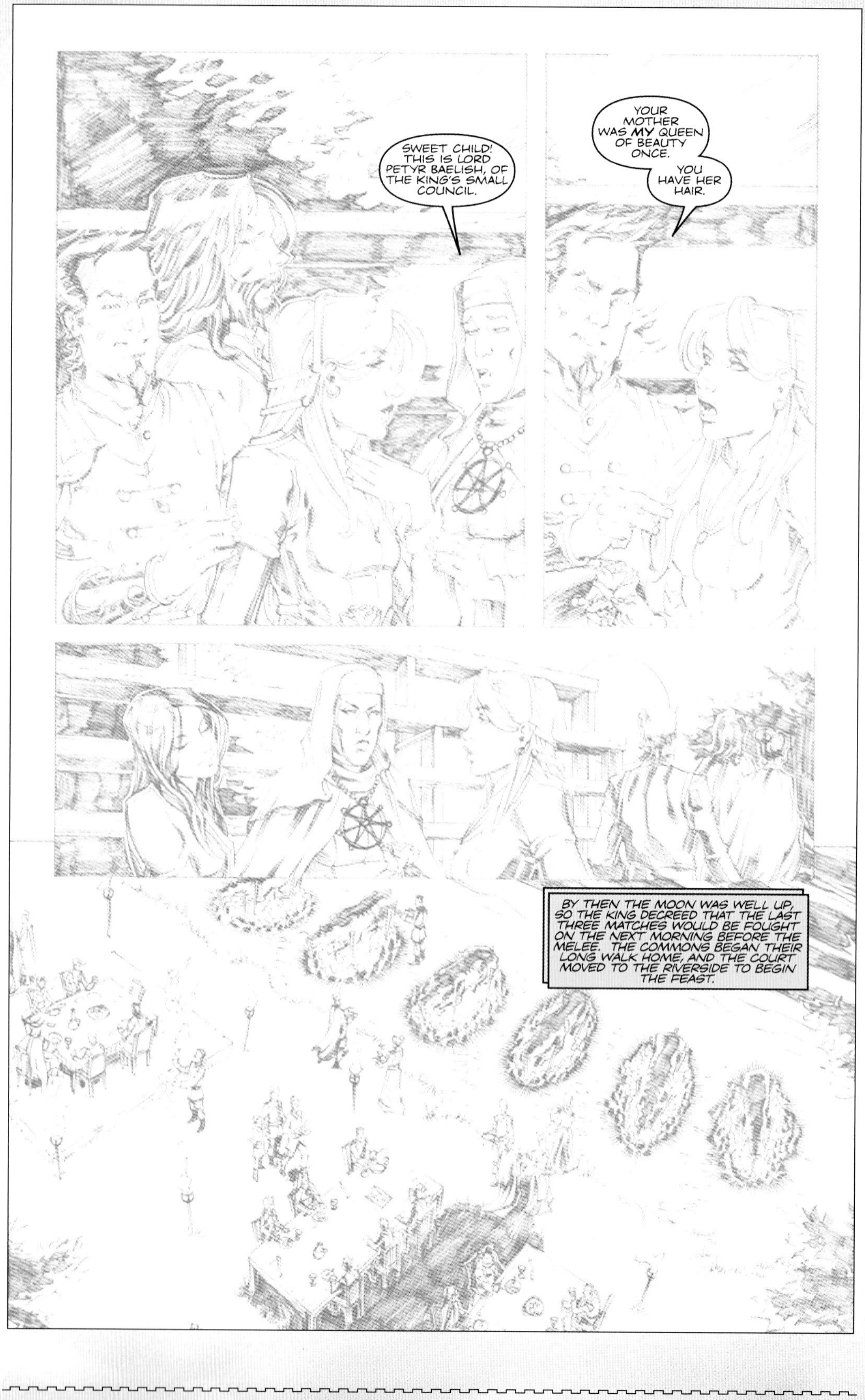
SWEET CHILD! THIS IS LORD PETYR BAELISH, OF THE KING'S SMALL COUNCIL.
YOUR MOTHER WAS MY QUEEN OF BEAUTY ONCE.
YOU HAVE HER HAIR.
BY THEN THE MOON WAS WELL UP, SO THE KING DECREED THAT THE LAST THREE MATCHES WOULD BE FOUGHT ON THE NEXT MORNING BEFORE THE MELEE. THE COMMONS BEGAN THEIR LONG WALK HOME, AND THE COURT MOVED TO THE RIVERSIDE TO BEGIN THE FEAST.

Mostly, this is the stage that we are catching typos and mistakes that Daniel and I both missed while going exhaustively over the script. Astute readers may already have spotted the autocorrect error on page 7 of the final script that both Daniel and I were incapable of seeing until the letters first appeared. It is easy, when you know how something is supposed to read, to blip over how it is actually spelled. But sometimes, in a different context, it can leap out. So here is where we realized that Thoros had become from Mount instead of Myr, and where that got corrected.

The only other change we made to the letters was to separate Petyr's two speech bubbles in panel 10.2, to add a bit of a creepy pause. Often in the script, Daniel and I will break one character's lines into two or more segments—partially to cut down the number of letters in any one individual bubble or caption, but also to indicate a pause or change in direction. We sometimes specify in the script where the longest pauses should be by instructing that the split speeches should be in separate bubbles, but mostly we trust Marshall to walk that delicate line between establishing the drama and not blocking the art, which he does so well.

And then sometimes—as in this case—something that we did not see necessarily needing a long pause suddenly seemed to when art and letters both came together. And just by moving those two speeches apart, we were able to add more emotional weight to that panel and to that moment.

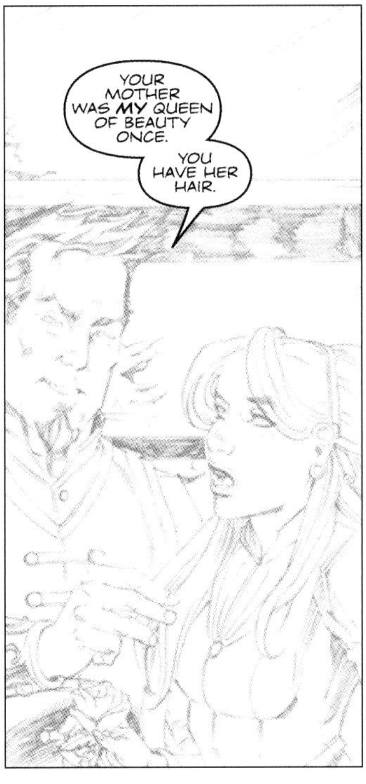
YOUR MOTHER WAS MY QUEEN OF BEAUTY ONCE.
YOU HAVE HER HAIR.

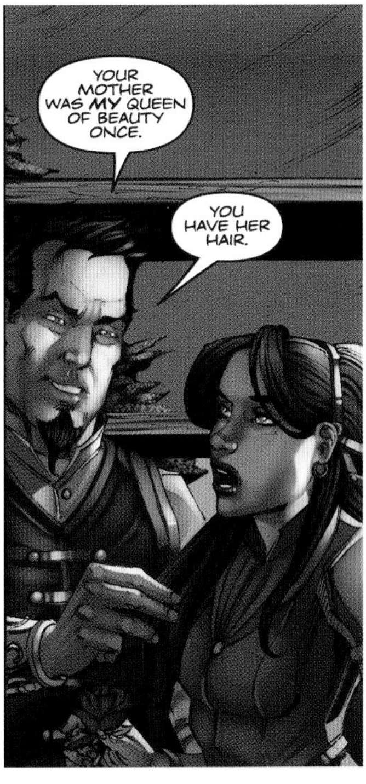
YOUR MOTHER WAS MY QUEEN OF BEAUTY ONCE.
YOU HAVE HER HAIR.

As for colors, Ivan's excellent work usually needs little to no correction. For the tourney scene, we had no comments at all, and here is what it looked like when it came in.

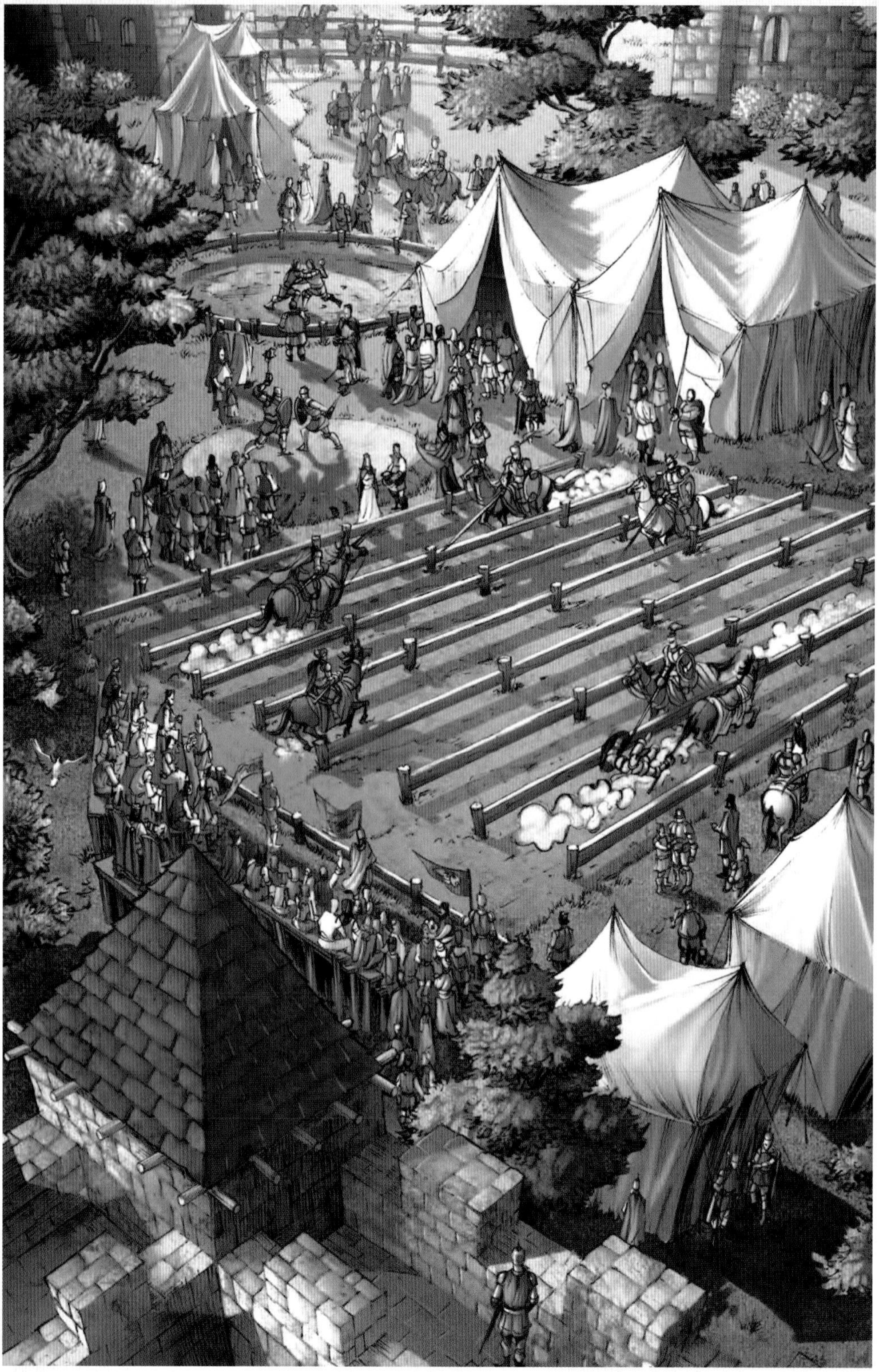

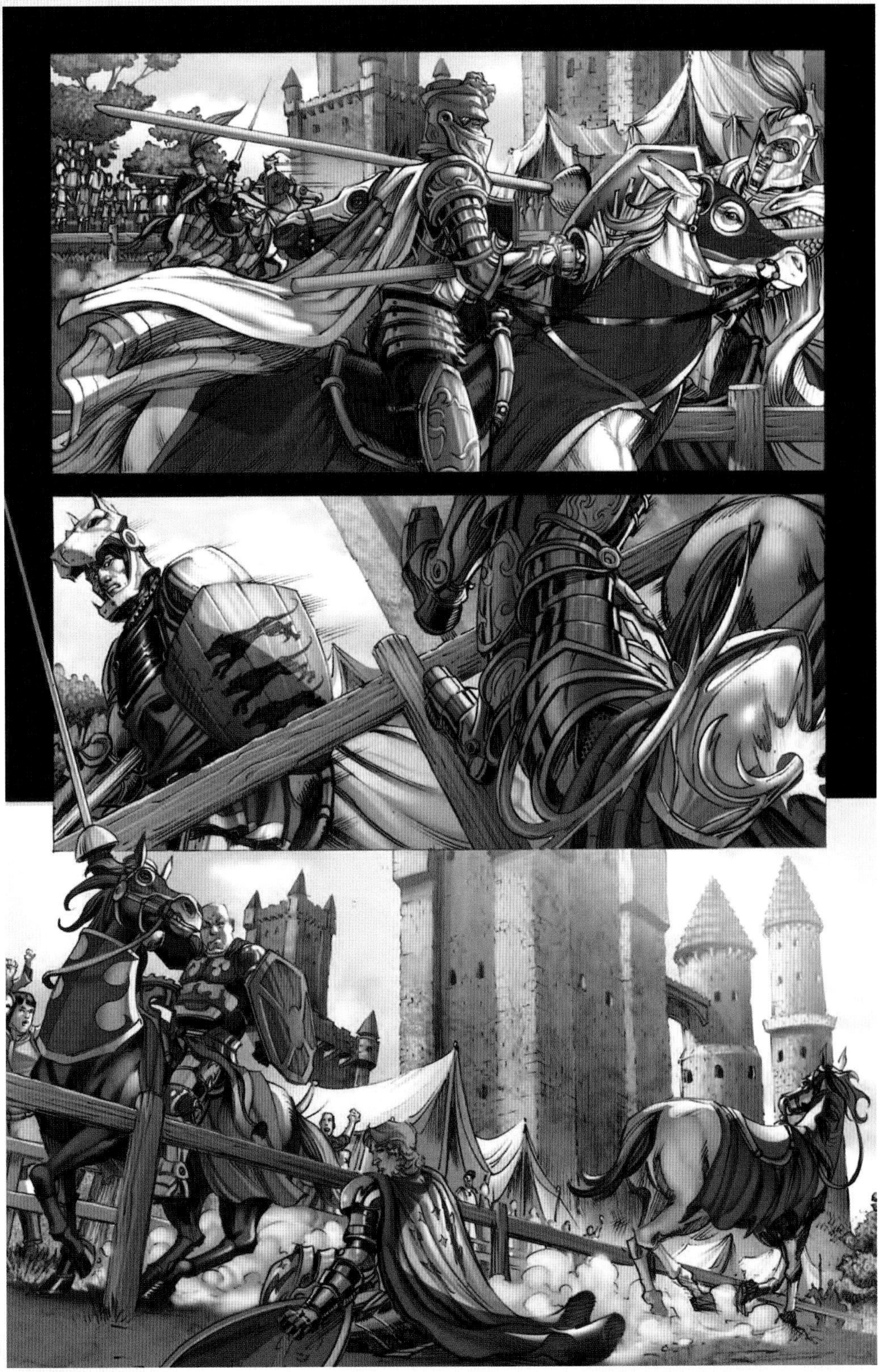

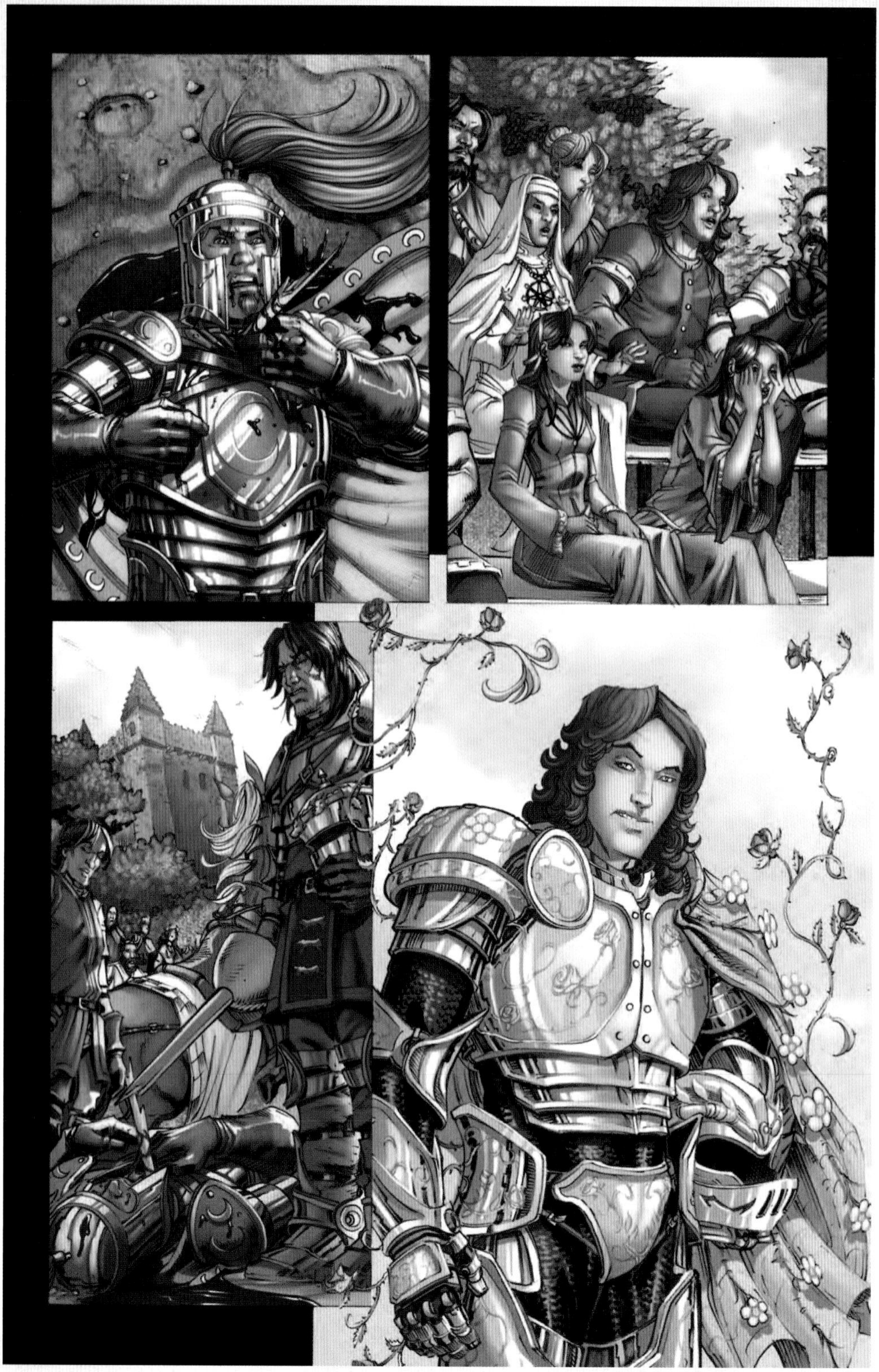

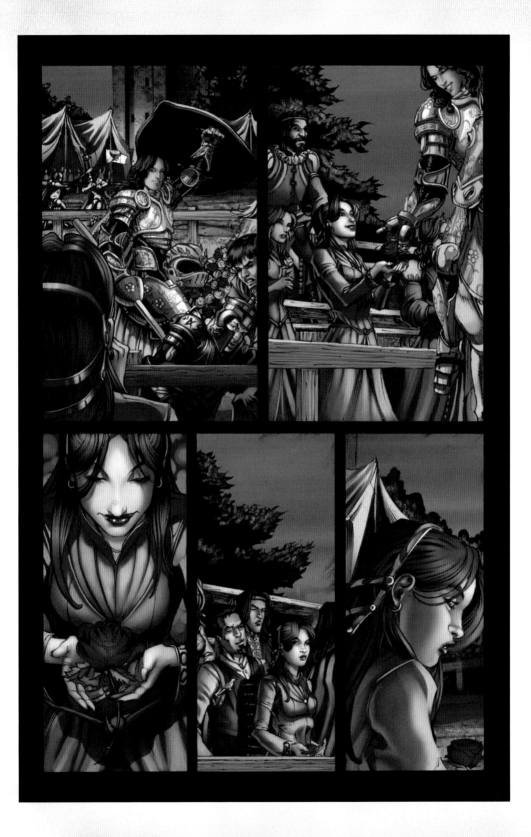

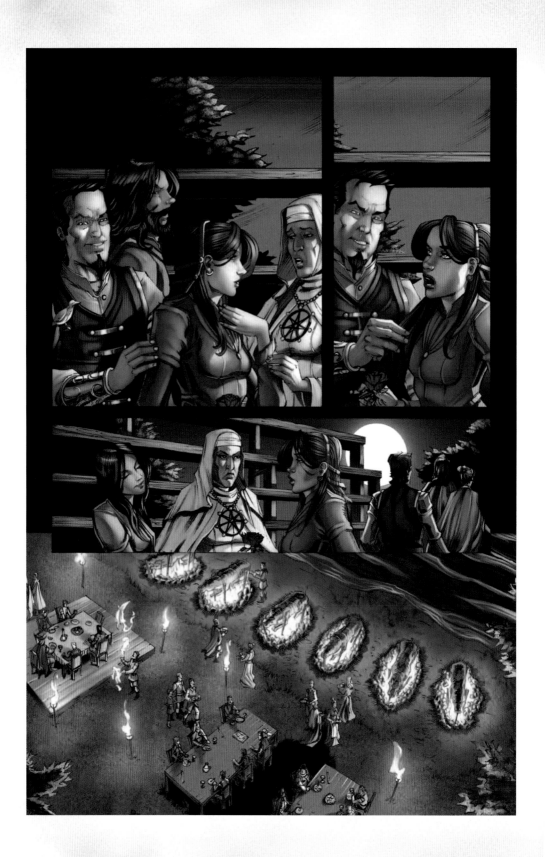

Our only color comment on this issue ended up being a heraldic issue in the Tyrion scene. Initally, the Bracken heraldry was showing a red stallion on grey-brown rather than brown, and the Frey heraldry colors were reversed, with a silver-grey castle on a blue background rather than the reverse. So we fixed that all up.

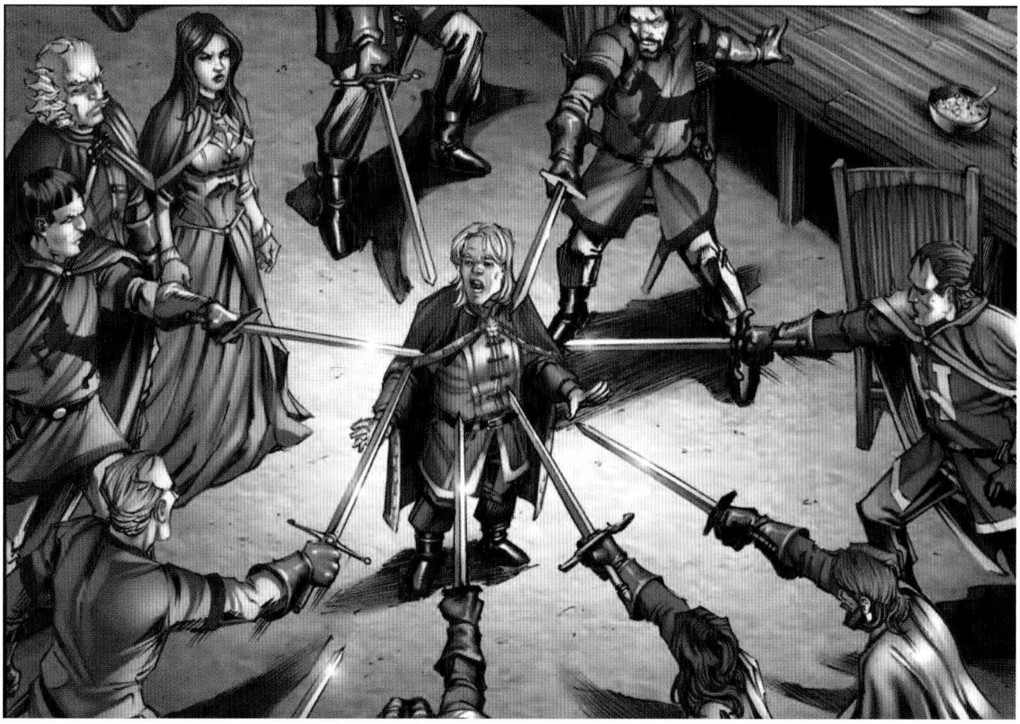

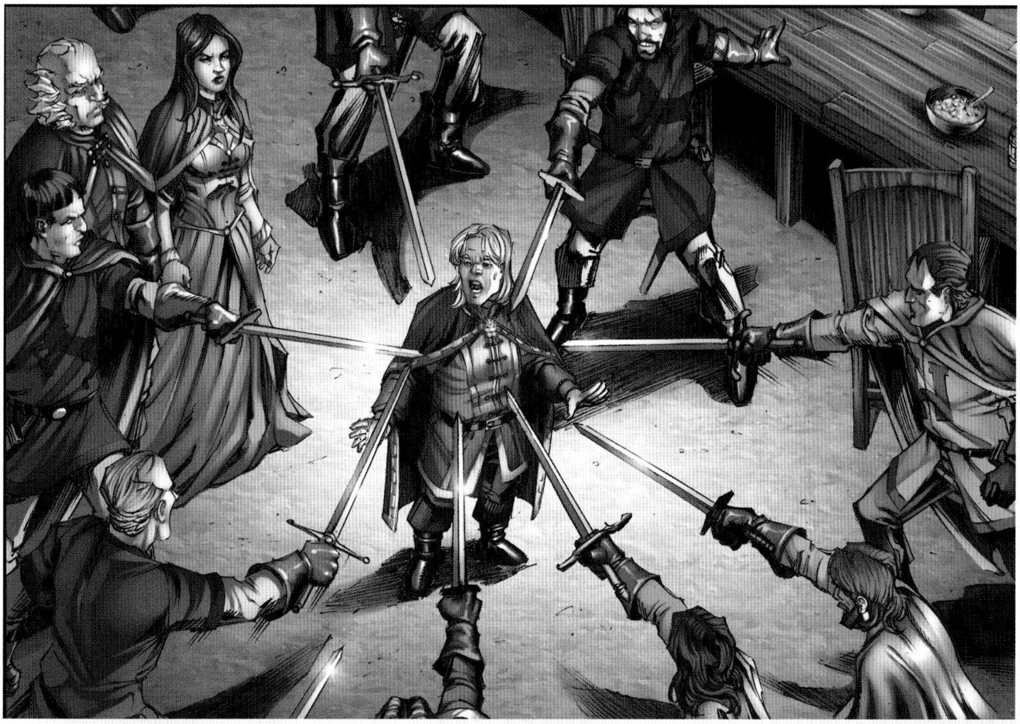

Jason Ullmeyer adds:

Once we have approved, corrected color files, we delete the older versions to ensure that no mistakes are made when assembling the final book. Then, once all colors and letters are approved, we assemble the book, double-check that all letters and colors align perfectly, give the book a final once-over, and send them on to the printer.

A little less than four weeks later, the final book appears in stores, then eventually gets folded into our compilation hardcovers.

The only thing left, then, is to give you a special advance preview of issue 13! Here is Mike Miller's cover and the lead-in to Tyrion's trial by combat....
Enjoy!

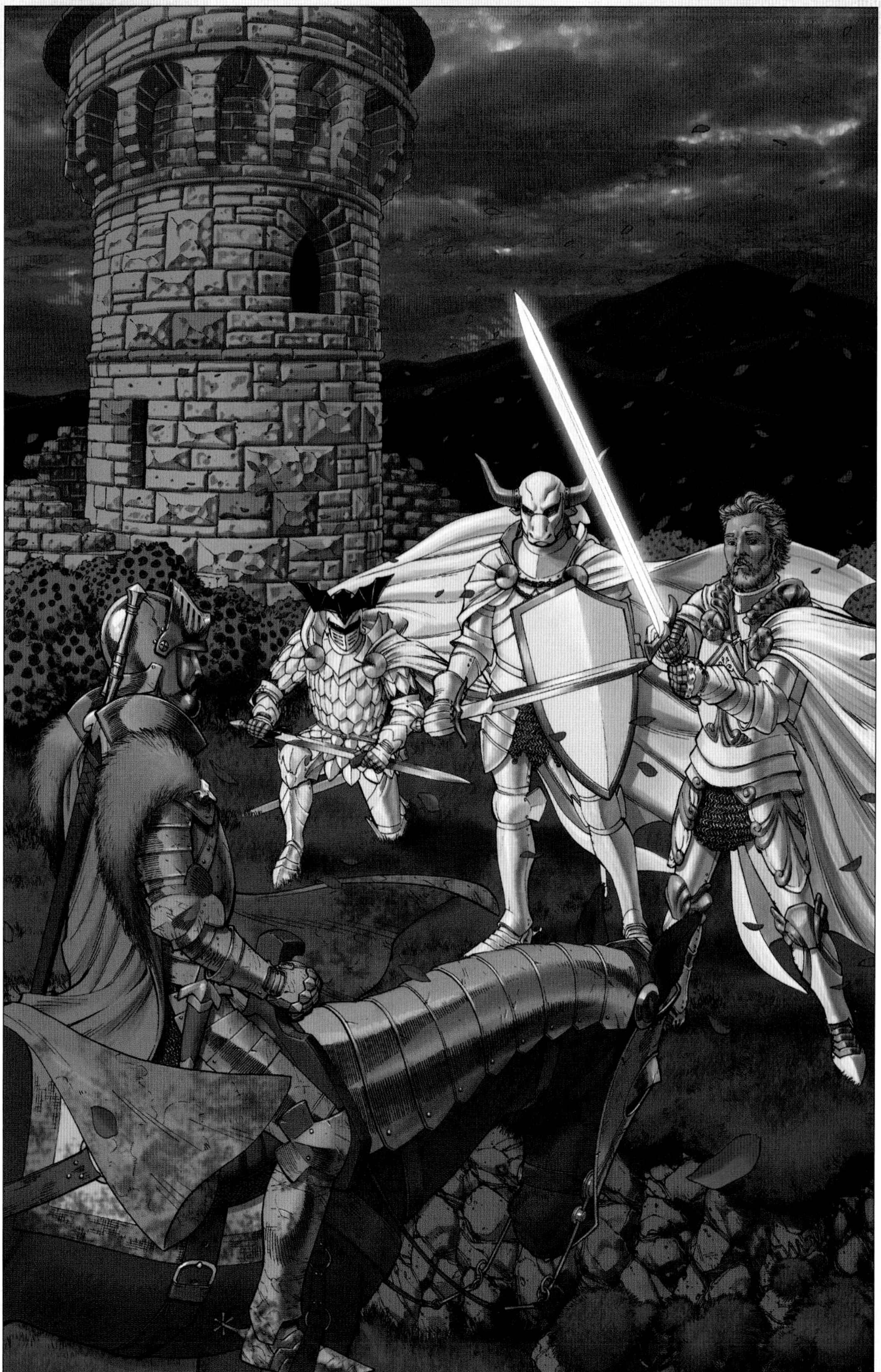

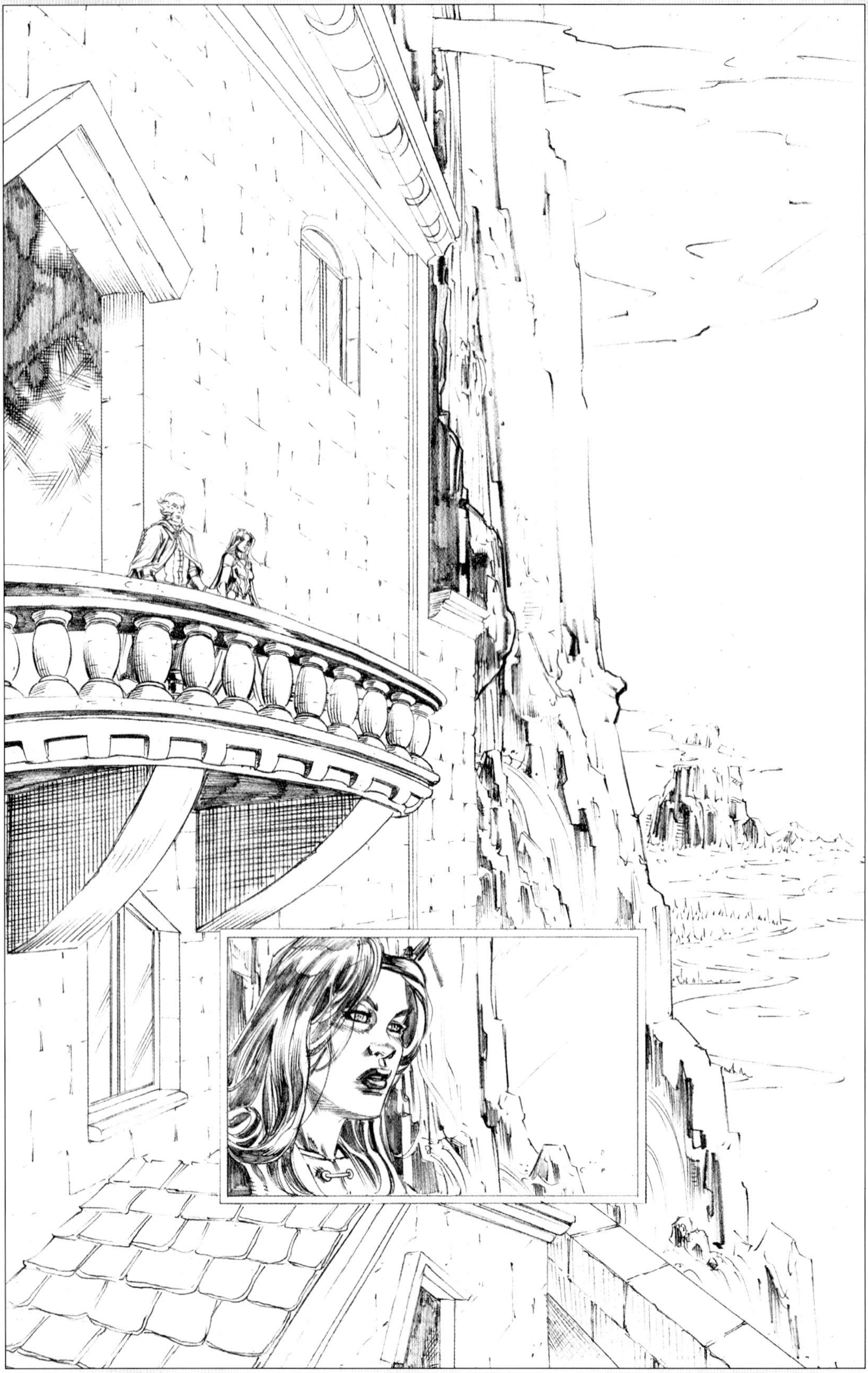

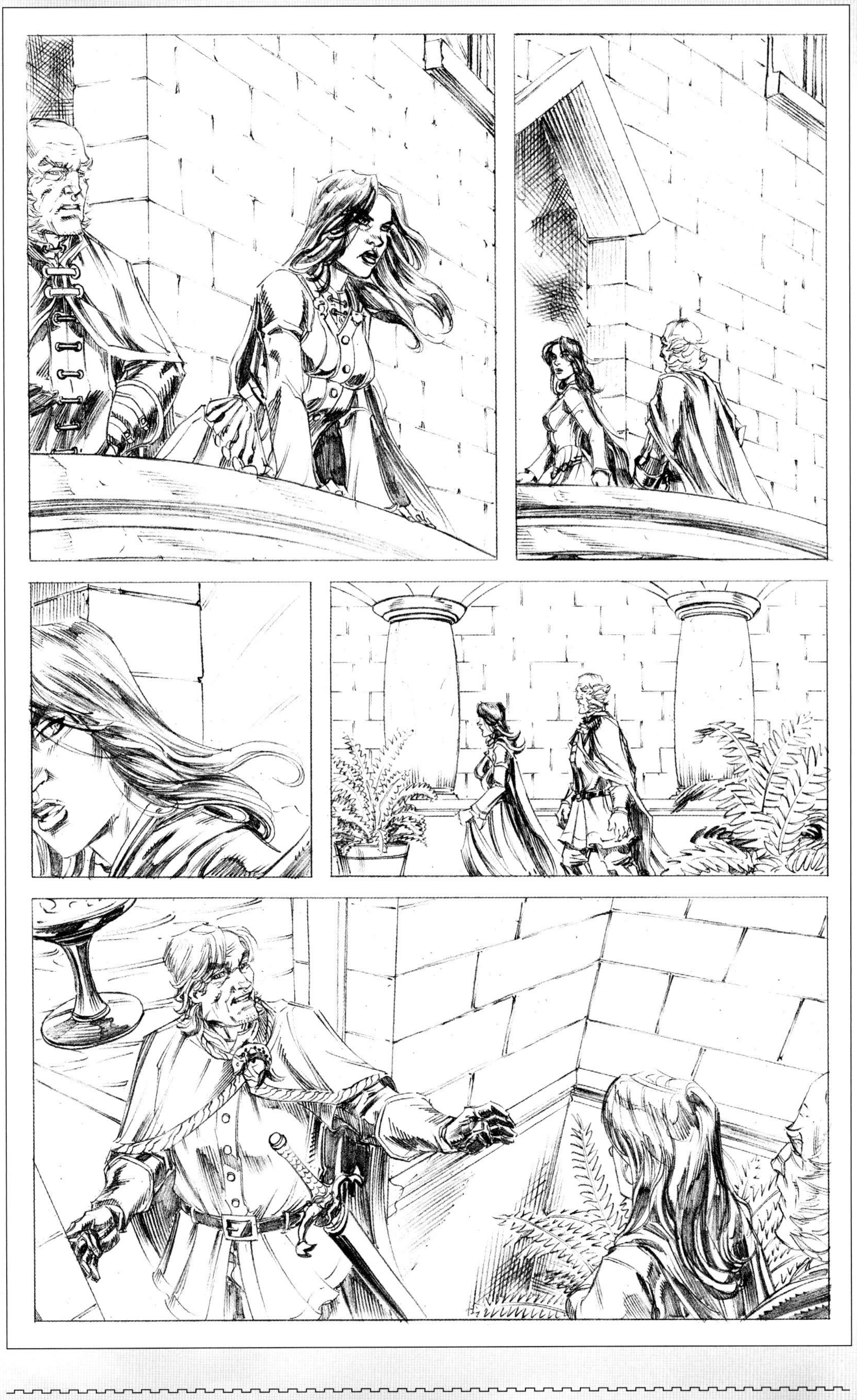

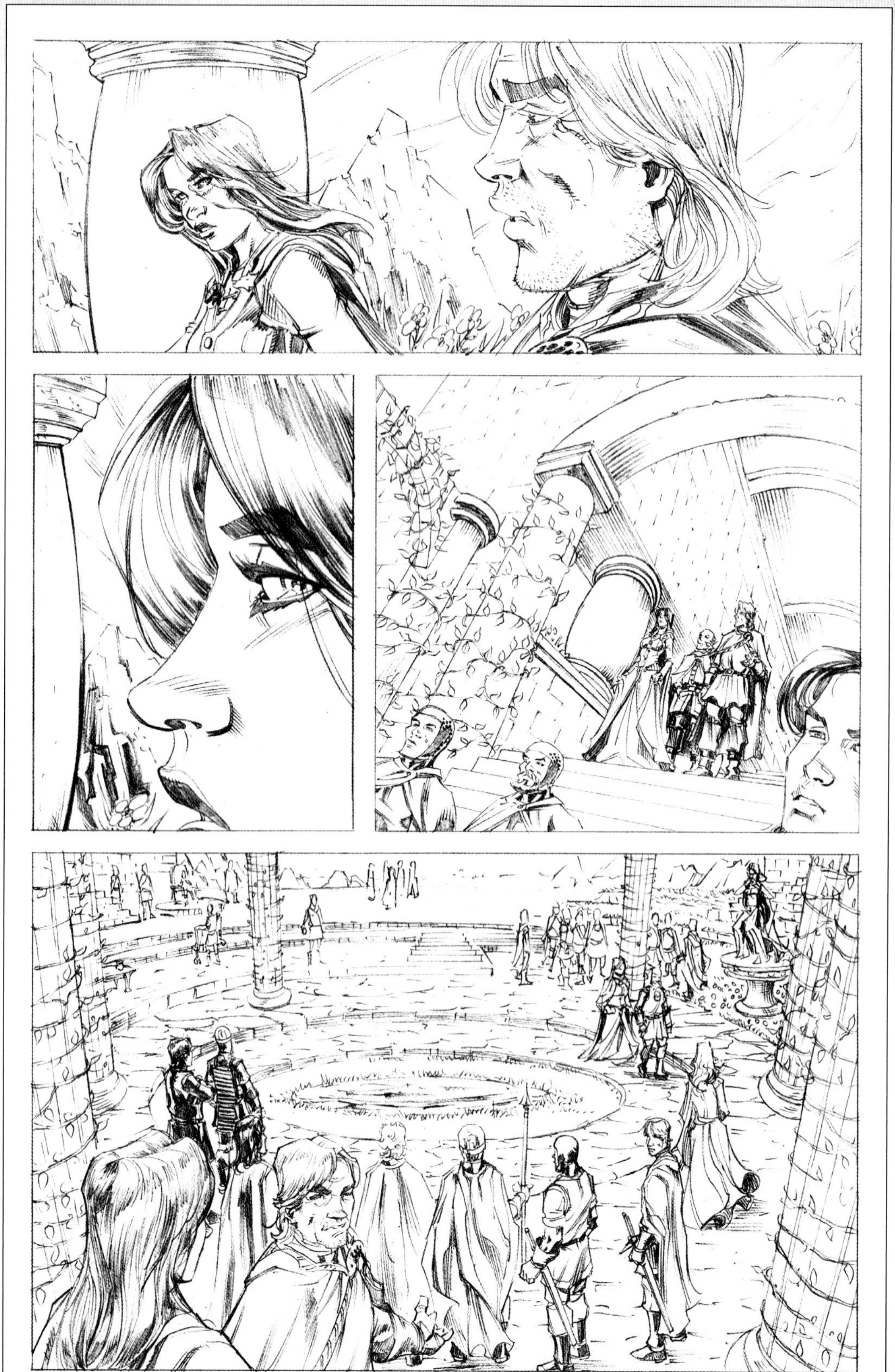

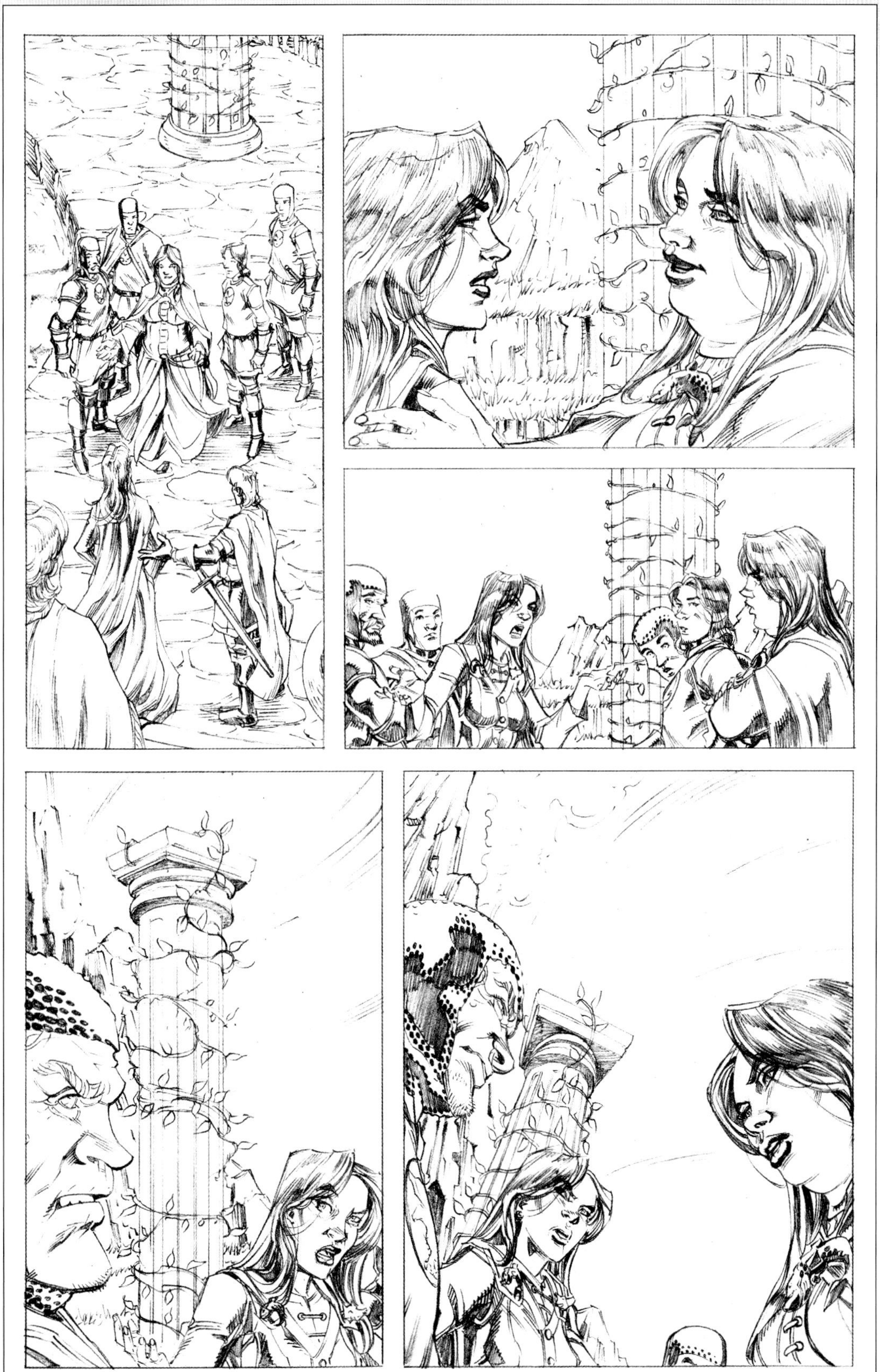

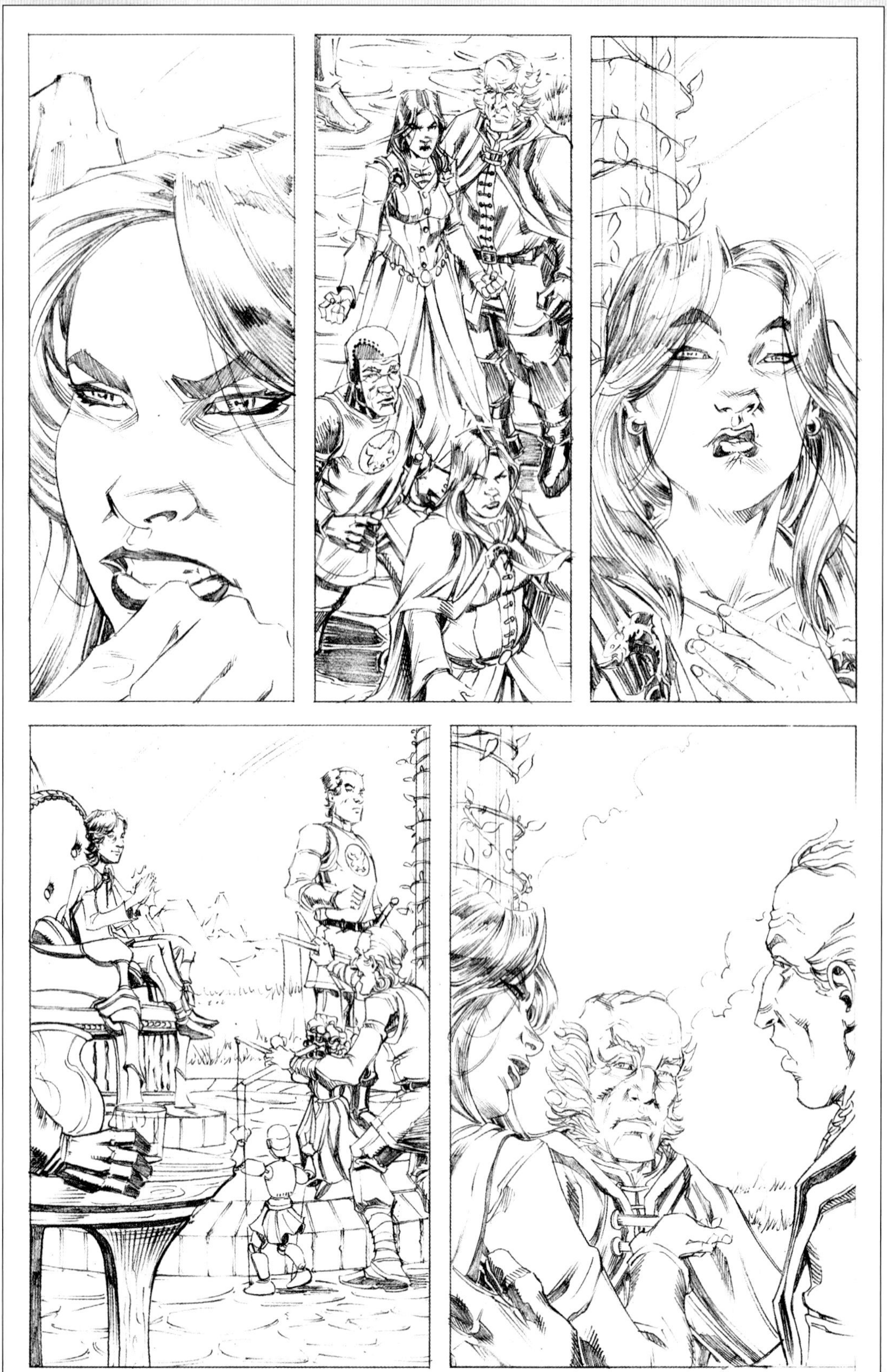

In A *Game of Thrones: The Graphic Novel, Volume 3*, we will take a look at the extensive gallery of character sketches Tommy has done to establish and distinguish the huge cast of characters that populates Westeros. I have a notebook containing hundreds of character sketches Tommy has created—especially since each issue introduces an average of about five new players whose appearances George must approve before they appear in the pages of the graphic novel. So I will share that with you next time.

In the meantime, we hope you have enjoyed Volume 2 of the graphic novels as much as we have enjoyed—and continue to enjoy—creating them!

—Anne Lesley Groell
    Executive Editor
    Random House, Inc.

We hope you've enjoyed this look inside the process and that you continue to have as much fun on this visual journey as we have!

GEORGE R. R. MARTIN is the #1 *New York Times* bestselling author of many novels, including the acclaimed series A Song of Ice and Fire—*A Game of Thrones, A Clash of Kings, A Storm of Swords, A Feast for Crows*, and *A Dance with Dragons*. As a writer-producer, he has worked on *The Twilight Zone, Beauty and the Beast*, and various feature films and pilots that were never made. He lives with the lovely Parris in Santa Fe, New Mexico.

DANIEL ABRAHAM is the author of the critically acclaimed fantasy novels *The Long Price Quartet* and *The Dagger and The Coin*. He's been nominated for the Hugo, Nebula, and World Fantasy awards, and has won the International Horror Guild award. He also writes as M. L. N. Hanover and (with Ty Franck) as James S. A. Corey.

TOMMY PATTERSON'S illustrator credits include *Farscape* for Boom! Studios, the movie adaptation *The Warriors* for Dynamite Entertainment, and *Tales from Wonderland: The White Night, The Red Rose*, and *Stingers* for Zenescope Entertainment.